IN A WORLD OF SORCERY ONLY ONE WILL RISE

Saranon glanced up at the dragons as they flew overhead. The hour of darkness covered them as she watched on. She waited as Pennie examined the stone. It formed part of the shield locking them inside the camp. Shouts rang out on the other side. 'Is that Galven?' Pennie asked.

She nodded in reply. A twig broke on the muddy ground. 'We have company,' she said.

A lone sorcerer. Just one, but that was enough to give them away. Pennie ran for fear of being caught, while Tasha stood gazing out into the distance, 'One day that will be us.'

Enter an epic tale of sword and sorcery. More than two hundred years ago a powerful sorceress freed her people then vanished. As time passed truth turned into myth and myth became legend. The time has come again. Saranon must claim her rightful place before Zyanthia falls.

www.chantellegriffin.com

THE LEGACY OF ZYANTHIA

THE LEGACY OF ZYANTHIA QUADRILOGY

CHANTELLE GRIFFIN

Published by Chantelle Griffin in 2019

The Legacy of Zyanthia series:
Book 1 published by Chantelle Griffin in 2013, 2017
Book 2 published by Chantelle Griffin in 2013, 2017
Book 3 published by Chantelle Griffin in 2017
Book 4 published by Chantelle Griffin in 2019

Interior layout by Chantelle Griffin
www.chantellegriffin.com

Cover artwork by Matthew K. Hoddy
www.spacepyrates.com

Catalogue-in-Publication details available
from the National Library of Australia

paperback ISBN: 978-0-6487305-6-9

Also available in hardback
ISBN: 978-0-6487305-5-2

Copyright © Chantelle Griffin 2019

For my sister

For all that has been before, for all the pain and sorrow, may you rise above them all. For the path less travelled brings hardship, adventure and triumph.

THE ZYANTHIAN REGION, TORDOREN

MADE IN THE IMAGE OF THE GODDESS

THE LEGACY OF ZYANTHIA BOOK ONE

CHANTELLE GRIFFIN

CHAPTER ONE

Rising from the ashes

The rubble caught between her fingers as Saranon peered down into the hole. It was not deep enough and the panic began to rise as Galven shouted from underground. She could not fail, or the time bought by the distraction would be lost. The cold wind swept through her tunic and she dug with her hands. It was no use the ground was too soft, from the rain that had fallen during the day. Tasha ran over, making no attempt to hide on the barren ground covering the low hillside. 'Get them out,' Tasha's voice was firm, 'Now!'

If she used her sorcery it would be detected in the camp and she would pay. Just as Galven and Jeremy had, for weeks they had been imprisoned in the sorcerer Keep.

It was by chance that Tasha found where they were. Saranon concentrated. The sweat cooled her skin in the wind that rustled through the trees in the distance. She held her hands out and willed her sorcery toward the hillside. Her palms ached as though they were on fire and the pain seared. Still nothing happened. Tasha watched in silence and then ran from sight. The guards sent up flares across the sky to signal the dragon riders. It lit up the darkness with a dim haze showing the desolate shabby buildings, that housed her and the rest of the Issola trapped in the camp.

It was all up to her. The cold air burned against her skin as she held onto her sorcery. Her eyes locked onto the direction of Galven's voice. She raised her arms and the ground ripped away. She fell backward into the undergrowth as the explosion hit its mark. The sodden earth disintegrated through the air leaving a heavy haze. She stayed low to the ground as the mud clung to her clothes. The cold soothed her hands as they ached. She glanced up as movement caught her eye. Tasha called out. The dull lights glowing through the camp were heading closer. Her heart thudded in her ears as she dashed the final distance. She skidded on the rough pebble surface behind the building.

She could just make out Galven and Jeremy in the shadows. If she stayed she would be found. Pennie signalled and she followed Tasha inside. She listened as the guards ran past the building. They fell silent as the guards shouted in frustration. Pennie peered through a slim hole between the wooden slats. Waiting until the guards had left. The sounds began to fade yet the lights remained. A great whoosh of air shook the building from overhead. Saranon glanced up through the small window. To see the underbelly of the dragon as it flew close to the ground. 'I want one,' she whispered in amazement.

Pennie snorted trying to muffle a laugh, 'You want trouble.'

'I can dream,' she said.

Tasha held her finger to her lips for silence. The cold night fell dark as the lights began to go out. There was nothing more they could do. She made her way to bed. She could feel the hard wooden crates through the thin straw mattress. She pulled the coarse wool blanket over her shoulders. Pennie fell asleep first, yet Saranon remained restless. Every time she closed her eyes she saw the image of her friends running in the shadows.

The walls of the building creaked in the wind, playing tricks with her mind. A man's voice spoke outside, 'Have you found them?'

'We'll flush them out tomorrow.' Lavena, the old sorceress that ran the camp answered.

It was a small comfort to know her friends had not been found. As her mind rested she fell asleep hoping they had made it.

Light shone through the small window trailing along the wooden floor, as the sun made its way over the hillside. The shadow of the sorcerer Keep Antavagon arched into view. The day broke warming the open room. She rummaged through the wooden crate, forming part of her bed. It was her turn to carry the small notebook and she wrapped it close to her chest using a ragged cloth. The bell swung as the guards made their way past. She pretended to get dressed amid the girls who scrambled before the door unlocked. The heavy chain from the guard's key hit against door and it swung open. They rushed passed before the staff fell across the last girl to leave.

Saranon winced knowing all too well what the pain felt like. Her bruises were a few days old. The agony of not being able to heal them without drawing attention was infuriating. The guard marched them across the worn pebble path to the old barn where they worked. The heavy crates were piled high near the main doors. Straw edged its way across the wooden boards. Cries rang out behind her and she fought the urge to turn. Pennie screamed as the staff came down on her, yet if Saranon turned she would be met with the same. A guard shouted, 'We found them.'

Lavena left and the doors shut behind them. Only then did she turn. Pennie was slumped near the wooden crates. Her arm outstretched, but her hand would not move. Saranon asked, 'Did she see?'

'No,' Pennie winced in pain fighting back tears.

Saranon looked back with a blank expressionless stare at Tasha. She placed her hand on Pennie's arm. If she flinched she would give it away. Pennie moved her fingers and Saranon walked away keeping her eyes on Tasha. The barn windows were high and long allowing the light to wash the space.

The footsteps from the guards at the other end marked the beginning of a long shift. She kept her head down and did her best to avoid attention. The notebook rubbed against her skin, but she dare not move it. She carried the full wooden crates across the open space between the wall and the bench. Some guards would let them eat the vegetables, but she could not chance it. She listened for every shout that rang out across the camp. She hoped that Galven and Jeremy made it. As the day blended into any other she began to lose hope, yet there was nothing she could do. They were on their own.

The toll of the bell for midday caught her off guard. She had been so intent on being busy that the morning had gone. The bright daylight shone as the three friends separated. Making their way to a stream that trickled through the camp. She picked up the coarse bread and ripped it with her teeth as she ran. Tasha stood close to the old tree overhanging the rocky bank. The sun shone golden across the ripples. The stream lapped against the pebbled edge. One day she would beat Tasha to their hiding place. She waited as Pennie scrambled through the bushes and doubled over catching her breath. She took care to remove the notebook and handed it to Tasha.

The stone markers were close. It was her duty to check the nearest one. She stepped along the rocks peering out of the earth. So she could avoid leaving a trace across the ground. There hidden in the scrub came the sickly glow. A faint green edge emanated around a stone almost as long as she. The sorcery continued without any hint of being broken. She reached out her hand wanting to touch it, but as she did a searing pain ran through her fingers. She held her hand there, determined not to admit defeat. It began to throb and she yanked it back. She made her way back as Pennie washed her face in the running water, winding down the stream. The other bank towered over them making a perfect hiding space away from the guards.

Tasha tapped the edge of the charcoal against the notebook as she gazed around. They gathered underneath the tree branches. Watching the sun glitter off the water as Tasha spoke, 'It will have to be soon.'

Saranon nodded. They had been planning their escape when Galven and Jeremy had been taken into the Keep. She had been there before, but the guards were on edge this time. Though none of them said it aloud they were the oldest group at the camp. No one knew what happened to the last ones to leave. It gave an uneasy feeling that made their escape all the more urgent.

The bell rang out cutting their time short and they made their way back through the scrub. Saranon took care to place the notebook back and wrapped it tight. She gave the cool water's edge one last look as the sun beamed down across the pebbles. She ran in line with the other girls piling into the straw covered barn. Gripping another wooden crate before anyone noticed her. The warmth from the spring air took the last chill out of the afternoon. By the time she had set the last wooden crate down, the pile of empty crates in the far corner stood as testament to the hard work. She wiped the sweat from her brow and took a breath of fresh air. The barn doors opened for nightfall.

Dinner was always late. It was a thin gloopy broth

that slipped off her spoon with the same consistency of water.

'Don't play with your food,' Pennie whispered.

She realised she had gazed at the spoon too long. Lavena was not looking and she breathed a sigh of relief. They washed up the wooden bowls before rushing into the building where they slept. The warm pebbles rubbed against her sore feet. She waited pretending to rest before Tasha tapped her on the shoulder. Pennie had already lifted the wooden slat. They squeezed through as the other girls slept.

Pennie had misjudged the guards. They hid close to the building waiting for the footsteps to pass. Her heart thudded in her ears as the steps grew louder. The guard was closing in on the corner of the building. Another guard spoke and the footsteps went away. They made their way along the pebble path in the dark staying together. The moon shone through the scrub, away from the buildings. They stayed close to the bushes hiding their shadows as they went. A magical glow fell over the stream at night and the wind rustled through the branches. Pennie unpacked a large handkerchief piled with food. She gasped at the sight, 'Where did you get that?'

'Shush,' Pennie said. 'You were so busy I thought you would need this.'

Her stomach rumbled in response.

As she ate Tasha spoke the words she had been dreading. 'I need you to break the stone.' A silence fell over the small group. 'I'm not able to do it and I know you can.'

She gazed down at the pebbles in the moon light as the stream lapped at her feet. Tasha was asking her to use sorcery, all that she could summon. She trusted Tasha, but it was a big task and she was unsure. 'Is there another way?'

Pennie waited before she spoke, 'I can check the connection again.'

It was all Saranon could ask. If she used her sorcery to try and break the stone it would summon all the Arthrose sorcerers in the camp.

They made their way through the scrub, along the rocks that broke through the surface. Pennie crept toward the stone marker as Saranon glanced around watching as she waited. The connection glimmered only for a moment and Pennie stopped. They hesitated, but only silence followed. Pennie began again, as the connection gave a dim light the wind rumbled with a whoosh. Lights flickered through the buildings in the camp. Saranon glanced up into the eyes of the first dragon as the riders flew overhead. For a moment their eyes met. She stared in defiance and the dragon flew past. The hour of darkness covered them as she watched on. She waited as Pennie examined the stone. It formed part of the shield locking them inside the camp.

Shouts rang out on the other side. The dragons flew toward the northern edge. A fireball of sorcery shot straight up lighting the night sky. 'Is that Galven?' Pennie asked.

She nodded in reply. A twig broke on the muddy ground. 'We have company,' she said.

A lone sorcerer. Just one, but that was enough to give them away and they all knew it. Tasha made the decision,

'Silence him.'

Saranon gave a curt nod and left running through the scrub. She circled in as the sorcerer tripped in the dark. He made a whimper as she braced her hands around his head. Her sorcery built up, it ran through without leaving a trace.

She stepped back as the sorcery flooded in. A voice called inside her head, but it was not her. She let go and the voice disappeared with it. Pennie almost ran into her, before heading straight back. The fear shone in Pennie's eyes and Saranon could not blame her.

Tasha stood for a moment and gazed out into the distance, 'One day that will be us.'

CHAPTER TWO

The end of the beginning

A pebble fell across the creek as the three friends hid, enjoying a brief moment as shouts rang out through the camp. The sounds brought with it the echoes of the only life Saranon had known. Her friend Tasha was not fazed by the possibility of being caught as they lay close to the edge of the shield. The stone marker shone bright within reach, but none of them dared touch it. The stone ward let off a sick glow visible through the scrub. Pennie had managed to scavenge the notebook that they hid, where no one would find it. Tasha now held it as her short pale wisps of brown hair glistened in the sun's rays, shining off the water's edge.

Saranon preferred not to keep notes, but Tasha insisted. Tasha made herself appear important with a serene stature that belied their predicament. Saranon listened although she tried not to show it. Her friends had been planning their escape, and as always it relied on her. She did not mind, it gave her a great sense of pride when her friends asked for help. 'Now,' Tasha spoke just above a whisper, 'I'm certain that a weakness in the shield lies here.'

Tasha pointed to a roughly drawn sketch, as Pennie eyed it with an unimpressed enthusiasm, 'So if you get it wrong we get fried.'

'What do you mean?' She asked Pennie and Tasha answered.

'No, if we time it right the worst that can happen would be a nasty shock,' then Tasha added 'and we would be stuck in the camp.'

'So nothing unusual then,' Saranon remarked, 'I'm in.'

They both looked at Pennie, who glared in a huff before finally giving in, 'Oh, all right.'

Saranon smiled there was something exciting about trying to escape. The thrill ignited her senses.

A sound carried too close to where they stood, and the small group scattered. Each made their way back to the main building from a different direction. Their meagre lunch break was over, as they scurried back to the hard work of the camp. Before she could dart in the building, the old hag hit out so hard across Saranon's back. She managed to stop herself from slamming into the ground. There were many reasons for wanting to leave the camp and no matter how much she tried to hide it, the thought glinted in her eyes. She made her way into the work shed, knowing it would be a long day before she could rest her weary head.

Long after the sun had left the sky, and the shadows had all but disappeared, Saranon made her way to bed. She longed for the day she could leave the camp. The thought filled her dreams with a never ending flow of images. All leading to one thought, escaping to freedom on the outside. She longed for the world as she imagined it, as the scenes filled the empty void with hope. It was a warm cosy thought that kept her snug, as she stayed in a deep sleep, resting her weary muscles for yet another hard day ahead.

The sky's murky grey clouds hung overhead, with an ominous gloom that wiped her dreams away. It filled the air below with a musty fog, gathering in a thick layer over the muddy grass which only added to the confusion in the camp. The old wretch in her fine clothes looked out of place, as she bundled Saranon up with the older children. They were taken into the depths of the mountain. Saranon had heard strange things whispered through the camp about what happened in the mountain. She went unquestioning as the other children did. A small group of rag tag tired and worn out youths. She knew Pennie and Tasha well, but that was all amongst the small group that huddled close together in the old coach. There was nothing to help cushion the ride as it jolted over a makeshift road. They travelled down into the deep darkness leading to nowhere.

The sky broke open with a great heavy rain, soaking the ground as the coach led the children inside. The large heavy doors shut behind them with a low groan that filled the air. The last of the sunlight slithered away out of the children's reach. They walked away in single file down the dirty well-worn steps. The sound of the droplets filled the silence, as they ran like sweaty perspiration down the chiselled outer walls. Saranon put her hand up to the wall, and it screamed at her. She flinched and snatched it back. The different screams filled her head and blocked her ears from the cries. Then she fell back down to reality as one of the caretakers shoved her back in line.

As they walked down the grimy steps they came to a large room where they split up and were taken further down. Her head filtered through the sounds she had heard. From somewhere through her pulsing heartbeat her mind put together the words, help me and she felt sick. The caretakers led her, Pennie and Tasha down to a room full of barred cells then pushed them in. The girls tried to get close to each other in the dim flittering light. This was not new for Saranon she had stayed like this before. When the caretakers had held her down, and marked her arm so that she would forever be recognised as an Issola.

She looked down on the mark on her arm, and wondered what she had done to deserve it. Tasha was trying to hold back tears, she hated the dark. Pennie put her arm through the bars to comfort her, as the two girls leaned on each other for support. As Saranon wondered what would happen this time, she rested her back against the wall. Her body felt limp as a faint presence entered her head and sifted through her thoughts as though she were not there. Her body fell forward and the contact broke as her head stung. Pennie and Tasha did not appear to notice.

As her hands fell forward she felt it crawling through her arms and down her hands.

Sweat poured down her cheeks from the pain, her hands felt so hot, she could not contain herself from screaming. The pain stung her eyes and she could feel herself go. Saranon woke up on the cold hard floor to find Pennie and Tasha staring at her, not knowing what to do. She could not move, her head hurt, and her nose had bled onto the ground. Everything seemed a world away as she tried to focus and as Saranon did she realised where she was. She laid her head back down on the grimy floor. Somehow a small ray of dull light had found its way through a tiny crack, to show that it was daytime outside. In the shock of sunlight creeping along the walls, the guards came to take Tasha away. The image did not register as her head still spun in a daze.

It was well into the night before Pennie reached over and tapped on her shoulder as she woke from her slumber. 'Can you feel it?' Pennie whispered.

'What?' she asked.

'I've been trying to find Tasha, but I can't sense her.' Pennie replied.

'Perhaps she wants to be alone,' Saranon knew she was only fooling herself.

'Please check,' Pennie always fretted when she could not sense one of her friends.

'All right, stop bugging me,' she replied.

The dark walls pulsed as Saranon gave in to the sensation, that she had been disciplined not to use, though luckily she had not let it get to her. She extended her energy, as she noticed it was easier to use and her reach appeared to be growing. It alarmed her, but there was no one here to talk to, except her friends who were none the wiser.

All she could do was accept whatever it was that expanded, and improved with every step that took her further away from what she had known. The bars faded into wavy red silhouettes through the expanding power of her mind. She did not notice Pennie as she stepped through the bars as though they were not there. The walls pulsated down like streams of flowing dark liquid with an almost rough feel on the skin. Yet she passed through with an ease that sent a shiver down her spine.

The floor seemed just a shadow of a memory underneath her feet as she pushed her hand against nothing. She stood up in the cool heat emanating outward and into the world. Saranon could no longer see Pennie, a sense of urgency swept over her, she had to find Pennie. She made out life forms of some of the guards that appeared in a faint form with a dull almost sickening dim glow. Up ahead she only just made out Pennie's light wavering form, it was far away. Saranon ran through the maze of forms ebbing through the shadows, but somehow that did not matter. She forgot Pennie for a moment and remembered her goal, to find Tasha.

It occurred to her that she had not sensed Tasha at all, as the worry inside her grew to an ever increasing panic. She had tracked Tasha down before this way, but this time something was different. Saranon's toes felt strange, she looked down, and her body seemed to be falling without the rush of gravity. A cold sensation thrust its way up her spine as she crumpled to a heap on the hard surface of the floor. The smell of blood came bursting thick and strong, hurting her lungs with a sickening dread.

As her sensations returned she could feel the taste of vomit in the back of her throat. Saranon's hand slipped on the wet floor and it was then that she looked up at the room. At the same time she stood her heart sank to the pit of her stomach. She realised there was no way out, she ran pounding her bloody fists on anything that looked like a way out. She could not cry, she did not want to, and Tasha would not have. Yet the tears blurred her vision as her breath caught up with her actions and she yelled out. She looked behind her and she knew that it could have, and should have been her.

The stench was overwhelming, yet she did not wipe the blood from her hands. Instead she went over and touched Tasha's forehead while wiping her own tears away. Saranon had to think and she could not. She knew deep down that this was her fate, and Pennie's. She realised she had lost track of Pennie. She leaned over the blood ridden patterns on the hardened surface of the floor. She could feel something calling her from far below, rising with a sense of urgency below Tasha's discarded body. It came closer, and closer, pulsing and rushing faster as it came. The walls started humming. Saranon had felt it before and she knew what it was. She leant over close to Tasha's face, 'This is for you. This is for us.'

Saranon reached out, and made contact with Antavagon. The great Keep had been dormant for so long, held back against his will, and now more than anything he wanted what was his. Without hesitation the central core hidden deep below embraced her. With it came the seething anger lying just out of reach. The great surge of energy from below rumbled through the building with a violent determination. It pulsated ever closer to her. This time Antavagon would have his revenge.

In the thrust of power flowing upward, she could no longer see Tasha's body. The Keep told her what she needed to know. Like a small silent rain, the tears were swept from their place on her cheeks, spiralling downward. Portions of the earth and the Keep appeared to rip free in the turmoil, sweeping her upward in a moment which seemed to take forever. She felt each hand grasp something solid and heavy, something not yet formed. The two swords formed through the air and the dust, her tears and the earth, two bond-breakers. The finest blades Antavagon could offer and he did so. In one small moment the Keep granted her the ability that so many longed for. Yet as Saranon held the blades she understood, strengthening her grip around them.

She held the most feared swords a sorcerer could use made of heart stone. The swords were a melding of the elements to form a solid material that resembled crystal, and sharp enough to cut through stone. The energy ran deep within and so did the thoughts of the Keep. As they filled her mind with an eager anticipation mixed with the darkness of dread. With the bond-breakers complete the sounds throughout the Keep rushed in and she remembered where she was. The sight of Tasha lay before her as a constant reminder as the Keep urged her on.

All too soon the swords were ready to use, Saranon ran her energy down the lengths of the Keep Antavagon. She knew what had to she had to do, what the Keep had called on her to do. With deadly accuracy the blades hit their mark; it was as though this was what she had been born to do. The guards had not yet registered the threat and fell quick underneath her, as she moved around with swiftness to her step. She could only just feel the bond-breakers; they were like extensions of her arms, doing her bidding. Too soon it was over, yet she knew it had just begun.

The power throbbed in her ears, as her eyes did not notice the real world. She became lost in the heat of her own energy, as it broke out in waves. She was able to make out Pennie and some of the children running away. There would be no one to run after them. The Keep whispered and she knew she had hesitated too long. The ground seemed to move and pulse in her wake as the memory of Tasha lay thick on her mind. She noticed her friend's blood still covering her hands, but that did not matter. What mattered now was clinging onto her power long enough to shut down the camp.

The guards were ready for her and the sorcerers held the dark sorcery close to their hearts. She could see and sense the taint as it wavered in the air. The dank smell was familiar to her now. Saranon's power washed over their fragile bodies, leaving nothing behind. They were no equal match for her. She had long suspected it, yet she had been too fearful to try. Saranon sensed the people, recognising other sorcerers that had been held in the camp. She could not understand why some of them were not leaving and it occurred to her they were still trapped. She pounded the earth so hard with her energy, that it ripped apart the buildings in its wake with such enthusiasm it frightened her.

This was no time to feel fear, as she remained calm and steady then moved on. As she found each tainted sorcerer her energy rippled inside her with a heightened enthusiasm as it wakened. The memories ignited by thoughts of Antavagon. She moved on bringing a path of destruction and the sorcerers ran, they all scattered in her path. As the buildings crumbled and the wards that had held so strong faded, the place became a shadow of what it once was. Now, it was Saranon's turn to answer, as her blows struck levelling the ground as she swept through what remained of the camp.

Saranon realised that the sensation she was feeling was satisfaction. A rough calmness settled inside as her breathing slowed. It was not what she had expected, yet the excitement still tingled within from a job well done. She soaked in the image around her as the smouldering shell of the building lay in tatters. She dreamed of this day, she had strived for so long to see an end, yet the meaning was hollow without Tasha. The memory of her friend held firm in her mind, and it darkened her thoughts. She had done this for Tasha, yet it was all too late.

Saranon stood surveying the camp she had just demolished. She had let go of the energy, and could feel its presence throbbing inside her, making it difficult to stand. The taste of vomit came back and she ran off to wash out her mouth at a nearby stream. The taste was foul, she realised she had not washed Tasha's blood off her hands, and spat the water out. As she washed her hands she washed away the last remnants of Tasha and the loss of her friend overwhelmed her. The Keep had told her what had happened, but it all seemed unreal and here she was for perhaps the first time in her life, unsure of what to do next.

'Saranon!' Galven shouted, 'Quick follow us, if you stay behind you'll be found.'

Galven was a sorcerer that Saranon had met from the first camp. He looked different, but she did not doubt his sincerity and followed at her own pace. Luckily she did not have to go far to see that Galven had reached help. Although riding on a giant black cat was not something she was able to contemplate in her current state. Out of the shock of it all she just accepted it as normal and hiked herself up behind one of the riders, a man with greying hair and a cold face.

As they left, Saranon saw that there were many other riders on misquew hidden near the river. As they took off and shot out into an open patch of field, this became clear. She had one of those moments, when she asked herself what she had done. For some reason her scrambled mind did not want to focus on any logical answer and she stayed in a state of bewilderment. She recognised a few of the other sorcerers, as her bond-breakers reformed themselves. The compact sized daggers sat one either side of her belt, looking as though they had always been there in two neat little pouches. One bond-breaker by her side had a crystal blade as clear as day and the other as murky as night.

Saranon's hearing faded in and out, she just managed to hang onto the man steering the giant cat. They came to a stop near a cluster of buildings part way up the mountain side. She almost fell as she came down. She was still trembling on her feet as Pennie rushed up and had to help her stand. 'I'm so glad you're here. You have to come and see the hall, it's so grand. I heard that the camps maybe closing forever, wouldn't that be great?'

Pennie was so excited that Saranon had not been able to get a word in as they entered the grand hall.

She had to admit it was quite breathtaking, but then she was still not feeling well. A sorcerer broke away from the side, and started walking toward her. He began talking to Saranon, 'You are not welcome here…'

Pennie turned around, and had a go at him, 'What do you mean? Saranon is one of us.'

Galven noticed what was going on and came over, 'Pennie is right.'

'Then you will explain where the bond-breakers came from.'

'The Keep gave them to me after Tasha died.'

'No!' Screamed Pennie and ran off holding back tears.

Galven explained, 'Keeps do not usually give bond-breakers to sorcerers.'

Saranon held out the bond-breakers for Galven, and he took them. 'They feel like they are yours, what do you think Max?' he handed the daggers to the man who had started all the fuss.

Max looked at the bond-breakers and then at Saranon. 'They are yours,' and gave them back before walking off.

'What happened to Tasha?' Galven asked.

'You don't want to know,' Saranon exclaimed.

Saranon found Pennie and together they consoled each other in the loss of their friend. More people were entering the hall, which filled her with hope that they would not have to go back. She could not stand the thought of going back. Pennie wanted to know what had happened, but she did not feel like talking. Her friend noticed a few familiar faces and with that Pennie was off. Leaving her to rest in a small make shift bed, one of many that were being set up. Galven came over, 'I talked to Max he's fine for you to stay, but he wants to talk to you later.'

'That's fine,' she replied.

'What happened?' he asked.

Saranon hesitated a moment then whispered, 'The Keep told me how to destroy the camp, and I did.'

Galven looked at her, 'But you couldn't have done all that Saranon.'

'I think I did.'

She followed Galven away from all the commotion that was going on. Along the way she noticed many faces, bewildered at the site of so many that had been held in the camp.

It was then that Saranon noticed something, 'I get the impression that you have been here for a while.'

Galven smiled, 'Yes. The Arroada managed to free me when I was moved from the first camp.'

'You could have told me,' she remarked.

'I thought you had enough to worry about.' He replied.

Galven took her to an area a little removed in the building, connected to the great hall by a narrow hallway.

The Arroada had a complex and advanced hospital the like of which she had not seen. The world felt dark and alien, closing in upon her as she let go of all the anxious thoughts that had clouded her mind in the camp. Galven did not appear to notice anything different, and she wondered how she could ever fit in. She was becoming her old self again. She could feel everything returning to normal as she took in the sounds and sensations of the small town on the side of Mount Eodarr. The sensations felt familiar as she reached out her hands and ran her fingers along the wall feeling the rhythm of the Keep. It spoke back to her vibrating through her fingertips, and sending words to her ears. She opened her eyes, and spoke the words that came to her mind, 'Aaron Wercaston.'

Galven looked at her a little unsettled. 'Galven, I would prefer to see Aaron alone,' Saranon spoke as she waited.

He nodded and with a stunned look Galven hurried away. Aaron was a greying well-built man who welcomed her inside the small room. Saranon sat down, she found the soft cushions and comfy bench rather unusual to sit on after the harshness of the camp.

Aaron smiled but looked concerned, 'What can I do for you?'

Tell him, whispered the Keep. Saranon did not know where to start. In the middle of all the confusion her mind was still hazy as she tried to think, so she began near the end. It was not easy letting go of something that would have cost her in the camp, something which cost Tasha her life. No amount of healing would wipe away the pain, and Saranon found herself crying. Aaron checked her over, 'You say that now you feel normal.'

'Yes,' answered Saranon.

Aaron stood up, and asked her to follow, leaving her in a small entryway while he left. She waited feeling like she was completely lost and annoyed, all at the same time. Aaron asked her to enter and she did, Max was there he spoke first, 'Saranon you have been given a great gift.'

'You mean a great curse,' Saranon said in a flat voice.

'We would like to find out the level of your sorcery,' Max asked.

She saw that Max was trying to be nice, but this did not suit his personality. He looked like someone who preferred to be outdoors and appeared to be uncomfortable in his surroundings. She went with Aaron to prepare, as he was explaining the process. It sounded quite simple, although she knew that did not always carry across to reality. Go into the room alone, relax and let her energy out so to speak. It sounded simple, but something told Saranon that this was going to be trouble, she had not figured out how. The Keep at Eodarr had gone quiet, not a good sign in her books which started to show through to feelings of agitation. 'Aaron, you are not telling me something,' she spoke.

Aaron laughed, 'I didn't say this would be easy.'

Saranon was beginning to wonder if she was up to this new challenge. Anything at the moment was better than what she had been through and she knew how to hold her own. The underground chamber smelt of dry acrid dust filtering through her lungs. She turned and Aaron had already shut her in. She was beginning to wonder if this was a mistake. She walked to the centre of the room and lay down as a small fog etched its way across the floor.

She thought its timing was too appropriate. She relaxed and was surprised to sense nothing that was not meant to happen. It would not be the first time she had been tricked. She thought that at least she should give the process a try before giving up. She still felt nothing, and could not understand what was going on. She got to her feet, and shouted, 'This isn't funny!'

Saranon turned around to try and open the door, only to be confronted with a smooth surface containing no remnant of an opening.

She pushed out with her energy so harsh it almost ripped at her skin, and felt like fire. She screamed, and could not see through her swollen stinging eyes. How could they? She thought this was nothing but a trick. She called through her mind and thought so loud she called to the

Keep. Saranon drew the sorcery up to her, and her down to it. She reached as far down as she could and yanked the energy so hard she thought she was going to break.

Saranon wanted to scream, but could not. It hurt to breathe and somehow through everything, she saw what she was looking for. She reached out, and touched it with both hands. She hit the solid ground with harsh thud that brought her back to reality. The floor of the chamber was ice cold and her hands were shaking as she tried to get up. There were voices behind her as the door to the chamber burst open, with a great boom as the vacuum ended. With help Aaron picked her up, and laid her down on a stretcher to take her away, through an array of muddled hallways. 'It's all right, it's over,' he told her in a voice that was far too calm.

CHAPTER THREE

Following the original path

It would be Pennie's fifteenth birthday soon. Her friend was a few months younger and had insisted that Saranon have a late birthday to join in the celebration. She was becoming aware that her friend had not come out of their ordeal as well as she had. Every now and then she would catch Pennie staring off into space, as solid and pale as a statue. It reinforced her view that if something was going to happen it was up to her to sort out. 'Get up!' Pennie shouted.

The light of the morning shone through the window, and into her eyes. 'You have to open your present,' Pennie was sitting on her bed.

It occurred to her that she had nothing for Pennie. So she reached over, and took hold of the crystal clear bond-breaker Attourin she had made earlier, then passed it to her friend. 'I want you to accept this.'

Pennie was so ecstatic she hugged Saranon, and ran off to tell everyone who was awake or soon would be with all the commotion. She stared down at the palms of her hands nothing could wash away the imprint of Mount Eodarr, the mark of sorcery. She kept the marks covered from sight, they felt cold. One a murky red and black, and the other on her right hand a mix of white and blue, with a smooth finish where the skin of her palms should have been. It had frightened Max to see them, but nothing seemed to astonish her. It was part of her hands and part of her. She did not see what all the fuss was about.

Her birthday morning seemed unusual with all the activity around the place. The air smelled sweeter as the sunlight warmed the room. She finished putting her jacket on and caught a glimpse of Mira's elegant long dress as the older sorceress swept by. Mira was a middle-aged lady who had kept her beauty well, though her greying hair betrayed her real age. She followed and Mira turned. There was something wrong. Saranon could sense it from the people around her. It was like a stale smell wafting through, spoiling the air that had only just reached her.

The sensation was strange, 'Have we been found?' She asked.

Mira smiled, 'No, you are safe here.'

Mira was one of the great Council members for the Arroada. The older sorceress had shown great wisdom which Saranon respected. Mira had managed to win support for closing the remaining detention camps scattered in the north. The older sorceress seemed to understand her friend Pennie. That took a weight off her shoulders, 'Are you coming to the party?'

'I would not miss it,' Mira replied.

With that she ran off forgetting her concerns, and went to help Pennie get ready for the event in the evening. The world was just how she had imagined it, and Saranon had not felt so relaxed for a long time. She wondered how such a short time could feel so great and feared that it would end. She had become impatient about waiting for her hair to grow, so she had made her brown hair long with her sorcery. It flowed down past her shoulders much to her satisfaction. With Pennie making sure the hall looked perfect the day soon faded away, while her friend had no problem meeting the guests. Through the excitement something caught her eye. Mira and Max were talking with a group of people. They looked her way, then Max walked off.

Before she had a chance to do anything else Pennie grabbed her hand. Her friend hauled her through the crowd so fast she almost knocked Galven's friend over. It was hard not to join in the dancing and soon she lost track of time. In the morning Saranon grew suspicious, something was going on. The sensation tingled at the edge of her senses annoying her even more. She would have preferred to know what was happening. She did not have much luck in that area and figured she would have to rely on herself to find out.

She had not been able to keep her thoughts from

Pennie, who declared that she was going to find out what was going on before Saranon did. In the clear open air of Felgrai she found time to leave the quaint little town in the edge of the forest and travel alone. Her curiosity had gotten to her so much that she would sneak out in the night. Max did not appear to suspect that she was travelling alone. With Pennie's help and listening to passers by she had managed to find a few places the public would be welcome to listen to what was going on.

The first time Saranon went into a gallery to listen to the politics, she found herself going with a sorceress by the name of Tina. Pennie had no trouble striking up a conversation. Without discussing too much she found that all three had something in common. She was so nervous. This acted to confirm to anyone who saw her, that she was a sorceress of no such importance and not worth paying much attention. The great hall of the Arthrose Council stood in a grand elegance that took her breath away as she entered. The delicate carvings, marble and gold were in stark contrast to anything she had seen at the camp.

She noticed that she was not the only one looking up at the ceiling and at the paintings on the wall. Taking the whole scenery in as she gazed about the grand room. It was so draining having to sit still through the meeting. She looked over, and noticed that Tina did not seem to have any trouble at all. There had been a few moments where she clenched the seat so hard from trying not to let her anger out. Saranon thought that no one had noticed. The sorcerer keeping order over the meeting had looked her way more than once.

She left the meeting with a firm realisation that they would continue to be a problem for the survivors of the camps. More worrying was the air of agreement that hung around the gallery with a sickening dread that ate away her hopes. The Arthrose Council appeared to have support. She clenched her fist, holding back a rage of thoughts as they spun through her mind. She did not understand, it seemed absurd that the camps would have support. She did not like to contemplate the thought, as her hope mixed with an edge of sadness. This was not what she had expected to find in the real world, in her dreams it had all been so easy after escaping the camp.

Saranon stood, and left the chamber. The night air was sharp and cold as she said goodbye to Tina. It was a long journey home from Dreggan. On the outskirts of the city the stars made out the path ahead shining on the buildings.

She came across the conversation of two sorcerers walking by.

'The sooner the Arroada are dealt with the better.'

'Don't worry, Aimen has sent a group down.'

The masculine voices faded with the shadows that had carried them. Her paranoia had not been for nothing as her heart pounded heavy in her chest.

The only thing she could think of doing was to warn the Arroada, she did not know the place well enough to trust anyone else. She ran to where her misquew was who had been dozing off, concealed from the surrounding world. She almost tripped as she heaved herself up. This was no time to be complacent as she masked her entrance through the lay-line, it would take time for her to return. Saranon made it as far as an outer post and rode past the agitated guards. No one here would be pleased to see her.

She managed to locate Jeremy, Galven's friend. He came out to greet her 'What are you doing here?'

'I went to Dreggan, and I overheard that the Arroada will be attacked. Can you warn them?'

The sorcerer nodded as he relayed the message. Saranon had no intention of making Jeremy's life difficult, as she sat listening to the gentle hum of the small Keep. Words formed in her mind, the Keep was already letting the Arroada know, but would it be too late. She stood up as Jeremy came back, he exclaimed. 'It is not safe for you to return, you can stay here.'

She did not like being in the dark. She wanted to stay as Jeremy had told her, but something felt wrong. She poured her energy out along the ground, the sensation came back thick and strong; the Arthrose. Her anger swelled from deep inside her, suppressed for so long, when she thought that she could do nothing to stop them. This time it would be different. Saranon left the fort, with Jeremy calling after her to stay. Whatever sorcery they were using to try and make her stay, it was not enough. She ran through the security shield that held around the building with no hesitation, or halt in her stride. Her misquew was waiting for her on the edge of the small Keep and she leaped onto the lay-line that would lead her to one place.

Her veins pulsed with the quickening speed. She felt cold, but somehow more alive knowing now that she had a purpose. The building ahead looked calm as she approached in the cool night air. The Keep lay almost serene as she strode toward and she wondered if it had always been like that. Saranon shook that thought away, the Keep did not notice she was there, if it had it was not giving her away. She entered the building, where would the Arthrose be? She stretched out her mind. In that moment she had been noticed, she had to act racing up to the main tower. The security seals were stronger and for a moment she doubted herself.

Her determination kept her going as she hid in the shadows waiting for the footsteps to fade in the distance. She did not make a sound as the thrill of the chase circled around in her mind. She knew she had to take care, if she moved with haste the moment would be gone. Then it would all be for nothing and she was not prepared to give in. Just as she thought it was too late, a noise emanated from the other rooms, as a mix of emotions carried through a wave of relief. Yet all this was short lived as she held onto a single thought. She had lost too much, it had all been too much, and now she would have her moment.

Saranon could sense a commotion rise as it rattled her nerves and she blocked the thought from her mind. She had to focus, she was near her goal and yet so far, all at the same time. She took a deep breath steadying herself as she let the energy rise. Seeping through like an eternal tide crushing the last of her fading nerves. Yet at the same time it stirred something from deep within, an unknown panic that she tried to subdue. The Keep stayed silent, it had no business here, as she expanded her senses through the wall and beyond.

As her head thudded with the pulsing energy she rose, this time it would be different, this time it would end. She threw her sorcery in a wild rage shattering the bulky door, as the seals broke spraying the burnt smell of ash in a cloudy haze. Saranon did not falter, her mind stayed on one thought and if she did not succeed she would lose more than Tasha. She managed to hold back her underlying rage as it seethed just below the surface. She moved forward with a blind stubbornness that drove her on.

The first blow came from the right as she blundered through the door, but the pain seemed irrelevant, it was a common friend. Their faces seemed to blur as she interrupted the councillors of the Arthrose. She had entered their most sacred place and for that she did not expect to live, but then this was not about living this was retribution. As her wild rage crept to the surface, the energy poured out demanding release. The blast struck in a curved arc that lit up the room as it seared through the air, while the sorcerers blocked as the tension showed.

Saranon could hear a muffled voice yelling to get something and for a moment silence pounded through the air. This was it, the only thing holding her back was she. She looked up at all the sorcerers around her and saw them in such clarity she could see the beads of sweat on their faces. The air buzzed around her, yet the image was crystal clear as her energy pulsed in her ears, muffling the noise. She was trapped in a moment as it slowed to a steady grace and she lashed out with her energy as they answered in return. On the edge of her vision a ripple blocked her focus and caught her attention.

An aging sorcerer began to approach with something hidden under his robe, and then she saw it. The Eye of Escora legendary Orb of Darkonia and made by Zeralden Hadenvar. The Orb shone with a murky glow absorbing the light from the air, as it pulsed with a radiant heat sweeping across the room. She felt herself falling into a trance that beckoned to her being from the edge of the darkness. The strength of the Orb pulled at her senses like a tight vacuum, Saranon tried to resist, but it would not let go. She thrust out her energy against it, yet the Eye of Escora absorbed the blows.

She could hear the voices around her fade as she realised the Orb was stripping her sorcery away and she winced. It should have hurt, yet she felt no pain. The Orb called, and she threw all the energy she had toward it. There was nothing left as the void filled her mind and an energy from deep within engulfed her in a raging flood, as it burst to the surface. She remembered to breathe as a gasp fell across the room in the silence. In the faint glowing light she stood, as the sorcery of old that lay within called to the Orb, and it answered in return.

For the Eye of Escora had been made for a purpose, one that Saranon was yet to understand. It called out to her as the faint glow intensified filling the room, and the noise around cascaded toward her ears. The pain creased in through the edges, yet it did not matter. As she stood she could see the wave of shock, as a recognition swept through the sorcerers. This time she had the Orb. She breathed as the dust settled, the Eye of Escora held tight in her grasp. The library at Felgrai had come in useful, there would be no more kneeling as she stood up and let go to the energy within.

The Eye of Escora was hers, as she held it in both hands the Orb glowed with a certainty she did not have. Yet the energy within pulsed strong as she let it flow into the Orb, it grew brighter with a wild radiance. Before she could do anything more the Orb boiled with a raging heat, the pain seared through, and she had to let go. As soon as she did, she knew it was a mistake. The explosion from the severed link to the Eye of Escora shattered through the room with a thunderous spray. For a moment blocked out any noise, as the ringing filled her ears.

She felt numb as she opened her eyes, and the haze cleared. The smell of ash lay thick in the air, as she wondered how she had managed to escape the full blast. The Orb was cool to the touch and dark as she held it in amazement, not wanting to let go. The sound returned to the room as her head spun, and she almost dropped the Orb. The deadening blast had blackened the edges of the room as she looked on in disbelief.

For a moment Saranon thought the only thing the Orb had damaged was the building. Then she came back down to earth, and the pain began searing up her arms. The place was a mess with the charred outlines the only remnants of the Arthrose, she coughed remembering to breathe. Stammering past the charred table she slipped on the paper scattered over the floor. She could sense movement heading in her direction, as she noticed the papers in front of her. The documents held details of people sent to the camps and she leant down as she felt sick. One paper near her hand had come loose from its folder. She pulled it all the way out, and saw Princess Antobathia's name on it. She shoved it in her pocket, and ran as the shouting came close behind her. It felt like she was on her last ounce of energy and her ribs ached as she ran.

The sounds grew closer and the panic as she moved with her heart thudding in her ears. She held the Eye of Escora not wanting to let go as she ran from the Keep, darting out into the cool night air. The breeze swept across her face as the sweat poured down her cheek and yet she carried on not wanting to look back. Even though the sounds had faded well into the background, she could still sense the sorcerers. They were in the distance searching as they drew closer. Saranon finally stopped, catching her breath as her lungs ached. She was overcome with exhaustion, but she had to go on. Near the outskirts of the town she could sense movement as a misquew raised its sleepy head. Its eyes shone bright as soon as it spotted her.

Without any hesitation she ran towards it as the air hurt her lungs with every breath. She sat on the misquew and raced onto the nearest lay-line which led east to Ollanthia one of the oldest Keeps from the days of

Zyanthia. If there was a time she needed refuge, it would be now. As the misquew moved, a pain ran up through her side and across her chest, she gazed down to the wound as the pain crept in. Saranon stopped the bleeding, but she knew it was not good. She began to think the only reason why she had found it easy to leave, was because no one thought she would be alive.

She groaned with a hint of annoyance at someone thinking she had passed away when she was alive, yet the thought had an appeal to it. If it meant that no one was chasing her she could relax and she was in no state to fight even with the Orb. The wound was sucking away the last of her strength as her hands became numb while trying to hold on. The misquew was giving her no comfort when it jostled around as it moved forward. The riding cat sprinted at a low pace, just enough for Saranon to hold on. Her eyes grew tired as the death of her friend Tasha plagued her thoughts, like a recurring nightmare that would not leave her alone.

The image haunted her still as she moved through the night, it made the victory bittersweet and she wondered if it was all for nothing. The lay-line faded way as she reached the end. Without any warning the misquew dropped her down, then vanished into the darkness. Before her stood a powerful Keep, even in the night its brilliance shone with the glow stemming from within. She forgot how tired she was as she made her way forward at a heavy pace. The feeling in her side was beginning to numb and she felt weak as she managed to move on.

Ollanthia was beautiful with its monumental well-kept gardens. It was like a small piece of paradise that even the most powerful people were too superstitious to disturb. Sweat poured down her back soaking into the blood on her clothes. She had been lucky, if it were not for the Eye of Escora tucked close to her side, she was sure she would be dead by now. The enormity of what she had done hit her and the tears ran down her face, glistening with the glow from the moon light and Ollanthia. She had to tell Pennie, her best friend would not be impressed.

Saranon steadied herself as she neared the outer gate, it was late and the guards did not like wanderers at night. Gus, an old stocky man she had met before saw her first; 'What've you done?'

Gus placed his hand on her shoulder and helped her as she almost lost her balance. He muttered, 'We'll get you inside.'

His arms were like stone, holding her up as they walked along. She was lifted onto a make shift bed as the surgeon started peeling away the cloth to examine the wound.

Saranon woke up later in the ward with an aching pain, Gus was sitting beside her. 'You were lucky,' he said in a stern low voice.

He looked tired and shaken, and she guessed that he stayed up the whole night. She had a dull ache, but told Gus that she was all right. She did not have the nerve to worry him more than she already had. The light streamed in bringing its warmth through the window with the morning light. The Keep began to come alive with the daily activities.

Saranon noticed the people walking past looked nervous. Then she thought it would not take long for the news to reach the whole of Darkonia. She hoped they had not guessed, but then it occurred to her that the Eye of Escora was with her, anyone who found it would know. Gus saw the panic on her face and pointed to her belongs underneath the chair, on the other side of the bed. She had to figure out how she was going to leave. A sharp pain pierced her body from her quick movement and Saranon realised she would not be able to go anywhere. Gus stretched out of his cosy spot in the armchair, and said his goodbyes as he headed off for a well-earned sleep. This was not what she had expected. Although the thought had crossed her mind, her situation could have been much worse.

CHAPTER FOUR

A promise to a friend

Saranon hit the pond's surface with a small flat stone and watched as it skimmed across the still dark water at a mighty speed. It was hard not to lose her temper with the Guardians of Ollanthia for running off with the Eye of Escora for safe keeping. She felt trapped and that was not a good place to be for anyone on the receiving end of her frustration. Pennie was due to arrive soon, after almost going off at John the Head Priest. The others had not known how to calm her. So here she was cooling down. She had been cooling down for the last few days after getting out of the uncomfortable hospital bed. The only surprise was that some of the residences began to look upon her with fear, not that there was anything scary about her.

She lay down on the grass calming her thoughts and lying still, as she sensed the Keep spreading down deep underneath the ground. It made a soothing sound, but that was not what she wanted to find, and she heard a sudden burst of laughter in her mind. Was the Keep laughing at her? She could not tell. Saranon heard a sound behind her that broke her concentration. The mirage that had been part of the hill had faded away as the Keep opened one of the passages into its murky depths. The door sounded like it had not opened for quite some time. Grime had built up around the edges, but the air inside was still fresh. The room appeared like a large foyer with stairs leading in many directions and she took the ones to the right going down.

If Saranon was not able to have the Eye of Escora she was going to find out more about Ollanthia. Her annoyance at being treated like an ignorant child faded as she slid deeper down. She thought she could communicate with Keeps better than people. At least Keeps were simple and easy to work out. The tunnels led down to the primary systems and the central core. The system transferred energy from far below the ground into the core and turned into a usable energy source. Most central cores were located deep in the ground where the temperature was warm, and this one was over a thousand years old.

The air was growing warm. Brushing along the skin on Saranon's arms it was a friendly welcoming sensation. She could sense the Keep, it almost wanted her to continue, as though it was excited to meet her. She continued her downward path. As the tunnels became larger and more elaborate with details carved into the walls. She ran her hand along the patterns. The Keep sang in her mind and she let it guide her way as some of the patterns lit up showing the way ahead.

The tunnel was deep, falling away into the ground, as she almost slipped on the wet moss creeping out from the corners of the stairs. All Saranon could think about was what she had done, something inside her knew she would have to leave Darkonia. There were few places to hide from the Arthrose. The tunnel led into an underground atrium with the light from the markings mimicking the light from outside. The Keep knew where it wanted her to go and led her into a makeshift storeroom. She ran her finger along the dust, the object underneath glowed transferring warmth to her cold hands. This was what the Keep had brought her here to find. The markings on the walls shimmered, and Saranon ran back up the winding staircase taking two steps at a time. The light rippled through the glowing marks like an imaginary soft breeze leading to the outside.

It was dark, she was sure she could not have spent that much time inside the Keep? John was waiting off to the side with several Guardians of Ollanthia. He looked half stunned to see her, but she did not seem to notice. All she saw was a group of priests that were starting to close in on her. If Gus had not told her that they were peaceful, she would have thought they were being hostile. John spoke, 'I do not know what the Keep sees in you. Your actions pose a threat to Darkonia we will find you safe passage to Alveron, after that you are no concern of ours.'

The words took her by surprise they were not as friendly as she had been lead to believe. Then she had not thought through what would happen afterward. The priests huddled together as they left her out in the open and once again Saranon felt the isolation press against her soul. How could she do this by herself? How could Tasha leave it all up to her? Tasha had always been the one whose faith in the future had been unwavering. Here she was wondering if anyone else would understand. Later she cried herself to sleep.

She was about to rush off to work on the project Ollanthia had given her when Gus interrupted. Pennie peeped around the door to the lounge room. She burst in with her head held high full of excitement. She lightened up the room as Gus disappeared down the corridor in amongst the exchange of greetings. 'Do you have any idea what you've done?' Pennie said, 'The Arthrose is in such a mess.'

'I thought you would be angry.'

'Saranon,' Pennie went calm, 'It appears that I was infected with a virus at the camp. So what do I care about the Arthrose.'

A tear escaped down Pennie's cheek as she sat quietly in the armchair, 'I know you have to leave, the authorities are not sure how to deal with you. If they figure out it was luck they will be here in an instant.'

Her friend looked so much younger than her, so small and fragile. To get so far and be told 'Sorry you do not get to enjoy life, that is for someone else' was cruel. Saranon knew that her health was okay and she could not help but feel guilty that she was not in the same situation. She took

Pennie to see what she had been working on, far below the ground away from the outside world. Just for a moment, they could be children again.

Pennie decided her mission was to help get her out of Darkonia and frequently left the Keep. Her friend had told her that there were people watching Ollanthia to see if she would leave, or to make sure she was still there. After all if Saranon could kill the Arthrose Councillors, what else was she going to do? Some of the people could be seen from the gardens. Gus always looked as though he could tell exactly where they were and had pointed a few out. For some reason she had difficulty picking them out, but it did not worry her. She was too intent on finishing the project that had begun, to resemble a bond-breaker, in the form of an elegant sword.

Perhaps Ollanthia knew what was waiting in the wings, after all it had seen a few battles in its prime. Although she had grown up in the camps she had not been in a position to fight back. It was a new sensation that made her feel as though she had control. She stood back admiring the finishing touches on her creation. She blew across the surface of the blade and the air sparkled. The hilt was just as fine, light weight and manoeuvrable. She held the sword and it made a small whistling sound as the blade cut through the air. A large dull sound whipped down the walls of the Keep and tingled down her spine. It took a moment for Saranon to realise the Keep was warning her.

She fled upward, and almost ran straight into the new comers. She rushed into another stairwell then everything went quiet. She could not understand why she was having trouble sensing them. The Keep told her someone was approaching. Saranon realised she would have to go back down, and try to get out another way. She changed direction, rushing as she fled toward a short cut. As the door was closing she caught sight of a dark clad man wearing the symbol of the Royal Darkonian Army, then the room went white in a flash. Somehow the Keep managed to close the door and down she went with the flash still in her eyes. She realised she was crouching and stood up. Her head turned to the great chunk that had been torn out of the wall behind. As her vision cleared she could make out one of the attackers through the damaged wall and ran.

The echoes of the wizardry blasting through the rest of the wall followed her as she went. The sound sending shivers down her spine as she quickened her pace. She still could not sense them as she made her way to the outer rim of the Keep. Her heart thudded heavy in her chest as the shouting drew near. The sinking feeling hit her stomach as she realised she was not going to make it. She turned around; she had to find another way.

John had been right it was too dangerous to stay in Darkonia. As Saranon stepped through, the door disappeared back into the wall. There were a few paths that led in the direction she wanted to go, but from now on she would have to be prepared. She started heading north and sensed something familiar the Eye of Escora. She turned and plunged the sword through the seal on the door. The blade slid through with ease. As she entered the Orb was in open view in the centre of the room, she was about to rush in, and the Keep stopped her.

There were shields surrounding the Orb, this was not the first time she had encountered such devices. She calmed her mind, relaxed her body and moved forward. The shields sensed stress, anxiety, and extreme emotions. As much as she tried the explosion had scattered her thoughts, and she took a deep breath. For days with the bond-breaker she had been practicing a heightened level of concentration, it paid off as she reached the Orb. Now she was left with the difficult bit going back and she let out a small sigh. She knew her concentration had started to waver. The ripple of the walls as she went through felt heavy and made her queasy. Her stomach muscles flexed as she passed through the last shield. She bent over before emptying the remains of her dinner on the floor.

Saranon hurried through as the door closed, she had to go up. No doubt that would be expected as she thought of the blast. She had to approach the task with care. These were people who wanted her out of the way. She held no grudge against the Darkonian Army, but if they were involved she would have to be strong. She did not know much about them, or their capabilities. Her palms were already sweating and she was still feeling sick. She heard noises and braced herself one last time before opening the door to the next level. The energy rose up inside her and out stepped Saranon.

She held the blade Tellembre as it swung with ease, glowing hot at the hilt. The mark of the old crest rested on the shoulders of her robes. The room was a blur with the only way out through the people that stood in her way. Before the blade met them there was a momentary look of horror. As she blasted a way through, hoping she would not have to use the bond-breaker. As the wizards regrouped she ran toward the exit, yet just as she cleared the last gap a blade swung out to meet her head on.

She held up Tellembre as her blade sunk through without hesitation. She flung herself over the scattered mess, with a momentary glance back. Her heart seemed to be pounding from somewhere else, yet on the outside her appearance was almost serene. The bond-breaker moved with ease in her hands. Saranon's next encounter ahead had heard the commotion hesitating in her wake. They seemed to blend into the background letting her pass as she moved onward and north to the outer perimeter of the Keep.

As she ran through a large foyer with several corridors tailoring off, a stench became heavy in the air. Saranon knew what it was, she recognised the sorcery from the camps. This time it would be different, she poised herself ready for the embrace. Her lungs filling with the heated air as the coils spun around, this time would be different indeed. The coils became tighter and she laughed on the inside. She had been waiting for this, as they pulled tighter pinning her arms close.

In the fraction between her heart beat she exhaled and the six sorcerers came in closer to strengthen the coil. Saranon's heart beat and the sound reverberated smashing the sorcerers' strands. That flicked back, spraying the harsh light all over the room. The shock of the rebound took out the sorcerers, leaving nothing but charred marks up the walls. She gasped yet she could not let the shock sink in, she was so close to the edge of the Keep. As she made her way through the courtyard, there was no sign of the trouble within.

Compared to that, the rest of the way was easy. She cleared the perimeter on her misquew, riding a long distance before slowing down. Her brow was sweating and her arms felt heavy with exhaustion, it was all she could do to stand up straight. She hoped the focus had been on Ollanthia, as Saranon did not want to run into trouble. She held up her talik, a small round disc that could open small enough to fit in the palm of her hand. She placed her thumb on the centre of the outside, it had picked up a signal from Pennie which she answered and then waited.

She started to shiver as her back grew cold from the sweat, she could see her own breath in the cool night air. The river running past refreshed her face as she bent down. The sound of Pennie's misquew came from behind. It was a moment before she realised it was not her friend she had sensed. Saranon stood up to find a wizard dressed in the robes of the Darkonian Army. She was too shocked to speak as they seemed to be appearing from everywhere. Jacob stared down at her with a calm composure, 'You have no place in Darkonia. You have two choices leave, or stay and die. Which one will it be?'

She held back her rage, how dare he trick her and he had used her friend to get to her.

She stepped closer, the soldiers had surrounded her but kept their distance. It was definitely a trap. 'If you cannot send your own message, do not use my friend. I am not staying now get out of my way.'

Jacob reached out, and held onto Saranon's shoulders, 'You have a lot to learn.'

She went limp in his arms.

Noise came to Saranon's ears first.

'What do you mean you couldn't restrain her?' Major Shenoff was seething.

Captain Jacob Assinden spoke with a calm tone 'It disintegrated. I would not have believed it had I not been there.'

'So you brought an Issola here and we have no means of controlling her.'

'The Arroada are certain she is not Issola.'

'What would they know? Saranon is your responsibility, if anything happens it's on your head. I don't want to see you until she is gone the Alveronians can deal with her.'

Saranon found herself in a large room, a fire warmed the air. The soldiers were intent on playing cards nearby. She thought she saw Pennie, but it could not be, why would she be here? Pennie leaned over, and touched her old friend's head to reassure her. She whispered, 'I'm sorry about what happened, I couldn't think how to get you out otherwise.'

Her mouth tasted like vomit and she realised she was thirsty. She sat up in a rush and scared one of the soldiers. An older one laughed and told him to sit down. The older one Roger introduced himself and gave Saranon a glass of water, 'That's some bond-breaker you made.'

She realised the bond-breaker was missing and Pennie told her she had stored it in a safe place. Her head pounded, she was not happy about her friend's way of helping, though Pennie had not let her down. So Saranon resigned herself to the fact that she was going to have to put up with a bunch of smelly soldiers for the rest of her time in Darkonia. Pennie explained what had happened as they strode outside. Along one of the open walkways overlooking the border it would not take long to cross. The problem was more timing, Alveronians were protective of their border and not that she had encountered any yet. Jacob stood higher up on a balcony keeping an eye on them.

Fort Grismor was a large well maintained fortress near the Qakrenarr Pass. It was one of three main gateways between Darkonia and Alveron. The two countries did not see eye to eye, the mountains and rough terrain acted as a natural barrier keeping the peace. Saranon walked up on her own to see Jacob, she was not thrilled about getting close to him after their last encounter, but this had to be done. She stood back, and produced the papers she had rescued from the attack on the Arthrose. Jacob glared down at her, it seemed to be the only facial expression he knew. He took the papers and she turned to leave. Jacob called after her. 'Thank you,' was all he said.

Saranon glanced back then returned to where Pennie was waiting. 'What was all that about?' Her friend asked.

'I found some papers when I was with the Arthrose.'

'You didn't tell me,' Pennie was not impressed.

'It's a form, admitting Princess Antobathia to the camps.'

Pennie looked at her speechless. Since the camps had fallen information had started flooding out about what went on.

Pennie looked serious, 'I wish you had told me earlier.'

Saranon changed the subject, 'I always thought you were suited to the army.'

'Thank you,' Pennie replied in a flat tone.

'So when were you going to tell me?' She asked.

'Do you know how much effort I had to go to, just to get this far?' Pennie raised her voice and Saranon laughed.

Something was gnawing at the edges of her mind it would not let her be and for once it was not the army. It was different to Ollanthia, but it called her just the same. She reached out and it grabbed hold of her even more. She slipped through the walls of the building. It was a smaller Keep than Ollanthia, but it was still a Keep and beckoned to her, wanting her to know. As she passed through the inner layers the army would be alerted, it would have to be quick. She was guessing by the trouble the Keep was going to that she needed to find out. Saranon was kneeling below the stronghold. She waited in the area above the central core where the Keep could communicate to a private audience, if it wished.

She had done this before and wondered if this was why the Keep decided to call on her in this way. It was a warning, a dire one and she knew she would have to act fast. Saranon turned to stand up and almost ended up in Jacob's embrace for the second time. Her look caught him off guard. 'I have to leave now, you are in danger if I stay. It was only meant to be a brief visit,' she looked serene and in control.

For a moment Jacob did not say anything, so she continued, 'Look after Pennie, and if anyone asks I am not Saranon. Your Keep says that if you say otherwise it would not bode well.'

Saranon was about to pass him when he spoke, 'How did you know that the Arthrose Councillors were using dark sorcery?'

'I could see their auras' she went to leave and Jacob hugged her, this time she did not go limp.

She looked up into his eyes and saw that he cared. 'Keep in touch,' was all he said before the Keep showed her out.

Fort Grismor had spoken with a firm tone the Arthrose were travelling fast, she had to make good distance and leave no trace. Saranon made her way back to her belongings and found Pennie sitting at the edge of the bed.

She stopped for a moment, and realised that her friend had packed for her. She hugged her old friend. It was too late for a long goodbye and she knew she had to go soon. She stood with her new robes flowing as she left the room. When Saranon walked by everyone stepped aside and let her pass. She strode out under the starlight in the cool still night. Her heart belonged in Darkonia as she glanced back, hoping this time would not be the last to set eyes upon her homeland.

CHAPTER FIVE

The path to the Summer House

The winds stirred over the damp grass, it was morning and Saranon made her way forward. As she lifted her weight from either foot and strode on. She had managed to pass through the skirmish at the border. She was trying to read the map that Pennie had given her, as the wind flicked at the edges in a playful dance. If the map was right, it would lead her east to a place called the Summer House. The home of Lady Ammera Alvere, a wise sorceress, who helped people on their path. Saranon did not exactly know what her path was, but it sounded like a good first step in this new land. The long winter had taken its toll, she did not have far to go and set up camp for the night in amongst the rocky base of the mountain range.

Pennie had packed plenty of food but she need not have as she was able to look after herself. If she had to buy anything she was good at finding discarded coins and the ground along the border was littered with them. It was not the most glamorous use of sorcery but practical. She used a few sova bags to carry her belongings, including Tellembre, in a small pouch attached to her belt, which also held her talik tucked to the side. She unpacked a sleeping bag and settled in for the night underneath the stars. The fine lines in the earth vibrated and Saranon opened her eyes. It was still dark whatever was coming this way was moving too slow for sorcery.

She stuffed her sleeping bag away and gazed around to see if she could find anything. If someone came across her she had dressed like an experienced traveller. It was uncommon for people to travel in these parts. The large game would rotate throughout the year in an attempt to get away from the local dragons. Saranon moved to take a look, she did not want to be caught off guard, even if it turned out to be nothing. She walked down and straight into the commotion before she realised. They had not noticed yet and she wondered for a moment what would be the best approach. A gruff deep voice said, 'I could have sworn one of them came this way.'

Saranon realised what a fool she had been, they had picked up her use of sorcery. She only knew one approach and that was to dive right in, 'One what?'

She was standing near the middle of the group and they all took a step back as a man made a light sphere so that they could all see. 'Is there any reason for disturbing my sleep?' She continued.

Jameson ignored Saranon's question, 'What are you doing here?'

Saranon produced a passport and permission form granting leave from Darkonia. 'Your outpost was receiving too much attention, so I was going to check in at the Summer House,' she answered.

She thanked Pennie for her smart thinking, her old friend knew she would attract trouble. Riddley looked over Jameson's shoulder astonished. 'You could have come back afterwards, instead of walking through,' he stated.

'That's not my thing,' Saranon tucked her papers away.

The sun was starting to come up and Riddley spoke, 'Well if you're going to the Summer House then you won't mind accompanying us.'

'Much appreciated, I'm terrible at reading maps,' Saranon said before anyone else could get a word in, 'Which is the best way?'

Jameson was not too sure about this, 'First we have to get our belongings.'

She followed the group back to their camp there were twenty in all. She found a couple of mazette dragons to play with and was so wrapped up in the tiny creatures that she just caught the tail end of an argument. The wizards were unsure whether they should travel with her to the Summer House. 'If it's too much trouble I can go by myself,' Saranon said. She walked toward them with one small dragon on her head; one crouched in arm and another on her shoulder taunting the one on her head.

The mazettes were the size of a medium scale birds

and quick to frighten. The sight drew the attention of the soldiers. She wondered what they were all staring at and looked behind her. She could be slow to catch on and was not amused. Jameson decided that they would go with her and she climbed up on an extra horse. Saranon could not think of anything to say, which made the first half of the journey uncomfortable. Every now and then she would catch one of soldiers staring at her and started to wonder what she had gotten herself into.

'So which part of Darkonia are you from?' Jameson said trying to make polite conversation.

'From the north, then I moved around a lot,' she answered. Saranon only had several weeks to get to know Darkonia and she hoped that she was not going to be quizzed.

'What do you plan to do in Alveron?' he asked.

That was a good question she had not thought of and said the first thing that came to mind, 'I was going to meet the Lady Alvere.'

Jameson shook his head in response. She did not know what to say and the rest of the journey hung in a strained silence.

Saranon could see the gates that marked the Summer House up ahead, she had read descriptions of the place from the library at Felgrai. She became nervous, not knowing how the Lady would receive her. It struck her that this was not her homeland as she felt small. Two large stone walls with no actual gate marked the entrance into the grounds of the Summer House. The group rode in on the horses which were beginning to lag, it was a good time for them to rest. She held her emotions in as they led her inside the building. She felt more when she heard Riddley talking with the guard and finding out that she was not expected. The house stood on a small yet powerful Keep, which meant if anything happened she would have an advantage.

An aide came and stated that the Lady Alvere would see Saranon. She did not have a chance to rest and followed the aide into a grand hall. Lady Alvere sat on an elevated platform at the opposite end. The last rays of light filtered through the windows and the light spheres on the walls began to glow as it faded. She walked forward to see Lady Alvere sitting in a clam stance with her eyes closed. The Lady opened them and stared, 'Is this how you plan to take Alveron, too cowardly to show yourself?'

Saranon was stunned, but the Lady continued as she stood close. 'You hide amongst our soldiers, is this how Darkonia takes what it wants?' Lady Alvere demanded.

Saranon was confused, she could not understand. Then it occurred to her that the Lady must think she was connected to the group that had fought at the border, 'I am not with the razen.'

'Of course you are not,' Lady Alvere spat the words out in haste. 'Now that you have the Summer House you will take everything else for your King.'

'No,' Saranon was aghast.

'You cannot fool me!' Lady Alvere shouted.

'I am not. I came here for your guidance.' Saranon's anger showed this was not what she had expected.

She walked away closing the door behind her. She could not go back so instead she found her way down to a small garden, and sat on the bench. What did Lady Alvere mean about taking the Summer House, it did not make sense. Pennie would have known what to do? She looked down at the marks on her hands, and took her jacket off. She stared at the fire mark on her right shoulder, the symbol of the fires of chaos. It had been used by the Arthrose to mark the Issola and a permanent reminder of her childhood. She decided that if Lady Alvere was not going to help, the next task would be to remove the fire mark. She had to find some way of changing the tattoo so it was not an obvious reminder.

Jameson and Riddley felt as though they had just been swept into the middle of a storm. Lady Alvere was so distraught, that Riddley found himself in the unusual position of trying to calm her down. Jameson had gone looking for Saranon and saw the fire mark as she repositioned her jacket. She knew Jameson was there, the Keep told her. She wondered if that was what the Lady had meant 'now that you have the Summer House you will take everything else'. She turned and looked at Jameson who realised that Riddley had sent him on a task far beyond his capability. This had not deterred the experienced soldier before.

He stood in Saranon's way, 'The Arthrose must have trained you well at the camps?'

She felt sick at the memory, 'All I came for was guidance and I was told that you would help.'

'I think you should relinquish the Summer House,' Jameson spoke.

'I haven't got the Keep! I can't relinquish something I don't have!' she exclaimed.

'If the Lady gives you guidance will you go back to Darkonia?'

Saranon stood close, 'I can't I've been exiled.'

Jameson looked into her eyes for a moment. He was a wizard and with one glimpse saw the truth as his stare softened, 'Then you'll need a place to stay.'

'Yes,' she replied.

'Wait here,' with that Jameson left a confused sorceress standing alone in the garden.

Saranon was beginning to wonder if there was a country that would not ridicule her. Jameson came around the corner, 'Lady Alvere will see you now.'

She was about to open her mouth, but thought better of it. She followed the soldier to a drawing room large enough to hold the Lady's personal guards. Lady Alvere continued to glare at her, 'Why would Darkonia exile its most prized possession?'

It took a moment for Saranon to realise that the Lady was referring to her. She thought a moment before she replied, 'Lady Alvere you are the first person I have encountered who does not think I am Issola.'

The Lady laughed, and Saranon did not understand why. 'There have never been Issola.'

'Then may I ask what am I?' Saranon asked.

Lady Alvere took her time she could not convince

herself to believe the girl did not know, 'You are the Angeon.'

Saranon looked puzzled and wondered if Lady Alvere had just made it up. Everyone looked serious, 'I'm sorry, but I don't know what that means.'

Lady Alvere was still unconvinced. 'The Angeon is Darkonia's answer to the Oracle. A sorcerer born with the ability to break down all defences and render a civilisation powerless.'

Saranon thought back to when she broke out of the camp and demolished several others. She had drawn so much energy from the Keep and it had not harmed her. Tasha had known she was unique and took that secret to her grave. She still did not understand. If she was supposed to be a weapon then why was she not like a soldier? It did not make sense.

She went off to bed after a long night. She was exhausted and drifted off to sleep. The Keep hummed away content underneath not minding her presence. The night was filled with strange dreams she kept waking, thinking that people were watching her. She ended up sleeping in the same room as Jameson, the only one brave enough to wake her. They both jumped scaring each other as he shook her shoulder. 'What's wrong with your eyes?' Jameson spoke.

Saranon took a while to focus it felt like she had been in two places at once then came back down to earth. Jameson said, 'It's almost noon.'

'Does Odana mean anything to you?' He did not say anything so Saranon continued, 'It tried to speak to me.'

'You should ask Lady Alvere,' he said with a stern voice.

When she came down to lunch Lady Alvere looked every part the serene figure that Saranon had expected. As they walked in the garden the Lady explained that Odana was an old temple and Keep, located north close to the border with Normisia. Saranon was going to let it be, but Jameson said that it would be a good idea for her to travel to Odana. The nearest place that could offer her proper training was in Serenphel to the far north.

Lady Alvere was polite as she spoke. The Keep sounded talkative so Saranon asked a question and received a reply straight away. No one noticed her brief silence as they walked along. 'Lady Alvere, I am not a threat. This is why the Keep does not react to me.' As Saranon spoke she could tell that was what had been bothering the older sorceress.

Everyone appeared so calm to her and she broke the silence in her clumsy fashion, 'Can you tell me who Odana is?'

Lady Alvere sat down on a stone bench with graceful ease, and she followed. 'Odana is one of the oldest Keeps in the Zyanthian Region and perhaps the largest. Most of his records are gone and we can only estimate his real size. You are not the first Angeon to enquire about Odana he was home for the Angeons of old. Much of our history is lost from the Dreshan Occupation. I cannot tell you what Odana's role in your future will be, nor can I say where it will lead.'

Lady Alvere showed the fear on her face from yesterday.

Saranon found herself thinking that the more she found out the less she realised she knew. It turned out that the people with the most information about the Angeon were the Armythral in Serenphel. A mighty organisation made up by some of the most powerful sorcerers in the region and the world. They preferred not to get entangled in the affairs of other sorcerer clans. Yet the Lady insisted on contacting them. Jameson knew the Summer House well and showed her around. It was reaching the end of winter and in amongst the strange land she began to realise how much she had missed.

At dusk Saranon left the house and crouched under an old tree in the garden. She managed to pick up a signal from the Keep strong enough to dial using her talik. She waited as the thin cool breeze played along her cheeks and fingertips. She almost dropped the device when a signal returned. She placed it on the ground and listened to the familiar sound of Pennie's voice. Telling her what had happened in the short time she was gone. She leaned her head back against the trunk of the tree. Her friend had not heard of the Angeon, but Pennie knew how to find out. Saranon trusted her old friend more than anyone else. Pennie wanted to know what Alveron was like, and started giving advice about a country which she had not seen.

Long after the call had ended, she sat with her eyes closed almost motionless. She could sense Jameson close by and gave no sign of recognition. She walked up to him, startling the man as he said, 'You're a long time out here?' He remarked.

'Has Lady Alvere made contact with the Armythral yet?' She asked.

'Yes, but they do not believe her. The Lady asked me to look for you,' he replied.

She sprinted back to the house, rushing into a circular room where Lady Alvere had opened a doorway to the Armythral. Saranon had seen projected images of people before, but not up close. They looked real and she forgot they could see her as well when she stood close to get a better look. Ryan looked back just as curious; his years of experience told him what he was looking at. Yet there had been no Angeon in Zyanthia since the Dreshan Occupation ended over 200 years ago. The Armythral had almost thought the gene wiped out, or so diluted that it would not produce another. He looked at Saranon, 'You will go to Odana.'

Lady Alvere showed concern, 'Ah you sure that is wise, you are asking something that we do not know the answer to.'

'Odana will be fine, he will know what to do, if she stays here it may attract attention,' he replied.

'I think she already has,' the Lady commented.

'I was referring to something else,' Ryan added.

'You can go now Saranon,' the Lady motioned for her to leave.

With that she left Lady Alvere with Ryan and his colleagues. She was not interested, after talking with Pennie she felt a bit home sick and Ryan would take her further away. She was beginning to wonder if this was such a good idea. She could see Jameson and Riddley with the others preparing to leave the Summer House. It was a beautiful old building rising above the trees in a quiet part of the forest, away from civilisation. It had served her well, but she was itching to move on. The Keep had told her about Alveron. She was quite comfortable letting Lady Alvere feel as though she was in control of the situation. The Lady had been quite clear about Saranon's travel arrangements which suited her. It was the quickest path to Serenphel in the far north.

She only half believed Ryan and Lady Alvere about being the Angeon. She thought of herself as ordinary in the world of sorcery. If it meant an education then she was happy to play along, after all she was not the one who had made the claim. Pennie had not been comforting, and all she had found out was that the bloodline of the Angeon was believed to be dead. This gave her no sign of what the Angeon was meant to be and Saranon did not like not knowing. It had been on her mind and intruded in her sleep. She had heard nothing further from Odana which was just as well. The soldiers were ready to go with their unusual cargo. Jameson took great pride in telling her about the plants and wildlife, as well as Alveron's history.

The landscape was foreign and it was written on her face as they made good pace. She could sense people watching them, a quick glance at Riddley and she could tell he knew who they were. The terrain was a bit drier than what she had seen in Darkonia. A horse was not her normal mode of transport and it felt a little strange. The group pulled off the track to a well-used camp site, as the stars started to arrange themselves in the sky. A fire had already been lit and a man heading towards the group returned Riddley's friendly greeting.

Saranon blended in with the group after having answered enough questions during the day to set the group at ease. Now she sensed a whole new group trying to pick her out. She was sorting out her bed for the night, in one of the tents that had been setup. She could tell two people were standing behind her. She stood up into the harsh stare of man younger and better dressed than Ridley, who was standing close by. Anthony stood tall against the girl, he was higher in authority. She started to wonder if Lady Alvere's words meant anything here. Anthony was from the security forces based at Odana and had been asked to escort Saranon through Alveron. She had the distinct feeling Anthony was not going to be as easy to fool as Max had been. This was not a promising sign for her late night deviations along the lay-lines. He did not look like he was thrilled about the experience either.

After that she stayed close to camp. She hoped that Anthony would keep a comfortable distance. She could feel his eyes staring at her and she was starting to get agitated, but no one seemed to notice. The morning was not much better with Anthony staying close, by now it was obvious Saranon's mood had turned sour. With every step closer to Qwezkin Fort, the nearest Keep, the feeling became stronger. It occurred to her that it was not Anthony that was changing her mood and broke from the party to ride ahead. He kept a close pace and almost drove his horse over the edge when she stopped on a rise. Saranon had lost all focus in her new chaperon to the point where she had become completely still.

She snapped out of her trance with Anthony shouting and holding her. She was not used to being held by anyone and removed herself from the embrace. She stared at Qwezkin Fort as Jameson asked if she was all right. 'I don't think we should go there,' Saranon explained.

'They know we're coming,' he said.

She was not convinced, but she could not pick up anything unusual about the Keep and carried on. Anthony appeared to lose all memory of helping her, and retained his cold façade. The ground changed into lush fields as they entered a small makeshift town surrounding the Keep. The sun had begun to set, and whatever had changed her mood was gone.

The large group entered into what appeared to be the main checking point inside the building. The foyer was on the south-eastern corner and swung around to Odana Temple in the distance. She wandered off and looked through the tall windows. 'Beautiful isn't it?' The voice came from a lady by the name of Jane.

Anthony and Saranon walked up to the platform where a better view could be seen. Up close Qwezkin seemed much larger, with the ground falling to the east showing below where they had entered.

She leaned over, and watched the dragons getting ready to work in the field below. 'What if I am not this

Angeon?' She asked.

'If you travelled to Serenphel the Armythral would be able to tell,' Anthony spoke.

'That's what I thought,' she mused.

Saranon lost herself in thought and the sky turned into night. She ran down the stairs, holding her left hand out to the wall of the Keep. It took her a moment to realise she was not getting any response. Then Qwezkin was the type of Keep that may not want to say anything. Before she went to bed that night it occurred to her that she should thank Anthony. While looking through her items she found a small protection charm she had made at Ollanthia and offered it in gratitude. He held the small piece in his hand unsure of what to say. He said a curt thank you, with that she drifted off to sleep.

CHAPTER SIX

An uneasy secret at Qwezkin Fort

Saranon woke while it was still dark, she knew she had to act fast. She was careful not to make a sound as she slipped out. According to the Summer House the library was downward and that was where she was heading. It was away from the main areas occupied by the Alveronian Army. Her palms were beginning to sweat as she touched the wall, she was almost there. The side door had several seals on it which faded in her grip and rearranged themselves so that she could enter. The smell was stale as she tiptoed over to an alcove and opened the locked door. She found what she was looking for, just a hand full of books on the Angeon. She did not have time so she held the talik over the books and copied the information which seemed to take for ever. Saranon hoped that the image she had left would be enough to fool Anthony into thinking she was still in bed.

She was heading through the main room when she heard a noise and darted out. In the hallway the air was crisp from a sudden drop in temperature. She touched the wall and felt nothing, all she could sense was silence. Then just as she raised her fingertips a jolt went through her and she was no longer Saranon. She ran following the source of the void, her glowing eyes were enough to keep people from hindering her path. She moved downward through the wall, and straight into danger. Her bond-breaker slashed through three dark sorcerers before the others had time to react. She glided between the sorcerers as they formed around her.

Before she had a chance to strike again, they had begun an attempt to leach her dry of her sorcery. It swelled up and out, ripping them apart and they tried to stop. Qwezkin's thoughts entered her head in a flood. The walls moved as the Keep latched onto her tormentors and sucked their screaming bodies into the Keep. Saranon realised there were people around her screaming and shouting. In the moment she was a fifteen year old girl again and turned to run, thudding straight into Anthony who took her out of the scene. The full impact of what had happened hit her when she saw the wounded, he led her through to a room to be checked.

When she was given the all clear they went back to a small lounge area, where Anthony spoke with his colleagues while she fell asleep. She woke to the smell of scrambled eggs and a hearty breakfast. The Keep sounded less angry, but it was not going to settle down. Saranon sat up and her hands were shaking. He placed her breakfast on a low table then saw the marks on the palms of her hands. 'Where did you get those?'

She realised she had forgotten to cover them up, 'The Arroada gave them to me.'

Harold was a big man who looked like he had just come from working on the Keep. The dirt still stuck to his clothes, as he intruded on the conversation to look at her hands. 'The Armythral won't teach you now. Those marks are given to a sorcerer who has completed more than just the basic training.'

Saranon blurted out, 'But I haven't had any training.'

She realised how naïve she had been. She began to feel sick as it dawned on her that the Arroada had stopped her from training elsewhere.

She stood up and barged her way out. She needed some space and the Keep was not leaving her alone. She heard Anthony in the background. She decided that if she helped the Keep at least she could get time to think, with that she vanished into the wall. Her anger matched the Keep's, as she realised she had come so close, only to have what she wanted taken away. The room fell down into the depths of the Keep far below the ground. Saranon knew Harold spoke true as she sat down resting her head on her knees, crying silent tears that only Qwezkin could hear.

The low hum of the central core started to reveal itself in the background and she stepped out wiping the tears from her face. She had submerged once before and had found the experience quite scary, as she did not like large volumes of water. This time she was filled with anger and the water surrounded her with a cool relief on her burning temper. Then she sank her head beneath and the transformation was complete. Saranon did not believe in mermaids, but if she had to describe her appearance unfortunately this fairy tale would be a close fit. In this form she could build up speed and go to low depths as Qwezkin lit the way. The Keep did not want the Darkonian to get lost any more than she did.

She followed the old lines down and saw the start of the chamber where one of the transit stations lay. She popped her head up above the water and moved at a swift pace. The ceiling, walls and part of the station were caked in gunk. This was where someone's dumped material had ended up. Saranon had seen this sort of thing before and was not afraid to tackle the problem head on with Qwezkin's guidance. She began to wonder if she did need training and the old Alveronian Keep scoffed at such a notion. The work went on for far too long, but at the same time it finished far too fast. She would have to go up and face reality, so she stopped awhile to admire her handy work. It was not the best job in the world, but it would do, and Qwezkin seemed to be satisfied. She asked the Keep a question and it answered while she left the hidden chamber behind.

Saranon had lost four days, she had food, so the time had not worried her. It was night time, and she was about to get ready to curl up into her bed to sleep. Anthony entered, he was smiling, 'There you are, come down and have some dinner.'

He told her that they had been looking for her until Harold realised that she was helping the Keep. 'I needed some time to think,' Saranon said in a calm tone.

He took her answer in his stride. She wondered if it would have made any difference had she said she had been plotting the end of the world. Then she thought better of it, with everything that had happened Anthony may not have taken it so well.

She stopped in the corridor, and the voices in the background seemed to fade away. 'Anthony, I was exiled from Darkonia for executing the Arthrose Council.'

He looked at her, 'I know.'

It was an awkward moment, but it seemed right to say it. Saranon's shoulders slumped down in relief as her body exhaled its secret. She relaxed in the large room with two crackling fires, one at either end warming up the thick stone walls. The scene was filled with the hub of casual conversations. The voices rose in snippets, floating up to her ears, broken by the occasional sound of laughter. She stayed for a while before the tiredness of the last few days flowed down her limbs and went off to a warm cosy bed.

The Keep had gone quiet again, but that was okay. She had the answer she wanted, and she was keen to go off on an adventure. Odana Temple, the beautiful old building lunged up through the walls of the mountain. It marked the corner stone of Darkonia, Normisia and Alveron. The Keep was some distance away, yet his presence was awe inspiring, and it captivated her. Anthony for all his experience, had not had to babysit an Angeon before and she was about to take full advantage of this. The open plain was too obvious so she headed down. There were a few old tunnels linking Qwezkin to Odana which were dangerous for the ordinary person.

Saranon saw this as an open invitation, after all, she had grown up in camps and all that hardship had to be of some use. She covered the great distance with ease, the tunnels were much quicker. She clambered up into one of the main chambers, its ancient columns reaching high above in a circular fashion. Her eyes continued straight up above and she felt her talik buzzing. With a sigh she picked it up and wondered if her life was ever meant to be peaceful. She looked down at her talik; it was downloading a massive amount of data at a fast rate. She could see the living energy of Odana in her peripheral vision it was much stronger than anything she had come across.

The groaning and creaking of the old Keep gave a strange, eerie sensation that tingled down her spine and made her hands quiver. She looked around still holding the talik in her hand, glancing at the shadows that moved in an unnatural fashion. The floor had been carved in some long forgotten pattern which made its way up to the tall ceiling. There were signs of grand images that had once detailed the walls, the only hint of colour stuck deep in the odd crevice. Saranon thought it was odd to find no dust, the air was fresh and apart from its age, the chamber was clean. She held her hand up against the wall. It felt warm with a distant dull hum which flowed through her fingers holding her in a trance. She felt someone touch her shoulders and she jumped, when she turned there was no one there.

She began to wonder if she had made a mistake coming here and turned to leave. She tried to open the door, but it would not budge. Saranon stood back trying to figure out what was going on and hid near a corner behind one of the columns, peering out. She could not sense anything and wondered what was happening. She tried communicating with the Keep, but nothing came back. In an instant the lights came on and it was not the Keep. Saranon knew that was not a good sign. She could feel her heart start to pound in her chest and her palms sweat. She was in another country, but this felt too familiar.

The air began to warm up and she knew she was in trouble as the sensation prickled up her arms. The sound of steps came closer toward her, conflicting with the sound of her heart beat as it beat hard in her chest. The shadows moved around her as they began to blur her vision, and she was pushed into the centre of the chamber by an unseen force. The patterns on the floor moved and she thought she had to be imagining it. She stood up and could almost make out twelve figures around her. She could not make out what they were saying.

Somehow her hearing along with her vision had become distorted and a single thought came to her mind. What if this is what happened to Tasha? She plunged herself down, ripping apart the stone floor with a force beyond all comparison. Her energy tore hard into keep breaking and melting the floor away with the steady impact. The Keep relented in agony and she fell into the darkness below. She could hear the boom of the floor breaking behind her and then she saw a strange glow that headed towards her like a sprawling web. Then something grabbed her and pulled her down so fast that everything became a blur.

She fell into a peaceful trance, somehow whatever had hold of her, felt comforting and much safer than the people in the chamber. Saranon kept on heading downward and wondered if it would ever stop. Tiny shards of reality started filtering through, whatever was above her had started catching up. She looked up to an awesome sight, made up of something that resembled an elaborate glowing spider web. The furtherest tendrils of the web shot out toward her. Its tiniest points fast trying to grasp the girl, her body jarred with the sensation of pain poised on the tips of the web. Her energy rang out with one final blast, disintegrating the edges as the web recoiled. It broke and shattered as it hit the edges of the tunnel.

The air grew warm and something deep beneath her rose up around, she could see the end of the tendrils begin to curl away. A giant dull hum spread out around her and the falling sensation along with the pain had gone. In all the turmoil she had closed her eyes. She held out her hands and felt around to get up, she realised there was nothing beneath her. In a state of shock she opened her eyes and found herself floating near the top of a massive underground chamber. Its spherical walls loomed down in the darkness extending off into nowhere. For some unknown reason the ancient walls had not heard about a little thing called gravity. The sparks of light crackled every now and then, from the grey clouds swirling in the depths below.

Odana had lived for 1227 years and for a small moment the Angeon saw him or thought she did. In the glimmer of the depths below in the midst of the whirlpool raging like a thunderous storm, its mass had revealed itself above. While keeping the swirling matter trapped beneath its grasp and then as just as it appeared, it had gone. Saranon's mind was overloading with the impossibility of what she saw, it had to be a dream that was the only way she could explain it. The age old core hurled an invisible force upward and hurled her back to the world of humans.

In the darkness that followed all Saranon could sense was the energy of the Keep, as it lifted her up with a might she could not comprehend. She held her eyes closed, not wanting to see where she was, but she knew she had to. She glimpsed the last remnant of Odana's work as he melded the floor back in place. The chamber appeared empty, as though nothing had happened. She stumbled as she tried to move, falling back onto the floor as she rolled over and stared up at the ceiling. It reached on forever in the darkness of the great chamber, as she peered up the shadows moved as though taunting her from a distance.

She was too exhausted to move as every muscle in her body ached and her head spun. The creaking sounds of the great Keep filled the emptiness, not letting her rest. Something brushed against her skin, but when she turned her head, nothing was there. An echo rang out from the distance, carrying voices with it as the sounds edged closer.

Saranon could sense the wizards approaching, but she was too exhausted to shout, as no sound came out. She never thought she would be so glad to see them, and managed a smile before falling into a deep slumber.

She was held in a troubled sleep. It stretched just underneath the surface of her consciousness. Her mind overloading with images of the great darkness and what lay beneath. Every time she tried to focus the image kept returning to the sensation of falling. She held out her hand to grab hold and this time she clutched something real. All at once her senses reacted and brought her back to reality. Saranon found herself gripping Anthony's jacket in clenched fists. As she realised what she had done he embraced her tight to his chest, not wanting to let go. She had the sudden thought that hugging a wizard was not the safest thing to do and ended the union. Anthony did not seem fazed.

It seemed like everyone had known what had happened except her. For the first time she saw members of the Mercidian Council, the Alveronian counterpart for the Arthrose. Lady Alvere had been the first sorceress she had come across in this strange harsh environment along the other side of the border. Saranon ached from her ordeal, as she stumbled around she realised there was something missing. She looked down at her hands and the marks were gone. Their meaning still remained a mystery. They had made her feel uncomfortable and for some strange reason she knew that they were wrong.

'Hello there,' a friendly warm voice spoke belonging

to Clara who was not much older than herself. 'I hear we missed the excitement.'

Saranon looked around to see a mass of bright red hair attached to Clara, the daughter of Flynn. Flynn was a gruff old man with a friendly smile, which Clara had inherited. Clara was more than happy to explain what had happened, as the two made their way around the commotion. They sat down on one of the large window openings, wide enough to sit on, and look out into the beautiful landscape. She was still feeling a bit queasy, and the story from Clara was not making her feel any better.

'The sorcerer clan believe they deserve a claim on several Keeps because they descend from the Otturin. They have been trying to reignite something which already exists within the Keep.'

Clara stopped to pause, 'Do you remember anything?'

'I remember being in the chamber. Then pounding, like huge continuous blows. I was trying to get away and then I fell.' Saranon shrugged her shoulders and sighed looking out the window.

Even though there was plenty of work going on around them, there was not much they could do. She did not feel like running off, she was completely exhausted and it was not fun anymore. She had gone along treating everything like one big adventure, which had been fine until this had happened. She looked around and even Anthony was oblivious to her presence which was far from the truth. The great old Keep creaked and groaned like an old fortress made by many hands rather than by sorcery, one of the signs giving away its age. In the end all things had to die. It seemed like a horrible thought, thinking back about Tasha. Clara was happy to do all the talking, which was fine, as her head still ached from the fall.

Her ears pricked up when Clara referred to the Regent, 'A what?' Saranon asked.

'A Regent, silly me I forgot. You don't have one of those in your country,' Clara was being cheeky.

This started a new conversation, as the day aged she could feel a cold change sweep across Odana. With the cooling of the air she shrugged it off. Clara had since gone with Flynn and she was left to her own devices, she had not gone far trying to blend into the busy background. Saranon was watching the tenants of the Keep, which included the army operating the big old Keep from small screens. The room looked somewhat like a platform of vibrant activity, with people worrying about things she did not understand.

A light from the corner of her eye caught her attention and she peered down. She had chosen a seat in the corner near a bench, but now it had a small light on it. She was filled with curiosity, 'Anthony, what's that?'

He came over, leaning over her shoulder. Without looking she sensed something was wrong. 'I'll let Riddley know,' he started walking away and added, 'Don't touch the…'

Saranon had her finger on the little light, and the whole bench flickered into life with strange symbols. Then she saw it.

She could understand, right in the middle, she placed

her hands near it leaning over. Strange three-dimensional patterns in long continuous streams flittered by before her eyes. The sensation stirred something inside. The word fell out of her mouth, 'Intruders.'

Riddley had managed to pinpoint the breach, he was not impressed. Anthony led her away from the unfolding drama and told her to get some rest. She thought that was rather a contradiction, but went anyway.

After the minor events of that night things went back to a mundane routine in the Keep. Saranon spent time with Clara and a wizard by the name of Derek whom she suspected was filling in for Anthony. Either way, the west was full of old ruins from where the three countries met and had been an empire with its heart in the east. The majestic stones that were fading underneath her feet, made her wonder what the Angeon would have been like back then. The information from the Summer House and Qwezkin had been useful, but it was still a small drop in a deep lake.

She asked, 'If this place was the centre of Zyanthia then would any great vault of knowledge be left?'

'I'm afraid not, the history we have left makes reference to your ancestors, but little more. Any information recorded by the Otturin would have passed to the Shalough, and they do not share.'

'They have chosen to restrict access. You could ask Lady Alvere.' Derek said.

Saranon was not so warm to the idea as the Lady had not exactly been forthcoming. There had been a lack of high level sorcerers in west Alveron and that had been a relief.

It had taken her longer to recover than she thought and she still felt weak, almost as if she were going backwards. The day had been long and her bones ached from a journey that should not have given her any worry. During the night her dreams haunted her, as they had since the incident. She could see herself falling, being dragged below. Then she was floating she opened her eyes only this time was different. By the thinnest thread she used all her strength to break through. At first she could hear herself screaming, then her consciousness caught up and she was gasping for breath. She remembered and her body reeled in shock. She tried to move and someone was holding her tight it took her a moment to realise. Saranon stopped screaming, but could not cope, 'I can't…' she gulped, 'I can't handle it.'

Anthony managed to hold her down until she sobbed, the commotion had woken Clara and Flynn's voice, told her to stay away. Flynn waited until she had calmed a little. 'If you do that again there will be serious consequences.' Flynn said.

'I saw the central core,' Saranon whispered.

The room fell silent. Flynn leaned down and in a gesture of kindness kissed her on the head. Her body was exhausted and out of need more than anything, she slipped back into sleep.

Her memories had rearranged themselves in the right place, Clara stayed close by her side. Saranon had spent most of yesterday down in the medical centre, only to find out the best thing was to do nothing. She was just going to have deal with it on her own. After growing up in the camps that was not a huge problem. She had the impression that if she had been anyone else, they would have bent over backwards to help. In a way she could understand fearing the unknown. The amount of energy she had let off in the Keep had been hidden by the central core from the outside world.

Anyone inside the Keep who could sense sorcery had noticed. Saranon laughed as she still saw strange looks as she strode by, she was not going to be able to hide in the corner anymore. Flynn had apologised, but in the same sentence he managed to make it clear that doing that sort of thing in the west was not appropriate. Odana lay close to two borders, Darkonia to the west and Normisia to the north. When she closed her eyes all she saw was the image. She had tried telling Clara, but the words would not come out. So she stayed in limbo waiting for the shock of it all to pass.

CHAPTER SEVEN

Odana Temple

The winds swept around the mountainside making hollow remarks. It rumbled down the massive air vents and into the body of the Keep. The structure was a fine-tuned mechanism with an almost seamless operation. A repair crew was sent down to fix the latest damage from intruders, who had managed to wreck some of the cabling, leading to the lower systems on the eastern side. The outer doors to the area were still working and had been locked. The Keep lay close to the border and this made it difficult to deal with breaches. Too much energy would draw the wrong sort of attention.

Still the occupants had become quite innovative; Saranon could not help but be impressed. The bulk of the Keep was well hidden in the mountain range and went unnoticed. There was a sense of urgency about getting the repairs done and she could see that they were not going well. Derek being younger had been put to the task of carrying tools backwards and forwards. The repair crew was so busy that at times they had almost asked her by mistake. For some reason asking, her was not considered appropriate and she did not question why. By the end of a hot day in the confines of the Keep, a couple of the crew showed their frustration. Their efforts had not gone as well as they had hoped.

The whole sense of formality had gone a few hours ago and it was starting to get late. Clara was talking to Shaun who was leading the repairs. This time he was a little calmer. Clara came over and said 'The area near ground level on the eastern side is down, which means we won't know if there is another attack. How do you feel about a long night?'

Saranon did not answer for a while, she felt like she was missing something and she was not the only one who could sense it. She knew what Clara meant, ever since she remembered the central core. There had been questions on how much access she had to the Keep.

In the sorcerer community it was like striking gold, but she did not see it that way. If she did have a higher level of access, then she was obligated to be careful how she used it. She felt like she was being coerced, but a breach of this scale was serious. The Keep would want it fixed, 'I'll have a look that's all.'

Clara restrained her excitement and Saranon wondered what she had gotten herself into.

The time had become late and with part of the Keep down, except for basic functions, the building took on an eerie feeling. In the silence the wind could be heard gusting down the large vents placing everyone on edge. There was a small tapping noise, Shaun cautioned Derek who replied under his breath, 'That wasn't me.'

She could see Shaun motion with his hands giving out orders, she had two choices stay in this world or step back into the other.

She called Clara close and unwrapped the jet black bond-breaker Odayour, the twin of the one she had given Pennie. It remained stable in the form of a small dagger. She passed it to Clara who for a moment did not understand, 'I made it, take it and go back, it's yours.'

'This is too much I can't,' Clara held it with such care. Anyone would have thought Saranon had given her much more than just a small homemade artefact.

Clara tried to hand it back, and Saranon reached out to stop her, 'I made it, I get to choose. It stays with you, now go.'

Derek stayed behind, he was too young for this, but then so was she. She tried to turn, but something was holding her back and she grunted in shear frustration. Then a thought entered her head and she leaned over near Derek, 'I want you to hit me.'

'What?' Derek looked puzzled.

She rolled her eyes before explaining, 'I meant wizardry, not your fist.'

He understood, but was not looking too keen on

the idea. He did not seem in a hurry to oblige so Saranon started walking toward Shaun. A searing pain thumped the breath out of her chest, she wanted to laugh and cry at the same time. She crumpled to the ground clenching her muscles and holding back a scream that pounded inside her head.

By now the area was filling with people who were positioning themselves to guard the area for the night. In the middle of this she transformed into her true self. Hundreds of voices flittered through her head which had been recorded in the walls of the Keep. She tried to contain the pressure. It was almost an invisible struggle in the darkness, but Saranon knew she had to let someone else in. Between clenched jaws she managed to call Shaun over, who was still trying to work by the small illuminated lights. She could not explain and hoped that the experienced wizard would understand. She translated the images and transferred them across through his skin in a painless process. The weight of it all was beginning to show.

Shaun held her and from somewhere she could hear him say 'let go'. The pressure turned off like a tap and she lay for a moment on the ground. Shaun checked her eyes, 'Be careful who you show that to.'

Then he engulfed himself in his work and the rest of his crew worked hard to get the area back on line. The work was going well. She sat near Derek who had apologised for getting a little too enthusiastic with the amount of force he had used. He became more relaxed and the two spoke as the others worked on around them. The power was restored with the growing flicker down the hall as the light came on. The pleasant sound of the equipment firing up filled everyone with a sense of relief.

Saranon went over to congratulate Shaun, when she noticed a small light on the control panel over his shoulder. She had seen it before and her puzzled expression caused Shaun to turn. 'Oh!' He signalled to the others.

For a moment she was expecting him to shout in frustration. Instead everyone around her flew into motion. Derek called her over and she stayed down close by. She could make out Anthony up ahead and she wondered why Flynn was not present. That thought faded as it dawned on her what the strange looking light had meant.

By now it was obvious Derek had been left behind to baby-sit as she let out a frustrated sigh. Saranon's senses were still prickling from the energy that had glowed so bright inside her. She turned to face him, 'Sorry Derek.'

Time was running thin as she melted into the background before Derek's eyes. The smell came to her first, the horrible stench of failure wafting up to her nose, crisp and sharp. A soldier lay wounded near her on the floor, but he knew not to make a sound.

She was further down at ground level the most vulnerable area. There were a few shouts from around the corner, but wizards preferred not to make noise so the shouting meant it was getting ugly. The intense energy raging nearby acted like an invisible door that had slammed shut. As she approached, the images which had crammed her head trickled into place. The small drops of reality washed away her fear. Saranon stepped through the haze as she noticed Clara, and tapped her on the shoulder. The two exchanged silent words and Clara followed her forward.

She could not help thinking that they were much alike. She knew the next motion had to be fluid and the adrenalin rushed through her relaxed poise as she ran out into the open area. Charging through the mass of soldiers, she could see Anthony ahead as he fell. She launched herself up behind him stomping his body to the ground. Tellembre in all its glory flexed into the great sword that she had made in chambers below Ollanthia. The blade sliced like a steaming knife into Anthony's attacker turning the sorcerer to dust. She landed on top of the ashes, her nostrils flared with excitement.

Saranon could sense the other attackers getting away. She stormed after them leaving Anthony and Clara behind. The two remaining attackers went down before they had made it outside. The thrill rushed through her veins and she realised it was the Keep's emotions she was sensing. She went back to find Clara looking at the markings on a sorcerer they had managed to capture. By the look on the soldiers who held their captive down, Saranon knew the sorcerer was going to pay a high price for his deeds. The mess was cleared up. As she learned that the Mercidian had been told not to intervene because it had been considered an 'ordinary' matter.

Flynn came down to meet them and hugged both girls the man was like a gentle giant, 'Enough excitement for you two!'

Sorcerers attacking were Mercidian territory. Flynn got straight into assessing the whole situation. Flynn had a lot of questions for her, but at no stage did he raise his voice or chastise her for what she had done. Eight soldiers had lost their lives in a small community that hit many hard and that knowledge lay behind Flynn's silent gaze. Saranon clambered up into the main area and could still feel the thrill of the Keep as she closed her eyes and went to sleep.

Eight dead was not normal for an internal conflict and it reflected the Mercidian's mistake. Flynn was trying to make the best out of a bad situation while doing his job. The girls had been allowed to talk about their ordeal and this helped ease some of the tension within the Keep. Saranon went to see Anthony who was recovering to find him chatting away with several friends. She sat lost for words, and Anthony placed his arm around her. It was hard to see him like that, knowing that she had stomped on him as well did not help.

In the silence of the wizard's embrace she heard him, Odana in the background whispering to her. Anthony's facial expression changed it was as though he heard the whispering too, they're coming. It was a soft spoken voice, but Saranon knew what it meant. She was too close to Darkonia and with the recent events it would be easy to know where she was. She did not want to leave, but deep down she knew she had stayed too long. Anthony saw the look in her eyes, 'You have to go, don't you?'

'Yes,' she replied.

He reached into a little draw beside him. He produced

a small wallet containing an Alveronian passport, 'You might need this.'

She was speechless and she thought to herself perhaps she should tread on wizards more often. The gift was much appreciated and she admired it for ages turning it backwards and forwards. It was held in a small suede wallet, died purple for the colour of Alveron, with a tiny silver clasp which closed together. Shaun who had been sitting close by spoke, 'When things calm down we hope to see you back this way.'

'Definitely,' Saranon responded with gratitude.

The afternoon sun shone in through the small windows high up in the long room as Saranon made an effort to enter in silence. A few coughs broke the air as she stood to the rear of the gathering, as the wizards said their final goodbyes to their fallen comrades. The funeral went on as she sighed underneath her breath with a heavy tone. The atmosphere weighed on her as the funeral gave a fitting end to those who had been lost. It brought home to her the reality of her own struggle.

Flynn explained to Saranon that Clara was so excited over having her own bond-breaker. She had given her new friend a massive status symbol. Now was perhaps not the time to tell Flynn that she had made another while at Odana Temple. She headed back to her room and Clara helped her pack with an enthusiasm that amazed her. Her friend advised her with great confidence on what to expect while travelling north. The Pendelon Plains were arid except along the Cravese mountain range. It was best to follow this to the north then go up through Magladen to Balquene.

The first part of her journey was filled with small farming towns. These were inhabited by wiccan and ordinary folk alike. The wiccan community were reasonable people and as long as she did not try to hide or cause trouble, they would be no trouble to her. Saranon had little to do with wiccan and was not as confident as her new friend.

Flynn became nervous even though the border was a short distance away. Saranon felt restless and so did the Keep, she did not understand what all the fuss was about. It seemed so simple, there was the border she would cross it and be on her merry way. Outside the sky was grey and murky the wind rippled through her cloak, as the weather reflected her inner frustration. A dark sullen mood caressed her fingertips as she held onto the outer wall, moving further down to her heart. The wind swept up over the lookout near the top of the Keep, blasting ice cold air across her face.

Saranon could feel the central core whirring deep below, Odana felt it and so did she. In a calm stance she turned to Flynn who had been gazing out, and spoke, 'You were right.'

Flynn gave her a confused glance, then a big roar shot overhead. In the brief moment that the massive body of the marmoz dragon loomed above, she ran over and pushed Flynn to the ground. It came so close she thought she could see the underneath of its belly. In the dense noise that cluttered the air she said, 'I have to go!'

Flynn nodded.

The next great dragon swung close and this time she clung on yanking herself up, while throwing both dragon and rider off edge. The beast tried to shake her by slamming his hulk against the side of the Keep. Saranon could hear the screams of the rider as he fell, though it was not far. She clung on with her ice cold fingers grasping the soft skin of his belly. The dragon thrust again, this time scraping his leg. In the realisation that the beast had hurt himself, she heaved herself into the saddle. The memories from the old Keep signalled for the dragon to leave. Its great muscular body jumped with immense grace into the air so fast, it took her a moment to realise where she was going.

His path conflicted with the other riders. This caused mounting confusion among the dragons around her. Saranon hoped this would be enough to help Flynn, because she was too scared to stop now. As if sensing her desperation the dragon continued flying into the night. Katholomu flew until he had made his way well across the border, to the south-east of Normisia. He landed in the outskirts of the large city of Dreverdon. The magnificent black dragon drank his fill then curled up in a shallow cave.

Dreverdon was a hub of civilisation where she found she could blend into the background. The busy streets passed her by as she crossed to the other side. Following the lay-lines north she managed to completely bypass several of the smaller towns. She headed into the second largest city Redadere. Her supplies from the markets at Dreverdon had faired her well. Now she had to restock and a nice warm bed was starting to sound good. Saranon found herself walking up to one of the many average looking taverns, and buying a room for the week. The food downstairs though nothing special tasted much better than her cooking and gave her a chance to relax.

Redadere was full of unusual visitors, so she fell right into place. The hard travelling had worn her out and she thought her stay would end up being longer. As she felt the throb of her weary feet underneath the table, she knew that sorcery was not going to fix it. The small bed upstairs was soft and cosy compared to the ground outside and she soon fell into a heavy sleep. Mrs Harper, a nice lady that had seen better years and had not lost her smile, ran the place with her older children helping out. The outer city was made up of swept cobble streets and close-knit buildings. Not the cleanest Saranon had seen, but the people took pride in where they lived.

The seaport brought in a decent turnover that flowed down through the city. The work was not easy, but it kept the city going and made it a vibrant place. As she looked around, it amazed her how a whole mass of people could embrace something so mysterious and unfathomable. The dark swirling green colour peering back from below the dock where she stood, did not appeal to her at all. The map showed no oceans between Redadere and Serenphel. So she could keep her feet planted on dry ground.

The main mode of transport on land was by cart. Not exactly as agile as the misquew and for her using the lay-lines travelling to large distances, was not a problem. The misquew were stubborn and proud. Clara the ever quick thinker had managed a novel way of delivering a message without addressing it to Saranon. It had arrived by mail and by the look on Mrs Harper's face, she was used to strange parcels turning up. The parcel had been addressed to her room number via Mrs Harper. She had spoken to Clara the first day and had taken great care to avoid the call being traced.

Clara wrote that Odana Temple had settled back down, but she should not come back anytime soon. The Shalough sorcerer clan had reacted in a strange manner towards Saranon's presence in Alveron. No one knew why and that was not a good sign. Clara had included a few contact details of people to call. Saranon's last experience while following her friend's advice, had not met with a warm reception. She had been a good friend, and perhaps she would be lucky the second time. She had tried contacting Pennie. Her friend was either too far away, or could not get a direct line back to Darkonia, which meant trying to make contact from a Keep.

The place was littered with small ones and the larger Keeps were well guarded. Walking up and dialling in the talik was not as easy as it sounded. For all its openness the city was well fortified and the port itself had its own complex set of rules. Mrs Harper's daughter Celia was more than happy to get out of her chores by showing Saranon around the city. She felt like she was being let into a strange and enchanting new world, as Celia introduced her around. It was not until she met one of Celia's older friends, a young man by the name of Jedd, the realization dawned on her that they were wiccan.

It was then that she remembered Clara's advice, since she was on her own she had to take care to treat the community with respect. A lone sorceress did not have the luxury of hiding behind a large group. Since she was some sort of anomaly, if she got herself in serious strife she could not count on anyone to come to her rescue. In Jedd's presence she hesitated then let the moment go by. If Saranon was alone in this new world then she would make her own rules and besides she saw no need to be high and mighty. She did not come from an influential background and did not remember much of her past, so there was no need to pretend to be something else.

Though the question had not been asked, she made little attempt to hide herself in amongst the wide variety of people in the city. She had not stood out as being unusual. Soon she realised why Mrs Harper had been so happy to let her go with Celia and smiled. She had been led astray, but not without her consent. Celia and Jedd introduced her to their community. What started out as the odd one or two soon turned into much more. Most of the people were from humble backgrounds. Though she had been isolated from the world at large, hardship was an understood language.

Saranon felt thankful for the fact that she had not been raised among the sorcerers, spread throughout Darkonia. She could not help but sense the irony, and wondered if the Arthrose had ever meant this to be. Celia and Jedd moved around her little room, glancing around at her belongings.

The sova bags included more than she had owned before in her life.

Jedd saw Tellembre fastened in its sheath in the dormant form of a dagger. He held it as he asked, 'This is an elegant piece of craftsmanship, where did you get it?'

Saranon could feel her cheeks growing red, 'I made it.'

Jedd looked at what he held with even more curiosity, 'This type requires skill are you sure?'

'I had some help,' she replied.

Jedd was astounded and she continued, 'I have been told that only a few can make bond-breakers.'

Celia liked the personal treasures that she had found while travelling from Dreverdon. She had grown a habit of collecting lost belongings hidden to other passers-by. Most of the objects were jewellery and small trinkets. Nothing she needed, but the camps had starved her of such fine things and now she found them cluttering up what space she had. Celia fell in love with a few small pieces and without much pleading made them her own. Jedd found Saranon's talik and to her surprise opened the seal unlocking it quicker than she could. He asked, 'This is state of the art how did you get this?'

'My friend Pennie gave it to me so we could keep in touch.'

Jedd played with it in his hands keeping it just out of Saranon's reach. Of course if she wanted to there were other ways of getting it back. Clara had warned her about using sorcery in Normisia.

'You have a lot of information stored in here,' Jedd

looked up at her.

'Yes, but I haven't been able to access most of it.'

Jedd looked as though she had just invited him to a challenge he was happy to accept, 'Leave it with me.'

Before Saranon could say anything the wiccan had pocketed one of her most prized possessions. Although she felt lost without it, Saranon hoped that Jedd would be able to decipher the information, the great old Keep had left behind in the talik. Her own attempts had led her around in circles and she was not one for being patient.

CHAPTER EIGHT

Mrs Harper's Tavern

The night air was warm and thin, with the smell of the ocean wafting in through the window. Tasha's death had left Saranon with a mix of disturbing dreams, which unsettled her senses as she tried to sleep. Her hands opened and closed holding nothing. Somehow the image had stayed with her much longer than any other and filtered through her mind and body. In her dreams she was resting on a stone slab and Tasha was leaning over holding her hand. She looked up into the shell of an old temple with a stream and garden visible from the openings to the side. Tasha had long fawn coloured hair resting on her shoulders, which slipped forward as she spoke; you have to go now you are needed.

She opened her eyes, she was already dressed. The stars outside shone bright as she made her way down the balcony and onto the ground. Her senses spoke to her in a language only she could understand. The weather was warmer this far north of the border, the sea breeze was a welcome gift blowing along her arms. Her senses were more alert than they had been for weeks. Odana had taken its toll, but now she was back to her old self. Saranon felt as though she could waste no time. She dashed across the shadow filled streets dodging the occasional passer-by. Her target was further away on the outskirts, as her silhouette raced through the air without leaving a trace.

Her pace quickened as the energy inside her came to life and ran burning through her system. In that instant she transformed and this time she was in control. Her senses had led her to an older building worn with age, as the first signs of what she was after came floating up to her ears. It pierced through an internal roar from the build up inside. Beautiful and serene the Angeon moved through the wall and down into the chaos below. The screams and sobs from the victims melted into the background noise as Saranon focused on the real reason why she was here. She could feel Tellembre stir underneath her hand, but this time she needed to leave no trace of any bond-breaker. This time it would be for real.

The last few occasions had been haphazard much to her disgust. She had used the time at Odana to concentrate her efforts on accepting what she had become. It had not been easy, then again it never was. The musty smell of sweat stained the air and made her feel queasy inside. This was only a minor distraction as she set sight on her first target.

The thrill made her too excited and again she lost control. Her hold slipped and with that she finished the task with too much haste. She had taken down the main offenders almost in one blow. Her only solace was that this would add more confusion to what had happened to them. She knelt gathering her thoughts in the night air, the victims were free with some injured. Though she could not go back and help them, it was too dangerous.

She cringed at her mistake, it had been an improvement, but still she had failed. It was taking longer than she expected, perhaps she would have to pay more attention to the information from the Summer House. She wanted to have some grasp over her true self before she arrived in Serenphel, so at least she would not be an easy target. The sweat grew cold as it travelled down her spine, and Saranon knew she had to get back. The warm air caked her clothes with sweat and soaked her hair. She thought that the task would be easy, but it turned out to be difficult. She felt her true self taunting her from the shadows, this was not her first encounter, nor would it be her last. Her limbs ached and by the time she made it back, the small bed could not have felt any better.

The first light beaded through the tiny holes frayed in a random pattern over the old curtain. She woke feeling refreshed, with no signs of what had happened during the night. The smells of a most hearty and welcome breakfast wafted up from down-stairs. With that, the previous events were all but forgotten. Saranon was in a deep ponderous thought when the outer world broke her concentration,

Celia came bursting in. By now she had become used to the fact that her room was considered a public space. Celia marvelled in surprise when Saranon was always expecting her spontaneous arrival.

The odd pair had become friends. Celia who had not travelled much was mesmerised by every mundane little detail of Saranon's journey. 'Am I looking at this wrong?' She exclaimed in frustration at the book.

'Of course you are. Sorcerers think of themselves as being different.'

'Then how am I supposed to figure this out, and don't tell me I need to ask a sorcerer.'

Celia held back a laugh, 'I think you need to act like one.'

Saranon looked up from the book, and frowned.

'Yes a bit like that, you find wiccan frustrating.'

'No, but you do party late into the night. I thought that was supposed to be for sleep.'

Celia held her head back in laughter, 'I had about as much sleep as you did!' and gave her a knowing stare.

She hesitated, 'Okay so I'm having a few difficulties.'

'I'm not picking on you. It's just that you saved Jedd's cousin,' Celia replied.

Saranon did not know whether to laugh or cry. 'I hope I'm not being noticed in the sorcerer world.'

'I doubt it, they're only interested when you do something wrong. The problem is they can turn a blind eye far too much,' Celia responded.

Saranon chose to change the subject, 'So how do I act

like a sorcerer?'

This seemed to open up a wide door, as Celia took full advantage of leading her to this particular question. She soon found herself off down the road to where Jedd's Uncle and Aunt lived.

The most esteemed Lord and Lady Karager were proud the owners of Bellington Castle. The grand building was perched on the rise of a small hill overlooking the city. The aged building had a simple splendour which made it stand out from a distance well before they arrived. The place for all its finery was quite welcoming, perhaps because it doubled as a learning centre and was full of life. The long corridors wrapped around the internal courtyard. This opened up to the cool breeze which skimmed along the surface of the pond and kept the atmosphere pleasant. Although the small community pretended not to notice, her presence was felt. She could already feel herself sticking out.

She had not seen so much in Alveron because she had been amongst her own. Now she was aware that she had been blessed in a strange way. It seemed that no matter where she went, as if by luck her path was never blocked, no matter how crowded the place was. This tiny little detail began to annoy her as it prevented her from blending into the background. She was trying hard to be respectful, but it was becoming difficult. Jedd who had joined them could see the frustration on Saranon's face and told her not to worry. They walked up to a small study nestled away to the side of the large lounge area.

Jedd was quite at home here, Celia had explained that Lady Karager was Jedd's mother's sister. Although Jedd's family were not well off that did not bother Lord Karager who welcomed them to work on the estate. Lady Karager and Emily, Jedd's mother were almost inseparable. So no one batted an eyelid when Jedd acted as though he owned the place. The small study was neat with fine yet simple furnishings from the window, she could still see the courtyard below. Jedd was in his element, 'What do you think?'

'Are there that many people here?'

Jedd came over to the window and smiled, 'That's only a small number.'

'I wonder if Indarin in Serenphel will be like this,' she pondered.

'I doubt it your kin make a habit of doing things in a different way. It's a wonder none of them have visited you.'

'I think I know why,' Saranon spoke with a hint of sadness.

Jedd looked at her, 'Being isolated from your own kin is not a good thing.'

Saranon knew what Jedd was referring to and knew that it did not make a difference. The Mercidian, as in Flynn, had left her with an important detail that her centre of learning was internally driven. This meant that it would be easy for her to learn at least nature had blessed her there. 'I'm sure I'll be fine,' she spoke.

Celia who had been quiet for a while, re-joined the conversation, 'He's serious Saranon.'

'So am I,' she spoke a little harsher than she meant to.

Celia gave Jedd a worried look, then Jedd spoke, 'If that is true, which I doubt, then your kin have made a mistake.'

With that the topic turned to Jedd's cousin Reida, who was still recovering from her ordeal that Saranon had rescued her from. The young girl had been injured and her parents had kept most people from seeing her. She wondered what would have happened if she had not been there, then left that thought behind. She could not become weighed down by sentimental things if she was going to be of any use. The most important thing was to figure out how to control her sorcery.

From what she heard Reida had been targeted and Saranon began to wonder if she wanted to know the sorcerers in Normisia at all. Even in her own country the attack had been sorcerer against sorcerer, not sorcerer against wiccan. Somewhere deep down she knew it was not right. It weighed on her mind as she wandered down the long corridors, careful not to bother anyone as she went. For a learning centre for wiccan, the place had an awful lot of information about sorcery, a whole section was devoted to it in the library. She led her fingers along the titles and realised she was looking at the Normisian part. She moved along kneeling down to find the Darkonian section, and found a group she had not heard of before, the Tarquerin.

She sat on the floor turning the pages, and Jedd slouched down, 'You can sit at the table if you like.'

'Oh sorry,' Saranon rummaged through the snippets

of information. 'I haven't come across the Tarquerin.'

'That's not surprising they keep to themselves,' he replied.

She looked up first at Celia then at Jedd 'Celia said you might be able to help.'

'Look a little further along,' he pointed.

She put the book back and then realised she had been staring right at the book she was searching for. The library was the proud home of many complete sets of texts for studying the art of sorcery. She was taken aback by the sheer volume of what she was seeing. She followed the line around the corner to the next lot of shelves. It was amazing, how wiccan managed to get hold of it was another matter. 'How do I know which one to choose?'

'That's the complicated part, I am afraid we don't know,' he commented.

The sudden enthusiasm changed to a hint of annoyance, as she poked her head back around the corner to look at Jedd. She asked, 'Dare I ask the question; how do I find out?'

'Well it's like this…' Jedd began.

'You mean I need to find out on my own,' she sighed.

This was not going well, and Saranon found herself in one of those awkward situations. The two had meant well and to let a sorcerer in this far, by the looks of some of the startled people around her, was quite a privilege. She held back the words she wanted to say and gave herself a moment to relax. 'I'm grateful for you allowing me access' there was a small pause. 'I know it means a lot.'

Celia's face beamed, 'I knew you would understand.'

Saranon felt like someone had opened a big door then slammed it shut in her face. She held back how upset she was, but Jedd could see it in her eyes. Sorcery was a complicated art and learning from the wrong book could be worse than not having studied at all.

She let out a sigh of frustration and resigned herself to being back where she started. The place was a hive of activity and so she let Celia take the lead while her dreams went stale inside. If she could remember her parents she would have somewhere to start, her lack of knowledge would make it all the more difficult. At least there remained a little ray of hope, her experiences would help progress her down the right path only at a much slower pace. Bellington Castle was some way out of normal travel and it was soon growing dark. The skies greyed outside reflecting Saranon's sullen mood. Being amongst so many wiccan felt a little peculiar, but she was in the company of friends. In the small room she shared with Celia she soon fell asleep.

In the early hours of the dark her dreams twisted again from the normal nondescript into a transverse harsh reality. The hollow temple was behind her as she stood near the water's edge. It flowed down with a peaceful tranquillity and somehow she knew not to touch it. This time she followed the stream, and heard a voice behind her. Tasha smiled, which way are you going? Saranon replied, I don't know. Tasha stood beside her and answered, well you had better decide soon the water's getting cold. She looked back, and saw that the stream had begun to freeze. I need to leave, she was thinking of the fact that she had wasted time instead of heading straight to Serenphel. Tasha pointed ahead, no; you need to decide which path you are taking.

In the distance Saranon saw the path fork not once but many times over, travelling in different directions. Some wrapped around each other and others went past the way she came. She half expected Tasha to disappear, but her old friend was still there beside her. Saranon spoke in her dream, why are you helping me? Tasha responded; you are too valuable to us. Saranon smelled a rat, us, who are you? Tasha spoke; you know who we are you hear us calling. Saranon gasped, that's not possible. Deep down she knew, but she had thought it was all her imagination. After all no one else she had come across had admitted to hearing a Keep.

She woke in a cold sweat, Celia was sound asleep in the other bed, so she tried to manoeuvre out of the room. Between hitting her toe while finding her slippers and the creak of the door, she was relieved to see no sign of movement from Celia. She cringed as the old boards on the stairs creaked as she made her way down to the kitchen to get a glass of water. A small light had been left on and she made herself at home. Her ears pricked up as a whimpering sound behind her made her jump. She almost spilled the water and placed the jug down.

The terrified young girl did not speak. Saranon gave her a large glass, half filled with water, which Reida grasped in both hands. Jedd's cousin had bandages hidden underneath her nightie and it reminded her of when she was back at the camps. She failed to understand the reasoning behind such cruel acts. The girl crinkled her sleeve and used it to wipe her mouth. Reida pointed to her bond-breaker. Saranon not thinking anything of it, took the blade out and transformed it into the long sword.

The girl seemed mesmerised. Without uttering a sound Reida reached out and brushed her fingertips across the flat of the blade. The bond-breaker lit up underneath the girls touch. Reida spoke in a soft voice, 'Will I grow up to be like you some day?'

She held back a hint of sadness, 'I think you're special being who you are.'

Reida stepped back and said in a small voice, 'I have to go now.'

With that the girl scampered like a little mouse off into the darkness of the hall and out of sight.

Saranon was not scared of the dark, but it brought back bad memories. Bellington Castle was a peaceful place, but not for her. After all even Celia out of jest, had commented on how unusual it was for a sorcerer to be invited to Bellington Castle. As she walked along she glanced out the window. Her eye caught on a shimmering image of a figure, just noticeable in the landscape behind it. She touched the door handle and her senses prickled. Somehow, she knew not to open it and went back upstairs ducking under the warm covers.

In the morning over breakfast, she told Celia, who listened with serious interest. Her friend talked about the wards protecting the building from intruders. Either way whatever the thing had been, it did not sound friendly. It took a while for Celia to convince her to travel a short distance across the estate to see some of the wildlife. In the end she thought if no one else was worried, then perhaps it was best if she just went with the flow. The scenery was lush and green with plenty of colour from the flower gardens as they made their way into the woodland. It was polite to limit the use of sorcery here, as it could set off wards and traps that Saranon did not want to get tangled up in.

Celia had gone a little further and was almost hidden as she bent down to pick something up she cradled it in her arms. As she walked over, its tail bobbed beneath her forearm, 'Here you go.'

Celia announced as she handed over the creature into Saranon's arms. She was unprepared for the tiny creature. It looked like a miniature dragon that had crossed itself with a multi-coloured parrot. Its beak nuzzled into her arm as it tried to hide, its back legs managed to break free. With a clumsy start it half jumped, and flew away. She was amazed, 'What is it?'

'It's a palafon,' Celia pointed to some hiding in the trees.

They were strange creatures that were just as happy on the ground as in a tree. She had to be careful where she stepped as the little dragons loved hiding in leaves and anything else that lay scattered around. She tried to catch one, at the last minute it jolted and then ran off at a fast pace. Leaving Saranon wondering how Celia had managed to catch one at all. She soon resigned herself to the fact that they preferred to be looked at, as she sat down on the soft grass keeping still. Together they explored the rest of the estate while avoiding the workers and people who had come to study. It was a fine day with most of the occupants and visitors outdoors. Celia had introduced her to many, but she was not good with remembering names. She had the distinct feeling that by the time she left, everyone was going to know her.

In a well-worn field a couple of small groups were gathering and chopping wood. They built two large piles for the nights festivities. By the way Celia and Jedd liked partying it was an integral part of being wiccan. Saranon enjoyed the events because of the wonderful spread of food. At the tavern Mrs Harper and Celia made cooking look easy, but her attempts were rather dull in comparison. Coloured ribbons and cloth were being hung up on poles and nearby branches. Now that she knew what to look for, she noticed a palafon trying to tear a piece of ribbon out of a tree. Celia glanced at the scene and explained, 'They like the bright colours.'

Jedd was helping oversee the arrangements with his mother Emily. She was a beautiful lady with fine features that outshone her ordinary clothes. From what Saranon could hear she also had a decent set of lungs as her voice carried over the band as it practiced. Emily was in the middle of yelling out to two young men who had taken a heavy crate in the wrong direction. Jedd waved from a distance and Emily turned to meet them with a pleasant smile, 'Hello, have you two come to help?'

Before she could answer and say no, Emily butted in. 'There are piles of ribbons and banners over there, if you get started now we'll be finished on time.'

Celia grabbed her arm so they could escape anything else Emily might think of. She was hesitant since she had left the camps, she had no trouble saying no to people and did not like being told what to do. Celia saw the look on her face, 'Come on it'll be fun, besides its better than some of the other jobs she's asked me to do.'

Saranon was still moaning after they had made it to the bottom of the first box. She wondered how in the Zyanthian Region she had managed to find herself decorating. She hung up the colourful pieces of material. When she had left Darkonia, this had not exactly been at the top of her list of things to do.

Celia pranced around as though she had been given the best job in the world, twirling around on her toes as she went. She wondered if this was the real reason why sorcerers rarely came to Bellington Castle. So they could avoid the boring and onerous task of decorating. She was trying hard to remain polite about the whole situation, when a third box was carted along and dumped near the second. She thought to herself, yes this was definitely the reason why sorcerers stayed away. An elderly lady called out to let them know it was afternoon tea. Both girls ran off to the tent where a wonderful array of smells, from fresh baked cakes met them.

Their task was finished and as Emily had predicted, just in time. They rushed back to their rooms to rest a moment before changing. Saranon was not into bright coloured clothing and had to be convinced to wear something different. In the end she settled for somewhere halfway. As the two of them made their way down the stairs, they encountered several performers all made up. She and Celia had to make their way through the maze and out to the fresh air, as the day was turning to dusk. The bonfires in the distance had been lit and the flames were starting to reach their height. The first band for the evening was getting ready. The two girls joined the growing formation of colourful outfits down on the grassy slope. Jedd managed to find them through the crowd and led them over to a good spot, close to the band and the food.

CHAPTER NINE

Celebrating at Bellington Castle

It was difficult to hear over the loud music and Saranon followed Celia's lead toward the outer ring of people to get some fresh air. They both lay down in a crumpled heap, as Celia stretched her arms and legs out in a butterfly motion. Saranon asked 'Does this happen at the end of every week?'

Celia cracked up laughing through her dry voice, 'No, just four times a year at each equinox and solstice. When you return you'll know where to find us.'

She was pondering whether this was good or bad when she could sense Jedd running towards them from the direction of the castle. At first she ignored it, but he seemed to be running fast. She began to get up and Celia saw her puzzled stare. She could see Jedd coming towards them, he plunged down and grabbed Saranon by the arm. She almost toppled to the ground trying to find her step. Without stopping he spoke, 'You have to come, it's important.'

Celia did not want to be left behind and was determined to follow. She became serious, 'What's going on?'

'You have to see,' Jedd answered.

They dashed in a clumsy fashion through the inner courtyard, bypassing a couple of serious figures to enter the main hall. Celia ran in ahead, her shoes crunched the scatterings of shattered glass. Before they had time to enter, the colour had slid out of her cheeks as she let out a gasp. Saranon entered, there were spots of blood on the floor, most of it had missed the rugs.

The cabinet had been broken into, with several objects missing that she had seen when she first came. She walked up and touched the back of the cabinet. It was enough to give her a vague impression of what had happened. She crossed over to the door and walked out into the dark night air. It had been a wonderful evening where, for a while, she had forgotten what she was, but this had brought her slamming back down to reality. Away from the castle she could raise her energy, without setting off the warning systems which protected the place. The fact that these had not worked, made Saranon worry even more, she was beginning to feel uneasy as she ran further away from the castle.

She walked through the scrub with ease, using her energy to quicken her pace. During her stay in Alveron she had learned to hide herself well. A basic process, yet she had much to catch up on. Further ahead she could sense wiccan, but that did not make sense. The prized artefacts had been well protected and wiccan would have detected their own. She crouched as she came closer to where two men and a young boy had taken a moment to rest. The two men were arguing and the bag holding their stolen booty had been left unattended. She thought that it was all too easy and stayed back.

Sitting on the cold ground in the dark she listened to the voices of the two men.

'If Lord Karager finds out we're involved, our clan will be done for.'

'He won't, not with a break in like that. He'll suspect the wizards like old Damon said.'

Saranon had heard about old Damon as he was referred to. In actual fact Damon was not that old. He came from a long line of leaders from the sorcerer community and should not be encouraging the theft of artefacts. She unsheathed her bond-breaker and transformed in silence. She used the dagger to take a peek inside the bag, and found what she suspected a tracking device.

She had little time and used some of the trinkets she had gathered to fill the bag, after she had lifted the artefacts out. As she headed away, she could sense a sorcerer approaching and went into full flight using her energy to run faster. She could feel the panic rise in her chest and before she could think, she saw someone up ahead. She slowed down, but not enough to avoid crashing into Jedd near the perimeter, her heart was still racing fast as they went inside. Lord Karager was waiting with several wiccan talking in hushed voices, which ceased as they entered the room. The artefacts were taken away for safekeeping. The shock of what had happened was still sinking in.

Lord Karager turned to face Saranon, 'You have done us a great service. I ask that you not speak of this again.'

'Damon was trying to set you up,' she blurted out in a rush.

'We know, this is something we must deal with,' he responded.

Even though Lord Karager spoke with a soft tone, his words resonated with strength. It left her in no doubt that he was not one to be crossed. In that moment she felt as though she had just been sidelined and her small triumph meant nothing. Yet this was not her world and she did not want to create problems. She left the small group behind. When she went upstairs she found Celia already asleep, she sat on the bed in the dark and stared out the window. Her head was still churning with the chase and it gave her an uneasy feeling that would not settle.

The sound of the night's activities crept in through the cracks around the glass in the window. Saranon decided that it was a good thing she had not encountered the sorcerer community before. Whatever it was they were up to she did not want to be caught in the middle. As she curled up in bed the events still haunted her. She lay awake for a while before her tired eyes closed, marking the start of a heavy sleep. The morning was a little cool as she and Celia got dressed and raced down the stairs to breakfast.

Unfortunately, they could hear Emily in the background looking for volunteers to clean up. The two sat near a corner so as not to be noticed through the doorway. This was a challenge in itself, as everybody else had the same idea.

As much as Saranon had loved the celebrations of last night, she was itching to have another look at the library. Celia had more important things to do like catch up with her friends. So she found herself in the midst of some peculiar sets of books. Along the way she had picked up a few tricks and now was a perfect time to test one out. It would take her too long to read every single book, even if she managed to copy them. She pulled out a few trinkets from Odana they were small and handy for transferring knowledge. Not quite as complex as a talik, but it would do what Saranon wanted. She glanced over her shoulder, there were a few people in the library, though no one was paying attention to her.

She picked up the first book and held it as though she was reading it. She held the device out, it was a simple transfer of knowledge to the device. If she went through all the books the compounding effect would make her drowsy. After last night it could be considered normal. The task filled the day, though it was better than expected. She had found something which excited her senses, a small set of books which had been tucked away near the top of the shelf. It was a full set of the Uvalen Code, a complex masterpiece describing the natural laws that governed sorcery. As Saranon slept that night she concentrated on that part, at first the text was rather strange, but it started to unravel.

The last few days she lay low, she had taken on too much, even though at the time she thought she could manage it. The result was that she looked unwell and did not stray too far. She was resting on a wooden deck chair when the Lord met her for the second time, 'Did you find what you were looking for?'

Lord Karager for all his harsh edges and large stance was a strange and elegant man, who showed the signs of a worried father. Saranon could not help feeling sorry for him, 'Yes.'

'You realise that one day you will wake up and all our struggles will seem insignificant.'

She knew what he meant, it was unusual for a sorceress to have so much to do with wiccan, 'I'm not so sure.'

'Just remember when that day comes, we will understand,' he spoke with a hint of kindness in his voice.

Saranon did not want to think of a time when that would happen and she hoped the Lord was not right. As Lord Karager left, his words gave rise to more unanswered questions for her to think about, but for now she would enjoy the time she had.

The journey was over far too soon as she and Celia packed for the trip back. 'Did coming here help?' Celia enquired.

'I think it did,' she replied.

'What will you do when we return?' Celia asked.

'Oh, I don't know I thought a tavern might be a nice

place to stay.'

Celia looked up at her and smiled, 'You mean you like mother's cooking.'

'That too,' she added.

Jedd joined them on the trip back he wanted to talk about what had happened, but held back. The great Bellington Castle faded in the distance and Saranon felt like there was something she needed to do before she left. The Keeps were trying to communicate with her and she wanted to know why. The strange dream had returned to haunt her through everything else and she wanted to get to bottom of it, before it became too weird. This meant spending more time in Redadere. She had made good time from Alveron and she wanted to make the most of her travels. Their arrival was late, but the fires were still keeping the tavern warm, which took the chill away from their cloaks.

As Saranon took off her cloak, she peered out the window, for a moment she could have sworn she saw the fuzzy outline of a figure, then it vanished. Celia had not thought anything about her last sighting, so she chose not to mention it. It was not long before she made her way upstairs. She was in the middle of getting ready for bed, when she had a change of heart and decided to take a look outside. The night air was sharp and crisp, but she was well dressed, this time she was ready for a chase. It was difficult, though she managed to find a glimpse of the silhouette. At this stage she was not sure if it was the same one, but she continued anyway.

She kept to the background, the figure was making its way back to Greddin Fort. The place had been built as a fortress. Only half way through someone had changed the plans, or at least that was what it looked like. For some strange reason the two designs worked and gave the Keep an imposing stature. The outer rim of the Keep was not a problem for her and she followed at a distance, just before the doorway the figure materialised. It was a wizard, which made sense, a wizard would not raise much alarm at Bellington Castle since there they were not a real threat. She was about to leave when the voice in her dreams revealed itself, come in. It was the Keep, but then Greddin was quite powerful and this was who she had wanted to meet.

Saranon chose to go in through a more discreet entrance around the corner, it led down. She had seen quite a few Keeps up close and this did not faze her. She made her way below the hustle and bustle that dripped snippets of noise down the large vents. She was looking at the indolin chambers which sat below the last part of the habitable area of the Keep. She placed her hand on the wall to try and find an entrance. A small seal lit up near her hand, identifying the area where she was, as part of the chambers opened up. She stood back unsure, and the Keep called, you are here.

Something was wrong, the place was almost lifeless. This should have been the busiest and most vibrant area, a place where the Keep could be itself with little interference. Saranon had done repair work before, and Keeps were not new to her so she took the opportunity to look around. At a glance it was not immediately obvious though she had seen this sort of thing before, so it was not a deterrent. She was going to find out what was going on, it would mean having to get dirty. She made a start in the dim areas taking down notes and measurements. It was a wonder no one above her had noticed, then stranger things happened.

Saranon had set herself a small task to begin with, but by the time she had been around the main area it had taken a while. Outside was still dark and she managed to slip out unnoticed back into a safe warm bed. The night's adventures had left her with a lot to think about, why would wizards be keeping a distant eye on her, at least she assumed it was her. The weather had turned outside into a dismal rain which darkened the day, now that she knew what to look for spotting the wizards was easy. During the day they tried to blend in rather than disappear. She had a list of things to get and Jedd had helped to point her in the right direction. At least with asking wiccan she would not raise any suspicions about what she was up to. The inner workings of the Keep were knowledge more likely to be held by wizards or sorcerers than anyone else.

The difficult part though would be making the tools, the process would be more obvious. Jedd's friend was an apprentice blacksmith who could provide a suitable location. It would be less noticeable since the kedrils looked somewhat similar. The Keep Greddin had been kind enough to pass on the information she needed, as each Keep was different. The workshop was a simple and grubby place, but Saranon had grown up in squalor so she felt quite at home. She set to work with the experience of someone who had made specialised tools for a Keep before. She was not good at making normal tools, but a kedril was a fine work of art, even if the finished product did not look as dainty.

Normal tools as she had found out were nowhere near as good when repairing a Keep. Celia who had become interested, set to work making a special leather carry bag. Most Keeps had their own kedrils which were tucked away in easy to find places often by the inhabitants. Yet as she had found out, Greddin had spoken the truth when he said there were none in the chambers. Saranon was a quick worker and made good progress, but there was still some work left to do. She stopped early in the afternoon, something had been bothering her, like a niggling feeling at the back of her neck. She packed up leaving the place as she had found it and searched around to find out what was causing her senses to go funny.

As she walked along the streets she could feel herself starting to slip into a trance like state, and tried to keep on the verge of falling in. Whatever it was, it had to be getting close, she placed her hand on Tellembre, it was warm with excitement. It knew what was going on before she did. Her senses intensified until she could work out what was going on and where. Saranon was heading towards the factories. To where a large old building lay hidden among the grimy structures. As she drew closer she slid near the edges, she could spot some wizards close by, they appeared to be here for the same reason she was. She could not find an entrance without being seen. Walls were not a problem as she had discovered earlier and placed her hand up to the brickwork.

There was enough leeway to allow her to go through unnoticed as she took a moment to calm herself. Inside she was in control, but that could change, and she did not know how long it would take. With no further thought she entered, unaware that a small edge of her robe, the last to go through had been seen by one of the wizards. The wizard rushed to enter the same way to no avail the wall was thick and Saranon was oblivious to what had just happened. Inside the story become clear, the wizards had been trying to deal with a group of dark sorcerers who had made this their den. She crept along trying to follow glimpses of movement out of the corner of her eye. This required concentration, in the space of a heart beat she felt herself slip and managed to regain control.

There were noises up ahead and she ran through a large room. Before she could make it back toward the door, a large strong arm, dripping sweat and holding a bond-breaker lunged around her head. She managed to duck around taking hold of the wizard's arm and sensed a sorceress to the left. She shoved the wizard's bond-breaker into the sorceress with the momentum of his own swing. The dagger pierced the sorceress wounding her in the stomach and she vanished from sight. The wizard did not look impressed.

Saranon turned to run and standing on the other side of the doorway were two of the wizards companions, they ran towards her. She sensed two more sorcerers. Before the wizards were able to enter the room, she had reached for both her bond-breakers, Tellembre and Corsavere. She drew them at full length. She used them to plunge deep into the sorcerers by each side. Her hands with the bond-breakers outstretched. Both sorcerers revealed themselves to the naked eye before falling on the floor, both dead.

All three wizards stopped in shock, Saranon took the advantage and ran after the wounded sorceress. As she ran she could hold on no longer and transformed into the Angeon only this time, she knew something was different. She felt in control, or at least she thought she did. Her senses lived for the chase and in this form the wounded sorceress was not hard to find. She had put Corsavere back in its hiding placc. It was a strange bond-breaker even to its creator. She was more familiar with Tellembre. The chase made her feel alive and even though she had more control this time, she did not feel like herself. It was as though she were looking through someone else's eyes. The sorceress was slowing down up ahead from the injury, Saranon approached her near the end of the alley.

The sorceress looked up knowing what she saw and what was to come. She did not resist as Saranon placed her left hand on the lady's head. She looked up at Saranon, 'You feel it too, it's only a matter of time. You will be like us,' the lady spoke.

Saranon let the sorceress's life drain from her in a quiet peaceful death. As soon as the last breath was taken the horrible marks that showed the path she had been chosen appeared over her body. The once elegant lady now looked haggard and ugly. She left unnoticed and did not feel any sense of empathy for the lady. Her choice in life had been made long before Saranon had set foot on Normisian soil.

As she transformed back, she wondered who was her real self, the one she had grown up with, or the new one she was yet to know. Either way something had changed. She felt a sense of satisfaction at her achievement. At the same time she was worried that she had just opened a door that could not be closed again. Her endeavours had taken her long enough. She forgot about the wizards as she went back to the tavern for a hardy meal and a good night's sleep. As she trundled off to sleep, the events of the evening gripped her in a strange nightmare that made her sweat.

In her dream she was running through the building, the sorcerers were still there and she was running to find someone. She went down in the basement, there was a locked door blocking her way she pelted herself against the door and it gave with a rush. There was blood on the floor and she saw Tasha's body as she had found it at Antavagon. Saranon jolted awake with a start, it was still dark outside, but she could not get back to sleep. She threw back the covers and started downstairs. At the top of the balustrade she could hear Mrs Harper speaking with a few of the older wiccan and stopped to listen.

They were talking about what had happened. Though from what she could make out, this time they did not know that she had helped. She decided it was safer to go back to her room. She opened the window and looked out on the world below. Sure enough she saw a strange outline of a figure across the road. She looked straight at it, but the blur hurt her eyes. She stayed sitting on the sill of the large window, which doubled as a door, until her eyes grew tired with sleep and she returned to bed. The rain had decided to make another morning miserable as Saranon made her way to the workshop. She was pleased with her work and lost track of everything else around her, while she concentrated on her goal.

The kedrils were easy for her to make, but for anyone else it would have taken longer. She had finished just after lunch, there were only a few. The small group did not look like much, but they were well designed for the task at hand. Celia had finished the case the night before and she placed them in with care as she cleaned up. Saranon headed off towards Greddin Fort. It was easier to go in the back-way near the dragons, she was less likely to be noticed. With a thought she changed the look of her clothes to blend in. There was a lot of activity around her, which was a good distraction, as she slipped past. She was about to open a concealed door, when she heard screams and shouting coming from inside the dragon pens.

At first she was going to ignore it, but the commotion was getting more serious. She stopped short of the entrance knowing that she would regret intervening. She flung herself into the situation with such determination that no one questioned why she was there. The stench of dragon's blood was sickening. One of the large males with a name tag hanging around its neck that said 'Splodge' had panicked. The dragon had wounded himself against some armoury, with two spears sticking out of his behind. One of the trainers who had been injured was trying to lie still on the floor. While several others not so experienced, were trying to calm the dragon. The great beast was stopping them from getting to the trainer.

It was an awful mess and before Saranon could do anything, someone else had been hurt by the dragon. Splodge was heightening into a mad panic. The dragon managed to storm past the first group of people, straight into her path. She held up her right hand, and touched the magnificent creature on the nose. It let out a low squeak that sounded like a sigh of relief then dropped its head and lowered it by her side. Another trainer who had arrived pulled out the spears. The dragon hardly noticed as its breathing started to return to normal. While the place was still a buzz with excitement and fear, she crept away hoping that no one would notice she was not supposed to be there.

CHAPTER TEN

An untidy welcome to Greddin Fort

As Saranon closed the door behind her she heard a man call out. 'Hey, where did that girl go?'

She cringed, and cursed her good nature. It was going to land her in trouble again, but she had plenty of time to think about that later. The Keep was relieved to have her back. The indolin chambers were calm and peaceful. This time she travelled down to take a closer look, it was not difficult to figure out where to go. The skada were the mechanical creatures that helped to repair the Keep. They had the misfortune of looking like large spiders and were leaving an obvious trail to follow. The problem with skada was their limitations. They were not smart and if anything major happened, they were not equipped to cope.

Saranon made her way trying not to tread on the creatures as they scuttled down the hall way. One she just missed it made some sort of angry gesture before carrying on its way. To her they were like living creatures with their own personalities made by the Keep. As she came to the end of the line she peered through to one of the substations that looked after a large section of the habitable areas. There were small signs of damage and she said out loud, 'It doesn't look that bad.'

One of the skada near her feet started jumping up and down tugging at the end of her trousers. She followed the little creature around the substation to where the engines were, that ran it. She peered down into the darkness in the opening to a large room. As she made out what was below she gasped. Two of the cylinders looked like ants nests from a distance, there were skada swarming all over them. Something had gone through the system that had made a giant mess.

Saranon looked at the skada that had climbed up on the rail looking for some sign that this could be fixed. The skada held its front legs together in a gesture that looked like it was expecting her to come up with a plan. No wonder she had not found any kedrils in the chambers, all of them would be in use on a job of this scale. the only entity big enough to fix this was the Keep itself. To do that the entire substation would need to be placed out of action. It was no small task, but delaying it would make the Keep more vulnerable.

All of a sudden her little repair job just got a whole lot bigger. She let out a moan of disbelief and the skada scuttled after her as she went. She stopped and kneeled down, 'I'm afraid I will have to tackle this from the other end. I am going to have to go up and change the system over to compensate for when this one goes offline.'

The skada hugged Saranon's leg, then wandered off back to work. She felt sorry for the poor creatures, but she had to leave and go upward. There were hallways that led up, but this would mean going through someone else's basement. The thought did not appeal to her. She did not want to go looking through other people's dirty laundry.

It was getting near tea time and if she did not return, Mrs Harper who had become quite fond of her, would wonder where she was. The pathway was clear and Saranon slipped out of the Keep unnoticed. When she reached the tavern she heard a few of the patrons mentioning what had happened at Greddin. Celia found her, 'Did you hear about all the excitement at Greddin Fort, a girl saved the life of a dragon trainer.'

Celia eyed her with suspicion, she did not know what to say. 'I thought it was you,' Celia whispered. 'There aren't many girls that can subdue one of Greddin's most prized dragons.'

Saranon wondered how the dragon had gotten the name Splodge and if that was important. It did not sound regal. 'Splodge?' She asked.

'Yes he was hand raised from a hatchling,' Celia explained.

She found it difficult to believe a creature that size had ever been small and with that thought, the two sat down for tea. She stayed up searching through her hand written notes and a few manuals she had found at Bellington Castle. The problem at Greddin ate away at her.

Now that she knew what was wrong, her mind was busy working on a solution. The end of the week festivities were finding their way through the floorboards to upstairs. Celia knocked on the door while Saranon packed her scribbles away and followed her friend downstairs. If there was one thing she could rely on the Harper's knew how to unwind. The music relieved her of her problems and that of the Keep. The air was getting hot inside and she went out onto the street where a few of the patrons had already gathered.

The night was cool and two of the patrons nearby had just decided to get into an argument over who had bumped who first. It was starting to get too noisy and ending up in a brawl was not her idea of fun, so she went for a stroll further up the street. She could hear the start of some heavy punching and Mrs Harper's voice ringing out behind her. It was calm and peaceful, a good night for thinking of how she was going to help the Keep. She looked up at the stars, and felt a strong breeze beside her, she thought it was odd. Two big sweaty arms gripped her and pulled her around the corner toward a waiting cart. Saranon tried to pull herself free, but this time she had been caught unaware. She kicked at the wizard as another hauled her inside, pinning her to the ground.

She knew they were blocking her cries from being heard by passers-by. She did not feel like crying, she just wanted to shout with anger and since she knew they could hear her she did not hold back. The wizard who had grabbed her blocked her in and her short temper was starting to fray at the edges. After being stuck in the camps a few wizards did not scare her as much as it might have. She could hear Celia calling out in the distance, on the floor near her she saw the emblem of the army on the cloak of one of the wizards. The men and one lady acted as though this was a normal everyday occurrence. The cart made a tight bend around a corner with the jerk of the moving wheels Saranon leaped and managed to jump free. Tumbling out, she ran down a side street, and used her sorcery to blend into the background.

The small group hardly made a sound, but she knew they were there and that they would know what to look for. Running with the wizards close by, could mean being found so she stayed put. She could hear the footsteps of the lady nearby then they faded. She waited through the night keeping awake. The sun was well in the sky and she had not heard any sign of the wizards for hours. Saranon made a move to stand up. Mitch who had been waiting, tackled her to the ground. He held her hands behind her. She was not impressed and for the second time she was bundled into the cart. This time she had to endure the bumpy ride all the way back to Greddin Fort, this was not part of her plan.

She could feel herself starting to heat up from the anger as she was shoved inside. Mitch kept her close, not wanting to make the same mistake twice, as the door closed behind them, Saranon could feel the wizards relax. The people around her looked as though they were used to seeing someone in her position making a lot of commotion. This time they would be disappointed. She was already assessing the surroundings planning a possible way of getting out. She was so silent that the rest of the party almost forgot she was there, after the language she had used in the cart. She was taken down to one of the holding cells, which looked familiar from her days in the camp.

Saranon was not the only one down there, an older sorceress had the cell opposite. 'We told you, you would join us,' the dark sorceress spoke with confidence.

She realised what she had been placed near, she examined the bars to no avail. 'You know it's too late,' the dark sorceress spoke.

Saranon turned and looked at the lady, but said nothing. Her only saving grace was that she had managed to save Tellembre which she often wore out in the open. Though sometimes she thought the bond-breaker had a mind of its own, either way she was not going to let the thing next to her know what she had. She was starting to wonder why she had been brought here, when there was a movement near the door. A more sinister wizard in long dark robes entered with two guards.

They approached Saranon and removed her from the cell, all the while she remained silent, like when she had been in the camps. They cuffed her hands and moved her forward as she was taken down to a lower level. She wondered if this was how Tasha had felt. The guards took her into a grimy room and made her kneel on the floor, one of them holding her head down. She could make out from the corner of her eye the one with the dark robes heading toward her holding something with a tool. He approached her and a searing pain etched through her skin as the wizard placed the thing around her neck. She did not move and she did not scream instead, she seethed in silent anger. They would pay she would make them pay.

The guard released the cuffs from around her hands and she felt sick, sick with anger and pain. The guards took her back to the cell, where the dark sorceress, Chevonne watched in fascination. Saranon noticed that the lady was wearing the same device. When the guards left the lady smiled, 'You will be like us soon.'

Saranon felt the device and she knew what it was, but she did not give any sign of recognition. One of the hazards of her previous life meant knowing too much about what sort of devices could be used against her. She had been foolish to think the wizards, or the army for that matter, would not resort to such tactics. The rest of the day went slow with her temper simmering underneath the surface.

As the light from the early dusk spread up the wall, the sounds of a commotion reached the cells. The dark sorceress next to her sat calm, Saranon could sense that the lady knew what was going on. The sounds outside went silent as her heart skipped a beat. When Chevonne's companions glided between the cells, Saranon hoped they would leave her, but they opened both cells. Chevonne laughed as they took Saranon out into the depths of the Keep. She tried to avoid being touched by the tainted sorcerers, but that seemed to make it worse as they held her so she could not get away.

The guards looked as though they had not stood a chance. She was led through a rabbit warren of corridors, before they entered a large open area. She could hear the sound of more tainted sorcerers before she saw them. One of them had a tool which removed the device from around Chevonne's neck, she turned to Saranon, 'Now you will become like us.'

She was shoved in the middle, as the sorcerers formed a circle around her trapping her in the centre. From outside the circle she saw real trouble heading her way, the head of the group was coming to complete the circle. Saranon concentrated as much as she could, but the device around her neck was holding her back.

Cornell approached without haste. This was not something that needed to be rushed. Saranon prepared herself, but it would not be enough. It was the best she could do and she needed to feel that she could do something. As Cornell joined the circle she gulped, this was not what she had planned. The first wave knocked her to the ground, she had to fight to resist the pull against her. Even if it tore her apart inside, she thought that would be a better solution and wondered if Tasha had made the same choice. The wave almost crushed her to the ground, but she managed to hold on, she had to hold on. The circle was closing in and she would have to try something to break their sorcery.

Saranon's breath was burning through her lungs and

she realised she was heating up. Sweat poured down her forehead and onto her cheeks. She looked down and saw charred remnants. It was all that was left of the device around her neck. She looked up no one had noticed, they were too busy satisfying their own means. The circle of sorcerers came ever closer and she could see the start of the third wave pummelling towards her in flecks of light. In that moment she stood up and reached out with her sorcery hurling the intensity of her energy out into the group. The explosion of the raging force fell almost all the members of the circle, except one.

Cornell opened up his arms as the wave of sorcery flared and aimed for Saranon with an immense force. She had time to see it coming and braced herself ready for the impact. Out of the corner of her eye she could see Mitch, running full pelt toward Cornell. Just before impact the wizard, Mitch took part of the blow. He managed to ram his bond-breaker home in the sorcerer's ribs before his injured body dropped to the ground. She could do nothing as she watched on helplessly. All she could do was try to block as much of the attack as possible, but the damage was already done.

Saranon held on under the strain as Cornell continued his attack, but as much as he tried to hide it, the injury had taken its toll. She held on as she summoned every last bit of her strength and hurled it with a renewed determination. The blow struck true as Cornell winced and fell to his knees on the floor. For a moment he waved his hands and she braced herself for another attack. Then without any warning he collapsed as the last breath left his body. She remained still, not ready to believe it was over. Yet as she waited she could sense that it was over, as she stood in open astonishment. Her body ached as she walked over to Mitch who was lying still, he was breathing which was a good sign.

Saranon opened one of her sova bags and took out a compact tray which folded out to be large enough to hold the weight of a person. She lifted Mitch up and floated the tray at waist height. He was still awake, but he was in no shape to argue. She took one last look to make sure Cornell was dead and knelt down to pick up the charred remnants of the device. When she got hold of that wizard, she would have a few choice things to say. So as not to make Mitch uncomfortable she pulled the tray along at a slow pace. She was not sure where to go and the Keep was being unhelpful. She did not blame him, but someone had to be at the other end giving orders. She could hear Mitch's laboured breathing and moved ahead with a sense of urgency in her step.

Unfortunately without the Keep's help, the place was difficult to navigate. At one stage she managed to get herself completely lost, until she found the trail of markers again above the doors. Saranon took a path which she thought would lead to the medical area, but she was not one hundred percent sure. She finally opened a door that led into the hub of human life, with people coming and going. She took a quick glance to see if any were from the army. If they were she could not see any sign and decided to take a risk. A lady approached her and asked her what she was doing. She thought that was obvious then answered and the lady went off to get someone.

While Saranon was waiting, she could tell Mitch was trying to say something, so she leaned closer. 'You need to go there,' Mitch managed to point to a corridor.

She was not going to stay and find out what was going on, especially as the only reason she had come was to help him. So she took off down the path that he had pointed out. As they were going she spotted the marks above the door that she had been looking for. From there made it to the medical area within the Keep. She slowed down as she entered the foyer and realised that Mitch was not the only one who had been hurt. Around her she could see other casualties waiting for treatment.

Saranon could see a lady by the name of Rachel in the middle of a conversation with the man at the front desk. Rachel looked up a little puzzled at the sight of her with Mitch and hurried the two in so that he could be examined. She waited on one of the benches as Rachel called over one of the doctors to look at Mitch. They were clouding their words so that she could not ease drop. She could tell by their tones that his condition was serious. She felt a bit small and useless. A lot had happened in a small amount of time and her mind was still trying to catch up. She was grateful for what Mitch had done, even if he had not intended to help save her. If he had not intervened Saranon was not sure if she could have dealt with Cornell on her own.

She did not like to admit it, but she owed him a great deal for what he had done. Even though she was sitting out of the way, she could tell people around her were staring at her and was yet to find out why she had been targeted. This combined with the attack inside the Keep gave an uneasy feel to the place and everyone seemed to be at the end of their nerves. The second doctor wheeled Mitch away, he was deteriorating fast and was almost conscious. Saranon wondered if her help would be in vain. Rachel brought her a drink and sat beside her. Rachel seemed nice enough, so she explained what had happened. She neglected to mention the part about the restraint that had been placed around her neck. She did not want to discuss that.

Rachel listened with sympathy, 'Do you know why the army is interested in you?'

She gave an honest answer, 'No.'

'So you don't know anything that could have attracted their attention?'

'I have difficulty blending in, I just don't know,' she exclaimed.

'It's okay. I know you are concerned for Mitch, you are welcome to wait here while he's in surgery.'

Saranon was shocked to hear the reality of how bad it was, 'Is he going to be okay?'

'I've seen Mitch survive worse,' Rachel answered.

Captain Mirshendy entered with a couple of officers. Rachel touched his arm on the way through and pulled him to the side, 'Are you missing a sorceress?'

The Captain spoke as he peered over her shoulder,

'You know I am.'

'She's not going anywhere,' Rachel replied.

The Captain looked confused and Rachel continued, 'She's attached to Mitch.'

'I have to deal with her,' the Captain spoke.

'I said she's attached to Mitch,' Rachel responded.

The realisation of what Rachel was saying started to show on the Captain's face, 'Do you mean to tell me?'

'Yes Jerald, that's exactly what I mean,' Rachel answered.

Saranon looked on, reading only their body language as the words remained muffled and she let out a frustrated sigh.

For a brief moment she locked eyes with the Captain and wondered if he had been the source of her trouble. She dangled the charred remnants of the hyrik that had been around her neck, catching his attention. He watched transfixed then without any hint of what he was thinking turned to leave. Rachel gave her an unimpressed glance before taking the object away. The lack of the hyrik did not seem to bother Rachel, yet Saranon had the feeling that did not matter. She could sense Rachel's energy, and was not about to annoy her.

CHAPTER ELEVEN

The help of a wizard

Saranon opened her eyes, and realised she was not at Mrs Harpers. The events of last night had left her feeling drained. The noise outside the room indicated that she had slept in she hurried herself to get ready and clambered out in a rush. She went over to the tea room. Rachel was there with a covered tray of breakfast for her. She rushed in, 'Sorry I'm late.'

'You are not late for anything. When you've finished Mitch asked for you.'

'He's okay?' Saranon spoke between mouthfuls.

'Yes,' Rachel replied.

She felt a little odd this morning, but she put that down to the attack last night. She wanted to make sure Mitch was all right before she left. Yet being at Greddin Fort presented itself with the potential to help the Keep, she would have to think about that. Mitch was awake in a room by himself. Saranon poked her head through the open door and he stared back, 'Is it all right…?'

'Yes,' he replied.

Saranon went with caution taking a good look to see if Mitch was okay and sat down next to the bed. Even lying down he was a big man. She looked at him and said, 'Thanks for helping me.'

Mitch did not answer instead he held her hand, the touch was strange and she realised what had happened. She felt sick, 'I'm sorry.' She stood up not knowing what to do, 'I'm sorry.'

Saranon held her hand to her mouth and turned to leave. Mitch spoke in a calm voice, 'Does this mean it was a mistake?'

She had to think about what she remembered on the subject, and what had happened, 'No it wasn't. I'm just sorry.'

She knew that to bond without good reason could be viewed as a great insult. She sat back down, 'I'm just sorry it had to be like that. I'm not sorry about the bond.'

'Now you're lying,' he replied.

'No. We haven't been bonded for long so you can't make that judgement yet,' she said with care.

'So now you're an expert,' he exclaimed.

'I didn't say that. I meant I did not expect to need the help of a wizard,' she was fumbling for words.

Mitch laughed, 'That's the first honest thing you've said.'

He raised himself on the pillow to sit up, 'How about we both keep quiet?'

'I can live with that,' she responded.

'Good, now are you going to hand that bond-breaker over to the army?'

'The bond hasn't sunk in yet has it?' She took the dagger out of its sheath so that Mitch could take a closer look.

He stared down at the hilt as he held it, 'That's less than six months old.'

'That's because I made it, it stays with me. No offence, but I don't part with that one,' she remarked.

Mitch handed it back, 'You are different to what I thought.'

'I hope that means I'm nicer!' Saranon was joking, but Mitch gave her a serious look.

She found the whole situation a bit awkward, but Mitch appeared to be taking it in his stride. Saranon cringed as he started describing a ceremony that would take place. It was beginning to sound like the bond was going to be more trouble than she expected. He held out his hand to comfort her, it was strange considering not long ago he had been trying to restrain her. She had not been involved in any wizard formalities and had tried to avoid them in Alveron. The little rituals were quite foreign to her and it had been easier to keep well clear.

She leaned over and placed her head on the bed trying to think of a way to get out of the ceremony. Yet she did not think that would be an option. Mitch looked up at the doorway and she could sense another wizard behind her. Captain Mirshendy was a little older than Mitch, who was only twenty-two. She found herself caught between focusing all her grievances on this man and seeing him as Mitch's old friend. She still held Mitch's hand as she sized up the Captain with an unimpressed glare. The Captain smiled, Rachel had been right, Saranon had become close to Mitch which could be used to their advantage.

She was not one to hide how she was feeling, 'What do you want?'

Captain Mirshendy walked over to them, 'I would like you to come for walk with me.'

She clenched Mitch's hand tighter and he broke the silence, 'I think you should go.'

She was not fond of being ordered about and she had not yet come to grips with the extent of her new responsibility. Yet the Captain may be able to answer some of her questions. She found herself in an uneasy situation as she followed him out to one of the small courtyards.

She took a quick glance around then turned back to face the Captain. 'Explain to me why I should not despise you for what you have done.'

Captain Mirshendy said nothing, so Saranon continued. 'If you had not brought me here none of this would have happened, or was that what you wanted?'

The Captain sat down so she did the same. She caught an insight to his thoughts, 'You only tolerate me because someone else does.'

The Captain showed no expression. She hung her

head with the thought, 'So where does that leave me?'

The Captain spoke, 'You pose a risk to us all. You cannot control yourself and you will spiral out of control unless something is done. In the mean time you will stay here.'

Saranon did not like that idea, but it would have to do since it would not raise suspicions while she assisted the Keep.

Her distain showed on her face, but she had to meet a compromise. 'Until you can prove that anything you just said is true, you don't lay a finger on me.'

Captain Mirshendy was not looking impressed, but she took no notice and walked off. Unfortunately Mitch was going to be bed bound for at least a few days and then there would be that annoying ceremony. Saranon found herself contemplating her next moves, while lying down in a large beautiful courtyard filled with a vibrant garden.

Its only misgivings were that the Captain, along with his comrades, had almost unlimited views of the entire area. The Tea Gardens as they were called, served a different purpose for her. It included several areas for easy access to the main workings of the Keep. She lay down staring at a little conduit which led up to a screen hidden amongst the bushes. She could hear a familiar clomping sound behind her. The Captain sat down beside her, 'You know everyone can see you through there.'

He pointed to a shiny black surface that covered the horizontal length of the wall. His body language was too hard to read. So she replied with a hint of sarcasm. 'There are more important things to worry about than wizards who enjoy interrupting my thinking time.'

The Captain started playing with the screen to her horror, 'Don't lose my work that took me ages.'

She was reminded yet again of all the reasons why wizards were annoying. As the Captain managed to flick through some of the readings for the vital areas of the Keep, before she closed it down. The two stared at each other in annoyance before the Captain broke first and asked Saranon to come inside. As she entered the inner stronghold it dawned on her just how alone she was. Everyone else seemed to fit into to a large group that sprang out of nowhere and she was left by herself. The Captain kept her close by, but she was intent on looking around. He sat her down next to Lyn, who did not look impressed. She was not sure whether she was on the verge of getting into trouble, or if the Captain was being polite. Either way it was hard to tell.

Captain Mirshendy opened up a large screen that came to lie along the length of the table. While Lyn exclaimed, 'Now I don't think that's a good idea.'

The Captain took no notice and changed the screen to reveal the blueprints in front of her. She was used to seeing Keeps in a different manner, so it took her a while to work out what was what, before making several variations. Lyn was not sure whether to be aghast or astonished, but she managed to blurt out, 'That's not what it looks like.'

Without glancing up she replied, 'That's what it looks like now.'

It was obvious that Lyn was not going to believe her and by now any belief Captain Mirshendy had seemed to have gone. Unfortunately, she was used to people not believing her. She spent the rest of the day in an off centre mood that kept everybody out of her immediate path. Though true to her word she did not wander far, Saranon would save that for later.

She found herself wandering down to where Splodge had just been brought in for the day. He had recovered and was quite placid as she reached out to touch the giant dragon. His trainer Mark who displayed a permanent reminder scarred across his arm, placed there from almost being killed by his favourite pet, had walked off without noticing her. Chelsea one of the handlers, had come in with a big bucket, soap and brushes. Saranon was about to say something, but Chelsea spoke first, 'I don't suppose you want to help?'

Saranon smiled, 'I'd like that.'

As she started to foam up the dragon's filthy coat she began to realise why Chelsea wanted a hand. It was hard physical work which Chelsea made look easy, as she climbed on top of the dragon with a bucket and scrubbed his back. She thought it would be best if she focused on his face first and laughed as she stood back to admire her foamy handy work. Chelsea's voice came from above, 'I wouldn't do that if I were you he doesn't like being laughed at.'

Saranon did her best to put on her serious face and apologised to the dragon.

A deep gruff sound left the dragon's lips, 'That's okay!'

She stared wide eyed up at Chelsea who looked just as shocked and asked, 'Is that normal?'

She had heard that some dragons could speak, but they rarely did so as they considered it to be beneath them. She enjoyed being down in the dragon pens everyone was busy and she could pretend the recent events had not happened. She was convinced that Captain Mirshendy thought the worst of her, even though he had been diplomatic. Saranon looked up from her ponderings and noticed someone trying to get her attention. As she stepped closer she recognised who it was. 'Jedd,' she whispered in amazement.

She felt a wave of relief fall over her as she ducked around the corner. He spoke in a soft voice, 'I haven't got long. Here's your talik and the rest of your belongings.'

He handed her a sova bag, she hesitated a moment then spoke, 'Did you unlock the information?'

'Yes, but I'm afraid I can't help you. My uncle says you've been bonded.'

The look on Saranon's face confirmed it, 'Thank you.'

'I have to go, good luck.'

She watched him disappear into the background. She held the talik close, as if it would somehow wind back time and take her back to Mrs Harper's tavern. For a moment she felt like running away from everything, but it would do no good. She went back and patted the dragon which smelled much cleaner. Chelsea was packing up when Mark came back to check how Splodge was going. He wandered up near Saranon, 'So you're the one causing so much mischief. What will you do with Mitch?'

She looked up startled, he was the mirror image of his dragon, all muscle and worn around the edges.

'I don't have a choice, it is my responsibility to look after him,' she grumbled.

'Yes, but there many kinds of looking after,' Mark exclaimed.

She was not sure where this was leading, but before she could think he had turned to leave and she started to follow. 'I wouldn't do that, when he ends a conversation it's over,' Chelsea spoke.

'What did he mean by that?' She asked.

Chelsea looked at her in disbelief then looked a little closer, 'You don't know do you? Not all bonded wizards are well looked after.'

'I don't understand, but what about the Uvalen Code?' She asked.

'That's only good if you have proof and sometimes that can be difficult. Mark had an aunt, who was mistreated,' Chelsea explained.

'I'm not like that,' she responded.

'You don't need to tell him, if you look after Mitch that will be proof enough,' Chelsea explained.

Saranon shook her head in disbelief and sighed.

Chelsea invited her up to the mess hall it was a grand old room, if she looked above all the marks at table height. They made their way over to where the dragon trainers sat. Unfortunately working with dragons could leave a slight smell behind. For all the wizard's efforts to be rid of it, it still clung in the air. The idea that the smell existed in the first place, meant that anyone who worked with dragons sat with no one else. Chelsea's colleagues now accepted her with hearty grunts of greetings between mouthfuls. The food was better than at the camp, but it was not the same as Mrs Harper's and she started playing with her dinner.

The place was filled with noise. A clanging sound behind her sent a shiver down her spine. She turned around to find several men in a heated argument. There was a brief pause, then one man went hurling into a table and the others for and against took that as their queue to join in. She could not understand what they were saying as they had clouded their voices. She looked at Chelsea who was worried, 'I think we'd better go.'

Chelsea leaned over, and touched Saranon's arm. What was being said came through loud and clear.

'That creature should be restrained.'

'That's none of your business.'

'Oh yes it is and they let her in here.'

She realised they were arguing about her and stood up. She felt an object behind her gliding through the air. She turned and stopped the dagger in the air without moving. There was a moment of pause as the man who held onto the dagger and the others, realised what would have happened. With an all in effort, the man was dragged kicking and screaming out the door. Mark who had not stopped eating through the whole event spoke to Saranon, 'Sit down, you're making a scene.'

Without any further encouragement the atmosphere became a little more tolerable. The group finished the rest of their meal in peace.

She left her strange new friends to check on Mitch who was still in a bad way. Even though he tried to hide it, Rachel was sitting next to him. 'Ah, my two favourite girls,' he remarked.

She felt a bit embarrassed while Mitch made every effort not to look in pain as he reached over and gave her hug. Rachel smiled, 'I'm afraid your new Hilazen is going to have a few more days resting. We heard about what happened in the hall, don't let that trouble you.'

'Thanks,' she responded.

Rachel stood up to go, 'I'll leave you two in peace.'

Mitch waved goodbye, then faced Saranon, 'Are you okay?'

'Yes,' she replied.

'You don't sound so sure,' he commented.

She was going to have to get used to someone knowing her too well. She held his hand in both of hers, 'I feel like I'm going around in circles.'

'Join the club, do you think I like lying in bed doing nothing?' he remarked.

'No. Mitch, are you able to tell me what's going on?' she asked.

'Ah, I was wondering when you were going to ask' he made himself comfortable.

'The Arroada sent a warning with your description. They told us they are the only ones who can look after you. The marks on your hands would prove this.' He leaned closer, 'If you had the marks you would be back in

Darkonia by now. The confusion may have saved you.'

'I thought they were trying to help me. Why would they do this?' she exclaimed.

'Because the Angeon is a powerful being and that scares people,' he answered.

Saranon knew that Mitch was right, but she did not want to admit it, if it were true then Odana had been her saving grace. Her mind started ticking over, 'But that still doesn't explain you.'

'We get on well with the Palascene. Besides, you were doing such a wonderful job cleaning up, that they thought it would be easier if we brought you in,' he spoke.

In the camps she had been one of many in a faceless crowd. Now the thought of being known across several borders was daunting to say the least.

In a short space of time she felt as though she had been thrust to centre stage and no amount of trying to blend into the background would fix it. He lay like a sleeping giant cramped into a bed that was one size too small. He had been honest with her and she felt like she owed him in return. 'Mitch something is wrong with the Keep. It asked for my help and I gave it my word.'

He did not look at her as though she were stupid, in some ways she wished that he did. Instead he gazed at her and spoke in a soft voice, 'Then you have work to do.'

Saranon lay in bed afterwards thinking about what Mitch had said. Her mind was restless and sleep was not going to be of any comfort. She waited a while for the outside noise to settle down. Then she crept down to the indolin chambers and the inner workings of the Keep. In the void of human voices, the soft ramblings of the Keep soaked up through the floor drenching the walls. The sensations made perfect sense to her as she went further down and entered the imbenik chamber closest to her. The Angeon inside intensified with every step as she moved closer to the altar and slid her body down onto the soft surface. She closed her eyes and reached out. Greddin wrapped itself around her in a warm embrace. Her restlessness was swept away replaced by the presence of the Keep.

Saranon was still herself, yet in that moment she was so much more it felt like being home wrapped up in a caring embrace. As she melded with the Keep she could reach further into the mess that had plagued it. In the darkness that surrounded her, she felt parts of herself that had remained dormant rise to the surface. At the same time she felt completely in control and lost in the haze. She opened her eyes and was startled by the sight of the Keep crisscrossing her body. It was gentle yet firm, she raised her arm and the embrace of the Keep moved with her. She rested her arm back down accepting that one of the strangest things came naturally to her.

When the embrace was over she stumbled, forgetting how to walk. For all that had happened it had not disturbed Mitch. Her body was ready for sleep. She made her way back through the corridors with the light from the stars trickling through the windows. 'You don't stay put, do you?' Captain Mirshendy's voice came as he appeared around the corner.

'I send my officers searching for you and you appear out of nowhere.' He grabbed hold of her and held her up against the wall in a cold embrace. Saranon made a small sound in protest.

'Jerald stop that at once! I said stop it,' Rachel had caught up to them, but the Captain would not let go.

The happy dream was over as she realised that Captain Mirshendy was not going to see the situation from her point of view. Before she had a chance to do anything, Rachel had broken the link the Captain was using to keep hold of her. Saranon breathed a sigh of relief as it broke and rubbed her arms.

She had been through enough for one night and if Rachel was going to take on the angry Captain for her, she was not going to complain. She could hear the arguing as they moved further away. She slumped to the floor with exhaustion and the tone of their voices changed. Rachel returned and led her off to bed. Rachel had tears in her eyes. It was hard to know what to say, so she kept her thoughts to herself. As she woke the morning light had been streaming in for some time, but Saranon was trying to ignore it. She was still drained from the night's activities and did not want to face Rachel or the Captain. There was a knock at the door, and Rachel sat down on the bed.

It was an awkward moment, and Saranon spoke first, 'I'm sorry about last night.'

'I know, I was wondering if you could do something for me. Captain Mirshendy needs your help and we both know he's too proud to ask,' Rachel smiled.

The idea of helping the Captain did not exactly appeal to her, but she had not intended to create trouble. If Mitch was right, not helping might do her more harm than good. Rachel continued, 'The Keep has been damaged. Jerald didn't realise you were helping until he sent a crew down to examine what happened. Can forgive him for me?'

Saranon let out one long frustrated sigh, 'I'll see what I can do.'

CHAPTER TWELVE

No easy task

The busy hum of work followed by the occasional sharp clanging noise greeted Saranon as she strode down into the chaos. Covers and lids had been removed. The innards of the Keep were visible everywhere. It was a strange sight to see. Keeps did not like people rummaging around underneath the surface, but this time Greddin Fort was content. It felt like a great sigh of relief stretching into every corner of the building. Captain Mirshendy spotted her and there was a moment of unease as he stared at her with the same cold expression from last night. Regardless of what Rachel had said she would keep out of the Captain's way.

Saranon looked in the other direction and saw two men looking over the makeshift plans she had drawn. It filled her with a sense of pride to be listened to, but it did not seem like a good time to shout with enthusiasm. The wizards around her were already on edge and like so many other things, it could be taken the wrong way. She knew how dangerous the situation was. Captain Mirshendy was keeping a close eye on her while she wandered around. She glanced back and for the first time saw a genuine Palascene, his aura was clear unlike of the others. A wonderful expression of shock creased across the Captain's face as he realised he was standing between the two sorcerers. He side stepped out of the way.

Saranon looked up as though staring into a mirror, and seeing a strange reflection of herself. Then with just as much silence the Palascene left. Normisia had only one sorcerer clan which was then broken down into structured groups and ranks. The Palascene preferred to do things their own way. She went over to Captain Mirshendy looking for answers, but he was not volunteering any. She had been around wizards long enough to know that they had a keen instinct for staying out of sorcerer business.

This infuriated her, as it meant if Saranon was going to introduce herself she would have to do it alone. By the sounds of it they already knew about her. She did not like the idea of forever being a few steps behind. She had a quiet chuckle when she saw Lyn using the drawings she had done earlier to supervise the work. It felt odd to be caught between and the thought made her skin itch. She was still sore from last night and in some ways she hoped that Mitch would be well soon so she could have some sort of privacy. At least the Keep had given up one secret, she now knew what type of sorcerer she was. That coupled with what Jedd had unlocked, left a sour taste in her mouth.

In some ways she was not sure if she should hate herself. Saranon started to think of what people who knew, thought of her, then stopped. If they did, then like the Arroada they could deny her the opportunity to make that choice. Yet the Arroada had let her go in their haste to be rid of her, frightened by what she had done to the Arthrose. Greddin Fort was a stubborn Keep, with an attitude to fight just about anything and if he was your friend he would be that for life. The job was not complete. Just seeing the looks on the wizards' faces, she knew they were cringing at the work fixing the mess would entail. Saranon had one of her bizarre ideas, to her it was normal. After all growing up around people who despised her was normal too.

She managed to track down Rachel who seemed to have a never ending supply of work. She waited a moment before she dropped her great idea into the world. Rachel's stunned silence let her know she was out of touch with reality. 'Do you know how lucky you were, not to be harmed before?' Rachel remarked.

It was the first time Saranon heard how Rachel felt about her joining with the Keep. Rachel took her aside and whispered, 'If you can do that again it will help the Keep, but if something goes wrong we cannot help you.'

She thought she should give it another try and perhaps she would learn more. She waited trying to calm her nerves and took a look around her, for the Keep, it was a matter of time. She had managed to help do the preparation work, but the bulk of it was still to be done and it would take more than one night even if it worked. She found Mitch and as she sat down she felt much older than she was, 'I may be gone for a while.'

'It's not a good time to leave,' he spoke in a firm voice.

'No, I meant I'll still be here just somewhere else,' she added.

'What's going on?' He asked.

'I think the Keep needs me,' she said.

When she saw Mitch again he would be back on his feet, but now was not the time to think about that. This time she knew where to go and what to expect, as the Keep wrapped around her in a warm comforting way. The Keep felt like an extension of her and vice versa. This time she did not need to waste time with introductions, the Keep knew why she was there and if it minded it did not let her know.

Everything seemed so distant, she came with the intention to help and that was what she was going to do. The Keep kept her safe in its warm embrace, protecting her from the outside world. Yet she knew it was not real and it could not last as her senses reached out into the building. Greddin welcomed her as it let her into his thoughts, observing her with a mild curiosity, as she extended her mind through the Keep. She could sense the central core below as it hummed in her mind, calling her from the depths below.

This time she was determined to heal the Keep, even if Greddin showed a small reluctance. As she moved further inward, something was holding her back. Yet that did not deter her as the two worked together to reform the damaged substation. The work was slower than she would have liked and she became annoyed even when the Keep reassured her. For Greddin Fort had a different concept of time and did not share her frustration. He reassured her as they worked and with every step, the Keep retracted his grip on Saranon.

For her it all felt like a deep sleep, only her mind remained active. When she woke it took her a while to realise how much time had passed. She had lost three weeks, Greddin Fort was back to normal, but she was not sure about herself. She hesitated before standing up, waiting for her legs to work again. Her muscles were sore, even though she had been lying down the whole time. Saranon had used a great deal of energy and the exhaustion hit as she stumbled before reaching the door. She placed her hand against the wall to steady herself as she caught her breath. Saranon hoped that what she had done would be enough.

Saranon opened the seal on the door and stepped out of the chamber. Mitch was waiting for her on the other side, she should have guessed. She had forgotten how tall he was, Mitch hesitated before helping her up to the habitable area of the Keep. She tried to say something, but he did not notice Saranon knew he was ignoring her. It was night time above ground and Mitch with all the care in the world helped her get ready for bed. She noticed her quarters had changed from amongst the wizards, to an area set aside for guests. The place was more welcoming and larger. Not that she minded the cramped little room, but bigger just seemed so much better.

He was being too nice, she was starting to suspect that something was going on, 'Mitch.'

She gave him such a strange look that he knelt down beside the bed, 'Did you forget about the ceremony?'

'I didn't spend much time reading,' she responded.

'Well, it's like this, I have to be nice for the ceremony,' he smiled.

'I think I preferred your old self,' she exclaimed.

'You know I can't be that,' he replied.

Saranon wondered what the others thought of her melding with the Keep, 'I hope I didn't get you into trouble, being away for so long.'

'No, but you gave the Palascene something to talk about,' he said.

Saranon curled up on the floor watching the dying embers in the fireplace. He sat down beside her, and placed his arm around her, 'I'm not going to get any sleep tonight am I?'

Mitch comforted her as the embers went out. She hated to admit it, but part of her needed him to be there.

She could manage, but Mitch seemed to make things easier. She wondered if it was like that with other bonds. He stayed and comforted her without question. The next day started with a loud clattering noise followed by raised voices. Her eyes opened into the bright sunlight streaming in from the early morning. She had almost forgotten what sunlight was like. It felt like a dream until Saranon dashed over to open the window, and the warmth came streaming through. As the Keep had instructed, she dressed in robes more appropriate for her kind. They were casual, yet still held an elegant sombre look, meant for one much older than she.

As she was fixing the finishing touches the door burst open and Chelsea burst through. It took her a while to remember who Chelsea was. There was a moment of awkward silence as the two girls stared at each other. 'People are wondering what you will do with Mitch. Sometimes bad things happen to wizards that get bonded,' Chelsea spoke in haste.

'I would like to say I can keep him safe, but I'm not sure,' she replied.

'Just say you don't intend to hurt him,' Chelsea asked.

'At the moment he is the last person I would want to…' she began.

'Good, now come with me,' her friend spoke in haste.

They tried to scamper past a few Palascene, she was held up with courteous greetings. Chelsea had moved on ahead before noticing that Saranon was holding a conversation. As she joined up with her friend, Chelsea yanked her arm, 'Do you know what you just did?'

'I was being polite,' she suggested.

Chelsea gave a look of exasperation, 'I meant that was too good, flawless.'

Saranon still did not understand. 'Be careful, you don't want to give people the wrong impression,' Chelsea added.

'In case you hadn't noticed, the Palascene have been

judging me ever since I arrived,' she replied.

'I just hope you know what you're doing,' Chelsea responded.

While the two girls were talking they managed to walk right past Mark who had been looking for them 'Hey!'

The girls turned at once and Mark continued, 'Do you know where I can find the owner of a large male marmoz dragon with a scar on his hind leg?'

Saranon felt the blood draining away from her face, 'I thought he had gone back to Alveron.'

'Right,' Mark nudged the girls forward until they were downstairs in the dragon pens.

The dragon that she had ridden all the way from Alveron was curled up in ball resting in one of the pens. 'I take it he didn't return home?' She remarked.

'Thanks to you, he doesn't have a home. Katholomu's previous owners do not want him back,' Mark spoke.

She reached out and touched the beautiful creature. Mark continued, 'I wouldn't send him back anyway, he hasn't been looked after.'

'Did you buy him?' Chelsea asked, 'You did.'

Saranon was wondering what on earth she would do with a docile giant that could kill at a moment's notice. Not the sort of thing one left lying around the home for guests to walk into. Nonetheless she did feel sorry for it, like her, the dragon had travelled far from home. 'I can look after him while you're here, but you'll need to spend time with him,' Mark spoke.

She could not help it, she felt a little tear drop escape

down her cheek. She wished there had been someone like Mark to come along and rescue her from the camp before Tasha had died. The dragon was as soft as she remembered, with muscles as hard as stone.

The marmoz were not the most favoured among wizard clans, due to their stubborn nature. Yet, at the same time, they were well respected for being fierce fighters. Saranon was unsure of what to say, no one had given her a dragon before. In fact no one had given her much at all. She was used to finding her own way. The dragon moved its head and she looked behind her to see Mitch talking with Mark.

She whispered to Chelsea, 'I'm doomed aren't I?'

Chelsea gave her a puzzled look. 'The ceremony,' Saranon said.

'Oh it's not that bad, well, if your idea of bad consists of a bunch old people droning on, then yeah.'

'That's not funny,' she remarked.

Mark's voice boomed, 'Hey, he's not a toy. I didn't say clamber all over him.'

Saranon and Chelsea stepped away from the dragon with innocent expressions across their faces. She was about to say something to Mitch, but thought better of it. Instead the two girls started running off in the opposite direction.

Chelsea had work to do, so Saranon kept her own company. Mitch had left her with some reading material. He had given this to her before she had linked with the Keep and now it was looking rather tattered around the edges. The dragon pens were not the cleanest of place, but they were kept tidy. An improvement to what she had grown up with. Saranon made herself at home. For all her good intentions, trying to understand the way wizards did things, was rather difficult. A few times she looked up at Chelsea wondering if she should ask, her frustration showing on her face.

The more she became frustrated the more Chelsea found the whole situation funny, 'Why don't you ask Rachel?'

'I wouldn't want to bother her,' she replied.

'Well don't look at me, I'm not going to help,' Chelsea grinned.

Saranon sat in a grump, tolerating her friend's amusement. She could not see the funny side at all. She finally gave in and wandered upstairs, there was a neat little staircase tucked away in the middle of a great arch. She turned to look at Chelsea, 'I'm going.'

'Of course you are,' Chelsea grinned while holding a dirty rag in one hand.

The staircase was narrow and was only large enough for one. She half ran to the top, almost pelting head first into a Palascene. Bianca did not seem to notice Saranon's folly, 'Were you trying to impress us by winning the Keep's trust?'

Saranon hesitated for moment before answering, 'I did not win anything.'

'That is not what I heard about your wizard,' the Palascene responded.

Saranon knew she was referring to Mitch, 'That was

different.'

'So you fall for the first man that comes along, whatever he is,' Bianca did not see any need to accept Saranon as one of her own. She walked away with a self-absorbed air of confidence.

Saranon could tell that had been no idle chat. The Palascene had been keeping their distance watching and waiting for signs of trouble. It drove her mad thinking about it, but there was nothing she could do. She was caught in a slow moving game and if she moved too fast, it could all come undone. Not that she was used to seeing things unravel, but this time it would be nice to succeed, and do things right. She did not have a clue about the inner workings of wizardry and it would be embarrassing to mess up at the ceremony. To her surprise Rachel for once had a lack of things to do and was taking her time tidying up the place.

'Rachel,' she asked.

'Yes Saranon,' Rachel replied.

'I was wondering if you could help me, you see I'm a bit stuck with these,' she pulled out the tattered bits of paper.

'Well for starters you will need this one,' Rachel pulled out a small booklet.

Rachel placed it on the table where they both sat. While Saranon was still frustrated she asked questions. Somehow it did not seem like a completely foreign language when Rachel explained it, which was a relief. For a while she was thinking she would have no hope of understanding and would end up making a fool of herself. It was difficult imagining having to put up with Mitch for the rest of her life.

There were some ways of breaking a bond, but from what she understood trying to undo the situation would only make things worse. For some reason wizards hated the thought of having a bond broken more than being stuck with one. It was an interesting concept which had helped give Saranon a bit of leeway. The bond had been tough for people like Captain Mirshendy to get used to. The thought of the Captain popped into her head as she realised he had joined them out on the deck overlooking the gardens. He came up and placed his hand on her shoulder, 'Now you are going to behave for the ceremony.'

'Jerald you are interrupting,' Rachel spoke.

The Captain looked down at the table, 'Oh.' For a second the Captain was lost for words, 'Carry on.'

Rachel was unimpressed by the Captain's attempt at backing out of an awkward moment. Saranon saw a glance she recognised, 'You two are going to be married.'

'What?' The lovers spoke at once.

The Captain realised he had given something away and went, leaving Rachel caught in the middle. Saranon continued on oblivious, 'You would make a nice pair, at least the Keep thinks so.'

The Captain who had not travelled far, ducked his head back around the corner. 'You can't say something like that,' he spoke.

'Why not?' She remarked.

'To begin with Rachel and I are not getting married,' the Captain added.

Rachel was aghast, 'Why not?'

The Captain realised what he had just said in front of his girlfriend, 'You know what I meant.'

'No, I didn't,' Rachael exclaimed.

'I just meant I think you both would make a nice couple,' Saranon knew as soon as the words came out that they sounded pathetic.

'It's all right Saranon just continue reading, the Captain and I need to talk,' Rachel stood up and left.

She was thinking herself lucky. She had avoided the complications of having a boyfriend on top of everything else.

CHAPTER THIRTEEN

The Host

It was a sleepless night that racked at Saranon's mind and kept her stirring well into the early hours. The past few days had flown by so fast that she had no time to catch a moment to herself. Between Rachel who had taken time off work, Chelsea, and Katholomu her time was all but taken up. She had been quite happy to let the time slip away. After all she had sacrificed three weeks to the Keep and what were a few extra days in comparison. Still for someone who was supposed to be in charge of her own life she was finding it difficult to stay focused on her agenda. She felt a tingle run through her arms and looked up to see Greddin moving a little in a strange manner. The faint flows of energy that she could see running through the ceiling had changed.

Her senses told her that it was not a good sign, but

she was still half asleep. It did not take long to prepare herself, as she went to pick up Tellembre she felt the Keep shudder. Now that was a bad sign, Saranon went to open the door, but someone on the other side did first. It was an elderly wizard, she could make out William Trazen in the first rays of day light and realised he had come to begin the ceremony. She was about to say something about Greddin Fort. Yet the look on the grand old wizard's face made her have second thoughts. The Cryzinelan wizards were strange. They were comfortable being open without giving anything important away. For all their friendliness towards her, she had been able to get much less out of them than their Alveronian counterparts.

They prided themselves on their differences. This could be quite frustrating as Saranon had found out on a few occasions. Chelsea had been a good friend, but for all her youth she let little slip. She felt awkward being chaperoned. William's arm felt like solid steel, as he held it firm for her to hold onto while he lead the way. She had asked Greddin about the ceremony, but unfortunately Keeps had a different take on human activities. Inside she wanted to let out a cry, staying calm and quiet was not her strong point. The urge to break the silence was tingling up her spine like a bad itch. The Keep had settled down, perhaps she had been overreacting and everything would be fine.

Of course it was not fine, her mind was starting to ramble through a hundred different thoughts cramming for attention. Saranon was trying not to sweat. Yet the last time the Cryzinelan had taken the initiative they had thought that abducting her was good idea. She wondered if the wizards would be more open after the ceremony. Then she sensed a familiar voice from the depths, it is time. Greddin was a wizards' Keep much to the annoyance of the Palascene, who had great difficulty using the areas within. William was leading her into a part of the Keep which was known as a wizards' only domain.

For Saranon it was like travelling, underwater not that breathing in water was a problem for a sorceress, but it just felt wrong. She took a deep breath and entered the large passage mindful that being here was not the safest place. The Keep had been matter of fact, when it stated that it was much easier for wizards in a stronghold to kill sorcerers. A lone one would not be much trouble. Keeps could live for hundreds of years and were used to humans having short life spans in comparison. Greddin would look out for her to a certain extent because of what she was. Still that did not help the uneasy feeling weighing her down.

It was hard not to let out a faint laugh at the serious faces, but she managed to control herself. The wizards greeted her as if for the first time, then William led her into a small chamber. As Chelsea had warned her, the ceremony involved a lot of reciting which William managed in a monotone voice. In any other situation it would have been enough to make her fall asleep. She was proud of managing to recite her own parts in a serious voice and hoped they could not tell what she was thinking on the inside. Mitch was not present for this part so she felt quite alone. She focused on William's voice. '…And do you accept the responsibility of guiding Mitchell Kregner in the ways of the Cryzinelan…'

Saranon was able to get through the first part without falling asleep. The second part involved dunking poor Mitch underwater to symbolise the start of a new beginning. Unfortunately she was rather small and meek in comparison. So it turned into a spectacle when she lost her grip on the smooth surface and got a dunking as well. She was upset about messing the whole thing up. She resurfaced to find William, Mitch and several onlookers roaring with laughter. The dunking had taken the serious edge off the rest of the ceremony and it had helped ease the tension much to Saranon's relief. Being drenched in the sacred waters of the inner stronghold was not an experience she wanted to be reminded about. Though in the Keep news travelled fast.

She had dried the water off, but when Chelsea visited her she may as well have been soaking wet. 'I can't believe you fell in,' Chelsea said with a cheesy grin.

'Well it wasn't what I was aiming to do,' she exclaimed.

Mitch was minding his own business sorting out a few gifts he had been given while the two girls chatted away. If the ceremony was anything to go by with Saranon it was going to be different, perhaps in a good way. He could think of a few sorcerers that would have had a bad reaction to being laughed at, but she had taken it quite well. He had been given some nice clothes and other items, all rather useful.

He stayed with her during the night curled up on the floor near the fireplace on a cosy makeshift bed. Saranon could not sleep she should have been able to after the day's events, but something was not right. After having been connected to the Keep for so long, she could feel its daily patterns were a little out of sync. As she stared up at the ceiling the energy fluctuated again. 'Did you notice anything?' She asked Mitch.

'No,' he replied.

She was not convinced that it had been her imagination and decided it would need investigating later.

She had become sick of staying within the confines of the Keep. She was longing to get out to enjoy the beautiful sunny morning and see her old friends who had welcomed her into their midst. 'Mitch, I don't mean to be rude, but I would like to leave Greddin and visit my friends.'

'That's fine William just wanted you stay in the town of Redadere,' he remarked.

Saranon almost fumed, 'You mean I could have done that any time!'

Mitch realised what he said and tried to back track, 'Well I don't think…'

'I'm getting some fresh air. Now did you want to join me?' She asked.

'It's best if I do just for the moment,' he added.

'Good, now are there any more surprises that I need to know,' she asked.

Mitch grinned, 'No.'

'Are you sure?' She snapped.

'I think it's time you got out for a while,' he suggested.

The two left the Keep and went out into the busy streets of the second largest city in Normisia. It did not take long to find Celia, or more to the point her friend found Saranon. Mitch blended into the background while the two acted like boisterous teenagers. Saranon found out that the wiccan had been worried about her, and with good reason. Celia was having trouble not knowing whether to laugh or cry as she explained what had happened. It appeared that the Palascene wanting to palm off the hard work to the wizards had backfired. At this pointed she noticed Mitch was trying not show he was listening, but she could tell he was interested.

Her wiccan friends loved gossip. Celia was in her element as she told Saranon the Palascene had not expected her to be so tolerant of wizards. This had led them to the dilemma of having to accept her in some form. This had disgruntled the Arroada who had sent them after her in the first place. This was all starting to sound too confusing. Yet she understood the part where the Palascene did not like being told what to do by the Arroada. She listened to how the whole arrangement had fallen apart. Of course this took the most part of the morning and the afternoon to explain, back in the privacy of Mrs Harper's Tavern. Saranon was surprised to find that Mitch did not seem out of place. He greeted Mrs Harper with a warm embrace as though they were long lost friends.

Celia noticed her puzzled look. 'We usually get along well with our neighbours, even if they have different ways of doing things.'

'You're not wrong there. I feel like the more I find out the less I understand,' she commented.

'Well you'll have to learn pretty quick seeing as Mitch will likely follow you anywhere. I never did find out about how you ended up with him?' Celia quizzed.

Saranon cringed while thinking about it, 'It's complicated.'

'That's all right. We've had more trouble since you left, more wiccan have gone missing. Jedd thinks they won't be coming back, it's pretty serious,' Celia spoke in a soft tone.

'If you want, I can stay longer?' She asked.

'I was hoping you would,' Celia added.

Mitch was fine with staying late and Saranon was looking forward to being able to relax if only for a moment.

When Jedd came in from a hard day's work she had trouble recognising him, the stress had made him look older. Celia left while the two spoke, it did not take long for her to figure out that the fluctuations within the Keep, may be related. It seemed that while she had been busy repairing the Keep, someone else had been busy trying to attack it. Taking control of a Keep was a lucrative prospect for those who travelled the tainted path. Yet a Keep, the size of Greddin, was usually safe. The sheer size alone and power behind it deterred all but the craziest. Perhaps they were going after a smaller Keep, but as Jedd said, they had seen no signs of anyone going after some of the smaller ones.

Saranon tried to enjoy the rest of the evening. Her

friends had no trouble doing so. It was getting smoky in the air so she went outside with Mitch following not far behind. He spoke first, 'So what do you think?'

'Well, I'm not sure to be honest it could just be…'

She was distracted by a fast moving cart coming their way. It looked familiar, 'Is that what I think it is?'

Mitch turned and waved as the Captain stepped down prompting them to climb on. She hesitated out of exasperation before squeezing between the Captain and Mitch. 'You owe me an explanation,' she glared at him.

The Captain was none too keen about having her that close but proceeded anyway. 'We're having trouble back at Greddin.'

'Mrs Harper said wiccan were going missing, and it had escalated in the last few days' Mitch spoke.

Saranon's brain worked overtime as Mitch, and the Captain spoke around her. She was trying to think back to her discussions with the Keep.

She was about to say something as Mitch turned toward her and whispered, 'We have to go.'

She gave him a disapproving look as the wheels of the cart rolled underneath. She took a last glimpse of Mrs Harper's Tavern before letting out a heavy sigh. She could feel a sense of urgency well up in him, as she tried to read his thoughts that remained forever clouded. For the third time she found herself in the cart moving toward Greddin Fort, although this time had she climbed in by herself.

She sighed in a mix of frustration as the great doors leading into the Keep closed behind her. The thought to scream and shout like last time was tempting and Mitch gave her a stern look as though reading her mind. Saranon could sense the energy of the Keep as it shimmered along the wall in an uneven pattern. The image made a shiver run down her spine, as she followed the Captain down below the habitable area. The air was dry as it hummed along with a faint breeze from the vents rising through the building. She stayed out of the way behind Mitch, as they approached a small gathering that appeared ready for anything. She wondered what she had just walked into.

Deep in the bowels of the Keep, Captain Mirshendy lead the team to check out some strange disturbances that had created a dead zone. No one felt comfortable when part of the Keep was down. For all the repairs that had been done, it had not gone anywhere near to fixing all the problems that sprang up. The Captain's troops were more than capable, but it was dangerous work. They stayed close together, this was no time to get lost. As they travelled closer to the area, the Captain realised that it had been flooded. It was not the worst problem, wizards were good at adapting, but flooding an area often hid other dangers. 'Can you send a sensor down to check it out?' The Captain asked his officer.

'Way ahead of you,' Nathan spoke.

The little beacon shot off into the dark water. Nathan waited near the edge, 'It's not sending back anything we're going to have to try somewhere else.'

'All right pack up and we'll move around to the east. There's an opening we can try there.'

Nathan turned away from the water to join the others. Just as he did something dark sprang out of the water grabbing his leg and yanking him down. One of his colleagues tried to get hold of his arm, but he was being dragged in as well. The Captain yelled for the second man to let go amid the turmoil. The last thing they saw was Nathan's petrified look as he went under without a trace. 'We're getting out of here now,' the Captain yelled.

There was no need to explain why as they ran back into the secure part of the Keep. Saranon could sense an odd energy rise from the depths and she needed no convincing to leave as she ran with the small group. The Captain walked straight into the control room where Lyn was running around in a mad panic. The information filled the screen as it was relaying back from the Keep. 'I just lost one of my men,' the Captain spoke.

'I know,' Lyn replied.

'Can you at least tell me what that was?' He asked with a sense of urgency.

'I'm trying as fast as I can,' she spoke.

The Captain stepped aside, 'I thought you knew what we were going into.'

'There's no way of telling in a dead zone, I just need some time to find out,' Lyn exclaimed.

'You had better have an answer,' with that the Captain walked away.

As the first light ran in through the open windows near where the Captain had been waiting all night, Lyn rushed in, her face paler than usual. 'I'm sorry I think

Nathan is being made into a Host.'

'How long do we have?' He asked.

'We've already lost four hours,' Lyn replied.

'So fifty-six hours remaining,' the Captain was not impressed.

He thumped his fist hard down on the table, how could he have been so stupid. Whoever was trying to take over the Keep had what they wanted. It would not be long before it would become impossible to stop.

Saranon caught the last few words, 'What do you mean?'

'I lost one of my men and now he's being turned into a Host for the Keep,' the Captain said in a flat tone before looking away.

This was all new territory for her. She was beginning to feel as though everything was fast spiralling out of control. Her stomach hit rock bottom as her mind raced, it was all happening too fast and she felt like she was being left behind. She left the control room, she would get no answers there, especially since it was so crowded. She would have to find another way to access the information she needed.

An awful pained sound came from behind, Saranon returned to see the Captain curled up on the ground, 'What's going on?'

Mitch whispered, 'Rachel has been taken.'

'We are in deep trouble, aren't we?' She exclaimed.

'You could say that,' Mitch replied.

It did not take long for the Captain to regain his

composure. This time, whatever was going on, it had become personal.

She wanted to reach out and help, but everywhere she looked the situation seemed to be have slipped beyond her. Captain Mirshendy saw her look and gave her a comforting pat on the shoulder, 'We'll get Rachel back.'

Saranon was not so sure. The Captain was preparing a small group to go out into the dead zone and she caught Mitch in the middle of getting ready. She gave him a disapproving look, but there was no point trying to stop him. If Rachel was in trouble he would follow the Captain anywhere.

She started getting ready to go with them, Mitch looked surprised and disgruntled, 'You are not coming with us.'

'It's all right' the Captain replied.

Mitch glared at her for intruding on his work then handed her a weapon. Saranon looked at it puzzled, 'What do I need that for?'

'For protection,' he explained.

She handed it back, 'I'm not going to need it.'

'Suit yourself,' he remarked.

Mitch was not going to get into an argument with her. If she wanted to go out into the dead zone unprepared, he was not going to bail her out. Saranon could not think of anything else to do and perhaps getting a closer look at the situation would help. From what she heard, it would be difficult to make it any worse. So, armed with that knowledge she stayed close to Mitch and travelled down into unchartered territory. She was used to hiding and a few times when the group had stopped she had blended into the wall. The first time it scared one of the soldiers standing next to her, but they had bigger things to worry about. The Keep was still operational, even though it was not much use as it could not be relied on.

This was the second time she had entered into a dead zone, the area where the Keep had lost control. Odana back in Alveron had remained calm. He had experienced many small glitches before and that was how he viewed them. Greddin was having great difficulty and had gone into a panic, which was not helping Saranon at all. Strange noises started muffling their way along to where they were and she listened. Unlike the mess in the control room some of it was making sense, 'Get back!'

She did not need to push Mitch out of the way, as the wizards cleared out of sight. The whooshing sound was now audible over the background noise. She had an intense urge to go out of her hiding place and deal with it, but she could not. Instead she held back a yell as a cold hard icy flame of sorcery whirled past them at phenomenal speed. The sound as it passed through, was deafening, she let out a yell that disappeared in the noise as she held on. Then it was gone.

Saranon crumbled in the silence that followed, Mitch bent down and picked her up. They had no time to waste and in true wizard fashion the best time to strike was after a great deal of energy had been expended by the enemy. She pulled at his arm and whispered, 'No.'

It was too late, whether she wanted to or not she felt like she was being pulled into the heart of a wasps nest. As the wizards attacked back, another ball of ice flew past only just missing the Captain, but that did not deter any of them. Instead the wizards went to action closing in as they struck back and the air soon filled with the hollow smell of wizardry. The smell burnt as it hit her lungs and made her gag. As much as she liked being on the same side as the wizards, it was beginning to have a few draw backs.

Saranon stopped to catch her breath and Mitch called out, 'Next time you should stay at home.'

'This is your home,' she said between coughing. 'And I'm not going.'

She ran after them not wanting to be left behind. The haze was thick, she could see two had been injured. She admired their strength, they were relentless. She wondered how she would have fared on the receiving end, then thought better of it. The Captain had sent for backup and she could make out a few new faces that had caught up with them. As she turned around, it took her a while to realise the only sound anyone was making was her coughing.

Saranon went closer to see what was going on. She could see several sorcerers and they had the one person that would make Captain Mirshendy stop. Rachel was kneeling on a small stone floor that stood out above a murky liquid. She recognised the liquid, sheal it could absorb almost anything including sorcery. Rachel was in the middle on a small island, just big enough to hold her. The wizards had rushed in and for the time being were an excellent cover.

They had managed a stalemate. While blocking the sorcery it created a beautiful deadly light works that crinkled across the air. Rachel looked over and saw her. Saranon knew she had to do something, the sheal was rising it was painful to watch.

Once it reached Rachel, her energy would be absorbed and flow into the Keep. At that moment one of the sorcerers managed to break through and two wizards disintegrated from sight. The sorcery hit Saranon with a wave of heat it filled her lungs and made her feel alive. She looked down at her arm and realised her body was consuming the energy. She looked up at the sorcerers and saw their faces as they realised they were in serious trouble. The three scrambled for the door, Mitch tried to latch onto the last one, but he managed to get away. Through all the excitement she rescued Rachel, and could only just hear her shouting.

Rachel grabbed her hand and shoved it in the sheal for a second. All the energy that she had absorbed drained with it. 'Ah! What did you do that for,' Saranon cried holding her hand.

'You absorbed too much energy,' Rachel responded.

Her hand throbbed, 'It's nice to see you too. Do have you any idea how much that hurts?'

'You wanted to come,' Mitch reminded her.

Rachel fell in behind where it was safe, while she clutched her hand in a grump. The wizards moved on, Nathan was still out there and time was running short.

CHAPTER FOURTEEN

Taking on the Dihan

Saranon's pulse was racing fast with both fear and excitement. The wizards around her were travelling fast and she was finding it hard to keep up. A glimmer of movement caught her eye and she realised the sorcerers were behind her. As she panicked she tripped over, the sorcerers muffled the sound so as not to alert the wizards and she was on her own. She could see Addison striding towards her. She could see a few sealed doorways and tried to go through one, but it would not budge. She kept on running, she sensed the sorcerer behind her preparing to attack. With all her might she managed to push herself through one of the seals. The blast of sorcery from behind just missed her hand as she plunged through.

Saranon turned and trembled as she tried to scream at what she saw, but nothing came out. She saw what had been done to Nathan, the seal was glowing and she realised Addision was trying to get through. Before she could protect the seal it had already closed and she was locked inside with the Host. She scrambled across the room to try and find another way out. 'I thought you would be pleased to see me again,' the Keep spoke.

The words came out of Nathan's mouth, but they were not his. She forced herself to look at what had been done, 'You look terrible.'

As Saranon listened to herself she wanted to take the words back. The Host laughed, it was not yet complete but it was aware of its surroundings. She forced herself to sit down beside it. She watched as the Keep melded part of itself to what was once Nathan. Once the process was complete Nathan would be part of the Keep and vice versa. He tried to hold out his hand and she held it. It felt strange and she almost dry reached. The Host seemed oblivious to her difficulties and relaxed. 'You look different,' Saranon spoke.

Nathan still looked human, he stared up with his jet black eyes giving away what he was and would become, 'I should hope so.'

Saranon felt a tear travel down the side of her cheek. There were a couple of loud blasts from the outside, 'What will you do?' She asked.

'You don't like my decision?' The Keep asked.

'No, I meant about them,' she spoke as she stared at where the opening had been.

'You disapprove, would you rather I give myself to the

Palascene?'

'To be honest I think neither is worthy,' she exclaimed.

Nathan laughed, 'Perhaps you're right.'

Saranon did not want to look away for fear of offending the Keep so the two remained silent as the process continued. In the corridor Addison was fuming as he realised she was with the Host. He hurled his sorcery full pelt at the locked seal, but only managed to knock himself back with the blast. The noise brought the wizards running back and he blocked their blows as he ran with the others. The wizards fell back leaving Saranon behind, she could sense Mitch moving further away and wanted to shout out but it would be no use.

The wall was stone cold and there was no way out, she had been locked in with the Host. She slid down onto the floor in a sign of resignation, it was all she could think of as Nathan lay in front of her. The process was slow she knew that all she could do was wait. There was no point trying to help Nathan, he was already part of the Keep. Trying to stop what was happening would kill him, and anger Greddin Fort. It took a great amount of energy to create a Host and the Keep did not always accept the offering. Either way, she wondered if whoever made him knew what they were doing. A short term gain came with all sorts of risks. Nathan would not be as easy to subdue as the Keep.

Hosts had a reputation for being uncontrollable and the description reminded her of herself. Saranon stood up and sat on the raised stone table staring down at Nathan, it was like waiting for the inevitable. Nathan was awake and spoke to her in a soft voice. Now that she had overcome the shock it did not seem so bad, but still she was having trouble seeing the dangerous side of it all. Perhaps it was just misunderstood like she was. She had had enough of being labelled by other people.

The Keep made a strange noise and she looked over her shoulder. Nathan grabbed her and shoved her onto the floor, the process was finished. Saranon tried to push him off, but he was much stronger, she shouted at him to no affect. He stared at her, then leaned down and kissed her, then brushed his fingers through her hair.

He whispered, 'Don't you want to play?'

'You and I have more important things to do. Now get off!' She shouted.

The Host hesitated for a while smiled and helped her up. Nathan took a few steps then turned and laughed, 'Did you think I would let you go?'

'You don't own me,' she said.

'I don't need to,' he replied.

'I helped you,' she snapped.

'Yes, you did. Tell you what we'll do…you don't like being kissed do you,' he smiled.

'Next time ask,' she glared at him.

'Someone's a little touchy, are you like that with Mitch?' He asked.

'No,' she replied in a harsh tone.

The Host took Saranon's bond-breaker Corsavere off her and she yelled, 'Give it back!'

He held it out of reach, 'Did you want it?'

'Nathan, give me the bond-breaker!' She yelled.

'No, I think I'll keep it,' he taunted.

'Nathan!' She shouted.

A shuddering noise echoed through the locked seal, someone was trying to get in. Saranon turned to the Host, 'Is there another way out?'

'Of course,' he replied.

The two made their way out through a narrow passage. While Nathan taunted her by holding the bond-breaker just out of reach. Behind them came a crashing sound as the seal broke and they ran even faster. The two scrambled into a large chamber, she stayed close to Nathan and he smiled, 'I thought you didn't like me.'

She did not answer, the sorcerers were catching up fast. The Host looked at her, 'So what's the plan?'

'I thought you had one,' she replied.

'You place great faith in me,' the Host retorted.

Saranon knew what he meant, the Keep was not designed to deal with this type of conflict and she felt alone. At least Nathan had led them into one of the main chambers where the Keep was stronger. Yet the connection was still down, and the place felt cold. She asked, 'Can you...'

Nathan was one step ahead, he had gone to one of the corners to try and bring the Keep back online. She felt her panic rising, she had no idea what to do and she felt small in the centre of the room. The sorcerers had taken the long way which was easier to travel. Though it would not be long and they would be through the door, Saranon tried to stay calm.

In the middle of the dead zone it did not take much before the giant doors gave way. At first there was nothing, then she heard the sound of their hollow laughing. The sorcerers were already in the room, she could see them. She looked up to where Nathan had been and there was no trace of him. She knew that no one was close, but losing sight of Nathan was not good. She ran to find him and hit a barrier of energy. She realised she was trapped, this was beginning to be a common occurrence. She had to get out, she placed her hands up against the barrier something was wrong.

It felt strange and she thought against trying to go through it. That would have been the straight forward option, but not doing so meant she was still trapped. There was definitely no sign of Nathan, as Saranon realised that the sorcerers had dealt with her. She sensed the other wizards approaching, Mitch ran up to the barrier and was about to do something. Saranon waved her arms to stop him, and he pulled up just in time, 'What is it?'

'There something different about the barrier, they've got Nathan,' she replied.

Captain Mirshendy spoke up, 'You saw Nathan?'

'You're trapped,' Mitch smiled.

Saranon turned to Mitch, 'It's not funny.' She turned to the Captain, 'Yes he was fine, but he ran off with my bond-breaker.'

Mitch found the whole situation amusing, 'Do you want some help?'

Saranon glared at him as he removed the barrier, she was not impressed about being shown up by a wizard.

The Captain thought out loud, 'So now we've lost a Host and your bond-breaker.'

'Yes,' Saranon said.

She realised that she had made a mess of the situation and Mitch was not showing her any support. She kept pace with the wizards as they searched for Nathan and saw that Bianca had joined them. She paid no attention to Saranon, but then she had expected that. They met up with a small group of Palascene and the problem became clear. Her heart sank with despair she wanted to help, but everything she seemed to touch was going wrong.

The Dihan who had been trying to take over the Keep, were so close to success. The desperation showed on the otherwise calm Palascene. She wanted to apologise, but there would be no apology great enough to make up for this. The Dihan had sealed off the area where they were holding Nathan and she waited as the group tried to find a way in. Bianca found a small weakness in the barrier, it was enough for them to go through. Saranon wanted to go with the sorcerers, but it was made clear that she had to stay behind. The Captain and Mitch were not impressed, there was no way they could make it through without trying to break the barrier.

She kicked her heel against the wall, patience was not her strong point, the Captain made it appear easy. A few strange sounds could be heard through the small opening, then a harrowing loud scream followed by stone cold silence. The Captain looked at Saranon, 'Perhaps you had better take a look?'

'I'm not going in there,' she exclaimed.

Mitch picked her up and shoved her through the barrier with her kicking. 'That could've hurt,' she said.

'Don't make me come after you,' he spoke.

She tried to get back on the other side, but Mitch stood in her way, 'I think you owe us a favour.'

Saranon knew that he was right. Although it did not make it any less scary as she made her way through the opening that led down a small creepy tunnel. The thought occurred to her that the Dihan would be expecting someone else to come, she hated surprises. The tunnel was deadly silent and she made slow progress. It occurred to her that Mitch may have been able to go through the barrier, but she was too far along now. The tunnel opened up to several different paths, she went left. Passing through another barrier before she knew what she had done.

The barrier remained silent she took a deep breath and moved on. She could hear people and did not know who they were. One of the Dihan was standing up ahead, there would be no way she could get closer without making a scene. She was caught between doing nothing and moving forward. If she went back now, Mitch would not be impressed. The possibility of something going wrong scared her, but then she had already done that. Her skin went cold. She had to remain in her current form, even though it would leave her blind to many things.

Saranon doubted whether anything she did would

make a difference, she would just have to try and hope. It was difficult to see, then with so much sorcery hanging thick in the air it was hard to make out anything. The sorcerer in front of her fell silent on the floor when she removed her bond-breaker. The movement was quick and fluid with a muffled sound. She found her way through the haze and what she saw did not look good. The place was filled with a strange light, which filtered through from the heart of the Keep in an open conduit covering most of the floor.

The Dihan had more than just the Host, the Palascene had been captured. She made it down to the conduit, Addison was lying in wait. 'Ah, so nice of you to join the party. Thanks for the gift.'

He held Saranon's bond-breaker Corsavere, 'Now the question is what I should do with you?'

Addison leaped back, floating above the conduit, she tried to get closer, but the energy was too intense. The sorcerer lashed out and she ran to find cover. The flare of sorcery prickled as it frayed along the edges of the blast. Saranon could see Bianca's frightened stare from the corner of the room where she was being held.

Saranon took a deep breath she had to concentrate and the energy running from the conduit was not helping. She tried to become the Angeon something was holding her back, she tried again and it only made her feel sick. She would have to find some other way to fight and then she remembered Nathan had kissed her. She could try to take control of the Host, but would it work? There was only one way to find out. There was a small conduit running up through the wall close by, she ran over and pulled the seal open. It was going to take all her strength and she was pelted backward with the blow. It had not worked, but that was no deterrent. Saranon was not used to giving up. She looked back, Addison was getting ready to fire again, she gave as much as she could, there was something blocking her.

She tried even harder as the blast roared over her head she ducked and stared down at the conduit in dismay, at least she had tried. Addison's screams cut through the air and she ran back to find that Nathan had broken free. Addison turned towards Saranon, 'This is your fault!'

He lunged towards her and Saranon could feel the Angeon rise though it did not strike out. Corsavere started burning out of control in Addison's hand and he had to let go. The Dihan joined their leader, and ran towards the Angeon. Their sorcery held the full blast of their fury as it hit her. Sparking with great intensity and causing confusion.

She could hear Bianca crying out to her as the Angeon disintegrated her opponents into ash. The conduit that Addison had opened, was still flooding energy through the Keep she walked toward the massive hole. Bianca yelled behind her, 'No!'

Then she dived in, the conduit sparked even brighter. Then in a brilliant array of light it began to close.

In the aftermath the Angeon lay motionless on the mezzanine near the ceiling as Mitch drew closer. He hesitated before kneeling beside her. The Angeon was still breathing she managed a whisper, 'I don't want you to see me like this.'

Mitch whispered back, 'You still won't accept me.'

'Do you want to be with someone like this?' She asked.

'That is my choice,' he spoke.

'I don't even want to look at myself,' she remarked.

'That's something you're going to have to deal with,' he replied.

'I'm sorry,' she added.

Mitch let out a tear and kissed her on the forehead before she changed back. Saranon could sense several other wizards who had come to help. They moved her back into the normal hub of the Keep. She was aching all over. She was well enough to walk, but Mitch had insisted that she endure a bumpy ride while the wizards carried her out. He stayed by her side as some of the Palascene tried to get close and shooed them away with small gestures. She did not feel up to speaking with any Palascene, at least not for the moment. It was difficult to face Rachel as she saw her again. She had no reason to feel this way, though part of her did not like people seeing what she was.

Even though Rachel had not seen it firsthand, there was bound to be talk about it and for that she shied away from her friend. Rachel was professional as Saranon lay in silence mulling over her own thoughts. It was a delicate process one which seemed to take forever. She was expecting Rachel to say something, but she did not. The silence began to eat away at her until she cracked, 'Are there many casualties?'

'A few,' Rachel replied.

Saranon cringed of all the people that could be annoyed with her it had to be Rachel, 'What have I done?'

'You hurt Mitch. I thought you wanted the bond,' Rachel spoke.

She closed her eyes in thought, 'It would be nice to protect him from everything, but I can't.'

'He knows that,' Rachel relied.

Saranon wondered when Mitch had appointed Rachel as his spokesperson, or if her friend had taken it upon herself to do so.

She sat up and her heart pounded in her ears, 'This has nothing to do with Mitch. Now if it is all right with you, I would like to see him.'

'You can't, he's thinking of having the bond removed,' Rachel replied.

Saranon stood in dumbfounded silence she did not think she was that bad. Then she had just saved the Keep and perhaps that was too much for the both of them. 'That's his decision.'

With that she left and went back to her quarters. Some of Mitch's belongings were still there and she realised she would miss him a lot more than she thought she would. She sat down on the small couch perhaps it was for the best, she had enough trouble understanding wizards as it was.

There was a knock at the door, Mitch let himself in he sat down on the armchair near her looking awkward. 'I don't want to be shut out,' he said.

Saranon stood in front of him and held her arms out toward him. She could feel the change take over her body as the Angeon within her came alive, 'This is what I am.'

Mitch did not look away but he did not reach towards her either. She placed her hands by her side. 'Are you sure you want to be part of this?'

'I already am,' he said.

She changed back and Mitch held her close and whispered, 'I was offended because you shut me out.'

'I know,' was all she could think of.

He accepted her response, 'I've seen worse,' he said with a smile.

Saranon felt like running for the door would be a good thing to do right now. He read the expression on her face and was far from impressed. She stopped to wipe the tears from her eyes, 'I've got a bit of a problem I'm going to have to deal with Nathan.'

'That can wait until tomorrow,' he spoke.

Mitch stayed dragging out the comfy makeshift bed near the fireplace. Saranon was too tired to argue with him about the importance of privacy. As she had not grown up with much, it was more of a luxury. Talking of her friends made her think of Pennie, she had not heard from her for ages. She hoped Pennie was having more luck than she was, not that saving a Keep was not a massive achievement. Her friend had been stuck with a bunch of wizards. If Darkonian wizards were anything like the ones here, she could be having all sorts of problems. Then her friend had always been resourceful, perhaps everything was fine. She would have to find out after dealing with Nathan.

CHAPTER FIFTEEN

Complications with sorcerers

The morning brought the noise clambering to her door as Bianca burst through interrupting her sleep. 'Control that creature before I put it in the dungeon!'

Saranon looked at her still sleepy eyed as she rose from her comfy bed, 'I take it you mean Nathan.'

'Of course I mean Nathan who else do you think I mean, your dragon!'

'Well…' She started.

'Oh for the love of Normisia just fix it.' Bianca slammed the door behind her, but Saranon knew she was waiting for her.

She got herself dressed and made her way down with Mitch following close by. Everything appeared to be normal and Saranon thought that Bianca may have made a mistake. Then she entered the control room and shouted,

'Nathan!'

The Host turned around in surprise and ran off leaving a mess behind him. If she did not know better she would have sworn that the Host had been sabotaging the control room.

She turned to Bianca, the Palascene looked like she had woken up on the wrong side of the bed, 'Oh don't look at me, this is your mess.'

Bianca wandered off while Saranon tried to find a place to start. She could hear Nathan in the background and went to investigate.

The Host eyed her at floor level as he raised his head above the hard surface. The boards had been removed in a haphazard fashion as Nathan climbed out, and made his way toward her. The Host smiled as he swaggered forward, eyeing her. Saranon began to feel far less comfortable standing so close to him, as he approached. She still did not know what to make of him, but for some reason he had become her problem. She turned to peer down at the gaping hole holding the threaded conduits. The Host took the opportunity to place his arm around her. Without looking at him she put her hand up to his face and pushed him away.

'I thought you'd be happy to see me,' the Host spoke beside her.

She groaned in annoyance, it was going to be a long day. She jumped down into the shallow hole. The Host lay on the floor peering down over her shoulder as he rested his head on his arms. 'What makes you think you can do a better job than me?' He asked.

'I was hoping you could open the panel over there,' she pointed to the wall behind him.

'Oh, so now you need my help?' The Host made the remark seem rather boisterous and sat up, 'I don't think so.'

Saranon gaped in open astonishment as Nathan continued, 'First you can do something for me.'

'I beg your pardon,' she scowled in annoyance.

The Host had disregarded the fact that she was helping him.

He leaned down, and hauled her up to the floor as she eyed him with suspicion. This was not going according to plan and the Host took great enjoyment from changing the game. 'I want you to do something for me,' Nathan spoke as he reached over to the table. He removed the shiny surface and took out the broken fragments of a tiny power source.

'I would like three of these, in their original form,' Nathan for once was serious, and she could hear the Keep's words as he spoke.

She let out a heavy sigh, 'All right, but I need you to help.'

Nathan smiled as he let go of shattered pieces, and grabbed her hands swinging her around as he went. 'Nathan!' Saranon shouted with a sharp edge to her voice.

The Host did not seem to be listening as he continued, then just as she was unprepared, he let go. She tumbled back toward the open conduit as she placed her hands out to stop herself.

A massive surge ignited at the end of the conduit. Sparks flew everywhere as she stammered backwards into Nathan's grasp. As the haze cleared in the air from the smoke Saranon stared in utter disbelief. There, near the edge of the conduit, were five tiny shiny new power sources. As the smoke wafted down through the corridor she waited for someone to appear and yell at them, but no one came. The Host saw her gaze, and commented, 'I closed the door.'

The vents took the last of the smell away, but it still lingered in her clothes as she opened the windows. She asked, 'How did you know that would work?'

The Host was picking up the spare power sources, pocketing them for himself as he looked back, 'You only see me Nathan.'

Saranon wanted to say it was not true when she only saw the wizard. To her the Keep was a massive entity, and one body seemed rather small. She gazed out the window as the Host fixed the new power sources in place.

She was missing a glorious warm sunny day and she lingered a little longer before going back to help fix the control room. The Host had not stopped fiddling about, instead he had moved on to the next area. 'What are you doing?' She asked.

'Do you need to ask?' the Host did not look up.

Saranon peered over his shoulder and understood what he was doing, 'Do you need a hand?'

'I wouldn't say no,' he replied.

The two worked while for rest of the day, Bianca was nowhere to be seen, which was just as well. She did not feel like being sociable while recovering from saving the Keep. There was a strange silence between her and the Host, one where each other knew how close the danger had come.

It was soon getting late and Chelsea visited to see what they were doing, 'Aren't you going to eat? There's a nice big roast in the hall.'

Nathan looked up, 'That's sounds like a good reason to stop.'

He walked over to Chelsea who was not sure how to react. People had been avoiding Nathan all day, but she was not that type of person. Chelsea asked, 'I assume you still eat?'

'Yes,' he stated.

'Is it true that you don't need sleep?' Chelsea asked.

'I'm still human,' the Host replied.

Chelsea thought of more than a dozen other questions to ask the Host before they entered the hall. She noticed that Mitch had made himself at home on a table with his friends, so she sat with Chelsea. Nathan became a little restless and went to lounge near the fireplace. She did not take much notice until she heard shouting. As she turned to look a crowd had gathered near the fireplace and a high pitched scream rose above commotion. It sounded almost unnatural, then a faint wave of energy hummed down the walls, and she knew who it was.

She ran, and barged her way through as the circle of people closed tighter not wanting to let her through.

Saranon paused letting her sorcery flow inside. Without hesitation the crowd parted just in time for her to see Terrance holding Nathan to the ground. The Host struggled before her as he screamed again and she stood watching in silence. It pained her to watch as the sorcerer held the Host down, then she saw the hyrik emerge as Terrance held it out above the Host's head. Nathan's eyes grew wild as he pounded against the sorcerer to no avail.

Saranon went pale as the sorcerer placed it over Nathan's head, she was too shocked to watch, yet she could not look away. Terrance extended his sorcery to seal the hyrik in place, as it shrank, a stale smell wafted up through the air. Without warning the audience cleared away around her. She stood alone watching in horror. The hyrik began to melt and bubble as it evaporated. Before she could say anything, Terrance jumped out of the away, as the last remnants fell to the floor. She tried to work out what had happened and then a thought sank in.

The small group of Palascene stayed around the edge in a circle as if waiting, not knowing what had happened. She scowled in disbelief and held out her hand to the Host who was still shaking from his ordeal. She turned to face Terrance, 'You deserved that.'

With that she went to walk away, but she did not get far as the Palascene made it clear they wanted her to stay. She was not impressed. She had somehow taught the Keep how to remove a hyrik, but then the Palascene deserved as much. Terrance showed no signs of his attack on the Host as he stood before her. She had missed out on what started the argument and the Palascene were not pleased to see her. Another sorcerer tried to pull him away, but Terrance would not let it be.

Terrance stared her straight in the face, 'You were supposed to stop this creature.'

'You were supposed to stop the Dihan,' she replied with a sharp tone.

'We have accommodated you this far,' he stated with a firm edge.

Nathan moved closer and started shouting. Without turning she signalled for the Host to stop. To everyone else's surprise he obeyed and sat on the floor without making a sound. The two sorcerers glared at each other, the room had gone silent amidst their arguing. Terrance looked at the Host and Saranon knew what he was angry about, 'You want the Host for yourself.'

'Don't be absurd,' Terrance had had enough and turned to leave.

The Host spoke in a soft voice afterward, but it filled a void in the room, 'I'm sorry for getting you in trouble.'

She smiled, this time it was not Nathan's fault. She flumped down on the couch as she felt the last of her sorcery slip away and breathed a heavy sigh of relief. Saranon had her own complications without having to take on someone else's. The Host was not the least bit worried, as he enjoyed the rest of the evening. Although she did notice all the sorcerers in the room now stayed away, they were reluctant to encounter the Host again.

Terrance had left in a rage and there was not much

that Saranon could do about it. She returned to the control room after that, the sooner the place was fixed the better. Captain Mirshendy came to join them in the room as they worked into the night. The Captain had been good friends with Nathan and while she worked, the two managed to have a conversation. She had taken several panels off the wall and had managed to squeeze into the gap.

The Keep had shown her what to look for, although she was having trouble locating it, 'Nathan, I think we have a problem.'

The Host pulled off another panel where she had crawled to, and poked his head in, 'Ah, I see.'

The Captain took a closer look, 'That's not supposed to be like that.'

'Given my new fan club I think we should finish here first,' Saranon spoke with a hint of sarcasm.

The Captain was quite calm, 'You have a way of making friends.'

It was past midnight before they could run the first test. Saranon was starting to feel the lack of sleep in her muscles. Her body was still healing itself. Nathan fixed a few small glitches without any complaint and finally made his way to bed. She sat in silence looking at the results of their work with the Captain, 'You look like you want to say something.'

'You need to leave,' he spoke.

'What?' She asked.

'You were right about Terrance, you need to leave Redadere,' the Captain added.

'You had this planned?' She asked.

'You have served your purpose,' he responded.

'I think you know why I haven't received any contact from my friend Pennie?' She asked.

'It was for the best,' Captain Mirshendy said.

Saranon was not angry, but she was not impressed either. She was still in a grump when she ran out to meet Mitch and Katholomu in the courtyard. Mitch was already sitting in place he reached down and grabbed her hand pulling her up before she could say anything. The dragon took off with one giant leap disappearing into the warm night sky. He was quiet behind her, 'So what do you have to say for yourself?' She asked.

'You didn't want to speak with me,' he said.

'Very funny, I suppose you and the Captain had been planning this, she said.

'That's unfair,' he replied.

'As I recall you kidnapped me,' she retorted.

Mitch remained silent and Saranon could not understand why. After all it was she who deserved to be annoyed by what had happened. The magnificent creature they rode on made good time into Gosbin. Normisia's capital was much larger and far grander than Redadere. Katholomu descended toward one of the outer Keeps as the morning light rose to the east. As they came closer she grumbled when she realised it was another wizard stronghold, 'No. You're supposed to avoid wizards.'

It was too late the dragon was already touching down. Several wizards in familiar uniforms came scurrying out to meet them. 'This is your fault,' she said as she turned to Mitch.

He had a big grin on his face, 'Come on, you'd better get down.'

The dragon lowered himself to the ground so that they could descend much to Saranon's disgust, 'What did you do to my dragon?'

Mitch spoke, 'Saranon this is not the place.'

Before he could say anything else she slipped down, and went over to the greeting party. The man before her looked like Mitch and was well dressed. She was about to say something when he spoke first, 'I see you could not stay out of trouble.'

Evan stared straight at her as though expecting something. Without saying anything further he beckoned them to follow him inside. As they passed by the decorated walls she turned to Mitch and whispered, 'You gave that up?'

'Yes,' he whispered back.

Then she asked Evan. 'Are you sure you're related to Mitch?'

Evan looked at his brother then back at Saranon, 'Yes.'

As the two brothers made polite conversation she peered out of the window in the small cosy room. She looked down to Katholomu who was taking no notice of her. She curled up in the chair and before realising it fell fast asleep Mitch woke her up, and she came too with a start, 'Did I miss anything?'

Mitch smiled, 'No.'

She could only just contain her excitement when she heard her friend Pennie was visiting. For now she had to wait, which was completely incomprehensible. As she thought of Pennie and how long it had been since they had seen each other. Saranon tried not to fidget, but the two wizards were beginning to bore her. As she looked closer she noticed Evan was wearing a familiar symbol on a small chain near his belt. It was the same mark from Ollanthia, a warped tear drop pattern and she wondered what he was doing wearing a Darkonian symbol.

The small object glistened in the sunlight, Evan noticed her staring, and did not say anything. As they left she had a chance to ask Mitch, 'How well do you know your brother?'

'That's a strange question,' Mitch commented.

'He was wearing a familiar symbol,' she spoke.

'We are on good terms with the Asdenard,' he knew what she was referring to.

She was not so sure about Mitch's answer, but did not press the matter further, 'So where is Pennie?'

Mitch was about to speak when her friend came running toward her. It was like a dream as they embraced so far from home. Tears escaped down her cheek and Pennie was the same. He had disappeared as they ran off out into the warm open air.

Saranon took a moment to compose herself wiping her face, Pennie looked a lot more relaxed, 'So how are you?'

'I'm fine. In fact I'm better than fine my health is

good.'

'How?' Saranon exclaimed.

'Could you believe it the Normisian's cured me,' Pennie said.

'Really,' she was astonished.

Pennie smiled and Saranon felt all the sorrow inside her trying to swell up again. They had been through some tough times and this was the longest they had been apart. 'Do you think I'll be able to return someday?' Saranon asked.

'Well if Jacob has anything to do with it, I would think so,' Pennie replied.

'How is he?' She asked.

'Why don't you ask him yourself?' Pennie spoke.

She was flabbergasted, 'They let him in Normisia.'

Pennie roared with laughter, 'He didn't have any trouble.'

Pennie had a hundred and one questions about her journey which was fine, except for the fact that it felt more like an interrogation. Her friend was a stickler for detail and any attempts to fob Pennie off, were met with a stern disapproving look. The hot afternoon sun pelted down between the trees near the outer rim of Zaidek. The great Keep for all its glory, was smaller than Greddin. The building above ground was similar, though it was in much better condition. The wizards kept a close eye on them without giving away too many signs. Saranon thought to herself that not much had changed. Off in the distance she could make out Jacob's tall slender frame, he looked as though he was in no hurry to meet her.

Pennie looked much better than she did last time, though the illness had taken its toll. Jacob was not hard to find, he was making polite conversation with Mitch much to Saranon's amazement. He looked different to the way she remembered, perhaps because so much had happened. The wind played in his hair and along his coat, but his eyes stayed focused. He looked out of place in the manicured gardens that swept at their feet, then so did she.

'I didn't think you were allowed out?' She asked.

He smiled as she screwed up her face in disgust. 'Did you think I would not find you?' Jacob spoke.

'I thought you didn't want to see me again,' Saranon remarked.

'I said you needed to leave Darkonia,' he replied.

'But…'

'You misunderstood,' he interrupted.

Mitch was trying not to crack up laughing she could sense it, but his lips remained unmoved. Pennie seemed not to notice, 'Now are you going to introduce me to your companion?'

'Ah yes, well you see it's like… this is Mitch,' Saranon motioned with her hands towards the towering wizard.

'My name is Mitchell Kregner,' with great sensitivity he reached down and kissed Pennie on the hand.

Her friend was taken aback by the gesture, 'Well you must be a special person to place your faith in her.'

'Yes,' he replied.

She opened her mouth to say something, but thought

better of it as Mitch stared at her. As he continued to charm her old friend she took the opportunity to take Jacob aside. He peered over his shoulder then back, 'You chose a Normisian?'

'It was an accident,' she snapped at him.

She kicked a lose pebble from the path in frustration then looked up at him, 'You've changed.'

'No,' he commented.

As Saranon left, her eyes were heavy with exhaustion as the sun began to set behind the hills. Zaidek was placed to look over most of Gosbin. The city dwarfed Redadere in size. The elegance of Gosbin's grand buildings far outshone the smaller city. Dinner was a strange experience, she had not stayed long, even though the wizards were happy to make casual conversation. It was small talk about nothing and Evan did not seem at all interested in answering any of her questions. She left Mitch who was relaxing and catching up with old friends, as she wandered down the hall toward her room.

'Saranon,' whispered Pennie from somewhere around the bend.

'What are you doing?' she whispered back.

'Hush,' her friend replied.

Saranon just wanted to go to sleep, even though Pennie would not be impressed. The two of them made their way through the labyrinth of pathways inside the Keep.

Pennie had mastered the art of snooping a long time ago, but she was not so light on her feet. Several times her friend gave her a cross stare for making too much noise. In the wizards' Keep they could almost conceal themselves. Wizards by nature detested the thought of not being able to know everything that was happening.

When they finally reached their destination her friend knelt down so that Saranon could take a peak. She asked, 'What are they doing?'

'I don't know, but it's a problem,' Pennie whispered.

'Why is that?' She asked.

'Because they want you,' Pennie replied

'Nonsense,' she remarked.

Pennie was in no mood to mess around, 'They will not let us leave.'

Saranon was not impressed, 'We can talk about this in the morning.'

'I'm trying to help,' her friend remarked.

Saranon could not see the sinister side of a bunch of sorcerers hanging around in a wizards Keep. After all, that was what she was doing, and besides the Keep felt fine. Pennie was one for worrying too much over nothing. In morning she would entertain her friend's idea and find out what was happening.

CHAPTER SIXTEEN

Partial acceptance

Saranon woke up with the bustle of everyday life, she looked around the room it felt empty without Mitch. She would have to face Pennie, it was a dreary thought, but she had brushed her friend aside last night. In fact she had been doing that ever since Tasha's death. She did not think Pennie was able to lead their small group which was now down to two. Perhaps they needed to recruit some new members? No sooner than the thought had entered her mind than a sorcerer close to her age ran toward her, he was Darkonian.

Richard grabbed her by the arm, 'Pennie's in trouble.'

'Hang on, what do you mean?' She asked.

'She did not return last night, when I went to look for her I heard that she had been taken,' he spoke in haste.

Saranon thought that Richard was not brave. The

more she heard the more she realised that Pennie had stumbled across something, 'You leave it to me.'

'We're wasting time,' he responded.

Richard followed her to where Evan and Mitch were. 'I do not see Pennie,' she spoke as she faced Evan.

'Did you think there would be no price for her recovery?' Evan commented.

'That was paid with Greddin,' she remarked.

'Ah, but you were the one who almost destroyed it. The Palascene are willing to teach you if you accept the hyrik that way we both get what we want,' Evan spoke in a calm tone.

Saranon hated his smile, but she knew that being a prisoner would cost much more. With a sudden jolt the Keep stopped. Right on cue the occupants of the Keep started going into a panic. She signalled to Mitch, 'I think it's time to leave.'

Mitch gave her a worried look as he obeyed they walked through the chaos to where Katholomu was. The majestic dragon lowered his head and stared her in the eye as he spoke one word, 'Coward.'

The word shook the ground like thunder making Saranon stop in her tracks. She wanted to argue with the massive beast, but dragons were known for being stubborn. It was cold, she looked up to see the weather had changed from calm to stormy grey and in her heart she knew it was time. The dragon had brought her here for a reason and now it was time. Her former self fell away in an instant vanishing in the cold wind which swept around her. It was a small price to pay to be who she was. This time it was Evan who came running flanked by wizards. Tiny pieces of ground began to crumble, falling away fast to create a rift between her and the wizards. It spread either side around one section of the Keep.

'Saranon you can't do this,' Mitch was terrified of what he was witnessing.

'Yes I can. Tell your brother to back down, and I will restore the Keep,' the Angeon spoke.

For a moment in the noise that roared around them Mitch remained silent, without speaking he did what he was asked. 'You have what you want,' he replied.

She kept her word, but did not change back. Instead she walked up to the wizards who fell back until she came face to face with Evan.

She caressed his face with the back of her fingers, and whispered so that no one else could hear. 'If you think I could take a Keep this size with such little effort you are mistaken.'

Evan did not reply so she made her way back into the Keep. Mitch interrupted, 'So the weather is not your doing?'

'You do not recognise your own Keep?' She answered.

Evan was not convinced, 'Are you sure it was the Keep?'

'Yes,' she replied.

They moved inside and Katholomu followed them in a rush, as the rain broke into a torrent. Saranon changed back as she looked out the window in disgust. The rain could be a soothing sound, but this was something different. Mitch shared a moment with his brother before joining her, 'This is how the Palascene punish those who go against them. If you want to help you need to make amends.'

To her surprise Pennie came running up to her, 'Can someone please tell me what's going on?'

'Where have you been?' She could not believe her friend would vanish.

Pennie shook some dirt off her clothes, 'I had to wait so I wouldn't be spotted.' She looked up at Saranon, 'Oh no, I know that look.'

Pennie waited for Saranon's reply, 'We need Bianca.'

'Oh no,' her friend responded.

Saranon stared at her friend, 'All right then, you figure it out.'

'But Bianca doesn't like me,' Pennie blurted out.

'I have faith in you,' Saranon replied.

'Oh no, you're not leaving this one up to me,' Pennie exclaimed.

Evan stepped in, 'I hate to interrupt, but if you could assist we would consider it a favour in kind for saving your life.'

Pennie knew what he meant, 'I will get to it then.'

Saranon wanted to follow her although Pennie could manage on her own. Before long she found herself with only Mitch for company.

'You did not ask before you threatened my brother,' he spoke.

Saranon was going to make a snide remark, then

thought better of it. 'So I'm expected to be civilised?' She exclaimed.

'That's not what I meant,' he remarked.

The rain gushed through the night the Keep muffled the sound, though she knew it was there as she drifted in and out of sleep. Mitch could not sleep either, 'Is there any reason why you asked for Bianca?'

'There's something odd about her,' she answered.

'You embarrassed my brother,' Mitch was not going to let the matter be.

'I'm a sorceress, that's what I do best,' she responded still half asleep.

As she rested, Saranon could feel Mitch staring at her. It made her feel uncomfortable, but there was nothing she could do to reassure him. The wizards had backed down and now she had to live with that. The morning was silent as she peered out the window to a bright clear day. She looked down and saw Bianca approaching with her entourage behind her. Pennie burst into the room. 'Saranon, Bianca is a master.'

'No wonder she looked down at me,' she commented.

Mitch invited himself into the conversation, 'She's too young?'

'You mean like me?' Saranon asked.

'You are an anomaly.'

'Hey,' Saranon noticed that he had developed an attitude since being at Zaidek. She was not sure if it was her or Evan who was causing it.

As if reading her mind Mitch gave her a wide cheesy

grin. She did not like to admit it, but it was nice to have someone else around.

Mitch remained silent though she knew he was not impressed. They watched as the rest of the procession was led inside. As much as Mitch wanted her to go and kept on staring at her as a reminder, she knew it was not a good idea. She hung back lulled by the distant hum of the Keep, and the sun shone down on the balcony where they stood. The wizards made the occasional glance up at her from the courtyard, where they hurried about below.

It was a waiting game and one Mitch was not comfortable with. The former soldier had been built for fighting and underneath the relaxed pose, he was frustrated. He finally broke his composure and sat on the balcony next to Saranon, 'What are you expecting from this?'

'A little leeway,' she answered.

'I still think you should have gone with Pennie,' he spoke.

The two sat chatting away while the world went on around them.

'They make a wonderful couple,' Bianca's voice hailed from the courtyard below.

Mitch looked down and knew that now was a goodtime to Keep quiet. Saranon was about to say something. 'There is no need to say anything. You are now linked to the Keep, which means you will not be able to leave,' Bianca smiled and then left.

'What does she mean?' She glared at Pennie as she jumped down off the balcony, in front of her friend in the courtyard.

'This way is best for all of us,' her friend answered.

Saranon ran off and Pennie yelled behind her, 'No don't, if you try to break it you will end up..!'

Her blood was boiling with anger, Mitch was right she should not have left Pennie in charge. She sprinted to the end of the Keep's territory, and felt the link. Pennie was right, but then so was she. She held out her hands as her energy surged through, as it seared against the link she could feel it weaken. She plunged herself through, it made a terrible breaking noise which bled back into the Keep.

As she opened her eyes, things looked normal enough, so she made her way down to the city it was silent. She moved around the street which lay empty, something was not right. She moved through the walls and into a building, then into another, and another. They were all silent with no people or animals and no sign of life except the vegetation which covered the landscape beyond. She wandered down to the shore where the water was black, this world was not real.

She stepped forward and as her foot plunged into the water, it subsided leaving a gap. The waves continued to wash ashore as though nothing had happened, whatever this world was she was not sure she wanted to be in it. The sand looked fine as she made her way back to the dune and strode along to cave at the far end. As she approached she could make out a small makeshift table. She picked up a book, but when she looked down at the writing she could not make it out. The words changed fleeting in and out, not wanting to make sense.

A breeze travelled through the air sweeping the papers off the table and into the air. As Saranon tried to catch them they disappeared, melting into the pebbles along the dune. As she stood up a figure appeared, waiting at near the end of the cave. She walked closer, and realised it was Tasha dressed in the finery that would have been hers had she lived. The two girls stood side by side and Tasha spoke first, 'I cannot stay long, you are in a different phase that is why you cannot see anyone.'

Saranon went to say something and Tasha answered, 'I am Tasha's spirit nothing more. The Palascene have committed a crime, they must know the meaning of sacrifice and you will bring this to them. Kill the boy, but leave the girl. Do you understand?'

'Yes,' she replied.

'The boy has chosen the path of destruction, he must be stopped,' Tasha explained. 'You can make your own way back.'

'What?' She asked in astonishment.

'You know how,' and with that Tasha faded into oblivion, leaving her alone.

Saranon was still stuck with no idea of how to get out perhaps the answer would be with the Palascene? Their Keep was further back from the coast, facing Elspy River, which swept through the middle of Normisia. The enormity of the unknown began to sag down on her shoulders as the distance in this phase made no sense. She reached the Keep in no time at all. The place was becoming creepy as she thought she could see shadows moving in her peripheral vision. Aneeda Keep shimmered as she entered into the strange world she reached out her hand. She touched the wall sensing all the life that ran through the Keep.

Something connected in her mind and the noise around her burst into her ears with a burning sensation after the silence. She held onto Aneeda trying to make sense of it all, a voice sprang out of the darkness, 'Are you all right?'

She turned around and Rianna gasped with recognition then ran away. Saranon stayed where she was, while her mind caught up with her body. The sorceress, Rianna returned with a blanket and Saranon realised she was sweating as she wrapped herself in it. Rianna's eyes were kind so she followed her to a warm lounge area.

Rianna watched her in silence as Saranon downed a pitcher of water before she stopped for a break. From the corner of her eye she saw Bianca enter the room and sit beside her mother. 'You embarrassed me,' was all Bianca said.

She was still groggy, 'It was…it was not your decision.'

She rubbed her eyes and put down her empty glass. Bianca glanced at her mother, Rianna, 'As a member of the Palascene…'

'No, no, you are supposed to lead. Tell me, what is your decision?' She interrupted.

Bianca remained silent and so Saranon walked over to her holding out something she had kept hidden in her hand. She passed it to Bianca and said, 'You know where to find me,' then left.

She heard Rianna gasp and Bianca ran after Saranon, 'Please tell me where you got this?'

Bianca held the small sacra seal in her hand, and Saranon stopped, 'I made it.'

'But you can't, you're not...' Bianca began.

'I'm not what?' She asked.

'You are not trained. Wait, stay for a while,' Bianca pleaded.

She was fast running out of options and with a sinking feeling agreed. As much as she could put on a show, she could not sustain her ability for long and at the end of the day Bianca was just one Palascene. In a way she knew Pennie was right, though she hated being trapped. Bianca smiled, 'I think you should return to Zaidek, I will meet you there. Try not to cause any trouble.'

Saranon knew it was a close escape and was ready for a rest from all the excitement, 'I will try my best.'

'Oh! By the way, your dragon is waiting outside,' Bianca said.

It was her turn to look surprised as she followed the Palascene to the courtyard. Bianca strode next to her and reached out to touch the magnificent creature. 'Now, straight to Zaidek and I expect you to Keep an eye on Saranon.'

Katholomu bowed his head much to her annoyance. She clambered up and without hesitation they were away. She whispered in his ear, 'Whose side are you on?'

The dragon made a rumbling sound like a stifled

laugh which reverberated through his belly and they began to descend.

The flight was over too soon, and she saw familiar faces rushing out to greet her as they landed. She clambered down with deflated excitement as Pennie gave her a worried hug, and spoke, 'Please don't do that again.'

Before she had time to answer, Pennie whisked her inside into a small cosy room and gave her a stern look, 'What did Tasha tell you?'

Saranon almost fell out of chair in disbelief as her friend continued, 'The wizards know, they told the Palascene. It's the only reason you haven't been pummelled out of existence. Now tell me.'

'Kill the boy, but leave the girl, she wants to punish the Palascene,' she spoke.

Pennie went quiet and put her head in her hands. Then after a brief moment recovered, 'Why do you always have to make things difficult?'

Saranon wandered off, being told off like a small child by two people in one day was more than enough. Zaidek was content whirring away in the back of her mind. She had the distinct impression that not much surprised it.

She walked back along the top of the internal courtyard retracing her steps. She could see the wizards training below. She made out two familiar faces Captain Mirshendy and Mitch. They appeared to be completely in their element and she felt like the odd one out. She was in no doubt that the wizards trained hard, compared to someone like her. They made it look easy, that was no small feat. Saranon cringed at the thought that she was staring down at the same people who had held her captive, not the nicest thought. The smell of old sweat wafted up and she frowned in disgust. Better leave them be, she thought.

'So are you going to come down and join us?' Captain Graddon asked.

She broke out of her self-absorbed thought. She stared down at the wizard standing by Captain Mirshendy's side. Jerald answered her look of dismay, 'This is Captain Hugh Graddon and the stairs are over there.' The Captain pointed.

She mumbled out loud as she descended, 'Why would I want to join you?'

Being down in the stench did not appeal to her as Captain Graddon replied, 'Because you are disrupting my officers.'

She was about to say 'yes I know', but the Captain continued. 'Now over there is the equipment.'

Without looking, Captain Graddon threw a staff Saranon's way, she fumbled and managed to catch it. She looked up at Captain Mirshendy with pleading eyes, but all the Captain could do was smile. 'Now you need to get into these.' Hugh pulled out some gear that matched her size, 'You can get changed over in there.'

She felt like shouting 'I am not a wizard', but she did not think it would do any good. So she went into the ladies change room and tried to find a corner to hide in. The whole thing seemed ridiculous and she almost tripped over twice as she mumbled under her breath.

She looked at herself in the mirror and felt ridiculous as she shrugged her shoulders. She placed her belongings in a sova bag then picked up the staff, this was not her day. Saranon grumbled as Mitch led her into the centre of a circular space, off to the side of the other wizards' training. Before she was ready, he clouted her side with his staff, the impact knocked the wind out of her lungs as she jumped out of the way. She was about to say 'that's not fair', but he moved so quick she struggled to keep up. He made her feeble attempts appear haphazard as he managed to strike her again. This time she was not impressed, using her energy to jump up and bounce out of the way, hitting him from behind with her staff.

Mitch did not flinch as he responded in kind he was not going to let her be. As he side stepped she managed to catch him off-guard. Yet the small victory was short-lived as his staff fell across her back with a dull thud. She was thankful they were not fighting for real, even though it still hurt. He caught her again and she only just managed to strike out in time to stop another blow. Mitch was enjoying the struggle, as her temper flared underneath the surface. He could be infuriating and she jumped out of the way.

Saranon was beginning to tire of the exercise, that and Mitch was winning. She thrust her way toward him and he managed to fend off every blow. He smiled in return at her annoyance as she leaped toward him, and he struck her again. She was not going to win and conceded as she held up her hand to stop. She was exhausted, as she turned to find they had become the centre of attention to a waiting crowd.

Captain Graddon was about to pat her on the back and she moved to the side. Jerald saw part of her back glimpsing between her trousers and top, 'Where did you get that? Mitch you didn't tell me about that.'

'I do not get that personal,' Mitch replied.

He was not impressed by the accusation as he stood close by.

Captain Mirshendy examined Saranon's back as she was starting to panic. She half whimpered, 'Mitch.'

Mitch leaned over, 'Ah, sir?'

Captain Mirshendy realised how big a fuss he had made, 'Most people don't get a scar like that, and live to tell the tale.'

Saranon gave Mitch a filthy look as he tried to cover his tracks. He grabbed her hand and whispered, 'Sorry about that.'

The two practised in the courtyard until it was time to pack up, she could not wait to get back into her own clothes. Mitch patted her on the shoulder with a hint of approval she was still annoyed at him for showing off. He was more than happy to gloat as several wizards praised him, which annoyed her even more. She could not wait to leave as she wiped the sweat from her brow.

As Mitch approached she rushed out to hand her gear back, 'Where do I put these?'

'No, you keep them for tomorrow. If you want I'll wash them?'

Saranon handed them over she gave him a stern look,

'What do you mean tomorrow?'

He smiled, 'You will be coming tomorrow.'

She did not like being ordered around least of all by Mitch.

Captain Mirshendy came up beside them, 'I'm afraid he's right, you can fight so you can train.'

'But…' She began.

The Captain came close, 'Do you know how lucky you are? You bring fear into the hearts of many, you will train with us.'

Saranon was about to burst into tears as she looked at Mitch. Then ran all the way up to her quarters and flung herself on the bed. The sun was just starting to set as she wiped her hand across the tears on her face.

She struggled, it had all been too much as the memory of Tasha clung on. All she wanted to do was run away, but she could not. She wanted to scream and instead she was left having to deal with the Cryzinelan wizards. She wondered if the Palascene had asked the wizards to look after her just to give them something to do, instead of annoying them. This was definitely not how she thought it would be, and sighed. Yet again she was stuck in a wizard's Keep.

Tea would be ready but she did not feel like going, she could always go down later. There was a knock at the door Mitch came in with a bag full of clean clothes, and something to eat. 'Did you get into trouble too?' She asked.

'Nothing I can't handle,' he replied.

He came over and sat at the end of the bed, 'We need all the help we can get.'

Mitch's words were not comforting.

Saranon stared up at the ceiling, 'Did I take all this on with you?'

'I'm afraid so,' he smiled.

'Wizards should come with a warning label, no offence,' she exclaimed.

'I hate to tell you, but sorcerers usually don't bond wizards,' he replied.

She wanted to say more and stopped herself. The last thing she wanted to do at the moment was end up in a discussion over something he knew more about than her. She resigned herself to the fact that she was not going to win the argument.

The bruises from the exercise taunted her as she tried to rest. Yet for all her scattered thoughts, it did not take long before she fell into a deep sleep. The only image that entered her dream was that of the black water at the edge of the beach. It lapped away with the pull of the waves breaking along the shore. There was no sign of Tasha, yet she could feel her friend's presence as though she had only just left. In that moment she waited and every moment felt as though it would last forever.

CHAPTER SEVENTEEN

The trouble with wizards

The place still smelled as Saranon walked through the courtyard, even though it was just a memory. It smelled of roses if that was possible. It was early in the morning, and Mitch had left over an hour ago. She could tell that he was content spending time with Evan. Pennie was busy as usual she had changed since Saranon had left Darkonia. Her friend was still the same, things had just become complicated. Captain Graddon saw her, 'If you keep standing around I'll find something for you to do.'

'I'm avoiding cleaning my dragon,' she commented.

'Ah, well I can always find something worse,' the Captain responded.

'I'll be fine,' she replied as she rushed off.

She had been neglecting Katholomu and went down to the pens to get some peace and quiet. The wizards took great pride in looking after their dragons and the place was kept as clean as could be. She was not sure what to make of Captain Graddon, he was different to Jerald. The fact that she was a sorceress did not seem to bother him. Katholomu, otherwise known as 'Kat' spotted her and sprang into life popping his giant head around the corner. The dragon was in a playful mood and when she stepped close he moved with astounding grace. He came back and rubbed himself up against Saranon before taking off again.

The game continued for some time before Kat rolled over, as if playing dead, wanting his tummy rubbed. His fur and scales were ratty and covered in grime. Katholomu's black colour hid his love of running through caves, and rolling around in the dirt. She groaned as she rolled up her sleeves, and grabbed a soft scrubbing brush. The dragon thought the whole process was fun as he lay there purring away half asleep. The murky water escaped down one of the many drains. As Katholomu stood up he showed off his elegant markings that stated his claim to fine breeding. In a seductive manner for any dragon that may be looking in his direction. 'That's a fine dragon you have,' Gabriel spoke as she patted Kat's glistening damp fur.

Saranon said, 'Thank you. You may want to remove your hand.'

Gabriel looked puzzled, but did as she suggested. She dried the dragon with her sorcery he looked content so she clambered down, 'I'm Saranon.'

'I know who you are. Captain Graddon is my uncle, and I've been helping with Katholomu.'

The great dragon moved over to a nice dry nook that fitted his size then curled up to sleep, with one eye open.

'Your uncle isn't scared of me?' She commented.

'His wife is a sorceress. Uncle Hugh says that it takes a great person to master a marmoz.' Gabriel spoke.

'I don't know about master, a pain in the neck is more like it,' she remarked.

The dragon smiled in reply as the girls wandered over to some of the dragon handlers having a break. It was getting late with the darkness dancing on the edge of the well-lit walls, while the stars were hidden behind the clouds.

'So you're the one that tamed Mitch,' Owen spoke over mouthfuls of a hot brew of coffee, the smell wafted up through the room.

Saranon was taken by surprise, 'I didn't tame him.'

Gabriel laughed. 'The rebellious son of the great Haiden Kregner and now you've placed Mitch in a higher position.'

'Have I?' Saranon was more than a little confused it did not make sense that bonding could give a wizard status.

Gabriel smiled at her bewildered look there were a lot of things she did not understand. At times she only just managed to muddle her way through. Owen and Gabriel seemed genuine enough, so she stayed until it was time to get some rest. The company was a nice relief from all the disapproval that carried her down.

Saranon made her way to bed trying not to disturb Mitch as she tiptoed past. 'It's all right I'm awake,' his voice travelled behind her in the dark.

'Sorry,' she had woken him a few times with her odd hours, 'Did you want to spend time with your kin?'

'Are you trying to get rid of me?' he asked.

'No, I just thought that you would want to spend time with your family.'

She could see that Mitch was thinking about it. He answered by rolling over and going to sleep.

The day was young and the Palascene had organised schooling for her. She was suspicious of the convenient way her schooling was organised. It ended in the early afternoon, when Captain Graddon expected her to take part in training. At first Pennie had been dismissive of the whole coincidence of the arrangement. Before admitting she had known for a while. Her friend had glued herself to the library and the many dull texts within.

Pennie had become obsessed with an Angeon who died more than two hundred years earlier. The great Zeralden Hadenvar whose legend lived on in mythical proportions. Saranon preferred to disassociate herself with the image. In comparison her life appeared meagre and dull. For once she was quite content to resign herself to having her life dictated. Beforehand the mere thought would have sent shivers down her spine, but for once things were as close to fine as they could be.

She was helping Pennie in the library when the lights of the Keep dimmed for a moment. Her friend could see the look on her face, 'It's nothing to worry about.'

She was in the middle of drawing cartoon figures of

her fellow classmates, when Mitch stared over at her handy work. 'I see you're ready to go on duty.'

'What?' She remarked.

Pennie did not look at all surprised, 'Captain Graddon's been training you so you can help.'

He placed a friendly hand on Saranon's shoulder, 'Come on, we'll be late.'

Mitch could not wipe the smile from his face as they walked down to training. With each step she was getting a little more agitated. The exercise did not help her mood and it went far too quick as she went with him along to the equipment room. It was a large hub of excitement as people were either gearing up, or returning items. No one seemed bothered by the fact that some of the items were rather deadly. He came back with a pile of gear including some garments for her. 'Oh no, I'm not wearing that,' Saranon exclaimed.

'It will help keep you safe,' he stated.

Sienna came up to greet them. She was a roughly beautiful woman with a hard edge to her features, 'Dressing her up won't make any difference.'

Mitch's eyebrows were starting to drop in an unimpressed look, 'Fine you decide.'

'It's okay,' Sienna hustled Saranon over to where the sorcerers' garments were kept.

At the end of the day she had enough experience for the glamour of working to have worn thin.

She bypassed a heap of items that looked too elaborate to withstand daily wear. Then headed straight for some hardy items, and yanked them off the rack. 'I don't think you'll need that,' Sienna tried grabbing one of the items as Saranon moved sideways and ducked around.

She had worn similar gear before in Darkonia when she travelled alone. It had served her well and she was not one to be concerned with fashion.

As she finished she strode out to skim past the weaponry and sized up a couple pieces before taking her pick. She turned toward Mitch, 'I'm ready.'

'Okay,' was all Mitch could manage as he prepared himself.

'Hey, you've…' Sienna took a closer look. 'I was going to say you put it on the wrong way, but you haven't.'

Saranon did not know what all the fuss was about. If the gear was not meant to be worn, it would not be there in the first place. She made her way with Mitch to the group and said nothing.

It all seemed straight forward as she kept up pace with Mitch. Patrolling was something that stirred the senses in her blood, but this time she stayed in line. She felt she had nothing to prove, except showing that she could be part of a team. For a while she had been part of a team in the detention camps, but that was different. Now she strode in a mix of pride as the warm night air set about with a stagnant stillness around the streets. She felt her palms tingle with the energy that was burning inside. Mitch could feel it too they were getting close. Then everything went cold, an officer went to look inside one of the buildings and Mitch stood behind near the door way.

There were muffled sounds from within and the wizards sprang through the walls.

Mitch hesitated, waiting for Saranon. She stood outside in the silence holding his stare then walked through the door. She could sense movement off in the distance, but it was all happening too fast. Her palms had gone numb with the cold, yet the air around them was warm. This time she had no urge to fight, this was a family home and something was wrong. Her mood was reflected in Mitch's face and she saw a couple of the wizards in the shadows. They remained almost hidden as if waiting for someone, waiting for her. She opened the door, and walked in. The stench hit her hard, but that was the least of her concerns as she looked down, she knew they were too late.

What she had sensed earlier, had left before they arrived. The body was covered and there was not much they could do. Captain Graddon spoke up afterward, 'You will have to move quicker,' he said as he passed Saranon by.

They moved on in silence leaving the place behind. As they moved on, there were a few of the normal squabbles that needed breaking up. Outside the Lady Jade Inn an older man had been beaten by a couple of youths. For some reason the Captain seemed right at home dragging the youths away. They stopped and had a short break back at the station listening to the drunken youths shouting in the distance.

The Captain kept a steady pace moving around, as a few strangers were given a friendly warning. The rest of the night was peaceful, much to her delight. It had not felt like a lot of work, but the sweat had stuck to her hair. As she was back in the safety of the Keep, she took off the heavy garments and jumped when she saw something move on her hand. There was a gale of laughter behind her as it dawned on her that the wizards had played a trick. She glared at Mitch who joined in before storming off to get cleaned up. He cornered her as she left, 'I'll be staying down in the dorm tonight, is that okay?'

'I suppose so,' she replied.

Saranon was still fuming and stubbed her toe while clambering up the stairs. In retrospect the night had been a disaster, she had not been able to keep up, the wizards moved in a completely different way. In reality she had held them back, it was not a good start, but then was it what she wanted? Pennie was too absorbed and had been quite content not to fill her in on what was happening. In Darkonia the long nights travelling had been relaxing and thrilling. Here everybody was happy to make fun of her, perhaps it was time to move on. The thought lingered as the warm night air lulled her off to sleep.

In some ways the night had drowned her sorrows as Saranon watched Mitch wander off with a group downstairs. He could look after himself, so that was the least of her worries. Zaidek had been silent since her arrival and she was beginning to feel a little claustrophobic. The Keep had extensive grounds which led into the open countryside. She hurried down to find Katholomu in the yard already waiting. This time the dragon needed no encouragement. Kat bounded off the ground to the surprise of several onlookers. The coolness of the breeze swept against her cheeks. Everything looked so peaceful from above, in stark contrast to the turmoil welling up inside. She rode the dragon down near the edge of the city that circled in Zaidek's wake.

The great waters of the Elspy River stretched down before her. Katholomu took a flying leap into the water and pulled out a large fish from the deep. Saranon sheltered herself from the wet barrage, as any attempt to remain hidden, faded away. The dragon seemed completely oblivious as he purred his way through the meal. She heard a rustle behind her and Gabriel came rushing down the hill toward her. 'Glad to see you've taken Kat out, he was getting restless.'

'What are you doing here?' She asked.

'This is a dragon stop, come on,' Gabriel gestured.

Katholomu followed as she walked at a slower pace. She was greeted by a temporary camp site with several dragons smaller than her own.

Owen was among the group, 'So the Captain let you out?'

Saranon's mood soured. 'It was only a joke,' he remarked.

'That's been happening a lot lately,' she wanted to shrug it off, but every time it hurt a little.

'Did you want to fly with us down further to Furly's Gates?' Owen asked.

She had heard of the great stone walls rising either side of the river. She wanted to be left alone, but Katholomu was already nudging her from behind, 'Oh, all right.'

The dragon nuzzled her hand with eager anticipation before she jumped on. It was strange flying in formation, though there was no effort on her part since Kat was doing all the work.

At least there was one consolation the day was beautiful and silent except for the breeze. A buzzing came from her talik destroying her thoughts it was Gabriel, 'What do you think of the view?'

It all looked the same to Saranon and she tried to sound enthused. The long grass wafted its smell up to greet her nose in a strong blast of wind. She sneezed into the dragon's fur as he landed, causing him to groan with dissatisfaction. She gathered herself before staring up, Furly's Gates looked much bigger now that she was on the ground.

'Come on,' Gabriel was already ahead of her, and she ran to catch up. 'You don't use much sorcery?'

She looked up puzzled as she caught up. It had never occurred to her that it was unusual, 'I guess not.'

'If you were one of the Palascene we'd have trouble getting you to stop,' Gabriel spoke.

Saranon did not know what to say to that and so kept plodding on. 'Hey, are you listening to me?' Gabriel asked.

She cringed, 'Yes.'

'So why don't you use your sorcery?' Gabriel asked.

Owen interrupted, 'If Saranon wants to tell you she will. Do you want to see the caves?'

Gabriel's stubborn look changed to excitement,

'Come on it'll be fun.'

Gabriel dashed in front of them and walked through the wall. Saranon hesitated. Owen held out his hand to her and she followed his lead.

Inside was dry and airy. Wizard lights had been placed throughout and lit up as they moved around. The place had been well used with little chips and dents marking its lifespan. A short distance in, the markings on the wall became clearer and Saranon could not keep her eyes off the ceiling. 'I thought you would like it,' Gabriel pronounced in a loud voice.

She reached out sensing the place, it was filled with a great richness. Something sharp came to her mind and she pulled back, 'What was this place?'

'It's where the Cryzinelan hid during the great invasion,' Gabriel replied.

The pictures on the walls fascinated her. She heard a sound through the walls, it was Katholomu, 'I have to go.'

'I'm sure it's nothing,' Gabriel commented.

'I'm sorry, but I have to go,' she replied.

Saranon rushed out through the maze to see another dragon attacking Katholomu. It blocked her from getting close. She tried to restrain it, but she could not.

She could feel the energy inside her grow as she hurled a blast which spiralled through the air, warping as it went. The dragon screamed in terror as the blast hit its side sending it flying. Knocking out several trees as it went, before disappearing. She ran over to Kat and breathed a sigh of relief when she saw his wounds were only superficial. The dragons gaze turned toward Mitsy, Gabriel's shazel dragon. The dragon had marks on her face and stomach, they were not life threatening, but the sight from the weeping wounds was not pleasant.

None of the wizards had come out of their hiding place so she went up to Mitsy and braced herself. The dragon let out a muffled cry of pain as Saranon placed her hands near the slimy wet mess and healed the wound on her belly. While trying not to dry reach at the same time. Dragon blood stank, there were no two ways about it she went up and healed the dragon's face. Mitsy gave her a confused look as she tried to wash the smell out of her taste buds with her flask. There was a strange rustle from the other side of the river. Gabriel and the other wizards rushed out of the cave and jumped on their dragons. 'Quick!' Gabriel shouted.

Katholomu was ready before Saranon was and as soon as she had scrambled up he was off. The dragon needed no one to tell him it was time to get out. They flew hard back to Zaidek Keep, the dragons needed no enticement, their fear driving them back all the way. Katholomu hit the ground so hard his claws scraped along the stone paving. Mitsy misjudged and pelted into his behind. 'Whoa there, how many times have I told you to slow down?' Captain Graddon spoke to his niece.

Owen piped up, 'Mitsy was attacked.'

Captain Graddon went over to Mitsy, 'She looks pretty good to me.'

'That's because I healed her,' she spoke.

The Captain said in a serious tone, 'Yes I can see that, thank you.'

Saranon felt her cheeks heat up with embarrassment, and she took Katholomu back to his pen. The dragon was thirsty and the water splashed over the floor as he guzzled it down with a ferocious speed. 'Well, at least someone's happy,' she said as she left him in peace.

Her ears were still buzzing from the energy she had released. As she thought back it had been a lot of effort to fight only a dragon, but she did not remember seeing another sorcerer. The whole notion that she had missed that detail was irritating, and it showed on her face. 'Are you all right?' Mitch asked

She jumped as he scared her, 'Don't do that.'

'Do what?' He asked.

'Jump out. I'm fine, but Owen mentioned something about Dihan and I didn't see anyone.'

Mitch held back a serious laugh, 'You'll see them soon enough.'

'Thanks,' she was not looking forward to more evenings. The thought of hanging out with a bunch of smelly sweaty wizards did not appeal to her.

Perhaps Gabriel was right, she had not been using her sorcery much. The days were nice and warm as the Normisian summer brought out a vibrant heat. Pennie was waiting down stairs she could see her from outside her room.

When Pennie saw her, she asked 'How are you going with school?'

Saranon pulled a face, 'Riveting.'

'I'm glad to hear it,' her friend ignored her sarcasm. 'I see you've been letting your wizard run riot.'

'I wouldn't call Mitch a riot,' she commented.

'Suit yourself,' Pennie spoke with a hint of amusement.

If there was one thing she missed at lunch it was Mrs Harper's cooking. The food was fine, but it could do with something extra. Since Saranon's cooking skills were close to nil she was not about to complain. 'Now you see that lady over there,' Pennie pointed across the room. 'That's your competition she's been with your wizard.'

Saranon almost choked, coughing up part of her meal. Her friend looked triumphant, 'You're not jealous, are you?'

She cleared her throat, 'I didn't need to know that.'

She went over to get ready for training, as she walked out she had difficulty keeping a straight face. A couple of times she lost her concentration and Mitch gave her a nasty bruise each time. Afterward he came up to her, 'You seem out of sorts,' he commented.

'Have you been seeing someone?' She asked.

Mitch went silent for a moment and sat down, 'I've been seeing an old friend, her name's Alyssa.'

He could not look her in the eye so she spoke, 'I just don't want to find out through someone else.'

'Okay,' he replied.

It was not the best outcome Saranon was hoping for, but there was little she could do. Mitch had been an accident and she was going to have to live with it. Still she had not counted on it being so frustrating, if Pennie was gloating at her then others were sure to know. Yet she had already given him space and to take it back would make matters worse. She knew she would not be able to sleep as she stewed in her own thoughts. Without saying a word she slipped away into the depths of the Keep. The noises were comforting in the absence of people. Zaidek was content whirring away pretending not to notice her presence. She found a comfortable position lying on a soft stone bed as it melded to meet the contours of her form and she concentrated.

The sounds of everyday life were recorded in the walls of the Keep, to access them required silence. It was easier to focus on Mitch since they shared the bond. Through the Keep she saw glimpses of Alyssa, but that was not what caught her attention. She opened her eyes, the hour was late, she could sense the being. It had interrupted her thoughts, but how could she get to it? Even though the Keep was friendly there were some places it did not want her to reach. Whoever it was moved faster than she could. Saranon was wondering if she should give up when she caught a clear glimpse, it was all she needed.

CHAPTER EIGHTEEN

The calling of Zaidek

Saranon transported herself beside the Dihan and thrust her energy against the sorcerer. It only just touched him, but the effect it had on the wizards in the room was instant. Several of them jumped out of bed grabbing weapons, lunging at the sorcerer dragging him down. He pelted them off with ease, but the distraction was all she needed. She ran Tellembre through the sorcerer's back only just missing one of the wizards. He stayed there for a moment as she held onto the bond-breaker. The sorcerer let out a small effort before collapsing into a heap on the floor. The sweat on her forehead soaked down her chin, it was then that she realised she was in a male wizard dorm.

The thought left her as she cringed at Mitch's voice, 'What did you do? You can't come in here!'

Captain Mirshendy butted in, 'Now that's a bit harsh.'

The Captain was sweating just as much as Saranon and a few of the others collapsed with exhaustion. One of the wizards was wounded and taken away. The wizards were not as keen to remove the sorcerer's body. Captain Mirshendy spoke to her, 'So you finally found a Dihan.'

Saranon was in no mood for jokes.

Mitch was standing beside her, 'You shouldn't be here.'

'I'm not sorting out your problems too,' spoke the Captain.

She cringed in disgust, she glared at Mitch as the room cleared and spoke under her breath, 'Did you have to do that?'

'Did you have to show up here?' He retorted.

Captain Mirshendy spoke, 'Hey, are you two coming?'

It was more of an order than a question.

Saranon grumbled as she moved into the common area where it seemed everyone had gathered. Mitch like the others had managed to grab some clothes and find a place to get dressed. The commotion had woken some of the others. Gabriel, not wanting to miss out looked half asleep. 'What's happening?' Gabriel saw her, 'You're not supposed to be here.'

'Yes, we've established that,' Saranon replied.

The officers were getting ready to leave and Captain Mirshendy popped his head back around, 'Are you coming?'

It was more of a command and without hesitation she got up from the table. 'Wait, where are you going?' Gabriel did not want to be left out, but the Captain gave her a disapproving look and she stayed. 'Since you were so keen on starting this, you can help finish it.'

Captain Mirshendy led her out into the darkness of the non-habitable area of the Keep. Then he merged into the background leaving Saranon alone.

She was not impressed by the wizards approach to merging. It did not help that she had trouble detecting them, even though she knew they were there. Although merging was as much a part of sorcery, she had not grown up with it and the method still appeared out of reach. She grumbled to herself as she went along, if the wizards were going to be of little help, she was just going to have to find a way to manage.

She could sense several things going on in the background, but as much as she tried she could not get a grip. There was a muffled sound behind her, and a wizard appeared falling dead on the ground, this was not good. She glanced around; the environment did not suit her at all. She may as well not be here, she had been running around to no avail. Saranon could not see and felt completely useless. A boom ricocheted through the winding corridor and she felt the shock run through her skin. She ran toward it. A cascade of stallic energy exploded into the air sending hundreds of thousands of tiny particles flying. The energy lit up the space before being absorbed back into the walls of the Keep.

It was all she could do to keep away the feeling of fright. Saranon had been close to Keeps, but this was different. That type of energy was not meant to get this close to the inhabitants, or above ground. The stallic energy excited her senses as she tried to hold on, it was a feeble attempt as she felt herself let go to the Angeon. As her eyes opened, she could see the voids in the energy. The patches glared towards her, with hatred spilling over from the Keep wanting to be rid of the source. Saranon struck through the gloom and into the darkness. The Dihan fought back filling her body with pain, but this only made her more determined and she struck harder.

As the voids weakened she could feel the excitement of the Keep as it spoke to her, finish them. Before she realised she had done exactly what Zaidek wanted. Then she had wanted it too, as she stared down at the dust that was all that remained of the other Dihan. Captain Mirshendy was the first to walk up to her, his eyes showed his uncertainty of her, 'You did well.'

The words sounded sour in his mouth as he turned and left her alone. As she returned Gabriel grabbed her arm. Before she could think about what she had done, and dragged her deep into the wizard stronghold.

'You were awesome,' she whispered with excitement. 'Come and stay with us tonight?'

'No, I can't,' Saranon replied.

'It's all right,' Gabriel said.

'Gabriel we need to debrief, you can catch up later,' Captain Mirshendy was serious.

She did not feel like chatting, she was just about to say something when she felt her legs going numb from the floor up. She could taste vomit at the back of throat, but could not bring anything up. Mitch caught her as she fell,

'Are you okay?'

'No,' she replied.

The floor started spinning and she could hear the Captain shouting as Mitch rushed her to the medical area. Saranon could only just see the colours were a blur that plagued her mind and made her head ache. She felt Mitch's hand not wanting to let go and could sense his frustration of not being able to help. When she finally came too, Pennie was staring down at her, 'Can't you do anything normal?'

Her head was still spinning and she did not enjoy being greeted this way as her friend continued. 'You came into contact with stallic energy and you look like you only caught a tummy bug. Do you have any idea how weird that makes you?'

The conversation was not what she had expected, she was in no position to talk back and felt robbed of what she wanted to say. Pennie had changed and the world had turned upside down. She cried as Mitch watched over in silence. Saranon was no longer alone, but this was not how she had planned it. Her silent thoughts were broken by Mitch's soft voice, 'I think your friend is jealous.'

After a while she sat up. 'I'm done with playing the patient. It was nice, but this place is starting to give me the creeps.'

She walked with Mitch back to the wizard's quarters. She stood by the door, 'This is where I stop and let you go to your clan. What will you do when I find mine?'

'A whole clan of Saranon's, I don't think so,' he smiled.

'Yeah right,' she knew Mitch was kidding.

She did not see how her friend could be jealous. After all she was exiled and she could not stay in one place for too long without attracting attention or causing mayhem. Mitch and Katholomu were nice, but they tied her down. Being free to do what she wanted came with life's little catches. In class she stuck out for all the wrong reasons, there was so much she did not know. It hurt her to think about it all at once, it came crashing down around the insides of her stomach making her feel sick. How could her best friend be jealous of this? It did not make sense when her life was such a mess. The Keep grumbled back through the walls at her frustration as she beat her fist against it.

Pennie stopped talking to Jacob as she approached the pair. 'We are returning to Darkonia,' her friend stated in a matter of fact tone.

'Is that because of me?' She asked.

'Don't flatter yourself we have out stayed our welcome,' Pennie brushed a cold shoulder against her as she left.

Saranon looked at Jacob for solace, but found none. Her friend was doing the one thing she could not, return home.

As she turned away from Jacob she saw something move out of the corner of her eye, 'How long has it been Jacob?'

'What do you mean?' He asked.

'How long have you been bonded to Pennie?'

He stood silent for a moment before replying, 'Darkonia is a dangerous place.'

Then he followed after Pennie.

Saranon did everything she could to fight the urge to run after them. If Pennie did not want to be part of her life, her friend was doing a fine job at keeping pace. She hung her head with the realisation that she could not sort out Pennie's problems before dealing with her own. She hated feeling useless, it was like a bad dream happening all over again. The sky was turning black to suit her frame of mind, filling with a chaos of clouds settling in for the rain. It tempered along the walls of the Keep soon streaming down ancient paths and crisscrossing the grounds. The wizards had been irritable since the ambush at Furly's Gates and the mood had washed off on her.

She guessed that would be the end of it. Pennie would go back to Darkonia, and she would be stuck here. Gabriel who had been trying to get her attention for some time called out below, 'Saranon, there's someone here to see you.'

She was so struck by her own thoughts that she had failed to notice Rachel and rushed down to meet them. 'I hear you've been helping my fiancé Jerald,' Rachel spoke.

'Yes,' Saranon said as she realised Captain Mirshendy had forgotten to mention that detail. Then the Captain was like that.

'Ah you ready for the big raid?' Rachel asked.

Her expression said it all she hated being the last to know, 'What raid?'

'Zaidek's power is being siphoned off, I'm sorry I thought you knew,' Rachel replied.

That would explain the occasional interruptions. She assumed she had just been having trouble communicating with the Keep, but this was not the case. She crumpled her nose in disgust and then smoothed her expression again. It was not Rachel's fault and she had always been kind.

For a moment she forgot her troubles and embraced her friend's warm conversation. As Pennie commented, 'You've changed since I last saw you.'

'I doubt it,' she responded.

Saranon could not help but feel frustrated, everything seemed to be going pear shaped as she managed to say goodbye to Pennie. It was a warm embrace given by two friends that meant it. Then her friend put on a cold face as she went out to start the long journey home.

The clouds above remained silent and menacing with few gaps of the clear sky breaking through. It was an odd eerie feeling, as if the rain had stopped to let Pennie pass back through the mountains and on to Darkonia. The feeling of home panged at Saranon's heart, though she did not want to admit it. She was losing a dear friend all over again to a world she was fast leaving behind. She had the distinct feeling that were she to return to Darkonia today, it would not be the same place she had left behind.

Mitch broke his solemn silence, 'Are you sure Jacob is bonded to her?'

She turned to where she could no longer see Pennie. Then spoke, 'Yes, but then stranger things have happened.'

He shot her a look; it was not the first time he had appeared to read her thoughts. She almost felt relief when she could sense the strain of the Keep underneath her. How she had missed that, she had no idea. Yet knowing it was happening was not going to solve anything, which led to the next misunderstanding. Saranon had thought that the wizards were going to deal with the problem, but no, this was the domain of the sorcerers.

Thanks to her wonderful lessons she did not think her teacher Mr Oakliff would be recommending her for the raid. After all there were some fine students who excelled at making her look like an amateur. The four sorcerers had been acting rather pleased with themselves of late, which seemed to fit in well with what Gabriel had told her about the raid. Katholomu was purring as she brushed his soft undercoat. At least she felt she was doing something useful with her frustration.

'Do you need a hand?' Gabriel asked.

Saranon let out a sigh, 'Sure why not.'

'I heard you won't be going on the raid,' Gabriel commented.

Again she was the last to know, Gabriel saw the look on her face. 'I'm sorry.'

Saranon was not looking forward to missing out on the raid. Yet she was not going to complain as Katholomu rubbed his cheek against her.

'He likes you,' Gabriel said looking up at the dragon.

'I don't know what I've done to deserve it,' she patted the majestic beast before he curled up to sleep.

'Thanks for saving Mitsy,' Gabriel added.

'That's all right,' she replied.

It had been a terrible windy day that had broken into a storm. Just part of Saranon's schooling had ended as she heard it thundering down on the earth outside. The wizards were busier than usual, with the sorcerer population that had been growing at the Keep over the past few weeks. The sorcerers were now gearing up for whatever she had been left out of. In a way she was content to be left alone. She would have had several arguments by now, as it was she was having difficulty staying out of the way.

Unfortunately training with the wizards had not taken a break. She was busy glaring at Mitch, who was content taking his time. She could have sworn he did it on purpose. He moved her along, 'Come on.'

Even though Sienna was a sorceress she just seemed to fit right in, and no one batted an eyelid, if only it were that simple. Saranon followed Mitch down into the lower part of the Keep. They may not come across anyone, but the damage needed repairing and this was more of a fix it mission than anything else.

Before she knew it she had been roped into helping the wizards mend the large cabling. By using fields to hold back the Keeps energy while they worked. It was boring so she tried to lighten the mood, 'So I guess you're looking forward to things getting back to normal?'

Captain Mirshendy looked puzzled, 'Can you talk and hold that at the same time?'

Saranon jumped about, 'Yes, I can do this too.'

Mitch glared at her.

The time passed so slow at one stage she had resorted

to counting wizards, but Captain Mirshendy did not see the funny side. When it was time to pack up she turned to the Captain, 'Don't get me wrong, I like to help. Next time can you pre-warn me so I can bring a book or something?'

'That can be arranged,' the Captain said in a flat tone.

'I think we had better go,' Mitch manoeuvred her out of the Captain's sight.

Saranon whispered, 'What did I do?'

'It's what you didn't do,' he explained.

'Hey!' She exclaimed.

She was looking forward to a good night's sleep. By the sounds of it the wizards had managed to do enough work on the cables not to need her help again. She thought that was convenient. In some ways she did not envy her classmates. She had managed to make it through her first proper schooling. Even though she still had catching up to do her marks were okay. As her teacher had said she would still be able to catch up to the level where she was meant to be. That gave her some consolation, although she did not think that would ever help her fit in. Zaidek rumbled beneath her and Saranon felt queasy. She ignored it and went to sleep.

The next day felt strange only everyone else seemed not to notice. She went out to see Katholomu who looked as though he was more alert than usual, 'What are you waiting for?'

The dragon made a sound for her to listen and she stepped up against the beast. Even if she could not hear anything it was not polite to say so. Katholomu pointed with a small flex of his claw in the direction of the sound she could not hear. She gave the friendly giant a puzzled look, but kept on trying. She was straining to listen so hard that when the siren sounded behind her she jumped and almost tripped over his claw. He waited a moment before retracting it.

Gabriel was motioning for them both to go inside. Kat moved and took his time. The dragon still managed to beat Saranon, 'What's going on?'

'It's the Dihan,' Gabriel whispered as she stood beside her. 'They've found out about the raid we have to stay inside.'

'And wait?' She asked.

'I'm afraid so,' Gabriel replied.

Great, she thought, now everyone knows. She let out a deep sigh. For all the kafuffle, not much had changed within the Keep.

She felt like finding a quiet place to sulk, but Katholomu gave her a disapproving glare. Between Mitch and the dragon she was finding it difficult to have time on her own. As she moved into the depths of Zaidek she felt dizzy, her eyes steadied and she realised it was not her. The wind rushed over her head when the air sat still. A pull of energy tingled down her spine as her senses stirred on the edge of a heightened panic. Yet she remained still, her eyes wide waiting for the first sign of movement when there was none. Something strange was happening. Saranon rushed and looked outside to a glowing orange crimson sky. It was as though the sound had been sucked from the air and then the roar came enveloping her ears.

The blast pounded every step of the way, forming a mountain of ash. Sorcery whipped around with a fiery gaze as it seared across the open ground. Crackling with a violent force as it went, as though taunting her from a distance. Her eyes stayed transfixed on the smothering clouds rising to block out the last remnants of sky. It shaded the Keep with an unnatural darkness that echoed her thoughts. She watched on, mesmerised, as her senses tingled, awakening inside. The sorcery raged within wanting to be let out.

She found Gabriel cowering with several others and spoke into the noise, 'I have to go.'

Gabriel's tear filled eyes looked back at Saranon and she mouthed the words, I know. Saranon raced toward the stream of light, but her limbs were taking forever to catch up. She made out a black silhouette on the ground in front. She thought it was Katholomu, but when she looked up through the haze she realised it was something else. At first in the glow it looked like a zennigh, one of the large cats she had come to know from Darkonia. Something was different as she approached it, for in the eyes shone the soul of the Keep. She had glimpsed an ockren from afar, but had not dared to get this close to one.

She stood in awe as she hesitated without realising. The great beast stared unblinking with sharp yellow eyes. It pierced straight through her, with an unwavering gaze. The embodiment of the Keep could be a dangerous creature and she was standing beside it. She looked down and realised she was touching its short course fur. Its unsettling eyes stared at her as if in anticipation. She trembled, she had not seen anything like what was happening and it scared her. Usually Saranon's senses guided her, but now she felt as though she were on her own. That was what she had wanted since she arrived, though it frightened her in the unsteady gloom that covered the sky.

The irony of the situation bemused her as she clambered aboard the strange beast. Zaidek had not warmed to her, but necessity dictated otherwise. As she gripped the ockren's short mane she could feel the undercurrent of the Keep sweeping through her. It almost willed the Angeon to the surface. The energy welled in like a torrent taking over her senses. Guiding her with a renewed urgency as the voice of Zaidek filled her mind with an edge of desperation. The rough raging sky dug deep into the untamed ground highlighting the sorcerers' plight. Saranon could feel the Angeon showing, but her senses still gave her no direction.

It was difficult to tell who was friend or foe as she steadied herself on the ockren. It felt weird under her skin moving in a different way to a creature made of flesh and blood. She somehow felt betrayed as the glow became stronger. Sweeping back her hair in the unnatural squall and the roar passed behind her. The deadly silence surrounded her like a plague thickening the air and making it hard to breathe. The hot stale air filled her lungs with the smell of the wounded Keep. It caked her clothes giving them an uncomfortable damp sensation close to her skin.

Saranon caught sight of Bianca up ahead and then she was gone. The earth trembled beneath her with the pain of the Keep, and the ockren let out an uneasy roar. She drove the beast hard into the fray. A blast of sorcery hurled her to the ground and the great beast howled in pain. She realised she was hurt, but she was still nowhere near the breach. She had to summon all her strength to rise up and go on. She caught the glimpse of another blast out of the corner of her eye and answered it with the age old power of the Angeon. Her energy surged ahead cutting a wild path into the throng. Saranon could make out Caleb and some of his companions making their way forward. To think she was going to miss out on this, now that would have been too easy.

The great beast heaved forward in protest of what was being done, leaving her no time to think of what to do next. The Dihan attempted to block her way, making the journey slow. If she did not pick up pace she would not have enough strength left to carry on. The pain coursed through her, and she knew it was now or never. She summoned the great power from the deep, the power of the great Keep, Zaidek. She pulled it up to the surface with every essence of her being as the Angeon struggled within. It was not enough as she surged her energy downward with such force. Then before she had time to pull back the flow, the great surge from the deep filled her mind with all the anguish of the Keep.

She could feel the ground start to melt below her with the pressure. Trembling as it sent ripples creasing through the surface of Tordoren. The foul smell became stronger, burning as it passed up through the acrid air. For one brief moment she lost her grip on reality, and the molten dark sheal spewed up through the ground. Searing the earth as it went like an open scar, sealing off the edges of the Keep. The ockren raced, excited to be so close to the Keep. Saranon moved it toward Bianca who struggled to hold her ground up ahead. She and the ockren swooped, and Bianca jumped on as the beast held the Dihan in his teeth, then flung him into the sheal.

She could hear Bianca calling to her, but she was still lost in the power that coursed through her veins. In a mighty leap the ockren spun them away from the rising liquid. For the first time in the raging anguish that had taken over the Keep, Saranon knew what she had to do. She turned and let out the full might of her energy sending the sheal and all the energy of Zaidek back deep underneath the ground. The surge ran through her with a staggering might, taking every bit of strength with it as it left a hollow vacuum. Yet the flame of the Angeon held strong inside her. The energy of the Angeon ran deep as it melded with the Keep. The great arterial cable which ran underneath healed with such smoothness. It left no trace of damage except for the wreckage above.

CHAPTER NINETEEN

The raging heart from the deep

As the Angeon turned, the great echo of rage swept in a bright arch blasting across the plume of clouds, as the sparks fell through the air. The impact only just missed. It knocked her from the ockren, as she managed to hold fast against the lasting remnants as they whirled by. She held on through the surge fighting her way forward as the Dihan struck hard. The harsh ash hid their forms in the distance, with only just a shadow making each figure out up ahead. Saranon raised the energy with a wild surge, as her steady hands held strong. The full might of the deep power of the Angeon awakened within, calling to be heard. The blast held true as it made its mark, out into the cloudy depths hiding the path ahead.

The Angeon, filled with the last determined thoughts of the Keep. She held on with a stubborn resilience not wanting to lose ground as she stumbled. The dim chaos swallowed the first signs of the blasts as they broke through, burning at her ears as she tried to focus. Just for a moment a brief figure stood out of the clouds, the first glimpse of the sorcerer she had seen through the haze. She held onto the image as her energy rose. All she heard was her heartbeat thudding hard as she hurled the raging blast through the broken haze. The surge burned across the clouds of ash searing away the sorcery that lay thick in the air. As the veil lifted Saranon could make out the figures up ahead.

She caught a glimpse as they disappeared, vanishing before she could run after them. As she made one final attempt she could feel the last of the Angeon slip away under the surface, as a cold sweat covered her skin. She screamed in an anguished fit of frustration, as she half collapsed beating her fists on the ground. Tears ran down her face, but the Angeon would not rise, and she cried out. Her aching muscles filled the void as she gave out an anguished cry she was not willing to admit defeat. Yet all the strength of the Angeon had locked itself deep within, and she pounded the surface of Tordoren one last time with her fist.

The Keep lay calm beneath not uttering a word. As the sheal cooled with a strength that would hinder any further attempt to siphon its energy. Saranon felt numb inside, it was not the victory she had wanted, as the Keep simmered just below the surface. The hurt left over from the fight mirrored her thoughts as she tried to make sense of it, the Keep was not ready to let go. She took a deep breath and the last remnants of the haze filled her lungs. Behind her the ockren stood with Bianca still showing the wounds from her ordeal. She stood hesitating, before clambered atop the guardian of the Keep. As the ockren turned, she took one last glimpse behind her. The Keep was safe, yet the victory felt hollow as she let out a deep resounding sigh.

The ground trembled with the changes beneath it as the Keep renewed its strength. It still seethed underneath the surface. The heavy wounds showed like a scar across the landscape, stretching far along the scorched earth. The chaos and injured people filled her ears, as the sky stained with the hues of the fiery blasts faded. Saranon could see the other sorcerers around her taking charge. The wizards that had been so long silent rushed forward to help. It was easy for her to ignore the dangers, after all she was a sorceress, but the wizards would have fared worse. She let Bianca down into the arms of the waiting Palascene. As she slid off the ockren's back it disappeared into the depths of the Keep leaving her alone.

She glanced around this was not how she had wanted it to end. She held out her hands in awe at what she had done, yet it was not enough. It was not what she expected as a weary tiredness set in over her aching muscles. The Angeon had risen then disappeared and somehow she had to make sense of it all. She breathed a heavy sigh as she let go of the frustration from within.

Evan walked over with a heavy stride. Saranon thought he was about to tell her off for interfering. Instead he looked concerned, 'You are injured, go inside.'

She wanted to say something, but the words would not come out. For once she was out of breath, which was just as well because she wanted to give Evan an ear full. As soon as she stepped in the doorway Mitch ran to her side, 'Come this way.'

He cleared a path among the chaos to the medical area where Rachel greeted them.

After some serious words, and waiting long enough to irritate her, she asked, 'What's going on?'

'I don't think we can heal that, you will be left with a scar,' Rachel spoke.

Great, thought Saranon it can go with all her other ones, 'I can live with that.'

Mitch helped her lean back, 'I'll see you when you return.'

She held his hand, 'Thanks.'

Rachel did an excellent job as she peered down at her arm the scar was only just noticeable. Mitch strode up behind her, 'Thank you for looking after my home.'

'Do you mean that?' She asked.

'It is an honour to ride an ockren,' Mitch's eyes looked troubled.

It was written all over his face like it was the others. The wizards were in awe of her, and afraid at the same time.

'Captain Mirshendy needs someone to help repair the cables.'

'Oh, all right I get the hint,' she grumbled.

She felt like she had just been roped into the most

boring job in the Keep, as she sat in silence mulling over the past events. She thought the Captain would be happy, but for some reason the silence made him appear uneasy. He hesitated before he sat beside her, 'I know you don't like this work, but I appreciate it.'

'Couldn't you get someone else?' She asked.

'We all have to do our part,' the Captain spoke from experience as he moved away.

Saranon's arm hurt she stared down at the faint scar left behind and rubbed it. Just as she was feeling sorry for herself a great spark flashed across her vision and for a moment she was unable to see. She guided herself by her senses then the roar of chaos came and the screams hit her ears. For a moment she thought she had done something then she sensed someone running in the distance, as the Keep howled at the intrusion. She felt faint as she realised it was a distraction, someone was trying to get into the Keep. She was torn between helping the wizards and running down to the central core. Captain Mirshendy bellowed through his pain, 'Go!'

Saranon's body acted out of instinct, and her mind took a while to catch up as she took control. It was all too fast she could sense it, there were too many. For a moment she slowed down overwhelmed with what lay before her. She could think of no other way to save the Keep. The reality scared her, and for a brief moment she would have given anything to be normal. The Angeon crept to the surface as though summoned by the Keep. It leaked through her skin as the floor opened up creating a chasm which swallowed her whole. The energy of the Keep threw her down which such force that she only just managed to hang on.

The central core heaved as her body melded and Zaidek locked everyone else out. The impact was instant as it sent a staggering shock wave rumbling up through the Keep, the sound echoed above as it rang out. In the depths below the Angeon reached out, but the Keep had been tampered with, and she could feel her hopes sink. Zaidek was so sure of himself that she felt she owed it to the Keep to try. The great engine whirred around her. As she reached out to the intense chaos pounding through the whirlwind that lay deep within the core.

If Zaidek lost his grip, she did not want to think what would happen. The struggle raged along the outer walls of the central core. The energy of the Keep ran hot through her veins, making her weep. It had to be close, but she could not see it. The edges showed on the periphery, but when she tried to pinpoint it she grasped at nothing. The sickening feeling came down her arms, as the tension grew taking over the thoughts of the Keep. It had to be somewhere, but Saranon still could not grasp it. All the while her head thudded in the great centre of the Keep. For a moment she wondered if she was enough, the sensation was overwhelming and flooded her with tears. The Keep beckoned her on pulsing with the need for revenge.

She felt the queasy sensation of panic and her whole body felt like it was going to vomit. Then a glimmer made its way through the whirling flow and she saw it. With all she could give she strengthened herself and surged out her energy to cling on. The energy of the Angeon raged in the core, lashing out in the haze as it locked on in a violent struggle. Saranon managed to hold on only with the help of the Keep, as it focused with an intensity that frightened her. The hard shell of the central core creaked and groaned under the intense pressure. She held on as the dark energy gripping itself around the Keep, and it raged against the Angeon.

Zaidek grew wild with frustration lashing out at the dark energy with all his might. The intense ferocity overwhelmed her, heaving her into the full strength of the Keep. The raw stallic energy coursed through her for a brief moment, as Saranon lost control. The Keep drove her energy forward with the full strength of many years of experience. It blasted through the hard shell of the core and melting new conduits as it went. The energy raged within as the Keep drove on with a ferocity that brought her close to panic. The waves reverberated up into the Keep, and tingled along her spine as she clung on with all her might.

The Keep held onto the taint with an iron grip and brought it into the intense energy rising up from the core. The dying dark energy screamed in her ears, as it lashed out in pain and anger. The last remnant of the sorcery forged from the Dihan, loosened its hold. Leaving a hollow vacuum that enabled Zaidek to rush in with a renewed force. Sorrow filled Saranon's heart as the Keep continued without hesitation. It killed off the external energy source, as the taint would have done to the Keep. She wanted to leave, but she was stuck until Zaidek scourged the last remnants away. Her body was weary, yet her energy beat on around her at a solid pace. This was not what she wanted, but the Keep ignored her distress. It showed no mercy as it lashed out along the furthest reaches. She started trying to disconnect herself. She pulled away from the core and nothing happened. She gripped with all her strength, and with a great reluctance the Keep let go.

She struggled to clamber out with the energy buzzing below. Most of her strength was gone and she had to find more to lift herself back up towards the habitable area of the Keep. The struggle was immense, but she held on with the whirling torrents raging below. In the darkness the sweat made Saranon's hands slippery. The crashing around her made her think of the turmoil outside, but she had to go on. The loneliness crushed in upon her as she reached the outer layer and realised she had farther to go. The Angeon slipped away as she came back to reality and the pain set in. It was a terrible feeling running through her muscles, but she had to go on. The way ahead was dark and grubby, the air smelled like charred ash as it filled her lungs with every breath.

As she clambered along Saranon found a rope. She clung onto it, and was dragged to the surface with the soot breaking off over her clothes as she went. Mitch held out his hand and hauled her up into the light, 'I thought you'd never make it.'

The light stung her eyes as she spun around. Part of the outer areas of the Keep had gone to rubble, but the heart remained standing strong against the smouldering sky. She clung onto Mitch, out of breath and exhausted. The landscape changed forever in front of her, with the heat still rising in steamy gushes from the ground beneath.

The last echoes of chaos still rung in her ears, as the sound of the central core lingered on as a reminder of where she had been. She gazed around at the haphazard mess as the wizards around her worked their way through the rummage. The main building stood strong underneath, like an ominous ghost hidden behind layers of ash. Her heart thudded in her ears as she took a deep breath and her muscles ached all over as she faced the small group of wizards.

Saranon strode forward, 'What have I done?'

'This was not your doing,' Captain Graddon spoke with a firm voice. He kicked the rubble away from his feet. 'I think you've outgrown this place.' He spoke with serious tone, 'We can look after Zaidek.'

She knew he was right, but she did not want to admit it. Mitch had always known that they would not stay. Compared to what had happened she did not think the scar was that bad, besides it was a war wound she could be proud of. The place was still a mess, although she was no longer needed by the wizards. Inside the Keep they had a great deal of work ahead of them to completely secure the Keep.

The Captain had already gone leaving Saranon annoyed. She had been quite content trying to avoid the whole situation, even though so far it had gotten her nowhere. She grumbled as she made her way down to the dragons. Katholomu was already thumping his tail in anticipation, which annoyed her even more. 'I hear you're leaving?' Gabriel said almost out of breath from all the rushing around.

'Yes,' she answered.

'It's about time,' Gabriel remarked

'What?' Saranon spoke before she thought, but Gabriel only smiled in reply.

She tried to take her time, but Katholomu knew what she was up to, and kept on nudging her to hurry up. Angry stares did not work on the great dragon, he shrugged them off. 'Are you ready?' She cringed at hearing Mitch's voice.

The marmoz dragon seemed to ignore her awkwardness as she clambered on, he was too busy scratching himself. Saranon sighed; they suited each other well. The morning brought with it a friendly heat that warmed the edge of the dragon's coat, making him glisten in the early sunlight.

Then she cringed as the dragon's claws scraped along the stone with a screeching sound painful to the ears. The noise was followed by a heavy thud as the dragon came to a halt. She opened her eyes; it was not the worst she had seen. It was enough to get disapproving stares from the others who were already making their way outside. To Saranon's surprise she saw Captain Mirshendy walk towards her as he came to see them off. The Captain waved as he spoke a short goodbye and she waved in return.

She laughed, she had come a long way, and could never have imagined herself in Normisia. The thought filled her with a great sense of pride, as Katholomu leaped into the sky with all the conviction of grandness. Mitch sat behind her, an odd companion, but welcome even so. The warm soft breeze blew in her hair as she clung onto the dragon's shoulder. Saranon smiled, she was free. A feeling she had wanted for so long.

RUNNING THROUGH THE RISING TIDE

THE LEGACY OF ZYANTHIA BOOK TWO

CHANTELLE GRIFFIN

CHAPTER ONE

The trouble with Magladen

Deep on the plains the shadows grew dark across the sky, Mitch was itching to be off but Saranon was not so sure. Normisia had provided sanctuary. Every day the northern border drew nearer she became more agitated. It was not so much that she did not like the place, but it felt odd. The dust crept into her boots making her feet grubby every time she went outside. The strange warm wind blew her hair into her face and became a continual source of frustration. The sky was even a different colour of blue and the land was poor with few people working the browning fields. The grounds around the Keep Zaidek had been lush and plentiful in contrast. Even though Saranon was not afraid the image loomed in her mind and played havoc with her internal thoughts.

The northern border was harsh and unforgiving; it

would be easier to follow the river up through Magladen. Mitch kicked the dirt beside him and grunted, his top which looked one size too small made his muscular arms stand out. Saranon could not help a small chuckle. He would be missed by a few of the ladies at Eggleston. A plain yet well sized Keep, blending into the background of the earthy hills. This was as far north toward Magladen as any Keep had been and withstood the elements which simmered across the border.

'Have you finished admiring the view?' Mitch spoke with a straight voice.

'Hardly, how do you feel about leaving tomorrow?'

Mitch just smiled and went inside, he did not seem adverse to adventure but she doubted the journey ahead. She needed to make it to Serenphel in time for the next calling that was weeks away. Then to get this far had been more than half a year, soon it would be her birthday and then the anniversary of Tasha's death. Her old friend still beckoned to her in her sleep and woke her at night.

She turned back to Brett the Captain of Eggleston Keep and her new friend Ingrid smiled. 'I'm afraid we can't go with you but I will help you make your way across. The people there are peaceful, but they keep to themselves.'

Saranon knew she was right; Ingrid had taken her along the border before. There had been little conversation and not much could be fathomed from the exchange. Yet try as she might, her dreams were going to be filled with the large forests that hid Magladen from the world outside. The pillow was soft as she settled down with one arm hanging out in Mitch's direction as he slept in the dark.

No sooner had she closed her eyes than Tasha was in her dream clutching at her hand, pulling her in haste. She almost tripped on the path wavering in front of her, we have to go. She knew her old friend was right even if her way ahead would not be easy. The first rays of light shining through the window touched her open hand. Something moved at the corner of her eye and Mitch was standing ready to leave. He knelt down and helped her up, not that Saranon needed help, but she had been dithering somewhat the last few days. He could see it written all over her face.

Brett held the horses at bay to let them pass through the ranks without a sound. As much as she wanted to take Katholomu he would draw attention and it was easier for the sly black dragon to fly alone. The border coming up was the easy part as they passed through the check point and into a windy dense oblivion. 'You seem right at home?' She asked.

Mitch did not answer, he was busy making ground. They could both travel using the lay-lines but the paths were vague and muddy, weakening at points and that was what she was unsure of. If they lost their way it could take ages to get back again.

The dense swampy land let out the odd dull sound from behind the undergrowth. Mitch had stopped up ahead. 'What is it?' Saranon whispered.

He signalled for quiet. She stood beside him and he pointed but she could see nothing. 'I don't see,' she whispered.

'Over there,' he whispered back.

She gave him a disgruntled look. She had a more detailed scan of her surroundings but drew a blank. She was starting to wonder if he was making things up. 'Look between the trees past that rock,' Mitch pointed.

She gave a sigh of exasperation and he added, 'They're clinging to the trunk.'

Saranon squinted and could just make out some odd shapes. That looked more like large stick forms wrapped together. Mitch whispered, 'They are firmadicide.'

'Oh,' her powers of observation were slipping. She wondered how she was meant to feel. She felt calm, which was strange at the moment given the presence of such a dangerous predator. She was thankful the odd gigantic stick creatures kept to themselves unless disturbed. A thought occurred to her, 'Are we encroaching on its space?'

He clutched her shoulder urging her to move on while he shook his head in mute disbelief.

'I was being serious,' she exclaimed.

He gave in, 'See over there are the nefrelle. We'll be fine as long as we stay close.'

'Are you sure about that, because I don't see how we could be safe…' She replied.

Mitch had picked up speed, no doubt to avoid the conversation which left her having to almost run to catch up. After a while he slowed his pace without missing a beat. Saranon was fit but her new found friend made the journey look effortless. His pace was sturdy over the lay-line which covered the ill trodden ground. She was thankful they had not reached the gap, which would be near night fall and she hastened her speed.

There was no sign of Katholomu but unlike people, dragons did not find the dense forest country heavy going. Instead it was a well-known sanctuary and if rumours were believed a place for larger dragons to hang out.She had spotted a few but they were different in build and looked a bit rough around the edges in an unwelcoming way. She felt as though eyes were watching her, then tripped over something running across her path. Mitch stopped her fall and the nefrelle ran out of sight, 'Can they do that?'

Mitch stayed close, 'Be careful.'

'I plan to,' she retorted.

The small furry thing was meant to have claws, small but sharp. As Saranon looked down she noticed a small scrape across her boot, 'Great.'

If that happened again, knowing her luck, it would tear a hole and she would have to mend it. They were trying to stay low as much as possible, at first she thought that would be easy. Yet lately she had been letting in to her energy in her sleep. Having to concentrate during the night was beginning to wear her patience, not that there was much to begin with.

A strange wave came over her and Saranon moved back near the middle of the lay-line, the distraction had taken her too close to the edge. The sun was setting on a warm day; she could feel the sweat drip down her back more from the effort of keeping up than the heat. Mitch was already making camp with a wry smile; he had not said anything about her clumsiness. The place had a good view, but tomorrow meant clambering over boulders and away from the lay-line. She felt calm near its edge but the thought made her shudder. At least she did not have to deal with people out here. The people of Magladen were a hard, down to earth kind. It was more the next stage that gave her a nervous stare into the beyond.

'You're scaring the wildlife,' he remarked.

'What?' She stared down to see the energy build-up underneath her hand. Several worried nefrelle peered at her in the distance.

Saranon calmed down, it was no use getting worked up before she had even started. The blankets they had packed were nice and soft and the calm night meant they could stay in the open. Mitch had mastered protection spells with years of practice that made her jealous. She gave him a look and he refused to be drawn in. The nefrelle kept a small and respectable distance before settling down for the night. When curled up they looked like small balls of fluff with silk soft fur. It was amazing to think that these tiny creatures could take on firmadicide.

A cool wind was creeping up from around the hill carrying a faint growling sound. Before she spoke Mitch did, 'Go to sleep.'

The growling sound continued in the background as she fell into a murky dream of being chased by firmadicide. The light filled the air and cast a shadow from his bulky figure. She scrambled up to find the campsite had already been cleared away and placed her hands on her hips in a huff. She was beginning to understand why sorcerers grumbled about wizards. She crammed her belongings in her small bag. The ground was not too moist underfoot as they began their slow climb over the rocky hills.

For once Saranon could show off, bouncing over the rocks as he struggled to keep up. She glimpsed Stragnar in the distance. Her heart pounded with excitement that was over the halfway mark through Magladen. The wind brushed across her sweaty skin bubbling with fresh hopes and ideas. A muffled sound clambered up her back, she turned around and she could not see Mitch. For a moment she forgot to breathe as she pummelled back to where he had been and almost tripped into the gaping hole. 'Are you all right?' She shouted there was no reply.

How on earth could she loose a wizard? She grumbled to herself. She shone a small light and could make out Mitch's tracker on a ledge, as she groaned.

Saranon latched a strong yet thin rope around a nice piece of sturdy rock. She tried to think of where she preferred to be at this moment, having a nice warm meal at a cosy tavern in Stragnar. The grime was sticking to her sweaty garments not that it mattered, a strange sweet smell began wafting up from the depths. She made herself comfortable on a small ledge and shone her light brighter in to the darkness. 'Oh,' was all she could manage as she found her lost wizard. He was huddled in a calm stance so as not to disturb the firmadicide in their nest. She took a deep breath, trying not to panic as she had been in worse situations. While standing with one foot on one ledge and one foot on another she made a strong hold for another rope to go down. She dangled it between her fumbling hands.

Mitch stood up with all the grace he could muster. He raised himself up, he reached up as if to hug Saranon, then dashed up past her. Leaving her last to get out, she put one hand on her hip in annoyance and started gathering the rope. She felt a small tug and yanked without thinking, a noise grew beneath her and she realised what she had done. She scrambled out grabbing chunks of dirt on her way out. 'Run,' she did not need to say it, as he was already someway ahead.

So much for getting a thank you, she thought to herself. The rustling sound grew behind her…it gathered momentum into a low chirping with hundreds of voices chiming in.

Mitch was using his wizardry to build-up speed, as she looked behind her the firmadicide were catching up. As Saranon was running she eyed a nefrelle stronghold ahead on the left. She was running out of options and slid down the hill straight into them. The firmadicide followed at pace and crashed right into the nefrelle. The two massive groups mingled back and forth. She was too worried at what she had done to look. Then she heard some awful munching sounds. She peered out from her hiding spot to see that the nefrelle were chomping away on a few firmadicide. The idea of watching made her stomach churn, so she backed away and pretended that nothing had happened.

At least this time it was not her fault. Mitch

was catching his breath in the clearing and waved in recognition. She wanted to scream, how could you do that, but the words would not roll off her tongue. So instead she resorted to an annoyed glare that did not phase him one bit. At least the next lay-line was close by or Saranon would be finding her voice after all that. To make matters worse, Mitch appeared to be laughing at her. The unusual pair made their way down along the windy path with time to spare as the afternoon sun shone on their backs. The way ahead broke into patches of fields as they drew toward the city of Stragnar. She could see signs of civilisation on the outskirts, 'What do you think they're like?' She asked.

'The patrol knows we're coming,' he commented.

'Just when were you going to tell me that?' She grumbled.

Mitch shook his head and moved on. For some reason the last league seemed to drag on forever. By the time they reached the small party of troops the last rays of sun were stretching over the hill tops. An officer by the name of Haywood was leaning up against a muddy old vehicle that had seen better days. 'You two took your time, were you thinking of bringing the locals as well?'

He seemed friendly enough and Mitch spoke for a while before they moved away into the Keep Karaden.

It was a smooth but fast drive with the occasional bump from the gravel road. 'So what brings you to these parts?' Haywood glanced at her.

She looked at Mitch for guidance but he was giving no hints away. She hesitated, 'We are on our way to Indarin.'

'Are you sure that's what you want?' Haywood asked.

Saranon did not understand the question, 'I don't know of any alternative.'

'It's all right; I just meant it's dangerous to be travelling that far,' he replied.

'I will keep that in mind,' she spoke.

'She doesn't have a sense of humour?' He spoke to Mitch.

'Hardly,' he remarked.

Great, thought Saranon, why do wizards have to think the same way even across the border? She muted a grumble under her breath, now she had two wizards smiling at her expense. The night time was creeping in with odd sounds through the darkness as they made their way into the Keep. Karaden made up the corner stone which protected the city of Stragnar; it was impressive in size. Haywood led them around the building to a large black sleeping dragon making happy snorts as he breathed. 'I believe this belongs to you.'

Katholomu looked cosy and almost gentle, curled up on a well-worn piece of ground in the courtyard. As she walked closer she wriggled her nose from the smell, the big dragon stank. She bumped into Haywood while trying to escape the smell. 'Don't look at me, we tried to wash him but he wanted to wait for you,' he grinned.

She turned toward Mitch. 'Hey, don't look at me either. He's your dragon.'

'Oh,' she exclaimed while scrunching up her face in disgust.

It was not the greatest experience Saranon had. She walked closer to the wonderful smell of food wafting out from the hall. She felt the warmth on her hands from the fire having Katholomu turn up unexpected did not seem so bad. She sat down on the cosy couch and scoffed down tea, as Mitch and Haywood spoke. Mitch stared as she slurped her soup and she tried not to make a sound, this was going to be a long trip. The calm night blew a gentle breeze through the open window. Even though she could still smell the muck off Katholomu on her hands, she was too tired to let it worry her.

The whirring of the great central core mumbled into a soft whisper as it reached the walls of the corridor. Saranon caressed the wall and the Keep seemed to respond underneath her touch. She let go and looked out to see no trace of the great black dragon. She was not surprised but a little disheartened. If she flew by dragon now she would stand out and dragons were few in Balquene. Mitch was looking unorganised and relaxed for a short stay, 'Are you missing something?'

She could not see his backpack anywhere as she snooped around the corner staring straight at a room full of busy people.

He smiled, 'We're not leaving today.'

As he spoke the clouds turned dark and a deep low rustle swirled toward them on the wind from the dark forest to the northeast. Saranon let out her own grumble in frustration. That meant it would not be safe to travel the lay-lines for at least a few days. 'You could have told me!'

She walked off in a grump and went down to investigate the surroundings.

The dragon had left his marks by flattening a few bushes and bending a young tree to breaking point where he had slept. One of the local drezen dragons, smaller in size, was pawing and sniffing at the ground before she curled up. Tassle looked tiny taking up less than half the space, they were quite strong and compact, purpose built for the rough terrain.

She was not so convinced about the wildlife blocking their path. From where she stood it looked peaceful. The Keep had dealt well with hazards but as she walked through the scrub she was less convinced. The path beneath her led on to the Pheneadin sorcerers' cove residing on the large estate. She had been informed that they were quite content to co-exist with the local Eudarin wizards. Yet the Pheneadin preferred to keep their own space in the giant shadow of the Keep. 'Hello there, we were wondering when you would arrive,' Elise spoke with a pleasant smile. She was a few years older than her.

Saranon looked up with a baffled gaze, for some reason having an inconspicuous approach did not work in Magladen.

The sorcerers had a beautiful set up, it was so light and airy compared to the heart of the Keep and large inside. As she stepped around with Elise guiding her way, she noticed how busy and tense people were. 'It's all right we're just getting ready in case the triden stampede,' her new friend explained.

Elise said it in such a calm voice that Saranon thought she misheard, 'The what?'

'Oh you haven't experienced that they tend to run in every direction except south over the border. If you stay long enough you'll get to see one?'

She opened her mouth in amazement but stayed mute. The thought of staying long enough to see a stampede of anything was not on her list of things she wanted to do. She wondered if Mitch had heard of such a thing. Around her a whooshing noise sprang up from beneath with a loud gush of warm wind. 'We are just making a few adjustments so the Keep will be ready, but you shouldn't have anything to fear.'

Fear was not what Saranon was thinking about, rather how long she was going to have to stay. 'When this stampede thing happens, how long does it take for the lay-lines to clear?'

Elise gave a soft laugh, 'Oh you will be able leave soon enough, besides you only just arrived.'

Elise took her down to meet some of her friends who were helping make final adjustments. As they worked, the sky grew grey drawing long dark shadows, the lights flickered in response. 'You will need to head back,' Elise spoke in a serious tone.

She did not need any convincing to go, the wind was picking up outside hurting her ears before she covered them. There was no sign of Tassle or any other dragons out in the courtyard as she looked ahead. The path gave views back up to the hills she felt a strange calming sensation from underneath the ground where the central core lay.

Something in the distance, a speck or two on the horizon caught her eye. She walked forward against the wind's steady breeze blowing at her hair. She placed her hands on her hips as she gazed at the dotted line. 'So you are, what is keeping me from my path.'

Saranon spoke underneath her breath in cold defiance, how such a beast could cause so much trouble. The triden were a large overgrown crab-like thing with fur on its back. Its dark muddy brown colour blended into the background, and the darkness swallowing the calm blue sky.

She stood alone as the others had already gone inside and shuttered up the grand old building. The leaves blew around her. The Keep stirred below thumping underneath her like a dampened drum chiming with her heartbeat in the small of her ear. Then it stopped and the ground cracked beneath her with a whip of excitement. Her blood stirred the Keep opened up in anticipation of attack. She scrambled for her talik as Mitch called, 'Are you going to come inside?'

'Why, are you scared?' She asked and there was no reply, 'I take that as a "no".'

Mitch was good at intruding on her thoughts. As the rising wind swept the ground around her, she wondered if it was all a lot of fuss over nothing. The Keep did not think so with a cold shudder deep from within. The might of the central core sparked upward through the great claws around her. Arching into the sky above, her scepticism was waning as the small dark dots on the horizon began to grow in number. The dots formed a patchy line along the otherwise peaceful hillside. The wind began to drop away and for a moment Saranon thought it was for nothing. The Keep took on an odd view with the barricades and the silence. The shadows broke to let in blue sky and she ventured out past the claws of the Keep into the meadow below.

It was a searing rumble that pummelled the ground as she looked up and saw what she had been waiting for. It felt like forever as the great dark mass heaved in slow motion caressing the lower hillside in a dark embrace and spewing forward. The temptation was too great as the excitement drew her in. All she could think of was that she wanted to be part of it and for the moment the part of her brain that kept her safe was staying silent. She lunged forward at pace letting her sorcery grab hold of her. She jumped up and rode a triden driving it forward with such exaltation she forgot all about the safety of the Keep.

Saranon rode hard, spurring the triden on to the head of the mass and leading it around into the dense forest beyond. She rode with all her might as the great tide of triden kept pace behind and around her. The great beasts stopped to catch their breath in a clearing and she almost felt disappointed it was over. Her hands were white with excitement and from holding on so hard. Her back felt sore, but as she walked away she still could not understand what all the fuss was about.

CHAPTER TWO

Hiding the Angeon

The rush of excitement still filled Saranon's veins as she left the mounting numbers of triden behind her. It had been breathtaking but now she had to get back to the Keep and some sort of normality. She looked in the direction of Karaden that from a distance did not appear to be affected. She shook her head in bewilderment. She wondered if it was just her who found the whole event rather strange and lacking in severity. The thought was not long to be pondered, as she was soon joined by Haywood who drove by. He was silent but not in a bad way, she figured there would be plenty of work waiting back at the Keep.

Haywood looked at her as if expecting her to say something, but Saranon was in one of her moods. 'You are full of surprises for one so young,' he smiled.

She did not know what he meant, 'Next time can we

avoid the whole incident?'

Haywood laughed but he did not say anything, she could see Mitch waiting as they returned. She strode toward him and in a matter of fact tone stated, 'I don't think I like triden, and they smell.'

Mitch kept a straight face as Haywood chuckled behind her, 'I don't like them either.'

Haywood came over and patted her on the back, 'You're more than welcome here anytime,' and with that he left her in peace.

'Is he all right?' Saranon asked Mitch.

'Yes,' he replied.

She was about to ask another question but had second thoughts it had been a strange day already and she had had enough of the wildlife. A nice hearty meal sounded good right now.

The Keep showed signs of strain as they walked along the main hall. It was more artificial and could be fixed which was just as well because she liked the Keep. It had a nice hum that reminded her of Darkonia and hoped that all her efforts would lead her back home. At the moment, that seemed a long way away and she sighed almost in disbelief. The food was good and the Eudarin wizards knew how to have a feast. Her normal response was to shy away but today it felt like a welcoming hug at the end of a hard day. Karaden hummed away underneath her fingers as she went to bed, tomorrow with any luck they would be on their way.

The first rays of sun hit the floor radiant and bright.

The excitement that had washed over Saranon had now been replaced with grumbling. She packed away her belongings for a second time, hoping for an early start to the day. The sunlight shimmered on the courtyard and this time Mitch was ready to go, finally she sighed in relief, 'Did I get it right this time?'

Mitch beckoned her on before Haywood could answer. A little further down the track Mitch explained that the young sorceress had managed to make a grand impression. She could see that he knew it was more by accident than by design. 'Well,' she said. 'I will take compliments even if it was an accident.'

The journey was easy going and the warm weather enjoyable for the rest of the way as they strode into their last stop. Before stepping over into what she had been informed was some sort of medium chaos. Mitch was becoming serious underneath his dark brow and she noticed he was tense. She had been given a set of instructions before making it thus far. She rambled about in her papers as they sat in the small courtyard of the last destination in Magladen. 'You won't need that paper in Balquene,' Mitch sounded much surer than he looked.

The tidings were small and neat. They reassembled their luggage including a few items that had been prepared at Haywood's request. Saranon heaved on a formal coat that felt almost weightless and tried on a few other garments to the guards' bemusement. She had not bothered with looking like a sorceress much anywhere, because she had not felt like one. It was an odd thought but the more time she spent travelling, the more she felt comfortable with herself. The ride on the triden had settled her dreams and she had slept well, it was a shame that would not last.

Tellembre that had remained silent by her side, was worn with ease. She was quite used to the two bond-breakers now, but still kept Corsavere hidden away. It resembled a small elegant dagger when at peace, but she knew it to be a tyrant when called. Through the whole journey Pennie had remained out of reach, but that meant her old friend was busy and did not want to intrude. Things were different in the morning, Mitch woke up a completely different person. His face was stern and he hung in the background, for the first time since Saranon had known him. It was amazing to think such a large man could do that, but he did so without effort.

They checked in to Balquene. Everything seemed perfect but the undercurrent was there, filling her senses. It had been a while since she had been under such tight scrutiny with such little interaction. The air smelled thicker with a whiff of distrust and she wondered if it would be like that for whole journey until Serenphel. As they left, a scene broke out behind her, something had happened and the guards circled in. She did not need to say anything as Mitch followed with haste. The lay-lines were well used and looked after as they arrived at the town of Salby and she breathed a sigh of relief. The mid-afternoon heat creased the sky as they trudged on through the dusty streets. The place was filled with a stale smell that cluttered the air around them.

For once Saranon did not seem to be the centre of attention, as a few stares found their way toward Mitch, who for the most part remained silent. The city on the fringes was well used to travellers as she made her way into the tavern. She was used to speaking for herself, but the calm acceptance felt odd as Mitch stayed in her shadow. It was a cool relief to move out of the warm sun. She toyed with her drink before saying something, 'It's my birthday today.'

'Pennie told me,' he said.

He produced a small bundle and passed it to her. Inside was a beautiful hair piece that reminded her of home as she held it tight in the palm of her hand.

In the evening the noise of the tavern began to grow and reminded her more of Normisia which put her at ease. She did not think she would ever be excited by the merriness of rowdy voices. She saw a few glances from a friendly looking face of a wizardess but appeared not to notice Mitch by her side. Saranon warmed to her company as Gezelda asked her where she was headed. That was an easy answer as Balquene was used to its sorcerers travelling to Serenphel for training. She glanced at Mitch every now and then but he looked relaxed. The sensation crept up her arm but she pretended not to notice. It was too soon after the triden for her power to surge again, yet another thing for her to worry about as she clenched her fist.

She needed some fresh air and Mitch left his place to join her outside, they moved away and he could see the look on her face. He went to say something but it was too late. The air moved around them and they had company. The wizards circled in with trained ability, she tried to reach out to Mitch but they had already taken him. She sped after them down the street and out of sight, sliding fast into the shadows as the energy within her surged with delight. The Angeon beckoned underneath her skin and it gripped tight from within her soul, burning her eyes. She could sense Mitch being hurt and she was taking too long to catch up.

Saranon moved further into the old Keep, near the north of the city. It had been built around but the disguise fell apart as her senses reached out. She was so close to Mitch now but still too far. The wizards were well locked around him as she cringed with the surge of the energy making its way up to her throat. She tried to hold it down knowing it would only delay the inevitable. As she listened to the voices, it became clear that Mitch was not welcome, she should have left him behind. The energy churned up inside her making her head spin, now was not the time to lose control.

Mitch was cornered in the darkness of the Keep and the deep murky edge of the sheal lapping up against the open floor. The intense energy burnt like fire up her throat and she ran in searing agony to the liquid edge, letting the Keep suck the excess energy out. The voices of the shocked disgruntlement of the wizards she had knocked aside in the process, sounded far away. Saranon took a step back and gasped as she broke away from the Keep and stumbled around to see stunned faces. That was not exactly what she had planned. An older wizard Bohdan spoke up in the array of silence, 'I think that is enough for now.'

His greying eyes stared down the fierce competition that had left Mitch with a few extra bruises. She stood beside her wizard, she felt a great weight had lifted off her soul but this soon filled with annoyance. Her sixteenth birthday was ruined, she grumbled as the events of the evening were forgotten under the docile faces. For once she was envious of Mitch who played along in a brilliant manner. It felt like she was the only one who was dismayed by spending time with wizards who could change their mood quicker than she could. In the large gathering room Saranon spotted Gezelda. Before she made herself hesitate, Mitch pushed her forward. He whispered in her ear, 'It's all right.'

Strange words from someone who was going to have a black eye tomorrow, she was in no frame of mind to argue, this got her nowhere with wizards. The light shone warm and lit up the room. Gezelda looked past her and for the first time noticed her companion, 'You chose strange company.'

'You have an odd way of greeting people, but I would prefer to enjoy the rest of my birthday in peace,' She remarked.

Gezelda smiled, she had not given much away. She wondered what would have happened otherwise. As if knowing Gezelda responded with an apology, 'We thought Mitch was travelling alone.'

The answer was unsatisfactory to her ears but Mitch

was making every effort to shrug off the chain of events. So she tried her best to put her sentiments aside. It was a shallow attempt, but he did not say anything. Saranon shivered as she looked on even though she did not want to fall asleep, her eyelids were falling as she grew tired. He put an arm around her and took her up to bed. The room was strange but large and well furnished, 'I don't want to go to sleep.' She spoke as she fell asleep in Mitch's arms.

The morning's first ray brought with it a massive headache, it pounded down the side of her face. He closed the curtains again, 'It's all right, I don't think the light is going to make any difference.'

He let the light in, 'That's good because you may want to see the view.'

Saranon clambered over to look down at the bustle and further onto the heart of Thaldar. They were on the outskirts of the city, but high up. 'How did we get here?'

Mitch did not answer as she sat on the large window sill peering down; the place was immense and alive with people.

She started counting, 'There are a lot of bond-breakers down there.'

'I know,' he replied.

A knock came from the door as Gezelda entered, 'A bit different from home.'

Saranon thought in a strange way it reminded her of home. Darkonia had entire cities filled with sorcerers and wizards, not that she had seen much. The wizard Keep Thrakin was almost dwarfed in the size of the city, which spread farther than she could see. The headache dispersed as they walked out through the maze of people, Gezelda had been polite but to the point. They could stay but the wizard clan could not help her through the maze of Balquene.

There were too many unknowns for a sorceress and it would be easier if they went alone. It was a bitter cop out, but one she was happy to accept, she did not want to travel with the people who had harmed Mitch for whatever the reason. The wizard had taken the whole ordeal in his stride much to her annoyance. The city was grubby, but full of life, as they walked through. She was still feeling miserable, caught up in her own thoughts, when a crowd drew thick around an open square. To her amazement she could see sorcerers using bond-breakers as she dodged being shoved to the outer rim. Mitch whispered, 'Perhaps you could give that a go.'

Saranon glared at him, then tried to peer closer as the noise of the cheers increased. Her breath slowed as she peered on, the whole thought of using bond-breakers for show had not even crossed her mind. Mitch grunted as she lost her balance and stepped on his foot, the thought brought her right back down to earth as she cringed. It was an unusual sight as they made their way through. The misquew kept on the edge of town, with so many sorcerers they shied away from the inner hub preferring to keep to themselves. She understood how they felt; the boastfulness and open displays of sorcery for fun were starting to get to her. She kept the only bond-breaker she had on her belt wrapped underneath her coat just in case a passer-by was tempted to ask her to show off.

The outer city came like a breath of fresh air on her dusty shoulders. The soft comfort of the misquew felt like home underneath her finger-tips. For once she did not mind the grime that came off the sleek animal's coat of silky dark fur. The northern outskirts of Thaldar turned into a more familiar green background. The forest rising up around the two as they rode inland. Away from the populated coast to the west, it was a small detour but Saranon wanted to stay as far away from attention here as possible. Balquene could be rather cumbersome to new travellers. The night was warm and kind with a cool breeze sweeping her hair back from her face.

She stood up on a pile of rocks as Mitch made camp in the open; it was a beautiful night so far from home. She could feel a small tear trickle down her cheek; it dried in the wind before she could wipe it away. The road was well used and she could hear some voices in the distance. 'Are you going to make some company?' He asked in a casual tone.

'What?' She asked.

Before she had a chance to turn back around, Maya made her presence known with Helen standing with pride beside her. The two sorceresses were not much older than she was. They were from Balquene, but grateful to the have another sorceress in their midst to talk too.

The pair had entered the Reanval competition in Craiden for the first time. Saranon tried to smile and sound enthusiastic. She sighed with relief that she was a year too young to enter the competition. Mitch gave her a funny look from the side lines, 'Yes, Saranon is most looking forward to when she will be old enough to join in.'

That started them chatting away and volunteering to help her with her skills. She wanted to kick Mitch, but he was too far away, if he thought he was being funny she did not appreciate it.

Knowing the basics would not be so bad and Craiden was on their path. She disliked, it but she knew Mitch was right, he groaned as they talked into the night which was fair justice in her mind. It was a distant mix of emotions that swept into her dreams. All she could see was Tasha in the empty square back at Thaldar holding up the bond-breaker, Attourin, she had given Pennie. She had Tellembre tight in her hand and they fought to see who was stronger. In her dream the air electrified around her as they clashed. Tasha matched her in strength and agility urging her on through the sweet warm night.

The morning felt strange with the fresh air blowing against her skin. Mitch had managed to distance himself from the high pitched giggling that followed soon after. It was odd to feel at ease laughing, but this was so far from the life Saranon had known, that she let herself relax. The cool water from the stream was a welcome relief from the heat rising over the hills and filling the clear blue sky. Helen watched Mitch with intrigue then giggled, as her faced turned red when their eyes met. Saranon's mouth opened in astonishment but before she could speak Maya did. 'It's all right, Helen already has a boyfriend you'll meet him at Craiden.'

Helen stood beside her and peered up ahead. Not another soul appeared but there was movement on the horizon as the company rode on with Mitch looking on from behind. She could not help but turn to check but he gave no sign, he was so quiet that she was starting to get worried. Silence was not the Mitch she knew from Normisia. Three groups passed them by. Each time their eyes met Helen and Maya it was as though a secret code had been exchanged and they went by their way. Each time Saranon wondered a little more about her new friends who were filled with excitement.

As the afternoon grew too warm for comfort they came to halt. This gave her a perfect opportunity to quiz Mitch who was reluctant to oblige by dodging her first approach. 'So what do you think?' She asked.

'I think that you've just made friends with Lady Davene's daughter,' he replied.

'You mean after all this time we could have avoided Magladen?' She said under her breath.'

Saranon gave him such a stare that he let out a small laugh of satisfaction for managing to annoy the young sorceress yet again. 'You and I both know the answer, now get to know your friends so we can have an easy trip back.'

She thought to herself, as if that was going to happen. If anything life had just become more complicated but they were travelling the same way. So it made sense to blend in, she was enjoying the company. Maya and Helen were content practising without any regard to the energy they were using. It splayed off the blades and every now and then part of the energy would escape past the shield. A rock blew past Saranon just missing her face, she turned to see both sorceresses gasp then giggle in all the excitement. Maya invited her into the circle and helped her go through the basics. She could feel her heart beat with excitement at the chance of learning and became embarrassed at showing off. Her cheeks grew red and felt hot as she tried to hide her nervousness.

The amount of concentration was draining, but deep down she was happy as it made it easy to skim away from the edge of becoming the Angeon. Here in Balquene she preferred to keep that knowledge to herself for as long as she could. As her mind turned to thinking she let go a little. Maya fell back and both girls rushed toward her, Saranon breathed a sigh of relief as she knelt down. For a moment her heart felt like it was going to beat through her chest. The small bruise healed as they watched but it was a sign that she was happy to accept. She banished herself to the sidelines to watch for the rest of the early afternoon.

The scenery changed as they moved further north following the lay-lines. Less people travelled along the alternate path, which made for good time as they arrived in the evening at Reneby. It lay on the verge of the great forest stretching east. Whereas to the west grew sprawls of civilisation meshing into large towns rising up from the cultivated dirt. It was an eye catching moment as they all stood on an outlook part way up the hill. The landscape appeared with a strange beauty as it filled Saranon with excitement, she had managed to make it this far.

As the night set in she could hear rowdy voices in the distance. The disturbance annoyed her but Helen and Maya did not appear worried so she tried to ignore it. Mitch was quiet in the background but every now and then she caught a glimpse of him looking up. The ground was hard underneath and she was left lying awake, wondering how lucky she had been not to cause serious harm to Maya. She knew that was the real reason she could not sleep, but blaming the ground was easier. Mitch reached over and patted her arm as if in acknowledgement of what she was thinking. The wind blew calm and the voices with them fraying into the back ground, at last thought Saranon, a little bit of quiet.

Something brushed against her skin and she expanded her senses as she turned out of her sleep in annoyance. The misquew made a funny low sound and she stood in a fluid motion. As her energy awakened with her it was easy to tell that they had company. Helen and Maya were still asleep but Mitch had crept over to wake them. The misquew felt uneasy, as she waded her hand through its soft fur she could feel the skin grow tense. A shuffle rang through into the clearing as an ominous sound reached her ears. Several figures dispersed and she ran between them and her wizard. Not thinking, as she slipped into the ever growing Angeon that came to surface with the thrill of excitement.

The Angeon gripped at the edges of the energy, heading towards them like a rushing wave. She ripped it to shreds, knocking the intruders back from the clearing. She chased, forgetting the need to hide. A heavy blow flew out from the side towards her as Saranon fought back through the night her energy strengthening in response. She chased to the edges of the wood none the wiser. Their faces were clear, but whoever the five sorcerers had been this place was well known to them. She could feel the sting of cold sweat drip down her neck. She changed back to find the misquew standing on edge in a large group as if to say 'and don't come back'.

She laughed then she reminded herself of what she had done now there were two sorceresses who had seen the Angeon. Her shoulders shrank low as she headed back riding a misquew in cold relief. It was little comfort to her self-pity. Of all the things Saranon had been told to avoid and she had walked straight into that one. She could see the clearing up ahead and Mitch waiting as he came over she spoke, 'I stuffed up didn't I?'

'No, but you may want to reassure your friends,' he replied.

CHAPTER THREE

On the path to Craiden

The three young sorceresses and Mitch clung to the path. They made their way straight for the big city of Craiden looking around them in a nervous manner. The bright warm day gave no inclination of the trouble the night before, as if mocking their uneasiness. For once he was in the lead, she threw a small pebble close by to get his attention and he did not seem bothered. Helen was still quivering from knowing their attackers, at least it was not Saranon who had attracted trouble this time. In some way it was a relief after bruising Maya, it would have been a fine start to a short friendship.

The subject changed to Mitch as she cringed. 'So how did you two meet?' Maya asked.

'I thought we were discussing the attack,' she responded.

'Ooh, it sounds like someone's avoiding the question,' Maya spoke and Helen chimed in.

Helen was still looking shaken, so Saranon gave in as she spoke of Cornell the Dihan who had tried to kill her and skipped over the location. She was aware that Normisia and Balquene had an awkward relationship and it would be better for Mitch if he came from the country side.

She could see him shake his head, 'And what happened after that?'

He spoke from ahead enjoying this version of events.

'Why is Mitch laughing?' Helen enquired with concern.

'I fell into the water in the Keep during the ceremony.'

The two sorceresses roared with laughter. 'I didn't think it was that funny,' Saranon commented.

'No, you're right it isn't.' Maya spoke trying to stop giggling.

Saranon felt like she had just dobbed herself in. For a moment she missed the fact that Mitch had stopped over to the right, it made Helen feel uneasy. 'I thought I heard something,' he waited for a while then continued on.

'The sooner we make it to Craiden the better,' she spoke her thoughts aloud.

'I agree,' Maya said by her side.

The eerie feeling returned, she was not sure if it was just her imagination as it pulled at the edges of reality. The thought played with her mind and put her out of the good mood she had been in. A storm grew overhead with one more night before Craiden it was not looking pleasant.

Helen and Maya led them to more comfortable quarters in a small town that was used to visitors. Saranon was relieved that the place was busy with tourists and people travelling to Craiden. She noticed Maya was still tense, 'Is everything all right?'

Maya whispered, 'We are still vulnerable until we reach Craiden.'

She knew what she meant but was hoping to relax, the food was much better and Mitch had pre-empted by ordering tea for her. As she took the tray the storm broke outside thrashing against the window and she was glad to be inside.

For all her ability Saranon did not like sleeping in the rain, the warm hearth in a dry crowded room was welcoming as she ate. Helen smiled as Saranon scoffed the food down in chunky pieces and without thinking tapped her on the hand to slow down. It was an old habit she was finding hard to break, but after the camps good food was appetising. Looking through the window Saranon thought she saw a shadow dart across in the gloom outside. When she looked closer she saw nothing and shrugged her shoulders. She licked the juice off her fingers at the same time. Instead of being disgusted Helen understood, 'I'm amazed so many survived the camps.'

She swallowed her food in one gulp as Mitch replied, 'We are fortunate that Saranon made it to Normisia.'

She coughed in disbelief. After the reception she received from the Cryzinelan it was strange hearing the words come from his mouth. The tavern was well set up for the weary traveller with the comforts of home. It was then that she realised that Maya was Helen's bodyguard. For a moment she felt clueless, with a stunned look on her face. Maya just gave her a knowing smile as she walked across the room getting organised for bed.

The company stayed together as neither one thought it safe to split up. Maya had the same uneasy look about her that Saranon felt earlier. A noise crept from the window near where Mitch was sitting, all three sorceresses jumped and he gave them a disgruntled look. The idea of travelling with adolescent girls that had been spooked by the wind did not impress him. She tried to make it sound more serious but he only grunted at her. The night was filled with sweet smells and music wafting up from below in the warm room. She pulled the blanket up she opened her eyes, there was a hand moving near the window.

She shook Maya's shoulder as she headed near Mitch who had fallen asleep on the long couch. She crept over, but before she could reach it the window blew open and an assailant crashed through onto the floor. Mitch moved at the same time in a cold embrace and held the young man pinned down on the floor. She stepped onto the couch with Tellembre ready in her hand but the night gave away nothing more. Behind her the room had become quite crowded as Lady Davene's guards had arrived. They came with the first rays of light breaking across the ground and bleeding into the room. For a moment Saranon was annoyed by the inconvenience. Then she saw Mitch's strained expression as one of the guard's carted the unwelcome intruder away.

He stood up straight beside her and dwarfed the other two men in the room. 'We came as soon as we could Miss,' spoke Tyron, his hair was still damp from riding through the rain.

As Helen spoke, Mitch led Saranon outside to where a fleet of dragons rested. The rozzen dragons shone with their well-kept coats gleaming in the early morning sun. 'I think you're new friend was out of her depth, she reminds me of you.'

'Gee thanks, that's reassuring,' she examined his arm, 'So how are you?'

'I'm fine,' he said.

Mitch's subtlety was lost on the young sorceress as she went up and inspected the dragon. Maggard turned his head toward her and rubbed it against the outstretched palm of her hand. The gentle giant was happy to see Helen as she approached them, 'I am sorry to have caused you so much trouble.'

She spoke with a mild sadness in her voice. She was about to say that she was all right but Mitch got in first. He smooth talked his way into hitching a ride with Lady Davene's daughter. Saranon was speechless and annoyed at him at the same time.

Afterward when they had a moment she took him aside, 'What are doing?' She exclaimed in total frustration.

'It would be easier if we travelled with Helen,' he answered.

'How? Have you thought this through? Why would I want to travel with someone who doesn't fess up about how much trouble she's in?'

Mitch gave her a sarcastic look but did not respond, so she continued. 'This is different, if I knew what sort of trouble I was in I would say something. I don't think it would help but I would tell you.'

'Really,' he smiled in surprise, 'I'll remember that.'

It had been an unusual day, Saranon was quite happy not being the centre of attention but she had been irritable. She chose to ride with Maya on the misquew rather than fly on the dragons with Helen. Riding a dragon had a different meaning in Balquene and she was not convinced that it was the right time to send that message. The well-built road was filled with travellers and unanswered questions of the night before. She could sense Mitch was already having doubts, but she did not have any other ideas. Maya reminded her a little of Pennie back home, interested in details and the way she held herself with confidence. Like her old friend, Maya was not one for giving too much away and expected Saranon to go with the flow. She knew how that had gone with Pennie in Normisia.

As the great gates of Craiden loomed overhead she finally thought of an excuse to part ways. Mitch had promised to check in with the local wizard clan, he gave her a grumpy look as she tried to remain serious and hold onto her tone of voice. As chance would have it, she did not have to wait long. She could feel her whole body breathe a sigh of relief as a familiar face came over. Fiona, Gezelda's older sister came to meet them. Parting them from the group, She could sense the urgency but Mitch stood back until she reached for his hand.

Saranon went to thank her and brushed her arm. Fiona jolted back in shock, 'Sorry you startled me,' she explained.

'There's no need to apologise,' Saranon did not want to disclose what she had felt. Fiona had been hurt and she knew that feeling too well. It stayed with her for a while and Mitch stepped closer, her palm was sweating and she let him go. News had travelled of her accidental union with Thrakin Keep through the wizard world, much to her bewilderment. For her it was just part of being who she was. Mitch warmed to Fiona but it was an uneasy truce, she poked him in the back and he was still tense.

After Normisia being in a wizard Keep did not appear strange, so when Fiona offered she accepted without hesitation. It was Mitch's turn to be annoyed, but she did not mind. There was something about Helen that she could sense in a few quick glimpses. They had been brief but all too familiar from her past. When they were alone Mitch slammed the door, 'What were you thinking?'

Saranon nudged the angry wizard away, 'Fine, you wander around here and if you want we will leave.'

'Is this pay back?' He asked.

She did not know how to respond so she left Mitch to check out the Keep alone. She held her head in her hands in disbelief then tried to get up.

The world became blurry and she knew it was the Angeon from deep within wanting to resurface, only this time was different. She would have to ask Andon Keep for help and leave Mitch for a while. Either way she was not looking forward to the next few days as the queasiness came over her in bouts. Her heartbeat pounded in her ears as she stumbled downward into the heart of the Keep. Andon was welcoming and Saranon figured it must be because of Thrakin. It would not be the first time she had heard of Keeps communicating to one another. Underneath the whirling buzz of people the energy struck through webbing over the surface of her skin. She would have to go down even deeper.

It was a long road down, the Keep was helping her but then she slipped into a hole which felt familiar and her thoughts turned to Odana Temple. Andon pulled her down deep into the heart below the chambers and straight down into the central core. The whirring sound was less intense as Odana, but familiar just the same. The tendrils pulled back and she floated. This time she was not in shock at the unnatural sight within the giant circular core ebbing downwards into nothing. In the glowing darkness the Angeon changed, forming new pathways across and within her. She let herself go floating above the great core which sparked with excitement in response. The core sent great shards of energy up to the surface.

The queasy sensation took over as she transformed and the Keep repaid her kindness to Thrakin. Inside the central core the mighty surging energy of the Angeon, paralleled the core within. The great walls were well fortified to absorb excess energy and hide the transformation. Saranon was not sure her nerves would hold up but from a distance she could hear the Keep soothing her thoughts. It was not the first time the central core in Andon had met an Angeon. The process took days to complete but Andon was pleased with his work, not that the world outside knew it yet. The energy settled with the pathways complete running without an undesired short circuit. That had been causing her so much trouble. It was a calmness that she enjoyed in the lulling hub reaching from below.

The climb to the surface was a grateful relief. She had all but forgotten about Mitch, the Keep told her that he was still around and the thought did not stop her from fretting. She went straight to where Mitch was and found herself heading toward the outdoor pool. That was not like him at all, so she ventured forward watching her step. Saranon could sense the laughter as she moved closer and realised she was stupid to think that he had been in trouble. Mitch splashed water at her from the pool and she stopped it without thinking. The droplets fell on the ground from mid-air. He looked at her from the water's edge, 'You've changed.'

'So have you,' she replied.

She approached Fiona sitting at the other end of the pool, 'How did you manage to get Mitch to relax?'

Fiona's face flushed with embarrassment. 'Ooh, right,' Saranon spoke, she should have known.

That explained why the Keep was not worried about Mitch when she had asked him. Now was not a good time to tell Fiona that he had a lady waiting for him back in Normisia? She took a mental note to remind him of this when she started dating. At least she would not have to worry about having an argument over staying at Andon Keep.

The Reanval competition would be soon, she thought of leaving while the roads were void of traffic. Yet a sorceress not wanting to see the Reanval would attract attention. In some ways it was a relief to have the decision made for her, but waiting gave her time for her thoughts to run idle. Mitch was occupied which gave her time to search the city. The place was fast becoming a beacon for sorcerers from the furthest ends of Balquene and tensions were beginning to flare. Saranon ducked out of an angry dispute not far from the Keep. She made her way to the Haveena Stadium where preparations were taking place.

As she moved among the slow moving throng of enthusiasm she heard a familiar voice. 'I thought I would find you here,' Maya spoke with an open smile.

The two of them talked as Maya showed her around and introduced her. It was strange spectacle with strong shields protecting onlookers from any mishaps. The thought of one failing, gave Saranon an uneasy feeling. It was not something she was accustomed to and trusting it did not feel right. She had two days of indecisiveness before she had to make up her mind to attend. Yet it sounded like Maya had already worked that part of her calendar. The flow of excitement illuminated around her and she was happy to take a step back.

She felt like she had to find her feet again after everything that had happened at Andon. She blamed it on the long journey when Maya noticed she was tired. She did not mind the company but the thought of attracting more unwanted attention after Reneby did not appeal to her. So she was quite content to be staying with wizards. After Normisia it was becoming a recurring theme for the young sorceress. Maya introduced Saranon to her cousin Kadin in the practice area. He was not much older and sweat poured off him as he held out his hand to shake hers.

She wiped her hand afterward but Kadin had a welcoming warmth about him. 'Maya tells me you had some fun on the way up,' he spoke.

She began to feel meek in his presence, 'Yes,' was all she could manage.

Afterward Maya burst out laughing, 'That's the first time I've heard you lost for words. If it means anything I think he likes you too.'

Saranon was trying hard not to blush in the confusion she had not expected to feel that way and returned to Andon not knowing what to say.

She almost bumped into Mitch while attempting to sneak in. The tall wizard stood in a casual manner blocking her way, 'Where have you been?'

'Haveena,' she said as she gained her balance.

He looked down at her in deep thought, 'I think we need to have a chat.'

The young sorceress was taken aback when she realised that Mitch meant a chat about boys. With all the travel Saranon thought it was a bit late. She could not help but see the irony in having him try to explain boys. It was all she could do not to cringe while he spoke.

She tried to change the subject, 'So how are you and Fiona?'

'What?' Mitch grumbled to himself without answering the question.

She giggled to herself it was enough to get him to leave her be. She could feel the buzz of excitement growing around the city and penetrating the atmosphere of the Keep as she slept. The glowing in her dream grew with the voice of the Keep and it woke her in the warm muggy night. She could feel a sharp pain running up through the walls hurtling from outside. If Saranon had to make a guess she thought the Keep was under attack. She raced downstairs and Mitch blocked her path, she almost leaped on him to get past but he pushed her back, 'Stay out of it.'

Every essence in her body was telling her she had to do something. Then having him looming over her creating an obstacle compelled her to wait. The force knocked several wizards down as she squirmed in frustration. She was not about to take Mitch on, especially when wizards were involved. The attack died down with the surge of energy from the central core strengthening the protection shields. He loosened his grip on her in resignation. Saranon slipped out of his arm and rushed down into the chaos. There were two blankets hiding the losses lying on the floor, as she glared back up at him in annoyance.

'Don't blame Mitch, he was trying to help. The Immaron would have increased their attack if they had known you were here.' Fiona spoke as she attended to some of the wounded.

Saranon felt useless for a moment before Fiona suggested that she assist with the wounded. It was not something she had experience with and her awkwardness showed. To her amazement it had a calming effect and she shook her head, it was going to take a long time to understand wizards.

Andon Keep hummed with delight as the sun broke into a bright warm day, sweeping away the pain of the night before. Saranon's frustration still creased her brow as she strode around the Keep checking the shield. Mitch spoke with a sigh, 'Why don't you visit Haveena? We can manage here.'

She was hesitant to leave but he shuffled her outside and she was not about to argue. She suspected the wizards were up to something and she knew her goal was Indarin so she went. The streets were void of any sign of disturbance. After a resounding huff she made her way up the slope to the grand Haveena Stadium looming over the productive city.

Kadin spied her as he was warming up with friends, Saranon had been looking for Maya but the distraction was welcome. The place was full of excitement and yet again she wondered if she would ever feel at ease with the display of raw power. She did not have time to think long as Kadin chatted away. He was quite at home with the prospect that she had travelled from Darkonia. This was much at odds with some of the strange looks she was picking up from the periphery. She was distracted by his smile as a surge of sorcery came down behind her. She turned and shattered the strange bond-breaker into obliteration with hers. Piping hot sparks flew into the air and around as Kadin stood transfixed in silence.

The show was over as soon as it had begun, as the sorcerer who had attacked her fled. Saranon pulled him down and pinned him against the floor, her temper plain on her face. The slow deadly embrace came to a halt with Maya screaming from the distance and she let go pulling back her energy. Regardless of what anyone thought, the blow would have knocked her out and it was not to be scoffed at. She seethed underneath the surface. It was ironic that everyone was rushing to the other sorcerer's aide but she felt little pity.

'You could have killed him,' Maya screamed at her.

'The feeling was mutual.'

Maya was astounded that Saranon had not faltered and stood her ground. The presence of the younger sorceress washed over the bewilderment. It transformed the small arena with a sense of awe. Kadin rushed from the side, 'Three of the shields are down,' then changed the subject, 'How strong are you?' He asked.

'One thing's for sure you won't be able to enter the Reanval.' Maya spoke as she picked up a broken shard from the bond-breaker. She peered at it in a frightened fascination.

Saranon shrugged as her attempt to stay out of the way soon vanished. Fear turned to excitement as Kadin's older brother Reece began organising the clean-up. He grumbled about the lack of time before the start of the competition. She stood watching him, not sure if she was welcome, but the sorcerer did not mind. 'Thought you'd bring some excitement to the arena for the day? I've been waiting for that to happen, the Immaron have been looking for a fight all week.' Reece commented.

Saranon was not sure what to say, she had been attacked and then berated for defending herself. No wonder Mitch had been so keen for her to stay away.

She had felt like she had taken one step forward and one step back. Reece could read her frustration and told her where she could find Kadin and Maya. It was a strange sensation as she walked inside the old stadium. It was as if time stood still inside the walls with the bright flags highlighting different areas and patrons. Saranon breathed a little sigh to herself and was about to knock when Kadin opened the door, 'I thought I would see you again.'

She became speechless and in the awkward silence he let her in. The room was filled with three other sorcerers of similar age preparing their gear in a relaxed manner.

It had not occurred to her that she had reduced tomorrow's competition. As the sorcerer who had attacked her was in no condition to perform and the sorcerers were happy with better odds. She was still calming down and talking about the Reanval was a pleasant distraction. This time she managed not to blush in Kadin's presence as she had the image of Mitch telling her to be careful, stuck in her mind. Saranon went to say something as she left but Kadin kissed her on the lips. She was so shocked that she scrambled back to Andon without saying goodbye. Her heart was still pounding in her ears as she entered inside the Keep.

CHAPTER FOUR

The Reanval competition

On the day of the Reanval competition the streets burst into celebration. It appeared that everyone was up early, just when Saranon felt like sleeping in. Mitch had urged her out of bed so she would not miss a thing. She was beginning to get jealous of the fact that he could sit this excursion out. His happy whistling did nothing to ease her mood. 'You look beautiful,' were not the words she expected to hear from him as she showed him her outfit.

She gave him a grumpy look as he continued, 'So what did you get up to yesterday?'

She was about to respond when he went on, 'I hear you had a lovely evening with a young man. Is there anything I should be aware of?'

'No,' she said in a meek voice.

'I told you to be careful didn't I?' He reminded her.

'Yes,' Saranon did not think this was fair, given that it was obvious Mitch was sharing his bed. Yet she was not about to say that and scampered off before he could say anything more.

It was easy to blend in, as she became swept along in the cheering crowd heading for the stadium. With many colours present denoting the popularity of the event. She was gliding along amongst all the excitement with a smooth stride all the way to the stadium. The second main arena was filling fast and she could just make out Kadin and Maya in all the commotion. The events were soon being called and the crowd settled in excited anticipation. For all Saranon's lack of understanding, the sparring was professional. She watched in bewildered awe at the sport. Kadin made third place in his rank which he earned with a swift graceful air. Yet the strength of his opponent in the last round had been exceptional. The crowd cheered with tense excitement the whole way through.

Maya had not been so lucky, making eleventh place with Helen making ninth. The two were competitive, but all that was put aside as they greeted each other after the game. The main stadium was reserved for the experienced. In amongst the games the lightning showed with energy glimmering off the vast array of shields. The sparks crackling at the edges made Saranon feel uncomfortable, but the people in the stadium shown no sign of distress. As Helen left the arena she used it as a quiet excuse to move inside but even that was packed. She waited a moment in two frames of mind wondering if she should see Kadin again when Maya caught her arms and beckoned her. Before she had time to ask, a thunder of energy ran through the place with a jolt, it shook the ground with such force then another. 'It's Reece,' Maya panted through her breath.

She looked up at the doors to the main stadium where they were headed and froze. She did not have much time to think as Maya urged her forward through to the arena. The noise was immense; it hit her ear drums with a tumultuous roar. People were already scampering in disbelief and running for the exits almost no one was left. If anything sorcerers could be counted on, it was for making a quick escape when not at the centre of the dispute. The shields were only just holding. She knew Reece did not have long as he struggled with every bit of his energy to hold of his attacker, this was not part of the show. At first Saranon was daunted by the task, but the sorcerer was losing ground and she had to try something.

In the chaos the glow came like a small ember folding in on itself with strength as it grew with immense force. She lunged forward with speed, breaking the hold over Reece. The ground shook with an all mighty rumble, the energy that flew out broke all the shields around the arena. The sorcerer ran, then tumbled as the air shook with the energy. He was pounced on and led away as Kadin rushed in to help his brother. A few brave people who had remained came out of their hiding places and cheered in relief. As she stayed by Reece's side watching him on the stretcher he spoke to lighten the mood, 'I think you've got a fan club.'

'I still don't get it,' Saranon spoke, and he laughed.

It felt like a long evening that dragged on before she went to see Reece with Maya.

The sorcerer looked much better than he had a few hours before. She breathed a heavy sigh of relief, for a moment she thought he would be lost. It was still a blur with the adrenalin running. Kadin had stayed by his side and as Maya, left she found herself speechless. It was strange to think that she had saved someone's life and she felt awkward sitting beside him in an odd silence. Kadin wanted her to stay and she was not sure whether to be flattered or embarrassed. Maya came by again, 'Well I think Reece is right.'

'What do you mean?' She asked.

'I think you've got a fan club. I've already heard at least two stories of a how a great sorceress saved the day.'

All Saranon could think about was how Mitch would react when he found out. She stood up, 'I'm sorry but I need to go, it's getting late…'

'You don't need to make excuses,' Reece said as he thanked her.

It was dark as she managed to make her way back unnoticed. What would Mitch think? She was starting to panic as she crept inside and almost made it to her room as she heard a familiar sound of footsteps beside her. 'Did you have an eventful day?'

Saranon could feel herself cringe 'I… there was an emergency… and…'

Mitch stared at her with his big brown eyes, 'So much for a peaceful journey.'

'I guess you heard,' she replied.

'And the rest of the neighbourhood, I thought the aim was to be quiet,' he remarked.

'Well, I didn't say much,' Saranon said.

'Hmm, I don't think you need to. Now come downstairs and eat something, while you tell me how you defeated an Immaron,' he suggested.

Mitch was patient but she could tell he was not impressed. 'Learning restraint is difficult, but it is an important skill to have. Make sure you think next time.'

He removed himself from any further questioning. He left her with that thought as she became annoyed with him, but then she had expected as much from the soldier within.

Saranon was still seething as she slept in the next morning, Mitch had not come along to rush her and she was thankful. She had too much to be thinking about after last night with Reece. It was going to be awkward attending the Reanval competition after that. It would be a relief when the four days of the competition came to a close. Not thinking she ran downstairs and almost tripped over Mitch startling both of them. He had been crying and her heart sank, 'I will try to be careful today.'

He looked at her in surprise, 'Fiona's missing.'

That had not been what Saranon was expecting and it took her a moment to digest what he was saying then let out a long sigh. She looked around at the panic that was beginning to envelope the clan. The competition would have to wait. Mitch dragged her along and into the thick of the search party getting ready, with the assumption that she would be going with him. She was about to remind him of their previous conversation, but he shot her a serious look and she held back. The competition had begun and there was almost no one on the street. At first she thought they were going to question people but no, that would be too easy.

As she ran to catch up she had the distinct feeling they were heading straight into trouble. The feeling crawling up her spine only added to the thought as Mitch slipped out of sight and Saranon had to find him again. It all felt like a lot of nonsense as she lost track of him again, she tried searching and could not find him. 'Oh, for love of Odana,' she exclaimed.

How could she lose a wizard? She thought to herself. The whole situation was beginning to wear her patience as her frustration grew. She knew what she needed to do but she was not ready to go there after yesterday and she felt trapped by her indecision. She stayed with the search party as they honed in on an area. She wondered if she was doing the right thing as she let the wizards lead.

It was the cold that struck her first after such heat outside in the midday sun. This time, Saranon showed no fear, as she was still bound by her confusion. In the dark she could tell what was happening and did not reach out as she heard Mitch's words deep from within. Corsavere had lain dormant for so long on her journey she almost forgot what it felt like in the palm of her hand as she grasped it. The edges of the trap rose. It unravelled just as fast as

Corsavere's blade sliced with such ease through the invisible edges. She thrust out her hand parting the grey mist as she latched onto an Immaron and held him down. The cold anger raged at the edges of her mind trying to break free as she held on.

Mitch's voice broke her concentration, 'You can let go now.'

She looked up and realised that the hard work had been done and all the wizards, bar Mitch had left. Saranon let go and the sorcerer ran without looking back, she was relieved to find her way out in the warm afternoon sun again with Mitch. For a moment there she had not been sure what to do if she had lost him, Captain Mirshendy would not be a forgiving person. As they made their way back to the safety of Andon Keep, she relaxed. Before Mitch reminded her that she would be missed from the Reanval if she did not attend the last part for the day. She only wanted to relax and calm herself after what had happened but she went.

The light warmed her heart as she grew excited to see Kadin again. She was still unsure what to do; Craiden was a confusing place to be. Saranon made it in time to see the last game and that the shields had all been fixed, Maya came looking for her, 'Are you all right?'

'Yes, I'm just a bit tired from yesterday,' she replied.

'No wonder, that was awesome.'

That was not the word she would have used. Yet she was not about to argue as they went back to celebrate with the other participating sorcerers for the evening. Reece was looking better as he sat in the corner and beckoned for her to come over. The sorcerer still looked pale and shaken in the evening light, Saranon felt out of place and Reece gave her a reassuring smile. 'I hear you had some more trouble with the Immaron.'

'It wasn't much,' she spoke.

'If you travel north through Estrard you will avoid most of them, few Immaron go there because of the Evergeldy.'

She was not sure what to think of going through Estrard, but was grateful for some friendly advice. Mitch had mentioned it before in passing. There were two main gates to Serenphel and the western gate could be found there. It was closer to Indarin but not the most popular travelled. Either way Saranon's excitement at the end of the Reanval approaching was fast fading with the sunlight. It was a long walk home and full of strange disappointment. She had not seen much of Kadin but then it was good since she would be leaving soon. Andon lay peaceful as she started to pack in the glimmering light. It let out a happy small humming sound that faded into the background as if thanking her from a distance.

She would miss the Keep after its most precious gift even though she did not know what to do with it. At least there was no longer the need to worry about ridding herself of an unwanted build-up of energy. She examined her hands, no marks yet, she was complete, her sorcery running well through her body for the first time. It was a grand sixteenth birthday present as she smiled in gratitude.

Now she just needed to find Mitch. He was in the Keep somewhere and was good at shading his exact whereabouts, if only she had such luck. In the wizard Keep, Saranon stood out straight away as she searched, it was tolerable given she was a visitor.

She rushed by to find him kneeling down in the garden and for the moment she thought Fiona had died. 'It's all right.' He spoke without turning. 'I think I owe you an apology.'

She sat beside him; in her heart she knew why Mitch was so solemn. She reached over and patted him on the shoulder. 'We have a long way to go and I need a companion.'

'If we were in Normisia…'

'But we're not,' she replied.

He appeared more at ease as Saranon wondered if it had been the right thing to ask Mitch to go with her to Serenphel. Then it was too late to begin doubting that decision. He leaned over and gave her a quick hug, before he disappeared walking off inside the Keep. Again leaving her even more bewildered than before. For a long time her dreams had been filled with the normal unravelling of thoughts. As she drifted off to sleep she could feel her old friend Tasha tugging at her arm, trying to get her to move. As she opened her eyes to the dream she could see Tasha urging her on into the darkness of the unknown. The light shone off her golden brown hair. Her friend pushed Saranon into the great shadows of grey swirling up ahead and colouring the ground beneath.

She gasped as she woke throwing her arms up and latching onto Mitch with stunned surprise. She could see he had brought her breakfast and that softened her mood. 'If you want to leave we can.'

'What about the Reanval?'

'We've stayed long enough,' he replied.

She agreed with him, as much as she was grateful for the last few days, Balquene did not sit easy in her thoughts.

The pair slipped away with Andon growing smaller in the distance. It dawned on Saranon that he had been rather keen to leave. When she quizzed him he confessed that Fiona had wanted to marry him. She burst out roaring with laughter as she almost lost her balance. Mitch gave her a filthy look. 'And you were worried about me.' She stated as she calmed herself down.

He grumbled under his breath as they travelled north on the misquew and she tried her best not to laugh every time she looked at him.

Half of her wanted to know what happened and the other half thought that it would just annoy Mitch if she asked. This left her with a small smirk across her face. The journey was so peaceful with almost no people travelling by. She was amazed when greeted by a few wizards going about their business with ease. A cool breeze came across and swept along to the west bringing with it small clouds crowding up the sky. Perhaps Tasha had just been referring to the weather in her dream it was a nice thought anyway. Mitch had setting up camp for the night down to an art. Her efforts took at least twice as long between grumbling and his mood lifted as she grew crankier.

She finally gave up and set up the tent with her sorcery. It seemed like a waste but her frustration was crowding her mood and if he grinned at her one more time she was going to snap. He handed her a warm cup of soup as he sprawled out the map and made notes, in theory they were running on schedule. Saranon grew excited at the distance they had travelled already her heart pounding in her chest. They moved further north and closer to land ruled by sorcery. That placed him out of his comfort zone and she was still finding her feet. They had been lucky so far even with Mitch's love entanglement, she laughed to herself one wizard was enough to look out for.

He peered up from the paper as if reading her thoughts yet another annoying aspect of wizardry she thought. Wizards were blessed with the skill, even though it was not her strength it did not stop her from trying. Mitch laughed off her pathetic attempt as the bond between them only gave him greater protection against her. Saranon's efforts amounted to naught. At Craiden he had communicated with the people at the great Indarin. The response to her struggle had been underwhelming. They had expected as much from a Keep as far away as she could imagine or at least as far as she ever wanted to travel.

As the night closed in her curiosity kept her awake, 'Mitch?' She asked.

'It's private,' he responded as if knowing her thoughts.

'How did you know what I was going to say?'

'Go to sleep,' he replied.

She giggled to herself in the dark and snuggled into the warm sleeping bag. In the morning light she could make out Faldarin Keep at Estrard in the distance. The city was a rising monument to the old capital that once ruled over Balquene and Serenphel.

An ancient rival to the old Zyanthia that Odana had been built to protect. It still shone as glorious as ever in a light misty haze forming from the night before. At the northern most edge she could make out dragons on the horizon and wondered if Katholomu had followed them this far. Large rozzen dragons with graceful elegant wings glided through the sky. She counted the silhouettes of two riders and grew excited at the thought of being among dragons again. She turned in a rush to leave and saw Mitch's worried look, 'They're scouting.'

'Oh,' Saranon's heart sank as she realised she had missed the obvious and let out a disgruntled huff.

She stayed close to him on the misquew. Then he told her to look where she was going for the second time after becoming too absorbed in the dragons flying past. Instead she sat up straight and concentrated on being inconspicuous. Mitch just shook his head as they moved on. The inner hub of the city had a different feel from the nice clean streets of Craiden. It was not exactly dirty, just old, but it made Saranon feel weary as they walked along. They had arrived at the southern rim in good time. The city sprawled out for a long distance on all sides with centuries of uneven growth making it look like a maze up close. He brushed up against her as he peered around a corner and moved away.

He said nothing and Saranon followed him as two sorcerers walked past with a purposeful gait. His mood had changed and after they left he whispered, 'They are looking for someone.'

With that her thoughts of an easy path into Serenphel began to wear thin. She wondered if dealing with the Immaron would have been a better alternative. The idea dissipated as the day grew brighter and the city opened itself up with an array of shops for much needed supplies. After their quick exit she had packed little and with Mitch spending more than her she guessed he had done the same.

She peered over at someone running past out of the corner of her eye and followed down an unmarked street. She was left wondering why she had considered it important as she turned around and saw nothing. As her footstep marked the pavement to go back, she heard voices raised and knew that it was Mitch. The scene happened so fast that she only just had time to see the sorcerers disappear with him. Saranon could sense the massive force around them and it was all she could do to watch. She wanted to do something but the tone of the conversation she picked up in the upheaval only reinforced the need to stay away. As the people around her steadied themselves back to normal, the shopkeeper spoke to her but with fear in the edge of his voice.

It was all she could do to stand still without quivering and she felt ready to burst into tears inside. It would be no use to Mitch now as she had to figure out how to get him back. Her heart plummeted to her feet in dismay as she felt like she was the only one who cared enough to sort this mess out. She felt numb as she went around trying to piece things together without being too nosy. In her case this was rather difficult and time consuming. She sighed in her own thoughts near the grounds surrounding the great Keep Faldarin. She could sense nothing and that was what worried her to the core. The Keep was not the kind of place for a wizard, even Mitch and she had to get him back, after all she was supposed to look after him.

The thought of failure hit her like a brutal force sneaking up behind her and churning her gut. The queasy feeling was the least of her troubles as she pondered what to do. The idea that the Immaron could cause trouble even from this distance did not please her but all she wanted to do was find him and leave. The glamour of the Reanval competition had worn off and had been replaced with a hard chilling edge. The great Keep's slow hum could just be heard above the silent sunset, sealing the sadness inside her heart at Mitch's absence. For everything Saranon had come from and everything she was going to be. She took a deep breath and entered the outer perimeter of Faldarin.

The outer area was teaming with wildlife that resided where people were not welcome. The smell of kultier rose ever sicklier from the depths. It was not a grand way to enter as she began wading through the sludge. Yet a direct confrontation without knowing the Keep was a risk she was not yet ready for. The large old tunnels with their worn inscriptions reminded her of Odana with the colour long faded. It was a beautiful site in an array of mess and stench as Saranon trundled through.

The haze and stench was all too familiar as she strived to find a connection to the Keep. It was old and well-fortified as she clung to the edge of the path rimming around a hollow pit. The light from above glimmered on the writhing bodies of the kultier below bouncing off the shiny scales from their shells. The hum grew louder a she approached the pit and held onto the slippery side walls layered with grime. As the central core roared from the depths below, the sound faltered just for moment then returned to a smooth rumble. Saranon looked down as she smiled to herself, if there was one thing it had in common with other large old Keeps it was the need for maintenance.

CHAPTER FIVE

Meeting the Evergeldy

The ravenous creatures ruled over the lower areas writhing along the walls. They crawled at any angle seeming weightless as they ran by. Saranon moved across as she felt something she had feared, it was Mitch and the sensation made her all the more frantic. She stopped a moment to calm her thoughts, she moved on trudging through the crowded tunnels. She noticed voices bellowing down from above in murmured tones. The sound ripped past her ears as the roar of anger and sorcery only just missed knocking her to the side it was all she could do to hang on. There in the silence lay her answer as she came to grips with the need to force her way in.

The Keep hummed with the absorption of the energy as it dissipated into the cavernous holes below. She reached to her energy within letting it saturate the surface as it glimmered in the dark. The magnification blocked the next blow and she could hear the voices in the distance move further back. The excitement ran a trail of sweat from her shoulder slipping down her back as she shivered. A window of hope opened as she managed to gain ground moving past the threshold of the Keep. Saranon stood just above the crossover. A bolt thundered from deep within only just giving her enough notice to duck as she clung to the ledge trying not to lose her grip.

She steadied herself just out of sight. Every breath raging in her lungs from the crackling energy left hanging in the air. In the darkness she soared and gave aim up ahead, her energy rippled through the halls. The response came loud and calculated in return, knocking Saranon back in full fury. The force catapulted her hurtling at great speed. She flew straight down into the murky undercurrent. In stark shock at receiving the force full blow the liquid sheal began to solidify. The substance bounded her with great strength back into the world of the living. The waves of the energy hitting the wall of moving sheal echoed with the sounds of chaos through the far reaching Keep.

Her energy magnified in the recourse and spun like a fine web around lifting her up. The Angeon inside her had changed growing into what she would become. The spark blew out into a dazzling light, outshining the Keep in the dim haze bringing with it the immense power of the Angeon. The roar shattered through the open air of the Keep. Bellowing as the old cylinder, one of twelve that had been holding on for so long broke in the impact.

She rose to the surface as the ash suffocated the clean air whisping through the tunnels. As the Angeon, she touched the surface of the main courtyard outside. The occupants of the building had already begun rushing out and as she looked upon them Mitch came running in her direction. He grabbed her arm and spoke, 'Move, just move.'

Saranon looked once more over her shoulder to see the Evergeldy glaring at her in a silent truce. She returned to normal as she ran by his side. She was beginning to doubt if he knew where he was going but she was not about to argue. He found a tavern on the edge of the city to spend the night, even after her hesitation. She was not about to argue as Mitch lay down on the soft bed and rested. His exhausted body soon drifted off to sleep. Leaving her peering out the window pondering what had happened.

Saranon stayed up with the energy still slowing down inside her body, she was not ready to rest. She could see one of the sorcerers below in the street looking up at her, out of habit she waved and he waved back. For a moment she froze still she had not expected that and Mitch was asleep leaving her in a quandary. She was mixed between guilt and excitement. She smiled at him at least someone would be getting some well-deserved rest. As the moon hid behind the moving clouds in the night sky, she lied down and fell asleep with the hum of the Keep still whirring in her mind. It was Mitch who woke first to the cool morning light. He snuck downstairs for a hearty meal, returning with a second breakfast as he nudged her awake.

Saranon placed her pillow over her head in protest at

the disturbance. Her muscles remained half asleep so Mitch put the warm scrambled eggs near her nose. 'I thought you were supposed to be sleeping in.'

'You have a new boyfriend,' he commented

'A what?' She asked.

She jumped up and slammed the pillow into Mitch for giving her such a start. She peered out the window and the sorcerer was still there, he looked up at her and waved then left. 'I do not have a boyfriend,' she glared at him and then felt pity for him, he was pale and weary.

She did not want to ask him about Faldarin as her heart sank knowing he had been hurt. She leaned forward and gave him a hug. Saranon closed the door as Mitch went back to sleep. He had assured her that he was fine and she was not going to argue, he was already cranky. The end of the Reanval had marked an end to the hot weather. The air still had warmth in it under the midday sun and the cool breeze was welcome relief to a muggy climate. The streets were filled with people and she could sense no sign of any sorcerers paying attention to her. This did not mean much, but today Saranon was not in mood for company as she strolled along.

The place reminded her of Gosbin with the Palascene and she wondered what Tasha would have made of it. Her arms itched and she stopped for a moment, the force from rebounding off the sheal in the Keep had left small grazes along her skin. Raynard stood beside her at a distance. The sorcerer commented on her arms and she looked up startled and annoyed at the same time. The Evergeldy knew who she was and she felt awkward not knowing what happened to Mitch. The sorcerer was not much older than she and held himself with a steady grace, almost in awe of her. They were caught in a moment each not knowing what to say. Then a gruff voice called for Raynard and Saranon said, 'It was nice meeting you.'

It sounded daft after she watched the sorcerer run off and felt her cheeks grow hot. If Mitch had not stirred her she would have been less embarrassed. This was not what she had expected as the rest of the day became ordinary in comparison. She hoped he was having a better day. As she went upstairs with her days pickings, Mitch was more alert, 'So how was Raynard?'

Saranon grumbled in annoyance, 'You didn't tell me you two had met and he is not my boyfriend.'

She placed the emphasis on 'not' as he passed her a letter, the invite was short and curt. 'So we will be going to Faldarin?' she asked.

'No, you will be,' he replied.

She frowned at him not saying anything, Mitch's look told her he did not have the patience to visit Faldarin again. She wanted to do the same and sighed knowing that could not be. The weather mirror imaged her frustration. The sky poured down with tepid rain tapping on the window sill. 'I'm sorry I cannot help you,' Mitch spoke.

The large gates of Faldarin loomed overhead as Saranon approached the Keep through the front entrance. This was a novelty after the last occasion. Before she had time to speak the gates were opened for her. The warm fresh breeze carried the moisture from the night glistening in the sun. The first glimpse was disturbed only by the lull in the hum of the Keep from the broken cylinder deep below. It mattered little to Faldarin who still had eleven remaining, to pick up the load but a nuisance nonetheless. The courtyard was calm as she strode up the steps to where Ardagh rose to greet her. Raynard's uncle welcomed her into the grand hall. The natural light shone through illuminating the peaceful surroundings with a white warm glow.

It was a tempered greeting as Saranon made her presence known and the air filled with a hint of reluctance. Afterward Raynard and his young sister Melissa came to show her around. She was left feeling as though the main question on the lips of her new acquaintances had not been asked. Melissa looked up to her with unwavering awe and kindness. It was flattering and made her feel awkward at the same time. In a quiet moment the young girl asked, 'Are you going to help fix the Keep?'

She smiled as the innocent question hit home and she knew it had meant to be asked all along, 'I will try.'

The recognition of her response spread across Raynard's face. He was about to say something, then refrained not wanting to disturb the moment. Melissa captured Saranon's attention guiding her from place to place. Melissa was busting with excitement as she introduced her new friend. Ahead of her lay a daunting task as the Keep gave up one of its secrets. The vast size of the broken cylinder laid beneath her as she peered down over the gloomy edge. Years of grime had smothered it with a slippery surface and the sight did not appeal to her. Underneath ran a myriad of cracks circling downward as the muck shifted revealing the rough broken lines.

It was hideous to think the Keep had been left teetering on the brink, perhaps it had been a blessing to occur now. The Evergeldy stayed out of her way except for Raynard whose interest kept him close, by his fidgeting it was clear he wanted to help. Between them they managed to set out a path and equipment for the gigantic task. Saranon groaned in anguish as it became clear she would lose several days off her journey. Melissa greeted them as she tried to sneak out the door and she felt she owed the girl an explanation. 'My wizard will be wondering where I am.'

'You'll be back tomorrow?' Melissa asked.

She thought that was a given, 'Yes.'

Melissa's eyes lit up with delight as she ran off with excitement.

Saranon's weary limbs carried her back to the tavern where she found Mitch who had already ordered tea. He looked up with a wry smile and shook his head at the sight of her slumping in the chair. 'You can always come with me tomorrow,' she suggested.

'No,' he said.

Mitch was in no mood to go there and she did not blame him, she was relieved to see him enjoying himself again. He was acting rather carefree and she suspected he knew something as she studied his face.

'You still can't read my mind,' he said in a matter of

fact tone as he ate a large warm meal.

Saranon was growing tired and had no patience for guessing games while she scoffed down her food in chunks. He motioned for her to slow down as she let out a noisy burp it was an old habit that stayed with her. The night was far more peaceful as she fell into a deep sleep and the turmoil of Faldarin faded. As the clouds of the dream world entered her mind she could see Tasha's hand reaching for her up out of the hazy mist. She leant down and grabbed hold, not wanting to let go as the spirit of her old friend reached toward her.

As she heaved Tasha out of the maze below it came together. She unravelled the whirring mass until she was peering down at the broken cylinder in the Keep. Tasha stood beside her enshrined in a glow of light. Now you know, with that her spirit vanished and she was left peering down at the gloomy depths of the broken cylinder. The darkness wrapped around her until a slight movement brought her awake, it was just Mitch so she drifted back to sleep. As she rose early in the morning he helped her prepared for the day with a worried look, 'Are you all right?' He asked.

Saranon replied but he was not convinced as he gazed at her with stern eyes then let her be.

He was avoiding asking her too many questions. Not wanting to be roped into an undesirable and awkward visit to the Keep. It mattered not with the task ahead looming over her as she focused on the image in her dream and hoped that it would be enough. If it had not been for Mitch the

Keep would be a comforting place, but the sorrow filled its walls soaking into the ground and covering her mood. The look in Raynard's face echoed her thoughts as he greeted her with a calm tone and a hint of prior frustration. As they left the habitable areas of the Keep, Saranon could see why the situation had become strained.

She peered over the edge and it was as though no work had been done. The weight of Raynard's gaze made her hesitate. In the moment, part of her wanted to rush in and the other wanted to pull back, not knowing what had caused it. The setback would be compounded if it happened again. She was about to drudge through the mess when Raynard pointed up in silence to one of the Evergeldy. She thought that he could have timed the interruption better before her hand squelched in the muck. They watched the sorcerer dart off and shared a silent moment of disgust as the events became all too clear. If Saranon was going to have any luck, it would mean completing the task in one long stretch. A friendly gesture of kindness was starting to fray her nerves.

She reached within and focused on unravelling the images behind her dream with her old friend in the quiet. Raynard left her to preside over the ever reaching darkness below. Faldarin preferred the silence as it hummed in relief. It had suffered and calling out a faint simple message beckoned to her for help. Saranon calmed her mind and then catapulted herself off. She hurtled at great speed off the ledge and into the soft thin web still gracing the inside of the cylinder as the Keep clung on in desperation. She slowed her descent into the darkness as the sparks of energy from Faldarin fell into place and held her in mid-air. The light glimmered in tiny droplets embracing her body.

The formation sealed the links in the cylinder sending it into a slow spin. Building up the energy inside, until it became so unbearable that she had difficulty clinging on. The burning sensation shifted along her arms. With a shattering of the tiny webs the force blew out sparking a massive expulsion. She shot up into the open air way beyond the confines of the Keep. Stunned silence racked her frame as it took a while for the air to fill her lungs. The crackling sensation of the fine energy particles dissipated into the sky. The Keep reached out its strength and grasped. It yanked her down ebbing off the flow in a fluid motion, leaving in its wake the figure of the great Angeon.

Raynard and Melissa stood out in the open courtyard on the steps. Their lone silent stand spoke volumes for the protection of their Keep. Saranon returned the energy inside her as she left the Angeon and Faldarin behind. The Keep whirred in gratitude with the mild hum piercing through the surface. She rose with the morning light with their belongings packed by the cheerful wizard the night before. It lifted her spirits to see Mitch in a pleasant mood. He was not the only one glad to leave Estrard. The calm cool weather spread across her face, as they glided through the quiet streets in haste to avoid too many onlookers.

Even as the two reached the northern edge, the peace brought forth by the morning remained uninterrupted. A familiar rustle ebbed from the thick vegetation on the outskirts of the city, followed by a deep grumbling sound. Katholomu reared his majestic head high above the trees. The beautiful sleek black dragon eyed Saranon without a hint of remorse for leaving them so long. He shook off the leaves and half a bush that became entangled around his hind leg. Then the dragon lowered his head, underneath her hand, letting out a low short purr before ending with a blast of air through his nostrils. Before she had a chance to ask, Mitch had already hauled himself up on the great giant. The dragon held out his arm for her to climb on, as she wondered where he had been.

The powerful hind legs leaped as they lunged into the air holding on with Katholomu fast gaining speed. The last of Balquene withered away beneath them, as they flew across the border gripping on tight as Saranon laughed in delight. The great beast did not understand the meaning of slow as he kept at full pace. He powered straight for Indarin leaving her to ponder if the dragon could have offered this before now. As the Keep drew near she remembered one problem, landing. The dragon was so big that the standard landing strip was far too small and heaving all that strength to a stop, was by no means elegant. She motioned for Mitch to stay down close to the dragon's thick soft skin underneath his scales and fur.

The dragon, Katholomu, hit the ground ripping up the dirt in a mighty spray and summersaulted with both riders clinging on. Kat landed on all fours with a pounding in the outer courtyard. The sharp talon in his wing scraped the side of the building with a horrible jarring. Running the length of Saranon's spine as she squeezed her eyes closed in a grimace. The open courtyard soon filled with onlookers as she felt her cheeks grow red. Mitch slid off with ease and greeted a wizard as though they were old friends leaving her feeling foolish on her own. The spin made her descent awkward as her shoe wedged between the scales and she gripped the dragon in a half fall on her way down.

The marmoz dragon eye-balled two wizards hoping to move him on until Mitch stepped in and explained. Ryan stood next to her motioning her inside and away from Mitch. She tried her best to compose herself. Her ears were still ringing from the tumble after Katholomu's spectacular landing. The crowd was slow to disperse leaving her in an annoyed state, grumbling as she went down the hall. It had not been the entrance she had hoped for and she shied away from the attention carrying forward with the occasional laugh. The greeting further inside the Keep was more sombre as Saranon breathed a short sigh of relief.

The Armythral were all too familiar with faraway guests. She felt as though she had missed out on the previous discussion. She had banked all her hopes on travelling to Serenphel. At least now the journey through Balquene had given her more than anything she had hoped. It made no difference as she met the Armythral. As a few remained unconvinced and her inability to show the finer points of what they were expecting only made the decision firm. She was granted access to Indarin just as any other and no more was spoken of the Angeon raging in the quiet inside. Saranon did well to restrain herself and hide her frustration as she thanked the Armythral for allowing her to stay.

She strode in a far corner of the Keep in sullen silence. Her temper flared beneath her skin and itched along her arms only recently healed from the Faldarin Keep. The Keep was bustling with sorcerers, including the non-habitable areas, as she travelled down. It was a calming blessing to know she was not alone and smiled in friendship as she strode past two sorcerers busy with repairs. She felt the humming of the central core below and moved further away. She slipped in the distance downward to the vast core hiding in the darkness. Indarin was bemused by the tiny visitor as Saranon glanced around the core. It was showing far more signs of wear than Odana for such a young Keep, in comparison.

The exclusion of sounds other than the whirring of the monumental core filled her with a calm sensation. She had been searching for this, as her body and mind relaxed into the Angeon. It did not last long as the Keep was interested in communicating with her. This time she was only too glad to talk to someone that listened. If anything, she knew she had made a friend out into the ever reaching darkness, as Indarin chatted away in a place where few had been. She felt at ease, away from prying eyes, even if the return journey meant re-joining the world above.

The quiet night up above saw many a person packed away in the habitable area. Except for a jovial soul by the name of Larry who had stayed behind to tidy up. 'You were gone a long time. Checking out the place?' He asked.

'Yes,' Saranon was not sure how to answer as she side

stepped the question.

The sorcerer smiled as he wiped the grime off his hands and followed her to the surface, 'So where are you headed?'

'I'm not sure yet,' she responded.

'I see, come with me.'

Larry showed her to the small reception that looked more like a casual meet and greet as he waved goodbye. She was unsure what she was meant to be asking but Sandra did not give her time to speak. 'So you'll be wanting keys to your room then,' she whisked around the desk and walked at a brisk pace.

She rushed after her up the stairs as the lights lit up the hallway with a warm glow. Sandra gave her a quick tour with all the grace of having done the same many times before. She left Saranon on her own to meet her flatmates. She felt like the odd one out, as it became clear from Todd's reading material, that all the others were studying the same course.

She went straight into her room taking a deep breath. Gathering her thoughts it had been a long time since she had lived with other sorcerers and part of her wanted to run and find Mitch. Her mind filled with images of Pennie and Tasha in the camps, as they came rushing to the surface. She wondered if it would be rude just to go back down to the central core and disappear for a while longer. After a while she opened her eyes where she sat. She peered out the door opening to the balcony which wrapped around a great many rooms. All leading out to a sunny courtyard with raised garden beds below. Todd popped his head out the window beside her, 'Are you going to come inside?'

Saranon knew he was just trying to be pleasant but at the same time it was overwhelming.

CHAPTER SIX

Dragon reunion

Saranon rushed out of the study to meet the snoring dragon cuddled up on the hillside with his head snuggled down in his powerful wing. After being so long without him, the attraction of the stubborn marmoz had not worn off. Katholomu lifted his tail, knocking over a large metal tin that flew high into the air. The tin rolled, clanging along the ground, as it tumbled. He rubbed his head up against her in acknowledgement. He raised his body from the ground, steadying himself with one foot on the side of the hill. If there was one thing the dragon could do, it was making everything else look miniature in comparison. She swayed while rubbing his head, as the dragon tried not to move in excitement.

It was a clumsy compromise and the humour was not lost on Mitch who looked on with a wry grin. She motioned with her arm for Mitch to come closer, but he was not tempted. He kept a respectful distance from the friendly giant. With a slight heave Katholomu almost toppled her over and she knew it meant he wanted to ride. This time Saranon lifted herself up not wanting to make the same mistake, with a great thump and whoosh they were off into the deep blue sky. The dragon soared through the ice cold clouds as they went. It was just what she needed after a frustrating day where she had almost torn her hair out. After being on her own for so long, the idea of dreary old text books and listening to a monotone voice did not engage her enthusiasm.

The only delight was that the work had not been difficult and with any luck she could move on after the unit was finished. The dragon provided a perfect excuse to let off some of her energy. As if reading her thoughts Katholomu dipped down near the edge of the Keep landing, near an outpost. As Saranon's feet touched solid ground she turned to the great beast, 'Now if only you'd done that the first time.'

He scattered off in offense, not wanting to stay for a scalding. The dragon was too big to chastise, as she watched him try to hide his bulk, then give up with an air of disgust.

The outpost, an end node with a direct link back to the central core, lay silent on natural ground blending into the scenery. Saranon stood within the short walls rising up at the corners creating a mental enclosure around the hard floor. It took greater concentration to engage the Keep at such a distance, but well worthwhile. As she gripped the rising energy with her own and immersed herself in its warmth. The walk back was a quiet one, until the thud of Katholomu's great feet shook the ground as he caught up and passed her making it a race. The dragon bent down for her to ruffle her arms around his chin. Scratching a cumbersome itch, then he leaped up deciding that was enough.

She shook her head in disbelief at the occasional agility the dragon displayed. After the brief introductions at her apartment, Saranon felt more comfortable. Yet she was still at odds with having to catch up on the basics that seemed to dull her mind. The Keep was not concerned, as it continued moving. Her knowledge grew through the central core and people business was not something Indarin was in tune with. She had already begun collecting a few handy resources suggested by the Keep. This had gained some puzzled looks when she asked for them, but nothing more. She noted in a small book the occurrences of the day building up a collection to take with her back home.

The next day brought with it a loud knock, as Hailey woke her up from a turbulent sleep emanating from her dreams. Hailey was kind and came from a family near the coast where her older brother and father trained dragons. Seth was much older than his sister and eager to meet the sly Katholomu who had formed his own reputation in the brief time they had stayed. The sleek black dragon was in the middle of rubbing himself in the dirt showing his soft silky belly for all to see. Seth kept his distance at first, then approached the great dark beast as Kat let out a loud snort, holding out his head in greeting.

To Saranon's annoyance the dragon urged Seth to climb on and leaped up in the sky leaving her speechless. Hailey burst into giggles beside her, she tried to talk and Hailey laughed louder. She went back and found Rasputen climbing on and rushing into the sky chasing Katholomu in a speedy haste. The large rozzen dragon was eager to keep up, exerting a great amount of strength with pride. Ahead she could see Kat was starting to play up and she urged Rasputen into a high dive speeding up as he flew. As they crossed paths Saranon let go and almost felt her heart go through her chest as it pounded. Before grabbing hold of Katholomu's shoulder and taking him down in a controlled glide.

The impact of the landing threw her straight into Seth's back as they both clung on. In the silence that followed they clambered down, Seth steadied himself then smiled, 'Can we do that again?'

Her mouth dropped wide open in disbelief, as he burst out laughing and patted her on the back. 'It's all right, I was joking,' he smiled.

A disgruntled Kat stared them off as they both flew back on the more dependable Rasputen. Who took advantage of the situation, by showing off. As she looked back she knew the grumpy dragon was going to be her problem later.

As they ventured down toward Indarin, Kat was already curled up pretending to sleep as though nothing had happened. Rasputen let out a snort and a low roar in protest, as he eyed the other dragon. Hailey rushed over as Seth told the tale and repeated it over lunch in the courtyard for any one passing to hear. Saranon was not sure whether to hide but her new friends urged her to stay. The thought of hiding underneath the table sounded enticing. 'Well,' exclaimed Hailey. 'At least you won't have to worry about what anybody thinks of your dragon skills after that.'

She sighed to herself and hoped it was true, but the grand entrance was going to be hard to forget. She was almost certain the dragon had done it on purpose. A steady breeze kicked up in the latter half of the day as she strode out of site to an end node and connected with the Keep. The first time had been awkward, but with every effort she was becoming familiar and Indarin was a gracious teacher. Saranon listened with care to every signal that hummed from the depths. It was a lonely challenge she had set herself and the Keep was willing to help.

The exertion aligned the Keep and distilled the sheal into its final form. Allowing the Keep to run and concentrate on other matters, like the state of the central core. Power diverted there could smooth over the superficial damage. For that the Keep was more than willing to oblige her. After all it was Saranon who was using her energy rather than Indarin's. As she slept that night a soft thud pattered across her window bringing her out of her sleep. She rose knocking a glass on the floor, Katholomu's eye levelled with her through the railing of the balcony and she climbed on. The dragon swished with timely grace making little sound in the heavy night air clouding the Keep.

The brilliant moon rose above hiding nothing under its warm grey light. Bursting down upon the dragons as Katholomu flew to greet them. It was then that she felt that she had been coaxed into something by the great dragon. She thanked herself for remembering to take her bond-breakers. There was no time like the middle of the night to get acquainted to the dragon elite. Holding nothing back, the dragons flew on with great speed through the spell of the dark. Flying fast into Espony and danger harrowing into the target with such force, Saranon had little time to brace herself.

She immersed herself in a solid wall of protection. Enveloping the group as Katholomu took the signal as his queue to plough hard into the building. The impact sprayed an explosion of bricks and concrete. That shattered into dust clouds in a harsh gust, wiping out the surrounds with a blistering force. The ground thundered with a concentrated energy, exploding on impact. All the dragons escaped from the rubble, fleeing away from sight. Leaving Saranon wondering what she had just been involved in. The dragon provided little comfort as he set her down in the courtyard. She thought of waking Mitch, but then that would need an explanation, one that she did not want to answer.

She could still smell the dust as she woke in the morning to a loud noise, for a moment thinking it was the dragon, as she readied herself. She made a small entrance, trying to discern what had happened catching fragments, as she walked to class. By the end of the evening it had become clear that there was no way anyone thought a person had been riding with the dragons. She breathed a quiet sigh of relief. If only Mitch would be that forgiving, she made her way to the northern wing and knocked on the door as he opened it. He was about to say something, then changed his mind after a moment, letting her through the organised mess. Mitch tried not to laugh as her tension slipped away into annoyance at the look of the bemused wizard.

Saranon was going to have to figure out how to deal with Katholomu on her own. She found the dragon curled up purring away with not a hint of acknowledgement of the incident at Espony. She sat near his arm staring at his sleeping face as the giant opened one eyelid. As much as she was agreeable to rescuing dragons from harm's way, she preferred to know. Rather than get taken along for the ride and dumped in the middle. She leant over almost falling as she hugged the warm tender dragon, he winked and her heart melted. The final exams of her first units came around quicker than she anticipated as Saranon fumbled dropping her sova bag as she went.

It was a relief to think that after this, she could start moving into the general subjects. Hailey had already suggested one that she and Todd were doing. Either way she would have to get through the next few days and she beamed with excitement. She joined the throng of many anxious sorcerers rushing in the hallway. The light filled the walls as she waited, her stomach feeling queasy, then her worrying faded as she flew through the tests. A small part of her wondered if Ryan had been right, but then the doubt fled her mind, in her heart she knew she was the Angeon. She breathed a sigh of relief with a few days off, Seth and Hailey had invited her to stay with them near Lethrill Bay.

The place was not far even though she would be taking Katholomu with her, she thought the company would keep the dragon out of trouble. Hailey rode with her brother Seth on Rasputen as she geared up to go on Kat, the head start did not bother her with the dragon's speed. The air was still warm in the autumn breeze as the dragon glided in, excited by the company, he stumbled before coming to a halt. The glimmering light sparkled across the water as Katholomu trampled in. The commotion brought Seth's team out from behind the cliffs. As the guards landed their dragons up on the grassy fields making their way down to greet them.

Kat shook himself off, blasting a fine spray over everyone before bounding over to nudge each of the five dragons. He skittered around Rasputen before flopping on his side. Saranon ran ahead with Hailey to her family's Keep, it was small in comparison to Indarin as the two settled in. The night sky stretched across the day. She joined Hailey and Seth for a late flight with the dragons, out across the cliff face. They flew over the regular rush of the waves breaking along the sandy shore. She loved the feel of the sharp night air brushing against her cheeks and neck as the last glows of the sun lit up the land below.

She could understand why Seth had chosen a life with

the dragons, as the feeling of freedom washed through her soul and tingled in her feet. Katholomu was more than eager to show off, swooping around and back, almost losing height as he heaved himself upwards. She laughed with excitement as his strong wings flexed in the wind. The beautiful promise of a new start from Indarin filled Saranon's heart with hope as she enjoyed the time away. The lights beamed in a line leading them home as her heart pounded loud in her chest from exuberance.

It was a swift come down with an exhausted thudding on the ground from Katholomu who walked off, leaving her for a nice warm grassy bed. She went inside to the warm cosy fire, shedding cool air from her skin. Hailey was too excited to eat as she stopped half way through to show her their proud ancestral home. The halls were garnished with elegant paintings and artefacts like a miniature museum. The history of Hailey's family made Saranon think of her own, a hazy labyrinth lay between then and now, clouding her mind. An absent tear trickled down her face before she wiped it away.

The night was filled with laughter, she and Hailey tried to stop but the more they giggled. Making small plumes of light then blowing them up into the air like tiny fireworks. For some reason green was a difficult colour to produce for her. It kept going purple or blue as she whined in disappointment. The small show lit up the open courtyard as Seth made an attempt to give advice from below. The sorcerer stayed near the light of the open doors, where he and Darren were cleaning their gear. Hailey only giggled even more when the next attempt failed and Saranon was just thankful it was not a serious matter.

In the distant dark Katholomu's head appeared around the corner with a low calm growl letting them know he wanted his rest. The girls ran inside squealing and giggling at the same time. She had not had so much fun in ages and fell into a contented sleep. The brightness of the day filled the room with warmth she had not felt in ages as she rushed outside, with Hailey showing her the way. An empty spot of crushed grass remained denoting Katholomu's presence nearby. The girls went to the shore to watch the dragons gleaming in the morning sun, as they fished. Kat had his head down on the rocks, scoffing a large fish while holding one end in his claws.

Seth was waiting near the cliff face and Saranon tip-toed toward him. Rasputen dipped his head to let the two small riders on as they flew north to the heart of the dragons' domain. It was difficult for her to grasp the concept that something so small and fluffy grew into a large scaly, grump of a dragon. The soft little creatures darted around their mother in the distance. Rasputen greeted the closest male baring his chest with friendly pride. The large male was not impressed about having young dragons bounding too close. He snorted, warning them to stay clear. The little ones were inquisitive with sharp teeth to match as she stayed out of the way.

Saranon was grateful for their kindness, as they showed no care at having people so close. A rustle up ahead sent a small alarm through the dragons and Seth motioned for them to leave. The sorcerer waited for Rasputen to take them up into the air before leaving a distance behind. The dragon flew fast with the skill of experience leading the girls straight home. As Hailey climbed down and looked back she could see no sign of her brother. She started to panic and Saranon jumped back on Rasputen flicking back into the air. At first all she could see were dragons below and wondered as the large dragon eyeballed the scene from a distance. Rushing in close to the wounded dragon Seth had been on. Taking her down hard for the ride, swooping in an outstretched form there was still no sign of Seth.

She could not return without him and jumped down not far from the wounded dragon. As Rasputen leaped up, the pelt of energy fired and as her stomach churned, she let out a massive shield blocking the move and providing Rasputen with safe passage as he flew behind her. The tips of the scrub caught alight with the roar of another blast and Saranon pounded it down in frustration. She was about to run after the culprit and almost missed seeing the guards swoop in with ferocity, lifting the air up in a great gust overhead. Rasputen roared with delight, as his fellow dragons flew past, rustling his mane up with all the fierceness he could muster.

Seth ran toward them and jumped on the dragon wasting no time grabbing the agitated sorceress in his arms, as they flew off. She was not impressed about being hauled off in midstream, trying to break free of his grip without falling off Rasputen. Both she and the dragon snorted in disgust at the same time, causing Seth to laugh and shake his head. As they landed back at Armeria, the sorcerer let her down then flew away leaving Saranon to grumble and shout after him. 'He won't listen,' Hailey spoke as she rushed to meet her.

She knew that Hailey was right as she shrugged her shoulders in annoyance at being dragged out of the scuffle.

It was a long and harrowing wait, wearing at her patience, as she stepped with a heavy stride across the open courtyard. She caught site of the great dragons coming in to land. Relief lifted the weight off her shoulders and Hailey rushed out with open arms to greet Seth. The weary travellers returned hiding their hard faces. Saranon looked Darren in the eye and saw a glint of something she knew all too well, she was about to speak but thought better of it. In the brief instant the guard picked up on her staunch stand and waited for Hailey to leave. The sorcerers sat around resting their aching muscles in the lounge near the courtyard, with the open fire warming the room.

Darren gazed in thought at her before asking the question burning through his mind. 'I get the feeling you have already seen death.'

Seth shot her an astonished look as she answered dispelling the illusion of innocence. A silence hung over the room as she hoped she would not have to explain, the momentary pause brought no relief racking at her nerves. With no way out trapped by her friendship with Hailey. She made a short response, admitting to her part in the fall of the Arthrose. After the words left her mouth, Saranon could not bear to stay a moment longer, the awkward stares were not what she had come to Armeria for.

She had come to Serenphel to move forward and her mind ran free with a mountain of turmoil. She strode with haste out in the calm night air to Katholomu who gazed at her stern brow. The great dragon had no intention of sticking his head into her problems but then he had included her in his. The dragon lay down his head beckoning her on board and they flew in the grey light of darkness showering over the land. The fierce mood of frustration covering Saranon seemed to leak its way into his thoughts. Katholomu led her far north into the tip of the dragon colony reaching into Espony. In the darkness she watched as the grip of the fallout from the fight lay wanton on the land.

In empathy she shed a tear in disgrace at the scene underneath the starlight and wondered if this would be her future. Without hesitation she glided off the dragon, Kat, with ease. She strode with all the magnificence hidden beneath the surface as the Angeon rose within. Moving out her energy struck itself deep into the damaged ground. Binding it together and reshaping the malformed land. The energy soared creating a rocky alcove emblemizing the northern boundary of the dragon colony. Noises drifted on the winds suggesting she would soon have company. She took flight on Katholomu leaving her masterful work for the eyes of the morning light. In the soon approaching dawn that crept ever closer as she flew on.

Saranon's frame of mind was calling out to return to Indarin. Yet a moving glint in the first rays of dawn caught her eye, as Hailey waved her downward. Katholomu rested a short distance walking to a stop beside her. Hailey rushed up and grabbed her arm. 'You didn't have to leave, Seth can be like that but I need to ask, did you see anything happen near Espony?'

Saranon leaned close, 'That's where I was.'

Hailey's mind ticked away as it came to bare on the same thought, 'It's going to be an interesting time at Indarin.'

Seth and his fellow guards were out busy for the day. This suited her, as she was finally able to rest her weary head in a stagnant dream, replaying the night's events. The sorcerer was waiting in the courtyard when she woke in the afternoon. His expression still glum and Hailey's mood was serious. 'Did you bring back the old ridge line?' He asked.

Saranon sighed in acknowledgement that this was a good time to leave. 'Yes,' with that she turned to face Hailey, 'I will see you back at Indarin.'

'Wait,' Hailey called out.

Saranon turned back as she was walking, to let Hailey finish.

'What he meant was, thanks for helping,' Hailey explained.

Seth's facial expression showed no sign of change. Even though it was a kind thought, at least she had not ruined her new friendship. Katholomu waited for her arrival near the front entrance eager to be off into the sky. The dragon took her back at a cracking pace across the warm afternoon curling into a cool breeze. Kat swooped over the crescent of the great Keep, shining the sun's rays off his wings at full spread, as he passed the tip. As the light faded Saranon felt a blast roaring from the depths sprawling upwards at such a speed.

She pelted her energy downward with intense frustration at being interrupted. Her annoyance steamed through the air. The marmoz dragon did not miss a beat nor flexed his muscles in shock as he landed in smooth formation and pride. Todd rushed out to greet her flinging his arms in excitement. 'Were you showing off?' He shouted over the rumble of the Keep, as it slowed down to a low hum.

'Of course not,' Saranon said in annoyance and the sorcerer burst out laughing in response.

CHAPTER SEVEN

Welcome to Serenphel

Saranon's grumbling mirror imaged the Keep's mood as she followed Todd in through the hall. The place seemed quiet as the sorcerer explained they had been trying to repair the Keep. An argument had broken out on how best to fix it, just before her arrival. She did not think much of the excuse for a jettison of raw energy flying at full pelt out of Indarin with impeccable timing. Todd saw she was not impressed, as he realised how lame it sounded. 'I'll go down and have look,' she grumbled.

'No, I don't think you should,' Todd exclaimed.

'If I have to put up with almost getting fried, I'm going to have a look,' she continued.

'Really I don't think…'

Saranon stared at him in disbelief…she was not about to argue with a friend and glared at him daring the sorcerer to continue. The lights flickered as she walked past down the flight of stairs. She stepped into the dim shallow light parading at intervals along the walls. After having to deal with the mess at Armeria she was in no mood to be told otherwise from a friend. She leaped into a flurry of shouting and animosity. The Armythral did not look at all impressed with her arrival. If that was how they treated guests, she was not sure if she wanted to know them on a bad day. As she stomped through making her presence felt. With one swift motion she walked straight through the sealed door sensing the astonished voices behind her.

The first glimpse did not appear to be as much. As she began trudging further in a close sound sparked her attention. Larry walked through the closed door behind her, 'Trying to beat me to it?'

'If I was going to end up toast I've earned the right to check it out,' she commented.

'Get a move on then,' Larry walked past her carrying his tool kit.

The sorcerer was unfazed by having a companion and had little hesitation giving Saranon tasks. She reminded him that she had come to observe first and moved in to see remnants of the overloaded line.

She peered down the giant crater emanating through the cracks in the floor to the giant hole below and clambered in. Larry made no effort to stop her as he worked away the tunnel was dark and deep, caked with the remains of charred ash sticking to her boots. The hole was enormous and she could hear the growl of the central core rising up through the Keep. Larry popped his head over the edge and shouted, 'We're about to get visitors, a few of the labs have gone off line.'

'I thought that was a good thing,' Saranon said.

Thinking that the Keep diverted power to support the damaged area would help make the repairs quicker.

Larry stopped a moment, 'You're definitely new around here.'

She liked the sorcerer, he had an odd simple charm about him but she did not want to find out what he meant as she examined the left over rubble. If time was short then it left her in a bind and the Keep cranky under her feet. She rose with that thought in mind raising the Angeon inside and spreading her energy out to sense the Keep. The energy burned, wanting to be let out in full force but Saranon hung on. Weaving it and wrapping it around the Keep and bringing the great line up through the floor as the Keep extended it upward with her help. The two worked as one to place the line back into its rightful position.

The section locked into the duct without a trace or seam showing on the surface. The keep glistened in excitement pulsating underneath. The energy ran warm straight from the central core up the line, just as a great noise overhead boomed. Larry held out his hand to haul her up and they ducked back through the sealed door without a trace. They stood in silence as the thudding and shouting grew louder, reverberating through the wall. Saranon stood for a moment waiting, but the shouting did not interest her and the Keep had settled. She turned to leave and Elliot stormed through unlocking the seal and opening the door.

'It's about time someone fixed that,' Larry spoke up.

'What?' Elliot asked.

'The door, I couldn't for the life of me work it out.'

Elliot gave him a strange stare, then walked on, after the sorcerer had left Larry spoke, 'It happens all the time.'

The whole event did not make sense and as she was about to say something the others giggled at more shouting coming from through the wall. 'You have a strange way of doing things,' Saranon exclaimed and Larry laughed.

She stood there not sure what to say as Larry composed himself wiping his gruff hands on the sides of his trousers. 'So who taught you to repair the Keep?' He asked.

Saranon hesitated wondering if he was serious, 'No one.'

Todd laughed then stopped as both glared at him, 'I mean there's no way you could have done that.'

She sighed in exasperation at the thought of a long night ahead. The older sorcerer eased off as though sensing her mood and she was not prepared to hang around.

The shores of Lethrill Bay had worn her out. A conversation was the last thing on her mind, as the image of a nice warm soft bed after a big meal popped into her thoughts. The sea floated in her dreams and the sandy shore reaching up out of the water. The Keep seeped through her memories, intruding on her inner most thoughts, murmuring thank you. The words struck into her mind compelling her to wake. It was a deep low rhythm that reached her fingertips as she caressed the wall with her hand. As Saranon opened her eyes she could see the cool rays of light dipping past the edges of the curtains and grumbled at the end to her sleep.

It was difficult to think of anything as she heard Hailey's voice and rushed out to meet her. She stopped in her tracks as she caught sight of Seth standing in the door. For all its grandeur and size, Indarin was becoming far too small for her liking. The sorcerer paused and then apologised as her legs almost collapsed underneath her in disbelief. She knew it would have taken a great deal of convincing for Seth to say those words and accepted his apology in a haze of embarrassment. It had not been the start to the day that Saranon had expected. She was left floundering through a haze of thoughts as she bounded straight into Gwen on her way to class.

The shock reverberated through her as she gave her a dark stare before moving on. A flash of images entered her head and she dropped to the floor, relief flooded through her as she checked to make sure no one had seen. She dashed in and plonked herself down near Todd, the only familiar face in the room paying no attention to his friend. 'Aren't you going to say hello?' Theron asked.

The question woke Saranon from her bumbling, 'Hello.'

Theron was expecting a longer conversation and Todd exclaimed, 'She doesn't know.'

She let out a big huff realising she was the last to know something and Todd let her out of her misery, 'Theron is a Prophet.'

'Yes,' Saranon exclaimed anticipating more of an explanation.

Todd laughed and shook his head just before the class began, leaving her annoyed for the entire lesson. She snuck away early rushing toward the library. The encounter with Gwen had ruffled her and she knew there was something she had missed.

The image haunted her in the dry stale air as her fingers fumbled along the spines of the books. Until she found the Eskardy, the sorcerer clan from Espony further north. She heard a shuffle behind her and jumped, almost dropping the book, to see Theron standing behind her. She peered around the corner, wondering how she had missed seeing him. 'Do you want to know what you are looking for?' Theron asked.

'No, I will find this myself thank you.'

'Are you sure about that?' He asked.

'Yes, thank you,' she replied.

'Do you know what I am?' Theron asked.

She thought it was a silly question given that she was an Angeon, 'Would you like to know?'

Theron was not impressed by her response, he was not used to other people having knowledge like his. Saranon did not have time to talk riddles, so she said it straight. 'You are the strongest Prophet at Indarin, now if you don't mind I would like to search for the information myself.'

With that she sat down and began flicking through the pages. Theron sat beside her, 'Are you sure there is nothing you want to know?'

'I'm positive,' she replied.

She smiled to herself as he left, while turning the page. Her thoughts were interrupted by a sorcerer grumbling at the Prophet for running off. The novelty of meeting him was lost on her. Saranon was not sure why and paid it no more attention as she read further back into the past of the Eskardy. As she read of a hidden time, she found the link she was looking for, a connection with the Angeon. If there was one image that Gwen had brought back to life it was from home. She closed her eyes to a faded memory from her distant past wrapped behind a wall of pain. She had too much to be concerned with to be awed by a Prophet with an attitude, if anything she found Theron annoying.

The only reason why she had refrained from being rude is because she knew what it was like to feel alone. She found herself wandering down to see Katholomu. Who was rolling around rubbing his back against a large sandstone rock with satisfaction. Mitch snuck up around the corner catching his breath, 'I heard you met Theron.'

Saranon shrugged in disbelief at all the fuss, 'Yes,' she said in a strained voice.

'I didn't think you would be over awed,' he commented

'Hardly,' she spoke and Mitch laughed.

Saranon's mind was still clouded with Gwen. She flew up into the still afternoon air with the fine breeze beckoning across a clear blue sky. The dragon had a purpose in mind and took her deep into the heart of Espony. He staked his claim by flexing his large graceful wings casting a shadow increasing over the land with the setting sun. She looked deep down upon the land in a sweeping gaze. It was hard to think the last Angeon had been here many years before. The hour was growing late and she had to return, something inside told her not to stay. The last rays of light beamed golden behind her as Katholomu jolted into the air with a mighty leap. He flew far too close to several buildings showing his massive span, before reaching for the heavens.

Her skin prickled with a strange delight. If Indarin was not forthcoming with answers, perhaps Espony held the key she had been searching for. As she clung onto the dragon, the night closed in around them and the great lights of the Keep guided them in with a brightness she had not yet seen. Kat kept to the outer boundary, as she strode in to see Seth, who had just flown in earlier. The sorcerer stepped aside to let her pass. This was not the Indarin she remembered. The Keep hummed running warm under her fingertips. 'What do you think?' Seth asked.

'What's going on?'

Seth explained that the Keep was being geared up for the next round of training.

Saranon was not impressed. She soon realised this would mean a barrage of sorcerers wanting to use the outer areas, including the end nodes. She grumbled underneath her breath as she went upstairs slamming the door behind her. 'Are you all right?' Hailey asked as she looked up from her studying.

She acknowledged her, as she searched through the books she had gathered in her room. To see if there was something she had missed. She was in need of another venue within the Keep, apart from the central core. This time she would have to look within the gaps as she grumbled to herself. One of the least disruptive places would bring her close to the Prophets' quarters. A scowl creased her forehead whilst in thought.

She stood up and took a deep breath at the uncomfortable change. The restrictions of learning were tiresome, she was going to need somewhere else to unwind. Saranon began tapping her fingers on the small desk in annoyance before drifting off to sleep. It took a few times for the message to sink in with her new friend Theron, that foresight was not something she considered to be a gift. The sorcerer was amused by her abrupt reluctance to ask him for anything, including a spare pen, just in case he misinterpreted. They had been practicing concentrating their energy to hone it in on a marker.

Todd knew it was Theron's weakness which was why he enrolled in the unit. For Saranon it was tedious and both her friends were getting frustrated. 'Why don't you try?' Todd asked.

She did not see any harm in helping Theron, so she walked down to the floor of the purpose built court. She stepped in front of the young Prophet who smiled at her and she whispered, 'If you know, don't ruin it for everyone.'

He smiled and shook his head. She unfolded her energy then compressed it down into a fine tube. She hurled it at break neck speed at the absorption pit at the other end.

The court flashed with the sparks of light, flickering

with intense heat. The dense padding in the pit lit up with a warm orange glow soon fading down to red and darker. She turned to Theron and said, 'Now it's your turn.'

'No, I don't think so,' he spoke.

The sorcerer was about to take a step back, but she grabbed his arm and stood behind him. Theron's nerves were starting to show as he gulped, she guided him wrapping her energy around his, for support. The sorcerer closed his eyes in concentration and then let go at the same time Saranon boosted his efforts.

The energy shone like a thick electric bolt arching across the room, thundering with a grand roar that shook the walls as it went. 'There,' Saranon stated as though the outcome were a given.

Theron stood in awe as their teacher Anne rushed down in shock. 'You didn't see that one did you?' He said.

The Prophet gave her an annoyed look as Anne met them in a flurry of speechlessness, as the three friends stared in stunned silence. Saranon made a poor attempt at guessing charades. That was met with a stern look by the older sorceress as the other two snorted back laughter.

'You are not supposed to exert yourself,' Anne stared at her.

'I wasn't.'

'She's right,' Theron backed her up.

Saranon glared at the Prophet, 'I do not need your help.'

'Well I could have gone further.'

'No!' She shouted.

The pair argued as Anne watched on in astonishment. Before finding a calm moment to change the subject, 'Someone needs to clean up this mess.'

She was referring to the excess energy now stored in the pit and Saranon knew it would have to be filtered into the Keep. Without hesitation she held out a web of energy opening the pores allowing the energy to drip-feed through. In a rather stubborn tone she spoke aloud, 'I have other things to do,' and with that she turned and left in a huff.

The arguing had wasted precious time alone with the Keep. She was not willing to stay around for the stunned silence that followed. Being taught at a slow pace was one thing. Yet, having someone tell her she was about to exhaust her energy when she was far from it, only darkened her mood.

The inner gaps within the Keep provided her with ample space to manoeuver. She wove her thoughts into energy cradling it in a delicate form. It was not the most ideal shape but it met the criteria. The place was an unattractive dead zone as it did not receive the full energy spiralling up through the Keep from the central core. It did not matter to her, who saw it as a large space to show off and relax without distraction. The small sound of her talik cut through the air interrupting her peaceful thoughts. As Hailey broke the silence and brought her back to reality. Saranon shrugged her shoulders and left the tranquillity for the busy habitable area of the Keep.

Hailey beamed with excitement as she greeted her at

the door, 'There is an Angeon at the Keep.'

'Really, where?' She asked, bewildered at the thought of another like her.

'I meant you,' Hailey laughed.

Saranon stood completely perplexed, then shrugged it off. Todd explained the three sets of consecutive readings that came from her talik. While helping Theron had verified what she already knew. She thought to herself how long it would have taken to find out otherwise. She left to find Theron as a thought crossed her mind, for a sorcerer he was immature.

As she approached she could hear raised voices and waited. It was not long before she grew impatient and burst in flinging the remnants of the broken seal. She had missed knocking back Ryan with the force in the process. The sorcerer had assumed that Theron had asked Saranon to intervene. Not one to let a friend down she answered 'Yes' before the Prophet could speak. 'Now, I have business to deal with,' Saranon spoke.

She carved through the web of sorcery covering the room with such force it startled everyone including Theron.

'You can't do that,' gasped Ryan.

'I never did understand that word,' she spoke as Sandra urged Ryan out of the room leaving Theron and her alone.

'Do you know what you've done?' Theron asked.

'Something you should have done a long time ago,' she spoke with annoyance. The young Prophet nodded as if reminiscing and she continued, 'No offence but can you leave that for later.'

'I thought that was what you were after?' He asked.

'No,' Saranon replied. She did not think she needed to explain herself but Theron's look said otherwise, 'I prefer to make my own mistakes.'

He laughed as though a big weight had been lifted from his shoulders.

'What I came to say is you did well today,' she exclaimed.

At first the sorcerer was a little quizzical, but he soon felt Saranon's steadfast response and became more serious. He sat down in thought, 'So do you think you will find what you need here?'

She was not sure what Theron was searching, for but answered, 'I already have what I need.'

Deep down she knew what she said was true, if she left today she would find a way to manage, it would not be perfect but it would be enough.

Her response unnerved the Prophet. She wondered if he could see everything while her sceptical mind answered for her. She peered around the room as they spoke, it was much larger than her own, a book caught her attention as she opened it and Theron stopped.

'You won't find anything about the Angeon in there.'

Saranon turned the page she was looking at and moved it towards him placing it down on the table, 'I was not looking for me.'

Theron read closer, 'I misjudged you.'

She wondered if the young man before, her ever had a friend, the Prophet stared at her but said nothing. If she wanted to there were a hundred questions she could have asked. Something inside told her that no answer would bring her any closer to the energy within. The understanding was mutual, if just a little awkward, as she left Theron in peace albeit temporary. As Saranon peered back over her shoulder, she knew there was one big unspoken difference between the two. There were a lot of prophets in the world of sorcery. She was left feeling alone as she vacated the inner sanctum of the prophets.

The Keep hummed in tune mirroring her thoughts of satisfaction at knowing all along the Angeon had come to stay. She laughed as she went down the hall. It left a bittersweet taste in her mouth, with one large unanswered questioned hanging over her, like a dark shadow. What was gained by not recognising the Angeon within? Saranon did not think the Armythral were the kind to concern themselves with fear of retribution. The sorcerers had placed great emphasis on her lack of significance in the world. Even now the fuss was muted within the Keep Indarin, as she pondered the thought late into the night.

The great Katholomu had curled himself up into a comfortable ball. He stayed a respectable distance from the glowing embers of the fire shooting up across the courtyard. The dragon was too big to sleep inside. If he concentrated, he could, but the moment he stretched his large heavy muscles the space would become far too small. She made a comfortable seat on his hind leg as she sat down facing his half buried head. Katholomu looked up and rubbed his cheek down her side in a welcoming embrace. While she patted him deep in thought, Mitch made his way toward her and the dragon moved his head away. 'Do you like Theron?' He asked.

'He's just a friend,' before she had time to add more Mitch was off again.

She thought of wandering after him in annoyance, but stayed in the dragon's calming presence, fuming to herself. He had a habit of picking the most inappropriate moment to intrude on her thoughts. The dragon's face creased with a slow smile rising up from the corner of his mouth. 'Don't you start,' Saranon whispered in disgruntlement as she stroked his head.

The night stars shone bright above her in a clear sky as she strode past listening to laughter escape through the dragon pens.

He caught up with her reaching for her arm, "There's a rumour going around that you and Theron are…'

'What!' She roared across the crystal clear night air.

'I'm sure it's nothing,' with that he left.

Katholomu let out a muffled grunt that sounded like a short laugh, covering his eyes with his tail. She grumbled almost stumbling in agitation as her annoyance at living in a large community grew. If there was any comfort with luck her time here would be short lived and she could return home to her own muddled life.

Helping the young Prophet earlier had left her muscles aching and it came back to haunt her while trying sleep. At the time Saranon had not taken much notice. Whatever had laid its path around Theron, was stronger than she had anticipated, not that it made much difference. She could already tell knowing Theron was going to be a nuisance and she laughed to herself thinking the Prophet could say the same of her. As sleep swept in an old dream returned. Before the image of Tasha and Pennie entered her mind she heard a woman's voice ruffling on the wind. It called across the breeze from the depths of home in Darkonia, a faded memory lost in the depths of her mind.

CHAPTER EIGHT

A new beginning

The morning began with the usual rush out the door and last check to make sure Saranon had everything. As she sat in her normal place near Todd, she followed his gaze to their teacher. Anne was fumbling with nerves and with all eyes focussed on her, she dropped the dragon sphere from the desk. As it teetered on the edge in slow motion she blew across the table. Letting out small glimmers of energy sparkling in the air, holding the Orb as it floated to the ground. 'Show off,' Todd whispered, and they all laughed.

As Anne gathered her composure, the rest of the lesson went uninterrupted. Saranon thought she was alone as she scampered off after class. Yet the heavy footsteps speeding up behind her, said otherwise.

She slowed down to let Theron catch up as Mitch's words from last night stuck in her head. 'I thought I might walk with you,' Theron gestured.

'I'm going to the dead zone,' she replied.

The Prophet stopped a moment. 'You are welcome,' Saranon said not wanting to miss a beat.

The sorcerer walked with caution by her side, as though in deep thought. The place was just as she had left it, with a few sounds echoing through from the rooms nearby. An awkward shaped space left over with pipes running through it, packed close to the walls.

It dipped down with different levels providing a flat platform where Theron sat with his study book in hand. She beckoned him down further to no avail. As the Prophet watched on, she called up the power from deep within transforming into the Angeon. Theron's patience was remarkable as he stood up afterward, 'Do you know what I think?'

'I would prefer not to,' Saranon spoke, 'I like to leave the future where it belongs.'

'Fair enough,' he spoke before he left.

She watched, staring at him as if warning him not to say any more, Theron only smiled in return. After the sorcerer was gone, she practiced alone. A few strange noises carried through the small vents breaking her concentration. Indarin still hummed in a smooth tone so she pretended to ignore the racket. She pressed on concentrating deeper. The Keep greeted the surge of energy with satisfaction and delight as it whirred away from beneath. As if in seconds, the power of the central core roared up around her in a massive whirlpool of strength. Saranon shot up floating above the ground, as the great mass of liquid sheal swirled around with great force.

The spasm of energy leaped around in shear tentacles sparkling with light, as the gas particles rose up from the heat. The Angeon embraced the strength of the Keep wrapping it around and through, as it spiralled higher. Then she turned it back down into the depths with such force, that it sealed cold across the floor. Whoever had summoned the Keep's energy, it had not been meant for her. The hall was quiet as she raced away and in no mood to find out what had happened. The light shimmered across as the great form of the large dragon brushed across the window. Katholomu nudged at the door with agitation as Saranon held out her hand. She clambered on, as he took off, whisking her up into the air without a moment's notice.

A storm was brewing in the clouds above, closing in on the sun in a slow elegant dance across the sky. The wind whipped down her arms as she clung on, while the great beast gathered speed, heading north. She cringed in disgust at the dragon's choice of direction. As if sensing her mood, he grumbled, heading downward near the steps of the cliff face enveloping the city below. This time Katholomu remained silent among the backdrop. As he urged Saranon down the hill with gentle encouragement. A glimmer came across the street, catching her eye as she strode down, the sun shone off the edges of a great building holding her attention.

The great hall rose above her having lived through the

time of Zeralden Hadenvar the last Angeon. The building showed its age well. The warm outdoor lights began to flicker and glow as she approached. The light illuminated her shadow across the courtyard. A small yet familiar pattern caught her sight near the entrance, reminding her of Odana Temple. A small shy voice spoke behind her, 'It's beautiful isn't it?' Kera stood smiling.

Saranon turned in surprise to see she peering over her shoulder. It was good to make a friend in such a strange place, as the two chatted away underneath the fading sky.

As she waved goodbye and made her way back, the streets were filled with a hub of night life. The casual conversations floating by reached her ears. Carrying with it the words that made her stop, she lingered thinking she had misheard but it was spoken again. The night was young and she need not be anywhere as she mingled among the Eskardy who were used to visitors from Indarin. If anything, the night allowed her a freedom she had not enjoyed at the Keep. In the excitement, she dropped her small sova bag, before she could pick it up, Gresham knelt down and handed it to her. She blushed with embarrassment as he smiled and left through the crowd.

The night gathered momentum and Saranon slipped away in the darkness. Finding the sleeping dragon curled up where he had landed. The thought of another Angeon rocked her to the core. As she rushed back to Indarin she wondered if the great dragon had meant her to find out. The cold brushed along her arms giving her solace, as the idea settled in, making her feel uneasy. The night wrapped around her as Katholomu landed with a thud across the courtyard. He bounded along melding into the dark background as he let his small traveller down. Why had she not been told of the other Angeon? The thought made her skin crawl, as she turned to see Mitch heading towards her with an unimpressed frown.

The wizard had stayed away while they had been at Indarin Keep even though she had missed his company, 'Something's going on.'

'What isn't?' She exclaimed.

'Are you all right?' He asked.

'There's another Angeon.'

Mitch stood there in shock at the thought of a second Saranon then regained his composure. 'So you've had an interesting day too,' she remarked.

'Part of the indolin chambers was flooded,' he explained.

She pondered a moment on what he had said and thought of the sheal coming up through the dead zone earlier. It made sense, but she had not paid it much thought. 'Did you want to stay in the wizard quarters, it's getting a bit crowded where you are?' He asked.

'I'll think about it.'

Saranon went to find Todd and Hailey, who were busy chatting with some of the lecturers and more experienced sorcerers, who were moving into the vacant rooms next to them. Chilcott was helping Anne move in two doors down. The thought of having her lecturer down the hall was not lost on the other two either, as Saranon tried to hide her annoyance.

'I know,' whispered Hailey in agreement.

The noise meant an early night was out of the question but her mind was running in all directions at the moment. Her eyes focused on Chilcott, one of the more experienced sorcerers and revered for his ability to break up fights. The older sorcerer stared straight at her with piercing hard eyes and an emotionless stare. She had seen him before, down in the imbenik chambers, but did not consider stopping to chat.

'What happened?' Saranon asked.

Anne spoke for him, 'The side wall of one of the eastern labs blew out and the blast broke the pipes. The area is being drained, but the clean-up will take a while, so here we are. Where have you been?'

'Espony,' she replied.

Anne froze, 'That was quick.'

'Katholomu wanted to go for a ride,' she explained.

'So you've been in Espony all this time?' Anne asked.

'I was with Theron beforehand, why?'

'We thought the habitable area was going to be flooded, but then it hit something and stopped. You wouldn't happen to know anything?' Anne enquired.

Saranon knew what the older sorceress was talking about as she left her and Chilcott alone. Todd ran after her smiling out of breath, 'So you met Chilcott, he's not big on words. So how did you stop the sheal?'

'What?' She was astonished.

'Hailey and I knew it was you as soon as we realised

where it was,' Todd explained.

She was beginning to wonder if it had been too obvious and Todd shook his head as if reading her thoughts. Hailey joined them a little way out, 'Sorry it took me a while to get away. Come on you have got to see this.'

The three avoided the main crowd gathering around the eastern section with a crew already well underway. Hailey moved forward to a staircase hidden in plain view in the wall near the side entrance and they snuck down out of sight. A tremble curled its way up Saranon's spine and she could see that Todd was not much braver, but curiosity kept him moving forward.

The voices dimmed as they moved along. The sheal had already started to retreat with signs playing across the floor beneath. Small amounts of sheal posed no harm to sorcerers, especially when detached from its source. They strode across without fear. The slow methodical lapping of the vibrant liquid penetrated through the room. They did not get far, as the sheal lay close to the underside of the floor, holding them back with a deep murky edge. Todd was disappointed, as he poked around to see if there was anything below the surface. The sheal gave nothing up as Saranon gazed around and through a small alcove. As she peered through Hailey let out a tremendous scream and she bumped her head hard.

The sorcerer looked alien all geared up knee deep in the water. Larry lifted his head piece up, 'What are you lot doing down here?' he asked, then spied Saranon. 'Get a suit on then come around, what are you waiting for?'

She and her friends were speechless. Todd grabbed her shoulder and urged them back up. She peered back as Larry sank back in the sheal without a trace. Her head still throbbed as she stopped short of running straight into Chilcott at the top of the stairs who stepped aside.

They joined the main crew as Chilcott spoke to Larry when he resurfaced sitting for a rest, 'I don't want any of them going down there.'

'The Angeon will be fine,' Larry spoke as he rested.

Chilcott stared at her with deep concern, 'I do not think you are the Angeon.'

Larry almost laughed, 'Come on Tony, she saved your hide earlier. Who do you think was in the dead zone?'

Saranon answered for him, 'Your fairy godmother.'

Larry burst out laughing as Chilcott look confused, 'That wasn't you.'

'Give it a break and let the girl suit up,' Larry said as he stood up.

When she came back Chilcott was gone, she let out a deep sigh. Larry heard her and spoke. 'He's had a couple of hopefuls let him down over the years, all talk and no spark. Come on I'll show you something.'

Hailey and Todd watched in pure amazement as she followed Larry down into the depths. The sheal made a strange gulping sound as it wrapped around her. It was eerie and silent, as Larry's form lit up in a small warm glow up ahead moving with ease as though it were second nature. It did not take long to find the problem with Saranon almost tripping into the gaping whole, as Larry held her back from the edge.

They walked along and she made out many tiny punctures across the surface, it had not taken much for the pressure to blow. Larry's voice came through loud and clear, 'I can mend it, but it would take me and a team ages, I thought you might like to have ago. Once it's sealed, we would have time to get a good look around before tinsel toes starts poking his head in.'

Saranon smiled knowing exactly what he meant. The sorcerer had always been kind and accepted her without prejudice. She set to work, while Larry stayed close pruning the area as the sheal slipped away.

Soon the liquid was well below her shoulder, as she opened her head piece the line slid below her waist and continued edging downward. In the distance she could hear shouting. She peered around the corner just in time to see Chilcott heave a blinding punch into Purton, who fell back against the wall. Chilcott caught her eye and stopped striding out with the sheal lapping at knee deep. He tripped and almost fell, regaining his balance in time for Purton rushing towards him. She stood there speechless as Purton tried to shove the other sorcerer under. She need not have worried, as Chilcott held his own soon gripping Purton's head under his clenched arm. Larry placed a hand on her arm and she jumped in her skin with fright.

'What's going on?' She whispered.

Larry spoke, 'We think Purton may have done it.'

'I doubt it,' she replied.

Chilcott looked at her, as Purton twisted his head out

of the close embrace. She finished her sentence, 'Not unless he's Eskardy.'

Larry spoke in a slow voice, 'Are you sure?'

'See for yourself,' she pointed.

Chilcott followed behind as they examined the underneath of the pipe Saranon had just mended. The jagged outlined still showed as a discoloured silhouette, he ran his hand along the line. 'Now do you believe me?' Purton said puffing as he steadied himself against the door.

Chilcott said nothing and the other sorcerer left wiping the blood off his face. 'I think you owe him an apology,' Larry spoke.

'Later,' said Chilcott.

'You do speak,' Saranon exclaimed.

Chilcott stared at her.

'You can't blame the kid,' Larry commented.

Chilcott tapped his fingers along the pipe in deep thought as he spoke, 'You are not the only Angeon.'

'Now, you don't break it to a kid like that,' Larry spoke.

'It's all right I know,' she interrupted.

'Did Theron tell you?' Larry asked.

'No.'

Larry smiled and nudged her out of the room while Chilcott examined the damage. They both heard him say, 'How could I have missed that?'

Larry let out a small laugh as he waved Saranon goodbye at the top of the stairs and went back to clean up. She was in two minds about going or following Larry then a voice spoke behind her. 'I wouldn't do that if I were you,' Purton was standing behind her, his face showed no sign of his earlier dispute. 'I owe you thanks,' he shook her hand in a gesture of gratitude.

Something almost no one had done, in that instance the energy still flickering in immensity reached out in a gentle caress. By the sorcerer's look of astonishment he had felt it. 'Chilcott's the one you want to teach you, I'll ask him when he's settled down.'

'Thanks,' Saranon was not sure whether she wanted to be residing next to two of her teachers, one was more than enough. Hailey rushed up to her, 'Wow, did you miss some action?'

'I saw enough,' she said.

Hailey was still dazzled by the fight as they found Todd sitting in the lounge with a glum look on his face. 'Purton is Todd's uncle,' Hailey explained.

Saranon stared in surprise, 'He's all right.'

'Are you sure?' Todd asked.

'Yeah, it looks like the sorcery used was from an Eskardy and he was fine when we spoke a moment a go.'

Todd was still stressed, even when he relaxed and she felt sorry for him as they stayed up chatting.

She placed her empty cup on the sink, it had been a long day and an even longer night as she wondered what Purton had meant. Things were beginning to get complicated; she tapped her fingers on the bench, the others had long gone to bed. 'You're picking up my bad habit,' the sorcerer spoke behind her.

Saranon turned to see Chilcott standing in the doorway, 'So you talk after midnight.'

She gibed as he continued. 'I'm swapping you over to my class, from Braxton's.'

The sorcerer left before she could speak again. Not that she thought much of Braxton's class, but the fact that Chilcott had known about the other Angeon annoyed her.

Then it occurred to her, she now had two of her teachers living next to her unit. Saranon groaned, too many people to ask questions when she wandered off. The silence the Keep had offered, was beginning to look a little frayed around the edges as she heaped up the covers and drifted off to sleep. Saranon's head throbbed as someone knocked on her door, in all the commotion, she had forgotten about hitting her head. Todd crammed his head around the door, 'Purton just said you got switched to Chilcott's class.'

'Yes.'

'Get up or you'll be late.'

'Oh no!' Saranon rushed grabbing her books and then wondered if she would need them. She hesitated a moment then left rushing straight past Chilcott. 'You're in hurry to get somewhere.'

She stopped and turned, falling into line with the sorcerer's graceful stride. He was a mirror of calm after the night before, unlike Saranon, who showed signs of lack of sleep. As soon as the lesson started she knew it would be no easy ride. She felt like she had just been flung up a few levels and had some catching up to do. Chilcott handed her a new text book without a second glance, it was twice as thick as her last and she let out a small sigh.

Hailey tapped her on the shoulder and pointed her to the page they were up to. She thanked the fact that her friend was already taking the class. At the end Chilcott spoke up in a monotone voice, 'Vandragamond, I want to speak with you.'

It took a moment for her to realise that was her, as the others piled out the door, he looked up with a steady eye. 'Purton thinks you are worth spending time on, you are not the first Angeon I have taught.'

He let the words sink in before he continued, 'Merrick Calthazard left a mess behind him.'

Chilcott rolled up his sleeve revealing a long scar running up his arm. 'You do this and I will have you kicked out of Indarin quicker than Katholomu can fly you to Espony, understood.'

Saranon was speechless, as the sorcerer gestured the meeting was over and she sprinted from the room. Hailey grabbed her arm as she spun around the corner, 'Hey.'

Hailey continued, 'I thought he knew something but I didn't want to say, I hope you don't mind.'

'No,' she replied.

The eastern wing of the Keep was still a shambles, as the last of the sheal was swept away leaving a shiny clean edge to the old surface. It was difficult for her to think that one substance could cause so much trouble. She strode down the open stairway to find Larry taking a break. 'I'm sorry I didn't tell you earlier,' he said.

It had not occurred to Saranon that he knew about

Merrick, but she accepted the apology. Thinking aloud she spoke, 'Chilcott said he made a mess.'

'Sure did, Tony was lucky to get out alive. The lad almost brought the house down, he was too hot headed and wanted everything now, but I'm sure you know the type.'

There went her plans of having a friendly meeting as the thought showed on her face. She did not doubt the finality in Larry's words as he stood up and went back to work. She peered through the door and noticed that someone had smoothed out her rough job on the pipe. Any signs of the cracks had disappeared on the gleaming surface. The old sorcerer smiled and said nothing as he saw her mind ticking away. The man hesitated with words on the edge of his tongue then stopped himself short. A sound came whistling up from the lower ground as Saranon stuck her head around the corner and she left the sorcerer alone. The steps were new as she entered a part of the Keep that would have been well occupied.

She marvelled at the detailed space below. The door of the lab was open so she let herself in, almost tripping over Purton's feet in the process. The sorcerer was busy fixing something behind the wall, 'Greetings Saranon.'

He called out without stopping. She assumed that gave her an open invitation to look around. As she traipsed through the large space picking up objects as she went. 'Can you pass me the kedril on the right?'

She handed it to him, 'You could have got it yourself.'

'I know, but I had to find something for you to do,'

he replied.

She gave him a stern look as the sound of footsteps approaching made her jump. She fell with a thump to see Chilcott staring at her. 'What are you doing down here?'

'She's helping me,' Purton explained.

The sorcerer mulled the words over, before moving on without a sound. Getting down to the business of restoring the lab as it had been. Saranon listened to the pair exchange short words and whispered to Purton, 'How do you two work together?'

Chilcott's ears immediately pricked up as his friend answered. 'Rather well.'

The sorcerer spoke without turning around, 'When will the engine be back up Mr Purton.'

'Another day I'm afraid,' he replied.

Chilcott came across to take a look as Saranon skittered out of the way, in his angst he knocked her flying as he pushed past. She slipped on the wet floor crashing to a full stop, slamming with both her hands into the control panel. 'Oh....' She exclaimed as both sorcerers scrambled in desperation to shut down the machine.

The terrible clanging sounded, then slowed as the machine whirred to a stop. Chilcott breathed a massive sigh of relief as he looked down, he had just hurled across the room.

'Why don't you go back upstairs and I'll handle it from here,' Purton suggested.

As Saranon motioned to leave, he added, 'No, I meant you.' He stared at Chilcott who understood and left. 'Sorry about that, he had three months worth of research ruined.'

'I can understand that,' she said as she brushed herself off.

It did not take long for her to discover how talkative Purton was, as she stayed to keep him company. Wondering every now and again when would be the right time to leave, as she kept eyeing off the door. 'It's all right you don't have to stay,' Purton said and she took it as her queue to hurry back upstairs.

The halls glimmered with light in the darkness, with almost no one in sight as she rushed by realising how late it was. The sound of muffled voices wafted through the corridors as she halted in her tracks and listened. It was her old teacher Braxton talking in the darkness. 'They don't suspect a thing, and everybody has been too busy with the clean-up.'

Another voice sprang out of nowhere, 'Then we had better get a move on.'

Saranon wanted to hear more but she could not without making a sound and would rather not have their attention. She crossed the large entrance and scampered to her unit, breathing a small sigh a relief as she reached the door.

CHAPTER NINE

A bloodline of old

The wind whistled in her hair as she saw the ground move beneath her feet, Hailey and Todd could not make sense of what she had heard. In the meantime, Katholomu had begun bending his weight, across the metal banister in agitation. The great dragon had almost taken off in one leap, but now he was rummaging through the clouds. Saranon was hanging on for all she was worth as he sped with all his might. The dragon grinned with excitement and flew faster. Just so she had to cling on the softness of his fur, between the thick folds of scaly skin. The muscles flexed as he pounded down on the side of a hill, skidding before coming to an abrupt stop.

The morning sun shone around Armeria as it glowed with a halo of light as the sun's rays reflected off the surface. Seth had been polite to her after the incident, but the image of a young girl who had not seen hardship, was shattered. After the sorcerer had settled down with that thought, he had become more comfortable. It was a weight off Saranon's shoulders, as Hailey had become a good friend. She could make out their forms in the distance flying high as Katholomu stood up straight. Assessing the dragons they were riding and letting out a low bellow. Rasputen responded with a deep low sound swooping across the valley as Seth glided in and down with the group landing in close.

Darren walked over, 'The place hasn't been the same since you left.'

'Pardon?'

Seth responded, 'He means the rozzen colony is doing well. Your dragon looks like he's itching to go, did you want to fly with us?'

Before she could answer Katholomu had spread his wings in eager anticipation, 'I guess that's a yes.'

No sooner than she had managed to secure a hold around the dragon's shoulders, than he heaved down. He rebounded with a mighty force up into the sky.

The other dragons followed suit catching up and fast taking the lead. Katholomu was more than ecstatic as he stretched himself to fly in perfect motion with deep concentration. The first stop rose up through the landscape as a weary outpost that had seen better days, came into view. It was a decent size as Saranon came into land on the edge, with Katholomu walking over. The dragon acted as though his clumsy landing and larger size were not noticeable.

Almost no attention was paid to such a common site as Darren and Seth checked in at their usual stop before heading further out. She waited outside, warming her face in the sun as her dragon waited. He shifted his weight as he curled his tail around the length of his body.

She left his side as she scurried around the outside to take a closer look. Saranon had not moved far away when the dragon let a loud snort, as if startled. The massive dragon did not have much room to move as she stepped around without seeing anything in sight. She placed a gentle hand on his forearm as the dragon stood poised and strong. Katholomu followed her with his eyes, as she walked away unimpressed at being left alone. As she peered off, she felt something rush past and held out her hand. A piercing jolt ran up her arm in a muted battle before she had it extinguished.

Katholomu jumped up flaring his nostrils to make a point, scanning the area with caution. While stepping forward with one arm poised ready. Saranon's initial shock had worn off as she searched around, wherever it had come from now showed no trace. Seth rushed out toward her, 'Duck!'

'What…' she began.

Another blast came forming out of the corner of her eye. This time she was ready and pulled in hard like a lead getting shorter. Its owner fell from the second storey window on to the muddy ground below.

The force of the impact was minimal as Talmon soon steadied himself. Clearing the dirt off in disgust, the sorcerer showed no sign of remorse. 'Why did you bring them here?'

Seth looked aghast and answered, 'Let's go.'

His face was stern as he stared hard in a silent standoff. She was not sure what was going on but hiked herself up on a full sized Katholomu who was not prepared to show such mercy. As they left, he flicked the sorcerer across the yard with his hind leg slamming him into a wall before darting off. Saranon deflected Talmon's last efforts as the gap between them grew too wide for another round.

The humour was not lost on Darren or Rory, as the first spoke up, 'I've always wanted to do that.'

'I doubt it, your mother would never forgive you,' Rory spoke.

Saranon had become lost part way through the conversation. With good timing Darren responded, 'He's my cousin.'

'Not that it counts for anything,' Rory added.

'I'm yet to be reacquainted with mine, so I wouldn't know,' she said.

Saranon had not meant the comment to carry as much weight as it did in the silence that followed.

Darren interrupted her thoughts, 'Don't worry, I'm sure you'll have at least one like that.'

The day grew bright as they made their way down to the shore. Scanning the far reaching dragon colony for signs of trouble, as Seth took Rasputen low to the ground. The dragon was showing off his might as Katholomu flew low to the ground fast behind and stormed ahead right over the top. Colderay followed with Darren gliding him with little effort. Katholomu grunted in disgust with so much friendly competition. They branched out in a wide formation along the shore. He dove down near Armeria in the cool midday sun breaking through the rising clouds.

Kat arched out stretching his limbs, showing off his full length. He was just a fraction longer than Rasputen, the largest of the group, as they rested. Rasputen flared in silence narrowing his eyes as he pelted Katholomu in the chest. They tumbled in a tight embrace, ending with Rasputen pinning the large dragon to the ground. 'Now you picked that argument, don't expect me to save you,' Saranon grumbled with a harsh edge on her tongue.

Katholomu tried to move, but Rasputen had the upper hand as he gave in and the two became friends. A large dot grew on the horizon as Levette brought Hailey down close next to Rasputen. Seth was about to say something and stopped as he saw his sister approach.

She looked straight past him at Saranon, 'I thought you were here, Talmon didn't waste any time getting sympathy.'

'I hope you didn't believe him,' she responded.

'Of course not,' Hailey rolled her eyes in disbelief. 'It's not the first time Talmon has done that but it might be the last if he has any sense.'

'My cousin, no,' Darren said with much sarcasm.

The company sat as they ate, her eyes were caught by a low glimmer to the south near the rocky coves.

As she turned she saw Seth transfixed in the same

direction in deep thought, 'What is that?'

The sorcerer finished his mouthful and pondered, 'Work. Why don't you stay with Hailey?'

Before Saranon could answer the small group had already risen on their dragons with Seth waving a small goodbye as he flew past. She felt as though she had just been cheated out of the action in her slowness to respond. As if reading her thoughts Hailey explained, 'He meant it.'

Saranon let out a sigh of exasperation at being left behind and tried to hide it with a smile. The pair walked for a small way heading back to Armeria. Katholomu pretended not to notice, after he had snuggled himself into a cosy spot. In a way she was relieved to be spending time with Hailey, it would give her dragon time to calm down as he warmed himself in the sun. The garden emerged up ahead, sprawling out on both sides, as a large thud raked across the ground bringing her to her knees with a heavy weight. Hailey clung to the open gate as she regained her balance, that was not what she had expected. Katholomu rushed in with a mighty leap, flicking Saranon up in a half summersault. As she heaved herself up on his shoulders.

The dragon bounded, twisting his full weight around. So close to Hailey's face the draft brushed across her shoulders. Katholomu flexed his muscles upward as he picked up speed. He flung her straight into the oncoming storm shattering across the darkened sky. The wind turned to greet them head on, as it rained out from the blows of sorcery flashing across the open sky. The ground thudded again with a mighty flash sending chills down her skin. The dragon persisted with his chase, carrying her with him. He began to roar underneath as if egging her on. The energy drew away around her in a massive rush, culminating at one point in the distance.

Saranon allowed her energy to intensify growing ever stronger in the void. She followed through with a mighty sound, as it catapulted at speed crackling through the air as it went. Her energy hit its mark with deadly precision that lit up the sky with a cold burning glow. Katholomu flew with speed knocking the opponent's dragon into the sea she plunged down with him, jumping off at the last minute. She plunged into the icy depths becoming disoriented until she managed to reach the surface. Seth and Rasputen dived down and plucked her with ease from the cold embrace. She clung on as the water below her flurried with dragon blood. Katholomu's head broke the surface as he gasped, treading water before jolting up in the air.

Seth grabbed her hand and pulled Saranon up behind him. He headed straight into Armeria with only four other dragons following. She did a quick head count and saw Rory with Darren on Colderay. 'I would have managed,' Seth spoke as they flew in.

She was speechless but she was not about to argue while riding on Rasputen, that would be asking for trouble. They dived hard into the grounds of Armeria, knocking down a small statue, as they went. Darren immediately slipped off his dragon and came to her side holding out his hand in a gesture of kindness.

She accepted as she looked back, but Katholomu

had long since disappeared. 'Your dragon looked fine. I wouldn't go after him though I couldn't say the same for his temper. So is he your dragon or are you his person?' Darren asked.

'I haven't figured that out yet,' she answered.

Darren's body language blocked Seth from making any more comments as he stood between them. Seth became disinterested and went to reassure Hailey who had come out to greet them. Saranon stood staring out to the distant ocean, absorbing the events and drying off the last of the water from her wet clothes.

'That felt like a different type of sorcery,' she remarked.

'He was using an Orb,' Darren answered.

The concentration of energy made sense though she had not dealt with an Orb since leaving Darkonia. They were difficult to use and viewed more as prized ornaments. The sorcerer noticed her elongated silence, 'Do you know about Orbs?'

'I've used one before in Darkonia,' she responded.

Darren reached into his satchel grasping a thick cloth, it unravelled, revealing a dark murky Orb underneath.

She picked it up in the palms of her hands and it glowed. 'The last one I held was the Eye of Escora, it was so pure that no matter how long I looked at it I could find no blemish.'

She held it up to the light and the clouds of imperfection showed in the faint glowing light from within, 'It looks like it was made in haste.'

'I think you're right,' Darren spoke as he wrapped it

back in thick cloth and carried it in.

As he handed his parcel over, Seth gasped in astonishment holding it up out of way of Hailey's grasp. The tug of war did not last long as Hailey outsmarted her older brother, 'This is the Orb of Throm.' She said as she peered into it.

The visible shock of surprise reverberated across the room missing Saranon completely. As Seth spoke first, 'Are you sure?'

'Yes, we need to return it,' Hailey replied.

'What?' Rory shouted, 'After all that are you serious?'

'I'm afraid so, it belongs to Gresham,' Hailey spoke as Saranon's cheeks grew red with embarrassment.

'How old is he?' She asked.

Seth sighed, 'If you've met him perhaps you'd like to return it?'

'Only briefly.' she spoke trying to side step the issue.

'It's all right, we'll handle it, I wonder if it was stolen?' Darren asked aloud.

'It would seem the case.' Seth said eyeing the Orb over in his hands before putting it away.

Everyone including Saranon was showing signs of a weary day in the afternoon sun. With an odd silence hanging over the sky as though mirroring their mood. It was not until she searched for Katholomu, lying low in the long withered grass, that she understood the extent of the damage. The dragon had a fresh mark from his opponent's claws stretching down his side; she held out her hand and healed the wound.

Katholomu's eyes met hers in a sad deep stare, she rubbed his cheek for comfort and he motioned her up on his shoulders. She took great care as she lifted herself up and he took to the sky turning back into the path of the original attack. He landed with all the grace he could muster, as his body still tingled from the fight. A small ripple of energy floated up from the ground, a left over remnant from the intensity of the energy that had built up towards her. The smell lingered in the air with no real sense of direction. She leant down running her fingers along the ground, sensing the past events with her mind.

A fragile picture flicked across her closed eyes as she scanned the area. Before she could stand again, something moved out of the corner of her eye. Any remnants of the sorcerer she had fought with, were long gone, but she was not alone, with another presence close by. Saranon peered over the top of several large rocks, her heart missing a beat as she recognised Gresham. The wounded sorcerer stared up unsurprised, 'I thought you would return.'

She stood shocked as his words sank in. Then without a second thought she bent down and helped him over to Katholomu, he sat down to rest, 'You got what you wanted?'

She did not like being second-guessed as she held his head in her hands and healed him. His presence muddied the situation, 'How did someone get your Orb?'

Gresham remained silent, so she filled in the gap, 'I have no use for it.'

The sorcerer steadied himself on his feet and climbed

onto Katholomu with Saranon behind him. The dragon was unimpressed at the newcomer, as he moved his head around to glare at the sorcerer. Gresham spoke, 'My friend wanted it.'

'Oh!' her heart sank as she realised whom the other sorcerer had been.

As Katholomu flew in, Gresham spoke under his breath, 'I guess he won't be bothering me anymore.'

The comment only made her feel worse as they landed. Seth relieved himself of the Orb and with it a whole lot of trouble, as Gresham accepted it back in an awkward silence. He led the sorcerer in and away from Saranon as she let out a small sigh of relief afterward. Meeting Gresham again under those circumstances, was not how she had imagined it. The idea perplexed her the more she thought about it. Hailey caught up with her out in garden, while she was brushing down a shabby and disgruntled Katholomu. Who was not sure whether to purr or growl at the attention.

'That went better than I thought,' Hailey said with a deep resounding sigh. 'Gresham is gone now if you want to come inside?'

She hesitated before pondering, 'What were they doing near the cliffs?'

'It's a weak point near Armeria.' Hailey answered.

She stood back from the dragon as Katholomu's patience grew thin. He scampered off in a great heap as she spoke, 'I was hoping it was something innocent.'

'So was I,' Hailey replied.

It was not comforting to know the intention, as

Saranon wondered if there was more going on. It would have been too easy to blame Armeria if Gresham had not made it out alive. Hailey gasped at the notion, before allowing it to sink in, neither was prepared to exclude the possibility. The offer of dinner had been too good to pass up as she sat down to dig into a hearty meal. She competed with Darren and Rory, who had empty pits for stomachs, after using their energy. She was about to say something, but no one was listening. So she gave up, as Darren scoffed a large chuck of bread smeared with the last portions of food from his plate.

As if stirring her he leaned over and said, 'So what were you saying?'

She stared at him in annoyance that was lost as Darren grinned. 'I was just thinking what would have happened if we had lost Gresham?' She asked.

'Then it's a good thing we didn't,' the sorcerer showed reluctance to give a straight answer as he disappeared from the table.

Katholomu was ready and eager for a night flight as the sky darkened around laying shadows on the ground. The dragon's dark colour blended in well as they took to the sky, as the breeze picked up over the ocean and carried its chill across the land.

The wind whipped along Saranon's arms as she went thinking of Indarin. Yet that was not where the dragon was taking her, as he veered to the north. Espony shone in the distance as he landed close in stark silence. She was hesitant to leave, but the dragon urged her on in a firm stance and she knew Katholomu was not about to relent. It did not take long to find Kera in the crowd. Kera spoke, 'Come with me.'

When they were out of the sharp cold air enjoying a nice warm drink, her new friend continued the conversation. 'Gresham said thanks.'

Saranon almost bit her lip in surprise it had not occurred to her, that the two knew each other. Kera explained that Gresham and Soren's family were related. There had been an uneasy resentment when Gresham's uncle had left him the Orb of Throm. She spoke, 'I'm afraid I'm not that familiar with Orbs.'

Kera laughed, 'The Orb is rumoured to be made by one of the strongest sorcerer's Espony has ever had, it's a bit late to want it now.'

She could feel herself blush, 'No, I didn't mean it that way.'

As the night drew on, there was one question that was being avoided by both of them, the other Angeon. It had plagued Saranon's mind earlier. Yet if meeting Merrick had the potential to disrupt her time at Indarin she was not so eager to find him. As she left, Kera spoke behind her, 'You are similar to my brother.'

'Pardon?' She asked.

'The Angeon,' Kera explained.

She looked down at her sitting at the table. For a moment regretted not having Mitch with her, not that he was inclined to say much.

She was speechless as she stared in disbelief at her new

friend. Part of her wanted to run, but curiosity stepped in holding her there in deep thought as Saranon sat down. It was difficult to understand, but it soon became clear that Merrick did not have much to do with his sister. In a way she felt sorry for her being forgotten. Then there were times when not drawing attention was something she craved. Kera smiled, as though in sympathy and appeared embarrassed at what she had just said. 'I thought being related to an Angeon would be a good thing?' She asked.

'He can be reckless,' Kera spoke a familiar tune.

'What do you mean?'

'He knows he's better than everyone else, I think you need to be careful,' Kera warned.

Saranon had grown to like her in the short time they had met and leaving her, carried a reluctant sadness deep within her heart. The cold night air wrapped around her with the clouds sweeping in, it was time to leave. The dragon had a way of letting her know what was going on, as she patted him, climbing up onto his shoulders. Looking back at the peaceful city, a fleet of dragons zoomed in across the sky. Before she had time to react, Katholomu leaped with all his might in the air as fast as he could.

A bolt of energy ran out, Saranon blocked but it fractured across the dragon's left wing. He went down in pain with a small thud, as he regained his composure before hitting the ground. It was all she could do to cling on as she slid sideways with the fall. She gathered her strength, glancing up to see the mighty dragon carrying Merrick. Without a second thought she poured all her energy into catapulting the sorcerer and his dragon as far away as possible. Merrick had not been ready. The force shot him back through the sky with such ferocity, that it left the other sorcerers riding with him in shock. Katholomu did not wait to be told, as he flung himself into the air heading south straight for Indarin.

Saranon's hands went numb as she trembled, still expecting to see something in the sky behind them, as they fled. The dragon landed with such force scraping his claws along the hard surface of the courtyard. Before she had a chance to move Mitch had climbed up yanking her down. They ran inside as Katholomu squeezed under the large opening into the foyer. He manoeuvred his way into the dragon pens before the giant door fell down into place. 'What did you do?' Mitch asked.

'Me?' She exclaimed.

'Well it always has something to do with you,' he responded.

'What about Craiden?' She asked.

'Ah…' He hesitated, 'That was different.'

Saranon scoffed at his remark, as they went further into the heart of the Keep. Her vision moved in slow motion as she noticed a wave of energy rippling through the Keep. 'What's happening?' She asked.

'The shields have gone up,' he replied.

'We're in deep trouble aren't we?' She asked.

Mitch stared at her, 'I'm glad you got the message.'

The walls tingled with a slight tremor. As they ran towards the centre he grabbed hold of her and pushed her towards an open door up ahead. She would not let go and they both hurled over the edge, down into the depths of the Keep below. Their fall slowed before they came to a stop in mid-air. The energy from the Keep provided a plateau, like a hard surface, at the focal point of the massive opening. Mitch took a moment to steady himself as he stood up towering over her, disgruntled by the situation. Indarin mirrored his mood as it readied itself in anticipation. The silence swept down the side of the large vertical tunnel as she tried to reassure herself. She knew he could tell of her immense panic starting to rise within.

CHAPTER TEN

Mercy

The dull thumping reverberated through from the edge of Indarin. It sent small shivers through her spine as Mitch stayed close. His fear crept through his eyes as he breathed. Another dull sound rattled down through the walls of the Keep at an electrifying pace hitting nothing. As he placed a hand on her shoulder, 'You need to stay away from the edge.'

The realisation hit Saranon as she peered upward. It was meant for her then another thought struck her, 'You were going to leave me in here alone.'

He hesitated as if caught out, 'Do I look like I want to be here?'

'And miss all the fun,' she glared at him.

Mitch groaned in response as she went and peered over the end of the platform and down into the dark abyss.

A massive spark of energy ran curling down the outside as the Keep funnelled it down, absorbing its strength along the way. 'Do you think I can do that?' Saranon turned to look up at Mitch for an answer.

'One day but not now,' he said it with finality in his voice.

He looked as though he were about to leap over at any moment and haul her into the middle.

Before waiting long enough to find out she strode the short distance back. As he was thinking aloud, 'Did you do something?'

'I knocked Merrick off his dragon,' she replied.

He cringed, 'I thought you were told to stay away?'

'Look, I'm not having this argument now,' she spoke.

As she stepped away losing her attention of where she was and fell back off the platform.

Mitch lunged, but he was too late and the energy around them was too strong for him to grasp her. She looked up and saw him stranded helpless above. Saranon tried to reach out to the walls, but the remnants of Merrick's energy made it a near impossible task. As she slid even further down only slowing the decline. If she could not go against the flow, there was always another option, as she placed all her energy into speeding up her decent.

She fell straight down to the full force and shield of the central core. If she were unfamiliar to Indarin, it would be a one way trip to oblivion, but the Keep already knew her. The energy seared through her as she plummeted through the shield with a mighty shock. Her energy creased around the giant sphere as she burst through. From the edges of reality Saranon heard the thunderbolt of the other Angeon crashing downward from above. It shook the building and sped down to its destination with precision. The melding of her energy with the central core spread far too slow. As she watched in horror as the bolt blasted its way through, just before she secured the central core.

The pain ripped through her mind as the Keep reeled from the shock and the ground above grew silent. The central core shone in disgust, flickering in the distance between its usual calm and irritation. Reaching up and increasing its efforts to heal the open wound. The fine cracks spread far, reaching out from the point of impact just above Saranon's head. The pounding had stopped as she tried to get out. Slamming her energy up against a hard surface that was not willing to give, or let her out. Panic started to cross through her mind as she remained calm on the outside and tried to think. The core was old and began healing the wound from within. Then it sent her hurtling up through a separate exit in the Keep.

She glided straight up through an opening leading to a familiar place, Purton and Chilcott's lab. The floor opened up with the raw stallic energy spewing forth, shocking Purton in place as he stood. The large gust was absorbed back into the Keep leaving Saranon lying on the hard cool floor in its wake. There was no denying the magnitude of the energy that flowed from deep within Indarin, it stained up the walls in a thin light spray. She took a deep breath and her lungs filled with pain from the harsh intrusion as she gasped. Purton found the strength to haul her up and he ran down to greet her calling for help as he went. He picked her up and rested her arm on his shoulder taking her above to the habitable area.

Anne was waiting and checked her over before letting her go into the waiting arms of Mitch, who was still distraught at what had happened. His face was pale with fright and Saranon knew he thought he had lost her. It was a sobering thought as she let him take her away from the growing excitement. She made out Hailey's face in the crowd and gave a tired recognition, she smiled in return. It was a fine mess, but she was glad to be out of the central core, as Mitch placed her down on a large couch in his room. The soft silence was a welcome relief as her ears still tingled from the harshness of the whirring, far below.

He sat beside her with both the colour and relief returning to his face. She smiled, but her voice betrayed her not making a sound. There was a small knock at the door that startled him. Saranon could sense who it was. Theron entered, skimming around the surprised wizard; he leaned over and said, 'I'm sorry.'

She smiled and managed a whisper, 'I've been through more than that.'

'She's right,' explained Mitch. 'You should've seen what she did in Normisia.'

The Prophet looked up as though he missed something important, then let it be. She knew that even Prophets could not see everything but with Theron, she would not want to guess how far that went.

He spoke, 'I asked the Keep to help you.'

'Thanks,' she was not sure what Theron meant, but she was grateful for any help she could get.

He left her in peace, but Mitch looked like he was going nowhere as though she would disappear if he left. She could not blame him and held out her hand, he grasped it between his hands until she fell asleep. It had taken all his strength not to dive in afterward, but he knew it would have been an almost certain death. His only hope was that Saranon had visited a central core before, a place he could only dream of going.

Mitch had left her too long in the care of the Armythral and if she had to stay at Indarin any longer, things would have to change. Part of him felt like he had failed but he knew for the Angeon, it was different and he would not be able to keep her safe. He picked up another blanket and placed it over the sleeping sorceress. He tried not to disturb her as he went to his own bed too weary to keep his eyes open any longer. The morning brought a loud harsh thud at the door after Mitch had been up for an hour. Chilcott stuck his head around to see if he had woken her up. 'I need a few helpers to mend the Keep and seeing as you are in my class now I thought you might like to volunteer.'

It was a lame excuse to see if she was all right, but Saranon did not mind, she had recovered and it gave her some normality to return to. Either way it was going to be a busy day. She ran downstairs past the dragon pens and through the main entrance to find her class already waiting. She was hoping to make a quiet entrance, but as she skidded through the door, that was the last possible thing she could do. Hailey handed her a spare kit. 'What's this for?' She asked.

'You'll see,' smiled Hailey.

They made their way through to one of the outer control rooms where Chilcott produced a series of large maps. Her heart sank as she realised they would be going around checking and replacing the small pieces that had been damaged. Saranon was about to roll her eyes in disgust, but thought better of it, the rest set to work without hesitation. She knew that if everyone helped the task would be done and the Keep would return to its old self. Rather than making the irritable humming noise that hung in her head, like a bad tune that would not go away. The door swung open and Purton came through with a large set of kedrils and a face that meant business. He yanked off one of the rear panels and checked the conduits behind the walls.

As she turned back, she could see Hailey beginning to lean forward near the main controls. She caught a small glimmer of a spark and yelled out. Hailey looked around in surprise. Chilcott noticed and grabbed a thick rag like shield. Throwing it over the broken tablet and disconnected it from the source. It glowed hot on the ground with a sharp, charred smell hitting the room. They piled out to let the air clear, it was a poor start to the day, but it gave Saranon a chance to look around as work progressed. Chilcott was undeterred as he motioned everyone back in. Without hesitation he went up to where Purton had turned his attention to the primary control panel.

Leaning over they yanked it apart, the pieces inside had corroded and Purton let out a small groan. The task was fast growing well out of their expectations and the frustration on Chilcott's face showed. As he turned to Saranon, 'The sooner you return to Darkonia the better.'

The words hit her hard as stone, she ran out of the room not thinking of where she was going. Within a short space of time it felt like everything she had worked toward was fast unravelling before her. She ran down to her retreat and almost slammed straight into Theron. The sorcerer looked as though he had been waiting for some time, his face showed great sorrow running deep mirroring the Keep.

'Do you know what happens next?' The Prophet asked.

'We are going to fix the Keep,' Saranon spoke with deflated enthusiasm.

Theron smiled, 'You understand.'

She had built up a short yet extensive knowledge of working with Keeps. Her practical skills showed as she began directing Theron. It was a long slow preparation, but they both knew it had to be done. They opened a small entrance down to the depths of the inner workings of the Keep. She had chosen the site well with easy access for one with experience. They climbed down into the ill-fitting tunnels holding the large conduits running downward.

As they looked along the length the damage was immense, it kept on running along and down the sides. For Saranon it would be tedious rather than complicated.

With the most pressing problem the exposure and leaks in the massive cables. Yet, if repaired it would reduce the damage. She groaned knowing she would need to do most of the work, 'Remind me to return the favour to Merrick one day.'

'Do you want to do that?' Theron asked.

'Probably not,' she half spoke to herself.

She headed down to where the ideal location would be. As they neared it, the sounds of voices travelled up, showing signs of fraying frustration. After Chilcott's cold remark, she did not think walking straight into that would be of any use. So they travelled to the second ideal location underneath. Theron inspected her choice, 'Are you sure about this?'

'It's a bit late to start having doubts,' she spoke as the young Prophet shook his head.

Saranon slipped down and the Keep wrapped around her on the soft stone bed, she could see Theron beginning to do the same.

'Are you sure you want to do this?' She asked.

'I know what I'm doing,' he replied.

She was not convinced, but she was not about to turn away his help either as the Keep recognised them both. It soon became clear that Theron was out of his depth although she did not mind. He had a calming effect on Indarin that made her wonder how long it would have taken her had he not been there. The true frustration of the attempt above came through as a fleeting glance. As she sped further down in the heart of the Keep with her energy trying to stay in balance.

The great central core whirred below in anticipation. She could sense Theron trying to reach out, but the pressure was too great and Saranon led him down with ease. She felt like a great connector linking Theron with Indarin deep underneath. She waited for him to catch up before leaping far ahead and straight into the task at hand, smiling at his surprised shock. This was a journey she had done many times before in the sanctuary of the Keep. The Prophet needed little encouragement but in comparison, he was leagues behind. Indarin did not appear to notice as it worked to mend the bulk of the damage left in the other Angeon's wake. The noise above them faded into a soft quietness enveloping the whole building.

Saranon's energy intertwined with the Keeps in a warm careful embrace. A jolt shuddered through separating the link to both of them. Theron gasped, the sharpness of the pain as it hit home before fading away. She did not show any sign of discomfort as her annoyance numbed the sensation. She sensed the sealed door and spoke, 'Someone's out there.'

'What?' He asked.

'They're trying to get in.'

Theron froze beside her looking around for another way out. Then he grabbed hold of her, jerking her backward before she regained her balance. The two ran as the seal began to give way, Saranon's heart thudding hard, whoever it was had been hidden from their senses. She grumbled at the thought of being stuck with a Prophet who was beginning to panic, as she tried to calm herself. She had managed to seal off another area as Theron knelt down on the floor not making a sound. It was difficult to tell how close the other sorcerers were, but for some strange reason she did not want to break the silence of her friend.

The Keep gave little away and for once she found herself wanting to ask Theron with the words sitting inside her mouth. Just as the words were ready to be said, she could sense the danger leaving and let out a frustrated sigh. All the while the sorcerer watched her as if knowing with his eyes, holding an uneasy truce waiting for the next step. Saranon moved over near the open door at the other end of the room. As she did, a surge of energy reached around with such force taking her by surprise. She reacted with the full might of the Angeon incinerating three sorcerers before she had time to gasp and take it all in.

She moved forward around the corner as her senses pricked up. It screamed through her body and her mind as she held back her energy at the last second. Chilcott flew around the corner straight into her path as her palms were still burning hot. The cloth on his arm seared away leaving a large gap, without a trace, on his skin. Theron came running to see the consequences and stopped short when he saw Chilcott alive. 'You knew,' Saranon spoke through gritted teeth.

'Excuse me but I was the one you almost killed,' Chilcott interrupted.

'Stay out of it,' she shouted as she turned her attention back to Theron. 'Have you ever heard of the Uvalen Code?

Don't you ever do that again?' The Prophet stepped back as she stepped forward, backing him into a corner. Chilcott was about to intervene but the Keep had a mind of its own and blocked him off sealing the corridor. This time it was the Prophet's turn to look surprised, as she waited before continuing. She spoke, 'You have a lot to learn before you become the Prophet your grandfather was.'

Whatever Theron had seen, it had not included this part, as she read the expression on his face, 'Next time say something.'

As the Keep eroded the wall and Chilcott stared at them, Saranon walked past fuming. She was in no mood to stay as Purton greeted her with a far too cheery expression. It was enough time for her teacher to pull her to one side and lead her away to his office. The thought surfaced in her mind to dart the other way, but she would still have to deal with the situation later. At the moment neither option was particularly enticing as she sat down in a chair next to Chilcott's massive desk. 'Do you know what I am going to say?'

'You shouldn't be alive,' Saranon said.

'No,' he replied.

'I'm being serious,' she said. The sorcerer paused as she continued in her pattern of thought. As she spoke, 'He wasn't looking and he only saw the version where you were meant to die.'

Chilcott wore a puzzled look on his face as the conversation dived into an area he preferred not think about. As a solemn expression overcame him, 'Whose idea was it to meld with Indarin?'

Saranon hesitated before saying, 'Mine.'

He sighed while glimpsing the hole in his sleeve, 'So now you are going to leave us with a Prophet who can meld with the Keep.'

In the silence it dawned on her that this was rather unusual, at the same time, she knew that Theron needed to know. It was a sensation that prickled at the edge of her senses and would not leave her alone. She found herself staring at an older sorcerer who seemed oblivious. His pursed lips spoke volumes as she rose in an uneasy deadlock and he spoke, 'Why are you pushing Theron into this?'

'He's already there,' she was in no mood to explain and left Chilcott to mull over his own thoughts.

The hall was dark and distant as she walked along exhausted. Almost tripping over Mitch as she entered her room, he was sitting down admiring the view of the sky outside. The night was fast taking over the day as he stood up, 'There's something I want you to see.'

Saranon was about to argue, but his stare said otherwise and she grumbled to herself as any hint of an early night vanished. He led her down underneath the dragon pens. Into a pile of grimy tunnels marking the edges of the former structure the Keep was built upon. It took a while to register that the place use to be a wizard Keep. She looked at Mitch with astonishment. 'This is why wizards don't like sorcerers in their Keeps,' he grumbled.

The walls still pulsed underneath her touch in a strange embrace, only just audible. The sound was hidden away amongst the calling of Indarin. 'Why would sorcerers want a wizard Keep?' She asked.

'Less work,' he replied.

She had heard and read about the reasoning behind such a move, yet it did not appeal to her. Trading less work for less control of the central core, did not sit well in her mind. Saranon focused her attention on following the energy paths of the Keep. She wondered why it had not been clear before then she had not been searching for the differences.

She placed both her hands to the wall surging out her energy to sense the Keep this time it was easy knowing what to look for. In a small faraway voice Indarin spoke thanking her. It was bitter sweet because there was still much work to be done. She stepped further down, it took her a while to see that Mitch had hesitated at the top of the stairs. 'I won't be following you down there,' he remarked.

'Are you sure?' She asked.

He just smiled and left, he had seen enough of the inner workings of the Keep in the last few days and looked quite content to stay away.

The novelty had almost worn off for her, but she went on regardless, the walls shimmered with a soft light sparkling as she passed by. A small circular symbol lit up on the floor and she followed its path to a large old door jammed shut with age. Saranon used her energy to heave the door half open. It was more than enough for her to fit through the wide gap as a strange sandy smell wafted up in a thick haze. She waited for it to settle before peering down onto the large head of a zennigh. The creature rose, with two gleaming amber eyes rising like two suns above the platform of the walkway. It pierced through the darkness with an ambient glow.

She trembled while standing her ground…the zennigh lifted its wet black nose up. Bumping it with a large dull thud into the railing, as it turned away, lying back down underneath where Saranon stood. She crept over and stared over the edge at the restful giant not making a sound. She stayed watching the sleepy giant cats moving part way down. The one that had curled up underneath her, lied with its head side on to the stairs. She reached out her hand and stroked its soft fur. A clamouring sound jolted through the door. She jumped in her skin as the zennigh remained motionless beneath her touch. Another jolt rattled even closer and Saranon slipped into the folds of the zennigh's fur.

The great creature seemed not to notice as the fur only just covered her. A sound rattled from overhead as she blended into the background. With the mumble of voices further down sifting through the air. In the dimness, if she listened she could make out a few words without giving herself away. It seemed like the perfect hiding place wrapped deep in the warmth of the zennigh. Then something sparked through the folds of fur encapsulating the large open space with light. The transition fell into place searing through the zennigh with such force. The sensation leaped through to meet with her skin.

It sent a sharp bolt of pain through and put an end to

the dull frame of mind inhibiting the zennigh. It bounded to life, pulling her with it. As it ran toward the emanating source she tried to untangle herself from the stubborn reality of being caught in its fur. In the frustration she used her energy and half hurtled to the ground as the zennigh leaped in for retribution. As Saranon steadied herself, she looked up and caught a tiny glimpse of a net. She yanked the zennigh to a stop with her energy. Creating a narrow buffer as the mighty creature stopped short with silent precision. In the glimmer of light from the failed net, she stood defiant. Braxton her old teacher glared back at her.

The zennigh moved its large paw in an unwelcome fashion forcing him to scramble in retreat. Saranon's cold anger hid the fear of standing in the midst of a zennigh den. As the large creature by her side, let out a harsh simmering breath in resentment. As if in unison the zennigh and Saranon peered at one another. For a moment, the creature gave her recognition with its piercing fiery eyes that went on forever. It curled up underneath the stairs in almost exactly the same place. With its front paws stretched out in a display of contentment.

CHAPTER ELEVEN

The other path

Saranon trembled as she crept past the sleeping giant. She took care to shut the large door behind her, before rushing off through the dim hall. As she ran, the fear and frustration soaked in as the anger left and now she was desperate to get to the surface. Rounding a corner she almost jumped and only just missed running straight into Mitch. He led her back to his quarters above the dragon dens. He felt her forehead as she slumped in the chair. She had a strange exhaustion creeping up from the edges of her fingertips. 'What did you do, hug a zennigh?'

Saranon blushed and he groaned in acknowledgement.

It was tempting to stay, but she would have to return. Braxton had courted the anger of the zennigh. As she stood, her legs hesitated with weariness and a heavy weight from the contact of the zennigh taking its toll. She grumbled in a bitter acceptance that she would get nowhere without a good night's sleep. Mitch appeared all too pleased to have her close. He had changed after the attack on Indarin and now he was showing signs of eagerness to leave Serenphel behind. If only for a small moment, before she closed her eyes. She drifted off into an awkward sleep with the smell of the zennigh still covering her skin.

A hand reached over Saranon's vision before the light did. Catching her attention in a short gasp, before she realised it was attached to Hailey. Her friend sat beside her, 'You didn't mention Mitch.'

She thought she had, but then she had been focused on training more than anything else. Mitch was not impressed by this new found attention showing few signs in the silence. Hailey asked, 'Why don't you bring him to Armeria?'

She cringed at the thought, but Mitch said nothing at her friend's suggestion. Before she had time to think Hailey dragged her out of bed with great enthusiasm.

For first time since she had fallen into the central core the Keep hummed away to a regular peaceful tune. She breathed a large sigh of relief. It was not the impression she had meant to make so far from home. Todd was waiting outside with two fine dragons ready. As Hailey began to apologise for Katholomu, the enigmatic dragon stepped out from a long sleep. The great beast looked every bit ready, as he rustled his wings half open in the wind that swept underneath rolling along the ground. The grass shimmered in the fresh light of the early morning. Hailey flew up with a graceful whoosh on her dragon putting Todd's efforts to shame. Kat took no notice as he slid into the sky with a great heave, his massive wings powering into a smooth glide.

The almost invisible aura protecting Indarin shimmered as they went. The dragons needed little encouragement to leave the large Keep behind, as they flew into the cool sharp air. Saranon soon forgot the troubles of last night with the large zennigh. The creatures were capable of taking care of their own and so her worry grew distant the further she went. Todd flew his dragon high and turned into a small summersault. Hailey's shouting screeched across the wind, yelling for him to slow down. He smiled and waved back; with Katholomu it was not a wise step to encourage him. She was having enough trouble holding the great dragon steady. With Kat's muscles belaying the itching tension underneath.

Saranon held her seat firm, feeling every slight move and tremor of the dragon's changing mind. Katholomu commanded all her attention as she steered him away from the group, as he wrestled under her weight. The thrusting wings veered off at a weird angle as she clung on, while starting to slip sideways. As she looked over the cusp of the dragon's shoulder, she looked up in time to see Todd's dragon catch the rocky hillside. The beast ploughed down into an awkward summersault throwing her friend clear in a dusty haze. The reaction from Kathomolu was swift as he thumped himself down with the full might of his chest thrust forward. He absorbed the scattered impact of the falling dragon.

Jadaro's head sprang up with a dazed happy relief, the scratch marks lying across the top of his thick hard skin. Kat was less than impressed holding a silent stare back at the younger dragon, as he backed off, giving Katholomu a graceful berth. Saranon wanted to go down and check on her friend. Yet the dragon's muscles lay so tense underneath his arched back she dare not move. If anything she did not want to lose ground if he struck out. Hailey clambered down, rushing towards Todd after waiting for the dust and Jadaro's pride to settle. As she watched on, a wave of relief curled down to her toes and Todd stood up. She was about to breathe out a large sigh, when Katholomu moved his weight, clouting the younger dragon around the ears.

The breath caught halfway and she almost choked, spluttering into the back of the dragon's fur. The reaction was instant as he tilted sideways and jolted her off, before heaving himself high above the ground in disgust. Saranon stumbled, then clambered herself up shouting and running at the same time. Her friends burst out laughing behind her. She turned with such an annoyed look on her face that it prolonged the response. Hailey composed herself and then suggested that Todd could fly with her, which left Saranon with Jadaro. The dragon was large but by no means muscular for a rozzen. She sized him up then clambered on.

He was steady to take off with an even balance, but he struggled in the winds running across. Half way between Armeria and Indarin laid the remains of an old Keep, with the outer edges left to crumble. Escreigh resembled more of a well-kept tomb, than a working Keep with parts left to run down with age. For Saranon it had been an area avoided more out of necessity, to stay focused on her training. The Keep did not have much to offer beyond a simple frame, with the central core having become worn and frail long before. Yet it had taken on a new life with parts still in use. The rest was an untidy rabbit warren with corridors crisscrossing in almost every direction.

The place provided a wonderful hiding ground and peaceful retreat. Hailey ran through it without losing speed. Todd was still a little shaken, with his nerves trembling in hesitation. This allowed her to Keep up as she peered over the ancient scenery. The place had been magnificent in the days of the old Angeon. Zeralden Hadenvar had been the Queen of Darknonia by marriage to the King's second son. The blood line had since disappeared until now. Saranon was still baffled by finding another Angeon in Serenphel. She ran in a rush as she realised she had fallen behind. The ground tumbled and she fell through the floor with a thump. Scrambling to hang on, as the floor she had been hanging onto broke away, before Todd managed to get close.

She tried to soften the blow as one break led to another. Before she knew it she was tumbling way below ground, holding her own weight so as not to land too hard. She finally stopped on a pile of rubble, on top of a dust ridden smelly old concrete floor; she called out to let her friends know she was all right. Saranon peered up and sighed, she had fallen two storeys below and the remains looked too unstable to try and get back out the way she came. Not that she wanted to try that way, as she looked around melting the cobwebs out of the way as she went. The situation only reinforced her view that Escreigh should be avoided as she mumbled under her breath, a large spider ran past.

She was used to dark and dingy places, but she did not like the idea of being stuck somewhere. As she focused her attention on working open an old door. Her muscles ached from the fall, even though she had created a buffer with her energy. A spray of dust blew out as the door sprang open and she stopped it from falling on her face. Inside the room was an old tomb. As she crept past, with common sense telling her that the occupants were long dead, but that did not matter. A light shone down from an opening above and the shock made her jump. Her hand felt something old and creepy as she grimaced, not wanting to turn around. Saranon pulled back and saw that she had disturbed the remains of an old sorcerer. There was an envelope underneath.

Without thinking she took the envelope and went over to the light where she saw a familiar face, as Darren and Todd peered down. Darren let a rope ladder down and she climbed up holding the envelope out to the sorcerer. She heaved herself out with ease at a fast pace, jumping back from the edge, as though it were going to cave in at any moment. Hailey spoke, 'It's okay this floor is quite solid.'

She was not completely reassured as she stood well

back. While Darren pulled up the rope and bundled it away, he spoke, 'I think you should stick to the main paths.'

No one was prepared to argue after and if there was any doubt Saranon's annoyed glare settled the matter. Her mood matched Katholomu's where ever he was. The corridor led to a far grander section still cared for, as Seth greeted them with a stern nod. He looked quite at home in the large area that had been converted into a sizable outpost. She slumped down with relief into a comfy chair before Seth called her over he handed her the open letter, 'It's for you.'

Saranon accepted the small parchment and was about to pocket it as the sorcerer stared at her, then she stopped midway and read it. She almost jumped in surprise the letter was for her, the Angeon.

A small hand written note from a faraway time addressed to the Angeon. It made her wonder what she had stumbled on underneath an old Dreshan Keep. Before she could put it away, Hailey had snatched it and read the letter, she smiled, 'I don't think it's for you.'

'Zeralden had auburn hair,' she remarked.

'Oh,' Hailey exclaimed.

Saranon did not like to admit it but this time she would need to ask Theron. The thought did not sit well and she wondered if another visit into the old Keep would reveal more. Darren eyed her quizzical look, but said nothing in the background as she took the moment to wander off.

The walls did not hum with the same vibrancy as Indarin, but it had been well built and many parts of the building still stood strong. This time she stuck to the more well-used paths, her arms and knees were still aching from the fall and she winced at the thought of another. If anything the place opened up another question, if the note was not for Zeralden, then was it meant for her or Merrick. She was not about to reach out and ask the other Angeon, in fact she had been hoping that Merrick had relented on his current path. A low whistling sound gathered around the corner, blowing a soft cool breeze from the depths below, if anything it was familiar.

The low noise brought with it, a small strange message from beyond it. It filtered through the air holding her attention, as she stood on the top stairs hesitating in mid step. The place lay quiet as she dived into the unknown. The gloom around broke with the small occasional glimmer of light. The energy channelling up from the central core in a last glimmer of strength, in addition to her small light showing the way ahead. A small shimmer waved through the air in a familiar tone reminding her of Odana Temple deep in the heart of the old Zyanthia. Escreigh's walls were coated with a thick layer of dust brushing against her shoulder as she flicked it off. The ancient Keep still had a warm vibrancy running through from a bygone era.

For an old Dreshan Keep it appeared calm and let her wander into the murky depths. The place had been home to Theron's ancestor, Octavious the Prophet, who had been alive in the days of Zeralden Hadenvar. For a mighty sorcerer little was known outside the lasting prophecies that remained hidden away at Indarin. Saranon, the Angeon knew full well from Odana that prophecy had little meaning to an Angeon. Who had the ability to rewrite history, by choosing an unseen path. She had hinted at the prospect to Theron, but he was still absorbed in his textbooks. In an absent minded moment her foot almost went over the edge of the floor which had broken off.

This was no place for scatterbrained thoughts but they were flooding in thick and fast. She tried to find another path. She made it through to the lower level; the old building laid intact, showing signs of weathering around the edges. An old shaft reached down into the darkness where something glimmered from the deep below. A faint movement caught her eye, as the shadow passed through with the beam of light as she threw it into the dimness with a dull thud. The soft sound returned, reverberating up to the cavity above as she peered over almost losing her grip. Saranon groaned as her curiosity sank in and she began looking for a way down.

She secured a rope and used it to lower herself down the columns that still appeared sturdy as she bounced off them. A faint familiar smell wafted up, mixed in with the dry stale air, as the dust resettled beside her hand. Even in Indarin, the great home of one of the most powerful sorcerer clans, all the textbooks she had read, said the same thing, stay away from ockren. Of course there had been no textbook saying this at Zaidek Keep in Normisia which was just as well. It would have mattered not to her decision to ride the great mysterious ockren. That had broken out of the Keep carrying the full anger of the central core.

Now she felt the hairs on the back of neck begin to prickle, as she began to have the timely sinking feeling of being the intruder. The thought did not perturb her as she drudged on with a muffled thud landing in the grubby ground. A sluggish sound rustled from a dark corner of the room. Saranon almost froze to the spot with surprise as a figure moved out of the shadows, with wavy fawn coloured hair. The image of her old friend Tasha transfixed her, as the figure of she, stood close. Tasha held out her hand welcoming Saranon who touched it, the sensation felt real enough. A tear escaped down the side of her face even if the figure was not real it did not matter.

She was about to speak but Tasha spoke first, 'I have been waiting for you.'

The words sent a chill down her spine as Tasha continued, 'You will defeat Merrick, and you must believe that you will.'

'What do you mean?' The thought of another encounter made Saranon's heart sink.

'You are the Angeon!' with that Tasha stepped back into the darkness.

A voice called out from above and she answered, but when she looked back her old friend was gone. As she climbed up the rope, the great golden yellow eyes of the ockren opened into two small faint lines, they shone in the dim light.

As she climbed up Darren grabbed her hand to help her up, 'Did you find what you were looking for?'

She was not sure how to answer; it was not what she

had expected. Tasha's image still played in her head in repetition and she only just caught Hailey's words as she spoke. The confusion rushed in through her ears. 'Are you all right?' Hailey asked.

The relief stretched across her face as Saranon gave a short nod and sat down with all the contentment in the world. Her mind strayed to one thought, the other Angeon. A small scowl crept across the corner of her face. In reluctant acknowledgement of the tension that had grown since her last encounter.

As Hailey grabbed her hand it was a welcome distraction to wander through the outer parts of the ruined Keep. The small group fumbled through the old shell, as she was coaxed into pretending to be a grand sorcerer of years gone by. The sun drew low in the sky as their laughter grew and for a few wonderful hours Saranon let the events plaguing her mind float on the wind. A large thud jarred through the floor as Katholomu landed sideways plunging his claws deep into the wall of the building. He peered at Todd and Hailey with indifference, then leaned forward pushing his head through the open frame.

Before his hand reached over to grasp her, she dodged and climbed up. The dragon was satisfied by the response as he flexed his body, retreating to the outside. He swooped his great wings the full length with an enormous rustling sound against the windows. He heaved himself up into the sky. The enigmatic dragon climbed high into the clouds above. They weaved their way through the picturesque landscape. Katholomu snorted the air out of his nostrils with a stiff blast of hot air, melting droplets in the cold sharp air. His wings itched toward Espony and Saranon held him back, he let out a knowing grunt from deep within the bottom of his belly.

The sound echoed across the sky in stark retaliation. Before finally edging the tip of his wing and turning with a hard almighty swing toward the towers of Indarin. This time it was her turn to groan, as the dragon came into a sudden dive skidding across the open courtyard high above the ground. The dragon held up his claws as he spun around to a stop allowing the momentum to carry Saranon forward. By the time she brought herself to a halt and turned, the dragon stood in complete innocence, with no recognition of what he had done. Without missing a beat, her voice boomed across the open rooftop in a grating tone. Just then the dragon stepped aside revealing Ryan standing behind.

She was about to say something, but she was cut off at the pass with Ryan telling her to leave the courtyard. It took all her energy not to respond, as the haven that Indarin once offered, was fast vanishing at every step. She clenched her teeth before wrapping her energy around her and taking the fast way down melding through the floor. The passage calmed her thoughts until a familiar hand reached out. Larry pulled her over, 'Hello, when could you do that?'

The question felt strange as she had seen others meld through the building before. Larry pointed a finger up, 'That there is sorcerer's stone it's designed to keep people out.'

His words sank in as Saranon peered up at the underside of the courtyard, 'Oh!'

The sorcerer smiled and patted her on the shoulder before walking off with his tools in hand. It was a short but kind embrace, a small gesture of recognition in an otherwise empty room. As she sighed, she peered up and noticed a small leak in the ceiling near the corner of the room. It blended into the dark background. She paid it no more attention before rushing down stairs for a well-earned meal as her tummy grumbled. If there was one thing she hated being late for it was tea. She quickened her pace downward to the large hall and landed on the cold hard floor with such haste that it made a loud thud.

The sound repeated with another thud reverberating through the walls, this time she realised it was not her. The smell of warm potatoes wafted up with the vibrant cooking vapour, as if taunting her as she turned and made her way up. The noise came again flooding through the air with a harsh dull tone as a resonating silence followed. Reaching above into the open wind, Saranon called out as she was greeted with nothing. She popped her head around without a soul to be seen. The sorcerer's stone was carved and worn with age. As she strode across, she breathed and a small sigh of relief escaped from her cold lips, it burst into the sharp moist air. A similar sound echoed through the walls of time and space and she knew where she had to go.

In a glimpse of light sparkling in the haze she moved into a different phase, the only one she was familiar with. A step to the side stood her old friend out of sight, as she turned to face a dark figure leaning over Ryan's wounded figure. The picture made perfect sense as she charged ahead, blocking the figure with her energy. She ran forcing the person to fall back away from the sorcerer. The cloak disappeared and Gwen stood before her. The shock caught her off guard and a great ball of thundering energy catapulted toward her. Before she could retaliate, Tasha stood in front of her and absorbed the blow, Gwen attacked again with the same result.

She sent bolt after bolt disappearing the instant it hit Tasha, it soon became clear that Gwen was tiring and vanished in retreat. Tasha held out her hand for Saranon to grasp, 'This is for you.'

A shimmering glow spread as the energy transferred to her. It dissipated just as the Angeon shone underneath. She peered down at Ryan, before pulling him back out of the phase and into the path of confusion as the sky trembled with a familiar presence. No amount of hiding in the confines of the Keep was going to do now, as the sky clouded in the grey tones of a sorcery deep within.

The enriched energy built up in magnitude, filling the air with a metallic hue. Saranon remained silent, listening in the absence of sound. As a great wave weaved itself back across the sky and the shadows grew even longer. In the distance a low piercing noise carried across the wind, winding itself around the palms of her hands as she flinched. The recognition hurt her ears, as it drummed an age old tone, shaking the foundations of the Keep. One more time she listened, reaching out for the curves in the energy purging out from the source.

The glow intensified in her hands dispersing through the frame of her body as the Angeon became complete. In a terrifying instant an age old prophecy came to life before Ryan's eyes. Only in the tense rumbling, this was not a question Saranon had asked nor had anyone answered. For if there was one thing that she had known all along the future could be rewritten.

CHAPTER TWELVE

Far reaching wound

The dark haze whipped through the harsh cold wind blowing the hair from her face. Whichever way she scoured the landscape, one thought rang loud and clear. The Angeon was breaking through, a sea of turmoil spun in the sorcery spinning itself around the Keep. The tendrils reached out in a steady motion, as if searching for a source. Sweat shivered down Saranon's spine as her energy surged from within. Only this time it held strong inside her small figure. The energy filled in upon itself, at regular intervals, while staying away from the edge. The smooth silence within created a mirror image of the world outside. Before she knew it, a strange pattern of energy reached out and grabbed hold.

A crack of thunder etched across the clouds heading for Indarin. A great heavy boom reeked through the air, cutting off all sound in its wake. As it ploughed down into the earth, a long glistening arc soared up toward Saranon. She stood in the middle of the sorcerer's stone, held out her hands, as Tasha had done. She began absorbing the energy in massive volumes. For a brief moment it appeared as though the sky were fighting itself with the clouds whirling in ambiguity. In an instant, she held on tight and yanked the energy back out of the ground. She sucked it from the air, before condensing it down into the stone beneath her feet.

In the turmoil a great thunderous sound reverberated. Ripping apart the air, as the outer foundation of the Keep sheared under the pressure. In an instant an eastern tower cascaded down, crumbling in on itself with chunks of the tower flying at a hurtling pace. In the dust that cascaded up from the depths, the build-up of energy relented and Saranon let go. As her hold weakened, her energy boomed across the distance, clearing the sky in a great gust settling the way ahead. The air felt grimy, as the debris cleared, leaving a solemn tone stretching far into the ground. The dying embers of the sparks from Indarin wept over the damaged tower. She searched the sky, but found nothing. It was quiet relief as the calm fell over the land in stark contrast of what had been.

A thought plagued her mind and she rushed beneath the courtyard, as she left, Ryan gave her a stern solid stare saying nothing. The corridors were wild with activity as Saranon grimaced, it could only mean the Keep had suffered damage. She was hoping it did not extend to more than the outside tower. A small shallow blast ran through, knocking Larry over, as he soon scrambled to his feet. He caught site of her reaching out and pointed toward the source. She staggered a moment before pulling a face and stepping in. The fine spray from the hair line breaks, made a light colourful mist of the energy pouring through the Keep. It hung in mid-air applying itself to her clothes as she strode past.

A familiar sound clanked from up ahead, as she caught sight of Purton trying to meld a large break together. The enormity of the task daunted her, as she staggered through, trying not to upset the work that had already taken place. The sorcerer grumbled as he worked handing her a kedril, without losing pace Saranon glanced at its unusual shape. She was about to put it down when he pointed ahead of her. The way was dim but before she could ask Purton, he had moved out of sight. She shrugged her shoulders in annoyance without complaining. As she veered to one side sliding around several small creases, revealing fine breaks. Saranon stepped through the doorway and looked out.

The last remaining pieces hung out into nowhere, as the broken floor vanished into the space where the tower had been. 'Did you want to go out and take a look?' Purton asked behind her.

She glimpsed the open wound below and her stomach churned in an unkind response. She wavered as she leaned over and then an unexpected push from behind, jolted her out into mid-air. Her fall was softened by the pulsing of the energy below, as she found her balance and landed below ground level. As she looked above, Purton's unwavering laugh rang out as he yelled, 'I'll see you later.'

She was caught between a surge of frustration and complete surprise. She wanted to say something, but no words came forth. It was not the way Saranon imagined she would help the Keep. Stuck with a few small kedrils in her hand, peering down at it in disbelief, she wondered how it could be of any use. The debris had slammed the floors together down on the main foundation, that had taken the full force. Protecting the lower levels with dust scattered everywhere. Before moving around, she gathered her thoughts. She cleared the small particles away leaving a clear surface to work with. Tucking the kedrils behind her, she clambered down to assess the base of the foundations smoothing them over.

Indarin rarely saw damage on such a large scale. Yet the tower had been old and further removed from the inner sanctum, the luck had not escaped her. A shadow fell from the side as she peered in the last rays of light, Ryan stood like a calm solid form in the shattered background. The bandages showed in a small slither underneath his cloak. The sorcerer's silhouette dragged along the ground in cold isolation. Saranon braced herself for a stern response, that seemed to hang in the air in anticipation. 'Who is your friend?' He asked.

At first the question drove past her thoughts in surprise at what he meant. The shock written on her face as the bright lights of Indarin came to life.

She sat for moment stumped for words, before Ryan

filled in the silence. 'Very well, if you don't want to tell me.'

'Tasha died in Darkonia,' the words came flooding with a great sadness deep within.

She could see Ryan's expression as he tried to work it out, the sorcerer sat down beside her on the rubble before he spoke. 'You don't do things the easy way.'

Saranon looked around her and answered, 'No.'

The sorcerer stayed for a while before standing in the cold night air that whipped across his face. 'This will be here in the morning, make sure you get some sleep.' he hesitated then turned back, 'Darkonia is lucky to have you.'

She was not sure where his words came from; she had not felt that way in return about the country of her birth. The place had been farthest from her thoughts. As she cleaned up, ready for a late tea in a warm welcoming hall filled with a great many people, staying up late in the night. Mitch's hand reached out and patted her on the shoulder. As he pulled her aside, he still appeared larger than life in a crowded room. His simple shirt showed signs of the dust that had blasted through the Keep. 'I think Theron needs you now,' he whispered in a low tense voice.

Saranon was not about to argue with his stern face, it looked like his day had been as hard faring as hers. She scoffed the remains of her meal down as she nodded in gratitude. She hoped the Prophet's problem would be easier to resolve, than a collapsed tower. The halls appeared silent after the day's events, with the echo still filtering through her head. She darted through and took a step back, as a large man towered before her next to Theron. Armand stood with a straight hard stare, as her friend hung his head saying nothing. It was an awkward moment as a thought dawned on Saranon and she burst out laughing.

She grabbed Theron's arm, 'Come with me.' His reluctance held him back for a moment as she spoke, 'I am going to answer your question.'

'What?' He asked in surprise.

'The one you didn't ask,' she replied.

The Prophet in waiting, gave her a puzzled look, as he moved in a relieved motion out the door.

'Are you feeling all right?' Theron asked.

'So you want to know why you have difficulty seeing me in the future,' she remarked.

The sorcerer stopped and glared at her as he whispered, 'How did you know that?'

'Odana Temple,' she replied.

The Prophet pursed his lips in a state of partial frustration. He stood in silence contemplating the conversation. Saranon took hold of his hand, yet the sorcerer stood where he was. 'You wouldn't want to miss this for the world,' she spoke.

A tiny glimmer warmed in Theron's expression. As he let go of his staunch pose, he still wore a look of uncertainty, as she asked him to hold on. With a dry gust of air rushing over the tunnel's edge, she pulled him over before he had time to let go. The might of the Keep hauled them down at an intense pace, with the giant drone of Indarin echoing around them. Theron clung on so tight, she could feel her fingers going numb under the pressure.

The regular pulse of the central core vibrated through the walls. The energy increased in strength, as they hurled deeper into the Keep. The Prophet had his eyes closed in anticipation and Saranon smiled as the energy bore down on her, while she shielded him from the blow. As the tremors grew louder, she could feel the time for her old self fraying away at the edge. A glow shone through from beneath the surface, as the Angeon wrapped around her outer form, in the darkness. The Keep's energy surged toward her sealing the transformation in an intricate mould. It created a shallow buffer as they descended.

Small shards fractured off the opening in the central core before them. It pulled the two down with a renewed force, sealing the gap without a trace. Theron gasped in the absence of a steady gravity, as the central core whirred below. Before he had the chance to gather his senses, Saranon lead him down further. An opaque shape glowed in the hollow light, bouncing in a hazy glow. She was certain if it was anyone else that had been with her, the reaction would have been far from calm. As it was, Theron remained in a curious state of awed silence, glimpsing down at the object below. The object was held in a giant dark silhouette forking out of a magnetic whirl wind of static clouds, held in an eternal cycle.

The sorcerer reached out, placing his hand through the soft glowing mass, pulling out the object held inside. A giant rumble headed up the dark spine from below as the Angeon lifted the Prophet up. A hike in the energy spored towards them as Saranon catapulted the Prophet out of the central core, before it reached them. The impact drilled searing pain into her head as she held herself against the flow. She stayed for as long as she could, as she transmitted the energy back into the Keep so that it could heal itself. The glow burned bright beneath the ground intensifying in force. This time she stayed in the form of the Angeon, letting the energy of Indarin pass through.

As the central core increased its capacity, she waited in the darkness. She projected as much as she could, back into the Keep. The sensation washed over her, the Angeon recognised it. As she felt it surge through immersing herself in the transformation. She magnified the energy upward, rebuilding the fallen tower as she went. The Keep embraced her sorcery flowing above. The warm sensation of the glow magnified in completion. The full transformation of the Angeon wrapped completely around her soul. Saranon was no longer bound by the confines of the Keep, as she reached upward flowing in an internal glow. She broke past the surface in a fiery blast. The rip melded, healing itself behind her as she landed beside the Prophet in waiting.

The Angeon held out her hand and he held out his in return as he smiled. A voice cut through the courtyard in front of the new tower. As Armand and Ryan ran toward them, in an almost frantic panic, as they stopped short of the barrier around the pair. Saranon waited in the calm of the buffer, but for Armand it was too late, his son had already melded with the Angeon. A low tone rang out piercing the night sky as Indarin glimmered in the darkness. The dull noise pulsated through the walls of the Keep as it shimmered with delight around the two. It brought Indarin into perfect alignment with the Prophet. As the Angeon let go, ending the peaceful connection the glow of the Keep stayed resonating with the Prophet's energy.

Saranon relinquished her role, returning to her old self as she stood back. She almost tripped over Mitch who beckoned her away from the gathering crowd. He had the tiniest hint of a smile curving the edge of his lip, 'You don't do things by halves.'

She was about to reply, but he turned the other way. As they stepped into the dragon pens with the giant Katholomu curled up on a pile of blankets. The dragon watched through a shallow slit below his eyelid, as the magnitude of the night set upon her. Mitch leaned a shoulder to lean on, before she thudded on top of her untidy bed. He sat down as though waiting for something to happen, at the end of a long day, all Saranon's weary body wanted was to curl up and sleep.

The shadows played on the ceiling as her heavy eyelids closed. The peace was broken by a soft noise as the wizard left the room and she smiled in her sleep. The first light of morning streamed in through the curtain, far too early. She remained oblivious to the outside world. A faint shadow appeared to block the light, as she jumped at the sight of Theron waking her up. 'Father wants to see you,' the sorcerer spoke.

She took a while to focus, then shooed her friend out of the room, before tripping over in her haste to get ready, grumbling as she went. She rushed out of the room and almost ran straight into Armand standing tall. As she searched the space she caught sight of Mitch sitting down.

It was not the sort of greeting she had expected after such a tumultuous day, and Theron offered no clues. The daylight splayed across Armand's face. He spoke in a firm and rational manner with the weight of the past days showing beneath his eyes. An awkward silence hung in the air, as Saranon pieced together the meaning of the conversation. A loud gasp escaped her lips in recognition of reading the information that Odana had left her and Jedd had translated. The shock did not appear to catch on to the Prophet standing before her, as Theron watched on. As soon as Armand stopped, she let out a bold laugh, 'That is not what I was expecting.'

By the look on the sorcerer's face her reaction had not been expected either. Yet it did not matter, after all as Saranon smiled she saw the clear picture. Merrick had not progressed to this level and the Prophet had let her know. As she pondered the thought, she spoke clear and precise, 'Theron I think you need to let your father know.'

The room fell silent in the space that followed as Theron stepped back, 'I thought you knew.'

Before Armand had time to lose his calm expression, Mitch stood up, 'I think what Saranon meant to say is, she knows she can return home now.'

'What do you mean?' Armand stood back in confusion.

'I am complete,' was all that Saranon said.

'No, I didn't say that,' Armand still looked confused.

'I'm afraid you did.' Theron spoke, 'Odana told

Saranon the signs to look for and you confirmed it.'

'No,' Armand was still in disbelief as he shook his head, 'It takes years, you misunderstood.'

'I knew before you told me but I thank you for the confirmation,' she smiled.

Armand stared at Theron hoping for support. Yet Theron offered none, 'I told you, but instead you believed Braxton.'

This time it was Mitch's turn to speak. 'We will stay until the end of the term, that should give you more than enough time to sort out Indarin.'

Saranon could not help feeling empathy for Theron. Something had gone astray in the lines of communication. At the end of the day she had to remind herself she had only come all this way for one reason. Whatever problems lay at Indarin these would need to be dealt with by the Armythral.

As Armand realised he was in the middle of a losing argument. He gathered his composure and left her standing with Mitch close by her side. 'I can see why Captain Mirshendy feared you,' the wizard spoke.

'Are you serious?' She asked.

He did not answer her question. Instead he hesitated near the door, 'Make sure you have your bags packed, we may have to make a quick exit.'

Saranon did not doubt his words as they resonated in her head, he had been quiet at Indarin, but he was no fool as he kept out of the way.

The day was off to a strange start as she gathered her

thoughts for the evening lesson. She liked Anne and the idea of having to say goodbye hurt inside, as she closed her eyes before bounding out the door. The day still streamed down a bold ray of sunlight through a clear blue sky. The cool wind that whipped at her feet belied the hint of the last days of winter. She was pleased not to be in Serenphel long enough to experience a hot summer. Todd stood with a satisfactory smug look at having beaten everyone else to get ready. Saranon scrambled to catch up dropping her bond-breaker in her haste, as it sliced a third of the way into the rock beside her.

Todd shook his head at his friend, as he walked off to be the first to try firing his energy out in the open. They had practised many times before, but the Keep had always provided a mental wall of safety. She wondered if her friend would be so keen out in the open air. She clambered on a ledge over to the side with a good view along the valley below. Wedged between arrays of rocky hills, it was a perfect platform that showed years of solid use. A small gesture showed Todd's nerves under his thick outer edge, as he steadied himself with Anne waiting by his side. The first blast veered to the left catapulting off the rocky side before fizzing out in the middle in a plume of smoke.

Todd steadied himself with some reassuring words. The second blast hit straight with a high arch that landed short of the goal. Theron clambered up beside her as they cheered the sorcerer on, for his third try. The effect was massive this time, the blast shot low and hard. It managed a fair length of the valley before disintegrating in the distance. Todd stood back to a barrage of loud applause as Theron skimmed down to take his place. The Prophet stood solid and true with three impressive blasts across the valley, but none came close to Todd's final mark. Todd gave Saranon a gentle push down, 'It's your turn,' he said with a friendly smile.

She had been so caught up in the moment, that she forgot and hesitated before reaching Anne who was waiting. She steadied herself taking a deep breath, surveying the valley below. From where she stood, it appeared so much larger and she could feel her nerves creeping in. Saranon focused her mind on the open target, letting her strength gather and well up inside, until it began reaching out. The sound of her heart beat ached in her throat, as she opened her eyes and let go. The cataclysm pulled at the edges as the sound followed in the gap left behind. The blast seared both edges of the valley and flew straight to the end without losing speed.

In the silence that followed a solitary voice rang out, it was Theron shouting for her to do it all over again. She let the build-up continue, before letting it fly with ease and accuracy across the valley, two more times. One after the other, straight as an arrow, all three shots hit the end of the valley. The sound echoed outside the valley in a sweeping gust of intense energy, roaring through, ripping the air apart as it went. Saranon smiled in acknowledgement, if there was any doubt that the Angeon was whole this plummeted the idea deep into the abyss. This time the Angeon rose, as she flew above and catapulted one final blast, as proof of what she had become. The sound roared in agreement back across the valley.

It took a while before she returned to her old self. As half the population of Indarin had gathered to watch after the first boom shattered the peaceful sky. Theron rushed down to greet her as they walked back, the sorcerer could not wipe the smile off his face. This time Saranon let it go, she had done what she set out to do and in the short space of time she had grown. Even Todd was lapping up the excitement, he held his head high as the crowd parted, letting them through. Theron paused at the sight of Armand peering down from the balcony. She gave him a small nudge, as she whispered, 'He'll have to get used to handing the reigns over some time.'

Theron gave her a side-ways glance and spoke, 'I'm not ready.'

'You were ready before I came,' Saranon exclaimed in a loud voice that hurled above the breeze.

Todd laughed, 'I wouldn't argue with her she's the Angeon.'

The group stopped then laughed as Hailey met them for a well-earned hot meal in the large hall. As the sun set on a peculiar day, she could not help but wonder what had happened to Merrick. Not a word had been said and this only played on her mind as she dabbled in her tea.

If it were her she would not have given up, the burden plagued her mind as Hailey distracted her from her gloomy thoughts. It was the second time her friend had asked her to describe what it was like to blast raw energy across the valley, but she did not mind. Anne had helped relieve a great deal of stress from her shoulders. She gave Saranon the opportunity to announce to Indarin the magnitude of her ability. Anne's warm smile shone through, her teacher was always straight forward.

As they entered their apartment Hailey had an inquiring look on her face as if she had been holding something back. 'What did the note say?' She asked.

She knew what her friend meant as she unfolded the small note and handed it to her. 'Is that all?' Hailey exclaimed.

'You don't need to say much if you use the right words,' Saranon read it aloud, 'To the dark haired Angeon, look after my heir. Octavious.'

CHAPTER THIRTEEN

Time for dragons

The sun shone bright as the morning warmed and the air filled with a fresh breeze. It had been a long tiring week and she was readying herself for a weekend at Armeria. Kathomolu snorted near the window in agitation, making it appear as though he had been waiting for hours, instead of minutes. Hailey tapped and opened the door to the veranda, 'I don't think your dragon will wait much longer, unless you want to fly with me?'

'I'm coming,' Saranon shouted as she peered out at Kathomolu as he curled his head over the railing and she climbed on. 'I'll meet you there,' she shouted and they were off.

The dragon wasted no time launching full pelt into the sky as the breeze flowed underneath his wings. If she did not know better, she would have thought he was running away as Kat gathered speed along the way. It was just as well with the activity below as a great many dragons took to the sky in all directions from Indarin. The great Katholomu grunted his preference to stay far from the crowd. It dispersed into the air sending all manner of colourful dragons streaking across the morning sky. A small shadow broke free as Levette; Hailey's dragon skimmed, gaining speed. Saranon's dragon pretended not to notice the elegant lady as she flew overhead.

Jadaro lagged behind in comparison, the medium sized dragon not yet grown. The dragon was dwarfed in the experience and speed of the other two. She thought he and Todd were well suited, though she did not like to say so. They glided back and forth among each other in the crystal blue sky as the warmth of the day broke over the land. Katholomu edged ahead as he dived down, dragging his heals across the ground in a sudden halt, as he closed his great wings behind him. The dragon kicked sideways at the last minute and Saranon clung on with both hands, so as not to fall off. This last offering had become Kat's new trick as he took pleasure in catching her off guard.

Hailey had already landed as she walked over trying not to laugh. Katholomu curled himself up in a tight ball with his back absorbing the full rays of the bright sun. The three were glad to be back at Armeria with its timeless atmosphere and the waves crashing in the distance. The faint smell of sea spray wafted through the air filling their lungs. Seth greeted them as they ran through the old gates at the edge of the garden before Saranon stepped inside. A flash glimmered to life in the protective markers surrounding the garden. Before she could ask, Hailey had spoken and Seth fobbed it off. She stared at her friend sharing an uneasy look, then went inside.

The old Keep still worked well and hummed with an unusual vigour underneath her fingertips. She brushed them against the wall. Whatever it was, Hailey had also noticed the change through the place. For the moment she followed without saying a word as she kept a watchful eye. She caught up with Darren and Rory, the pair were at a peaceful ease, calming her suspicious mind, as the thought passed. Rasputen filled the courtyard with his giant frame as she stepped out. She had to negotiate her way around the dragon that was just as stubborn as hers. As Saranon moved too close she trod on his tail, the dragon arched his back in an unimpressed response.

The dragon remained unwilling to move, as Hailey and Todd found their way around the giant who flared up his mane. Seth tried to sooth his beast, as Rasputen half stood, his wound showed underneath. Hailey gasped in horror, 'What happened?'

Darren did his best to skirt around Hailey's bold stare without answering the question. It created an awkward impasse, before Seth asked the three to leave the courtyard to allow the dragon to rest. Before anyone could argue, her friend tugged at her sleeve and they dashed away from Seth and Darren.

The strange mood followed them through the Keep, clinging like a stain in the air as they went. Hailey showed signs of being unimpressed by the response, but neither was about to annoy Rasputen. Saranon followed her friend down to the cool shore's edge as the sun shone down. She peered back toward Armeria which shone in the warmth of the day. Whatever had bothered the Keep appeared to be far gone, she ran along as she realised she had been left behind. The wind blew deep off the water's surface, sending a chill down her spine. She looked back over the water and thought there had been something there, but no trace remained. She ran almost clambering into Hailey who stared down at the ground. Revealing massive scorch marks running parallel along the earth.

The scorched path continued off centre towards Armeria and disappeared without a trace near the Keep. The three stood in silence as Todd reached down rubbing his fingers in the charred dirt, while Hailey remained frozen to the spot. The thought made Saranon giddy as she stood on the spot where Seth and Rasputen had defended Armeria. Hailey ran home with a look that concerned her, as she ran after her. It did not take long for the shouting to start with Seth standing next to his wounded dragon. The outburst made her cringe and before she knew it, her friend had dragged her into the conversation. 'Tell Seth he just can't go around taking on an attack like that on his own,' Hailey spoke.

She could feel her face go red with embarrassment under the stern eye of her friend. Unfortunately Saranon knew it was not that simple and offered Hailey no relief, as her friend stormed off in a huff and Todd ran after her. She sighed and grumbled to herself as she stared at Rasputen bathing himself in the warmth of the sun. The sanctuary of the garden felt awkward with the large dragon curled up in a restless mood. He stiffened his claws scraping them along the ground in a grating tone, as he lowered his head further down. It was a peaceful moment, before Seth urged her away from the sleepy dragon. The sorcerer made no attempt to convey what had happened, other than the wounds on his dragon.

The silence hung in the air as Saranon passed through the narrow corridor. Up to where Hailey was searching through the draws of an over-sized desk. Before she had time to ask anything, Todd held some papers up behind her. Hailey reached over and snatched them from out of his hand with a satisfied smile, as she flicked it in her hand. Footsteps sounded from nearby and she jumped. While her friend stuffed the papers away and pretended not to notice, as they dashed out of the room. She caught site of Darren before they fled down the stairs via a second staircase. Hailey stopped to catch her breath in the open doorway as she glided through.

She grabbed Saranon's arm with a jolt and whispered with a sweet determination, 'Come on.'

As she peered up Todd had already raced ahead. She let out a small groan and ran after them while a hundred small thoughts flittered through her mind. Almost every one of them, ending in a place called trouble. Levette and Jadaro were easy to find. They played with Katholomu who relented to the two younger dragons chasing each other in the long grass. Hailey climbed on Levette beating Todd who had been given a head start.

Before Saranon had time to think Katholomu decided that he would close the distance. He lifted her up on his head and shoulders, while showing off with a long smile. The dragon flexed his head to reveal his sharp back teeth, before bunching himself up for a massive leap into the sky. The wind swept across her arms in an agitated tone as the sun warmed the air. The bright light shimmered across Katholomu's dark body, as he swept his wings to go higher. She found herself looking down upon her companions, as they sped inland. Hailey swooped ahead and down into the crux of the valley, Levette landing on the steep incline.

As Jadaro matched the daring manoeuvre his foot gave way on the ground and tumbled. She watched with a bubble of air caught in her throat. Todd managed to jump clear but the dragon tumbled further down the hill. He cascaded into a mass of greenery, flattening a path before diving into the undergrowth. A horrid sound roared up from below, bouncing off the rocky incline and echoing with a deep grumble through the entire valley. The sound swept away all of Saranon's thoughts in a heartbeat, all except one Ferridge, the dragon of the other Angeon. Jadaro's screaming echoed across far too clear in the still air. Katholomu had not yet landed as she looked on with a steady sinking feeling.

Todd made it to Levette, but as the dragon launched Ferridge lurched out of the depths with Merrick in clear view. Without so much as a prompt, Katholomu veered in sideways, locking his claws around Ferridge's. Bringing the dragon down hard with a mighty crash, as Levette needed no encouragement making a mad dash out of sight. Saranon braced herself as she struggled to get some distance between her and the fighting dragons. For a moment she lost sight of Merrick and a deep rumble flew above her head, hitting the rocky edge behind. She would have to leave Katholomu to fight his own battle, as she ducked half slipping down the slope.

A warm haze heated up the air as she made her way to the bottom of the valley in the distance. It became clear she had stumbled into so much more. As she stared across and into the bulk of a massive construction site, a thought rushed into her mind. The other Angeon had begun the early stages of building a central core. She did not have time to think, as a thundery bolt flashed across the sky. Leaving her only just enough space to block the hit, as it sent sparks cascading out from the impact. Saranon could see several figures in the distance rambling together and deep inside, her heart hit rock bottom.

She had come so far and she did not know what giving up meant, when there was no way back she would just have to move forward. The decision brought tears to her eyes as the reality meant facing another Angeon. She held her breath deep inside as she cried, she wanted to scream out as she stood on the verge of frustration. The air stemmed up around her as she took on her true form. The pure elegance of the Angeon long trapped inside her fell into perfection as the paths within her lay complete. She floated in the air with the sheer force of the energy holding her up as the attempts the other sorcerers made melted away from her being.

The energy spawned within searching far into the ground in the shallow edge of the deep ravine waiting for a new central core. Merrick responded with a cold hard bolt searing through the air. It exploded into a multitude of shards above the gaping hole in the depths as Saranon stood her ground. The fierce intensity of the energy below began to rise as Merrick pushed the massive force towards her from a great well of strength. The ferocity of the onslaught caught her off guard. As part of it trickled through at the edged sending a searing pain deep into her lungs. The sharp exchange sent shards of light and energy catapulting in all directions. In the tiny fragment of calmness that followed she held her grip.

In a moment between her breath and the solemn sound of her heartbeat she returned fire. The blast struck deep and hard cascading into the ground and across the land with a spray that cut so fine as the ash of charred dirt fell. The hole collapsed into a molten dark mass beneath her. As Merrick fled and any sign of other life soon disappeared in the panic to escape the rupture in Tordoren. The molten lava ran hot and fluent creeping into the deep cracks eating away at the valley. She sent a chilling surge deep into the earth pummelling down the rising disaster as it leaped to the surface.

The sheer pressure strained the edges of her being as the land shuddered with the competing forces. A last defiant rumbling tremor stretched across the depths and beyond the valley. As Saranon landed on the solid edge of the hillside looking down a familiar figure wandered over inspecting the site as he went. Theron had flown up to meet her dragon curled away from the damage. 'I don't think I need to tell you my father won't understand,' he spoke as he surveyed the valley.

'No,' she replied.

'Good then I won't,' the sorcerer gave a faint smile as they stared in awe.

She shook her head in disbelief. As Katholomu shook himself out of a large clearing and curled up beside her without any sign of his latest struggle. She dared to think how the other dragon had fared. As her eye perused the valley it focused on a sobering sight as the fallen clump of Jadaro's dead body peeked out from behind a clearing. She was not sure how Todd would react but then it had been inevitable. Katholomu leaned over his head and brushed it sideways against her. As a tear ran down her cheek but in her heart she knew it had all been too late.

The Prophet glanced out surveying the view before adding, 'You do know if you can break a Keep you can also make one.'

'Is that a hint?' She asked.

Theron laughed at her response and went to leave. 'Oh no, you're helping me with this one,' Saranon said.

Before the Prophet had time to respond, Seth landed with the wounded Rasputen and Darren with Colderay right beside him. The remaining four sorcerers in the group were quick to follow, as Seth glanced over the edge and into the remains of the valley below.

'Just a normal day really,' she said trying to make light of the situation.

Theron kept a straight face beside her, 'It's a good thing I didn't ask you to show off.'

She kept back a quiet laugh that ended up sounding more like a snort as the sorcerers surveyed the damage in silence. Darren kept a serious tone as he spoke first, 'Seth told the Eskardy, that he hoped their new Keep, would fall into oblivion.'

'That's the polite version,' Seth commented.

'Yes I know that,' Saranon spoke.

They gazed on in silence as Seth clasped his hands on his hips staring down at the mess, 'Is there anything left of him?'

'Who Merrick? I think Theron could answer that one better.'

'I would prefer not to,' the Prophet spoke.

'He's still around,' she said as she looked over to where the sorcerers had fled. 'So who's going to tell Todd about his dragon?'

'You can, in fact you can help clear this whole thing up,' Seth spoke in a disgruntled fashion.

'Seth!' Darren chimed in.

'No, if he's going to start an argument he can wear it,' Saranon spoke to Darren before she turned her attention square on Seth. 'If you had been honest with me, this would've been different.'

Theron broke in, 'She's right.'

'Thank you,' Saranon answered.

'But it would have been the same outcome,' the Prophet finished.

'Thank you,' she spoke a little louder and glared at him.

Seth changed the subject, 'I'll tell Todd about his dragon while you two sort out this mess.'

'Me?' The Prophet exclaimed wide-eyed.

Katholomu lifted his head and yawned at the commotion. As his empty stomach let out a loud growl, that reminded her it was teatime and the thought of food was too hard to resist. The dark sky blanketed the scars in the earth below, as they made their way back to Armeria after Theron had gone. The sticky sweat from her dragon saturated her clothes, as she clung on until they arrived to a quiet Keep.

The silence hung in the air like a dark cloud around her, before Seth broke the atmosphere, 'It's good to have you back.'

Darren smiled and then shook his head. They ventured inside the dim hallway with the warm smell of a large feast filling her nose with a deep breath. It was not until Saranon had entered the room proper, that a wide-eyed familiar face popped around the corner. Hailey gave her a big hug, filled with relief as she exhaled a breath full of tension and her shoulders finally relaxed. 'I'm sorry,' her friend whispered in her ear.

'Don't be, next time your brother should speak up,'

she exclaimed.

Hailey let out a soft laugh that took the edge off the silent vacuum in the room, 'That's a tall ask.'

It was with some delight that the two friends found ways of annoying Seth across the table. The turmoil of the day built up in Saranon's head. Her eyes grew tired and she tiptoed from the room as the hour grew late and her arms grew heavy. A few hollow sounds stemmed indoors through the gaps, but as her head hit the pillow, none of that seemed to matter. A hand crept across her vision in the morning light and she woke staring out at nothing. The image stayed with her as she bounded down the creaky stairs.

The murky start to the day as the clouds gathered outside, did not appeal to her mood. She entered the outer yard to find Katholomu in immaculate condition. He looked every bit the pure thoroughbred in his fearsome prime. As he arched his back casting a faint shadow on the ground as the wind picked up. She hauled herself up on his hard shoulders. As the dragon leaned down and bounded with magnificent force into the open sky. The clouds parted as though in anticipation, letting the great dragon pass. The immense scar did not take long to find heaving up from the ground below. No amount of denial could hide it as the sunken dirt revealed the cataclysm of destruction.

The broken, dying signs of an ambitious dream held up for all to see in a dismal embrace, as the ground still trembled in the eerie silence. A small gathering on the hilltop viewed the damage. As Saranon recognised Theron and brought Katholomu down close by. Not a word was spoken as she landed and met the group while Chilcott peered over the edge. 'You have an unusual way of doing things,' the sorcerer remarked.

As they watched, Levette brought Hailey down by their side, the smaller dragon was quite nimble and did not miss a step. 'Well, I think we have everyone here,' Chilcott spoke with a firm certainty in his voice.

Hailey stood surveying the scene, for the first time her mouth gaped in awe. It was greater than she had imagined, as she stepped behind Saranon not wanting to get too close. Chilcott did not appear to notice, as he held out a small glimmer of light, that shot out to stretch like a thin spider's web resting with great care over the valley. He motioned for Hailey and Theron to follow suit as each mesh crisscrossed and reinforced the last. The fine lines sparkled under a shady sky, holding under the soft breeze as a chill ran up her spine. She stepped forward feeling a small surge grow stronger. As the power stirred within, as if knowing the moment had arrived. Still she hung back waiting for Chilcott to prompt her as a moment of uncertainty swept over her mind.

The Angeon dived forward embracing the web and sending a massive surge melding the energy deep into the damaged ground. The sorcery removed the last signs of construction of the central core forming the earth as the energy saturated through. The last rays of sparkling light from the faint web disappeared as the great scar healed through the valley floor. A shallow mist rose up covering the surface of the valley as Chilcott looked on. The sorcerer gave a long worried gaze over the valley, before returning to his dragon. For a moment he hesitated and then thought better of it as he launched into the sky.

Hailey rushed up to her side, 'He knows something.'

'I think a lot of people have,' Saranon responded.

Hailey stared over at Theron, who was pretending not to notice, the Prophet remained calm in the light. Katholomu grew impatient, as he came over beckoning her as she replied. She climbed on his back before they flew into the grey sky. A cold shiver ran through her as she realised she had not seen Todd in the distance. Indarin grew larger as she made her way, swooping down to the dens. The pavement was scarce of dragons on what should have been a busy day.

Instead of stopping in the courtyard Katholomu veered his head in the dens. He angled his body inside the large opening taking care not to scrape his wings. As he did so, Mitch came out to greet them, holding up his hand to help her down, as she slid off the side of the dragon's shoulder. He looked as though he had not slept at all, but the shabby appearance suited his rough features. He whispered in her ear, 'The sooner we get back home the better.'

Saranon wanted to believe in that thought. Yet with Merrick still out there and without the beginnings of a new Keep, a sinking feeling made her doubtful.

In stark contrast the great halls of Indarin were filled to the brim with the usual hub of activity. The Keep showed no sign of the drastic events outside. She almost wanted to scream out in protest and instead settled for a small grumble as she sighed. The end of the term was fast approaching and she had so much to do before then, as she rushed off into the busy hallway. A small solemn figure sat in the apartment as Todd waited for her arrival, Saranon closed the door. His drawn face appeared pale in the afternoon sun, as it streamed through the large windows decorating the room. She could feel the space grow tiny as an awkward silence clung to her throat.

Todd smiled, though his eyes were filled with a deep sorrow, as the two embraced in a warm hug. The sorcerer steadied himself as he pulled himself together with a deep sigh. 'I've got another dragon, Hailey picked him out.'

She could not help a muffled laugh, if Hailey had anything to do with it the dragon would be built for speed. 'His name is Kadvere,' Todd stated.

The name sounded familiar, as a thought fled through Saranon's mind, it was good to see that he had another dragon to care for. Her friend was attached to the great beasts. With an insatiable love for flying whenever a spare moment presented itself.

CHAPTER FOURTEEN

Vision Eternal

The storm hit the Keep hard, as the rain wiped out any memory of what had been. Mitch stood like a dark silhouette peering out across the courtyard. As the smell of damp wet dragons wafted through the air, she realized the horrid smell was coming from Katholomu. The dragon had moved himself into a corner and no one was game enough to confront him. Mitch pretended not to notice until a voice echoed across the distance. Hailey's words cut through the air, 'Saranon, that dragon stinks!'

'I think you'd better clean him,' Mitch added.

She had been avoiding it because every time she had been about to clean Katholomu, he had gone out into the rain again.

The dragon eyed her with a knowing stare as she went up to him. His dirty grubby skin needed a wash. As she sighed in defeat and called him, for a moment she thought he would not move. At the last minute his tail lifted and he stretched, flexing the might of his muscles. As Kat strode over he flicked something heavy near Saranon, it clanged and rolled out of sight before she had a chance to see what it was. Mitch picked it up. 'You can look at it afterward,' he spoke as he wondered off, without giving any hints away.

She grumbled as she started scrubbing the dragon that was easy to bathe when he was in the mood, but it took longer due to his size. She watched as the miniature mountains of dirt came away from his feet and claws and wondered what the dragon had been doing. Katholomu always loved the feeling of being dry again. He purred with a loud rumble of satisfaction revealing his shiny teeth. The dragon wasted no time heading straight for the opening again, dashing outside as Saranon shouted after him. She stopped herself from going after him and stared at Mitch who smiled in return. 'Here, you might want to look at this,' he said smiling as the faint musty smell of wet dragon left the air.

She had almost forgotten how annoying Mitch could be, as she stared down at the remains of a seal, for which the image had no meaning. Now that the dragon had made himself scarce Saranon was left holding an awkward puzzle. The weather eased with a fine rain spraying through the opening with each gust of wind. She held the seal in her hands and she realised she had seen the pattern before. She fled down into the depths of the Keep, as the small lights lit up along the corridor penetrating the darkness.

She pursed her lips as a cold wash of anger fleeted through, scowling across her brow. Saranon kicked something small in the dim light as she made haste and swung back to see the small object tumble beside her.

The tiny object looked like a broken kedril, as she rolled it over in her hand she was about to fob it off. A small glint caught the corner of her eye, it was not the type of tool she was used to and she knew why. The path led to a few different tunnels which did not make much difference. She just needed to get down as she let herself slide through the floor. Falling down as she slipped, half catching the floor below. Before meeting the harsh familiar stare of two piercing yellow eyes lighting up the large room. The elegant ockren stood far too close, for comfort. She peered beyond it to the open door containing the other part of the seal.

The great magical beast created by the Keep itself, showed no shyness in the faint glimmering light. Saranon stood in a slow steady motion as she stared at the creature. It wrapped itself around as it brushed past with its skin tingling at the touch of her hand. It whipped its body round to face her at an angle, shining its eyes past her soul. The path to the door way was now clear, even though she hesitated with her heartbeat resounding in her throat, as she made small slow steps. Her fingers touched the edges of the frame and she yanked them back with the shock of pain. The charred remains of the blast still clung in the air with the seared end of the door showing.

The amount of energy spent for such a feat did not make sense. Then Saranon had to remind herself she had an unusual way of gaining access to the Keep, one that was not open to others. The seal, the remains of which she held clumped in her fist, would pose an obstacle for a majority of the sorcerers she had seen at Indarin. She stuck her head around the doorway and jumped in surprise, almost hitting her head on the frame, at the sight of Purton staring at her. 'Most people usually don't try and walk away from the prize,' the sorcerer said.

'Pardon?' She asked.

'Go look behind you,' he pointed.

Saranon gave him a puzzled look after staring out at nothing, behind the ockren, 'I don't…'

'Look harder,' Purton suggested.

She was beginning to get annoyed and fumed with a deep sigh let out underneath her breath. In stark contrast the ockren smiled baring its teeth. Purton pointed at the altar not straying far from the doorway. It took a moment for her to recognise it since it had been so long. Without hesitating she walked over to the altar running her hand along its edge. The image of Antavagon ran fresh in her mind as she took a step back.

A moment of silence hung in the air before she raised her hand to the open doorway. With all her might she used her energy to rebuild the door with a new seal sturdier than before. She took one small look admiring the new frame before she strode through the closed door. She appeared next to Purton who had been waiting on the other side. 'What did you do that for?' He asked as she appeared astonished.

'No good will come of anything behind that door,' Saranon spoke as she strode up the hall.

Purton was about to say something, but thought better of it changing his mind mid-way. 'There will be repercussions,' he spoke.

'Mm…' She was caught in thought as she turned to face him.

At that moment a flurry of activity fell through from above as several sorcerers, including Braxton, rushed past. They started with a barrage of verbal grievances at the sight of the sealed door. The only words Saranon waited to hear, were the assumption that the Keep had foiled their efforts before leaving. Purton's mouth dropped in silence as he followed, saying nothing. Waiting until they were well clear of the commotion.

'Are you going to tell them?' He asked.

'There is no difference between me and the Keep unless you want to?' She eyed him.

He backed away from the question as he whispered, 'You really are playing with fire.'

'Is that warning meant for me or them?' Saranon spoke, as she left Purton with that thought.

The recognition of the altar stirred back a range of vengeful feelings creasing though her skin and shaping her brow. It was a sight she had blocked, out to such a point, that she had only just noticed the altar's existence.

A myriad of tones from the past, flashed over, her making her mood even darker than before, as a fork of lightning boomed across the open sky. A thought entered her mind and she knew where she had to go. Her old friend Tasha would be waiting in the place between time and space. The one person she trusted more than anything. Tasha had seen the altar before the one that linked the phases, but that path was not one she chose to venture, she would have to find another way. She darted into her apartment making a mess, while trying to find one thing. Corsavere, the bond-breaker was easy to lose track of.

She had not worn it for ages. As she looked up, Hailey peered at the mess and moved a clump of clothes, revealing the smooth dagger still hiding in its sheath. Hailey's words hit hard as she spoke to them, 'I'm coming with you.' Her friend continued, 'This isn't just about you.'

Saranon felt as though she had missed the first part of the conversation, as she stood in bewilderment at the statement. Todd peered around the corner, 'I'd like to say the same but I think I'll leave this one alone.'

'Theron said you mended the seal,' Hailey explained.

'Theron talks too much,' she grumbled aloud.

She was not so sure about having company, but Hailey was not about to give in and Saranon knew she would need help. She handed her friend Tellembre, the bond-breaker was well designed and easy to use. A smile lit up her friend's face in acknowledgement, if anything went wrong Hailey would need to defend herself. A sad thought, which did not let go as she tried to shake it off. The shadows grew deeper, as the light faded with the culmination of clouds sweeping up what was left of the delicate blue sky.

They rushed off to find a weakness in the frame of

light shrouding the Keep in a fruitless task. As the light outside gave way to the genuine darkness of night. As the last glimpses of sun shot through the sky splaying across the open floor of a narrow corridor, a tiny glint sparkled. Saranon held on, dragging it to her holding her breath in excitement and with a small nudge a door way opened. Before she could speak Hailey had rushed forward, gone in an instant with her following close behind. A shear shrill met her ears, through a stifled strain, as the phase settled itself with two new occupants. She could see Hailey up ahead as far as the eye could see, they were the only two people here.

She moved down towards the seal, to be certain it held just as well in this place. Her friend followed with her hand near the hilt of Tellembre in anticipation. The eagerness glinted in the corner of her eyes as she walked on. As she approached the seal in the dismal silence, she held out her hand and touched it, the binding held strong as she sensed it. The look on Hailey's face was clear disappointment, as they searched around finding nothing. She stayed a while managing to convince herself that they had done enough. While feeling as though there was something left undone. As they made their way back, it was far easier to break out of the phase, with a breath of relief as they stood in the real world.

A sharp pain stretched across Saranon's vision as it slammed into her body. Hailey wasted no time making ground to hurl Tellembre in full display. Hailey struck the blade hard up against the might of Braxton's bond-breaker.

The effort gave her a moment to steady herself, at the sight of what had just happened, taking it in with every breath. As she gazed into the background, she saw what she was looking for, as Tasha drew her finger with such smoothness under her chin and pointed. Saranon knew what her old friend wanted her to do and she raised Corsavere drawn in the form of a sword and brought it down. In the last instance Braxton twisted and braced himself. He held his bond-breaker against the steady force.

For a moment they were interlocked as Hailey's screams cut deep through the air, she clung on in a cold grip. Her eyes were cold with the knowledge that the sorcerer would not live. She arched her arm under, in an all mighty swing and the blade hit true underneath as Braxton's body fell to the ground in a still motion. His robes covered the wound as he went. The shock reverberated up her spine as she let the sensation pass over her and let the bond-breaker down. Ryan came rushing to watch the last of the devastating scene, as he covered the body and stared in shock at Saranon. She did not flounder under the strain of his eyes, as no amount of pressure would have prevented the inevitable.

She clung to her bond-breaker as the sparks of heat from the clash of sorcery simmered in the air, the embers fading to the floor. If it was not for Hailey standing between them she would not have been so calm in the failing light of the evening. Ryan glared at her before turning away; it was a hollow defeat which she knew remained unresolved. The energy inside her settled as the immediate danger, now lay in a heap on the floor. She could not help but wonder who else had been involved. She did not expect such a blast of the seal to be done by Braxton alone. The thought weighed heavy on her mood as she retreated to the sanctuary of her small apartment, with Hailey staying close to her side.

A rattle ran across the window making Hailey freeze to the spot, as a familiar voice soaked through the wall. 'Well, are you going to let me in?' Mitch wasted no time summing up what he saw.

Saranon's bond-breaker filled the narrow coffee table in its full sword length. He picked it up admiring Corsavere's blade with a keen eye. He gave no inclination of relinquishing the prize as he looked up at her. 'I haven't seen it close up since you've always hidden it away,' he exclaimed.

Leaning over to take Tellembre as Hailey stood back in a silent response. Her friend handed the bond-breaker back. It appeared small in its dormant form as Mitch eyed the second prize in Saranon's hand. He swapped the bond-breakers over as she placed Corsavere away. Mitch held the bond-breaker for a while. Before asking the question that had been plaguing his mind, 'Which one did you use at Antavagon?'

'Neither, Pennie has one and Clara has the other.'

He smiled as Hailey spoke first, 'You made others?'

'I don't know what Ryan was more concerned about, you or the bond-breakers?' Mitch interjected.

Both sorceresses looked puzzled. 'Why would he be so interested in them?' She asked.

'Because he can't make them,' he replied.

Hailey stared in disbelief as the thought crossed her mind. Ryan was powerful and the inability to make a bond-breaker would not go unnoticed. Saranon was not convinced, but Mitch did have a point, Ryan had been staring at the bond-breaker and not her. She did not feel at all like settling for the night. As Mitch strode with her through the corridors, he had his own bond-breaker which he wore at his side. The dull brown glint and rough edges belied a sturdy blade, she was not so keen to parade hers about.

There was one place she wanted to revisit, a place where she could let her thoughts run free. Mitch had spoken of a memory she had kept silent deep inside. One she still struggled with, as she reached the door grabbing his hand as she went. The place was as she had left it, the eastern tower which had been rebuilt. It felt smooth and cold to the touch as she knelt down in the courtyard remembering Tasha, as she had seen her friend last. She could feel the anger build up as the memory of blood staining the floor welled up inside. Mitch placed a comforting hand on her shoulder. It was not a perfect night as the faint drizzle and grey clouds blocked out the clear moonlight.

Random patches broke through the sky as the wind whistled past enveloping her warm cloak. It did not take long for a call to carry thick across the breezy air with a harmony that rang true. Saranon broke from her silent stare and turned upward to face Ryan across the courtyard. The sorcerer stood tall with a firm determination as he faced her in the cold night air. The only sound came from the external draft wrapping itself around the tower as the two met in silence. Mitch stood close by, in a reassuring stance, not far from her side. The cold wind divided them as Ryan spoke, 'You have no idea what you've done.'

She stood a moment, before answering. She was in no rush as the words left her cold lips, 'Protecting the Keep, which is what you should have done.'

The sorcerer glared at her and was about to say something. As Saranon interrupted, 'The Armythral have allowed their own to harm the Keep far more than Merrick could. There is no reason you can give to justify those actions, none. So do not stand there and tell me otherwise. I have seen the results first hand, with the death of my friend Tasha, whose spirit still walks Tordoren. The seal remains.'

Her chest heaved with the strength of her words as they resonated through the air. She was prepared to fight even if it was not what she wanted. A figure grew out of the shadows not far from where they stood, as Anne slipped away, the hood of her cloak fell as the wind caught the edge of the material. The older sorceress stood between the two facing Ryan as she spoke, 'You knew there would be consequences now let Saranon be.'

Ryan could see he was getting nowhere and with one last hesitation he left into the grey dark night. It took her a moment to recover from the encounter and calm the flow of the fiery sensation inside.

The energy continued burning strong as she turned to

meet Anne's sorrowful eyes gleaming in the darkness. The wind whipped across the surface of the ground. The older sorceress faced her and sighed with a deep and meaningful purpose, before suggesting they go inside. The walls of Indarin hummed with a quiet satisfaction. The lights beamed overhead as she strode onward. Mitch fell in place by her side as her mind ran with a torrent of dark images from the depths of her past. The seal had been broken in the Keep. It did not feel like Saranon had seen the last of the turmoil that had encapsulated Indarin. The mood scowled a crease across her brow, as it darkened her frame of mind.

Her pace quickened with a sharp edge as she headed closer to Theron's quarters, the sorcerer sat resting as she entered. It took a moment for her to realise they had been expected, the thought annoyed her as she gazed at her friend. Mitch found an excuse to leave and she envied his ability to fade into the distance. The skill escaped her the more she tried, though it had not stopped her trying. The Prophet asked, 'Is there something you want to know?'

'No,' she replied.

He appeared astonished at her response before she continued, 'I know where this is going to lead.'

Before Theron had time to answer after his bewildered look, she interjected again, 'I think you're in danger.'

'I know,' he said.

Saranon was not satisfied by such a quick response. For a Prophet Theron had a habit of jumping to conclusions, which frustrated her, as much as it reminded her of herself.

There had been a time when she would have let that be without a response, but the memory of Tasha lay thick upon her mind.

She grumbled to herself when she realised that the Prophet would not budge. She swept out of the room and marched down the hall. In her haste she had left her coat behind and muttered under her breath before turning back. The small oversight was the last thing she needed at the end of a long and arduous day. Without thinking twice she slammed the door backward almost taking it off its hinges. A hard dull thud sounded instead of the deep whack of wood on wood. She swung Corsavere out in an easy grace far too quick as it came within a hairs breadth of Ryan's nose. The blade flashed in front of his horrified look as he stepped backward.

The sorcerer regained his composure and half threw Saranon's coat at her, 'Leave.'

'I think you misunderstood,' she placed her coat back on the chair. 'This is my place.'

Theron who had waited without saying a word spoke up, 'This is her place.'

Ryan looked at her and then at Theron with a cold gaze. He left without uttering a word with the other sorcerers in the room. In the silence that followed the Prophet spoke first, 'Nice blade.'

'I think so,' she said in an inquisitive tone with a question trapped at the end of her tongue.

It was not the first time the Prophet had neglected to mention the current situation as she grumbled to herself in deep thought. 'You realise you will be expected to stay the night,' Theron spoke.

Saranon had no time for mind games, but there had been something going on and she was intent on finding out more. She eyed the Prophet as he proceeded to prepare a spare bed for her, 'You can be inconvenient sometimes.' She commented.

'Really,' Theron answered in an amused tone. 'I thought you wanted to visit?'

The idea had crossed her mind, but the Prophet tended be get on her nerves after a while, as she gave him an annoyed stare in response.

'Is this your way of saying you're scared?' She asked.

Theron returned her annoyed look, as he threw a pillow in her direction. She had more than enough to worry about. Yet wherever she went, somehow she ended back at the same point, with the Prophet at the centre. 'What do you know about Ryan?'

The sorcerer went silent, 'I thought you were not going to ask that.'

Saranon corrected herself, 'I meant you know him, not everything is about what you see.'

Theron looked a little hurt. For all his secrecy he prided himself on his ability and the sorcerer made a point of not wanting to be interrupted by glimpses of the future. Her friend sat and spoke in a reminiscent tone. She listened while checking over her bond-breakers and belongings with small relief. Ryan sounded as much ordinary as any powerful sorcerer could be, in a place like Indarin. Theron gazed into the rays of light beaming through Corsavere, 'Your father carries a blade like that.'

'I thought I said… Oh never mind,' she grumbled.

She only had vague memories of her family and with a common surname she had not had the best of luck finding any leads, even with Pennie's help. She handed over the bond-breaker for Theron to have a closer look. He appeared to want to say more, but instead kept it to himself. Saranon began to wonder if she could keep from clouting him over the head, if he continued to pull irritable faces. He hinted at something then changing his mind. She sat making herself comfortable on the chair opposite. The Prophet handled the elegant bond-breaker.

He stared at her with a quiet gaze, 'What was Odana Temple like?'

'Magnificent,' she exclaimed.

'You do know, Odana never fell,' Theron spoke referring back to the days of the Dreshan Occupation.

It took her a moment to realise what he was saying. If Odana Temple had withstood the invasion, it held an unbroken history of Zyanthia, including the Angeon.

CHAPTER FIFTEEN

Final Hurdle

A tiny thought entered Saranon's mind as she hurried down to the dragon pens. The morning was cool and brisk running goose bumps along her skin. Katholomu was panning his tummy to the first rays of light breaking through and warming the hard surface of the courtyard. She sat close to his warm thick skin as the dragon purred away. His belly rumbled with a low deep sound, reverberating through her hand as she stroked him. She fumbled around until her hand touched the circular talik. Thanks to her friend Jedd she had been able to make a slow and steady start on reading the information it stored. Odana Temple, the great Keep at the centre of the old Zyanthia had transferred portions of what it knew. Now in the grasp of her hands it seemed even more real.

If there was no need to search any farther than what

she had, then in theory the small device held the key to the door that she had been looking for. Saranon closed her eyes in excitement, which she held back. For what she had already read did not make sense and the Keep was not human, the way it saw events would not be the same as she. Katholomu pulled his head around on his long arching neck, rubbing his ear on her back. He poked an eye around staring and pretending not to notice. The dragon flopped sideways curling his tail around in front of his mouth in a sleepy stretch. Unfortunately the more she searched, the less she found, which gave any hint about why there would be two Angeons.

She thumped her hand up against the dragon in irritation and he gave a short grunt of annoyance. At least for now Saranon would have to concede that the world had granted two Angeons. The thought did not rest easy, even though part of her liked the idea of not having to be alone. The sky fast reached the middle of the morning, when a voice stretched across the open air. 'There you are, I thought I'd find you here,' Hailey spoke as she grabbed hold of Saranon's hand.

Her friend showed little fear around the large marmoz dragon as she patted his long nose, Kat moved his head.

They rushed in just before the class started. An air of anxiousness continued to cling around her as the dust settled with Braxton's death. Her friend Hailey had been taking the liberty of helping to fill in the gaps in the short space of time thereafter. Still it did not rest easy on her mind and dragging a friend into an old score linked to her past, was not the most comforting sensation. She had seen the fallout in her past and was not convinced her friend knew the type of consequences involved. She managed a meek smile as Hailey caught her looking her way. For his part Chilcott remained completely focused on the task at hand.

After a brief moment she did the same, either way the quickest way to end the mess would be to finish her lessons. A small spark flicked across her desk as she looked up to Hailey's smiling face. She sighed to herself as the class finished and a familiar tone rang out just as she was a step away from reaching the door. 'Saranon we need to talk,' Chilcott could make the simple sentence send a chill down her spine.

He was like a gentle giant lying dormant and no one had the nerve to annoy him because he had the ability to back up a threat. She tried her best to appear at ease in his presence, but the attempt required some effort which showed on her face.

'Mitchell tells me you dealt with a similar matter in Darkonia,' Chilcott spoke while tapping his pen on the desk.

Saranon was not used to anyone calling the wizard by his full name. She was even more surprised that he had taken the time to speak with Mitch. All she could manage in return was a blank expression. The subject was one that she kept hidden deep within her mind. Chilcott continued, 'If you wave that bond-breaker near me you had better have a good reason.'

'Yes,' she spoke with an exasperated shrug as she stood up.

'There were other ways to deal with Braxton,' he said as he eyed her.

She stopped, placing one hand on the desk. While peering down at the old scar that creased along Chilcott's arm only just poking out of the edge of his sleeve. 'I wish there was but I think you know that,' Saranon spoke as she left.

The conversation had placed her in a rather foul mood as she stormed off without hesitation. The lack of seriousness conveyed to the broken seal brought an old anger from deep inside. The memory of Tasha had haunted her dreams. Chilcott was a sorcerer who could take care of himself. Still she wondered if he knew the depths of the darkness which lay hidden in a foolish desire.

Hailey beckoned her out of her momentary pause with the memory fading, as they headed for the dragon pens. Her friend grasped Levette, her beautiful rozzen dragon, as she made her way onto her shoulders. It was a temporary sweet relief that Saranon allowed herself to be drawn into, as she climbed onto Katholomu and they swept past the old courtyard. Her dragon knocked several garden tools before launching high into the air. She cringed as a few faint shouts followed in the wind. Kat was not one for delicacy although it was more for display to show off his enormous size. She let out an all too familiar sigh as they flew across the sky.

In the distance Colderay and Rasputen flew with pure

elegance. Holding their riders high as Hailey waved to her older brother. Katholomu saw it as a signal to show off and immediately flew close to Rasputen as the dragon growled and snapped at Kat's wings. Saranon just managed to stop Kat from taunting the other dragon again, as they flew within a tight formation. She continued to struggle as Seth shouted out for her to hold on. As she was almost ready to take her dragon down, he settled as though nothing had happened. They glided a moment before coming to rest down in the valley. The damage still showing in creases along the ground, the only remnants left from where Merrick had been.

Darren landed Colderay much closer than Saranon would have liked, as the sorcerers showed no fear from what lay beneath. Hailey stayed near the edge with Saranon who had no desire to be nearer. The memory had been set aside after the discovery of the broken seal which continued to plague her mind. It filled her dreams with a misty darkness. A small section of the ground crumbled under Darren's foot and Hailey jumped where she stood. The sorcerer stumbled before regaining his balance on the uneven earth. 'What will happen when Merrick returns?' Hailey asked.

Her mind was far away, the thought had not been her main concern and the question drew her into a different direction.

'I don't think the Armythral are ready for him,' she spoke with deep honesty.

Her friend responded with a knowing silence. It was the answer Hailey did not want to hear, the unspoken fear that had spread through Indarin. She figured it had been there long before she had arrived, if Chilcott's scar was anything to go by. What seemed like a pile of rubble and dirt held Seth and Darren's attention for a long time. Although the sorcerers refrained from asking questions, their glancing eyes spoke otherwise. Saranon stood near the edge. The dragons were in a world of their own as they exchanged snorts and grunts before appearing silent.

A jarring sound cut through the air. Katholomu sent Colderay shoulder first into the rocky hillside, followed by a horrid screech. She scrambled onto Kat's shoulders climbing over his left wing and holding on as hard as she could. She jolted the dragon sideways with her movement and clung on tight as a shallow scratch mark appeared on his right arm. For all his temper Katholomu was reluctant to lift a finger unless taunted. Colderay nursed a massive bruise down his left side before scampering backward. Her dragon raised his chest in triumph and let out a deep growl of satisfaction. She clung on gripping the mane around his neck.

Seth and Darren wasted no time darting along the rugged ground to help calm the giant dragons as Katholomu gave them both a stern stare. The slitted eyes of the great dragon shone through in a menacing tone. He let out a muffled grumbling that bellowed through the harsh cold wind. Before another word was uttered, Hailey had taken Levette into the air and away from the disgruntled male dragons. Darren showed great ease in calming Colderay down. In an all too familiar manner which suggested this had happened before. Katholomu sat letting the chilly air run through his thick coat cooling his sweaty skin.

Saranon dreaded the thought of having to wash him again. She wondered if it would have been simpler to have a female dragon that had an aversion to rolling in the dirt. Just as the idea entered her mind, Kat wiped his sweaty shoulders along the ground. He gave little time for her to change sides. She let out a small grumble which went completely unnoticed. As the great smelly dragon now covered in patches of dirt launched into the air and headed toward the dragon pens of Indarin. Katholomu stopped in the courtyard, flopped out his legs, and bent his head over. He drifted straight to sleep as she tried to nudge him awake. She did not want to leave him all dirty and smelly, but the dragon had relaxed giving all his weight to stay in place.

A small crowd of wizards watched, hovering around the doorway of the pens. Saranon gave in as she left the smelly snoring heap of a sleeping dragon to clean up. Mitch stood near her as she rinsed her hands, 'You do realise you're going to have to clean that in the morning.'

She gave him an annoyed stare, 'Yes, why, are you volunteering?'

He did not look impressed, 'It's your dragon. How are you going?' He asked.

The question seemed odd after everything that had happened. 'Normisia is looking really good right now,' she replied.

He smiled, 'I wouldn't bet on that.'

Mitch had a way of saying a great deal with few words, the eagerness to return to his home land shone in his eyes. It was the only sign he displayed as he left her alone. The warmth of the large dining room shone bright, it was nowhere near the size of the great hall. Yet, what it lacked in grandeur, it made up for with a welcoming atmosphere and a view that spanned out over the resting dragons. The last rays of the fading light melted with the glowing lights to create a vibrant glow as Saranon ate after a long day.

She waded through the flowing corridors to find herself at the front door of her apartment. As she opened the door Todd opened it from the other side. He shuffled her into the room, 'Have you seen Hailey?'

'Not since this afternoon,' she replied.

'She left a strange message with Seth and he hasn't been able to find her.'

Saranon woke from her tiredness with a start as she realised Hailey could have been missing for hours, 'I have to go.'

The thought crept in and once it was there she was unable to shake it. Hailey would be ideal for the one thing that the Armythral had allowed to go too far. She ran then with a mighty leap transformed as she fell through the floor of the Keep, dropping several levels as she went. She slowed to a halt just missing an ockren, as she fell into the darkness underneath the great Keep. The course hairs of the creature rippled across her skin in an unnatural motion. As she peered around the seal was still intact, but the eyes in the ockren spoke of unease. The Angeon searched, finding almost no sign running her fingers over the wall and then a faint murmur tingled through to her spine. A hole had been blasted through the wall hidden by layers of sorcery.

She traced her way back to the sealed door. The one sealed by the Angeon which she could pass through, just as she took the first step, a weight tugged at her jacket. Saranon turned to see the ockren pulling her back and pointing its head in another direction. A part of her knew the ockren was right, whoever was in there would know that she could walk through the sealed door. She drew Corsavere, taking it from its sheath, as she closed her eyes, drawn in the depth of the memories that lay just beneath the surface. In full flight she swung herself through the wall, as it faded around her with ease. The bond-breaker rose without hesitation, as she drew Tellembre from its hiding place.

Two sorcerers fell, hitting the floor in unison, as the sparks began to unravel. An all too familiar scream cut through the air followed by the next. The Angeon moved on, without as much as a glance toward Hailey screaming at the sight of her own blood. As the last sorcerer hit the ground, the Keep moved like a living being pulling the remains through the floor. No sign was left except Hailey and the Angeon. Saranon hid her bond-breakers before kneeling down to embrace her friend. She allowed her sorcery to weave its way through. Healing both Hailey and the Keep and she wiped away the last signs of blood from her friend's hands.

In the calmness that followed, a sound crept in from

outside. She stayed silent as voices raised shouting through the still air. To her surprise the Keep refused to let anyone in as Hailey gathered her composure her face belied the fear in her eyes. A shattering motion broke through the wall. The sorcery from outside found its mark in the damaged wall breaking through the Keeps defences. Indarin howled in anguished pain at the intrusion. Its voice no longer silent, as Chilcott came face to face with Hailey and Saranon. The fierce look in his eyes said he was in no mood to be messed with, as he examined the room and a few small remnants left behind.

Before the sorcerer had time to say anything Seth managed to break through with desperation. As he hugged Hailey in his arms and she began to cry. Darren moved a little slower behind him gazing over the sight and taking every care to help Hailey as she left with Seth. A small movement caught Saranon's eye along near the altar. The Keep was beginning to retaliate against the intrusion. 'Go, go now!' She shouted to Chilcott and Darren, 'Just go!'

The older sorcerer took a moment to react, as Saranon looked him in the eye, 'It is not your time to die.'

He was about to say something as she cut him off, 'I will see you again.'

Just as the two sorcerers left, the surge of energy from the Keep reacted to the intrusion like a virus spread around the altar. It hesitated then spread through the whole room. Then it reached the Angeon and she hoped that she was right as she held her breath. The energy spread through her joining her with the Keep, but then she had met the Keep before. In the exchange of the raw energy surging between her and the Keep, the pulse cut through. It disintegrated the last remnants of the ill-fated attempt to take over the Keep.

Indarin's anger spilled forward as it sealed the room anew. The Keep hurled the Angeon out before the last part of the ceiling hardened with a new seal. The thrust catapulted her back to just outside her apartment. The Angeon slipped away and a familiar voice carried across the corridor. It was then that she remembered Chilcott had an apartment close by, as the sorcerer's firm, still voice cut through the air. Saranon turned around to see the early rays of the morning sun shining through the window. 'I said are you coming to class?' The sorcerer repeated.

She took a moment to realise her perception of time had been distorted. As she followed Chilcott spoke in a straight tone, 'We missed you in class yesterday.'

'What?' She gasped as her teacher smiled.

She ran to catch up as the sorcerer strode on and stopped as she noticed Hailey sitting at her desk. As she sat down her friend leaned over and whispered, 'You've been gone three days.'

Saranon grumbled at the thought, it was not what she had expected. The time lag made sense as Indarin reeled at a repeat performance. The Keep had showed little sign of its deep seated anger at the betrayal of a hand full of Armythral. The intense ferocity of its determination belied its mood. Three days lost meant Indarin had made the seal well and it would only take a short time before reality sank in and someone noticed.

Part of her could not wait for the class to finish, as she rolled the pen over in her fingers. The agitation showed plain on her face, as Hailey smiled in recognition. On another occasion her friend would have laughed. Yet the jovial mood had slipped away from her eyes replaced with a quiet sadness. A rush of stomping came from behind the door as Ryan slammed it open, staring straight at her. 'You!' He shouted.

An immediate reply sprang into Saranon's mind. She remained tight lipped at the sight of the exasperated sorcerer. Before he had a chance to step much closer Chilcott grabbed his arm from behind and yanked him back.

Ryan swung at his opponent as the class fell away, trying to avoid the fight, Chilcott managed to pin the sorcerer down. Hailey made for the door after the other students and motioned for Saranon to follow. As Chilcott shouted for her to stay she shot him an irritated glare. Before the sorcerer could say anything she spoke, 'You seem to be doing that a lot lately.'

He looked up as the two men broke up their arguing, neither one appearing a winner, 'Yes.'

Ryan steadied himself as he realised he had chosen the wrong time and place to take out his frustrations.

It was not the ideal meeting place but she knew that with Chilcott there, it would be safe. The underlying tone of Ryan's voice cut through the air, 'You planned to seal off the altar.'

'Indarin planned to seal it off, are you going to go after her?' Saranon added after a moment's silence, 'I would have done the same.'

She was about to say more, as a scream resonated behind the closed door. The sound curled down her spine as she recognised who it had originated from. Chilcott allowed her to pass unheeded, as the sight caught her off guard.

Sandra, a solitary figure, held Hailey close to her blade. The bond-breaker was raised within a finger's width of her pale, white skin. The Angeon reached up inside and the dagger flew, like metal attracted to a strong magnet, across the void. Sandra stood in shock, before she scrambled out of sight and her friend fell in an exhausted heap, before Seth ran to pick her up. Saranon held out her free hand to Ryan, 'Come with me.'

To her surprise the sorcerer did not hesitate as they slipped out of phase with the real world. Out in the courtyard a lone figure wrapped in silken white stood in silence. Tasha's beautiful warm hair flowing around her face, the figure did not move. 'This is the result of the Arthrose, it will wound your Keep more than my mirror image can,' Saranon continued.

She held up her hand reaching out to Tasha's hand as her old friend did the same. They clasped hands as Saranon added, 'This is not what the Arthrose had planned.'

As she spoke the words, Tasha combined her energy with the Angeon. The strength of the meld rippled out as the Keep responded in kind and they returned leaving

Tasha behind. The energy still pierced the air and the sound of Indarin rang through the air. Saranon spoke, 'This path is not for you.'

She relinquished the Angeon and the Keep settled, as its hum blurred into the background. Ryan stood quiet, before Chilcott swept him to the side with a friendly seamless motion of his arm. He left her in a mist full of cloudy dreams, merging into the edges. It was not the response she had been looking for. Yet, at least the sorcerer had taken it in, a small consolation as she trudged to the small apartment. The door opened as her hand reached out and Seth's face appeared, with a weary look, similar to her own. His presence gave her a start, even though she half expected to see the sorcerer. Saranon glanced around for her friend, who had gone to sleep. Darren's eyes followed her around the room, as she shut the door. He was sitting without saying a word, but it did not stop the feeling that there was something he wanted to say.

As she walked past Seth pulled out a chair for her to sit down, 'We need to talk,' he spoke as he sat nearby. 'I am hearing two trains of thought, one says that we lost our best chance to protect Indarin and the other says we almost lost the Keep. In three days the Keep has been sealed far stronger than any of our best and the only form of sorcery intertwined with the Keep is yours.'

Saranon knew it was not the outcome she had hoped for, as it left little hidden from view, even though it meant Indarin had been healed. She would have preferred the cover of secrecy which now seemed to be seeping away with every moment.

A hand reached across near her shoulder. As she looked up to see Hailey who had woken with the noise, 'Why are you persecuting my friend?' She stared at her brother.

Before Seth spoke she did, 'I lost an old friend the same way, the path led to ruin and it would have been no different for Indarin.'

She could sense Hailey flinch at her words, as her face paled and she left with Seth following shortly after her. Darren asked, 'What happened?'

'Antavagon wanted revenge and I was only too willing to give it. It wounded the Keep and I wounded the Arthrose.'

The sorcerer sat in thought, before he spoke; 'Now the stakes are higher.'

Saranon knew what he meant with the other Angeon so close, it was not what she had expected to find in Serenphel. The room grew silent when Seth re-entered with a sorrowful stare, hidden deep within his eyes as he sat with his head bowed. 'When I first saw you I did not think you were able to kill a sorcerer,' he spoke to her.

'I saw my world fall apart, I do not want to see it happen again,' she replied.

'What are you going to do when Merrick comes?'

She had hoped that day would not come before she left, even though the time was fast approaching, it did not go fast enough.

CHAPTER SIXTEEN

Time to stand

The morning sun broke through the narrow slit between the curtains. Marking a golden crease across the sheets as Saranon tried to sleep in the early dawn. It flittered along her fingers as she raised her hand before a shadow faded past. She startled as Mitch's face became clearer into view. He was a solid figure who managed to achieve an awful silence when creeping into places. She remained reluctant to leave the cosy warmth of the blankets wrapped around her as she stared in annoyance. 'Ryan wants to see you,' he spoke.

She was in no mood to face him, but if she managed to find an excuse to avoid him, it would only prolong the agony.

Mitch ducked his way out of the room to wait in her tiny little apartment which appeared rather crowded.

She peered around the corner before shutting the door. She scrambled together a few things, almost forgetting Tellembre. It sat on the table in a dull frame, its pearl white finish gleaming just below the hilt. He was well dressed in comparison as she eyed him, thinking of how shabby she looked. It was not the start to the day she had been expecting and being outdone by a wizard in even simple matters brought a crease to her brow. He nudged her out into the corridor when she did not move fast enough, 'Have you forgotten?'

'What?' She snapped back.

He gave her a wry smile as he fell in step beside her, 'Your exams.'

'Don't be silly that's a week away,' she responded.

'You lost a few days remember.'

'Oh…' The thought did not sit well in her mind even though she had studied.

It was not the first time she had lost track of time and he revelled in the opportunity to remind her. Even though she had studied, the idea rattled in her head as it signified the passing of time and the reality of returning home. The Armythral were engrossed in the second Angeon albeit one not to be over looked. She had been far more concerned about the reception waiting for her in Normisia.

For all Mitch's steadfast commitment, the initial welcome had not been warm. Hence staying there was bound to be problematic. The thought stuck, shading her mood on what by any account should have been a tremendous moment. The excitement bubbled in the air from hundreds of sources. The next generation of sorcerers prepared themselves in anxious anticipation. Saranon groaned as all the activity seemed to slide off her when all she could think about was Normisia. She turned to Mitch, 'I suppose you will be happy to be home?'

He showed no expression as he moved along the corridor, 'We have a long way to go yet.'

He gave a short bow as he turned leaving her at the door. The small gesture was a little out of place, amid all the frenzied excitement. She breathed a heavy sigh as she knew it was now all down to her, all this way for a few tests and it would be over along with her time in Serenphel. She reached up and touched the door. It opened and she took a deep breath and entered the room. The air was dark and chilly, she knew it to be an illusion but the steady heartbeat pumping through her chest said otherwise. The energy seeping through the walls, electrified the corners of the room, intensifying as she moved forward. It was a simple, yet elegant test 'just reach the other end of the room'.

Hailey's words still clung in her head, an idea she had not yet fathomed. She had fobbed it off while trying to hide the seriousness of the matter. The first barrier passed through her with only a flitter. As she moved forward she held out her hands for the next, making her stomach queasy, as she pushed through. The fine array of the flows of energy glinted off her hair in a faint enigmatic glow. The third and fourth barrier held a little stronger than the last, still they did not bother her any more than the second. Saranon stood before the fifth barrier and reached forward. It felt sharp to the touch as a prickling sensation ran through her hand, but she was not swayed.

She did not come here to fail and with a mighty effort she forced her way through. The barrier stung with precision as she passed through. The sweat clung to her skin as she remembered to breathe and opened her eyes in preparation for the next one. The touch of the sixth felt like ice, as it sent sharp cold shivers in a needle like fashion down the length of her spine, but she was not deterred. Saranon was no stranger to the feeling of pain and she pressed on as the icy barrier pressed against her heart and then let her pass. The seventh barrier showed no mercy, as the razor sharp edge stung to the bone. Clinging, before letting go, as the searing sensation flashed through her mind.

She stood at the far end of the room with her eyes closed from the memory of pain, a voice shouted through an open door at the end. 'You know you don't have to go through them all,' Chilcott stood in front of her holding out his hand.

She took a moment to steady herself before following the corridor, it felt like a breath of fresh air. She inhaled its welcoming warmth as it wrapped around her. The intensity of the moment passed as she peered at her lecturer in stone cold annoyance and grumbled as she left. Saranon only just made it around the bend as Hailey leaped out, almost knocking both of them to the ground. 'So how did you go?' Her voice was filled with excitement.

'I think I over did it,' she spoke.

Hailey broke into gales of laughter, 'We were

wondering if there would be anything left of the test after you went through.'

She was not sure how to respond as Hailey moved her along, 'Come on.'

She felt like saying something but the words appeared all jumbled inside her head, as she ran to catch up. As she ran an image grew out the window to her left, it struck out behind the clouds, then as she peered again it was gone. The image played in her mind as though it had been pulled from her imagination. Her friend would have to wait as she turned off toward Theron.

The Prophet had been silent since Hailey's rescue, far too quiet for her liking as she sensed him avoiding her. The sorcerer had sat his test early, not that it mattered with the amount of training he had been given. She held her hand up to knock as a voice spoke from the other side, 'Come in.' Theron spoke.

It was not the sort of reception she had expected as Saranon entered the room to see the sorcerer gazing away. 'I think I just had a vision,' she spoke.

'What?' The sorcerer asked.

'I was looking out the window to the north and I saw a large grey blob heading this way.'

As soon as the words had left her mouth she realised how silly it sounded, but the Prophet was not laughing. Theron turned toward her his face, pale and drawn in the light, 'I think you know what it means.'

'No, but I can improvise,' Saranon did not like riddles at the best of times and his response annoyed her even more as she stood to look at him.

'If we're in danger you're supposed to say something,' she retorted.

'Are we?' He asked.

'You're not helpful,' she said as she walked away stopping mid-stride at the door.

'Oh, when are you going to tell Hailey?' She asked.

'Tell her what?' Theron hesitated.

'That you like her,' she replied.

The surprise spreading across Theron's face said it all, as Saranon smiled with glee. Her friend may be a Prophet, but he was still hopeless with girls. There was one name that escaped a mention, the other Angeon. The thought filled her with a twisted dread even though there had been no sign of him. For the moment at least he had stayed away, she felt so close, yet so far, from returning home.

It remained on the edge of Prophet's lips as he refrained from talking, when his eyes portrayed his thoughts. After their last encounter she was not looking forward to dealing with a sorcerer whose past she did not understand. The Armythral had been careful when discussing the other Angeon. The gaps in their conversations spoke more than their words. 'If you are expecting Merrick, I have a right to know, he is my kin,' Saranon exclaimed.

'You have a strange way of referring to the other Angeon; he does not share your sentiments.'

She sat down staring at him with open arms, 'I met his sister, what makes you so certain?'

'You will fight,' Theron was not used to being

questioned.

'I have fought with my best friend, is that the only thing you see?' She enquired watching him.

The Prophet hung his head saying nothing, as though in shame before continuing, 'He wants you dead.'

'Who doesn't?' She asked.

'No one here…' The sorcerer began.

'Look around you, I am not what people expect and I am not to be tamed,' as she spoke the words, Theron's legs gave way as he dropped to the floor.

She knelt and held the Prophet as his eyes went cloudy the great swirls revealing the essence of time. The whole event did not last long as he stared at her and whispered, 'You know.'

It was not the answer Saranon had been looking for as she grumbled underneath her breath and left.

Still she was not about to argue with the Prophet she had not asked much of him. Yet if Merrick did return Indarin was at greater risk with her presence. Two Angeons in the same place made for a difficult task for any Keep, no matter how great. With any luck Merrick would not appear, even if the image suggested otherwise. For now she had other things to focus on, as Mitch greeted her near the dragon pens. 'If you are looking for Katholomu, he's been gone since the morning,' he said.

He had an irritating habit of reading her immediate thoughts. 'Besides I thought you would be getting an early night ready for tomorrow?' He continued.

'I made it through today,' she exclaimed.

'Don't be too confident,' he spoke as if staring would somehow make her go and rest.

Mitch could be annoying at times as she relented and let him be, as she made her way up to her apartment. A barrage of shouting hit her like a wave, as she opened the door. Seth stopped as she entered the room. 'Did you know about this?' He asked in a hoarse voice.

Saranon looked at Hailey's sullen face. She wondered if it had anything to do with her conversation with Theron, before she could respond Seth answered for her. 'A storm is coming and the only one the Prophet told is my sister.'

She was relieved after having misplaced her assumption. 'It's about time he had a girlfriend,' she remarked.

Hailey's cheeks went bright red. 'That still does not excuse what happened,' Seth spoke.

'No, and I'm sure you would know what it's like to bear a great burden upon your shoulders,' Saranon said with a hint of sarcasm.

'The Prophet is not there to tell all, when there are some things better left unsaid. If I have to make it clear Merrick is mine to deal with,' she stared up close at Seth who was much taller. 'Not one of you is to get involved understood,' she spoke with a firm grace.

Seth hesitated a moment before responding, 'If that is your will, but let me know if you change your mind.'

'Do you really think you can defeat Merrick? He has more experience than you,' Darren raised the question that Seth did not ask.

Saranon breathed a heavy sigh before she responded,

'Is that what bothers you? You see a girl, when I have spent many years fighting for my life, I am as ready as I will ever be. Now I think you owe Hailey an apology.'

Seth's stubborn eyes did not sway under her glare at the feeling of being left out. He frowned as he shook his head. The inability to help played on his face. 'Take care,' he said as he leaned over and gave her a short embrace hugging her in both arms.

The warm gesture caught her off guard; she was not quite sure how to react as he laughed. Hailey gave her a small smile of approval as her face looked more relaxed.

'I'm sorry,' Seth said with a genuine vindication to his sister.

'Now that's resolved, Mitch expects me to get some sleep,' she spoke with relief.

'Merrick is going to come for you,' Hailey said with an urgent tone.

'Yes, I know.'

Saranon would have preferred to be gone by the time Merrick arrived, she started packing the last of her belongings. Yet the hope of avoiding the other Angeon was starting to dissolve before her eyes, as the light dimmed outside. She held Corsavere in her hand. The memory of Odana Temple stayed with her as she touched the smooth edge before hiding it away.

The temple plagued her dreams even as far as Serenphel with the image of the central core greater than any she had seen since. The blade felt cool underneath the soft caress of her fingers, a reminder of her stay. The ancient Keep of the Angeon of old from a country long since gone and only remnants remained. At least for now Odana would have to wait with her time at Indarin drawing near. The place was not as she had imagined, but she had persevered for her own sake. The place grew quiet as she peered at her talik, fondling it in her hands. It had been a while since she had heard from Pennie. Her friend limited their lines of communication while she was in Serenphel.

A quiet knock sounded on the door as it opened to reveal Mitch, 'I think you should come with me.'

'What happened to an early night?' She shouted as she caught up to him.

'Things have changed,' he spoke as he opened a door in the exam area. 'You will be doing the test early.'

For a moment her mouth hung open in clumsy astonishment, it was not what she had been expecting, as Mitch disappeared. Her long drawn out sigh filtered through the air, as she held out her hand and stepped inside. The darkness engulfed her, as she plunged and slipped into nothing when the floor gave way.

The hard surface vanished into the walls as if it did not exist. For a moment the fear rose up into her dry throat, with her voice caught in mid-stream. The ice-cold water wrapped around Saranon as she sank deep below a vanishing surface. The impact came down hard upon her body, chilling her heart and crushing the air out of her lungs. The sensation spread like a sharp pain, as her toes began to numb in the darkness, she tried to reach up and hit a solid surface with her fist. The panic rose inside her, followed as she hunted for a sign of a way out. Just then something rose from beneath her, gripping her leg and pulling her down.

She tried to concentrate so she could breathe underwater. Yet her technique was still clumsy and the creature pulled her down too fast. She tried to start again, but the cold filtered through to the edges of her mind as she tried to stay warm. With an almost angry reluctance she gave in, transforming into a mermaid. The grip of the creature below slipped as it slid into the depths and she grumbled at having to move forward in another form. As she rushed through the depths of the tunnel, her lungs pumped the oxygen through her body. Her mind returned to a calmer state even though she was still trapped in the swirling dark depths. She had been unwilling to transform and the mere fact that she had been forced to use it, placed her in a murky state of mind.

She managed to find a small pocket of air, before plunging down in the depths of the unseen. A faint light glowed out of the corner of her eye, as she rushed towards the first target with a cranky determination. The sooner she was away from here and on a dry hard surface in the warm open air, the better. The icy darkness played host to an obscure obstacle course, which only blackened her mood the further she went. One of the large grey creatures, a gentle giant of the murky depths with incredible strength, brushed too close. As Saranon bounced off the quadmar's fin like arm, it turned staring at her through piercing eyes showing no emotion. The look was cold grey, as they locked eyes for an instant, then it moved out of reach.

It made her mermaid form pale into insignificance as she quickened her pace. A faint glow lit up from below and she groaned knowing that it would mean travelling deeper. She edged her way between two of the creatures as they swam by angling down to pick up the target. As her hand reached down, she felt something pass near her side. She swallowed as she turned to see a quadmar blocking her path, its great tail masking the way out. She froze, still not making a sound, as the shock of her predicament tingled through her spine. The thoughts racing through her head, as she tried to distract the graceful beast without bringing it to temper.

She flicked its fin and the quadmar moved a little sideways, yet it was not enough. She waited, trying to gather her thoughts, then with one quick move the great creature slid clear. The exit was in sight and she wasted no time darting through as the quadmar's tail fin swished higher. The impact catapulted Saranon forward and upward before her head broke the surface of the underground cave. She leaped out, while transforming back into her real self and her soaking wet clothes. She edged her way a short distance from the murky, marble edge. Breathing out her exhaustion as her excitement floundered. She preferred to admire quadmar from a distance and on dry land, rather than a step away.

As if in mocking the creature closest moved and made her heart miss a beat as she held her breath, before letting it escape. She smiled in a quiet relief with no desire to move and dried her clothes with the warmth of her energy. It did not take long for the warmth to wipe away the ice cold memory of the dark pool that lay beside her. As she turned peering down with satisfaction at the thin cylinder targets clumped on the ground. She stood up with a slow stagger catching her breath as she peered at the water's edge. The time below had passed with great reluctance, making just a few hours feel like a whole day had passed in her absence.

Saranon looked around her. The place remained silent as she strode away from the murky pool. Her hand took hold of Tellembre at her side, as she peered around the empty rooms, when the area plunged into an eerie silence. The only sounds emanating from the water and echoing along the cavernous walls behind her. The corridor felt like a hollow tomb, as the walls gave away nothing in return to the soft touch of her fingertips. As a stranger, the Keep had spoken little with a wave of small gestures, but not even that sprang to life along the stale surface. It was not the greeting she had expected as she searched around, not even the Keep gave an answer to her inquisitive mind.

The quadmar stared back from a watery grave as she contemplated going back the way she came, but the water was not appealing. A quick flitter of movement rippling along the liquid surface only confirmed her thoughts. Saranon used her energy to call out but no reply came as it struck out to meet nothing in the dim light. Off in the distance of the darkness a small faint tone ignited a familiar spark inside. As something deep within recognised the source and her energy grew flaring to the surface. Still no other sign came and she wondered if it had been a mistake, as she returned to the sound of the dark pool of water.

The quadmar making tiny ripples, her only company in the vacuum of silence echoing throughout the Keep. The strange sensation sent goose bumps along her arms as she looked upward hoping for a response in the void. A voice cut through the air with a harsh undertone. 'In our mind we fear what we most dread, but you are something else, it would have been better if you had not been created at all.'

Merrick's soft tone filtered through every direction.

His voice touched her ears, as though he were standing right beside her. Saranon's senses had gone numb as she stood not far from the icy water, not knowing which direction to take, as the voice gave no sign.

A cold rush of air swept past from above. She looked up to the open door, when it creaked, echoing through the underground chambers of the Keep. The air wavered around her as the light from Indarin shone down the walls. For once the quadmar remained silent in the dark pool. As Saranon peered into the murky depths a hurtling force of energy shattered the moment in an instant. She dived for cover as it just missed. With the heat narrowing down on her back, radiating with ferocious intensity from the source. The impact hit hard as she clung on to solid ground. She tried hard not to breathe in the fractured shards of energy catapulting off the edges of the blast.

In the frame of the vacuum that followed, she lashed out from an awkward position. She fell back near the water's edge with the blast from her own energy. 'Surely you can do better than that,' Merrick's words rung in her ears with a mocking grace.

An array of light broke the surface, glittering in a needle like fashion along the walls of the building. Growing in magnitude as it ripped through. She dove to the side only just missing the second blast, as it melted through the wall behind her, leaving a horrid mark. She swallowed, as the sweat poured off her skin and she managed to send a resonating blast back through the open tunnel. The sound speared out in a spiral, caressing the walls and leaving charred marks as it split the air.

It took a great deal of strength and she was losing ground. Saranon bent down to the icy pool and as the next blast thundered through, she dived. The icy depths greeted her with its chilling tone, as she transformed for the second time in the same day and the thought made her cringe. A voice rang out loud and clear sending a chill, filled with darkness, from above. 'You were not meant for this world!'

Merrick's words resonated even through the water as she darted away. She was running out of time, but she needed to find a more suitable location to take on the other Angeon.

CHAPTER SEVENTEEN

When the end turns anew

Saranon clambered into a quiet place to transform back before climbing up and away from the dark pool. The walls of the Keep, still gave no sign of what had taken place. Indarin felt like an icy tomb with no sounds of life emanating through its corridors. It chilled her to the spine, as the silence followed, cutting through her senses with a sharpened edge. In the end, the message was still the same. A dull numbness returning nothing, not even a peep as she ran through the emptiness. She searched for a glimmer or a hint of just a glimpse, to guide her, as she sank in the realisation that she was alone.

If the other Angeon had succeeded in one thing, it was finding her. Then she had been here before with Antavagon in her past, waiting just below the surface. The images hidden under all the layers, that had been placed with care, as Saranon had merged out into the world. The Keep waiting deep in Darkonia, with the hope that one day she would return and if not Antavagon had exacted his toll in a fearsome rage. As he let the Angeon loose on the world in a defiant form of retaliation, before returning to a quiet state, away from prying eyes. As the window of her past played in her mind in a rhetorical form, she listened for any sign of Indarin, as she moved further in toward the heart of the Keep.

If the other Angeon was looking for someone easy to prey on, he had sent her back to where her journey began. She saw the images flooding back, the memories that told her the Keep was there, waiting for her. No matter how much she wanted to pretend. Underneath the surface, lay a predator forged from the coldness, similar to that of the other Angeon. Merrick had control of the Keep but the image he had created was too smooth. It slid into the background with a perfection the Keep did not possess. A shadow of the character held within the structure of the building, belying its natural being.

As she touched the surface running her fingers along the wall, the old memory prickled up her spine. Antavagon the prison in her homeland, had held years of anger waiting to be released. In comparison Indarin was so much larger and so much more, even for an Angeon holding such a Keep, would be short lived. An echo of a whisper ran down the windows shattering the peace, with a hollow sound resounding at the source and she knew what had to be done. As the soldier inside took over, she raised Tellembre in her hand. The bond-breaker sang a sweet faint song filling her head through the empty madness. In a slow subtle form, the fierce brutal flow of the Angeon ran seeping in and saturated her skin through every edge of her being.

The pale blade of the bond-breaker shone with the impact of the first silhouette of morning. Breaking over the horizon and etching its way along the land. The immature light revealed an intense calm in the centre, void of its ferocity in the absence of the Keep's ability to fight. Her steps penetrated the awkward silence spilling down the halls in every direction. For a moment Saranon fooled herself into thinking she was alone, when she was far from it. The false image mattered not as she made her way knowing the path well. Her blade sang with a metallic chime the only other sound to cut the air.

She headed down, turning her back on the sun's golden rays of light, that broke through the windows giving a false glimmer of hope. When the real light lie deep within and now Saranon had to fight, as she broke the plain cold seal, from the old gateway to below the Keep. The path to the old source of power where others feared to follow in the footsteps of the great, and now it would know the Angeon. As she strode in the darkness of the mighty Keep, it laid dormant, she had one mission to make Indarin speak. She pummelled through the underground passages. Each time she hurtled herself forward at the next barrier.

The iron grace of Tellembre breaking deeper with every step as Saranon lashed out with a cold embrace of the energy inside. This time she would not sit side by side within the central core, this time she would give it a voice. The thought held her in a clumsy trance as she lashed out with hard intent. Small sounds scratched the surface of her attention as she turned around and held so tight onto the Angeon within. As she peered around, she stared straight into the eyes of Purton lying curled up and in pain on the floor. It was not what she had hoped to see and it made her hesitate as she took the image in. The sorcerer gave her a rough smile through his pain, as he lay half stretched out near the wall.

The memory of him stayed with her, as she moved on with a purpose as the picture of his face played in her mind. There was only one way out and that path lead down as she drew on her energy intensifying its strength along the way. The power of the Angeon reeled within writhing in wait as the sensation of the central core became stronger. The two sources whispering to each other from afar as the barriers fell away. The distance shortening as she managed to reach the place near where she and Theron had melded with the Keep. It appeared cold and grey almost lifeless to the touch. The stale air wept with the stains of moisture dripping down along the surface of the walls.

Saranon reached down with a power untold, ripping the floor beneath her as it melted and cracked under the pressure of such force. The seconds passed like hours before a mighty roar filled the vacuum. The stallic energy poured out with a trembling thunderous blast, flooding all the way from the core. The energy enveloped her soul mingling with her energy, before it took her whole, into the deep. The blast that followed was enough to shatter a million minds. It took hold exploding through the Keep like a fireball raging through its connections. The intensity took Indarin by surprise as it succumbed to the overload. The raw energy pulsated throughout, wrapping around the edge of the Keep, with a flood of renewed strength.

The clasps holding the Keep to silence melted away as the energy flooded through at a mighty speed. Crackling along the conduits and saturating the building. An intensity engulfed Indarin, a great power combining with the core. As it climbed, it let out an unwavering source, giving the Keep new life. In the darkness of the depths, Saranon held on for all she was worth and more, as she pushed herself to the limit and then further. She grabbed hold of every essence that made the central core move, driving it harder and faster, washing away the pain of the Keep as she went. In the only reality which was hers, as she held on in the darkness.

Shining bright beneath her like a sun in a black sky. The charge spurred onward and upward strengthening Indarin as it surged through. A glimmer came from the distance, a hazy shimmer she recognised, the other Angeon. In the darkness, through the pain, she cried tears for everything she had been through, she was not alone. Yet the world had condemned her to be that way and she knew it would have to be. Whichever way, there was one thing she held certain for all she was worth, Merrick could not escape, not this time. A great surge from beneath inside the central core fired up skyward taking the Angeon along with it and out into the blood red sky.

The flames mingled with the early rays of a sunset filled with the rage of the Keep. It gave the sun a hot orange glow burning its way across the land. A mark deepened on the horizon, a blemish on an otherwise golden image. Penetrating the auburn colours of the setting sun in a cold embrace as it shifted across the sky. Saranon regained her composure long enough to stand facing the other Angeon from afar. If not now, then time would not present it again as she held on to her source. She drew down upon the Keep's energy and steadied herself as the energy raged within waiting to be let out.

A numb hollow sensation wrapped around her as she grasped out searing through the pain. The blast of her sorcery impacted with a deadening blow. Catapulting across in a great wide arc as it melded with a force just as strong, striking out, slicing hard as it cut through the air. The pressure crackled sending out sparks across the sky. It hit the ground with a deep roaring anger, thudding into the surface of Tordoren. She held on in the intensity as the energy ignited into a hurtling torrent, as it pounded with shear force, creating a cataclysm across the open sky as Saranon held her ground. Standing with all the strength she could gather from within and hoping that what she had done would be enough.

The great roar from the Keep below, filled her ears as it held on gathering speed. The charge flowed out in an ever widening circle filtering through the air as it reached her, holding her up strong. With Indarin fierce as ever she aimed all she could. Concentrating on Merrick as the fragments from their energy sparked across the sky. Her hands throbbed with the impact of the force as she crept closer in a steady stance moving forward. It was not the way she had wanted it to go, as the other Angeon held his ground. It would have been better not to take the sorcerer on, but the choices had already slipped away. This time it was not so easy to leave and the thought of losing her friends compelled her to go on.

She had held her ground, before the other Angeon and the pain was no stranger as it sank in. The only time Saranon had known the full extent of her power. As she faced a bleakness which overcame her, when the ground she had gained, diminished. The arc bowed off centre as the two sources of energy missed. Merrick's energy hit the Keep with a thundering impact, rocking the ground and hurtling her to the side. The momentary shock ran through her as she peered upward. She moved without hesitation steadying herself on the uneven muddy surface.

The glimmer of hope faded into the deafening roar heading her way. The energy struck through the vivid sky lighting the way with a deadening brightness. Consuming the background noise in its wake as the world grew silent. The pressure hit her on impact as it shattered through the air. Blasting its way around, shrieking past her ears, as the time drew near and Saranon knew she had to choose. The anguish rattled through her mind as the pounding force stemmed up from the depths. A blinding premonition from a time long since buried in the grave. The flawless energy flowed from her deep into the ground as it hurled outward crashing through the earth. Her energy locked around the other Angeon in a cut throat embrace bringing the sorcerer ever closer.

A harsh cold edge ran across the torrid sky as the air filled with a blinding rage colouring deep into the cuts carving up the ground. A harrowing howling stifled in an intermittent sound as it broke through the hurtling wind. It took every moment to strike out against a merciless hold grappling through the rubble. The intertwining of the forms of energy melding as she held out, as Merrick struggled at every turn. The ground of Tordoren rumbled as she dragged the other Angeon closer. The earth before her crumbled, spreading out, as it went in a steady cascade, plummeting into the waiting dark as she used her strength to stay in place. As the widening crevasse travelled toward her, creeping ever further along the open field.

The other Angeon lashed out as he stood near the other side of the crevasse. The blow caught its mark as Saranon faltered on the edge of the pummelling chaos beckoning for her to fall. Merrick rose in the haze with a vicious grin reaping the reward of his success as he gained ground. She stared in a cold, unforgiving manner across the divide. She clung onto the edge as she flailed over nothing before steadying herself. The other Angeon grasped the moment of his strong hold, as he rose widening his arms in a cold embrace as he seized control. She bit her lip from the shear grit of her teeth as she held on and then let go leaping into the void. The jolt ran like a shockwave wrapping around

Merrick's legs and dragging him down with the force.

His rage howled, cutting the air, as he catapulted off the edge and into the writhing darkness. The other Angeon's cries pierced from above. Screeching through in an anguished and unrelenting tone, before the earth absorbed the sound. As the outer form slipped away Saranon became the Angeon of old once born again, but alas it came too late. For all she could do now was the one act she would see through to the end, as she took hold of Merrick in a final embrace. His screams arched upward to the sky beyond, as she took him down into the darkness inside Tordoren. The Angeon of old clasped on with all her strength in the shimmering light as her energy burned bright and beyond.

She held on in a tight embrace taking the other Angeon down deep into the ground, as the energy carved its way through. The heat pounded through her body with a vibrant flow, keeping Merrick's attempts at bay as he struggled. The harsh determination stayed in her mind as he struggled. For now the fighting seemed useless, as her sorcery held in place, not letting go from the path she had chosen. Any sound from without soon evaporated, as they fell further down. The noise which encroached around them resonated from her sorcery. The grip grew tighter as they went deeper into the darkness.

Her energy broke through the bonds and tore through the other Angeon's skin in a fine array as it held in place. Merrick gasped in shock as he could scream no more and the earth began to shatter in around them in a torrent. As the tendrils of Tordoren wrapped around them, a grip from the darkness half woke her from the hypnotic trance. A grip so strong, it bound around her, hauling her upward as the ground caved in pulling with a heavy grace. The last rays of a crimson red dusk spread across the land sweeping the ground in a shadowy silhouette. Saranon blinked in the light as the dragon's great wings carried her above the whirling turmoil and her body cried out in pain.

CHAPTER EIGHTEEN

An elusive Prophet

Chilcott watched as the dragon lay Saranon down as Kat stepped back curling his tail half around letting his wings drop. The wind raced howling in a cloud filled sky as the darkness of night washed the ground, racing at a heavy pace. The sounds of life began to emerge from deep inside the Keep as he waited, but no movement came. The winds beckoned low across the tower trickling the light bearing of rain, faltering as it swept across the land. Chilcott walked toward Saranon as the dragon lowered his head and nudged it to the side, beckoning for her to wake up. No sound came from her as the dragon stayed waiting in the evening light fast fading into darkness. Katholomu let out a mournful sound as if knowing the exacting cost of the attack.

Chilcott waited acknowledging the dragon's pain.

Kat stood so close his mighty claw tapped the stone, but a hands width from Saranon's flowing hair as it soaked up drops of rain. He leaned over sheltering her body from the burdening storm as he arched the tips of his wings out as the rain pooled. The echo of voices carried through the air as Chilcott stood beside Katholomu. The great dragon peered up without moving. Hailey's voice rang out behind him. 'Saranon!' She screamed.

Chilcott remained still as he held out a hand only to halt Hailey from rushing in, 'But we have to help her.'

'Go back inside,' he commanded.

Hailey hesitated in the dark and a silent tear escaped down her cheek, as she realised what had been said. In the dying light of the sorcerer's gaze as Chilcott stood in the still night air, the breeze whimpered to a halt. A heavy thud grew louder from the open door as Mitch made his way rushing past in the late night hour. His sleeve caught on the dragon's claw. As he stooped down underneath Kat's great wing and reached out taking a moment to lift her from her place of rest. The bond within him held a glimmer of hope inside as he paused before Chilcott. The sorcerer made no effort to move, as he guarded the dark open sky, waiting for the turmoil to ease in the field below.

Katholomu lifted his head after Mitch had darted from view. As he took care to curl up near the sorcerer's side peering out into the distance. Chilcott raised a hand brushing the dragon's soft leathery skin. The flames of light around the perimeters began to light up the Keep, with an eerie glow, bouncing shadows off the walls. Kat arched his head as faint noises flared through the still soft air and the sorcerer bade him to stay. The outer skirts of Indarin came to life with a reassuring surge of activity bellowing through the fragments of light. A few steps carried their sound across the open air as the sorcerer turned his head with a great reluctance.

He sighed in silence as the young Prophet joined him on the outdoor terrace overlooking the land. 'At some stage you will have to own your decision,' he spoke in a rough round voice to the Prophet.

Theron peered out over the wall's hard edge, unwilling to provide a reply to his teacher's advice. Chilcott strode to his side with a firm stance as he peered into the darkness. 'There is no room for complacency at Indarin, for whatever reason you had now is not the time to hide,' he spoke.

Theron swallowed as he closed his eyes, 'I did it for the Keep.'

He laughed, 'You are a braver man than I.'

He patted Theron on the shoulder before taking his leave to the well-lit halls inside. The echo of movement rallied down the long sweeping corridors amid the sorcerer's presence. It caused a stir in the murmur of voices as he travelled past. The sound of chaos gave way to a practical vibrant tone, as he ventured below to the medical area. He stood, closing his eyes for just the whisper of a moment, in the silence between the rushes of noise. He held his hand forward moving the door as he went. Purton's friendly smile peered up through a crowded room, as his friend waved, but it was not who he was searching for in the wake of the turmoil.

He strode past with a purpose to every step, as he moved forward through the fray. A small gathering of whispers passed near the door as he opened it ajar and peered in to see the pale image that lay waiting. Chilcott knew that every moment from here in, counted as Anne remained calm with determination. Mitch waited saying nothing at the scene playing out before him, as Anne and Rasine stabilised the Angeon. He began to ask, then hesitated in the moment, as Saranon opened her eyes peering at nothing. Mitch sat beside her, but she did not utter a word in the soft surroundings. Chilcott moved a little closer and her eyes stared straight at him piercing through his soul.

'How did you survive?' Saranon spoke through a dry swollen mouth.

He knew she was referring to the scar on his arm a reminder left from his encounter with Merrick, 'He missed.'

Chilcott held her hand. It was cool and clammy with little strength left. Yet she held on with a stubbornness that shone through. As he left, Purton joined him in the hall looking half his old self, 'There's no use worrying about Saranon when we've got a Keep to sort out.'

'That is not what concerns me,' he replied.

Purton looked into his friend's troubled brow, 'You mean Theron, don't you?'

It was not like Chilcott to keep secrets, though he was one to leave out words. The ones he was thinking in the foremost of his mind as the hours bled into the long night. His eyes grew tired, but the power of sleep evaded him in the dim light as the Keep fell into a familiar hum. The purr of the great centre core filtered up through the tiny vents to wash away any fear left in the hearts of the Armythral. Every sense that fled along his old bones told him that there was a business left undone. He peered into the soft lamp light flooding over a cram filled desk.

The Prophet had given no sign away, as the end drew near and the Keep along with its occupants had been unprepared. Regardless of the merciful outcome the lack of foresight was obvious. The gaping void plagued his mind, as he rubbed his brow in irritation. A soft knock woke him out of his thoughts as Anne beckoned for him to follow her lead. A rush of shouting pounded through the great hall as they entered. It broke a sultry deadlock when Armand and Elliot backed down. 'How did I know it would resort to this?' Chilcott spat the words out in distain.

'Theron needs to be punished,' Elliot rasped with conviction.

'There will be no passing of judgement until the job is done. If you are not resting for tomorrow's shift, there is plenty of work around here. I will hear no more of this,' Chilcott's voice shouted echoing off the ceiling, as it boomed through the air.

He waited to see who would stay for the night shift, with few rising, to the awkward challenge. As Armand stayed behind, his face filled with a heavy weight. The sorcerers worked through the night and into the first harsh rays of dawn. A golden glimpse pierced the crisp air to creep across the land. The sun reached out its insidious gaze, stretching upon the fierceness of the battle, raking a path toward the Keep.

It echoed the call of a lack of sleep among the weary eyed in the face of the grim task ahead. Indarin held well its own, in the morning light, with most signs of damage proving to be superficial. A small blessing, as the peace filtered through with an eerie groan, as the wind wrapped itself around the Keep. Theron stayed close by his father's side, with every attempt to remain out of the way. It only made the obvious more abundant as he attracted the attention of others. At first Chilcott saw no reason to question the young man. As he had seen many a young sorcerer make mistakes, but as the tension grew, his thoughts turned. Armand was an old friend and he had known Theron well. 'You may have kept a silent air, but all those faces out there will expect an explanation,' Chilcott spoke.

Theron peered over at Chilcott with knowing eyes, 'I will not shy away from what I did.'

Armand stood strong as he spoke to his son, 'You need to reach out, and hiding behind a righteous tone won't find you any friends. You will speak in the great hall when this is done.'

The sorcerer would hear no argument after his decision was made, at some stage his son would have to grow up and defend himself. Now, would be as good a time as any as the day grew strong and vibrant around him. A distant tone called out across the open sky harrowing the mournful end of a plagued era. As Chilcott tried to forget, the scar on his arm, would not let him. His eyes caught Theron's as he looked up and the Prophet said nothing, as the sorcerer gave him a firm stare.

The weariness was settling in on Chilcott's shoulders, with no good reason to stay longer, he made his way back to his apartment. Anne had placed a large warm breakfast on the table in anticipation and he smiled, she knew him too well. As the afternoon sun raised its head through the slit in the curtains, a thud and shouting reverberated into the room. He dashed out to the commotion. The sound blasted into the corridors as Todd pinned Theron against the wall amid Hailey's screaming. The scene appeared familiar as he stood between the two and bellowed in a deep low voice, as Todd backed down. The Prophet left in the moment with no need for any further encouragement.

He faced Todd with the signs of a skirmish showing on his face. 'You have lived with Saranon for months. You know Theron was not involved.'

'But he could have done something?' Todd exclaimed.

Chilcott let out a bellowing laugh, 'I don't see anyone here brave enough to tell the Angeon what to do, now clean up those marks. Don't make the same mistake I did.'

He uttered his last words with a solemn tone as a bitter warning. The day was almost gone and he meant to check on the Angeon before the day was through. It was a sobering journey down to the medical area, as Mitch sat in silence watching over the sleeping sorceress still as pale as before.

It was too early to tell the damage done, as he held her hand in a loose grip. He waited, without wavering, in trust which was more than he could say for himself. The Armythral believed that the Angeon were just another form of sorcery. Yet his instinct from the first time he had met Merrick as a boy, told him otherwise. For all the talk of the other Angeon's death he was not so convinced. He knew only too well that a sorcerer who does not want to be found can disappear. Only time would tell as the evening passed. The voices for Theron to answer to the great hall, haunted every step growing louder into the night.

For all he was worth the Prophet had stayed out of the way as if avoiding the inevitable, before being thrust to centre stage. For now, the matter grew far from Chilcott's thoughts, as Purton caught sight of him and handed him his set of tools. In a Keep this size there was always work to be done, as he smiled to his old friend. It would be a comforting relief as they walked into the deep stretches of the building. The pleasant sound of the humming Keep ran underneath the caress of his hand. It offered a small relief to calm his thoughts. He laid his hand into cleaning out the gunk that had matted along the conduits, filling the grates.

Purton chuckled, behind him in a familiar setting, he was quite at home in the bowels of Indarin as he hummed in tune with the Keep. Chilcott frowned without uttering a sound or losing pace with the work at hand, as his friend continued smiling even more. In the midst of the moment a sharp rush of footsteps raced towards them. As Anne almost threw herself into Chilcott's arms, 'Theron is missing.'

Purton sighed as he packed up, 'It's started,' he exclaimed.

He had been hoping and his heart sank in the recognition of the impact of Anne's words as she spoke them.

He strode up above, quickening his pace toward Armand's chambers where his friend greeted him with a solemn stand. 'They took him, Ryan has him and I want him back. I've called a meeting in the great hall and I want you there.'

Armand did not need to ask, he had supported Theron from an early age. It was not the form of resolution that he had been hoping for, but now the path had been taken he would stand by the young Prophet. The decision had spurred the Keep into action as the details spread rife. Armand was right to call a meeting so soon, even if it meant little preparation, as he gathered a few belongings.

Chilcott's bond-breaker Shehoarth sat in its case in silence, a token of his youth now gathering dust on the shelf. His own energy might have been more than enough to see him through the years, but he was no fool and wiped off the dust as he held it. The great irony of having to defend himself from his own clan, did not rest easy on his mind. The room lay clear, as he stood for a time waiting for the great hall to fill, before making his entrance. He had earned a great deal of respect and there was no need for grandeur. A small hand caught his attention from the side as Rasine beckoned him closer, 'It's Saranon, she's missing and so is the wizard.'

'What?' Chilcott whispered in disbelief, 'Let me know if you find anything.'

The astonishment drained from his face as he entered and sat near Armand. He said nothing in a room with abundant ears listening for the slightest sound. Armand was a grand speaker who took his time. Armand captivated the audience, holding back great strain and the love for his son to emphasise his point. As Elliot stood opposite and began, a slow yet steady cheer crept into the crowd. Chilcott knew he had made the right decision to bring Shehoarth. The mood told him it was going to be a long night as he clenched his fist out of sight. Elliot's furious tone cut deep as Armand demanded to see his son and Ryan standing by Elliot's side finally relented.

As he took his leave, the silence clung thick with tension pounding through the air. It was not an easy task as a few from the audience beckoned and jeered. The great hall was familiar with the peace and quiet of daily business. Yet the unusual events made the undercurrent electrifying with intensity among the clan. A shaken pale face emerged as a band of sorcerers kept a close circle around Theron, who held his head to the ground. He stared at his feet as he walked. The pain shone in Armand's eyes, as the ferocity of his emotions pierced his lips.

In the moment Ryan smiled, knowing the impact cut deep as the crowd responded in a loud roar and Elliot spoke strong. 'We were placed in harm's way because a Prophet, a boy, would not share his knowledge. This Keep has suffered at the hands of a fight, which does not concern us. People have lost their lives, when we had the ability to prevent it. Instead we are left with a child who thinks that playing with people's lives, is a game.'

The words cut deep, but the growing support in the crowd cut deeper still. Chilcott began to wonder if the chance had been lost to get Theron out unscathed. Anne gave him a worried, knowing glance as if reading his thoughts.

He grimaced as Elliot went on and Ryan chimed in with a lashing tone before Armand could stand his ground. At best, Theron would have to be reprimanded in the strength of support and any ground lost, could not be regained. It would be held against the Prophet forever more and with his youth that could well be a long time. Armand held his ground rivalling back a slow growing support, but it was not enough and he carried on. He looked at Theron but the Prophet hung his head not looking him in the eye. If anyone was going to save him it would be Theron himself and now was not the time to play the victim.

Chilcott lost track in his own thoughts as Elliot's words caught his attention. 'What have you to say in all this Mr Chilcott?'

He stood up and took the stand with a firm vibrant tone. 'I remember finding a sorcerer trying to drain the energy from an Angeon and when I went to intervene I was prevented from doing so. Yet when that Angeon broke free, that sorcerer screamed for help and his screams rang out through the lower levels of Indarin. You created a monster and now you want to blame a boy for the consequences. If you want to talk about punishment I would start with you,' Chilcott spoke with conviction.

Elliot's face burned bright red with anger, as he shouted, while Armand smiled in response. Elliot's fury showed in his words echoing across the great hall with a bitter rasp. Chilcott's speech held ground as Ryan and Elliot worked hard to regain their support with a waning crowd. He would not admit defeat, even if it meant, reaching a compromise. Either way Chilcott had hit his mark and returned to his chair with a knowing glint in his eyes, as his achievement took on a life of its own. In the long rain of events, a change so discreet occurred, it was almost lost in the array of words. The person presenting themselves as Theron stood up and transformed.

***

Saranon, the Angeon, rose in her full glory with a small smile of satisfaction creeping across her face from the looks of surprise. The change was so subtle it caught the sorcerers around her off-guard, as she used her energy to move them aside. She took her place at centre stage for all to see, as she set her tone hard against the background. She had no fear of the Armythral in the midst of the damage done. The only feelings running through her head all led to loss and pain. In that moment Elliot uttered unfathomable words, 'You should have died with Merrick.'

'I did not kill him so pray tell me, how is he dead?'

Saranon shouted with some bemusement to Elliot in the great hall before lowering her tone. 'After what Chilcott said I doubt the other Angeon will ever stray far from you. It is a pity, I always wanted a brother.'

She almost stated the last sentence through mocking eyes as Elliott grasped the meaning of her words. The Angeon spoke as she stood in the centre of the great hall first turning to Armand. 'Theron is safe, but this is not his fight and I told him not to come. Now Ryan you have something that belongs to me and I want it back.' She spoke as she stared right into the sorcerer's eyes.

Elliot turned to Ryan, 'What is she talking about?'

Ryan began to look worried as the meaning of her words sank in, he tried to run in a mad dash that came to a sudden halt, as she reached out. The panic in his eyes was visible, as she held him down and out of view of the crowd that were now standing on edge. As Elliot looked on in horror he realised that Ryan had stolen part of Saranon's energy. He looked like he was about to jump, but stayed almost captivated not able to veer away. Ryan breathed his last breath, before she covered his face, she peered up at Elliot. 'I hope you choose your friends more wisely.'

She continued. 'Now I have a different kind of score to settle, as I said before and I will stand by my word Theron is your Prophet now and in the future. His ability to keep silent saved many of your lives and many more including Indarin. It takes a brave man to speak the future and a true Prophet to know when to remain silent. Theron has done this and more, you have Indarin, the other Angeon is not in the position he once was and I will return to Zyanthia. May Odana help anyone who stands in my way.'

The Angeon stared around the room to a sea of faces in open silence as Armand stood, 'I think I can speak for all here, when I say you have our leave.'

As one group, all the sorcerers in the great hall in unison, rose as Saranon walked toward the door. Mitch released the handle from the other side opening the doors their full length to reveal one lone figure. Theron stood smiling as she approached. He held out his hand in recognition. 'You have my leave and my gratitude, if you ever come this way again you will always be welcome at Indarin,' Theron smiled.

A loud cheer echoed through the hall as Armand rushed to greet his son in open arms too scared to let go in the moment. She looked at Mitch's wide grin filled with excitement at the prospect of returning home to Normisia.

It had been a long time and the thought of being among wizards was appealing after being around so many sorcerers. With any luck Pennie would have made progress searching for her parents. Something which had plagued her so far from the country she had still not reconciled with. It was tempting to think that when she returned that would somehow change, but inside, she knew the damage lay too deep. The wounds along her back, a constant reminder of a childhood lost in the dark void. It had been left forgotten in the edges of Darkonia and the gaping memories of a life before. She did not anguish at her lack of knowledge of the past, for she had not been the only one to feel the spiteful wrath.

As she stood in the courtyard looking back at the majestic Keep, standing stronger than ever. The wound running along the earth caught her eye, as she gazed over the land. 'I hope I do not have to do that again.'

He stood by her side, 'You are the Angeon, I don't think you get to decide.'

She looked at him knowing the truth of his words. It was not what she wanted to hear. Then Mitch had never been one to soften the blow when he spoke. 'How did you know about Ryan?' He asked.

'It took too long to recover,' she smiled as she beckoned him to follow. 'Now where did that dragon go?'

Mitch smiled as he strode toward the dragon pens. He still managed to be annoying in subtle ways. She hesitated before following. The yard showed no sign of Katholomu. She peered around the corner to see his great paw sticking out sideways, as he slept curled up near the open door. The large opening revealed his head just inside, completely relaxed as Saranon walked toward him. She felt his coat; it was smooth and soft and smelt fresh, Mitch smiled beside her. The dragon moved with a calm resolve as his head came close to hers and he looked straight into her eyes.

'What do you think?' Hailey's voice sprang from behind the dragon's head as she beamed from ear to ear. 'We thought we would help and I don't think anyone could stand the smell any longer.'

'He looks beautiful,' she replied.

'I'm glad you like it, Seth and Darren helped, and I

just wanted to say thanks.'

Saranon patted Kat's head as he raised his shoulders. He stretched his muscles and hind legs before shifting his weight and lowering his head to step outside.

He glimmered under the early evening sky as the wind caught his wings and he bent his head back waiting. She clambered up his side, sitting herself close to the top of the dragon's shoulders. Mitch followed, placing himself into position. Katholomu lifted his great form up to meet the night stars shining down. He motioned for the dragon to go. Kat heaved up into the dark sky, swooping up in a wide arc, turning mid-air. Then flying up at a great height leaving the Keep Indarin far behind.

DEEP IN THE SHADOW OF THE FALLEN

THE LEGACY OF ZYANTHIA BOOK THREE

CHANTELLE GRIFFIN

CHAPTER ONE

Across the border

Saranon raised the fine glass to Lady Davene. The most powerful sorceress in Balquene entered the marble courtyard. The Lady's flowing burnt orange dress trailed over the polished mosaic floor. The tiles added to the vibrant colourful scene and a warm breeze ran over the shallow pool. It came through the open columns leading into the grounds that surrounded the grand mansion. It was a wonderful way to celebrate the end of training. Yet she continued to struggle with her sorcery. A fact she tried to hide in a country that once belonged to Dresha, an empire long gone. It disintegrated with disappearance of the last Angeon, the only link to her ancestry.

Maya broke through the crowd as the feast was brought to the table. The centre piece was positioned at the end of the courtyard. Music played they strode out into the afternoon sun. 'What do you think?' Maya asked.

'It's beautiful,' Saranon said as she gazed upon the low fields on the edge of the grounds.

'Does it make you want to stay?' Maya asked waiting for her to answer.

It was not the first time she had been asked, and her response remained the same. 'I have to return.'

'A pity,' Maya exclaimed.

An awkward silence fell and she made her way into the busy room. As people danced to the soft music and sat on the cushions by the walls. The table had been laden with fruit in front of the deep colours of the fresco. She gazed up in awe. The mansion had been untouched by the ancient war between Dresha and Zyanthia. She wondered what it would have been like if Zyanthia had not fallen. Yet there she stood, one of two Angeon when there had been none for more than two hundred years.

A glass fell shattering across the mosaic floor as the wizard moved away. Saranon caught a glimpse of his tall muscular frame. Then she came face to face with Lady Davene. 'You have outworn your welcome,' the Lady's voice cut through the crowded noise.

She stood between her wizard, Mitch, and the Lady as the blood began to run down his arm. If Saranon spoke she would regret every word. She held Lady Davene's infuriating glare and gave a swift nod in a partial bow of respect. It was more than the Lady deserved, but she was not about to risk it. She had gained a momentary truce when her wizard's life was at stake. She hesitated long enough to allow Mitch to make good distance. He headed toward the marble columns surrounding the sheltered courtyard.

Balquene was no place for a wizard. She glanced around the room reluctant to take her gaze from the Lady. The setting sun ran its golden fingers along the polished mosaic floor. It sprawled over the scenes of victory and spreading her shadow toward the heavily laden feast. The party was over and all eyes were on her. A large frame eclipsed the sun. Covering the courtyard in darkness as the great dragon came into view. Katholomu stepped forward and the crowd fell in a hushed tone. She waited as the lights of the sorcerer Keep flared glinting of the dragon's eyes. She bowed once more before the dragon raised her on his shoulders. He made for the sky in a mighty swoop his wings outstretched their full length.

Mitch stayed silent as she concentrated on leading the dragon Kat south. She glanced back and Mitch answered, 'They are not following.'

She was not convinced and signalled for the great beast to fly on. They increased the distance from the stronghold of the sorceress Lady Davene. After a time she asked, 'What did you do?'

There was no response and they flew on. Mitch spoke, 'It's what I didn't do.'

Saranon stifled a laugh and gagged. 'I…' She cleared her throat, 'I'm glad you have standards.'

She could not help but laugh at the wizard's predicament. He was seven years her senior and it was last the thing she had expected.

The low torrid ground with its stark remnants of grass vanished into darkness. The sun disappeared over the horizon. Katholomu lowered his descent toward the low rocky hills, that marked the outlying area of Balquene before the border. The wind swept around the sparse hillside breaking the evening warmth. The great dragon hid as best he could, lying low to the ground but there was little cover. She rested underneath his wing. As Mitch scanned the horizon in the fading light that remained. It was not the end to her journey that had expected. She pulled out her small sova bag that fitted inside her pocket. The bag grew larger and she reached inside for the map. The border to Normisia was close and they had been told to return via Magladen. They could still make it west to the wizard Keep Karaden.

Mitch peered down at the map lit by a small sacra seal over the pebbly ground. The ink stood out on the thick parchment as she ran her hand over the border with Normisia. 'We cannot go there,' Mitch said.

She did not intend to but spoke her thoughts aloud, 'We may have to.'

He crossed his arms in fierce stance. He would follow her if she went. They both knew the border between Balquene and Normisia was out of bounds. The closest the two countries had ever been to reaching an agreement. It remained an unspoken stalemate. If they flew across the border they would meet the Imperial Normisian Army head on.

The sky was clear as they settled in for the night.

Kat's muscles remained tense underneath his sprawling pose. Taking advantage of the sun's heat left behind in the large boulders. Mitch leaned in, he was about to speak and stopped. An awkward silence fell. 'You could have waited until after dinner,' she said.

As her stomach grumbled, reminding her that she had not eaten. He took out some bread from his pack and broke it in two. 'That is not what I meant,' she said.

'I know,' he replied.

She rested against his shoulder drifting into a shallow sleep. It was so difficult to read the wizards thoughts. It resembled a twisted haze and she gave up, sorcerers were not designed to read minds.

Mitch woke her up. The sky was pitch black. She could just make out the dragon's silhouette, as he crouched off to the side. She could sense the sorcerers approaching from the north. Mitch could not ask her to do what they both knew. She clambered onto the dragon sitting high between his shoulder blades. Mitch sat close behind her. Saranon could sense the sorcerers panning out. Soon the path to the west would be blocked. She had to make the choice. She took one last look out into the dark expanse as the sorcerers made ground. She signalled for Katholomu to turn. He leaped into the sky heading south, straight for the border. The great dragon flew hard and Mitch clung on. He whispered, 'Thanks.'

She concentrated on the horizon. There was no sign of Mitch's homeland, but it would not be long. She could feel the tension in every beat of the dragon's wings as Kat picked up speed. She held onto the thick folds around his neck. The great beast moved with a precision that belied his bulky frame. The low hills rose and fell. They revealed the final outposts guarding the edge of the border. For a moment there was nothing then the Balquene side sprang to life. Fires flared up lighting the night sky. Yet it was the only sign to great them as Katholomu headed toward them. Saranon lowered her head as the dragon flew toward the border at speed. Mitch remained silent soon they would be there.

Katholomu flew into darkness, Normisia stayed quiet underneath. It created an earie void. The only sound came from the wind sweeping past the great dragon's wings. She began to relax yet Mitch remained tense. She glanced down over Kat's shoulder unsure if her mind was playing tricks. There appeared to be a line of movement along the ground. She pointed and Mitch spoke, 'Hold on.'

A haze radiated along the ground sweeping through the open field. It crept through the air. The movement pulled at the Kat's wings and he struggled to gain height. A line of wizardry sparked through the night, the barrier expanded as they approached. It was too late to turn back. She steered Kat straight into it. The night sky whirred to life as blasts of wizardry pummelled through the air. She dare not look as the dragon swerved, and they made it past the first barrier. She glanced down as a blast roared up through the dark sky. It was heading straight for them. She raised her sorcery from within. Before she could attack, Mitch struck out at the blast. The impact imploded, knocking the dragon off balance and he dived toward the ground.

She lost her grip and fell, rolling as the dragon skidded along the dusty plain. She just managed to soften the fall before hitting the rough surface. A cloud of dirt filled her lungs and she coughed. She tried to stand and her legs collapsed hitting the hard earth. Her head spun and the dust settled. Katholomu stayed low to the ground leaving a trail of dust behind him. Mitch held on until the dragon came to rest then ran toward her. 'Are you hurt?' He asked.

Her mouth was dry and no sound came out. A line along the ground moved as the wizards emerged from the dark. She stood still waiting as they closed the distance. The cryzinelan wizards were Mitch's clan. Though it had been made clear they had to return via Magladen.

They greeted Mitch and the tension swept away before it changed in an instant. The soldier kicked Mitch to the ground and her temper rose. She hurled her sorcery to form a shield and the soldier flew backward. She had had enough. The line broke and wizardry sparked along the shield as she knelt to the ground. The urge to fight back grew and she gritted her teeth under the strain. The wizards stepped away and a silence fell. All she could hear was the thud of her heart in her ears. Mitch held her and it was enough to calm her thoughts, the sorcery slipped away. A dragon rider plunged to the ground landing behind the line of wizards. The wizard rider approached as the line fell back to let him through.

She glared at him as the wizards protecting the border circled in. Mark's voice rang out in the dark, 'Saranon!'

She flinched at the sound. Mitch stood up, 'It was my decision to head south.'

She shouted, 'No!'

'You were warned,' Mark said.

He marched Saranon over to where Katholomu watched. He stood close, 'Welcome back. Now get on the dragon before I change my mind.'

CHAPTER TWO

A wizard's welcome

Saranon peered over the dragon's wing. She watched the barren ground change into a sprawl of green fields below. The great beast Katholomu responded to Mark's commands. She fumed at having to relinquish control. The wizard Mark took delight in flying Kat toward the Keep Hedavin. They drew further away from the northern border. The aged dragon trainer directed Kat with ease. 'I know how to fly Kat,' she exclaimed.

He chuckled, 'I'm sure you do, but you were to return via Magladen.'

'I already told you we met with Lady Davene,' she retorted.

'That does not give you permission to cross the border with Balquene,' he said.

Saranon glanced over at Splodge. Mark's dragon was

terrifying in the air and on the ground. 'How come Mitch gets to ride your dragon?'

He chuckled again, 'Splodge does what I tell him to.'

'Like when he almost killed you,' she responded.

Mark became silent before he replied, 'You have a lot to learn about dragons.'

Splodge flew close to Katholomu, the two glided back and forth through the sky. The warm air gave the first hint of spring carrying with it the scent of blossoming trees. The hill hiding Hedavin in the woods came into view all too soon. Saranon slid down the marmoz dragon as they landed. 'Wait there sorceress,' Mark said.

She watched Splodge swooping in from the sky, 'He's a bit close.'

Mark pushed her flat to the ground as the dragon sped down over them. She asked, 'Did you tell him to do that?'

'Don't be smart,' Mark replied as he stood up.

It was all she could to not to laugh. The wizards could read her immediate thoughts. She caught a few glares as they landed. Normisia brought back mixed memories as she gazed at the woods closing them in. Mitch was seven years older and towered over her. The wizard made no attempt to hide his joy at returning. The Cryzinelan wizards gave him a warm welcome. In stark contrast to the way they greeted her.

Mark patted her on the shoulder, 'It's good to have you back. The border with Balquene is off limits.'

'Thanks,' she replied with a flat tone.

'Now, you get to wash your dragon,' he grinned.

Saranon began to remember how annoying wizards could be. She strode around the stone courtyard amidst the undergrowth of the woods. She had left so much behind and it haunted her still. Tasha left her a hard task and she had failed, leaving Normisia far behind. Mitch had accepted the bond of a Hilazen, as though it were intended. She rubbed her arms and longed for a warm bed.

She paced with a hint of caution as the wind stirred with a widening rustle. It wrapped around the length of the building and they approached. The leaves fluttered as they hung to the trees in the woodland. The giant Keep Hedavin appeared empty with no one in sight. The graceful Keep lay with its true magnificence hidden. It gave the appearance of a sleeping giant. The Keep lay covered by the scrubby, woodland forest that wrapped around. The roads were narrow with worn stone. It fed the illusion of a small building nestled in the hillside. She waited as a small creak emanated from the door. She glanced up at the massive dragon in a playful mood. The image masked his quick temper and restless mind. He ducked his head between Saranon and the open door.

The black marmoz dragon frightened the occupants on the other side. Saranon admitted that this was not a difficult feat. Even when Katholomu was being cheerful, she was not sure which mood was worse. Mark Staragen bought the massive beast as a gift. This was after she had saved the wizard from being squashed by Splodge. Kat raised his claws and the door slammed shut so hard, she thought the handle would fly off. 'Now you've done it,' she hissed.

Kat stared at her with his black sorrowful eyes. She nudged his head to the side and gave an exasperated sigh. A small gap broke, showing a crease along the edge of the door. A familiar voice filled the air, 'Oh for goodness sake Jerald, open the door.'

Saranon let out a giggle at hearing Captain Mirshendy's first name. Saranon's friend Rachel had a warm and tender voice. The memory of the wizardess melted away her fears. She raced to peer over Mitch's shoulder. Only to lock eyes with the stone faced Captain. Who, for reasons she did not understand, was blocking their path. Rachel's beaming face shone through. The wizardess raced over giving Mitch a warm embrace. For an awkward moment Saranon and the Captain stood next to each other. The thought of hugging him did not interest her.

Captain Mirshendy had never once warmed to her and he kept a respectable distance. Rachel broke their silent gaze as she greeted the sorceress. She led them further into the confines of the Keep. Saranon followed Rachel's lead. She could feel the Captain's eyes watching her all the way along the corridor. Rachel leaned close and whispered, 'He's been busy and it's not you this time.'

Saranon was caught halfway in a relieved sigh when her mind caught up to the response. 'What do you mean it's not me?' She asked.

Rachel laughed, 'You are not the only sorcerer who can cause trouble.'

It was a strange form of compliment. She thought no

more on the matter when a hearty smell wafted through from the kitchen door. For an instant the wizard Keep felt like the most appealing place. Even with all its strangeness. She relaxed her weary muscles and filled her empty stomach. Mitch had managed to disappear, she could not blame him. This was his home and now he was in the company of old friends. A gruff sound reached her ears through the warm air wafting through the windows. She peered out from the balcony to watch Kat standing over another dragon.

The beast did not take much to stir and his size was enough to scare even the largest opponent. The wizardess, Gabriel, waved and shouted for Saranon to join her in the courtyard. It was not the sight of her friend that worried her. It was more the thought that Gabriel's Uncle was Captain Graddon. The man had been irritating and she hoped that he was not around. Even though her muscles ached from the ride, she went out to meet her friend. While Katholomu rested, curled up the sunniest spot he could find. The courtyard's size was hidden by the lack of boundaries. The growing shrubs covered the edge wrapping around the paving.

Gabriel was only just younger than her. With as much enthusiasm as anyone could have. She had shown Saranon through the hills of Normisia further south with her dragon. Mitsy's medium size was far smaller than her personality. Gabriel smiled, 'Thanks for bringing back Mitch.'

She peered around eyeing Mitsy. The beautiful shazel dragon recognised her with a warm welcome. 'Did you come all this way to meet us?' Saranon asked, it would not have surprised her if they had.

The wizardess broke out laughing, 'Don't be silly, I'm learning how to train dragons.'

It was not the reaction she had expected, but it was good to see her friend all the same. Even with Gabriel's constant questioning about her travels, well into the late evening.

Her weary body longed for the lure of a nice warm bed as she left the warm fire in the great hall. Gabriel had not been the only one wanting to know what had happened. She had sensed quite a few of the wizards listening in. Saranon opened the door to her apartment. She froze at the sight of Captain Mirshendy talking with Mitch. The Captain ceased the conversation and left and she gave Mitch an annoyed stare.

As she glared the wizard appeared serene, for now she would let it rest. Her weariness caught up with her and the sight of a soft bed was too appealing. The starry night shone through the open curtains with a comforting glow. It echoed the pattern of her homeland to the south. Darkonia seemed so far away. The memory of Tasha made its way back into her restless thoughts. The words of her friend from the grave still clung in the air, Kill the boy but leave the girl. She had let the boy slip through her grasp in the battle. If she had not, then Bianca would have died. A silent tear fell down her cheek for she had done neither of what Tasha's spirit had wanted.

A small comfort remained in knowing her friend Pennie was alive and well. Residing in the homeland, where she could not return after what she had done. Pennie was always resourceful. She had little doubt that if anyone could find a way to help, her friend could. The image relieved her tension. Every time she woke with mixed dreams of Indarin Keep in Serenphel. The country seemed so far away. Yet it plagued her still, seeping through her thoughts. The sorceress tried to push them away. It was an uneasy battle that kept her mind from a peaceful rest into the early morning. When she tip-toed out of the room in a clumsy grace.

Saranon half tripped as she clambered through the doorway. The dim glow darkened the silhouette of the wizard as he sat peering into an empty glass. The sorceress stood up straight, 'I take it you couldn't sleep either.'

Mitch smiled before making an excuse to go to bed. Not that there was much left of the night. The thought of a day without the wizard was appealing. Before the first rays of dawn broke through she had made a large breakfast. The journey had been far more tiring than she had let on, but it was worth the speedy return. The thought of having to face Merrick Calthazard again frightened her. Fighting the sorcerer in any form had been a good reason to leave Indarin. The second Angeon still filled her dreams with unease. She had been the one to spare him. Yet she did not think he would be so grateful for such a deed.

A small creak sounded from the door. She stood up to poke her head around the corner. Only to see nothing, before it opened further in the dark. This time she crept forward, the silhouette of a figure stood near the door.

Bently peered around whispering in a low voice and gave her fright. The tall lanky wizard was one of Captain Mirshendy's officers. Before she had time to berate him he had already spoken, 'The Captain wants to see you.'

She was not impressed and the thought of meeting Captain Mirshendy did not appeal. She followed in an awkward silence through the wide corridors. They wound along the outer rim. The high windows revealed the stars from far above. It did not take long to find the hub of wizard activity. She was led to a room via an open corridor on the edge of a magnificent internal courtyard. It was simple yet elegant with an aged feel where the stone worn. The place was well kept with a hint of pride. They made their way down the open stairs joining the internal balcony to courtyard. The surroundings were lit by a stream of lights along the columns and wall. The glow beamed from the energy of the Keep.

An opening, hidden in the outer wall covered over by the hill, displayed the fading stars outside, as the early morning drew near. The place shone with the sun's first light awakening the Keep. As she walked into the room her surprise turned to annoyance. The Captain who stood there, was not Captain Mirshendy. To begin with he was taller. What Captain Mirshendy lacked in height he made up for in strength and ability. The absence of an explanation, came as a reminder of an old scar that stayed fresh in her memory. Captain Tredeer stood in a welcoming gesture that felt too smug. He was almost the same height as Mitch and behaved as though he were an old friend. The sorceress hung back in hesitation then sat down.

She listened to yet another wizard trying to tell her what to do and kept a pleasant face. Saranon had to remind herself to slow down when she closed the door. She tried not to show her eagerness to leave, as most of the morning had been wasted. Captain Tredeer was someone she did not want to meet again, he was far too vague for her liking. She went down to the Captain she had intended to see. She bordered on a dislike for Captain Mirshendy. He was straight forward and for all his attempts, did not hide how he felt. She let out a short laugh at the thought of finding the wizard's company welcoming.

The noise of activity brought Hedavin to life. A warm vibrant movement of people bustled past. Great care was taken looking after the Keep that showed its age. In simple classical forms that noted every foyer or small entrance. The place was void of lavish colour. Yet the dull light hues suited walls and reflected natural light deeper still. The long hollows holding the opening, let in an abundance of warmth as it neared midday. She made her way down to a voice she knew well. Captain Mirshendy stood in the midst of a room filled with activity. The place was called a room, yet it was space, between other rooms. It had been adapted and filled with connections back to the inner workings of the Keep.

Panels shone with the energy from the central core below. It provided valuable feedback to the habitable area. Saranon had assisted Captain Mirshendy with fixing Greddin Fort in southern Normisia. The central core was a fascinating thing for those who saw it. She was aware that the wizards could not visit. The amount of sorcery required was mind boggling. Then careful preparation to build the structure that sat above. First the central core, then the imbenik chambers and the indolin chambers. Then last of all the habitable area which could be used by many. The giant conduits ran the stallic energy away from the liquid sheal. This fed through to the smaller pipes running through the Keep.

Once complete, the whole structure could last for centuries. People sometimes forgot there was a central core deep beneath. It lay hidden under the many layers, until something went wrong. Work was well underway with looking after the Keep. Captain Mirshendy only acknowledged her with a glance. She stepped sideways out of the way, stumbling as she put her hand out near a control panel. The sequence showing on the screens caught her eye. Her curiosity was short lived as the sorceress was asked to move.

She was about to say something when the power cut out, before flickering back to life. The pulse felt strange underneath her hand and she pulled back. She leaned against the wall and a sound sent shivers up her spine. The wizards around her responded with haste. She sped past to look out at a vacant space seeing nothing at first. In the ambient void the small sound clicked past, echoing through the floor. As she peered toward the source, two sorcerers emerged from the air. One held their prize, a wizard who still struggled to break free. The sight caught her breath and for a moment everyone froze as the shock set in.

The wizards around her moved forward in a lunge, only to hit a shield. The sorcery maintaining the shield came to life with electrifying speed. Two wizards made contact as it threw them backwards. The captive wizard made a small whimpering sound. Saranon peered through the shield. She glanced straight into the eyes of the sorcerer standing free. He moved close to the other side of the shield. Smiling with a haunting laugh as his eyes lit with a cruel delight. While their eyes met she held out Tellembre. She brought it forward with a smooth motion as she held the sorcerer's gaze. The bond-breaker was cool to the touch as she brought it out, hiding the heart stone blade.

She stabbed its blade at full length through the shield. The sword, made of heart stone, hit home with a final certainty and the sorcerer sank. The mark of the Dihan showed faint on his neck. The wizards took no time to run through as the shield faded. The remaining sorcerer vanished from sight as he fled. The captive wizard gave a thankful nod as he was freed. She gazed his way holding the bond-breaker as her nerves steadied within. Tellembre had a pearl finish, made at Ollanthia Keep in Darkonia. She let it sink back into the form of a dagger before placing it back out of sight. The energy she exerted was minimal, but the nuances of sorcery still escaped her. She turned looking at Bently, 'You failed to mention you had a problem.'

The tall wizard made an attempt to hide his expression. 'I didn't know we had one,' he replied.

The response did little to please Saranon's temper,

which lay just below the surface. Bently's words were the most the wizards were prepared to let slip. The Keep steadied itself into a peaceful rhythm. As she left to find the sorcerer quarters.

She had not expected to meet the Dihan, the Keep had given away no sign as it hummed away. Yet she was troubled by the attack. The sorcerer she had struck with the bond-breaker was Dihan. A chill fled down her spine, her first encounter had been horrendous. It was the reason for the bond with Mitch. The wizard had saved her life from being taken by the Dihan. For that his energy had linked to hers. The Dihan who had taunted the wizards did not appear to be the same and it plagued her mind. The sorceress passed through the internal foyer with its slender columns and light hues. As she peered up at the hexagonal ceiling a familiar voice spoke beside her. 'Beautiful isn't it?' Caleb asked.

The sorcerer looked far more mature than the boy she had first met at Zaidek Keep in Normisia. He stood tall with an air of confidence, yet his eyes gave away his youth. For her brief schooling in Normisia, Caleb had been a fellow student. It was an awkward time as Saranon had struggled to fit in. She smiled in response as Caleb showed her around. At least this time she did not feel like an outsider.

The warm winds of spring blew through the open windows. Carrying the fresh sweet smell of the rambling open garden as Saranon stepped outside. Cradling in amidst of the shrubs covering the edge of the path, she found Katholomu. The great marmoz dragon appeared well camouflaged amidst the shade. His dark coat belied his true length. Hedavin Keep was flanked by a vast team of dragons. The dense woodland covered the true scale of the place and its operations. Saranon wondered how the Dihan sorcerers managed to make their way into the fold. The response she received from the Keep would have been perfect. That was, if it had not been for the attack.

Kat rustled in the undergrowth. Then he stretched out grabbing hold of the first floor balcony. He flexed his wings partway open shifting them to a more comfortable spot as he stood. She held her hand out, placing it over his powerful claws. His tense muscles moved in a smooth motion. The dragon appeared for more content than he had for days. His sharp eye gave away his true composure. She stepped out onto his shoulders. The dragon etched his mark toward the sky in one fluid motion. He circled around in a massive arc mapping out the grounds of the Keep.

Katholomu had no interest in stopping. He gathered speed. He steadied himself on a high perch on the hillside covering part of the Keep. The dragon stretched his body low and the sorceress did the same. Blending into the darkness of his scales and fur, she held her head close to his. The steady sounds ran down from the Keep. She listened unsure of what had raised the dragon's attention. Two raised voices carried just above their location. It marked the end of a short argument with no sense. Still she stayed close to the great beast. He lowered his shoulder and she slid off. The dragon had less subtle ways of getting his point across.

She was not about to argue as she climbed a little higher.

She clung on and lifted her head over the small rise. Peering just above the top of the stone wall embedded half hidden in the hill. The low scattering of shrubs spread across the rocky ground as it met the wall. Then it led down offering little view of the open platform. At first the sight did not yield anything. She began to dismiss Kat's enthusiasm. Then the sun caught an object glinting back toward her with its own spark.

The clump of stone lay on its side with a faded glow, yet the energy should not be there. Saranon eyed it with great suspicion as she stayed close to wall. The cool stone numbed her cheek as she stayed still. She was caught in disbelief. The Keep should have registered the syphoned energy source, yet it did not. As silence filled the air she moved over the wall. She made her way down on the narrow steps on the other side. She glanced around as stood close enough to reach out her hand. The energy gave off a heat that infuriated her. It was too hot for a contraption that was less than half her height. The device had well fused with the Keep, she could remove it on her own and it did not make sense.

A change in the breeze made the hair on the back of her neck prickle and she caught her breath. She dashed toward the dragon scurrying over the wall as she went. She tried not to lose her grip as she half fell onto the dragon. For once Katholomu did not make a sound, not even a tiny grumble as he usually did. She leaned back into the warm folds of his side, as she stood looking out over the vast terrain. The haphazard forest trailed into the open fields. It surrounded the dense city in the distance. A city placed in the heart of nowhere. The warm breeze whipped along as a steady sound filtered up from the hillside. She clambered along and peered over the edge. Captain Tredeer's hand leaned forward with a silent speed. As he ascended, climbing at a steady pace.

Saranon gave the wizard a stark look of disbelief. She was not impressed at having her momentary thoughts interrupted. While the rest of the small group made it to the open ledge. The sorceress had wandered far from her discovery. She felt no burning desire to share as she eyed the wizard with a steady stare. The Captain, who she had only just met, was becoming less tolerable. The sorceress did not recall Captain Mirshendy being so annoying. Yet it had been some time since she had been in the midst of wizards. The dragon behind her gave no hint as he bathed in the sun's warm light. The Captain urged the sorceress to go with them as they climbed higher still.

She felt as though she had just been coerced into an awkward arrangement. She began to miss her solitude. After the final climb she stood, drawing in a long deep breath. The top yielded a full view of the surroundings. The fresh greenery blossomed after a cold winter. The wind whipped at a fast pace through her hair, as she stood admiring the view. Further down, she spotted the familiar shape of Captain Mirshendy near the dragon pens. She could sense him more than anything. The wizard had a habit of standing out from the rest, now that she knew him well enough. Captain Tredeer brought her back to reality. As he asked her about the journey to Indarin Keep in Serenphel.

Saranon had expected this. Still the tone made her even more uneasy as she responded. The conversation had taken far too long, as the afternoon grew dark. Her polite restraint was beginning to wane with fading light. Captain Tredeer made it sound as though he had only just begun. They returned to the Keep for dinner. For once she had lost her appetite, she returned to the apartment to eat alone. Except for Caleb she had not laid eyes on a sorcerer since her arrival. Yet that did not bother her after Serenphel.

Raised voices made their way through the open door. She peered out half listening out of sight, as the words reached her ears. The bold claims of Captain Tredeer had trickled down through the Keep. It was then that the anger rose, as she realised she had been tricked. The Captain had been quick to claim he had a hold over the sorceress. Saranon made her way down a narrow staircase that led below the habitable area of the Keep. Hedavin hummed away in a regular tone. It grated on her nerves since the reading it gave was false. She waited for the right moment to slip undetected along the corridor. The Keep responded with no sign of trouble which unnerved her even more.

She found the nearest panel and held out her hand searching through the Keep. The thought of having to deal with an annoying wizard, made her more determined. Yet the information Hedavin gave up took her by surprise as she let out a small gasp. The shuffle of feet broke the silence close by and she hid, not wanting to be found. The wizard could sense the slight disturbance even though the Keep gave nothing away. He lingered a while before moving on. The sorceress let out a sigh and relaxed. Things were becoming far more complicated as the Hedavin gave up an unexpected name. Major Kellaway, the wizard who stood at the centre of her annoyance.

The Major was encouraging Captain Tredeer, although she did not know why. Saranon knew where to head. There was one person she was after, but she would have to ask the Keep first. Hedavin did not like sorcerers in the wizard stronghold. It would mean a bitter compromise, but one she was willing to make.

For the time the Keep remained silent. She waited holding the frustration back from her face. The sorceress knew she would have to wait as Hedavin decided, it was not an easy ask. Her mind rattled over what she would do. Yet if the Keep accepted, there would be limits to her options. Still, extreme measures were not on the path she was willing to take. So the compromise would serve her well. Etching out of the darkness, came a tone from the heart of the central core. She smiled in response as she made her way to the wizard stronghold.

The dark pool lay in an internal courtyard. Light shone from above with a graceful opening skyward. The wizards worked at their fighting technique around pool in the centre. The place filled with daily life. The Major practised near the water's edge, stepping toward the pool. A sharp short cry rang out, as she pulled the Major under the water. On the surface, the wizards looked down to see the Major caught in a struggle with her. The wizard, Bently, ran into the pool. As soon as he entered the water the image on the surface broke away around him. He dived under staring into nothing and stepped out. 'They're in the surface,' he spoke with haste to Captain Mirshendy, who stayed close.

The Captain leaned down. He plunged his hand in, stopping short of the surface. He took hold of the Major's leg, dragging him with help back out of the pool. The Major's deep gasps for air echoed in the silence. Saranon raised her head from the water's edge. 'Next time send someone other than Captain Tredeer,' her harsh words cut through.

Her statement carried the deep anger inside as she ducked under the surface.

The wizards huddled around in shock and amazement. Major Kellaway shouted at Captain Mirshendy, 'She's your problem.'

A sigh escaped the Captain's lips. She watched on as the Captain began to search the stronghold. The Captain called out, and the sorceress replied. She had perched herself high. Not far from his gaze, as the wizard peered above toward the balustrade. Bently moved without hesitation, he stood in position behind her without making a sound. Captain Mirshendy gave a grim smile, 'This is a wizard stronghold. Go back to your room. We will discuss this in the morning.'

Saranon was not about to argue. She made her way

with ease past a rather grumpy looking Major, who spoke only with his eyes. In the silence the only sound that escaped, emanated from the walls of the Keep.

She stopped herself just before colliding into Mitch who stood in the doorway. The wizard was in no mood to argue. He stayed with a steady restraint, the frustration gleaming from his eyes. 'Next time, tell me if you have an issue. The Major will not forget,' he spoke, with a firm tone that needed no reply.

She was not about to step headlong into an argument. So she tried to veer away from the conversation.

She had almost slipped through the door to her room. As he spoke, 'Were you standing up for Jerald?'

Saranon felt her face go red. As she heard Captain Mirshendy's name and the words stuck in her throat, 'Well…'

The wizard smiled in disbelief. He patted her on the back, 'Sleep well, no doubt we will have an early start.'

She hoped Mitch was wrong, but the chances of that were non-existent.

CHAPTER THREE

The disparity

The vibrant light from the first rays of the sun swept through the curtains of the window. It hit Saranon's eyes with a vengeance and she knew she had overslept. The slight disturbances of footsteps rocked across the floor from the lounge. It suggested that she was last to rise. She sat rubbing her forehead as an almighty headache loomed into place. The thumping sent a shake down her shoulders. Mitch rose as she entered the room, with a knowing expression. He said, 'You didn't think the Major would leave you without a parting gift?'

The wizard's odd sense of humour was half expected. After a moment's hesitation she picked up the toast. Mitch watched with a slow smile. She was about to leave. Then he spoke, 'Captain Mirshendy has asked you to patrol the perimeter with Gabriel.'

Before she uttered a word she thought better of it. She did not particularly want to meet the Major twice in two days. Katholomu had been getting restless. Without a second thought she responded, 'You're coming with me.'

The wizard looked speechless for once. Then she added, 'You know this place better than I.'

He agreed on one condition, that he rode his own dragon.

They went out into the clear morning light. It played through patchwork of trees shrouding the courtyard with a shadowy rim. A robust male shazel dragon sat steady near the opening of the dragon pens. His crisp elegant mane gleamed with a rugged pride. The dragon lifted his head in anticipation. Mitch reached out his hand as Holdvar beckoned him to ride. The wizard took his place on the dragon's muscular shoulders. The beast eyed Saranon as if tempting fate. He made his mark on the open sky with a sturdy, defiant grace. Leaving little doubt in her mind the two were well suited. She eyed Katholomu in the distance and wondered what the dragon said about her.

The mighty marmoz dragon was a fraction too big for even the largest of dragons. His size alone would have made him undesirable to train and he had a temper to match. All his elegant marks of fine breeding were smeared in a thick coat of dirt. Giving away the dragon's favourite past time. His dark coat shone black from a distance. Yet on close inspection the colour was deep dark brown. His wingspan terrified most, dragons and people alike. The size of his claws stretched along the ground. All together the great beast looked spectacular until he moved, giving away his clumsiness. There was also a sense of unreliability for the dragon could not always be found. This amazed her, for his size alone would be difficult to hide anywhere.

She climbed up his shoulder sitting comfortable, on top of his thick sturdy neck. The fresh winds swept across her face as the great beast launched into the sky. She leaned forward as her headache hit hard. She managed to steady the pain while the sun pelted down with a warm glow. Kat flew in a smooth formation following Holdvar's lead. A familiar pain etched its way across her stomach. She lurched forward closing her eyes. The sinking sensation grew as she tried to hold it back. Katholomu bent back his ears and twisted sideways as the sorceress vomited. The dragon made a quick dive low to the ground without missing a beat. He flew upside down and threw the sorceress to the ground.

Saranon tumbled down the rocky hill. She grazed both her arms before coming to halt while Kat flew off leaving her far behind. She managed to sit, holding her heading her hands. The dragon was in no hurry to return as he skimmed through the sky with an easy grace. He curved around in an arc giving her a cursory glance as he glided past. He taunted her for such indignation. She could not blame him as he circled again. He held out his claws as he skidded down the hill, digging in as he slowed to greet her. Katholomu gave her one final look before rubbing the back of his neck down her top. He wiped the last of the vomit on the sorceress. She glared at him while removing her jacket.

Katholomu let out a low grumble. Then side stepped the sorceress when she tried to get back on. He lowered his head near her, and took a sniff before allowing her to ride again. The sorceress could not blame him. As she reached for Kat's shoulder a sound scraped out from the Keep. It bolted through her senses more than she heard it. The dragon curled his tail around him, waiting in the soft winds. She ventured out toward the disturbance. In amongst the scrub she could see the signs of the outer areas of the Keep. It revealed just above the surface.

She reached out touching the panel that gave every appearance of an ordinary rock. A door opened with a distinct hissing sound. The air felt hot and humid as it rushed against her face. The place appeared almost deserted. She instinctively brushed her hand against the wall of the Keep. A muffled response came through piercing its way into her thoughts. It was small, but it was enough.

The fear hidden in Hedavin's response gave a sense of urgency. As the pressure rose deep beneath the surface. The anger swelled within her. The concentration of energy made sense filling her mind with a whole new picture. She left the outer region. The door closed with a tiny whisper of acknowledgement from the wind. There was no trace behind her of where she had been.

Katholomu strayed from his vigilant watch to let her clamber aboard. The great beast heaved his wings into the air and glided along with ease. She could spot Mitch waiting out in the open, with a wave of his hand the dragon dived down. He flew at a dangerous speed ploughing deep into the muddy ground. Kat rolled his chest in the dirt before Saranon managed to climb down. She swung sideways and leaped off. He asked, 'How are you feeling?'

As she stared at him he gave a knowing grin. 'I'm fine,' she snapped.

'You could apologise to the Major?' He suggested.

The headache dissipated, but that was not what darkened her mood. She stood beside him. 'The Keep is in trouble,' she spoke in a grave tone.

Mitch did not budge, he eyed her before he responded, 'You have a lot to learn.'

She was not about to argue with him. Yet the sensations from the Keep had said otherwise, and she knew where that led. A shadow appeared across the sky. Gabriel landed Mitsy close by with a graceful ease.

The wizardess smiled. She scouted the terrain with a thoughtful gaze, 'So what do you think?'

She was not sure how to answer, 'I think we need to take care.'

Gabriel laughed, 'You were the one that picked on the Major.'

Saranon grimaced at the remark. Their journey led them down toward the edge of the city. Mitch showed a reluctance to go any farther, so she did not press the matter.

Upon returning to Hedavin she slipped out of the way as he walked on. On the surface Hedavin felt smooth to the touch. With a methodical hum that should have denoted a functioning Keep. The day's events had ignited her suspicions after the death of the sorcerer.

As she returned, the apartment felt warm and welcoming. The small balcony held the gaze of the mid-day sun. She took a bite to eat and sat peering across the grounds with its mass of foliage. A sound from the kitchen made her jump as Mitch smiled. For someone so large the wizard could be rather quiet and put her own efforts to shame. She glared at him in annoyance, 'So how is Captain Mirshendy?'

A creak escaped from the room behind them, and the sorceress spun around. She breathed a sigh of relief and sat back down while Rachel joined them on the balcony. 'If you want I can take you to see Jerald?' Rachel asked with hint of sadness.

The expression was lost on Saranon. She bounded forward in eager anticipation, hoping that the Captain would be more forthcoming. Rachel had helped her at Greddin Fort. The Cryzinelan wizards had been intent on capturing her. She was still unsure if that idea had been put to rest. Either way the wizards found it awkward having to deal with her. Yet that did not bother Rachel as the wizardess smiled in return. She shared a warm moment as they passed through the large passageways. They walked further as the corridors became less grand.

The plain walls changed with the appearance of an odd layer of grime. That squished in her fingers as she picked at it. A stale smell wafted under her nose and she flung it to the ground. Without warning, the sounds of voices floated up from beneath. She found herself standing near the bottom of the stairs. She stared at a group of wizards in the midst of cleaning up. The gunk clinging from wall to wall had all the appearances of a murky cesspool. Yet it did not have the pungent odour. It took a while to make out who was who in the dim light. Bently raised a welcoming hand and invited her down into the muck.

The sorceress took the whole site in with an astonished awe. Rachel stood calm and perplexed, waiting for something that Saranon could not figure out. Then Rachel was gone, making her way back up the stairs. She faced the small band of wizards in silence, it was hard to tell what she had just entered into. 'Right, well then,' was all the conversation she could manage. She walked toward the mess in bewilderment.

She stood for a moment looking into the swirling mess. She moved toward the edge. The sorceress peered below while a bubble broke the surface of the murky sludge. She watched as it faded in slow motion and grimaced. It was not the outcome she had expected. As she breathed her lungs could feel the grime sifting up through the air. The stale smell sank into every part of her clothing. The wizards were clearly overwhelmed by the task. It was not the response Saranon was hoping for. She saw Captain Mirshendy avoiding her gaze in the distance.

Such an abundance of muck spilling through the innards of the Keep did not bode well. As she stood thinking she could feel several pairs of eyes watching her. While the wizards worked away at the task. She walked further into the confines of the Keep. The sorceress trudged with a heavy weight on her shoulders as she thought. The screens she had found were showing only a weak connection back to the central core. This explained the build-up. There was not enough energy for Hedavin to maintain the flow. Any attempt by Hedavin to clean up the mess would have to be setup manually.

She let out a groan as she realised that would mean wading through knee deep muck. She had to get to the other side of the open drain where the levers were. The bridge still held, though it was covered under the rising sludge. Saranon searched the pile of equipment for suitable gear to wear. The return journey did not take long. She cringed before stepping down into the sludge. It felt as bad as it sounded. She squelched her way across and heaved up to the other side. The levers were easy to find, but not marked. She concentrated, reaching out her senses to look for some direction from Hedavin. In the glimmer of an instance she found it and moved the levers in place. She poked her head around the corner, as though expecting something to occur, but nothing did.

A sorcerer called out, wanting her to get out of the lower area of the Keep. Saranon's work was done. Yet, she made it clear to Weylin she was not impressed as she made her way back up the stairs. The fresh air hit with a welcome relief, as she washed down her gear, peeling it off her clothes. The smell lingered, even after changing.

Her heart warmed at the sight of Rachel, who always seemed to have enough time to speak to her. She asked the wizardess about Weylin Druyard. The sorcerer had been put out by her presence below the habitable areas. Rachel smiled and responded without answering the question. It was a sign that Saranon was on her own. Still she did not push any further, as the wizardess would have told her if she could. She sat biding her time in thought. A commotion rang through the main doors of the medical area.

Her eyes transfixed on the pain held in the wizard's face, as he was wheeled past. The image locked with her thoughts. She sensed the bond of a sorcerer running deep inside with the pain. The sorceress had seen too much, she ran out before Rachel had time to stop her. She ran to find Mitch, almost instinctively. Just to reassure herself that he was all right. The frustration showed on her voice as she spoke, 'Have I ever treated you ill?'

'Well…' The wizard hesitated.

'I was being serious,' she exclaimed.

'No,' he replied.

The mood had gone stale as she entered the great hall for dinner. There was definitely a distinct tone left hanging in the air. It filled the gaps of silence funnelling its way through the conversation. Like a pause that had been left too long. Saranon managed to find Gabriel across the crowded room. The wizardess seemed unaware of the fuss.

Her friend spent most of her time with the dragons, so she may not have known yet. She waited until her friend had eaten before mentioning it. Gabriel's stunned look answered for her. Mark eyed them from the other side of the table. He hushed the conversation with a stern look. Saranon thought he would say something. Instead the he stood and room fell silent as he left the great hall. It was not the response she had expected. Her mind began processing the information. Gabriel leaned over and whispered, 'No good comes when that happens.'

She agreed with the resounding statement, as she too left. This time no one noticed as she scampered from the room. The Keep lay in silence as she tried to reach out. She had not expected much given its current state, but a little sign would have been nice. She searched around away from the medical area. She circled back through via a more discreet path. As she drew close Saranon expanded her senses. The glimpse shot through with resounding clarity. The pain pierced her mind in an instant.

She opened her eyes not realising she had closed them in the shock. She could sense the wizard breathing in a low ragged tone and she had her answer. The wizard was bonded and he fought with every breath to hold on. The sound of footsteps crept close by. She ran from the scene before anyone could follow. As she returned, the sanctuary of her apartment was not as appealing. She flicked the light on and almost jumped. As Captain Mirshendy appeared from the dark shadow washed along the moonlit wall.

The Captain glared down at her, 'Stay away from Rowan. You are here as a guest.' He spoke with such a stern voice that Saranon was taken aback. It was not what she had expected. 'The bond needs to be broken,' she responded.

'Do not interfere with the Cryzinelan,' his voice was final as he left. She was not ready to admit defeat, but she did not want to meet the Captain head on. She almost jumped at a rustling sound behind her and stared at Mitch as he froze. The wizard vanished into his room before she could talk. She opened the door and she peeped through the gap, the wizard sat not uttering a word.

She asked as she stared straight into his eyes. 'Would Captain Mirshendy let you suffer at the hands of a sorcerer?'

Mitch had not expected the question. He answered, 'No.' The wizard spoke after her, 'Don't go near Rowan.'

'I wasn't planning to,' her words drifted as she left for a restless sleep.

The bed did not feel anywhere near as comfortable. While the wind played through the branches of the trees. The shadows moved along the walls irritating her. She reached out searching for something unknown.

Sleep caved in and a sharp image broke through the surface, as a hand reached out and pulled her in. The rush was so sudden it left her breathless as she hit the ground in an ageless dream. She stood near the running water that made no sound. She looked up to the fallen ceiling marking the edge of the ruins. A figure stood in the centre facing away, as the sun shone through. Tasha's fawn coloured hair sparkled in the light breaking through the roofless structure. As Tasha approached Saranon turned to see a man lying on the altar. He hardly moved except for a ragged breathing. Tasha turned to face the man, he does not have time.

Saranon faced her old friend who showed no sign of the death that had taken her. Then Tasha's lips moved and the words prickled down her skin, kill the boy. She knew what it meant. She had left the task undone. Tasha had always been the leader and now more than ever she felt the burden she had run from. The sorceress knelt down on one knee as she had done when the task was hers to bear. Tasha reached over and tapped her shoulder. The shock ran through Saranon's body pulling her awake and into the dark morning.

She steadied herself, while wiping the sweat from the back of her neck. She crept out, to see the corridors void of life at such a dismal hour. The only sound haunting the darkness came from the rustling breeze. Saranon dashed out into the open. It swept away the last remnants of sleep as her mind cleared. In the distance a sound made its way through the air like a small mumble. As she ran through the darkened edges of the woods more voices travelled. The sound was ever so low among the swaying leaves.

Saranon crouched out of sight. The hidden door into the Keep lay wide open. Tellembre twitched by her side. The bond-breaker hummed with delight, sensing the events before she did. A dim light stretched up ahead. It roamed from the gathering of sorcerers in the cover of darkness.

As the sorcerers parted she caught a glimpse of Edan. The sorcerer stood near the centre. A movement caught her eye. The faint sorcerer's light shone upon the boy's face. Tasha's words were still strong in her mind as she held her breath. The glow flickered as the boy moved. The build of a sorcery stirred from the ground. As the vapour rose its tentacles skyward. The spiral grew taking form and Saranon stood. The last remnant of fear left her eyes as she stared out in the distance. Tellembre's pearl blade sang as she drew the blade and it formed into a sword. The bond-breaker made at Ollanthia was light and durable, fitting snug in her hand. She honed in on the boy's face. She had let Tasha down in the battle at Zaidek. The blade swung as she held it by her side.

The sorcerers began to close in a tight circle. Around the trail of sorcery as it lit its way into the sky. She raised the pearl blade and it shimmered in the light. Saranon swung in tight as the first two sorcerers turned to face her. Their eyes stayed with the bond-breaker. Her energy rose with one purpose as the blade swung. Then the blast followed through. It hit the sorcery swirling from the ground and deflected. The blast hit the sorcerer to the left of Edan. The sorcerer took the full force as he crumpled into a heap. She sensed the wizard Rowan and her face went pale. Captain Mirshendy had told her to stay away.

Edan disappeared as the group of sorcerers broke away from the huddle. She grimaced as she lost sight of him. The two sorcerers next to her regained their composure. They hurled their sorcery toward her. The blasts spiralled before she managed to block them. A cataclysm of sparks radiated through the air. The sorcery settled to show the place had been abandoned. Tellembre shone as she fumed. She had failed Tasha again, and she would have to face the Cryzinelan wizards.

She swung Tellembre high in the form of a sword, and staggered back. Tellembre came to life in the darkness of night before the dawn. Her heart pumped loud in her chest. Katholomu swooped down following the glow from the bond-breaker. His mighty claws dug in hard as he ground to a halt. His wings stretched their full length to lessen the impact. The dragon lowered his head and glared into her eyes. She transformed the blade back into a dagger and Kat lifted her up onto his shoulders. His coat was smothered in grit and blood, yet she did not question him. Her mind was filled with the silence of knowing she had failed again. The great beast grunted as he leaped into the sky. She patted him and the blood soaked her hand.

'We have both been busy tonight,' she spoke to the dragon and he snorted in acknowledgement. 'Perhaps I should have gone with you?'

Kathomolu gave a low chuckle that rumbled through his belly, and coughed. 'Great, even my dragon won't fight with me,' she grumbled.

The dark silhouette of Hedavin loomed overhead and her heart sank. She would have to face the wizards.

CHAPTER FOUR

End the night

The grey sky hid them and they made their way to the dragon pens before the morning sun broke. Saranon waited for the dragon to stop instead he squeezed under the gate. She clung on as she shouted. Kat ran toward the pool of water with a flying leap. He rolled and she managed to jump clear plummeting straight into the water. The great beast ducked his head under and scooped her up. He placed her near the edge. She wanted to shout at him, but he needed a bath or there would be questions. 'You owe me,' she said as she picked up a scrubbing brush.

'At least you don't have to face the Cryzinelan,' she said as a thought struck her. 'Please tell me you don't.'

Katholomu snorted in disgust.

The dragon showed enormous patience as she dried him off. Taking care to pick out the last signs of what he had been up to. He curled up in the courtyard welcoming her to rest with him. She was exhausted and accepted knowing she have to face the wizards later. The air filled with shouting as the great beast gave no sign of his hidden guest. The shallow hint of dawn splayed through the tiny openings. She remained silent, well after the commotion had passed. Mark's voice cut through the air urging the dragon to move. At first Katholomu gave no response. It only prompted the wizard to walk closer as he shouted. Kat stared the wizard down in a bemused fashion before uncurling his large body.

Saranon knew Mark Staragen well from Greddin Fort. The wizard was the best dragon trainer in Normisia. A reputation the wizard did not need to boast, he was also stubborn and irritating. The only reason she had warmed to him was because he had bought Katholomu for her. It was an act of kindness that left her baffled. The wizard had a grim presence and she was sure he could back up the unspoken threat. She climbed up onto the dragon's shoulders. She stared down at Mark, before the great beast launched into the grey sky. She was in no mood to answer questions as the night's events weighed on her thoughts.

Katholomu landed on a nearby hill before he lost his footing skidding to a stop. His sheer size made the landing difficult to judge. She patted the great beast. Then stared down into the valley where she had been the night before. The deep forest hid the area from the sky, as she stood with the wind sweeping through her hair.

A dark figure overshadowed the sky, she peered up

to see Splodge's underbelly. She could recognise Mark's dragon anywhere. He dived down beside Katholomu, giving a friendly nudge with his shoulder. Splodge stood his ground showing off his height, before letting Mark slide down. The wizard was one of the few Saranon had not argued with. His statue and appearance gave him a stronger presence than any other she had met. He was almost the same height Mitch. With a stocky robust built that gave the impression he could withstand anything. 'You need to return to the Keep, Mitch is in trouble,' the wizard spoke with a gruff rigid tone.

'Are you sure?' she asked completely stunned.

'He is blamed for Rowan's death,' Mark responded.

'Mitch wouldn't do that,' the sorceress spoke, still in shock.

'Then I suggest you return to the Keep,' the wizard's answer was final. He stood waiting for Saranon to move first.

Katholomu saw no need to rush. He waited before bolting into the sky, toward the open courtyard. Gabriel ran to meet her before she was stopped by a wave of Bently's hand. Captain Mirshendy's officer stood strong as the sorceress strode towards him. 'Come with me,' he spoke in curt voice.

The silence faded into a dull chant of shouts, emanating from the wizard stronghold. Saranon did not have much time to wonder, as a searing sea of eyes fell straight upon her. Then the shouting began as the realisation came too late. Bently strode behind her blocking her escape. She made her way to the front of the audience. The crowd parted with a great reluctance. None were brave enough to block her path.

She almost landed into Captain Tredeer, side stepping at the last second. She spied Mitch kneeling down on the platform. The chants grew around her before the Major's voice cut through the noise. Her mind was still catching up as she looked around. In amongst the crowd Captain Mirshendy stared back. Major Kellaway's words rang out. He boomed over the crowd as he stood on the platform near Mitch. He ordered the sorceress to stand on the platform before her. The crowd waited in eager anticipation.

She stepped forward turning back to face the Major. A hush fell through the crowd of waiting faces as Saranon waited. The buzzing silence lingered too long. As she braced herself for what may come. She remembered the agreement she had made with the Keep. She held back a smile, eyeing the Major as nothing occurred. Captain Tredeer broke the silence with his rage. The Keep would not harm the sorceress. He lunged toward her, as the Major ordered Captain Mirshendy to take Saranon and Mitch from the hall. Captain Mirshendy wrapped his strong arm around hers. They ducked away as the mood in the crowd changed too frustration. To her surprise the wizard took them back to his quarters in the wizard stronghold.

She could contain herself no longer and smiled. As she spoke, 'I always wondered what you did for entertainment.'

For once the Captain did not growl. Instead Mitch filled the gap, 'This is serious.'

'Did you kill Rowan?' She asked.

'No,' he replied.

'Then what is the problem?' the sorceress exclaimed as she faced the Captain.

Captain Mirshendy was about to answer when Rachel rushed through the door. She beckoned them to follow, as an array of harsh voices rose from the corridor.

Before Saranon had the chance to ask, the wizards ran ahead. They left her bewildered as she caught up. She peered around the wall, her mouth dropped at the sight of a sobbing wizardess. Cynthia, the Major's daughter, turned and looked her way. The Major's humiliated face told her more than she needed. Cynthia had ended Rowan's life.

She stood close to Mitch, and whispered, 'Will they do the same to her?'

'No,' he whispered in return, as the room fell silent.

The Major looked up at the Captain, 'We'll have to find another way.'

Captain Mirshendy nodded his agreement.

'Ah…' Saranon was about to speak up as Mitch read her thoughts.

'You didn't,' he exclaimed.

'I was only told to stay away from Rowan,' the sorceress glared at him.

Cynthia broke out into a painful sob as she realised the sorcerer was dead. Rowan would have survived. 'Take them from the room?' Major Kellaway addressed Captain Mirshendy. The Captain ushered Saranon and Mitch away. 'Tomorrow I expect you both to help with the clean-up,' the Captain spoke to the pair. Their mouths gaped in silent protest.

Saranon turned to Mitch, 'This is your fault.'

As the two exchanged short words, neither noticed Mark wandering up behind them. He said, 'I have two dragons that need cleaning, go and sort it out.'

Mark had not stopped moving as he moved them toward the pens. Mitch made his way down the stairs. She was not so convinced, 'Katholomu was clean this morning.'

'Why don't you take a look,' Mark spoke as he stood at the top of the stairs.

She was not about to argue any further as another person approached. Mark began shouting. She hurried down toward the dragon pens. Saranon almost ran into Gabriel who looked relieved to see her. The wizardess was a fraction younger even though she was an apprentice trainer. She had a natural gift for working with dragons.

The horrid smell of damp dragon stuck in her throat as she tried not gag. Gabriel smiled, 'You haven't seen Kat yet have you?'

It was a knowing comment more than a question. The sorceress did not need to wonder much longer. The great dragon was hunched back rubbing an itch on his shoulder. He kept dropping clumps of gunk. It had matted across his fine coat, and taken away all its shine. If she did not know better, Saranon would have sworn the dragon had done it on purpose. He had trudged through the mess the Captain asked her to clean up. Her mouth gaped, then she shut it, as a putrid smell caked her tongue. The dragon turned around and grinned.

Kat wiped a grubby cheek all the way along her side, making sure not to miss any part of her clothing. The wet substance sank through the fabric. She cringed as it stuck to her hands and she pushed the dragon away. Gabriel tried to stifle a laugh as she stepped back. The sorceress held out her grubby arms and her friend let out a short squeal then ran. Gabriel could not get away fast enough. As Saranon made her way to the change room covered from head to toe with muck. She winced at the thought. She hurled herself into the giant task of cleaning the dragon.

The sorceress looked up after dry reaching for the second time. To see Katholomu standing, soaking wet. The hose rinsed away the bulk of the smell, as she lathered his rough skin. It foamed with the sweet smelling liquid over his hard scales. The dragon did not mind being clean. For all his love of dirt, it was an excuse to find another way of getting grubby. He swished his tail along the ground in a curved arc. The sorceress groomed around his ears. Katholomu's ear twitched but she took no notice as she brushed up his markings. A gentle hand reached up and patted the dragon. Saranon almost fell off with surprise at the sight. Rachel had appeared without making a sound.

'Thank you for helping with Rowan,' the wizardess had been crying. Yet her eyes shone true.

'Will Cynthia be okay?' Saranon asked.

'Yes,' Rachel responded. The weight of a heavy day filtered through. As the wizardess asked the question she had come for. 'How is it that you were not affected by the

Keep?'

Saranon smiled as she glided down off the dragon's silky back. 'I made an agreement with Hedavin,' she said.

'You were lucky,' Rachel remarked and welcomed her to an evening meal.

The sorceress scoffed into the dish. Captain Mirshendy joined them with a thud as he sat down. The Captain glanced at her, 'You made the Major look like a fool,' the Captain spoke.

'Jerald,' Rachel responded.

'He has more empathy than I do,' at no stage had the Captain lost his harsh edge.

It was as close to friendship as she would see from the Captain. So she kept the response to herself. The night was growing dim as she left, with her weary muscles calling out for sleep. As she went into the apartment Mitch gave her a warm hug of appreciation, 'Thanks.'

'You could've cleaned my dragon?' Saranon suggested in astonishment.

'He's your responsibility,' the wizard smiled.

A tear escaped falling onto the pillow as lay awake in a warm bed. Rowan had lost his life for nothing. She hoped tomorrow would be more welcoming as she left.

A figure blocked the light. She blinked opening her eyes, letting in the morning light. She remembered where she was meant to be and groaned. Mitch smiled he did not have to say anything, as he waited. 'Why do wizards always have to be annoying,' she muttered under her breath. She followed Mitch downstairs.

'Well, you are in wizard Keep,' Bently's voice startled her, 'Did you sleep in?'

Mitch turned around and smiled with a soft chuckle. She was about to grab some equipment when Bently shook his head. They stepped into the underground chamber. While her mind took a while to catch up with what she was seeing.

Saranon peered over the hard edge into the darkness. She made out the trail of muck that had receded to the depths below. She was about to ask the wizard how, when she recalled her previous visit and smiled. The mess had been dissipating since she had manually engaged the Keep. It picked up a higher level of waste. Bently slid down and walked along the lower ledge. They followed as the sorceress tried not to touch anything grubby. It was impossible as she wiped her sleeve. Up ahead she heard a familiar voice. Captain Mirshendy gave a nod of recognition between orders.

The Captain appeared far more relaxed and at home in the slimy belly of the Keep. The wizards worked hard to open the doors. They washed out the grime from the chambers underneath. She peered around the corner, and stood stunned. The roaring sub-station whirred away underneath her feet. She knelt down, peeking over the edge. 'Impressive isn't it?' Bently spoke next to her before the Captain interrupted.

Impressive was not the first word that sprang to Saranon's mind. As she took note of the load the sub-station was picking up.

'I need you to go further down,' the Captain spoke in a flat tone.

'I can see why,' the sorceress answered without taking her eyes off the engine.

'If this is not fixed there will be another Rowan,' the Captain spoke. The other wizards fell silent.

The sorceress felt the weight of his words on her shoulders, she stood up and nodded. Mitch peered over the edge next to the Captain. He stared out into the gloom just as Saranon fell into knee deep muck and shouted.

She could hear the wizard laugh with nervous relief from above. As she waded out to the other side and cleaned herself off. She trudged along, trying not slip as remnants of the grime squelched beneath her. It covered the base of the lower floor and pooled in the lower areas. A sound crept up from the pipes leading deep underground. She caught her breath, then letting out a sigh into the silence. She steadied herself climbing downward along a stale dry passage. A musty smell wafted from the opening and prickled up the back of her neck.

Saranon froze, before stepping into an alcove. The large sealed doors were lying in her path. The sorceress stood in the alcove of the great archway. The doors blocked her entrance down to the central core. She held out her hand and it felt hot to the touch. As she examined the seal around the doors the stress lines showed. The weakness embedded in the tiny grooves. She stood back in awe as the Keep held the pressure at bay. It remained locked within the central core. A small tapping sound echoed from above.

She moved away and started back to the surface.

Captain Mirshendy was waiting in the silence, 'We have to leave.'

Before she could speak, Mitch whisked her out of sight. A familiar sound crept through the space and the colour drained from her face. They darted away in the midst of the confusion. A warning prickled at the edge of Saranon's senses. She ran in front of the wizard as the sorcery hit in a fit of rage. It melted, trickling down as the sparks hit the barrier. It faded, as she shielded Mitch from the blow. The heated shouts from the other wizards reached their ears. The group reunited in the ambush. The Captain's cold harsh stare glimmered in the light, as a scream cut through the air.

Saranon recognised who it was, as she peered beyond the group. She could just make out Cynthia, made visible in a moment hesitation. In the verge up ahead she could make out Captain Tredeer. She cringed knowing that the sorcerers who attacked had the advantage. Just as an attacker spotted Captain Tredeer's hiding place. Saranon ran with all her might. Time slowed as the pain seared through. The familiar agony that coursed through her and an old memory came to life. As her energy resonated with Hedavin she sucked the energy of the Keep in. She churned it out with immense force.

The Keep let out a violent thunderous roar. The wind whipped through the air and shards of Hedavin with it. The sparks broke across the walls in an array of light. For in the space between time and nothing the Angeon held out her hands. She grasped the energy. The pain melded with the air and the smell of fear pulsing through the pressure. The blades formed from the whirring haze. The brilliant razer-sharp blue of Normisia, called forth in two strong bond-breakers. As Saranon raised them Captain Mirshendy leaped forward. He took the one to the right, wielding the blade as he sheared through his opponent. Captain Tredeer took the one in her left hand. The sorceress could not raise her voice amidst the dim haze. The two Captains had finished their work.

She was in no frame of mind to argue over losing her new bond-breakers. She walked over to Cynthia and held out her hand. The wizardess stood in amazement at the scene. As the other wizards cleared the area, with almost no sign left of the disturbance. In the silence that followed Cynthia asked, 'Does there have to be another Hilazen?'

Captain Mirshendy did not answer, his hard stare spoke for him. Mitch stayed by the sorceress. As Captain Tredeer led Cynthia away, 'I thought you didn't like him?'

Saranon was not about to argue with the wizard. Yet he could be infuriating, 'Of course I don't.'

Then she realised she had spoken the words too loud.

CHAPTER FIVE

Company

Mitch was still laughing to himself after Saranon's outburst, much to her disgust. The sun shone bright at the start of a new day. The glimmering rays belied the subtle tone, that had swept through the Keep from the day before. It was not what she had wanted in many ways. Captain Kane Tredeer had begun boasting of his acquired prize. At least Captain Mirshendy kept his hidden from sight. Although there was a distinct jovialness to his step that appeared out of place. She smiled shaking her head in disbelief. A thought had crossed her mind to take the bond-breakers back. Yet Mitch's glare suggested otherwise. The wizard had become good at answering her sudden nondescript thoughts.

The fresh air flowing around the grounds outside swept beneath her feet. She strode toward the dragon pens and a familiar sound rang out. Only this time it was Mitsy the shazel dragon, who had a rough elegance about her. The dragon greeted the Saranon before expecting her to follow.

Mitsy skittered around the corner disappearing with a short flick of her tail. She was full grown but the size of a teenager compared to Kat. She woke Katholomu who lifted his sleepy head with one eye open. The dragon had been sunbaking on his side and he stretched out his body with a vibrant shake. Saranon stepped back and Kat had already stooped down. He picked her up, tilting her onto his large shoulders. The sorceress smiled as Gabriel's voice echoed nearby. She asked, 'I thought you would like to go for a ride?'

'That sounds great,' Saranon smiled in return. The clear blue sky beckoned from above.

It was good to feel the air move. Even if the dragon's launch made her stomach squirm as he bounded for the sky. The wizardess, Gabriel, glided along with ease as Mitsy flew in perfect formation. Kat grunted beneath her. They flew to the edge of the bustling city, where the two dragons did not appear out of place. It had been ages since she had the chance to roam through Normisia. She let Gabriel lead the way. The street was clean with a rough edge. She reflected the hardiness of the people living in the north.

Saranon rushed ahead in the maze of shops and activities. It took her a while to notice that Gabriel was not following. She looked around then went back reaching out with her senses. She narrowed down her search walking up to the corner of a building. In the alleyway stood a sorceress she gasped at the sight. Bianca shushed her as they stood in silence. Saranon could not see the point of staying in the dreary alley. Bianca disappeared into the wall, leaving the sorceress alone with Gabriel. Before she had time to ask, a sound came from along the ground in a slow hiss.

She reached out and dragged Gabriel into a rear entrance of the building. They listened to the sound of soft gravel footsteps approaching. Then it stopped. The sorceress did not need to tell her friend to be silent, as they stayed hidden. The sound resonated from their breath, as every minute felt like an hour. When the footsteps had headed away she breathed a sigh relief. Bianca stood beside them as Gabriel let out a small gasp in recognition. 'What are you doing here?' The wizardess asked.

'It's all right they're gone,' Bianca said.

She tried to sound convincing, with the doubt showing in her eyes. The thin smile did little to reassure Saranon, who saw the signs of a hidden fear. 'I think now would be a good time to head back,' she spoke her thoughts aloud.

'No,' Bianca said with a strained voice, 'How about we stay a little longer?'

'Okay?' Gabriel responded hoping for more of an explanation.

Bianca smiled as they crept outside with the fading light. They stepped into a warm welcoming air. A complete contrast to the last few hours. Saranon stayed several paces behind in an agitated state as she surveyed the area.

She remained unconvinced that the trouble had vanished, but her senses revealed nothing. Gabriel was intent on having fun as she joined a group of friends. From the edge of her energy Saranon felt something. She grabbed Bianca's arm, 'You need to go.'

Her tone was so final that her friend did not argue, as the three of them made it back to the dragons. Bianca sat atop Katholomu. The scent of sorcery that had been picked up earlier grew stronger. She motioned for Kat to go and the great dragon wasted no time. Mitsy followed in unison. Saranon stayed, watching them as they grew distant in the sky.

The air buzzed around her as she glanced back not seeing anything. The Angeon crept to the surface with delight knowing what it had been called for. The energy of old ran through her. A sound sparked her attention in the dim shadows of the late afternoon. It spread across the ground from the buildings. The sound grew as the wind rushed around her, sweeping a steady path. Growing in the hollow drone as a figure appeared in the distance. The sorcerer came closer with every step. Saranon was waiting. As she did the figure blended into the background leaving behind no trace.

She stepped forward toward the last trace. The air prickled against her skin as the cold set in. Damon stood in the shadows as she waited, she could sense him. Damon raised his sorcery from the ground as it twisted around. He strode forward facing her. Saranon let out a gasp as he stood too close for comfort. 'Stay out of my way,' he waited for her to back down, then shook his head. 'I gave you a choice.'

'Another time,' Saranon replied.

She raised her sorcery to remove the barrier he had placed around her. It took more effort than she expected, yet she shrugged it off in Damon's presence.

'Very well,' he spoke.

He raised his arms and the ground trembled, Saranon was thrown back. She managed to buffer the fall before slamming into the dirt. She stood catching her breath and braced herself. She created a barrier to give her time. Damon could sense the shield and he flinched. He gave one blast that shook the shield just enough to frighten her. She took the warning and fled. 'Run, run while you can girl,' Damon's voiced echoed after her.

It was not what she had wanted, but then there was no point chasing Damon as her senses reached out. She ran to the nearest lay-line, and rushed to the Keep Hedavin hoping her friend was safe. She did not have to wait long to find out. She made it to the apartment, where Bianca was talking to Mitch. He appeared at home with the Palascene sorceress in his presence. He was far more comfortable than he was around her. Bianca stood to thank Saranon. While avoiding any direct questions about who had been following her.

Saranon felt a great reluctance to push the point. All the while Bianca's calmness made her feel more on edge. At Zaidek the Palascene sorceress had been scathing at times with her remarks. The sight of the same person with sadness haunting her eyes ran shivers done her spine. Her friend changed the subject, 'You are lucky to have Mitch.'

Lucky was not how she would describe the wizard. The word irritating was more appropriate. Bianca laughed at her expression as the thought showed on her face, 'I need your help.'

'I guessed that,' Saranon looked up from making the bed. Her friend watched in amusement.

'I need a Hilazen,' Bianca said.

As the words left the friend's mouth she almost fainted. She asked, 'Why in Tordoren would you want that?'

'My kin want me to bond a wizard,' she replied.

Saranon froze, as all her thoughts escaped in the stillness that followed. She was not sure what to say in the awkward pause.

She said the first word that entered her head while her mouth gaped, 'Oh.'

'Do not tell anyone.' Bianca added, 'Not even Mitch.'

'Well that makes it difficult. Is there anything else?' She asked with a hint of sarcasm.

'I would like some toast,' Bianca's request reminded her not to ask silly questions.

Mitch was keeping busy in the kitchen. She almost ran straight into him and the wizard side-stepped. Saranon changed her tune as she waited for the toast. The wizard could appear uninterested as he lingered. She darted back to the room where Bianca sat. Her friend showed no hint of their conversation. She settled down into her warm cosy bed and turned over. The rain crept through the quiet night, lapping at the window.

The restful sleep turned into a rampant dream. All

she could see in the image was a figure running. As she chased the figure ran farther away. She was left alone as she caught her breath and turned back. She was under attack. She flung her arms to hold off the surge of energy as it catapulted toward her. Something moved in the real world above her head. She opened her eyes with a start. Her energy raged just beneath the surface as she reached out her senses. She walked over to the large window and peered out into the darkness. No sign came so she eased her way back into bed. Whatever had alerted her would have to wait as she drifted off into sleep.

The sound of rushing water woke Saranon, as she remembered she had a guest. Bianca looked far more like her former perfect self as she left the room. By the time Saranon managed to run out to the lounge room Bianca was gone. Her heart skipped a beat with panic before Mitch reassured her. He led the sorceress to the main control room, like the one she had seen at Zaidek. At the threshold of the door she stopped glancing in. Bianca and Captain Mirshendy were deep in conversation.

For a brief moment Saranon saw a small spark of energy between them. Then it was replaced by a sense annoyance that swept through her. The Captain was calm and polite around her friend. Just as she was about to speak Mitch asked, 'You two have become good friends?'

He knew the pair had clashed at Zaidek. As she tried changing the subject, 'So what are we doing here?'

'We need to gain access to the lower areas,' he answered.

She was not convinced with Bianca not having to brave the grimy chambers below. He spoke as though reading her thoughts, 'The controls are our best chance.'

The scowl remained on her face as she let it go. She peered down at the screen running the length of the bench. She ran her hand over it to search through the information. A shadow passed over and she glanced up to see Cynthia.

The wizardess tapped on the control panel, 'Mind if I help?'

She felt a sadness knowing Cynthia's loss and nodded. If anyone would be able to help the Major's daughter could. Cynthia saw her cringe as Bianca's laugh cut through the air. The wizardess asked, 'What did you do to annoy the Captain?'

'I don't know,' Saranon answered while Mitch coughed interrupting them.

Cynthia smiled at him. As the sorceress retorted, 'You became my Hilazen afterward so that doesn't count.'

Mitch coughed again, and she glared at him. Cynthia laughed, shaking her head. As she went back to work and remarked, 'It's like all the accesses are jammed.'

Saranon felt like hitting her head against the screen. She refrained from acting on the thought. The wizardess was trying to help. She glanced sideways to find Bianca had discovered a way into the maze. Captain Mirshendy greeted it with jubilation.

The Captain's reaction annoyed her even more. As Cynthia broke the silence, 'You don't like him do you?'

She turned to answer, 'I'm not sure.'

Her response was not what Mitch had expected. Before he spoke Bianca began showing them how to gain access to the system. With a way in, Saranon did not need much encouragement. Cynthia watched with excitement.

The paths that lay hidden underground came to life. It showed in sequences cascading along the screen. Still it held a few glaring disadvantages, as she began plotting the way in her mind. No doubt she would be expected to make the journey down. Bianca's voice chatted away in the background. She sighed as her friend gave the appearance not being in trouble. There had been no sign of Damon since to her relief. The morning progressed with a graceful ease. Cynthia's conversation came to a mute halt as she peered up.

Captain Mirshendy had lost none of his hard edge. Even with the new bond-breaker sitting by his side. The Captain gave no sign of appreciation. He suggested proceeding with another attempt down in the Keep. All the while staring at Cynthia as the fear shot up through her eyes. Saranon pursed her lips together as the Captain spoke. He appeared as though the fate of another wizard had been decided. The silence gave away far more than his words. As she eyed Mitch with a knowing glare, 'I don't look so bad now?'

'Well…' He began.

Saranon thumped him on the arm before he could answer. His laughter only annoyed her more. The midday sun in the garden offered a refreshing change, as she moved away from the group. Spending the afternoon in the control room did not appeal. She strode toward the dragon pens. Gabriel was grappling with one of the dragons. She intervened and held on to the dragon's hind leg as the beast admitted defeat. 'Thanks,' Gabriel called from the other side.

A loud snort ran warm air straight down her back as she turned to see Splodge. Mark's dragon, Splodge, was hard to miss. He had the same no nonsense attitude as his rider. The beast had a soft spot for her after their first meeting at Greddin Fort. The dragon had almost killed Mark. Being trapped between two dragons gave Saranon an uneasy feeling. She heard voices from across the courtyard. Gabriel poked her head over the dragon Dredger, 'Are you hiding from something?'

'Hard work,' she answered.

'You've come to the wrong place,' before Gabriel laughed.

Mark motioned for his dragon Splodge to leave and he spied the sorceress.

'Why aren't you with Mitch?' He did not wait for a response. Before making the firm suggestion that the dragon pens needed cleaning.

Saranon was still trying to think of a response when Mark had left. 'I wouldn't bother he's been out of sorts,' Gabriel added.

Dredger was more of a hindrance than a help. She used a small amount of her energy to push the dragon out of the way.

The beast did not make any attempt to snap at them.

Gabriel laughed at the sight before diving in to give a hand. The place wafted of a musty smell, although it looked far tidier than it had before. She had to find a solution for both the wizard clan and Bianca. She mused over it as she rinsed the floor. While trying to avoid soaking Splodge as he lay to the side watching the spray of water. She placed the bucket back on its stand and peered around in search of Gabriel.

A sound drew her attention from the corridor. As she stepped into the Mark's office finding no one. A paper caught her eye on the desk and she could not resist the opportunity to peek. She let out a gasp, as the muffled thud of footsteps approached and she ran outside. Mark's booming voice echoed in the distance. She was too shocked to take any notice. Saranon ran straight for an end node of the Keep. As she reached it she fell in a weary heap and collapsed out of breath. The sorcerer's stone had a dull finish resembling paving. It was smaller than the end nodes she had seen at Indarin. She rested her legs trying to think as the image stuck in her head.

She drew a heavy breath, as a light breeze blew around her. The afternoon shadow grew into a murky glimmer of evening. Thoughts whirled around her head. She had to help Bianca. The air trickled with an unseen stillness by the natural sky. Her senses began to prickle at the edges. There was no time to waste as she made her way down in the confines of the Keep. She touched the wall of the Keep, and sent a faint signal hoping that it would reach Bianca in time.

If her idea did not work it would be too late. The sorceress could sense the wizards in the background, keeping their distance. A figure emerged up ahead and she smiled with as Bianca met her in the outer region of Hedavin. Bianca spoke, 'It's good to see you.'

Saranon whispered, 'I think you should bond Jerald.'

Her friend let out a small gasp. The wizards revealed themselves from the background. Just as she had expected the Captain approached first.

Captain Mirshendy's eyes pierced the darkness as he went for Saranon. She was ready for him, and in no mood to yield to the wizard as she gripped him in a tight hold. The other wizards closed in. As Bianca cried out, 'I can't do it, I can't do it,' and sobbed slipping to the floor.

The hesitation of the whole group was instant. As Saranon turned to the Captain and retorted, 'Well you're no good.'

She loosened her grip, and tossed him to the side. The Captain did not go far as she stared him down in an attempt to negate a second round.

'What's going on?' Captain Mirshendy's mind did not miss anything. It bought a temporary truce.

'Bianca needs to bond a wizard and I thought you would do,' she exclaimed.

The Captain's jaw dropped. To Saranon's amazement he approached Bianca and held out his hand. Before she had time to think Bianca and the Captain bonded. She was speechless at the sight.

Bently stood beside her. As she noticed the wizards

had blocked the most obvious path of escape. She eyed the wizard as he led them off to the wizard stronghold. They peered down over the balcony. Listening as Bianca and Captain Mirshendy explained what had happened. She was so focused on the pair that she only sensed Mark when he stood right next her. Saranon did not know what to say as he listened. Bianca was accepted into the midst of the Cryzinelan.

Mark leaned over and whispered in her ear, 'I was meant to be bonded to you.'

The words cascaded through her brain like a torrent as her face went pale. All she could manage was a whisper, 'Why?'

'Because you can access the central core,' his words were so definite. That it made her wonder if she could enter the core under pressure.

She turned, the wizard walked away without saying anything more. Yet what he had said was enough.

Saranon was so bewildered that she lost track of time as she entered the apartment. Mitch took on a scary appearance when he was angry, he slammed a mug down so hard it almost broke. 'I'm sorry,' she spoke assuming he was angry with her.

'It isn't you,' Mitch explained.

'Are you sure?' She asked.

The wizard managed a smile in return.

She stood watching him for a while before sitting at the table. 'I couldn't stand to have more than one wizard.'

Mitch nodded staring before looking up with eyes

that showed a heavy burden. It was not what she wanted as she her thoughts turned to the central core. 'I may be gone for a while,' she said.

'Are you going to spend time with your friend?' He asked.

'I meant Hedavin,' she responded as she eyed his knowing look.

The pair sat in silence as she thought of Captain Mirshendy and Bianca. She wondered who her friend was afraid of. As the night crept in, Saranon began feeling the harshness of the day. It rested heavy on her shoulders. The Captain had given her a thumping bruise that would still be there in the morning. She wondered what the Cryzinelan had been thinking and what lay below in Hedavin.

CHAPTER SIX

A virtuous ground

The branches clipped the window in the night breeze. As the moon still shine outside. Saranon had not bothered to close the curtains. Her dreams had been filled with darkness from her days in the detention camps. She felt the marks in palms that were no longer there. Mark's words still clung in her head and echoed through her ears. She reached for her bond-breaker, the dagger stayed in its dormant form. She opened the door jumping with fright. In the darkness stood a figure, Captain Mirshendy, his silhouette form stood like stone.

It was not the first time the Captain had snuck up on her, as she caught her breath while he spoke. 'Mark should not have warned you,' the wizard said with a firm stance.

Saranon's mouth gaped before she closed it. 'You don't get to make that decision,' she retorted and headed past the

Captain.

Bently materialised out of the shadows and blocked her path. She eyed him while her anger rose to the surface.

Her energy surged escaping from her hands. It stunned Bently as he clambered to the ground. Silence followed before the Captain pinned her to the wall in one swift motion. The Angeon waited just beneath the surface calling to be let out. Saranon held it back as the two stood face to face. Letting go of her energy could kill the Captain, and that was not what she wanted. The Captain was not gaining any ground and she laughed right in his ear. 'I'm not the little girl you first met,' she remarked.

The Captain knew that he had met an impasse. He was reluctant to acknowledge the fact, as he kept hold of the sorceress. A door opened and she sighed as Mitch made an appearance. 'Can you tell him to let go?' she asked Mitch as he stared with a curious smirk.

Before he had time to ask Captain Mirshendy eased off a little. Her head was still thumping and she could sense the headache was unnatural.

The wizards were caught in a power play without words. She felt as though she had been left out of the conversation. Saranon felt like running for the door, but Bently stood in the way with a bemused look. The Captain began to speak then his legs crumpled. He collapsed with bewilderment as Saranon's headache went away. She knelt down, 'You forgot about the bonding.' she said as the wizard still showed signs of weakness.

Mitch helped lie his friend down on the couch as

the sorceress lifted his feet off the ground. 'So what have you decided?' She asked the wizards as they appeared inexplicably dumbfounded. 'Well my plan is to get into the central core,' she spoke as she stood up. '...And that does not involve Mark.'

She stated the last words as she leaned over Captain Mirshendy.

She waited for a moment expecting some kind of response. Yet the Captain gave none as she eyed Mitch, 'Can you make sure he stays out of trouble?'

'What makes you think it's going to work?' The Captain asked unconvinced.

'Because you are not going to be in the way,' she retorted.

She wanted to add a whole lot more but stopped herself. She closed the door and a face appeared from around the corner, she let out a blunt cry. Bianca smiled, 'You didn't think I was going to let you go alone?'

'How do you...?' Then she remembered the Captain, 'Never mind.'

Bianca smiled with an air of confidence. They went in search of equipment to ready themselves. Her gaze flittered up the wall. They approached the small foyer created by the merging corridors. The graceful columns lined the perimeter making the space warm and welcoming. It held a simple elegance with a plain finish as the lights of the Keep shone around the edges. Her heart raced inside her head but she dared not show it as she followed. The last trace of anger slipped away as she focused on the ladder leading down. She tried not to lose her step.

She ran her fingers along the wall, and a soft sound resonated from beyond. It was so faint she almost missed it. The thrill of meeting the central core crossed her mind. Before the enormity of what it meant sank in. She began to ask a question. Bianca motioned for quiet while listening in the darkness. They were not far below the habitable area. The muffled sounds of life echoed from above. A sharp sound rose above the rest and Bianca let out a gasp. Her friend stepped back and almost knocked her flying as she hung on.

Saranon peered around the corner, the open room appeared empty. If only she could hear the Keep. A shadow stretched along the corridor and a glimpse ran along the periphery. Her senses found nothing. They continued downward until all signs of life above had vanished. The shimmering warm glow from the array of small lights led downward. It formed patterns in the dark and they followed.

The remnants of the grime caked itself to the edges of the floor. In a murky trail building as they went. The soft dry air began to creep up from the outer rim of the core and Bianca began to relax. Her shoulders slumped in recognition as they sat in the depths of Hedavin. A tiny clink sparked Saranon's attention as her friend laughed aloud. She smiled in response, still wondering how she would enter into the central core. As though reading her thoughts Bianca answered the question. The easiest way would be through there. Bianca pointed to a small opening that ran parallel with the arterial cable.

The access point was one of the least used by sorcerers. It was located near the Cryzinelan. The walls were still smeared with grime. She cringed as her hand slipped in the substance and wiped it off. It revealed the broken body of a small skada. A mechanical spider that repaired the Keep lay covered in the muck. Hedavin had been awfully scarce of the little critters that worked in groups. She turned the metallic body over. Running her hand along the charred edges left from sorcery.

The hollow remains crumbled away in her hands as the fragile shell lost its shape. She placed it back as her hand touched something solid and hidden in the grime. She wiped it clean as a small emblem protruded on the fragment. As she held it up to the light it moved and almost fell as she caught it. A tiny spark of sorcery flowed within the fragment as she recognised the mark.

Bianca did not notice as they went on their way following the pipes. For such a large Keep little energy flowed through. Saranon tapped the edge of the gauge hoping it would move. Instead it stayed below halfway. She was being left behind and rushed to keep up. She slipped, diving over to the side. Both hands squelched along in the grime. Her shoulder caught the side of the wall and she winced. A flash of golden raging light boomed overhead. In a fiery instant, the surge of sorcery drove a wedge between them.

The crackle roared past with a deafening tone. Saranon managed to shield herself from the blast. The heat radiated through the room as she gulped. The hot air hit her lungs and she wanted to cry out. Her heart pounded hard as she stretched out her energy. She reached out to the Keep but it did not answer. Her breathing slowed as she waited, searching in the dim light for a sign of the assailant.

She could sense him in the darkness. She closed her eyes and winced. She had run away in the chaos at Zaidek Keep. As she understood with a rising dread what Tasha had meant. She tried again to reach out to the central core and no response came. Saranon breathed in the warm air. The last remnants from the sorcery faded in the distance. She took in a deep breath and the Angeon rose to the surface. The energy swirled as it coursed through her body.

The sorcerer Edan stood at the opposite end of the darkness. He held up his hand as a fireball flared lighting up the room in a smothered embrace. The sorcery sparked outward as it wrapped around the Angeon. It dragged her in to the centre of the room. He stepped out from the darkness taking aim as she floundered. His sorcery stormed through as a ceaseless source. The blast struck her, catching Saranon off-guard as she staggered to her feet. The shield around Edan held its strength as he ran forward. The air crystallised and shattered in the intense heat. She held out her arms to block the full blow. The wave of energy slammed her back to wall and the air rushed out of her lungs. The pain edged its way through her muscles as she clenched her jaw.

Edan sealed off the way ahead and her only chance to enter the central core. She stumbled and Edan struck.

The blast fractured through her shield and hit hard sending her to the ground. The pain seared along the surface as the Angeon took hold. She ran as the pain faded and blasted her way through. Her energy smouldered around the edges of the seal. Edan retreated further into the Keep. The Angeon raised her hands as the energy flowed. Spiralling as it lit up the underneath of Hedavin. It scorched the edges of the walls as it honed in, hitting Edan with enough force to knock him down. He staggered as she caught up.

Edan's eyes held a stubborn stance. In the darkness Tasha's words rose, kill the boy but not the girl. Something inside the Angeon snapped as she closed the gap and plunged both her hands around the hilt of Corsavere. Her bond-breaker shone a deep sea green in the darkness, as the blade in the form of a sword rose. He saw it in her eyes. The Angeon held the embrace with a cold strength. Shouting rang out from behind her as her focus fell to one task. The blade struck home.

There in the last essence as Edan's strength flowed the dark sorcery. The Angeon saw him as he truly was. The fear rose from within, yet she did not let it show. Edan gave a small gasp, but she did not loosen her grip. Tasha's words played in her head. She understood the message that had been sent from the grave. In the distant haze Bianca's scream cut through. As the exhaustion showed on her face, she did not want to admit it had taken a toll. It was not the ending Saranon had planned. The effect was instant as the marks of the Dihan marred the dead sorcerer's hands. The dark sorcery left its trail plain to see. She covered the body with her cloak. She showed all the care in the world as she whispered a final goodbye.

As the web that held the Keep unravelled, the shriek from the core below rang out. It pierced through the air. Bianca stood motioning for her to go on. Saranon wasted no time as she turned. The Keep cried in pain and that was all that mattered. As she trudged through the darkness the Keep gave off a dim light guiding her way. The pain screeched at her ears as she tried to remain calm. Yet the Keep was having none of it as it called, demanding her attention. It pinpointed her every move bellowing with an urgency that made the hair stand on end. She wasted no time as Hedavin urged her on ever closer to the pain.

Her heart thudded as she could only guess what lay beneath. Yet she had to go on in the eerie darkness. The sounds of the Keep filled the silence with a dread that filled her mind. She stood at the edge as the sounds bellowed up from below. She peered down into the resulting chaos. The sparks of stallic energy flew up arcing out from the deep. The heat rose through her hair at a constant rate. The stallic energy blew hot and sharp with razer precision. The energy swirled in the void before falling back into the Keep. Saranon, the Angeon, closed her eyes. She took a deep breath with the memory of Odana Temple pulling at her mind. With cold precision she leaped off the rim, diving straight into the darkness.

As the first wave hit her it jolted her back with the sudden impact. She dived further down a sheer drop. Then hit another arc of the Keep's energy. The pain seared through with an agonising slowness. Saranon reeled from the shock as she sank further into the darkness. She peered ahead and a massive ripple formed like a bubble with an eerie surface. The stallic energy held in a moving formation beneath. The Angeon rose with all her strength. Guiding her sorcery deep and she fell through. The sparks shot up around her and it was all she could do to hold on. She forgot to breath and gasped in the hot substance around her. It burned through her lungs as she writhed in a silent scream.

Before she could blink she found herself floating in a dense fog, with no up or down. The sparks lit up the murky clouds with sudden flares. The light glinted through the distance in an eerie motion. A heavy clunking sound resonated from the side. Saranon gasped at the sight of the central core. The dense storm held in a gigantic shell with no meaning of gravity. The stallic energy light up the air. It called with a shattered voice searching through the hidden nightmare. Help me, it called out in muted disbelief at the tiny visitor. The voice echoed inside her mind as it faded in a muffled tone. Before calling again and again like a steady tide. The Angeon managed to move with the strains on the Keep magnified in the core. A dark shadow moved closer as the cold touch of the Keep wrapped around her leg and dragged her in.

It was all she could do to keep from gagging in the filthy air. The tendrils of the inner core sucked her inside. The Angeon dropped with a short thud as gravity found itself again. The Keep had miscalculated the location of the floor. The control room lay hidden in the rod that struck down into Tordoren. Saranon stood as the Angeon left and made her way over to the controls. The small circular compartment wrapped around the solid core. Shaped like a massive impenetrable rod. It led into the hidden ground far below the surface. The core captured the arcs of energy from deep inside Tordoren. The energy was concentrated before sending it up through the Keep.

The sorceress reached for the nearest control. It moved as if not wanting to be held and she almost stumbled into the seat beside it. The room was cramped as she sat upright catching her breath, filled with apprehension. Her fingers felt numb from the decent. They still ached while she tried to figure out the controls. The sweat beaded down her back as the air grew warm from the charging of the central core. The power surged at an uneven rate sparking through the core. It crackled around her as she watched through the windows. Even in the confined space it was beginning to be unbearable.

Saranon tried again with the controls as they moved in an unfathomable rhythm. Yet somehow she had to figure them out. She rested her hand on a bar and leaned over for a closer inspection of the levers near the floor. She tried to move them, but it would not work, a deep crackling sound rose from below. The sparks blew a wave of light flashing pulsing through the windows. It shone through the slits in her fingers. The roar began with a low rumble resonating in a deep tone, as she opened her eyes and remembered to breathe.

The heat in the air hit her lungs as she lurched forward in a violent cough. Without warning three of the controls moved all at once. She froze waiting and listening, as the harsh wind tunnelled around the core. It bellowed with a menacing call as it whirred in the background. The flashes of stallic energy broke through leaving trails criss-crossing the harsh grey fog. The charge compounded in on itself. The air whistled again from below in the depths of Tordoren. The sound of the crackling clung in the distance.

Saranon's heart beat faster as she recognised the chaos below. She stood peering close to the window and tripped. The controls moved for the second time. The ball of light grew beneath her and she caught her breath. She gulped letting out a small whimper. The charge curled itself up the surface of the rod. It circled closer with every breath. The thunderous roar of pure stallic energy gained speed. The sound became louder as it swept toward her. The crackling buzz reached her ears, turning into pounding bellow with no pause. The solid rumble carried the heat far above, glowing with an electrifying intensity as it neared the control room.

She tried to concentrate. Yet the swirling inferno held her attention with a fatal beckoning. She knew she had to break free and time was slipping away. The crackling roar thundered through the floor. She felt herself lift as the sound around her became deafening. Hedavin spoke inside her head, I've got you. The white wall of energy hit, with an enveloping blast that shook every part of her body. For a moment the world stopped as she held out her hands and felt nothing. The panic hit with a jolt as the air rushed out of her lungs. The Angeon woke with a power so great she absorbed the energy.

In the insufferable moment the Angeon linked with the central core. As the massive clouds of energy poured down, condensing between her hands. The last traces of energy stemmed into the inescapable stronghold. A small sphere formed. The Angeon floated in a trance. She had lost the ability to move her limbs as the energy coursed its way through. The beautiful shiny Orb formed as the energy condensed, glowing from the continuing flow. The last particles wrapped within sealing the surface of the Orb as it cooled to the touch. The air in the central core brought with it a sudden chill.

Saranon stood waiting for her legs to catch up as the Angeon slipped away. It left behind darkness amidst the low humming of the central core. She peered over the edge of the controls in the small room. The whirling clouds of stallic energy had tipped upside down. They lay at a safe distance around the base of the rod. The Keep was at peace as it lulled to itself in a reassuring tone. The pressure had eased as she stepped back. She melded into the main rod of the central core, falling out the other side. Hedavin wasted no time as he spurned the little visitor out with all his might. The central core was content to be left alone once more. The force pelted her upward. The Keep sighed with the last signs of disgruntlement washing away.

She could sense from his mood that Hedavin would not be so easy to fool a second time. The journey finished as she came to a stop. She lay on the floor of the imbenik chamber above the central core. Saranon sat alone as she clasped the Orb in both her hands. It was smaller than the ones she had seen and wondered what to do with it. A gruff voice called from above. She tried to call back, but her voice was too hoarse. A figure reached down. She recognised Mark and stepped back almost slamming sideways into the wall. He shouted something, but the words were fuzzy in her head.

Saranon looked up at him with tired eyes and he shook his head as if reading her thoughts. She caught her breath, and clambered to the surface. The throbbing in her head made it difficult to grasp the flow of conversations. The words muddled in and out. The group of wizards crowded around as she recognised Captain Mirshendy. Without saying anything she placed the Orb in his hand. A stunned silence collapsed over the space. Major Kellaway strode up to inspect the Orb. He mulled it over in his hands. The Major studied Saranon's face before returning the Orb. 'The fun is over, now let's get Hedavin back on track,' he said.

She looked at Captain Mirshendy, who whispered, 'You did well.'

She smiled as the exhaustion shone through her eyes. Mitch guided her away from the hive of conversations blurring into one another. As much as she was itching to stay and listen, all she wanted now was a warm soft cosy bed. Before she could lie down a thought entered her head, 'Bianca.'

'She's all right,' the wizard whispered as he tucked her in.

Sleep crept in like a flood taking over. The sweet hum of the Keep was the last sound she remembered. A dream swept through her tired mind as a hand reached out. She looked up to see Tasha waiting on a windy path near the river. Her old friend held the Orb in her hands it glowed with a warm radiant light. She held out her hand, but she could not touch it. Tasha was too far away as she spoke, not yet. Saranon tried to reach for the Orb again, but Tasha moved farther away. In her dreams she ran and ran.

Then with one final leap she hurled herself forward catching the Orb. As she did she fell down a massive hole carved deep into the ground. Then she saw the large ockren. The essence of Hedavin stood, wrapped into an unnatural large panther like creature. It had sharp yellow eyes piercing through her soul. The creature bent its head forward until the tip of its nose almost touched the Orb. Its breath blew over her cold fingers. Saranon stood in silence not wanting to move as the ockren circled her in a slow stance. She backed away out of the cave and onto a sandy beach near the black ocean.

The waves crashed on the shore around them as the wind echoed along the dunes. A distance hung between them, then the ockren leaped in a fluid motion toward the sky. Saranon held the Orb up above her head shielding herself from the ockren. A jolt ran through her body and she woke with a gasp. The energy of the Angeon flared to the surface. As her eyes opened they made contact with the sorcerer in the room, Damon lunged in. She grabbed his arm in a powerful lock as he began to wince. Before she could concentrate he was knocked to the ground. It took her a while to realise Mitch had entered the room and a wave of relief swept over her.

CHAPTER SEVEN

The unexpected

Mitch held onto Damon with ease as Saranon's room became crowded with wizards. She darted out into the lounge room. She almost stumbled straight into Captain Mirshendy. He glared at her then stepped aside taking charge. Damon began rambling protests while the Captain clung onto him with a firm grip. She stayed out of the way not wanting to be the focus of attention. She kept close to Mitch waiting for the voices to fade in the hallway, before relaxing.

The dawn was breaking as she dressed. She followed Mitch down to the stronghold of the Cryzinelan wizards. The internal courtyard warmed with the morning light. While the Keep returned to its old self. The wizard clan appeared stronger than ever. To Saranon's amazement Damon spoke to the Major as a friend. Then he left the stronghold. Major Kellaway smiled as he spotted her gaping mouth. There were many things she did not understand, and letting Damon go was one of them.

She stood in astonishment as the anger dissipated. If it were not for the group of wizards she would be tempted to run after him. As though reading her thoughts Mitch stayed by her side. He could be annoying at times. She cringed while Mitch pretended not to notice. Her arms still ached from holding the sorcerer. When a wizard walked over and blocked the light streaming down from above. The Major was a tall man with a stubborn look as he gazed down at her. He leaned over and asked, 'Did you mean to kill Edan?'

The question stopped Saranon's thoughts from roaming as she stared back in defiance, 'Yes.'

It was a small reply that meant so much as the Major mulled it over. She swallowed and bit her lip. She was not about to tremble among so many wizards. The dragon pens did not seem so welcoming anymore. She went out into the warm courtyard, breathing a sigh of relief. As she stared toward the sky an array of small dots grew just above the horizon. Katholomu lying at the edge of the clearing, lifted his head. The dragon clambered as he uncurled himself. He arched his back in a long stretch that filtered through the whole of his body.

Up ahead the skies broke to make way for three riders flying in fast with their dragons. She watched in quiet anticipation as she turned an inquisitive eye toward Mitch. The wizard stared up into the crystal blue sky. He spoke in deep thought, 'I think it's for you.'

'What do you mean?' She snapped in annoyance.

'It's Pennie,' the wizard replied as smile touched his lips.

'You're making that up,' Saranon spoke.

She tried hard to glimpse the image in the distance. The wizard chuckled which only made it worse as she checked, trying to gauge a sign of any sort. He patted her on the shoulder, 'Why don't you go to the roof and take a look?'

She agreed as her dull walk turned into a quick run. She covered the last distance with ease up to a vibrant roof top. She came face to face with Captain Mirshendy. Bianca stood near the edge of the low wall. They watched peering out in the direction of the dragons.

She strode toward Bianca as she gazed out over the clear sky. Her friend looked on as Saranon asked, 'Do you think it's Pennie?'

'Of course it is,' Bianca quibbled.

She stared at her friend in annoyance, 'You didn't tell me.'

'I did not think I needed to,' Bianca replied.

The pair stood in an awkward silence as the gracious beasts swung overhead. The dragons flew down gliding into the courtyard. Pennie's blonde hair caught in the sunlight. She peered upward and straight at the sorceress.

Saranon made her way down to the dragon pens. Hoping she would not see Mark, which was almost impossible. Pennie stood tall and proud not far from

Captain Assinden. The Darkonian wizard held himself with a great ease so far from home. In a way he reminded her of Mitch. No words were needed as the two friends embraced. A familiar voice spoke behind her. 'I hope you're not going to stand there all day. The dragons need to rest,' Mark's voice was gentle, but it still made her cringe.

Pennie laughed as they sat down, 'So you made it back from Serenphel? I half expected you to stay, but then I heard about Merrick.'

Saranon grimaced at the sorcerer's name. It was not an easy memory to stomach. She had completely recovered from the ordeal. 'I would prefer not to think about it,' she replied.

'That's okay, I've got something else for you,' Pennie lowered her voice. 'We've got a problem.'

She leaned closer as her friend explained without giving too much away. Pennie was good with that. Yet as Saranon's mouth gaped she figured her friend need not have bothered. She mulled over the words in deep thought. Pennie waited with an endless patience. 'Well, it looks like I'll be going home,' she said.

'You'll need to stay close to the border, on the other side. If you get into trouble you're on your own.' Pennie replied.

The last part was said with such seriousness by Pennie that they both laughed. Captain Jacob Assinden gave a stern stare as he watched on. Pennie waved it off with a flick of her hand. Before she turned to her friend, 'I'm sure you'll be fine.'

Saranon breathed a huge sigh as she looked at the wizard, another reminder of home. Before she could think on it anymore, her friend changed the subject. The gesture was made to gloss over the raging problem. It did not go unnoticed. Captain Assinden gave away a small sign of annoyance that creased along his brow. Saranon had not forgotten his strength as she stayed at a distance. The talk turned to Pennie's birthday just gone. With her friend describing a party of such grandeur that she found it hard to imagine.

She smiled wondering if her friend's effort had turned into a tall tale. She tried not to interrupt. It was wonderful seeing Pennie so content. The small scrape of footsteps behind her brought her back to reality. She turned at the thought of Mark being there. She jumped off her chair so fast she almost lost her balance. Captain Mirshendy spoke, 'I need to have a word with you.'

Pennie did not flinch at all as she stared at the wizard in a serene fashion. She gave nothing away under her gaze.

The Captain strode with a sturdy step then came to a halt. He gazed out of the large window in a meeting room that opened onto views of the garden below. 'You cannot travel to Darkonia with Pennie,' He said.

The edge of his voice filled with a finality. Before she had time to ask him how he knew. He continued, 'We have received word of the Keep your friend is here to discuss. If you go there you need to stay out of Darkonia.'

Saranon's heart sank as she admitted to herself. That it was too early to return to the land in which she grew up in.

The deed was done she had taken down the Arthrose Council for hunting the Issola. Even in exile the threat still lingered. If she went into Darkonia the Arthrose would find her. Then she filled with annoyance at the wizard for being so knowledgeable. Yet he appeared ready for that response. A smile crept at the corners of his mouth. She placed her hands on her hips, in a silent defiance. 'I've arranged for you to travel with someone else,' the Captain said.

His words shocked her out of her stagnant mood. 'What do you mean?' She asked.

'Wait and see,' the Captain smiled then left her alone to wonder.

Her life appeared to be decided for her yet again. The temptation of crossing the border into Darkonia filled her with excitement. She went to find Mitch who to her dismay was engaged in a conversation with Mark. He stood beside Katholomu. The dragon had a rather suspicious looking full belly. She wondered where he had plundered the amount of food required to leave him in such a state. Mark explained that the beast had helped himself to three breakfasts. Scoffing all the food down before he had time to shoo the dragon away. She could believe Kat had done it, as he showed off his belly in the sunlight with a sleepy smile.

'Well he won't be flying anywhere with that on board,' Saranon spoke. She grimaced as Mark stood beside her.

'Do you want to know how close you came?' He asked in a low voice.

She knew what he meant and shook her head as

her cheeks began to feel hot under his gaze. He walked away without needing to say anymore. Her heart was still pounding. When Mitch broke into her thoughts, 'Have you been to Taria?'

'I beg your pardon,' she hissed, the wizard knew full well about her past.

'I meant we're going there,' he replied.

Saranon rolled her eyes in disgust at yet another wizard telling her what to do. She fobbed it off by reaching over to the great dragon and rubbing him under the chin. Kat obliged her by kicking in the air as Mitch side stepped to avoid contact. The great beast nuzzled his head around her. He did so in a comforting grasp while pretending to be asleep. The sun warmed his coat with a glistening touch. She reached over and hugged the dragon. He seemed not to care enough about his gruff image to show concern.

Mitch let them be, he had far too much to do to worry about. He shook his head in dismay. A voice cut through the open courtyard as Saranon glanced around. Not wanting to be disturbed. Damon stood on the edge of the stone paving, his face pale even in full light. She remained calm on the outside. Every essence of her being told her to run. She stood transfixed as though turning away would be worse.

The Palascene sorcerer, Damon, gave an eminent glare. He moved closer wrapped in a cold silence. Katholomu retracted behind her, experience told the dragon not to intervene. Saranon's first instinct was to step back then she stopped in midstride. Reminding herself there was no need to give the sorcerer ground. Yet his eyes pierced with a raging intensity. His anger quelled only by an air of superiority, as he approached. Damon raised his arms without a halt in his stride as he closed in. She could feel the energy rip through the air in front of her and held her ground.

The energy of the Angeon rushed through her as she met Damon's sorcery head on. She watched him hold under the strain. The build-up of energy spurred against him. He cringed then relented expecting the energy of the Angeon to consume him. Yet as he stood unharmed his smiled waned. This time it was Saranon's turn to smile knowing she could hold back the tide of the Angeon. Without any warning a large dark matted scaly tail swept the sorcerer off his feet. The dragon sent him flying high into the air.

Kathomolu stood up heaving his giant chest in victory. His strong tail curled up beside him. He bent down in a casual stance as Saranon gaped in amazement. She was too shocked to tell off the dragon who gave her a quizzical look. 'Well I guess that's one way of dealing with him,' she responded in awe.

Pennie ran to the courtyard peering out to where the sorcerer had landed. Trying not to laugh she said, 'I was about to give you a hand, but I can't beat that.'

A small laughed escaped Saranon's lips as Bianca rushed out. Damon walked off with a slight limp toward his quarters. Bianca smiled, 'If he bothers you again let me know.'

After a small cough she agreed, even though she

thought it would not be needed. The sky began to grow dark as they went inside for a heartfelt feast. Pennie enjoyed sitting with her as they laughed again. Captain Mirshendy had asked about the day's events.

They giggled with delight. As the Captain realised Damon deserved the consequences of his actions. It made a great tale as they ate. Just as Saranon took a breath and regained her composure. A hush fell on the crowd at their table as a wizardess entered the room. The Captain wasted no time introducing himself to the new arrival. Zara had travelled a far distance with a buoyant smile. Zara had an adventurous air around her full of enthusiasm. She headed straight for the sorceress placing a gentle hand on her shoulder.

Saranon looked at her in surprise, wondering who she was. As the Captain spoke, 'Zara will be taking you to Taria.'

It was more a statement than a request. As Pennie filled in the gap, 'Zara is Lord Glyrondagar's sister. Her clan can get you close to the border with ease.'

Her friend spoke as though she had known all along. Then she was used to Pennie making arrangements. As she looked around the table she noticed Mitch gazing up at the wizardess. She felt like the odd one out.

Mitch spent the rest of the night chatting away to Zara. Saranon found an excuse to leave. She tried not to sound annoyed at the situation. She was about to step out of the path of a sorcerer, he appeared out of place. He looked straight at her with a calm grace as he introduced himself.

The Denowan sorcerer known as Garth Arbidan explained that he was bonded to Zara. He would be accompanying her to Taria. For a sorcerer Garth seemed rather meek and quite. He was content to wander in Zara's shadow.

To her surprise the sorcerer explained that there were few of his clan in Taria. Saranon could not imagine a land full of wizards. Then Normisia felt like it at times as she peered around the room. She left feeling perplexed and tried to block her thoughts out. Her head hit the pillow with a welcome sleep. The dreams of the night before clung in a faded bubble. She glimpsed them from afar, drifting further into a restful slumber. Later in the night two sets of footsteps made their way around the apartment. The moon shone bright through the open curtains with a soft welcoming glow.

She sat up with the morning light. She stared around an empty room, checking under the bed to make sure it was safe. Not that she thought someone would hide there. Yet finding Damon lurking around before had unnerved her. Clanging noises sounded from underneath the door with the making of breakfast. Zara helped lay the table with a comforting smile. She was too shocked to say anything and Mitch was not offering any answers.

Before any words came to mind a hearty breakfast was laid out in front of her as the three began to eat. The toast was warm and the butter melted as she took a bite while eyeing him with suspicion. 'Are you ready to head south?' Zara asked waiting for a response.

She swallowed a mouthful and coughed, 'Where are

we going?'

'To my home,' the wizardess replied.

Saranon stared at Mitch, 'Are we going to be staying at a wizard Keep?'

'Isn't it wonderful,' Zara smiled.

She did not look impressed. She thought about having to get to know yet another group of wizards. Garth would be there for company. He seemed far more interested in talking than being a sorcerer. Mitch leaned over. 'You are welcome to leave the table,' he smiled.

Then he indulged in a conversation with Zara. She rushed out the door and realised she had forgotten to ask when they were leaving. She was in no hurry to go back and glanced out over the balcony into the open courtyard below. A familiar voice made her smile. As Rachel approached, 'Sorry I haven't had a chance to catch up with you.'

The Captain's voice interrupted her thoughts as she stared beyond her friend. He appeared to be caught off guard by her. He stood beside Rachel holding her with his arm. The sorceress peered down at the bond-breaker, she had made for the Captain, as it glistened on his belt, 'Have you given it a name?'

He smiled as Rachel answered for him, 'Stayer.'

Saranon spoke to the Captain, 'Do you think the Keep will be attacked again?'

His mood darkened with an eminent sadness. For once he was at a loss to hide his thoughts as she looked on. 'Hedavin has a long memory,' as he spoke the words he leaned over. He gave Rachel a soft kiss before leaving the two in peace. Rachel watched him go, 'Thank you for looking after him. We haven't much time since you leave tonight.'

Saranon's mouth dropped open in astonished disbelief. Yet she could not stay annoyed for long. Rachel had taken the day off to spend with her. The wizardess was a welcome relief in a storm of chaos. They made their way down the stairs. It took a moment to realise she was heading toward the dragon pens. She had been trying to avoid Mark, which was much harder to do than she thought. He seemed to appear almost everywhere.

It was as though he knew she had been trying to stay away. She was not angry with him, but at the whole notion of not being asked which annoyed her still. Rachel stepped aside and before Saranon knew it she was staring straight at Mark. Who appeared undeterred by the whole passing of events. In fact he looked quite comfortable. He was at home as he patted her on the head while she ducked to the side. He gave a knowing smile, 'You have nothing to worry about.'

She was not convinced, as she spotted Gabriel in the background. She found an excuse to runoff, darting past as he let her leave. Saranon surveyed the pens. To find the dragons glistening in the morning light through the open doors. 'They're ready for when you leave,' Gabriel explained.

'Wow,' she was impressed at the sight of several clean, sweet smelling dragons.

She knew the hard work would not last long.

She stared up at Katholomu whose eyes darted across to the open air. 'Mark did most of it, I think he felt sorry for you,' Gabriel spoke.

Mark patted her on the shoulder. Making Saranon jump with start, 'What do you think?'

She smiled and agreed. Hoping he would not do that again as he continued, 'Ready for your big debut?'

'Pardon,' she asked.

'You are going to Taria. The wizards don't have many sorcerers to contend with,' he spoke.

'I thought I was already,' Saranon exclaimed.

'Perhaps,' Mark replied in deep thought.

As they spoke Rachel patted Katholomu. The dragon appeared eager to comply as he rolled his head. The great beast was good company and Saranon was looking forward to the ride.

'That dragon cost me a good amount, but I knew someday the favour would be returned. You earned him when you took care of Hedavin,' Mark Staragen spoke.

The wizard showed a genuine respect. She peered up at the great beast as he lapped up the attention. He looked almost comical, knowing full well his short temper. She could not imagine life without the dirt loving, cranky and opportunistic dragon.

CHAPTER EIGHT

A careless grandeur

A warm wind blew with the sun's rays in the late afternoon as Saranon looked at Pennie. They both smiled with the thrill of excitement. The thought of being close to Darkonia pulled at the heart of her emotions. She still did not know who her parents were even though she was a Vandragamond. With any luck she would find out more. Her friend had tried so hard to search for them while she was gone. She was grateful, but now seemed like the right time to go. The sun lost its' strength with the last of the afternoon fading away.

The dragons preferred the cooler weather of night and she could not blame them. Saranon clambered aboard as Katholomu leaned down. This time she would ride alone, with Mitch and Zara riding together. Captain Assinden went with Pennie which left Garth to fly on his own.

The sorcerer was quite at home with this. As he urged his dragon forward with a mighty jolt upward into the fading sky. Saranon and Pennie followed. The two wizards made up the rear of the diamond formation. They flew southwest to the edge of the border near Taria.

Her heart pounded with a happy tune as Kat covered ground with ease. Way underneath his massive outstretched wings. She let the wind fly free whipping at the wisps of her hair. The beast appeared to absorb the excitement as he flew hard without a break. They glided down onto the Pendelon Plains, in south-east Normisia. The dragon's smell had soaked through her clothes by the time they landed. She clambered down as the wind sent a chill along her skin. They had stopped near a small township. She ran into the tavern where the owners were expecting them. Saranon was so relieved to have a warm bath and clean clothes as she sank into a soft bed. Taking no notice of the morning light as it broke outside.

The smell of baked bread wafted under her nose. Captain Assinden brought them a hearty lunch. He woke them from a restful sleep. It had been a while since the sorceress had been spent time with other Darkonians. Yet she still held a small grudge at the Captain, for tricking her before she had left for Alveron. The warm bread melted the butter that dripped down her hand before she caught it. He started to whisper in a low voice, but stopped as the door creaked open.

'Ah, you're awake,' Garth said. He sat down near the Captain, ' There's something I need to tell you about the

Glyrondagar. They are good at dealing with sorcerers so take care.'

Saranon choked on her mouthful of bread, as she coughed to clear her throat. 'I thought you would understand,' Garth replied. As he patted her on the back, '...And don't say I didn't warn you.'

His voice sang out as he left them in peace. She could not see how the wizard clan could be more annoying, than the ones she had already encountered, but Garth meant well.

She calmed her thoughts as she stood up and scrambled her things together. Captain Assinden had already packed and watched in an awkward silence. 'We have tried hard to find out who your parents are. Whoever knows is not giving anything away. It may be more than wizards that you need to worry about.' He spoke.

His voice carried a firm certainty as Saranon tried to brush it off. 'I can guess that I am about to walk into trouble. So if you don't mind I'd like to finish packing,' the sorceress eyed him as he bowed and left.

She could not bring herself to trust the wizard. She rushed down the stairs and almost knocked Pennie over in the process. 'Are you ready? We're all waiting for you,' Pennie beamed.

Her friend gave a large smile full of excitement to have her friend back. Saranon knew how it felt as her nerves gave way to a sense of excitement. She rubbed her hands together in anticipation. Katholomu gleamed in the dry afternoon sun glowing orange along the horizon. It tilted toward the call of the evening sky. She clambered up onto the dragons shoulder. Riding high on his back as the giant took one big leap showing off in full swing. He opened his massive wings with a rush of the wind beneath.

Her breath filled with enthusiasm as the darkened sky hid the border into Taria. A welcome chill crept along her arms as she held on tight not wanting to let go. Kat roared with excitement as he tasted the wind. He moved on at an impressive speed waiting for the other dragons to catch up. The hills rushed by beneath them in a blur, as she looked on, hoping for a glimpse of the Keep Ardaguar. Even though she knew it was far too early, it still did not stop her from hoping. The breeze swept through Saranon's hair as the other dragon's kept up. Katholomu paced himself for the last leg of the flight.

Pennie's dragon Veradae swooped close to the side enticing Kat to race. He called on with a renewed strength to fly ahead. Ardaguar Keep came in sight, a beautiful towering fortress over the grand landscape. The terrain was filled with the low lying hills that ran all the way through the border. The great dragon circled the open sky. She peered over the top of an open arena, that hung silent in the early hours of the morning. Katholomu glided in sliding along at ease. Then he ploughed his legs forward to a sudden stop. With a small tilt he dropped the sorceress down before she had the chance to protest.

The dragon shook himself spraying musty sweat in all directions. Saranon used her energy to shield herself just in time. She had not been so lucky before and was not about to be left with the stench that took hours to fade away. Zara ran up behind her, 'Come on you'll be late.'

Saranon asked, 'For what?'

The sorceress could not imagine being late for anything, but sleep, as she tried to catch up with the others, following behind. As she reached the entrance all the lights were on sparkling along the walls. The foyer opened up onto a great hall filled with trophies along the walls.

She was so overcome with the sight that she failed to hear the footsteps right beside her. Lord Dackren beamed down, his bulk towering over the young sorceress. The Lord did not look much older than Mitch. Yet his face was weathered and it displayed hints of more than one good fight. Lord Dackren smiled as he used his size to intimidate her. Saranon took a step back, he followed as Zara tapped him on the shoulder and he stopped. 'You are welcome here Vandragamond. There is one thing I want to know, where do you fit in?'

She stood in silence while trying to fight the urge to step back a good few paces. In fact the other room was starting to look appealing. Pennie spoke up as she let out a sigh of relief. 'We do not know, but if you are offering to help that would be appreciated,' said her friend.

Lord Dackren glanced her way with piercing deep brown eyes. He responded, 'If I help you, you will let me know.'

The last words sounded like a warning, and she was not about to argue as the Lord left them in peace.

Zara seemed oblivious to the whole drama. She showed

them to their rooms and wished them a good rest. Saranon did not want to sleep, but her tired eyes said otherwise and the bed was so cosy. Before she knew it her dreams were filled with the wild whisperings of the Keep. Ardaguar spoke to her with a tight grip. It tried to pull her down below the habitable area in her sleep. The Keep spoke the words in her head with a background whisper wrapping around her. It tried to drag her along on an unknown path. No matter how fast she moved it was far too slow for the Keep's liking. It called ever louder through the dream.

Saranon sat up gasping for air, as Ardaguar's voice faded in the distance. The knocking that had broken her sleep stopped, as she shouted out. A wizard's voice extended through the closed door. 'It's Killian, my sister asked me to tell you it's lunch time. If you want anything you'd better hurry up,' he spoke.

She wondered who the wizard was, then shrugged it off. She ran downstairs as the thought from her mind. The large row of tables held a gathering, that filled the air with the rumble of many conversations. She wound her way through the jubilant crowd.

A few wizards glanced her way, but she tried not to notice as she made her way through. Then she darted off with a small arm full. She juggled the food while finding her way to the open courtyard. The sun beamed down with its full might. As she glanced around to spy Mitch entangled in Zara's arms. It was almost enough to make her choke as she turned the other way. Across the courtyard a sorceress a few years older than she, stared back. Triona hesitated before walking away without saying a word. Saranon was tempted to follow. Yet just as she did a large welcoming arm gripped her far too close for comfort. Lord Dackren grinned down at her.

She managed to nudge her way free as she stared at him in a constrained silence. The Lord was a little too close for comfort. 'You'll want to check out the disc this afternoon,' she could smell his breath as he spoke.

'No,' she answered.

She was not sure what it was. She wanted to steer clear of anything Lord Dackren was involved with. 'That's a shame, perhaps I can entice you later,' he grinned as he left.

Saranon did not feel like eating the rest of her lunch as she ditched it in the bin. Killian stood beside her and asked, 'Do you want to check out the disc?'

'No, I'm fine,' she replied.

Killian smiled as she turned to look at him. 'I meant just to have a look, I don't fight on it, like my brother,' he added.

'Well that's reassuring,' she spoke, wondering what it was.

'No, I really mean it,' he continued.

Killian tried to reassure her, as he walked while keeping a respectful distance between them. She sighed as she relented. Wondering what she had gotten herself into. They left the bright courtyard for the more subdued light of the Keep. Killian brought her to a large room and the ceiling lifted high above. It allowed for tiers of seating wrapping around the walls. In the centre a circular stone pattern swirled along the floor. The anti-climax was astounding as she realised the carved stone floor was it. She attempted to sound interested as he waffled on about the history of the disc.

The dim lights above in the high ceiling gave the great room a dark atmosphere. Saranon walked over to the rough walls that had stood for so long. She ran her fingers along the edge as the Keep spoke. I see you, she flinched, recoiling straight back in Killion's arms. He smiled, but said nothing as the sorceress composed herself. Zara followed through the open doorway. The wizardess had an air of pride as she relaxed in the small row of seats near the disc.

'So would you ever part with Mitch?' Zara asked.

'Pardon?' Saranon exclaimed. She felt like she had just been dragged into an unspoken conversation.

'Have you ever had a lover?' The wizardess asked in a low whisper.

'No,' Saranon replied hoping she would not have to answer any more questions.

She began wondering if she could find another seat. A flurry of activity filled the room with a crowd gathering in around them.

Mitch leaned over from the opposite side of Zara. He whispered, 'Lord Dackren is up against Crevan, the ambassador for the Vandragamond.'

Saranon sighed with a lack of enthusiasm. Then she tried her best to look interested as the crowd went quiet with a hushed tone. She glanced through the faces, but could not see Pennie anywhere. Garth whispered a small greeting from the row behind. He waited in eager anticipation. She watched on as the crowd of wizards gave a deafening roar. Lord Dackren entered dressed for the occasion. He beamed with a jubilant pride and waved.

A second deafening cheer rang out and reverberated around the room. It was then that she noticed a small gathering of sorcerers. They made their way out to the opposite side of the disc. Crevan stood forward, a tall solid man almost the same size as Lord Dackren. With no hesitation he strode onto the disc. Crevan scouted the audience. He locked eyes on her before returning his gaze on his opponent. The Lord was more than eager to oblige as they stood for a brief moment. Eyeing each other across the centre of the disc carved into the floor. Then with a flash of wizardry the sorcerer was pelted back. The two were locked in an intense struggle to gain power over the other. They were intent on defeating their opponent.

Saranon's jaw dropped in a mix of surprise and horror. While wondering why anyone would do that for sport. Garth leaned over, 'You can breathe now,' he said in a gentle tone.

She gave him a smile, and then watched on in astonishment. She tried not to flinch when a streak of energy flashed along the edge of the disc. Both Lord Dackren and Crevan appeared to be enjoying every moment. It gave them the opportunity to show off their strength to a crowd that cried out for more. She looked around at the nearest exits and contemplated the idea of creeping out. With Zara by her side she doubted it would be well received.

The pair on the disc locked close together for a final struggle. Then it was over as Lord Dackren stood, he flung his arms up in victory. To her amazement Crevan stood up unscathed. Yet he looked jittery on his feet as he shook hands with the wizard and left to his side of the disc. Jack, a sorcerer not much older than Saranon eyed the wizard with contempt. Lord Dackren shouted out to the crowd daring anyone else to come forward and fight. He eyed Saranon and gestured, but she stayed right where she was. Jack Heath stepped forward onto the disc, 'I will take you on.'

He stood proud beyond his years, with a certainty that left no doubt he was ready. The Lord eyed him with a cool smile, 'So you think you're ready to take on the Lord Dackren?'

He shouted his last words raising his fist high in the air as the crowd roared in delight. Jack Heath stood silent waiting for the noise to subdue. Then he stepped up to the centre of the disc. The sorcerer did not hesitate as he struck first. The Lord had expected as much. Before Saranon could blink the two were engaged in a heated exchange.

The crowd watched on in wide-eyed awe as Jack lost ground. It was slow to watch as she winced at the sight. The Lord looked as though he was using every last bit of strength. The strain showed across his face. Yet Lord Dackren stood his ground and the crowd grew tense around her. The spectators began to stand as a low chant hummed through the air. A great creaking sound caught Saranon's attention. As she turned back to see the circular disc had tilted, dipping at Jack's end. She gasped as the end of the fight became clear. She stood up in a wide-eyed horror as the two locked in a power struggle. Jack moved closer to the lower edge of the disc.

Her whole body froze with shock as the disc creaked again and dropped. It tilted even further into the dark abyss. Jack stepped back as the Lord pushed him ever closer to the edge. Then the great disc tilted, and for a moment she lost sight of the sorcerer. Saranon rushed past Mitch's fleeting hand as he tried to hold her back. She ran and shouted, 'For the love of Odana stop!'

It was too late, the disc tilted at a sharp angle dropping the sorcerer clean off the edge. Jack grasped out with his energy and managed to grip a small ledge down in the darkness.

Saranon stood at the edge glaring at the wizard as he heaved himself up to the middle with ease. Then with a great groan that echoed off the walls the disc began to close. She felt her heart sink to the bottom of her toes as she tried to think. She reached out with her energy and Jack wasted no time as he formed the second half of the link. She hauled him up as she held her breath. With the disc closing behind him he darted away from the edge. He stood grinning beside her and held out his hand. He took no notice of the astonished gasps escaping from the crowd, 'I'm Jack Heath.'

Saranon was astounded. That he had just waved off the fact that he only just made it out of the dark tunnel. She shook his hand without speaking. The spectators began to fill the floor with a wave of excitement. He darted away and disappeared from sight. As she glanced around for a brief moment she locked eyes with Lord Dackren. She too left, not wanting to be caught up in the action. Mitch grabbed her arm and led her away as he spoke, 'What did you do that for?'

'You could've warned me,' she said as she yanked free of his hold.

He peered down at her, 'You're going to see more of that around here.'

Saranon was not sure what he meant and she did not want to find out. She ran off in search of Pennie. As she turned around the corner, a familiar face peered back at her. Jack smiled, 'I thought I might find you here.'

He was starting to get on her nerves. She refrained from making a comment as he led her toward the sorcerer quarters.

Triona opened the door to greet them as they entered the place. It was pleasant enough, yet it was smaller than the quarters set aside for the sorcerers at Hedavin Keep. Triona was around same age Jack. Crevan was twice that with a short crop of greying hair to match. It was a strange sensation wandering through rooms meant for the Vandragamond, the sorcerer clan she had been separated from for so long. Saranon was not sure if she was meant to behave like a visitor or one of their own. The turmoil was visible on her face as she found an excuse to leave.

She made her way back to the room she shared with Pennie. It was empty, but she did not mind as she slumped onto the bed. A silent tear dropped down. The urge to throw an object against the wall felt right. She lacked the energy to carry it through. She peered out the window and leaned on the sill. Ardaguar held an air of confidence, one that sided with the wizard clan. Yet the Keep itself, felt odd as she listened. She reached out her senses in the gaps of noise stemming from the courtyard below.

She searched the Keep with her energy, but the further she went the stronger it felt. It did not make sense. The thought tapered from her mind as the smell of tea wafted up from the kitchen. It mixed with the warm night air. Pennie welcomed her as they made their way to the table at the centre of the room. It was wonderful to hear her old friend laugh again. Mitch approached her and whispered, 'Lord Dackren wants you to sit at his table.'

He left assuming her compliance was a given.

She made her way over to the table, the Lord filled the large chair with his size. He leaned forward with an air of arrogance. From what Pennie had said the façade belied an intelligent man underneath. Lord Dackren tapped for an ale as he kept a careful eye on her between conversations. Killian sat beside her quite content to blend into the background. As she listened to his brother's bragging. Saranon did not believe half it, but preferred not to say so. The Lord continued with an eager audience.

As she finished her meal, Lord Dackren turned his attention to her. He asked, 'What of you sorceress, how many have you killed?'

Saranon hesitated not knowing how to answer. As

the Lord leaned forward and continued, 'The border is no place for a soft heart. Interfere with my fight again and I expect you to answer for it.'

She could feel her cheeks grow hot as all eyes turned to her. The Lord was not someone she wanted to face as she found an excuse to leave. Her words sounded meek even to her own ears, but it was better than having to stay and listen.

A flurry of footsteps followed her down the hall she could sense who it was before she saw him. Killian smiled as he stopped, 'Did you think my brother would let that go?'

Saranon glared at him in silence. 'Sorry I'll start again, let me show you around,' he showed no signs of relenting.

Ardaguar Keep was massive in size and stature. As much as she wanted to wander by herself, she would not know where to start. Below ground the Keep's voice would be stronger to guide her.

Killian spoke and it took a moment to break out of her train of thought. As he repeated himself, 'Lord Dackren wants to know who you are. There are many who went missing.'

She was speechless at the thought of what that meant. Pennie knew that not everyone had returned from the camps. Yet she had been hesitant to discuss it. Saranon slumped on the floor as the tears ran down her face. She asked herself, 'What have I come back to?'

CHAPTER NINE

Aspirations

The large entrance leading out into the hall loomed overhead. The place was filled with a grandness Saranon did not understand. She made her way up the stairs. The Keep beckoned, but she was not ready. Exhaustion set in. She could feel it all the way down to her fingertips as she moved through the doorway. Pennie sat in cold silence while she turned to greet her, 'It's getting worse.'

'Garduend Keep?' She asked.

'Yes, what did you think I meant?' Pennie spat the last words out with a hiss.

She hesitated not wanting to annoy her friend. Pennie replied in a soothing tone, 'I need you to look into it.'

Saranon did not like taking orders from anyone. Her friend was the only exception. As she rested on the bed, the silence of her dreams swept her away. In the darkness the whispers of the Keep Ardaguar spread out around her. In the early hour of the morning she woke with a start. The moon still covered the sky in shadows creeping across from the corners of the room. She made her way down stairs.

She crept along the creaking floor, while her leaving did not go unnoticed. A soft rustle escaped from around the corner just as she was confronted. Lord Dackren stood over her in a menacing tone, 'Where are you off to girl?'

He leaned too close for her liking as she replied and he remarked, 'You are not going alone.'

Before Saranon could muster an argument he began giving instructions to his right-hand man. Ben Waterworth wasted no time gathering the clan's best fighters.

She was reluctant to ask the wizards to stay behind. Even though all she wanted to do was travel alone. Somehow Lord Dackren managed to look even scarier in the darkness before dawn. As he hiked himself up on his dragon Ember. She was a sleek dragon with a large build. While Saranon clung on as Katholomu leaped into the sky before she was ready. She managed to sit upright as Kat flew at full strength. He made haste catching up with the wizards who showed no signs of slowing down.

The warm night air ran through her hair as they dived in close to the border. Lord Dackren had landed near the side of a hill, as she rushed to keep up. She looked straight ahead through the night sky. To a row of shimmering lights in the distance, the Lord turned to greet her, 'This is as far as we go.'

Saranon waved a short thank you, before darting off.

She fled into the darkness to the end node of the Keep Garduend. Her feet touched the stony edge. She hesitated with the realisation of being in Darkonia.

The thought evaporated as she remembered why she was here. She searched out with her senses and no sound came back. The only thing she could hear was her own breath. When she leaned down to touch the stone it felt wrong. The sensation felt like a heavy burden, sitting underneath the surface, held back by an invisible barrier crouched just below. In the distance a sound caught her attention, but it was just a misquew. Its sharp eyes stared with a warm glow as the large riding cat curled up to rest near the edge of the stone.

She found an entrance leading back into the Keep. As she placed her hand up the shield around it held strong. The misquew stretched out in response as it rose to greet her, before wandering off. She hesitated before following. The creature had an agile stride glancing back before sitting down near the bushes. Saranon peeked through as the bush prickled along the palm of her hand. The misquew laid down closing its eyes to rest once more. She moved the branches away from the stone and read the marker. It did not make sense, but then not much here did.

She walked further and a jarring pain ran through her leg as she stubbed her toe. She held her breath and nothing stirred. Saranon leaned down to find a large metal ring. It fitted around both her hands and she pulled. A cloud of air sprayed dust away from the side and she coughed trying to mask the sound. It was a vain attempt, yet by the look of the entrance it would not have mattered. The air was musty and dry with no sign of any sorcery guarding it. She ran her fingers along the wall. A bulging sensation reached out as she pulled her hand back.

The Keep felt unfamiliar as she glanced around. All the sounds of the normal running of the Keep were mixed up. The Keep lay empty while she moved about expecting someone to notice at any moment. The hair at the back of her neck stood on end and her heart pounded. She continued her descent into the depths of the Keep. Garduend rumbled around her in an eerie tone.

The place filled with a sadness that penetrated her mind and darkened her thoughts. There was not a soul in sight except for the empty mutterings of the Keep. She clambered downward and the oddness dawned on her. There was no flurry of skada, no sound of sleeping zennigh, not a peep. The Keep was void of the creatures that protected it. In the silence it was just her and Garduend. Saranon stepped further down aware of the time outside. This was not the place to contemplate what had happened, she had to move fast.

The strange clanking sound from below became louder. She jumped out into the dark cavern where the main conduit should have been. Her energy held her as she made a slow descent to the bottom. Peering down a gigantic tube filled with nothing but a shambled mess. The last remains of the conduit tying the Keep to the central core had wilted. To all but a thin tube charred at the edges. It glowed hot with the inability to shield the energy pulsing inside. She was able to protect herself from the heat as she walked along with a purposeful stride.

The conduit dipped down a long shaft, she stood at the edge holding on in thought. All the conduits would not last long. An idea crept into her mind one that would have scared her had she not helped Hedavin before. The Angeon enveloped her then she reached out with a tight grasp. She seared all the main conduits from the central core. The blast pounded out reverberating up through the walls. If no one knew she was here that would need to change, as she used the blast to catapult the energy upward. The deafening roar split through the conduits as the stallic energy poured out. It drenched the walls so hard the damage rang out behind her.

Saranon ran out the door closing it behind her. Not wanting to hear any more with the last traces still ringing in her ears. She turned to go and hesitated. A large figure stood in the first glimpse of light spraying out from the unwelcome dawn. Edred the administrator stood strong. The Vandragamond sorcerer was more than twice her age. Her eyes grew wide and she ran. The last traces of the Angeon shielded her from the sorcerer's blow. The energy faded, but she took no notice as she ran back to Katholomu. The dragon picked her up in a sideways scoop and flung himself hard into the air.

The great black dragon looked magnificent in the light of day. Yet that was not what she wanted, as her hearted thudded. A small glimmer up ahead revealed the wizards who had been reluctant to stay. She grumbled in annoyance. Kat gave a deep low growl in return. The dragon did not think much of acts of cowardice and had let her know more than once. The warm sun creased across the sky with its full rays just as they hit the ground. Katholomu held out his wings in a seething manner. He whipped his steel like talons hard against the Keep Ardaguar.

The effect was spontaneous as one wall cracked, with dust flying over the courtyard. The dragon moved his head in an ominous glare daring any of the wizards to challenge him. Saranon landed with a heavy thud as she swung down from the tense beast. Shew ran inside, in a lame attempt to hide. She slowed to a walk as she realised it would be useless. Mitch reached across grabbing her arm and pulling her out of sight. Before she had a chance to say anything he held a finger to his lips.

They both listened. She wanted to shout at the wizard. As the exhaustion wrapped around she reconsidered. Crevan's voice spoke over his talik. As only half the conversation was grasped while the sorcerer walked by. The small circular communication device fit in the palm of his hand. Saranon frowned, 'I think it's about Garduend.'

Mitch gave her a look that said otherwise, 'So how did you go?'

She muttered under her breath. He smiled before responding, 'You'll do better next time.'

She was hoping there would not be a next time. She had the distinct feeling that would be unavoidable. As she walked away the sorcerer at Garduend had looked familiar. She had seen that face somewhere before. She was deep in thought when an arm circled around her shoulders and she flinched. Lord Dackren began talking as she removed his arm from around her. 'Now,' spoke the Lord into her ear, 'When am I going to see you on the disc?'

She cringed before answering, 'No Lord Dackren.'

He gave a ruthful smile and winked as he left her in a state of mortified bewilderment.

The Lord was starting to get on her nerves. She was not sure how much more she was could put up with, as she shook her head. Saranon went outside in the golden sunlight. It streamed down just before midday, as Jack caught her attention. Now that was where she had seen the face before. Jack Heath looked like a younger version of the same sorcerer. He waved again with a warm smile, 'Lord Dackren won't rest until you fight him on the disc.'

'I know.' The reminder annoyed her as she added, 'This is your fault.'

Jack shrugged his shoulders at the accusation. As the smell of lunch wafted passed and consumed Saranon's thoughts. She had not eaten breakfast amid the rush to return to Ardaguar. Afterward she returned to her room. Resting on the small couch as her exhaustion took hold. The warm breeze glided through the window and she fell asleep. Her dreams were filled with a large gaping hole, as she let go, falling deep into the ground.

She landed at the end of a long journey down. Embedded in the soft dirt of Tordoren, a small shining spark glimmered. In the dream she reached out pushing the dirt away so she could hold the spark in her hands.

She held a solid form of life, warm to the touch. Then something grabbed her and she woke up. Pennie stood over her smiling, 'You almost fell off the couch.'

Saranon glanced around the room making sure nothing else was going to jump out at her. 'What's happening at Garduend?' She asked.

'I'm afraid we haven't been able to get close to find out,' Pennie explained.

An unknown problem in a Keep with a detached core spelt even more trouble. Her friend look at her while she was searching for an answer, it was not forthcoming. Pennie could read her face and the sadness welled up in her eyes. Saranon hated seeing her friend this way the internal torment made her heart sink.

The moment was broken as Mitch entered in a rush. Catching his breath while leaning against the wall, 'You're needed.'

He looked straight into Saranon's eyes and nodded. She gave him a quizzical stare oblivious to his reference. As Pennie rose taking her queue without hesitation, 'It is time.'

'What do you mean?' She asked.

'You entered the disc, now you will fight,' her friend explained.

She gave an exasperated sigh. Her mind ran through several arguments. Pennie's expression displayed an answer for them all. 'I'm not sure which one of you to blame for this,' she spoke in anguish.

Mitch stepped aside without saying a word. Saranon

strode down the corridor in a sullen frame of mind. A flurry of sound stemmed from the grand two-storey foyer. A familiar grunt from a dragon filled the air. Katholomu turned his head sideways staring straight at her.

The shouts grew louder as a group of wizards tried to move the great beast out of the main doors. The dragon paid no attention as he lowered his neck and she leaped on. For once she welcomed Kat's disregard. He twisted his body easing through the open doors. He jumped up high into the evening sky as the darkness of night wrapped around them. The voices of the wizards shouted through the wind. No one followed after them. The dragon flew too hard she could sense he had a purpose. She clung on tight as Katholomu swung a hard left, into Darkonia.

She peered down as the ground changed below. The low hills parted into a clearing then Kat swooped fast and smooth in the silence. Up ahead a dragon stirred on the outer edge of the hill, greeting them. She moved through the group of dragons with ease. She realised they served the Vandragamond. She moved closer listening to the sorcerers as she hid. They spoke in low voices and she recognised Edred Heath, the administrator. He stared right past her and she hoped he did not notice, it was all she could do to stay still.

A booming voice echoed in the darkness above. The harsh tones came from the sorcerer that towered over the rest. He said, 'Take the path down below, she's had enough fun. Next time you want a divorce, warn me.'

'Yes, sire,' Edred, the administrator answered with a

dry tone.

Lord Shakar stared off into the distance straight through her. Then his eyes locked on and he shouted, 'Gallagher!'

Allard Gallagher moved off from the side. Saranon wasted no time running toward Katholomu through the low scrub.

She clung to his shoulder as a sound crept up behind her. The dragon lunged. Gallagher stepped back as the great beast took off with a mighty roar. She was too shaken to understand the dragon's sense of delight. He swooped onto the nearest hill across the northern border. The dragon landed with a sudden pelt. The jolt threw her forward as she used her energy to slow her descent. The hard ground stung her hands as she left it too late. Katholomu stood arching his shoulders up to full height. He spoke the same word he had said before with a deep growl, 'Coward.'

It was one word and as much as Saranon tried to argue, it amounted to nothing, as her voice fell flat. In a last effort she shouted, 'I'm not a coward.'

The dragon laughed with the sound rumbling. It ran through his entire body from head to toe. Then he lied down in a casual stance staring at her with bemusement. She tried to stay angry, but the great beast pouted and her heart melted. She clambered up over his shoulders. 'Let's go, I have a wizard to fight,' she grumbled.

The dark night swept in around them as a light rain took the last of the heat from the day. The disc did not enthral her in any way. Lord Dackren had not left her alone since she arrived. Continuing to hide from the problem was not going to work. She smiled as she patted the dragon. Ardaguar came into view and she cringed at the thought. Sometimes it would be nice to be someone else. Katholomu glided down in silence sweeping through the night air.

The dragon flew low along the ground. As he headed straight for the place Saranon wanted to avoid. The beast ran along slowing as he went. He ducked straight into the great hall with the disc and he slid her down near the edge. She did not want to leave the comfort of the dragon. He stayed with the same expression reminding her of what he had said. She jumped as she realised she was not alone. A solitary figure stood in the shadows. Lord Dackren was hard to forget. As he stepped close to the outer rim of the disc, 'I didn't pick you for one to run away.'

She grimaced at the cold remark then walked onto the disc, 'I don't run.'

He grinned, 'We'll see.'

The Lord was no stranger to taking on a sorcerer as he moved with a graceful ease. Saranon watched in fascination, but she had little time to think. The first bolt hurled across the disc. The Lord's energy shattered as she shielded the blow. From that moment she locked her attention on the Lord. She moved forward hurtling her sorcery with certainty. Yet the Lord cut through it in lightning speed. He smiled in delight at her shocked expression.

The shards of energy ricocheted off the edges of the shield around the disc. They lit up the hall with a magnificent array of light. She struck hard, but it did no good. Lord Dackren shielded himself. 'Are you going to call on the Angeon?' He taunted.

She grimaced at his words as she tried to concentrate. She kept pace as they moved around the disc exchanging blows. A movement caught her attention at the corner of her eye. The noise and light had brought other occupants from Ardaguar to watch.

The Lord struck again more specific as if honing in on her. Saranon held her ground as she dodged the full impact of the blow and moved closer. The Lord smiled, consumed by the challenge. He circled in anticipating the end and this time she let him. In the heat of the excitement part of her wanted to see what the Lord could do. He lunged hurtling his energy hard and fast. Saranon gasped and in the gap between her thoughts Katholomu coughed. She turned to face the dragon only just escaping the blast. It lashed through, lighting up the shield in an almighty spray of light.

She rushed forward in the skirmish. She tried to grab hold of the wizard, but he was too agile and darted out of her grasp. He grinned as they moved around the disc. It had not been long, yet her body felt heavy from exhaustion. She refused to give in and she recognised something just for a moment. The Lord lunged in close with his energy and Saranon took hold, dragging him to the floor. She stared straight into his eyes and whispered amid the cheering crowd, 'Let go.'

'No,' he groaned through gritted teeth.

The latches holding the disc in place came free with a metallic ringing sound. Piercing through the crowd as the people roared with delight. 'Relent, and I will spare you the indignity,' she whispered to the Lord.

His attempts remained futile as they remained locked in a silent battle. He sighed, 'All right Vandragamond, I'll give you this one.'

The Lord ceased his fight, and the disc stopped its slow swaying. It returned to its permanent holding.

A roar stemmed up through the crowd so loud it hurt her ears. As they both stood Lord Dackren spoke, 'You have won this one.'

The words were not endearing, but for Saranon it meant an end to being hassled. For that she was relieved as she managed to catch her breath. Mitch found his way through the crowd and held out his hand, 'Come on.'

She followed as they darted away. The thrill of the excitement still buzzed around her head making her feel giddy.

Zara greeted them in the large entrance. With a warm smile, 'My brother rarely loses.'

Saranon was too exhausted to speak as she left for her room. A rose hung from the handle, she picked it up as she went inside. Pennie was studying and stole it from her, reading the note attached. Her friend burst out with laughter, 'I think you have an admirer.'

'What?' Saranon's face went red with embarrassment.

'See for yourself,' Pennie handed her the note.

She fell back on the bed, 'If it isn't one, it's the other.'

'What are you going to tell him?' Pennie asked.

'I'll think about it in the morning,' Saranon sighed.

Pennie burst out laughing, 'At least it's not Lord Dackren.'

She threw a pillow at her friend who would not stop laughing.

CHAPTER TEN

Rising to the challenge

A harsh round a shouting pierced through the open window. Saranon resisted opening her eyes to the morning light. Her body felt like a sack of potatoes as she lifted her arm and winced with the pain. She tried to figure out how the wizard had caused the bruising. Pennie glanced out to the courtyard below, 'Wow, you have to see this.'

She was not amused as she moved her aching shoulders and slid out of bed. The ranting had ceased, but the figures stood in plain view.

Saranon's head throbbed as the harsh light stung her eyes. Jack Heath seemed attracted to trouble. As Crevan walked away her friend made a sly comment, 'I don't think all is well.'

She was not convinced and paid no more attention to the idea as she ran downstairs. Jack was still standing in the courtyard. As he spoke, 'I understand you've been to Garduend.'

'Who told you that?' Saranon asked.

Jack gave a sad smile, 'It's everybody's business to know about the Keep. I was wondering if I could go with you?'

She wondered why anybody would want to go straight into a troubled Keep. She agreed to the request. There was something about the sorcerer's determination that changed her mind. She was not sure what she was getting into herself. If Jack was familiar with the Keep it could be of some use.

She sensed someone approaching and blushed. Saranon had forgotten about the rose as she turned to meet Killian. He greeted her with an open bow and she could feel her cheeks grow red as he asked to walk with her. Her mind went blank and she could think of no reason not to, so she accepted his company. He was not much older than her.

The mystery of Garduend Keep still racked her mind. She almost lost track of Killian's words. He had a quiet manner though he was not shy, Lord Dackren would have made sure of that. He was intent on showing her the beautiful gardens that surrounded the Keep. They were hidden away throughout the many courtyards. The blissful rays of the sun warmed her face as they meandered along the path. Saranon took the opportunity to quiz him about her homeland. A tear trickled down her cheek as she wiped it, hoping Killian would not see.

'I could not imagine what it would be like without my kin,' he spoke with a hint of sadness.

She sensed something, 'You do know?'

He hung his head in shame before answering. 'I was held by Lord Shakar when my father angered him,' he spoke.

Saranon was not sure how to answer.

She held out her hand and he held onto it not wanting to let go. Neither of them knew what to say. Part of her did not want it to end, but then she had no idea what she was doing. At best she managed a small goodbye before leaving him behind. When she was out of sight she smiled as her cheeks grew warm.

A still air hung over the warm afternoon as she looked for a distraction and found none. Pennie was meticulous in her method of packing as they prepared for the inevitable. Her friend had been too absorbed in the details to ask her whereabouts. It was just as well, because she was not sure how to approach the subject. Instead she found some of her belongings and pretended to be busy. Pennie's voice made her cringe, 'Will you stop doing that! I need those boxes packed over there.'

She gave a meek smile while helping.

Saranon followed her friend all the way down underneath the Keep. They passed through the grand foyer. A large simple staircase led them to the armoury below. The lower Keep was more spacious. Only the great columns broke the immediate view. Pennie strode with a purpose. They stopped while two wizards opened the massive doors to a large room.

'Wow,' Saranon exclaimed in awe.

She stared at a room full from ceiling to floor of weapons. 'See anything you fancy?' Her friend asked.

While examining a tool she had just picked up. She had travelled to Indarin with what she had and saw no reason to change. Yet the offer was enticing. She hesitated in thought then left the room and all its glory behind.

Jack stood ready though a little nervous around the edges. It was the first time she had seen him show fear. The late afternoon was still light. This meant swinging around the long way into Darkonia, then back toward the south of the Keep. Pennie had been plotting the path, not wanting to lose time once they were in the air. Katholomu glanced at her as she entered the courtyard, this time he was calm. She held on tight as the great dragon flew hard into the sky.

The ground swirled past below, but she paid no attention as the wind picked up. Kat flew with a majestic grace. They surged over the border straight into Darkonia. It was a fair way in before they needed to turn. The air filled with the flight of dragons missing one another as they went. She was relieved to see that many did not have riders. The last thing she wanted was to be spotted. Pennie showed no hesitation as she bolted through the sky with a purpose. Jack blended in with ease.

Still the anxiety made her queasy and she wished she could be like her friends. The untouched hillside beneath them broke down with the signs of settlement. They stayed on the outskirts flying at a swift pace. Before she knew it, the dragon dropped into a glide, hitting the ground running. Then he arched his great body to a mighty halt. The muscles tensed and she clung on closing her eyes until Katholomu came to a rest. Pennie landed closer still to the Keep's edge. Saranon followed as the strange noises emanating from Garduend resounded through the air.

A snapping sound came from close by but her companions paid it no attention. She quickened her pace not wanting to be left behind. The Keep had an odd stillness that crept over them, with the looming darkness of night. Her senses prickled at the edges. She felt the crisscrossing energy of the Keep leaking through. The path they took along the edge of the forest felt dense. The energy wafted up through the ground. Jack reached over taking his time to read the inscription. He used his energy to shuffle the words around. Something creaked from behind the door and she jumped.

Pennie gave her a stern look before making her way inside. The air was musty with a slight acrid smell, that tasted metallic on her tongue when she breathed it in. She held out her hand. A strange sinking feeling stemmed back through her senses. The odd sensation made her tingle and her eyes locked with Pennie. The taint was something they had seen before. Saranon did not want to admit it, but she was scared. The only thing that had stopped her fear at Antavagon was a deep wild rage. That she had released after Tasha's death.

Tasha's face still haunted her from the grave even though she did not want to admit it. Jack found a hatch leading down to a substation. He knew the layout, the Keep was so faint and it would be easy to become lost. A spark grew from up ahead as she caught her breath and braced herself in the glow. She could just make out her companions as they managed to dodge the blast. It rippled past as the blow hit hard. She staggered back as the last remnants swept through. In the distance she could hear Pennie and Jack running away. She hesitated then darted after them.

Part of her wanted to stay behind. As they escaped out of the Keep, another blast pelted down the passageway. It seared the sides of the building. Kat eyed her with suspicion before whisking her up onto his shoulder. The dragon had no intention of taking her back to Ardaguar. He circled out of sight landing close to the Keep Garduend. Saranon watched in anguish as her friends flew through the sky disappearing from view. Katholomu stood his ground. The dragon lived to fight and he would not back down, much to her astonishment.

She patted the dragon's sturdy shoulder then clambered onto the grass below. The still night air closed in around her as she plucked up the courage to move forward. In the dim light the distant voices travelled to her ears. She crouched in the darkness. It was beyond her how the large dragon could blend into the background. Yet Katholomu did it with ease much to her annoyance. Dragons were so common, that even if he had been seen she doubted it would draw attention. She tried not to make a sound and waited in the shadows on the edge of the Keep.

The voices became people. She watched on as two travellers arrived holding a strange glowing bundle. A sorcerer came out to meet them, then all three darted inside. Saranon hid for what seemed like hours. Then she gathered the strength to climb onto Kat. Her mind filled with unanswered questions as the dragon flew into the air. Just as they picked up speed her thoughts were broken by a stirring of noise on the ground. Katholomu wasted no time leaving Darkonia behind as she clung on tight. The wind whipped around her with a vibrant energy of its own. She could feel the strength of the dragon. He moved with a powerful grace, with the excitement still buzzing in her head.

Saranon wondered what she would have done if Katholomu had been shy. Then she could not imagine him any other way. The great dragon glided into the warm open courtyard of Ardaguar. Jack waited, he was a tall lanky figure and stood back as the dragon came to rest, 'I let you down.'

'What do you mean?' She asked in surprise.

'I know someone at the Keep, and I didn't want to see anyone get hurt,' he explained.

It was not what she had expected, but then she could not blame him.

'I saw something. I was wondering if you could help?' She asked changing the subject.

He smiled, 'I'll see what I can do.'

Jack led her down below the habitable area of the Keep. It was warm and dry with a soft flow of fresh air.

Then he sat dangling his legs over the edge of floor. The warm dark mass of sheal shimmered, swirling below. If she reached too far she could touch it, but it did not scare her. Saranon sat near the edge leaning up against the column waiting to see what he would do. He projected the sheal and transformed it into an image. Asking her if it looked like what she had seen. She shook her head and he created another. This went on as she tried not to laugh. Then her voice stuck in her throat as she waved out her arm and almost lost her balance.

Jack whispered something under his breath. She was too busy staring at the image. She was caught in a trance as it sparkled with an eerie glow. He gave her a knowing look, one she did not expect. He explained, not wanting to stare at the image as it melted back into the sheal. Somehow Jack knew that next time she could not take him with her. He looked heartbroken in the midst of so much unsaid.

A clicking sound cut the Keep's hum short. It startled both of them as they glanced at each other. She had heard the sound before. Her mind raced through the possibilities. The low hum filled the background once more. It did not quell her suspicions. Jack spoke, 'Let me show you something?'

He reached out his sorcery weaving it into the sheal as it glowed fusing into a sphere of light. Jack brought the sphere around holding it out toward her. She was mesmerised by the light.

Saranon had not seen anything like it and the sphere of sorcery intrigued her. She held out her hand and it responded, 'How did you do that?' She asked.

Jack smiled, 'You need to find that out on your own.'

They made their way to the door as a small trail of bubbles popped along the surface of the sheal. She glanced out of the corner of her eye. She stopped as it held her curiosity then left for a well-earned sleep.

The beautiful stars twinkling in the night sky had vanished. They faded into the brilliant mid-morning sun. It played through the open window, reaching the dull carpet. Saranon felt half asleep as her eyes played tricks on her with the light. She blinked and the message was still clear there, marked by a pattern in the shadow. As she stepped towards it, the lines vanished. She lowered her head to the floor trying to trace the source. Pennie opened the door and burst out laughing, 'What are you doing?'

When she explained Pennie smiled, 'It may be one of the wizards.'

Saranon was not so sure, but she did not see any harm in following the instruction. She made her downstairs. It seemed an odd way of communicating. Her annoyance showed on her face as she went below the habitable areas of the Keep. The great doors had been left open with voices echoing above the hum of the Keep. The substation whirred with a strong steady sound. She was not sure if she was meant to say something, but the wizards appeared to be expecting her. Killian strode through the door, 'Beautiful isn't it?'

She was about to complain about the message on the floor, but before she could he walked away. Killian smiled,

'I wanted you to check something for us.'

'Who is us?' Saranon asked.

'The Glyrondagar. We think something is wrong with the Keep and we thought you could help,' he responded.

It did not matter which country she was in, wizards had a habit of finding ways to be irritating. The small group stared at her in anticipation. Until she relented, 'All right I'll take a look.'

She had nothing better to do while waiting to gain access into Garduend Keep. She sat down near the control panels. It was a short way down, positioned near a main connector between the conduits. It was below the spider's web of small connections above. Saranon started flicking the buttons. She froze as Killian slid in the seat beside her. She could feel Killian's eyes boring into the side of her head. He waited with a hint of excitement.

She was tempted to clout him for leading her astray and thought better of it. She immersed herself in the task at hand and listened to the Keep. It hummed along as Killian waited. She moved the levers, switching connections before Ardaguar was ready. Saranon listened to the gaps between, the missing notes in the hum of the Keep. She tried to concentrate as Killian's hand moved across the controls, breaking her concentration. 'Will you stop doing that,' she exclaimed.

Just then an audible clunk broke the silence. The hum of the Keep whirred into action. 'Did you hear that?' he asked.

'Shush…' She held her finger to her lips.

She waited then moved the levers in a different sequence. This time the clunking rattled deep within the Keep, echoing up through the floor. The Keep tried to engage, but it could not. The hum broke into several false starts and the colour drained from her face. She worked the control panel creating a surge from the depths of the Keep. The great roar echoed up. She held her breath as the stallic energy whirred the Keep into life.

Saranon gasped and she stepped out catching her breath. Before she could blink Killian had leaped into action. He wasted no time directing the wizards around them to locate the source. Then turned to her, 'Are you coming?'

'Are you mad?' She asked in exasperation.

He gave a faint smile, 'Maybe.'

She trailed after the wizards. Ben gave her a sideways glance in acknowledgement as he darted ahead.

She had the distinct sinking feeling of rushing into something unprepared. The sensation sank to the pit of her stomach. The uneasiness made her lag behind, no matter how much she tried to keep up. A small clinking sound skittered along the floor. As she turned around to see her talik bouncing down the corridor. She leaned down to scoop it up. A high shrill escaped through the air. Saranon shielded herself from the blow of raging light. The energy sparked along the top of her shield as she dared to open her eyes. The air was thick and metallic. It left a sharp taste in her mouth as she searched through the spray of light.

Her talik buzzed in her hand, but she ignored it. The

air crackled around her as the energy dissipated. She showed no fear as she strode forward toward the shadowy light. The only sound came from her rapid heartbeat pulsing up through her ears. The haze dimmed the way ahead as she searched with her senses. There were figures nearby, but she had no way of telling who was who. Wizardry arched through the air giving the sorceress a small glimpse. It was all she needed as she honed in on her target.

The roar from her energy was electrifying as it cleared the air in an instant. It absorbed the other sorcery. Crevan's eyes became all too clear as they filled with an intense frustration. His blast erupted shaking the ground. Saranon met the sorcerer's blow in kind as Crevan struggled while losing ground. The wizards kept a respectful distance away and she eased off as he stood in defiance. Her mind was still racing, trying to catch up. The wizards reacted before she did, using their energy to block the blow.

Saranon had had enough. She held out her arms absorbing the blow and combining it with her own. The result was pure hot vengeance as Crevan fell limp on the floor. Ben Waterworth ran up to check and gave acknowledgement that he was alive. Her voice sounded hoarse and remote as Ben smiled in response. He remarked, 'Crevan has been syphoning the Keep's energy for himself. We had it narrowed down, but we needed to know which one.'

It still did not make sense. She was willing to accept his judgement after having been attacked. 'Perhaps you need to join the night watch and get some practice?' Ben suggested.

'I'd like to see you take on the Keep's energy,' she coughed.

'That's not possible,' Killian spoke.

'Next time warn me,' she spoke with a tired voice.

Ben smiled, 'I will add that at the top of my list.'

CHAPTER ELEVEN

The old world still burns

It was not long before the whole of Ardaguar was abuzz with the news. Jack's hands trembled as he tried to hide them he was still shaken by the events. Saranon could not blame him, but at the same time she was not about to give the wizards any ground. Lord Dackren's voice boomed across the room. It felt like she was the only one strong enough to answer. She found herself shouting at the Lord. He stared at her, 'I suppose you want me to shower you with praise?'

'Some respect would be a start,' she spoke aloud with a hint of annoyance.

Her body still felt the effects of the fight as she stood her ground, staring the Lord in the eye. Lord Dackren was not about to budge which infuriated her even more. She had been refused access to the lower levels of the Keep.

She could always ignore the Lord's word, but she did not have time to get caught up in a dispute. She was about to say more, then stopped. She did not want to get bogged down in the Lord's antics. 'I expected you to be more forthcoming,' Saranon grated her teeth in frustration.

Lord Dackren took genuine pleasure in his position. He enjoyed telling sorcerers what to do in his Keep. He leaned forward, 'For a guest you make many of demands.'

Pennie broke through the crowd. She stood in front of Saranon, 'We are indeed grateful for your hospitality. As you can appreciate we will leave as soon the matter at Garduend has been resolved.'

To her amazement Pennie bowed and grabbed Saranon's arm. Pennie yanked her down in a clumsy bow, guiding her away from the Lord's gaze.

'What are you doing?' Pennie hissed.

'You can't blame me for that,' she retorted.

Not wanting to start an argument with her friend. Pennie glared at her in astonishment. Then let out a heavy sigh, 'We'd better go before one of you starts round two.'

She did not think the statement was fair. Her head still buzzed from the confrontation. If she had known helping the wizard clan would land her in trouble. She would not have bothered helping.

The room offered little escape from the sentiments of Lord Dackren, that echoed the mood of the clan. The sensations running through the Keep did nothing to calm her mind. Pennie left as though making noise would provoke her frustration. She leaned back on the bed and closed her eyes. A knock broke her rest as Mitch entered, 'I think you'd better come downstairs.'

He left before she could ask. A noise erupted through the open foyer and it only meant one thing.

She ran along the upper level which joined up to the balcony around the stadium for the disc. She could sense who it was, before glancing down. Jack Heath stood on the side of the disc closest to her. She felt awkward as she looked around and found no other sorcerers in her midst. She sat down preferring not to be the centre of attention this time. All eyes focused on the fight below. Sparks flew bouncing off the shield around the disc. The roar from the audience erupted with excitement.

The noise and the sensations running from Ardaguar changed. She could tell the Lord was starting to close in. This time she would have to leave Jack to his own fate. The thought did not sit well with her. Then a tiny spark of wizardry flickered from the corner of her eye. All her irritation narrowed in on the culprit. Her sorcery reached out extinguishing the wizard's work. He tried again without success and looked around. By this time she was well hidden. The wizard was growing frustrated as Saranon remained calm. A loud gasp of astonishment rang up through the crowd as Lord Dackren lost to his opponent.

She darted away in the commotion with a smile of satisfaction. She should have guessed the fights were rigged. She made her way downstairs where Mitch caught her still smiling. 'That was not what I had in mind,' he exclaimed.

He guided her out to the courtyard toward the disc.

Saranon could not understand what the problem was. She glanced at a rather shaken Lord Dackren. The Lord focused on her and their eyes locked. He glared at her. As he moved away from the disc, 'You've just made a sorcerer even more arrogant.'

She leaned close and could smell his breath on her shoulder. As he fumed, 'You were not going to win that fight, at least this way Jack thinks it's fair.'

Lord Dackren looked as though he was about to say something as the sweat soaked his top. Then the conversation was over as he strode through the crowd. She stayed out of his way with no intention of fighting the Lord again. Jack clasped her shoulder from behind and she jumped. 'I didn't scare you did I?' He grinned, 'I've wanted to beat him for a long time.'

Mitch stared at the younger man and responded, 'I hadn't noticed.'

Jack smiled, 'Perhaps next time I'll take you on?'

Mitch gazed from Jack to Saranon then walked off. As she spoke for him, 'I don't think you should, he took down a Dihan.'

'I'm impressed. I need to talk to you about Garduend,' this time he spoke with a sobering tone.

He changed the subject when evening had fallen on Ardaguar. The drunken spectators spilled into the warm night air. They had no inclination to rest. The pair made their way over to a quieter courtyard where the stars lit their way. Together with the small glowing lights along the ground. He looked as though he was about to say something, but stopped. Then tried again as she wondered how long it would take. Jack fumbled around with his hands and let out a sigh. The first hint he had ever given of an inner turmoil. Saranon stared on in bewilderment as Jack Heath began to make sense. Her fragile smile turned into a deep frown.

Footsteps rushed towards them and Jack stopped. He behaved as though nothing had happened as he greeted Pennie. Her friend grabbed hold of her hand. She did not have time to react. 'We need to go now, if we're going to make it to the Keep,' Pennie said.

She tried not to stumble as she ran along the shadowy path. Katholomu snorted in the dark and pushed his way into greet her. The dragon shifted his shoulder sideways scooping her up. She clung on while he took off with a jolt, leaping up into the beautiful still night sky.

She clambered around on the dragon's back and saw Pennie catching up. Her friend wasted no time taking the lead. With Kat following so close the wing tips almost touched. Veradae snorted in disgust. She was almost as large as Katholomu with a sleek black coat. Pennie headed across the border as Saranon's mind raced, full of jumbled thoughts. She left out of the discussion yet again. Blind trust was one thing, but she was beginning to feel as though she had been left well behind. The warm empty night gave her too much time to think. The still air uttered few sounds as the sleepy darkness shadowed her mind. It was not the Darkonia she had entered before.

Without warning Katholomu veered away from the

small group at a sharp angle. She did not try to stop the massive beast, if she could feel the sensation then so could he. She surrendered to the dragon's flight. If not a little bemused by his instinctive decision as she held onto his shoulder. A faint series of lights broke along the hillside. She could feel the great beast beginning to descend. He lunged out his hind legs absorbing the blow. Kat reduced his short sprint to a walk as she stayed low near his shoulder blades. This time she let the dragon lead and the warmth of his skin gave her comfort.

A damp sensation gripped her skin as it dawned on her she was hugging a sweaty dragon. She cringed in disgust. The dragon was searching for something. She was beginning to feel silly clinging to his back. A movement caught her eye in the distance as Katholomu leaned forward. A moment of sheer jealousy ran through her body. As she felt more than heard the dragon rumbling a happy purr deep within his throat. She reached out her senses, and recognised who it was, 'Galven.'

She jumped in surprise not expecting company as he answered, 'Saranon.'

His voice was filled with relief, 'We thought we'd missed you.'

It was an odd statement. 'What do you mean?' She asked.

'Come down,' Galven spoke in a soft tone as he plucked her down off the dragon.

She would always remember him as one of the unfortunate. Branded an Issola like her, and taken to the detention camps. Since then he had changed so much. There was no sign of the scared little boy as she stared into his eyes searching for an answer. He moved forward crouching low, and she did the same. The Keep was still some way off, but there were signs of activity below in the shallow valley.

She watched comprehending what Galven wanted to show her. There in the valley, gathering in their numbers. They were some of the most powerful sorcerers she had ever sensed. They were trying to shield their whereabouts. It was clear that someone else did not approve of the goings on at Garduend. A branch snapped underfoot nearby and her heart leaped into her throat. As she stared into the eyes of the administrator, only a few strides away. Galven grabbed her arm, and they ran. They melded straight through a stone wall before Saranon had time to blink.

While they waited Galven explained as Saranon spoke aloud, 'He looks like Jack Heath.'

He gave a soft laugh, 'Jack is the administrator's son.'

'Are you telling me we just ran for our lives and we didn't need to?' She asked.

'No,' he remarked as he walked down a small path leading deeper into the hillside.

It was wonderful to see Galven again. Maybe someday they would be able meet under ordinary circumstances.

They went down into the small Keep hidden underneath the hill. As she followed along, hoping to avoid getting lost. She glanced at a few familiar faces in the narrow passages. Galven announced an end to their journey. He presented her with a small unassuming doorway. Saranon stepped out into the warm night air, bidding him a short goodbye. Garduend was becoming far too busy. She wondered if she would still be needed when a tall dark figure stood in her way. The administrator loomed over her, and she froze in an odd silence.

'You seem to have misplaced your dragon?' Edred, the administrator spoke.

Saranon looked around her, but there was no sign of Katholomu anywhere. He stood so close this time there was nowhere to run. The soft noise of footsteps behind her only confirmed her situation. Gallagher went to hold her arm. He stopped short as her energy blocked him. 'Don't be stupid girl,' he remarked.

Instead she walked ahead of him, 'Suit yourself,' he commented from over her shoulder.

As they approached the small camp she could make out Pennie and the Captain. Still there was no sign of her dragon.

A large figure approached them in the dark. The sorcerer strode with a fierce pace, showing all the signs of his stature. Lord Shakar's glare cut through the faint light webbing its way around the camp. Without warning the night moved. The Lord sent a blast of his energy toward her, cutting into the air. The Angeon rose inside her shielding the blow. To her astonishment the Lord stammered backwards. As he held his ground the Lord wiped a streak of blood from his chin. 'Don't ever do that again,' Lord Shakar spoke.

'I should say that for you?' Saranon almost shouted the words as she spat them out.

Gallagher tried to tackle her and she gripped his hand. She crushed it with her sorcery until he relented in a shriek of pain. She turned her full attention to Lord Shakar, as they exchanged a verbal argument. Both were prepared to back the exchange with their sorcery. The Lord unsheathed his bond-breaker holding Evermoor in the form of a sword. The blade shone in the reflection of light. It was then that Saranon remembered. The words told to her by Theron, the Prophet in waiting. The blade was like hers. In an abrupt shock she burst out laughing. It was not the reaction the Lord had been expecting.

She smiled realising that Lord Shakar was none the wiser. Captain Assinden's calm voice intruded, 'I think you'd better tell them.'

Mitch was not the only wizard who could read her immediate thoughts. She said, 'I don't think that's necessary.'

She was annoyed, but at that moment the Lord stepped so close. She could feel his irate breath as he glared at her. She held out Corsavere in all its brilliance, gleaming in the form of a sword. She held it up with the ambient light radiating along the blade.

It glowed in a brilliant sea green. The same colour as Lord Shakar's bond-breaker. In the soft glow Saranon saw his expression change. The Lord nodded in acknowledgement as she was left alone. She placed Corsavere away by her side. Gallagher leaned over her shoulder, 'Welcome to the clan.'

'Thanks,' she whispered back, although she was not sure how she felt.

Her would be father had wandered off without uttering another word. So she followed Gallagher to meet her friends. Pennie gave her a giant hug that almost bowled her over in midstride. 'That was great,' her friend said so that no one else could hear.

She looked up in the background to see a large shadowy figure sprawling into view. Katholomu barged his way through claiming a warm spot near the open fire. 'I take it that's your dragon,' Gallagher asked.

He gave the massive beast a gentle pat of affection. 'I think it's a mutual agreement,' she was not convinced the dragon was her pet.

Kat treated it as a convenient arrangement. Gallagher laughed, 'It always is.'

Everything in his body language gave her the impression. That he would not take her on again. 'How do you know Lord Shakar?' It seemed a silly question as soon as she asked.

'That answer is not for a young sorceress,' he explained.

Before she could ask again Pennie interrupted. Her friend said, 'How do you plan to deal with Garduend?'

Gallagher walked over to her friend. 'You'll see,' he spoke.

As though it was a given and strode off leaving the pair bewildered. She wondered why there were no guards around them. Pennie laughed, 'Do the Vandragamond need them?'

In a more serious tone she whispered, 'I should have known there was something odd. That the clan didn't know you.'

She was inclined to agree as Captain Assinden stayed close by. He did not appear fazed by the whole ordeal. Katholomu looked far more content. He would have blended in with the other dragons if it were not for his size. His attitude showed with a small curve at the edge of long jaw.

The still night air caught an odd conversation as she remained quiet. 'How could it happen?' Lord Shakar's voice carried in the dark.

'With your lifestyle anything would be possible sire,' the administrator replied.

Saranon gave a small chuckle as she listened in. Then another voice broke into the conversation. Pennie whispered, 'That's Garridan, Lord Shaker's son.'

She peered up at the great dragon resting. She strode over to the tent before Pennie could say anything. Saranon felt the energy shielding the place. She warped it as she went through, out of annoyance. Wondering how she could have heard the conversation. As she entered the occupants looked none the wiser. She made no attempt to greet them as she searched the room for an answer. The administrator coughed, 'People do not snoop in the Lord's tent.'

She spoke aloud, 'Why could we hear you?'

Lord Shakar glared at Edred, the administrator. He moved quicker than she had seen before. Once Edred knew what to hone in on he made her attempts appear feeble, as he produced a small device. Placing it in a dense black box, 'That was a delight for the evening. I wonder what else they heard.'

Saranon found herself standing near Garridan who gave her a sympathetic smile. The resemblance was there as she gaped in astonishment.

'You mean Hollie, your ex-wife has a name,' the Lord shouted.

There was an awkward silence. Before Lord Shakar spoke again, 'Garridan look after Saranon and our other guests.'

He stared straight at her, but that was as much acknowledgement as he was prepared to give. All she wanted to do was find a warm place to sleep, like Katholomu who had since rolled onto his side. Garridan showed them to a tent then left. She was not about to argue and Pennie relaxed after he had gone.

The events of the night crept through into her dreams as her mind fought them. It was no use too much had happened and the images flashed through. She was left hanging in limbo with a sea of unfinished realities sneaking in. She imagined what it would have been like growing up in the north. Then every time she managed to cling onto an image it vanished. The torment kept her from falling into a deep sleep as her eyes slipped open. A figure moved by her bed.

She jumped upright as Captain Assinden knelt down. He whispered, 'I didn't want to alarm you, Lord Shakar has gone.'

She raced to get dressed then ran out into the night air and ran toward her dragon. Faeryn stood up and was almost about to stop her. Katholomu arched his body up to its full height. He broke into a run with a massive leap into the sky. The dragon's mood mirrored hers as she fumed.

The air swooped over Kat's wing. She clung in tight to his shoulders in the silence that followed. Garduend had given up nothing. The frustration ate away at her as the dragon tilted preparing for the descent. A faint row of lights made their way across the fortress of the Keep. It was an eerie glow that held her full attention and her stomach churned. All her senses honed in on the Keep. Kat spread out his wings and floated the remaining distance to the ground. The grassy hillside hid them with a scattering of trees. The dragon hid well, yet she was sure she could be seen.

There was no hint of the dragons marking Lord Shakar's arrival. She wondered if they were here. She crept forward and a small hum emanated from the Keep. It was more than she had heard before, yet still she could not sense any words from Garduend. Saranon entered the Keep as the clanging began in a faint chaotic rhythm. A shiver ran down her back and she ran further in. The door was blocked and she pounded at the seal. A chip flung to the side thudding against the wall yet still it held. She pounded her energy again and the seal shattered around her. The opening appeared and charged through.

Faint voices travelled along the Keep haunting her from

a distance. The clanging came again reverberating upward from the deep. The walls shuddered and she ran. A voice screamed up ahead, but it was too late. Saranon ducked as Gallagher's blade swung full circle. She ran as the room filled with the Razen sorcerers from the Keep. Gallagher was too far away and the sorcerers were too many. They were blocking her path to the Keep. She caught her breath and turned as the Razen sorcerers honed in. Isen Quinn's voice rang out above the noise as he attacked Gallagher.

Saranon dare not look as she ran. The group of dark Razen sorcerers moved in as the room fell silent. She leaped toward the second sorcerer as the attack began and lost her grip. The thud was eclipsed by the pain catapulting into her side. The sorcery edged through her shield. She tried not to scream, the path lay up ahead and she ran using her energy to hold the path. As she turned into the corridor she hesitated, her path was blocked. The panic rose, she hurled her energy against the wall. It hit too hard and sparks screeched into the air cascading past. Then the roar bellowed from beneath and she froze.

The sound terrified her as she realised what she had done and screamed. The stallic energy rose and the Keep shuddered. There was nothing holding it back. The sorcerers behind her fled as the clanging filled the air. The raw stallic energy swelled upward. Saranon's mind raced, she wanted to run, but if she ran it would catch up. The horrid gurgling sound deepened, there was no escape. The floor creaked and she could feel the stallic energy flooding the lower levels. The crashing grew louder as the energy of the Keep grew close. It was almost upon her and she closed her eyes.

The wave hit as the energy pelted through scrambling her mind and the world grew dark. The sound of the Keep blocked her ears and she clung on as the wave swept past. Then the rush was gone and it slowed. She wanted to open her eyes, but the fear held her back. She stayed hidden in the sea of stallic energy until she could hang on no more. Saranon reached out. Climbing above the surface and made her way to the upper level. The walls still held as the Keep creaked. She reached out grabbing hold of a balustrade. She pulled herself out of the lower level as the mass of energy stagnated. It turned to a darker shade.

Gallagher caught sight of her as he held his blade free. He motioned for her to follow, and she glanced up. Her whole body screamed and her head throbbed as she ran. The chaos filtered through her ears as Gallagher headed straight toward the fight. She gasped as his blade hit into the attack of the Razen sorcerers and she hesitated. The Keep made no sense, the lower level was flooded and she had no way to communicate with it. Before she had time to think a bolt of sorcery swung to close. She held up her hand as it hit, watching it dissolve. Gallagher glanced in amazement before returning to the fight.

The Razen sorcerers regrouped as shouting rang out. Lord Shakar's voice boomed overhead. Gallagher fought hard but gained little ground. They heard Lord Shakar in the distance. He shouted back at Saranon, 'Cut a path.'

'What?' She shouted above the noise as her shield held

against the attack.

His voice was blunt, 'Use your bond-breaker.'

Saranon fumed and used her energy to blast a gap toward Lord Shakar. Gallagher ran through and she followed. He ran into the shield blocking the room and fell backward gasping in pain. The Razen sorcerers behind them were gathering. With no way out they would be trapped. He gazed at her with the same thought and she moved toward the shield. Saranon held out her hand. The stallic energy held inside her, ran along the shield's web, it flittered and she ran through. The shield faded to a dull glow. Holding on with utter defiance yet it was enough to let the Vandragamond through.

The small group of Razen were closing in on Lord Shakar as the shield lost its strength. Isen Quinn glanced at her with eyes that pierced straight to her soul. He was an even match for the Lord as they fought. Lord Shakar's bond-breaker, Evermoor, flared as he kept Isen grounded in the fight. The Razen closest to her broke away and she held out Corsavere to its full length. The bond-breaker sang as she charged. The sea green blade made from the heart of Odana Temple. It slashed through the nearest bond-breaker. With a piercing sound that made her skin crawl. The Razen sorcerer who held onto the remnants of his blade ran as the group broke away.

The only Razen sorcerer left, stood fighting Lord Shakar. Isen shouted as he fled into the depths of the Keep. Lord Shakar waited, lowering his blade. Saranon thought he was calling off the attack. Instead he signalled to

Gallagher and they parted in separate directions. Leaving her to wonder what was going on. She stared down at her blade as the dark night held on.

CHAPTER TWELVE

A fight for the worthy

Sounds creased through the Keep from the deep as Saranon ran to catch up. It was all she could do as she moved toward the direction of the bond-breakers. Evermoor made a hiss as it swung through the air. A stale burning smell greeted her as she ducked. The blast of sorcery whooshed overhead, heating up the air as it went. She slid across the ground as it hit the floor. The sound from the impact reached her ears. The floor lifted with a jarring crack and silence followed. She could feel the floor rise, as she jumped it, came to a halt above where she stood.

Her heart thudded in her ears and she ducked as the sorcery scorched the wall where she had been. The heat flickered past as she winced. Saranon tried to breathe, but the air had been wrenched away. Panic rose inside and she tried to scream, yet no sound came out. She concentrated as the clang of the two bond-breakers ahead reached her ears. She saw Isen Quinn's face. The Razen sorcerer thrust his blade against Lord Shaker's, his eyes locked with hers. She opened her mind to the energy within. The draft echoed into a gust as she blasted through the shields that blocked her out. Before the shield broke apart she braced herself moving forward. The energy hit, the pain reached her lungs and she gasped. The air flooded with sparks in as the shield fell.

The sorcery sparked in wild arc as it shattered and the Razen sorcerers ran. All except Isen Quinn. Lord Shakar's blade fell by his side. Isen stood for a few moments before he dropped to the floor. She ran forward and Isen held up his hand as the colour drained. He let out a cold laugh that sent shivers down her spine. Lord Shaker picked up his bond-breaker. The Keep creaked again from the deep but he did not run. He stared straight at Saranon, 'We are buried.'

'What?' She asked.

Gallagher met them, 'The Keep fell, we are buried and so are the Razen.'

Saranon's face went pale, 'We can't be.'

She was not about to believe the unthinkable. Yet, she could not determine where she was in the Keep. Lord Shakar smiled, 'Shall we finish the Razen?'

Gallagher gave the first hint of a smile that enjoyed pain and nodded as they began to leave. Saranon stood aghast, 'Wait, are you giving up?'

Lord Shakar smiled and held his hand on her shoulder,

'You were never meant to live.'

Saranon stood in shock as the Lord revelled in the cold words as he spoke them. 'How dare you?' She shouted, and he backed away.

The Lord continued, 'You should have died at Antavagon. Now you will die at Garduend.'

Saranon fumed, she wanted to hit the Lord, but at that moment the Keep rumbled and slid. Only this time she could sense it drop. She drew her bond-breaker Corsavere, 'One day I will take you on, but not this day.'

She swung her blade close and drove it down into the Keep. The floor began to meld with the blade as it seeped further into the walls. She watched Lord Shakar and Gallagher leave. As she spoke, 'Not this day, this day is for Garduend.'

The slow rumble of the stallic energy crept higher with an eerie drone as the Keep rumbled. She waited as she remembered Antavagon. The Keep had reached out to her, clinging onto life. Antavagon had survived, yet the sounds that crept upward were from a dying Keep. She steadied herself waiting as the sounds grew louder through the gaping hole beneath. The sparks rose as the Angeon surfaced from within and for a moment all became calm. In the darkness she heard a voice and Garduend spoke in the void.

The Angeon reached out to the dying Keep as it held on to the last spark of life. The central core was boiling underneath. It melted deep into the ground as it broke apart. The stallic energy flowed without a guiding source, and she clung to the wall. The Keep spoke over and over, let go, yet she held on. The shell of the core cracked deep beneath as the Keep held on in its last moment. She concentrated and the stallic energy narrowed just a fraction. She focused as it relented to her and the Keep creaked as it shuddered upward. The Angeon held on under the strain as the building moved toward the surface.

A boom rattled from below as the shell of the core fell in. She held out her arms as the blast catapulted toward her with the last rays of energy from the Keep. The hollow sound rang out in the void as the vacuum filled the gaping hole. The building began to groan under the stress. The eerie echo from the pressure droned around her humming the sound of death. Her concentration waned under the weight as she held her grip with every ache. Then the crashing came as the building crumbled above her. Her heart skipped a beat as the explosion followed and it was all she could do to hold on. Saranon strained under the pressure as the building began falling in on itself. Then a sound came from below, the last sound the Keep ever made.

In the numbness that followed the Angeon reached out. She compressed the last of the energy that was left. The Keep had given it to her, the last and most concentrated energy left behind. She held onto it so tight. That before she realised it the last remnants of Garduend collapsed in on itself. She could feel the energy writhe in an uneven swirl as it compressed. She held back the collapsing building in a deafening stalemate. In the dim haze that followed the clouds and misty vapour unveiled the Orb. She gasped though the sound was completely absorbed in the chaos around her. Her astonishment melted away into panic as she scanned around. She spotted a small opening in the distance.

As the energy subsided she grabbed the massive Orb. She floated back to the ground stumbling before she could run. The building crashed in behind her with nothing left to hold back the pressure. Saranon went to shield herself from the blow and the new Orb in her hands glowed. She ran, and thanked the Keep as she went. She held the last precious remains of Garduend in her arms close to her chest. She rushed to find a way out. The sky was filled with a charcoal ash. A mix of clouds not fit for daylight as the shadows met her in the croaky outside air.

It was all she could do not to choke as she held onto the energy of the Orb, clearing her way and the air ahead. Saranon could sense the Razen sorcerers in the distance and stared down at the Orb. She could not let them take it. She ran along the hillside heading toward the end of the smoke and dust that clung in the air. As the rocky forest became clear up ahead. She found the last remnants marking the edge of Garduend. She leaned down, her hands were so numb that she struggled to move the Orb. She stared at it in amazement, it was the largest she had ever seen. 'Goodbye Garduend,' she whispered.

Then she used the last strength of the Angeon to send the Orb into the ground surrounded by a seal. She hoped it would be enough to keep the Orb hidden. The dust began to settle she took a deep breath and ran toward the Razen sorcerers. The explosion left a blackened crater confronting her as she drew near. Deandra Lythen stood near the edge peering over the ruins as she glanced up. There was no sign of the Vandragamond. She wondered if Lord Shakar had ever intended to deal with the Razen. Deandra laughed aloud as she catapulted a blast toward the sorceress. Saranon blocked as she stepped back with the impact. Deandra waited with an amused smile then she attacked again. The blast hit Saranon in the back and she fell into the crater. Hollie Zimmerman stood where she had been peering over the edge.

She tried to aim but the two Razen attacked, sending her down into the crater. Deandra laughed and Saranon dived back into the remnants of the Keep. The hollowed out cavity creasing across the ground arched back into the rocky hillside. It left more than one trail to follow as she hid. The pain arched through the numbness as sensation returned. The dark caverns in the crater held an eerie tone as a draft flowed through. She could sense the Razen moving closer as the cold set in. The Keep was gone, it offered her no protection, as she glanced around. She would have to face the Razen head on. Saranon took her bond-breaker Corsavere. She held it up to the dim light it glowed as it sang through the air.

She held the bond-breaker firm in her hand as the Razen advanced. She could only just sense them as she waited in the silence. They were closing in and still she waited not daring to make a sound as she hid her location.

Yet it would not work for long as the sorcery of the Razen cut through. She sensed them searching and clenched her fist. Her shield had almost faded and she lunged toward the nearest Razen. Hollie ducked as the blade hit straight into the rock wall. It just missed her shoulder. Saranon tilted the bond-breaker toward her neck. Holding the blade before it touched Hollie's skin.

Deandra came up behind her, 'You won't win.'

The Razen sorceress blasted her in the back. The pain seared through and she winced. She relented taking her bond-breaker. Swinging the blade toward Deandra as Hollie made her escape. Deandra stepped back and Saranon advanced as she struck a shield. She swung Corsavere as the blade carved through, yet the shield held a moment too long. She could sense a blast building in magnitude as it rushed through the tunnels. She was too close. The air drew back in a vacuum as the sorcery rushed forward, then nothing. A giant flood of sorcery roared from behind. She found herself standing in the middle. The sorcery melded in a frozen embrace as each blast neutralised the other.

Deandra and Hollie had long disappeared by the time the energy settled. There remained an unsteady stillness. Saranon glanced outside. Edred, the administrator, loomed over her and held her arm, 'Come with me.'

It was not a tone to argue with as his dragon emerged from the hillside. Tarketh snorted with a sense of purpose. The mighty marmoz dragon leaped above the looming clouds. Edred held on behind with a tight grip. As he steered away from the last pounding plumes marking the end of the Keep. The air dissipated into an open sky with a warm dry stillness. Silence followed the rest of their journey. The dragon swooped with an elegant grace before touching the ground.

The Keep was the tidy home of the administrator. A lone figure came out to greet them. Tom was a taller version of his brother Jack, if that was at all possible. Edred, the administrator motioned for them to go inside. The sky filled with lurking dragons and their riders. She went out to greet Katholomu, now covered in a grey mucky coat of ash. He rubbed himself against her until she was completely covered. The dragon had an innate ability to let her know he was not impressed at being left behind. A rumble broke from the sky above. The dragons circling above broke into two clear packs.

As Saranon approached the open grounds a dragon broke from the clouds sweeping fast. She turned in time to see the claws reach out toward her. Tom struck first, the bolt of sorcery knocked the rider off-balance. She ran past him to the Keep as the group of riders were upon them. Hollie rode the dragon in the lead. Yet she did not strike as she landed between Saranon and the Keep. The Razen sorceress stood facing Saranon with a hard face. 'You were inside the Keep when it died,' Hollie said.

'No. Do I look like I was?' Saranon said as she tried brushing of the muck that Kat caked her in.

The tender soft stance that Kat had shown a moment ago vanished. His great body flexed. He jumped the last distance as his mighty claws dug into the other dragon's side. Katholomu eye-balled Hollie as he held the other dragon, pinning it down with ease. Hollie became uneasy as her dragon screeched out in pain, 'We'll see.'

She made the statement as Kat let go, then flew back into the open sky.

The dragon lowered his head and gave a low deep chuckle as he stared at Saranon who was as dirty as he. She frowned at the great beast, 'You do realise that we are both in need of a bath.'

The dragon snorted in open defiance at the suggestion. He stretched out his muscles in a show of strength and size, before curling his tail by his side.

The administrator's house was deceptively small. As part of it lay hidden underground in a maze of corridors. She made her way along to the dragon pens. Saranon rinsed her hands under the warm water. Katholomu lowered his shoulders to fit under the archway. A clump of dirt scraped off, it fell onto the ground spattering her from a distance. Then the dragon threw himself into the waiting pool. He soaked her from top to bottom. She snapped at him. He replied by rubbing her with his drenched shoulder before returning to the pool.

'You can have a bath in there if you like?' Tom suggested.

'Don't encourage him!' She shouted in haste.

Tom grinned at the sight trying not to laugh, 'The bathroom is that way.'

Katholomu lifted himself in one fluid motion out of the pool. He shook every drop of water out. Tom laughed as he held back the spray with his energy. He said, 'You had better go before you get soaked again.'

The dragon smiled looking pleased with himself, before squeezing out under the archway. He flopped on the ground with a hearty rumbling purr. That reverberated down his body. The bathroom was too small for a marmoz dragon and she washed in peace. There was no one about so she took the chance to peek around and crept upstairs. It was the first time she could remember being in a Vandragamond Keep. She felt a pang of sadness for Garduend it was not what she had wanted.

Saranon crept along to an open door and looked inside. It was full of books along one wall. She leaned over to pick one up and saw Jack Heath's name on a piece of writing near the desk. A sound caught her attention and she turned, knocking the ink all over his work. She froze unable to think, then used her energy to remove the ink spill from the writing. She gave a relieved sigh as she held it up to the light, with no mark to be seen. A creak of the door made her jump, and greeted Tom as she went red with embarrassment, 'Ah…'

There was an awkward silence. She made her way to the bright open room leading out to the courtyard. The meal on the table steamed as Saranon remembered how hungry she was. She dived into the thick stew. It was the first time Edred the administrator appeared at ease. She wondered if it was a facade. A tingling sensation stopped her from relaxing. She peered out the high glass windows to the sweeping view of the low mountains. She tapped her spoon against the bowl waiting for the tension to ease. Tom glanced at Edred then at her, keeping an uneven peace. She glanced up and the sky filled with a dark terror. She dropped her spoon and pushed Tom to the ground.

A crash came shattering through the window as she turned to the site of the blast. A group of dragons swarmed overhead with the sound screeching through the sky. She ran out into the courtyard looking for Katholomu, but he was nowhere to be seen. She scrambled back toward the Keep as the dragon riders circled in. The shield held as the Razen sorcerers blasted against it. She scrambled to the edge of the Keep trying not be seen. Then a great whir came overhead as her friend Galven rode his dragon toward the group. He hurled his sorcery toward the Razen. It was enough to send the dragons in every direction.

She could sense the Keep underneath as it rumbled away deep underground. She let her energy reach out and the Keep answered. She clung on to the energy of the Keep. The razon sorcerers who had attacked her friend were now in retreat. A sickening feeling reached her stomach as the dragons regrouped. They swooped down through the sky and the sound gave an eerie tone in the grey clouds. She stood her ground as best she could and kept the energy within her. The dragons came close and she could see Deandra. She raised her arms to the sky the energy flooded through as she aimed high.

This time it hit singeing the dragon's side. Deandra answered with a blast of sorcery. She managed to block it with the aid of the Keep. Deandra fell to the ground as the dragon rolled in pain. It screeched as it tried to get up. Then the beast ran toward the nearest pond not thinking of anything else. Its screams chilled her before it finally calmed. She hesitated as Deandra fled and she was too shocked to go after them. Even though the Keep held, it did not feel safe as she returned.

The grey sky darkened overhead as the night set in. Edred the administrator stood in the alcove waiting as he allowed her to pass. A great crash rumbled through the sky. She lost her balance and glanced back to find the sorcerers gathered once more. She could see Katholomu in the distance as one of the dragons struck out, her anger flared. She ran toward him. She gathered her energy preparing to strike. She ran as a new fleet of dragons gathered on the horizon. They loomed from the darkness toward them. Lord Shakar flew in close. She could sense him, but could not see his face. Deandra's attention swerved toward the newcomers. Saranon took a chance and blasted her energy toward Deandra.

The Razen sorceress retaliated before Saranon could shield herself. The Lord blocked the Razen's sorcery. Then without warning he turned his full attention on her. His dragon Dregora swooped close. This time there was no Keep to stand in her way. She held her bond-breaker Corsavere. In the form of a sword, high above her head to challenge him after what he had done. The Lord stepped down from his dragon holding his bond-breaker by his side. For a moment he watched waiting for her to move. She was frustrated by his calm stance and her anger swelled as she raised the blade. Her swing fell short as she raised her hand and used her sorcery to follow through. The Lord staggered back as his face showed a hint of surprise. Yet it soon turned into a cold harsh glare.

He raised his hands and his sorcery strengthened. She could see the Razen sorcerers flee and only then did she begin to panic. She stood back and let out a gasp. When she realised she had stepped back toward the administrator. Her sorcery swelled from deep within and the Lord laughed, 'That will not work.'

Saranon glared at him as she fumed, yet he did not relent. Lord Shakar aimed for her. She absorbed the energy before he had time to think. He began to raise his arms again, the second blast hit and she absorbed it. She waited for him to close in. Yet at the last moment he pulled back as though sensing what she was prepared to do. 'Perhaps another day,' He said.

Lord Shakar smiled in a manner that took away any trust she may have had. 'You let the Razen escape,' she glared at him.

The Lord laughed, 'They will not get far.'

She struck out catching him off guard and held his arm, there was nothing. Gallagher whispered underneath his breath as he put back his bond-breaker, and stepped away. There was no sign of the energy she had absorbed. It was not the first time Lord Shakar had been lost for words. He waved his hand toward Edred, the administrator. Edred leaned over. 'It appears you will need to leave,' he spoke. He gave her a map for the Asdenard Keep, Endorell, 'It would be best if you stayed there.'

Saranon felt like she was being passed off, but said nothing as she left. She wanted to put as much distance as she could between her, Lord Shakar and the Orb. The Razen sorcerers would already be searching. It would be best not to draw attention. With the map in hand she darted out of the courtyard. Tom ran after her, 'Wait, aren't you going to say goodbye?'

She smiled and waved as he grinned. He gave her a small present, it was a book, 'In case you become lost,' he explained.

She was not sure what he meant, but accepted it with gratitude.

Katholomu met her with a calm gaze as he let her climb on. He was watching the sky with an anticipation that made him tense. The shadows of darkness crossed the evening with the smell of ash. The dust was still thick in the air from what remained of the old Keep. She closed her eyes as the image flashed through her mind, yet she would have to forget. Saranon motioned for the dragon to go and he flung himself hard into the still night air. The tiredness rolled in as she managed to keep awake. The great dragon darted down near a small cave well worn by dragons. He took her into the heart of a dragon colony.

It was the first time she had seen so many marmoz dragons, yet she was too tired to be scared or excited. She took the dragon's suggestion and setup camp for the night. After she had lain down the dragon wrapped himself around her. She was thankful that the dragon was clean.

Katholomu closed his wing over her in a small cacoon. She wondered how long the sweet smell would last.

Saranon drifted off to sleep, a familiar face haunted her dreams. No matter where she was Tasha found her, waiting just beyond the darkness. Tasha's spirit came to visit across the void holding out her hands. Saranon could not make out if it was a warning or an invitation. Her dream held the image, yet it did not answer her question, as she fell into a deeper sleep. The image of her friend faded into a deep resounding darkness.

CHAPTER THIRTEEN

Friendship of old

Saranon found herself staring out at several sets of small eyes. The three infant dragons began losing their shyness. One small dragon, the same size as her, stuck her head into the sleeping bag. This provided a cue for the other two who felt as though they had just been left out. She heard a sharp rip, as her sleeping bag was torn into shreds. All three young dragons froze at the sound. Then realised there was no danger. The last remnants of the sleeping bag became even smaller.

She sighed as any hope of saving her sleeping bag evaporated. It was too difficult to be angry with three of the cutest creatures she had ever seen. They revelled in the attention. The landscape was beautiful, untouched by people. It had an array of paths well-worn by the dragon inhabitants. Saranon stood out in the open contemplating the map to Endorell. A giant snort of warm air rushed down her back. She turned her head to see the largest female marmoz dragon she had ever met. She walked away trying to avoid doing anything to draw the dragon's attention.

As she sidestepped backwards she felt something large behind her. She glanced up in a silent horror, as a male marmoz dragon bent his head down and glared. Saranon wanted to scream as she remained silent. She stepped away and glanced around, hoping not to bump into any more dragons. Her heart sank as she walked along she would have to dart through the crowd of dragons up ahead.

Saranon began treading over the uneven ground. Every small move or grunt from the dragons made her quiver. She took her time, with more than one set of eyes keeping close attention. She made her way to the end of the group letting out a sigh of relief. As a low rumble of a dragon voice bellowed behind her, 'You're welcome.'

She stared in astonishment. As the dragon near her curled up into a tight ball with one eye left open. She had just wasted more than an hour when the dragons were content to let her pass through.

She wanted to say something, but the sheer scale of the group gave her an uneasy feeling. She unfolded the small map before choosing a pleasant spot to sit down. The map was well drawn, yet she was having a difficult time locating any bearings to go by. She felt awkward heading deeper into Darkonia. It was not a place where she could ask for directions, given there would be people searching for her. There were several lay-lines nearby. Yet without knowing where she was going it could be dangerous to become lost. She trudged on. The open paths were silent and a welcome relief. A faint light beamed from her talik as she opened the small circular device. It had picked up a faint signal from Endorell, as she changed direction.

Saranon strode along feeling confident with her decision to avoid the lay-lines. She followed an old path that had seen better days. It was overgrown with scrub amid the sparse trees. As she looked up to the beautiful clear sky a spark of wizardry whizzed up into the air. Endorell Keep was a wizard stronghold and she was not bothered by it. As she trudged along the path a few buildings became visible in the distance. She bent down to check her map.

She stood up and turned just in time to see a large ball of wizardry heading straight for her. She reacted using her sorcery to snuff it out. The wizardry burst into a cloudy haze raining tiny sparks over the ground. The sound of muffled voices reached her ears before she saw anyone. As the sparks settled two groups of annoyed wizards appeared on either side. Captain Verkin shouted, 'This place belongs to the Asdenard.'

She was not sure how to respond to the wizard. Yet before she could Roger spoke up, 'Saranon was sent here by the administrator.'

Captain Verkin was a large man who looked much taller as he stood beside her. 'You don't look like you could cause that much trouble,' he said.

Roger smiled, 'Believe me she can.'

The Captain was not impressed. He did not give her

any welcome as he walked in the direction of the Keep. Roger waved her over as they marched together in unison. 'I thought you weren't supposed to return?' He said with a wry smile.

'That was not my fault,' she grumbled as she ran to keep up.

Endorell Keep was mighty indeed. Its great buildings and walls loomed high into the air with a statuesque grandeur. The wizards slowed as they entered the vast courtyard. They were be met by a few quizzical stares at the sight of Saranon. 'Wait here,' the Captain spoke to her and Roger.

She rested on the stairs leading to the main entrance. She took in the view from the raised platform. The Keep was well spread out with its own town huddled close. The buildings were followed by sprawling low hills. The open fields were broken by the rocky ground and small forest. A firm hand leaned on her shoulder as the Captain reached down, 'You are expected.'

He walked away, assuming that she would follow. The wizard moved so fast that Saranon ran forward when he stopped. She almost ran into the Host Matthew. After her last experience with a wizard bonded to the Keep she backed away. The Host's dark eyes watched her. Captain Verkin made a small bow to the Host then turned to leave. She called out, 'Wait, where are you going?'

'I said, you are expected,' then the Captain left.

She was not sure how to respond to Matthew. She stood there in stunned silence as the Host spoke first. The melded part of the Keep just showing above the neck line made her shiver. She knew it was not painful but it looked out of place. Matthew was calm, in complete contrast to the way the Host Nathan had been at Greddin Fort. She was not prepared to let go of the uneasy sensation whirling away in her stomach. She waited for the moment he would change as she listened. The Host wished to show her around the Keep and she accepted.

Endorell was a massive stronghold by any comparison. The wizards around her knew it holding an air of confidence. The few sorcerers she saw welcomed her, yet the whole scene made her uncomfortable. She had been exiled from Darkonia and the sentiment could not have vanished. The old detention camps had not been forgotten. Pennie had not spoken of any forgiveness for what she had done after breaking free. Yet here she was in a small piece of tranquil paradise. The Royal Darkonian Army had made Endorell its headquarters.

She wandered off, thankful to be away from the Host's company. She peered over the balcony taking in the vast landscape. 'Beautiful isn't it?' Galven asked.

She almost jumped and gave him a scornful look. While he continued, 'The Asdenard will give safe passage until the Razen are finished.'

'I thought that was finished?' Saranon asked.

He replied, 'It hasn't begun.'

She found her room and flopped down across the bed letting the breeze fill the air. Her tired eyes woke with a clunk near the open window. She sat up to see Roger making himself comfortable sitting on the sill. 'The Captain wants to see you,' he spoke without giving anything away.

She gave him a puzzled look before stepping over the sill. Following him along the balcony in the afternoon as the shadows began to creep.

A rowdy sound echoed from below as they made their way down through to a great hall. There was an abundance of food to choose from, yet she still felt uneasy. Captain Verkin sat through the whole meal without uttering a word. She wondered if he wanted to speak to her. As the table began to clear she rose and the Captain motioned for her to sit. It was the last thing she wanted to do. The Captain gave no hint away as he spoke, 'I don't know what you've done to Matthew, but it has to stop.'

She asked. 'Pardon?'

'You heard me,' the Captain spoke with a firm tone.

Saranon wore a puzzled expression, with no idea what he was talking about. The Captain showed his annoyance. She glanced around hoping for a sign of help and found none.

Captain Verkin leaned forward clasping Saranon's hand. He said, 'You have no idea what I'm talking about?'

She felt uncomfortable underneath his gaze. The Captain led her away from the table, 'You are a novice.'

She grimaced at the response, after everything she had been through. He continued, 'Your visit here will not be long.'

The wizard left, yet he did not answer the question. Leaving her to wonder why Matthew was being nice to her.

She peered around and she spotted Galven. She wanted to throttle him for not helping.

He quizzed her about the Host without giving anything away. Saranon was not impressed and found an excuse to leave. She left the window to her room open to the night sky. A small welcome breeze offered relief. She knelt and placed a small ward on the windowsill. She glanced up to see the Host standing on the balcony. Matthew stood silent for a moment then he spoke, 'I knew you… from before.'

She gazed up at him, unsure what to say as the Host struggled to find the right words. He sat on the windowsill peering at the tiny ward. 'I wanted you to stay, but it was before…' Matthew trailed off.

As he turned away staring out at the night sky. 'You mean before you were a Host,' Saranon filled the gap.

He nodded without looking at her. It was not what she had expected, but it would explain his odd behaviour. 'I called out, but the Asdenard didn't listen,' Matthew spoke in the breeze.

From the thoughts of the Keep that melded with his mind, she felt the weight of the Host's words. She hung her head without uttering a sound in the silence that followed. The Host stood composing himself. He tried to shift away from the Keep's emotions and left. The hour was growing late and too much had happened in one day as she climbed into bed. Yet her mind would not calm itself. The remnants of Garduend washed over her dreams. A lone figure stood haunting her. The sorceress turned in the radiant light with her long dress flowing.

Tasha her old companion through the dark days. A memory from the detention camps returned in her dreams. She stood more elegant than she had appeared in life. Saranon walked up the slope to greet her friend. Tasha held out her hand pointing to the land below. In the distance she saw a large holding with an aged castle rising up from the landscape. Yet as she focused on the building it was gone, disappearing into the embers of her dreams.

The sound of the door crept into her precious sleep as she tried not to notice. A voice followed. 'Are you awake?' Galven whispered in the faint morning light.

His shadow moved overhead and she open her eyes, 'Can it wait?'

'Acwellen has disappeared,' Galven spoke in haste.

Saranon did not understand the significance of his tone as she mumbled her way out of bed.

The morning light filled her head with a stubborn ache, as she rubbed the sleep out of her eyes. Galven shook his head upon seeing her emerge from the room. Her head still ached as he explained along the way. A familiar thread tugged at her thoughts, the Host had been too calm. A small group had gathered by the edge of the habitable area. They were dwarfed by the size of the great entrance into the indolin chambers of the Keep.

Captain Daina Ressinden was busy as she held out a tracer device, larger than a talik. The doors below were open with two officers not far from the entrance. 'Ah, just who I've been waiting for,' Daina said as she spotted the sorceress.

Before Saranon had a chance to say otherwise the Captain held her arm. They walked down the stairs. 'If you don't find Verkin's son, he will turn you into ash,' Captain Daina said.

'What?' Saranon gasped.

The Captain smiled, 'You heard me, now give me your talik.'

She handed over her talik not sure what to expect. As the Captain calibrated it to the tracer, and tossed it back. 'If you pick up anything don't wait. Just go in and get him out,' the Captain instructed.

Before Saranon could reply the Captain had moved on. She wondered if it was Captain Ressinden who would turn her into ash.

The chambers were warm, and she wondered if the talik would pick up anything. She trudged through the underground corridors trying not to become lost. She leaned down and used her sorcery against the jammed door. It refused to budge as she sensed the Keep willing it to stay shut. There were other ways to get in to the lower chambers. Yet that would mean going further out from the wizards.

The Keep and the Host did not want to talk. She felt like there was something she was missing. The confusion hindered her thoughts. She stepped back as Captain Verkin rushed down shouting as he went. The Captain was in no mood to listen as he ranted with an incessant desperation. He hurled a blast against the door, the wizardry shattered and she stepped away. The Keep had shut them out, and she needed to reach Acwellen. Captain Ressinden rushed down with her officers to calm the scene. Captain Verkin's shouts ran through the air.

If the Keep would not let her in she would have to find another way. Saranon took a few steps back then she held out her arms, leaned backward and fell. She let her mind clear and the energy wrapped around her. She melted straight through the floor, in a freefall as the energy softened her landing. She felt something soft and furry underneath and opened her eyes. The soft sweat purr of the zennigh trickled through. The giant cat was so large its fur covered her. She sat upright trying not to wake the creature.

She slid down the zennigh's back landing on the sandy floor. The creature shifted closing the gap between her and the wall as she ran out of the way. The walls of the imbenik chambers were older than she expected. She leaned close to the Keep that did not want to be heard. There was something there as she sensed the walls, something else.

A tiny ripple that caught in her mind as the Keep came to life behind its vale of silence. Endorell gave a tremor from above as it reverberated through the walls. She ran trying to hide from the flow of stallic energy from the Keep. She stopped running as all the walls appeared the same. She ran back, but there was no trace of the zennigh. She was lost. Panic began to swell up in her throat as she tried to quell her rising thoughts. Saranon ran, and glanced around at the blank walls.

The heat filtered through the dry air and she searched for her talik. As she fumbled a small glow appeared it was the small book Tom had given her. She opened it and the pages changed to a show a moving map. A wall moved on the map and she heard a faint noise and smiled. She was in a moving maze but she still had to find a way out and Acwellen. The walls moved again. Soon she would have to choose, she held the book in one hand as she moved with haste.

The Keep had annoyed her long enough, she raced to move ahead of the maze as it closed in around her. A way out revealed itself on the page. Yet as soon as she made her way there the walls moved back around her, to form a large room with no way out. She hit her fist against the wall and felt the Keep's reaction. She wondered what that meant as she looked at the page again, yet there was still no way out. She put the book away it was no use against a stubborn Keep.

The wall opposite moved as she ran toward it, and she stopped. In the alcove Acwellen laid on the ground almost still. She slumped down beside him and wondered if he knew. It did not take long for the wizard to wake up as he panicked looking for a way out. Saranon watched in an awkward silence as desperation set in. The wizard used his energy to blast against the wall. It was not enough. She was not about to argue with an angry wizard as she watched on.

She waited until the wizard stood exhausted. She asked while he caught his breath, 'Has your father met me before?'

Acwellen turned acknowledging her for the first time. 'If you help we can both get out,' he said.

'I don't think so,' Saranon exclaimed to his amazement. 'Has your father met me before?'

The wizard who was not much older stared at her, 'I have.'

Saranon could not hide her astonishment. Acwellen read her thoughts, 'Fine, I'll tell you, but then we are getting out of here.'

She nodded in agreement, not wanting to change the subject. 'Oriana requested sanctuary for you, but the Asdenard would not give it,' Acwellen explained. Saranon sank to her knees. 'Your mother came here before we knew what was happening.'

A large crack began to form down the ceiling and it spiralled out. Saranon and Acwellen gazed in silence. A jarring sound rang out as wizardry pelted from above them, and they ran. The labyrinth moved as the blast fell through. Saranon slammed her fist against the wall as it blocked them away from the blast. 'We're safe,' Acwellen said.

She was not so sure, 'Really?'

A rumble made its way from underneath as the Keep stirred. She could sense the wizards breaking through and pushed against the wall in frustration. Acwellen did not look impressed.

She felt the Keep whirring underneath, it wanted her to follow. She hesitated as the floor began to melt away. Acwellen panicked, the wizard could not enter the central core. She ran and dived through as the hole vanished behind her. Endorell Keep reached out pulling her down into the central core. The vast shell defied gravity. She floated above the unnatural storm spiralling up from Tordoren. Endorell reached out and her mind blocked the Keep. It rumbled from beneath then it gave her what it had held onto. A memory of what was, what will be, and what should be. She saw the Angeon, but it was not her. The image was Zeralden Hadenvar, the last Angeon.

She recognised the walls of the great hall in Endorell, a cold silence hung in the still air. The walls were charred and in her hand Zeralden held the Eye of Escora. The Orb glowed, yet the Angeon did not need it as the night wrapped around. All she could see on the ground were remnants of the Dreshans. The army had occupied Zyanthia. Zeralden placed gave the Eye of Escora to the Keep. She stood back, the energy flowed through. The energy of the Angeon glowed, it glowed beyond all reason and then the image was gone. Saranon gasped. 'You had the Orb,' she spoke to the central core and it spoke back. You and I are the same, its voice lingered in her mind.

She stared in disbelief. As the stallic energy lighted up the swirling storm trapped in the core. It sparked rushing up the great rod embedded in the unseen depths. She could feel the panic rise as the Keep continued. The rumble blasted upward igniting the rod. Instead of sending it through the outer shell the Keep sent it toward Saranon. The shock rang through her ears as the Keep rumbled hurtling her to the surface. The light of the Keep shone as she reached out to touch the surface of the end node. At the farthest part of Endorell. Her hand brushed against the sorcerer's stone to make sure it was real. She was alive, yet the Keep had known.

She stood up, bathing in the sunlight as it streamed down. Perhaps, just once, she could be who she was. Saranon reached inward as the Angeon rose, this time she let it go. The energy grew beyond what she dared to hold. The creases of energy glowed as it concentrated. She held out her hands and let it flow back into the Keep. The moment of peace lasted for only a short glimpse as the voices of wizards rang out. The group approached her and Captain Verkin spoke, 'Where is Acwellen?'

Saranon stood on the end node unswayed by the Captain's tone. She stood in the centre as the stone surface retracted into the Keep. She floated above the gaping hole as Captain Verkin stood near edge. The stallic energy rose in a soft wave that filled the morning air. It brought with it the wizard. Acwellen was overwhelmed with awe as the Keep closed the end node underneath. He touched solid ground. Saranon stepped from the stone's surface, moving away from the elated wizards. She flinched as she watched Captain Verkin greet his son, Acwellen. Her greeting had been far different.

She hung her head and walked away, perhaps one day she would feel the same. Her senses reached across the grounds of Endorell as a figure approached. Mitch had made it to Darkonia. The wizard still managed to astound her, though he did not look impressed. Saranon was in no mood to talk as she attempted to ignore him. 'When were you going to tell me about Lord Shakar?' He asked.

'You didn't come all this way for that?' She replied.

He placed his hand on her shoulder, 'Lord Shakar is dangerous.'

Saranon glared at him. 'I'm serious,' he said.

'You are too late,' she did not want to elaborate.

Mitch fell silent. He could read her immediate thoughts but gave no hint of what he thought. The grounds belonging to the grand fortress of Endorell softened its edge. With the grass fields and low shrubs. The long walk gave ample time for a crowd to gather as Captain Verkin followed them. For the first time she saw the Captain smile as he passed them. She stopped at the top of the stairs leading to the main courtyard. 'That wizard knew my mother, Oriana,' she spoke to Mitch.

He nodded in silent agreement before adding, 'Do not hassle the Captain.'

The thought was tempting and Mitch gave her a stern look.

CHAPTER FOURTEEN

Acquaintances past

Saranon dodged the wizards who were excited to see Acwellen again. She had managed to clear the commotion when Galven picked her up in a tight hug. He lifted her clean off the ground. She wanted to shout at him. He had put her down with a large grin, 'I just thought I'd share in the excitement.'

Saranon could feel her cheeks grow hot with embarrassment.

As she waited a moment it became obvious that none of the wizards were going to thank her. She let out a sigh. She managed to sneak her way in to the kitchen before the lunchtime rush. She munched on a piece of warm toast. If there was one thing she could say about Endorell, the food was delicious. It reminded her of Mrs Harper's Tavern in Redadere. As she reminisced, a sound crept along the floor breaking her concentration. Captain Verkin stood near the doorway while he spoke, 'I forgot to thank you.'

Saranon was not impressed by the attempt to appease the Keep. She wanted to shout at him in the silence, but instead nodded a curt reply. She stared up at the wizard who appeared reluctant to move. As he added, 'Stay away from Matthew.'

She almost choked on her toast while the Captain walked away.

The Keep itself was welcoming in stark contrast to its occupants. She placed her hand up against the wall sensing Endorell. It lulled in the background. A small whimper escaped from the darkness at the end of the stairs. She made her way down while no one was looking. The distinct sound of the zennigh drew her as she peered around the corner. Saranon smiled at the sight of the young creature. The kitten was as tall as her, as the zennigh glanced back with deep amber eyes. Before she had a chance to reach out her hand it purred and she stood mesmerized. A voice drew her attention as Galven called out and when she turned back the zennigh was gone.

'Back to the wizards I suppose,' she spoke aloud.

'You'll be gone soon enough,' Roger said, startling her.

She tried to work out where he had come from, and he smiled without giving an answer. She was too astonished at being caught unaware to argue. As she ran up the stairs hesitating and stared back into an empty space. Galven waited, a solitary figure. He gazed out the window toward the rugged terrain below. They headed off to gather some equipment before heading out.

He appeared edgy though Saranon was unsure why as she followed him. They left the main building along an uncommon path. It took her a moment longer to catch on to what Galven was up to. A misquew waited in the shade as he motioned for her to go. He patted the riding cat with a heavy hand on its back and it leaped into a steady run. She leaned down and held tight to the misquew. It padded along with its soft paws not making a sound.

It was dangerous to stay in Darkonia. The ground cover hid the full strength of the sun as the misquew avoided open ground. Saranon kept her head close to its fur as she glanced around hoping that they were alone. She sensed an end node just as the creature stooped to let her down. She patted the misquew feeling the sweat along its back. She wiped her hand as the creature left. The end node looked as though it had hardly been used. Yet the Keep reacted when she reached out her senses, opening a door to let her in.

Kaythar felt solid and sturdy, filling her mind with a flood of conversation. She brushed her fingers along the walls. The Keep knew she was being sent here. She enquired as to why. The Keep let out a chuckle that ran along her senses as it responded to her question. Answers given by a Keep did not always make sense, but she thanked him all the same. The Keep appeared quite pleased to be visited by the Angeon. She was not sure the occupants would be as enthusiastic. So she kept to the less travelled path leading below the habitable area.

Kaythar talked away even in the silence. It encouraged her to go below the indolin chambers. She smiled as he continued to talk and the image of a bond-breaker filled her head. The Keep was talking so much because it wanted something. Still, after Garduend it made a pleasant change. She listened as Kaythar chattered away in the background. The Keep felt alive and well looked after as she opened the door, trying not to make a sound.

The room was laid out with the equipment needed to refine a bond-breaker. A few skada rested under the bench, the only hint that the room had been prepared in a rush. She leaned down and held one of the mechanical spiders in both her hands. It gave a sign of recognition. She patted it as though it were alive and tucked it under one arm. She rummaged around the room. The Keep was silent, then it began chatting even more. Saranon held the spider level with her eyes. 'Well do you think I should create a bond-breaker?' She asked.

The skada moved in response nodding its head and she let it run across the ground.

She placed a couple of tools on the table with a clunk. She froze in surprise forgetting the need to be quiet. She waited to see if anything had been heard. The Keep reassured her, she set to work while faint noises echoed from above. The lower chambers were warm and welcoming with a hint of age and dust along the stone walls. The strength of the Keep showed in the well-kept skada who tried to pre-empt her. In truth it had not taken much for the Keep to convince her. Saranon had been itching to make more bond-breakers. Hiding away in Kaythar seemed like the perfect opportunity.

The Keep came across with a thrill of sheer excitement. Reverberating into a faint hum along the walls and she smiled as she worked at a steady pace. Kaythar was not eager for her to meet the occupants of the habitable area. She was not willing to meet them. Before long the sorceress had five blades ready. With great care she carried each one from the pool of sheal where she had made them. The potent liquid energy running through the Keep lay silent. Absorbing any noise she made when lifting the bond-breakers out. The fine blades shone in the light, with the heart stone well formed from the elements. The Keep and her energy condensed into a solid mass.

She wrapped them up after one last gaze. She took them back to the quarters that had become her temporary home. As she made the finishing touches leaving two behind for the Keep. Saranon patted the skada that had kept her company. It was a small gesture, yet it was a relief after the end of Garduend. She slipped the three new bond-breakers into a sova bag. It shrank back into a tiny pouch. Then she made her way out into the warm night air.

She followed the lay-lines. Hoping that the advice the Keep had given her would be enough to make it north over the border. The warm breeze played at her cloak as she tried not to draw attention. There was no one there, but still she had to be careful. Travelling along the lay-lines was common this far north. The night air broke with the occasional sound. Each time she glanced around trying to assure herself it was nothing. The night grew late and she managed to find a small alcove for some much needed sleep. Her weary muscles told her how far she had gone.

Even though the lay-lines quickened her pace it did not ease the toll of the journey. She used her energy and a tiny sacra seal to conceal her location. She curled up in a comfy sleeping bag. The morning light broke long before she woke. She pretended not to notice the brightness of day. Her muscles were still weary from the night before. The warm air rustled through the branches of the trees. There was a short gap in the lay-lines up ahead as she scanned the area.

She hesitated wondering if she should risk being seen. The safety of the sacra seal remained as she stayed close by. Preferring to wait as the movement passed. The small snap of a dry twig caught her attention as she looked up to see a misquew. The creature lay there. Unaffected by her attempts to remain hidden from the outside world. She was reluctant to shoo it away, hoping that no one travelling by would notice.

Another sound emanated through her senses. As she waited ever so still, hoping the travellers would pass. Saranon could sense a group of wizards scouting the area to the south-east. The group was in the direction of Kaythar. She could hear the voices as they closed in, they showed no sign of noticing her. Though it was clear they were looking for someone. A larger group appeared behind the first. She sat while the misquew rolled over bathing in the sun's warm light. It stretched out its paw ever closer, as she held back a surge of panic.

A few voices became raised and she recognized Captain Ressinden's voice through the clearing. She shouted at the Captain from Kaythar. Her tone carried with it a menacing threat as her opponent refused to back down. Saranon found herself in an awkward position. She watched the Asdenard ready to fight amongst themselves. Her chances of leaving soon were dwindling with every moment.

Before she could wonder what would happen, Captain Verkin rushed in, igniting a massive shield, it forced the wizards from Kaythar to step back. The open threat had an instantaneous effect. Saranon gaped in disbelief as Captain Ressinden tried to gain control. The wizards nearest her were intent on each other. She stayed in the protection of the sacra seal. The misquew stood up from its rest to sit right beside her. She felt sorry for the creature as she patted its shoulder. The misquew rubbed its head against her in gratitude. She froze realising how stupid she had been.

She glanced around to see if anyone had noticed and there was no sign. The arguing dissipated as the voices faded. She was beginning to think she would have to wait until nightfall. The first of the evening shadows stretched across the fading light. As she leaned down to pat the misquew goodbye. She picked up her sacra seal. She tucked the three bond-breakers, in the form of daggers, under her arm. She surveyed the landscape one last time before heading out into the open.

The north of Darkonia felt like a country she had never known. Yet she had to remind herself she had been here before. Acwellen's words stuck fresh in her mind as she mulled them over. The Keep Endorell had met her mother. Kaythar had given her some old directions albeit in its own language. She headed out towards the lay-line. The warm breeze swept along providing a cool relief. Saranon held onto her belongings as she covered the last patch of ground. Then the air changed as it took her a moment to realise it was not the lay-line.

The ground rushed away beneath her feet as she was thrown backwards. Before she could land she reached out her energy. It shielded the blow of her descent. Shouting rang out around her, the confusion set in and she panicked. She let the blast of her sorcery scorch across the ground. Breaking the distortion, as soon as she did it she knew it was a mistake. The energy would act like a beacon for any sorcerers close by, as she mumbled under her breath. The words of a wizard cut through as he screamed, 'Stop, I yield just stop!'

Saranon stared on as Captain Edevon crouched close to where she stood. She gaped in amazement unsure what to do next. Captain Ressinden smiled with a calm sense of satisfaction. 'Don't mind him, you are coming with us,' he said.

She spoke the truth, 'I can't.'

Captain Verkin spoke, 'The Arroada know she's here. Leave before I change my mind.'

The Captain spoke the last sentence as he stared straight at her. Saranon could feel the sorcery stir in the distance, she had to go.

She handed the bundle of bond-breakers over to Captain Daina Ressinden. As she spoke, 'I made them at Kaythar.'

The Captain whispered the words, 'Thank you.'

It was not the grandest way to give the Asdenard the bond-breakers. Yet it would have to do as she ran straight into the lay-line. She hoped that she had enough time to cross the border. The night air took away the heat, replacing it with a breeze. That did nothing to sweep away the agitation from being caught unaware. As it was she could not help thinking she had left the journey too late. She hoped, in the silence, that nothing else would come as the darkness settled in. Every sound made her nervous as she quickened her pace.

She hoped she could make it. The lay-line ended as the large head of the dragon rose into view. Katholomu saw her expression. He grunted with a loud snort then picked her up with a twist of her neck taking off for the sky. The great beast wasted no time with a strong flight. Straight for the shadow that was Ardaguar. The Keep shone in the moonlight with a grey silhouette. Marking the end of her journey as the dragon swooped down. Mitch climbed part way up Kat's shoulder, and held her in a firm embrace. He helped her to the ground.

Saranon went to walk and stumbled as the wizards around her burst out laughing. Mitch whispered, 'They know you took on Captain Edevon.'

She picked herself up, trying to block the laughter out. As she headed toward to her room and slammed the door too loud. A headache sank in as her head hit the pillow, yet she was too tired to sleep. She stayed awake in the dark when a noise disturbed her. She looked up to Pennie's silhouette in the light. As her friend crouched down, 'Captain Edevon is here.'

Saranon sat bolt upright. Pennie giggled, 'That's the least of your worries.'

'What do you mean?' She asked.

'You gave him a bond-breaker,' Pennie explained.

'I did not,' Saranon shouted and her friend glared at her. 'I did not,' she whispered, and Pennie giggled.

Saranon could not sleep before, she was not going to be able to after that. Pennie's laughter taunted her. As she closed her eyes and tried to count dragons to fall asleep.

The face of a dragon stuck in her mind and she stood up in annoyance. She tip-toed to the water jug, as a torrent of glass exploded behind her. The shards from the window shattered through the air. Saranon caught the motion with her sorcery and slowed it down almost to a stop. She stared at the bloody object as it rolled along the floor. The dragon's claw had been broken clean off with the toe still attached. Before she could think Pennie grabbed her arm and they ran.

An explosion thundered from the courtyard, vibrating through the Keep with a deep rumble. It left her with no doubt they were under attack as she stumbled and tried to catch up. A flash broke across the night sky. The thunderous sound roared again, with an unwavering tone. She stopped at the sight. Pennie ran down into the heart of the Keep and Saranon hesitated. The Glyrondagar swarmed in a mass near the breach of the outer shield. Lord Dackren's blade burned in the raging dark as shouts rang out. The wizard clan was losing ground, as the smell of charred dragon choked the air.

The Razen surged forward. She could almost sense the stolen sorcery wrapped in their souls. A blast rang out through the depths they were heading for the core. The wizards gathered holding on with all their strength resonating from their sheer numbers. Saranon ran toward them, and Lord Dackren hit the ground. The blast of dark sorcery ran through as it spiralled out of control. Saranon leaped into the blazing night sky, and met the blast head on. The impact evaporated as she glided through holding Corsavere high. The bond-breaker shimmered. She used her energy to take down the first Razen sorcerer mid-air. She landed on firm ground and the Keep reached out from the depths below.

The impact sent a shock-wave splitting along the ground as the sound caught up. The night went dark as all the light from the Razen sorcerers went out. Saranon could sense the wizard clan charge in the dark. They ran past with only the sound of their feet connecting with the ground. Screams rang out up ahead and she circled in. Lord Dackren had regained his senses and raised his blade toward the Razen sorcerer. 'Ardaguar belongs to us,' the Lord shouted as his blade swept through in a long arc.

The wizards lit the sky as Lord Dackren turned to face her. 'Saranon, the Keep belongs to us,' he repeated.

She stood silent for a moment, 'It is not the Keep you sense,' then she let go of the Angeon.

The Lord's bond-breaker fell to the ground in disbelief, 'For the love of Odana.'

He regained his composure. He held her close, 'I know why the Emperor of Normisia wants you.'

'What?' She asked, but he left without an answer.

Mitch ran up beside her and gave her a hug that shook the air out of her lungs. She tried to speak and he let go. Even though it felt like such a short time had passed, she was exhausted. She managed to make her way back inside the walls of the Keep. Pennie had cleaned their room yet neither wanted to be there. They made their way to the quarters of the Vandragamond. Jack welcomed them, this time she did not have any effort drifting off to sleep.

In her dreams Tasha waited grabbing hold of her arm, and beckoning her to follow. There was haste in Tasha's movements, as though she could not move fast enough. Saranon ran after her friend and stumbled, as the ground moved underneath. She glanced up, and the horizon that shook as she lost sight of Tasha. Then something stirred, something deep beneath the ground. The reverberation hit the surface of Tordoren like a flood. She placed her hands over her ears. The sound rang out, only this time she knew what it was, as Tordoren called from the deep.

No amount of blocking it out would make it fade. She closed her eyes wishing the dream to stop. Yet it went on long after mocking her without remorse. The darkness that followed filled her dreams with a hollow resonance. Every time she searched she found the same answer. The one she had been hoping to avoid. No matter how much she ran, the flood was there. It waited just below the surface beckoning with a slow march. It called, without whispering a word from the silence that crept with it. Washing away the hurt and leaving a solitary numbness. Lady Alvere had warned her, the Angeon has the ability to make or break the world.

CHAPTER FIFTEEN

The quest begins

The light streamed through with the brightness of the mid-morning sun. Saranon was still wrestling with dreams that had haunted the night before. Pennie popped her head around the door. Her friend smiled, 'Nice to see you're finally awake.'

It was not the response she was hoping for. The sorcerer's quarters were like a small labyrinth. As she made her way through, Pennie tried not to laugh. The sun was far too strong and only added to her headache.

A bustling hub of jovial voices greeted her ears as she entered the corridor. She rushed down to the great hall. She arrived in time to see Lord Dackren waving the new bond-breaker about with a steady sway. He kept his ale steady in the other hand. She gaped in amazement as he just missed slicing the table in half. Lord Dackren staggered and smiled as he caught sight of her. She glanced at the door, but he was closer. He placed his mug down then scooped her up in the same arm and planted a moist kiss fair on her cheek. Without thinking she pushed him away and he held her even closer.

He grinned before letting her down and she breathed a sigh of relief. She darted away and a voice spoke from over her shoulder. 'I see Lord Dackren thanked you,' Ben Waterworth remarked.

She was about to say something then changed her mind, 'Yes.'

'It was not as bad as it looked, we only lost two souls,' Ben spoke as they walked. 'I was wondering if you would come for a ride.'

His request caught her off guard and she nodded in response.

Captain Edevon was waiting near the dragon pens, 'It's time to return to Darkonia.'

'What do you mean?' Saranon asked.

'The Razen have not been defeated,' Ben explained.

'We must leave,' Captain Edevon answered.

Ben Waterworth nudged her toward Katholomu, 'See you in Darkonia.'

With that he climbed up on the grandest marmoz dragon Saranon had ever seen. Thrack was the same size as Katholomu. They followed the Captain and his dragon into the blue open sky. She had so many questions to ask as her mind raced, yet all her thoughts closed in on one, the Razen.

Captain Edevon took her back the way she came. They flew the rolling hillside straight to the Keep Kaythar. Katholomu glided with ease keeping less than a wing span between them. The dragons sped towards the Keep, and skimmed along the open courtyard. Then with the last momentum, ran into the stronghold of the Keep. As the great doors lowered behind them she stayed firm atop the dragon.

Ben Waterworth extended his hand, 'You can come down now.'

It was not how she wanted to arrive back in her homeland. After all the trouble Galven had gone to help her leave. She made her way down from Katholomu's shoulders. He was calm. For an absent-minded dragon he understood an awful lot, which made her wonder.

The hum from Kaythar was more distant as though focused on something. She turned her attention to the wizards who greeted Ben as they would an old friend. The walls of the Keep held strong, yet the marks from the damage were clear. The far tower to the north had been obliterated. Only the broken remains scattered along the grounds hinted to its location. Saranon strode closer to see the outer sheen on the rim. The light reflected off the stone seal covering the once hidden floor. It was testament to the enduring Keep that the seal held stronger than ever. Yet it made her shiver to think of what had been.

The marks scorching the ground lay fresh as the pungent smell filled the air. The shallow forest surrounding the Keep gave an overbearing silence. She gazed down at the seal. Captain Edevon approached. The sun beamed down on his bare arms showing the bruises of the night before. He stood in the silence transfixed by the seal, 'If I were to make a bet I would say you know where the Orb is.'

Saranon glanced toward him and her eyes gave away her secret. 'I thought as much,' he said, 'Do you know how many people we lost?'

The Captain left the question without pressing further.

'Not enough' she replied.

The Captain was aghast. 'The Razen do not have your Keep,' Saranon explained.

She glanced across the open courtyard to the distant fields. 'You stand the same distance away from Validain as does Ardaguar,' she spoke.

'That we do,' the Captain replied. 'We defeated them once, long ago, they care not to remember.'

She wondered why the Vandragamond would take an interest in the wizard clans. Then let the thought be.

'You haven't seen wizards take on sorcerers. Have you?' The Captain strode by her side, 'That is a sight to behold.'

Saranon was not sure she wanted to stay to find out. Yet as she passed through the corridors one thing was clear. The Asdenard were preparing for battle. She found Ben in the control room overlooking the fields beyond the Keep. He stooped over a map that made no sense. 'You certainly make an impression,' he said.

'What?' Saranon asked.

'An Orb that everyone wants and you have no need

for,' Ben mused.

'Is that why I am in Darkonia?' She asked.

'The Orb belongs to the Asdenard. The Keep was theirs before the Razen destroyed it,' Ben replied.

'The Orb stays where it is,' she spoke in a firm voice.

Ben laughed and the tone caught her off-guard, she had not expected his reaction. The shadows grew as the sun set across the still landscape. Kaythar was not where she wanted to be and the wizards made her feel on edge. Everywhere she went their eyes were on her, the one who had the Orb.

For once Saranon found herself in the unusual state. Where the Angeon was no longer the issue and she wondered how important the Orb could be. She had not spoken of its size and she had been the only one to set eyes upon it. The night air swept across the open grounds mixed with a warm breeze. Katholomu was resting, content in the dragon pens. She wanted to shout at him, all someone had to do was offer him a warm bed and food. This did not bother Kat in the slightest, as he taunted her with one eye creased open. He rolled over on his back and gave a rumbling purr of affection. Then he flopped over whisking his tail around to encircle her.

She was not impressed as she crossed her arms and he laughed in a mocking gesture. 'What's so funny?' She snapped, and he laughed even more.

Captain Edevon spoke and sound of his voice made her jump, 'Even your dragon can tame you.'

Saranon's face went bright red. The Captain stepped

closer as Kat relinquished his captive. 'Bring me the Orb and I will demonstrate. You are no match for the Asdenard,' the Captain spoke as though she were an unruly child.

'I am not here to fight you,' she said.

The Captain smiled then walked away. She glared at the dragon that pretended to be asleep. The smug smile showed underneath. Night covered the Keep as the lights warmed the outside walls with a soft glow. She was not ready for sleep. The wizards had not slowed their pace and the Captain had left her in an agitated state. She had seen the underneath of Kaythar Keep. Yet in the habitable area the wizards held it strong. They had been blocking her access to the inner workings of the Keep.

She went down to where the wizards trained, the open room sat just below the main entrance. The Captain greeted her by throwing a staff her way. She caught it with great reluctance, training with wizards did not appeal to her. Captain Edevon nodded and she saw no polite way out of accepting. The wizard was quick he left several bruises before she managed to make a mark. He stopped and gave a short bow in acknowledgement. The Captain ceased much to her relief. 'Most sorcerers use their energy to win,' he explained.

'I told you I am not here to fight,' she repeated.

A thunderous roar shuddered down the columns making the building shake. 'Well, not you…' She added.

The Keep came to life as the wizards rose to the challenge, only this time they were prepared. Saranon ran out onto the courtyard to watch the Razen attacking from above. The wizards streamed into the sky as they rode on their dragons. A gaping hole opened as the courtyard moved. It made way for the wizards riding the misquew. The large riding cats ran without fear. She found herself standing in the middle with the Keep on one side and the wizards on the other. The Razen sorcerers swooped in from the sky. Their dark sorcery pelted against the shield protecting the Keep.

The Razen wanted Kaythar with the Keep then they would have an unbeatable stronghold. The wizards fought, picking at the edges as the shield began to flicker. The Keep had not been able to recover. Saranon ran away from the protection of the wizard Keep, she had to protect it. The Razen dragon riders continued their attack against the Keep. Kaythar gave everything it could to hold the last remnants of the shield. Soon the wizards would be on their own. She ran as the energy surged from within. Floating high above the sky as the Angeon revealed itself to the world.

The Razen sorcerers changed their aim and blasted their sorcery toward her. It was all she needed as the energy was absorbed and cascaded downward. Kaythar latched onto the Angeon. The stallic energy rose from below the Keep surging upward from the central core. The Angeon held the energy as it flowed into the shield. It pummelled through the air with a solid tone. Her frustration showed as she remained caught. Holding up the shield for the Keep, rather than taking on the Razen. Yet as her anguish showed, the wizards rushed forward eager to hold their fort. Captain Edevon charged into the fray. She lost sight of him as the wizards surged ahead in an almighty wave.

The flanks held strong against the Razen sorcerers yet neither was giving ground. The Angeon began to feel the wane of the stallic energy crashing from below. She held on hoping that it would be enough. The wizards crashed forward as a Razen sorcerer fell under the stampede. The dragon it had been riding shrieked in pain. The wizards downed another Razen. The screams cut through the air piercing at her ears. Yet still she held on as the stallic energy creased through and the hold began to slip.

The wizards divided the last of the Razen sorcerers. She could only just sense their movement as her hold reached the end of its grasp. The stallic energy ebbed back through the ground with an impenetrable sound. It filled her mind as it fled. Saranon glanced up at the rolling sky and freefell, until her energy cushioned the final gap. She lay back expecting to feel the ground and gasped as she fell into Ben's waiting arms. He stayed by her side as the last cries rang out, marking the end of the attack. Darkness covered the night sky as a chill set in. Time flowed again as the events caught up with her weary muscles.

Mitch ran to her side from the battle's edge, his face showed the pressure of the fight. She had not seen him go and she had just been able to sense him as she held onto the shield. 'They were after you,' he said with a grim tone that made her shudder.

Saranon strode toward the battle where the Razen sorcerers had fallen. The wizards stepped aside to let her pass through as she went. Athera stood in the middle. The wizardess showed the signs of a weary fight and her eyes shone with a fiery temper.

The ground beneath revealed the ashen scars from the defeat of the Razen sorcerers. It filled the air with an acrid trail of smoke hovering with a heavy weight. She gazed over the maze criss-crossing the boundaries of the Keep. 'We need the Orb,' Athera said what the wizard clan was thinking.

'No,' she answered with a steady determination and left with all eyes on her.

Mitch ran after her, his expression said it all, he was not impressed. This time as she entered the Keep Kaythar welcomed her. It opened the great doors that led below the habitable area. Mitch followed behind her. The sparse foyer opened to many corridors and all were silent. Saranon fumed as she leaned down near the pool of sheal. The liquid stallic energy resembled water at a glance. She removed her shoes and waded in. As the last of the stallic energy left, she made her way up to the solid floor. She rested near the liquid's edge. 'The Orb is not for the Asdenard and is not for the Vandragamond. It was made for the Angeon,' she spoke.

Mitch listened, but the wizard did not change his stance. 'The Asdenard will guard it,' he said.

'An Orb so large even I struggle holding it,' she said.

Her voice echoed through the corridors. A small pebble came loose and drew her attention. She sensed Pennie along the corridor near Mitch. She changed her open astonishment, before he had a chance to investigate. 'It's only Pennie,' she explained.

Wondering how the sorceress had managed to make her way into the wizard's Keep. 'I'm stuck,' Pennie's voice called out.

'Of course you are,' she rolled her eyes as she stood up.

Mitch observed Pennie trying to pull something through the wall. It was clear she was not stuck, but the object she was trying to bring through would not budge. He melded into the wall, and handed the empty staff to Saranon.

'What is it?' She asked.

'It's for the Orb of Garduend,' Pennie snatched it back.

Saranon produced the small Orb from Hedavin and placed it in the staff. 'Very funny,' Pennie said with a flat tone.

'The real Orb won't fit,' she explained.

Mitch took the staff, 'You put it in a Darkonian staff.'

'Does it matter?' She asked.

'Yes,' he replied.

Saranon tried to remove the Orb and he waved it out of her reach. 'It belongs to me,' he said.

Pennie was about to argue, but Saranon shook her head. The Orb was Normisian and she was not about to take it from him. Pennie folded her arms, 'You have to get the Orb.'

Saranon grimaced. 'It was formed from a wizard Keep, and belongs to the Asdenard,' Pennie explained.

'Wizards,' she grumbled and Mitch stared at her.

The last thing she wanted to do was expose the Orb of Garduend, yet it appeared she did not have a choice. As they headed to the habitable area Mitch's staff gave way to confusion. Before Captain Edevon confirmed the Orb was not from Garduend. The presence of the second Orb only made the tension worse. Everywhere she went all eyes were upon her. The evening was late. The exhaustion of supporting the Keep set in as she made her way to a heavy sleep.

A jarring scratching sound filtered through her mind. As the morning light shone in, Katholomu's claws scraped across the floor. He had managed to open the window and his forearm stuck through. The dragon twisted his paw sideways clasping her in the blanket. He dragged her out the window. She scrambled up his arm and yanked at his ears, while shouting at him. Kat curled his tail around he batted her away from his ears. Pennie came running to the courtyard and burst out laughing. Saranon swung down off the dragon while shouting at him.

'I asked Kat to take you to Garduend,' Pennie explained.

'I don't need help,' she snapped.

'All right then, but you need to have the Orb here in three days. The Asdenard will not be forgiving,' Pennie replied.

Before she could respond Mitch tapped her on the shoulder. 'I will come with you,' he spoke as he steered her away.

She felt unprepared as she spied the staff strapped to his pack. 'Where are we going?' She asked.

He stared down at her the wizard towered over her when up close. He was not about to be dragged into conversation. The cloud of silence hung over them as they crept toward a lay-line at the edge of the Keep. She was reluctant to travel through it, but Mitch did not hesitate. The Orb lay hidden near the remnants of Garduend protected by the seal from her energy. She shuddered to think what the Razen would do with it.

A warm breeze met them at the end of the lay-line. They were still some distance from the ruined Keep. They stood in the sheltered hillside marking the entrance. Mitch raised the staff as he glanced around. A warning blast rang out and he used the staff to shield the blow. Saranon ran up behind him as the Vandragamond circle in. She could see no sign of Lord Shakar and waited. Andwyrdan made his path through the legion of sorcerers that gathered around them. The eldest son of Lord Shakar stood tall with the same menacing glare. 'Hand over the Orb of Garduend,' he said.

'It belongs to the Asdenard,' Mitch spoke.

Saranon gasped, then regained her composure, 'Hand it over.'

She eyed the staff and Mitch gave her a disapproving glare. For a moment she thought the wizard was going to take on Andwyrdan. He relented and threw the staff toward the sorcerer.

'You are coming with me,' Andwyrdan spoke. The

Vandragamond circled around them in a tight group.

Mitch remained silent as they entered the camp hidden in the hill. The fresh dry air whispered through with light from above. The band of sorcerers were not well organised. She wondered how long they had been there. Equipment lay scattered all over the floor. Faeryn was caught between telling her what to do and apologising for the mess. Saranon began making a mental map of the place as she went. Faeryn showed them to a small room with scant furniture. She sat on the bench and watched Faeryn leave.

Mitch stood inspecting the wall for any sign of an opening. She wondered if he was still cross about handing over the Orb from Hedavin. 'Look I… Get down,' she screamed the last two words.

The blast of sorcery thundered through the wall. It sent rock and dirt in every direction. Saranon shielded Mitch from the damage. As the rubble settled she glanced out to the sky, 'I found a way out.'

Mitch ran grabbing her arm as he went. She heard the Razen behind her, but there was no time. If they stayed to help she would lose the opportunity to uncover the Orb. She ran ahead and he followed. She struck down at the dirt revealing the seal and placed her hand on it. The solid seal twisted open and the Orb glistened in the sun as she held it in both hands. Mitch gaped in amazement and stood back, 'We have to return it.'

Saranon opened a sova bag and placed the Orb inside. Mitch was about to protest then he changed his mind.

There were more elegant ways to transport an Orb. Yet it had already attracted too much attention. The path to lay-line was clear and they ran toward it. Shouting rang out from behind, but she did not turn back. The lay-line offered a pleasant relief from the fighting. They reached the end too soon. Captain Edevon greeted them flanked by the wizards of Kaythar Keep. 'Hand over the Orb,' he said.

Saranon took out the tiny sova bag and let it expand before she reached in to reveal the large Orb. A hush fell upon the crowd and Pennie ran through, 'I can see why you didn't want to use it.'

The Orb for all its magnificence could be too dangerous to use. She had had enough of dealing with it and placed it in the Captains waiting arms.

The Captain treated it with care. She hoped that it would be as safe with the Asdenard as it was guarded by the seal. The wizards gathered around as they led her into the great hall of Kaythar Keep. An air of sadness clung in the room. Saranon remembered what little time she had spent with Garduend. For all the damage it had been graceful in defeat. Worthy of the final remnant she had created. The moment slipped past as music brought the hall to life. Mitch brought her a steaming bowl of soup and she sat near the open fire. The flames danced with the music. She wondered how long it would take for Andwyrdan to discover that he had the wrong Orb.

The evening filled the sky as she followed the trail of lights toward the dragon pens. A dull thudding spread from underneath the door. As Katholomu heaved it up out of the way and squeezed underneath. He took care to make sure the last wisp of his tail was clear. He let the door fall to the ground with a sudden thud. The dragon opened his wings to the warm breeze.

Katholomu waited holding his head high in the air, listening in a poised stance. Then it came, the eerie call in the distance a hollow sound that grasped her soul. The sound clung in the air long after it began fading with the sun. The sensation left her cold as a chill ran down her body. Kat nudged his head forward and she clambered up his shoulder. The dragon waited in anticipation and a voice called out. She turned around while holding on tight. 'Are you ready?' Ben asked from below as he patted the dragon's side.

She wanted to express her annoyance. Katholomu leaped into the air with jolt as she held on. The dragon paid her no attention gliding through the sky with ease. Saranon fumed at being led into something she did not understand. The warm night air did little to soothe her. The sorcery in the air became apparent. It trickled through like a dry wind brushing against her skin. The sensation prickled along her arms. Her mind registered where it came from. The Razen sorcerers were heading for Kaythar. She could sense the dark sorcery as they drew near.

The dark haze spread along the ground and then she saw it or she thought she did. It moved with the wind and Kat moved with it. He swooped side on and gave a small flinch of discomfort, yet he went on. The darkness grew in haphazard patches criss-crossing the ground. She let go, falling from the sky as her energy softened her descent. She saw the underbelly of the great dragon as he flew past. The great wings pounded the air into the ground. For a moment all time stood still. The dark sorcery leeched across the ground covering Tordoren.

The whooshing of wings rushed against the air behind her. She glanced up to see Mitch land beside her. 'What are you doing here?'

'Getting back my staff,' he explained.

She was not about to argue as the dark sorcery began to spark. It glowed in lines scattering the ground. It appeared as though a section of Tordoren had shattered underneath.

CHAPTER SIXTEEN

In the great hall

Saranon wondered how Mitch could remain calm. The faint lines deepened in the ground. The surface split from beneath, she dropped down losing sight of her companion. The sky lit up above as the corner markers flared forming a shield over the dark sorcery. She was being trapped in. She tried to rise upward and the dark sorcery sparked into life. It expanded like an open wound tearing deep into Tordoren.

A hollow screech stretched across the withered sky burning her ears, a piercing sound. So shrill she clenched her teeth as it reverberated through her body. The patterns of shadows came to life. They moved underneath the full light of the golden yellow moon. A haze of smoke wrapped around it in a smothering embrace. The smell of charred dirt filled the dry air. The shadows moved above in an unnatural path, vexing her from a distance. A chill ran down her spine mirroring her thoughts.

The chill ran deep as the smell of the deadening of Tordoren lay thick in the air. It filled her lungs with the remnants of the seared earth. An angry flame sparked in the distance rising above the ground. It shot out without warning as the air absorbed its glow. The rip of the blast hurled closer. Narrowing the distance as her energy surged into the gap. Its strength hit with a staggering speed. It hit with a heavy jolt pounding through the air. The explosion lit up the sky with a thunderous boom whipping along the hillside. The air beat hot with an acrid sound reverberating across the night sky.

Saranon reached down, as the energy of Angeon rose, seeking Tordoren below. She called out through the open wound willing for an answer in the silence. Dark sorcery flared from above. Mitch responded in kind keeping the Razen at bay. A well began beneath as the first sensation rose, she could almost feel it yet it was there. Tordoren rose from the depths searing the dark sorcery as it went. She allowed the energy to rise within. The Angeon broke through the dark prison. Sparks lit up as the links shattered, pounding along the open ground.

The Angeon rose into the night sky as the dark sorcery dimmed, creating a void where she had been. Mitch managed to hold on as the movement settled. She could make out the Vandragamond up ahead. They rushed toward the Razen under the cover of darkness. Andwyrdan led holding the staff high as he closed in. The Razen struck and the Vandragamond blocked. The staff began to glow and she held her breath. Andwyrdan's sorcery spiralled outward from the Orb with a crashing force. It sent the Razen back. The Angeon glimpsed Hollie and Deandra in the distance, then they were gone.

The lines of dark sorcery came alive as they lit up the sky. The lines connected in a pattern around the Vandragamond. If she did not act soon the Vandragamond would be trapped. The Angeon let her energy run into the ground. It ran along Tordoren searing through the dark sorcery as it went. The explosion shattered the ground as the two forms of sorcery collided. The Angeon held out her hands as the energy strengthened into a burning sphere. Then it sheared through the air. Screeching as it expanded toward the front row of the Razen. The night went dark for all except the Angeon whose energy glowed from within.

Andwyrdan turned and raised the staff toward the Angeon. Mitch yelled out and used his wizardry to drag her down. The blast of sorcery flared past just missing her in mid-air. She managed to soften her descent and the Angeon left. Mitch grabbed her hand and they fled. Shouts rang out behind them as the Vandragamond turned their attention to her. 'Next time let them die,' Mitch said.

Saranon stopped and ran toward the Vandragamond. 'What are you doing?' Mitch asked, shouting above the noise.

She was already in front of the group, they surrounded her as Andwyrdan stared her down. 'That does not belong to you,' she said.

Andwyrdan held up the staff and broke it in two, disconnecting the Orb, 'This is a fake.'

He held the Orb in his hand and it began to glow. Saranon shouted, 'Hand it over.'

Andwyrdan laughed, 'You are not Vandragamond, it won't be long and you will die.'

Saranon fumed as the Orb grew stronger Andwyrdan aimed it at her. She caught the blast and absorbed it, then drew the Orb toward her. Andwyrdan refused to let go as it became too hot to grasp. He screamed and let go, the Orb flew toward her. She used Andwyrdan's energy from the blast to form a new staff stronger than the old. She held the staff high and the Orb grew so bright, the sorcerers had to look away. She brought down the end of the staff, it hit the ground with a thunderous crack. As the last of the dark sorcery scourging the ground, lifted up to the sky, the energy crackled across the sky as it fled. It sent millions of tiny sparks raining downward.

'At least I know how to hold an Orb,' Saranon shouted.

The Vandragamond ran from the commotion. Mitch stood beside her. 'We have to leave,' she said.

She gave the staff to him and he smiled, 'You had to annoy Andwyrdan.'

He said no more as they rushed toward Kathomolu who was busy rolling in the dirt. The dragon shook himself and grinned as they clambered up. He headed north at hurtling speed and she had to stay low to hold on.

Ardaguar Keep came into view with the morning light, as the sun's first rays hit the Keep. She could see the troops gathered in the grounds. A great cheer rose as Mitch held up the staff and the Orb glowed. If she had wanted to make a discreet entrance any chance of that was gone. The dragon gave an almighty roar, before skidding across the courtyard. Whipping his tail around as he came to a stop in the opposite direction. Ben Waterworth came out to greet them, 'The Vandragamond have attacked Kaythar.'

Saranon's weary eyes revealed her exhaustion. 'This is not your fight,' Ben added.

She was in no frame to argue with him, but the frustration showed. Ardaguar welcomed her with caution, it was a wizard Keep and remained guarded. The faint whirring hum from the central core filled her mind. As her head slumped on the pillow she fell into much needed sleep. The black sea in her dream filtered into a clear stream as she followed it from the shore. She gazed into Tasha's eyes, the image of her friend stood over her. 'I have let you down,' she whispered.

Tasha leaned in close and answered, no. A space nearing eternity lapsed in the silence that followed. The image of her old friend stood over her in the dream. She tried to block out the last remnants of the attack, until the sound faded. In the warmth of the afternoon she managed to stumble out of bed. She landed with a thud on the floor yanking the bed sheets with her. Ben ran to see what all the noise was and burst out laughing before he kneeled down. He lifted Saranon to her feet. 'Not so nimble after the fight,' the wizard grinned as he helped her up.

The Keep was silent with few people as she glanced

around. Katholomu made his presence felt by flicking his long tail in the air just outside. He moved his head to stare eye to eye with her. She did not need the dragon and yet he followed her. He gave an amused smile and a deep rumble from his belly that sounded like a chuckle. As the sun's rays crept lower in the sky she faced the dragon. Katholomu pulled himself up in anticipation. Ben waited near the doorway as she clambered on Kat's shoulders. He spoke with a firm resolution, 'I cannot go with you.'

Saranon turned to face him, 'I know.'

The dragon itched to reach the sky as he steadied his legs and jolted forward. She clung on tight to the fold around his neck and nestled herself close to his skin. She glanced down at the broken earth along the surface of Tordoren. The scorched remnants stared back at her. It was a stark reminder of the strength of sorcery used in the attack. The night was settling in fast as Katholomu spread his great wings across the sky. Through it all Saranon could pinpoint where she had been holding her own ground. A chill trickled down her spine. If Andwyrdan could not control the small Orb, she did not want him to get the Orb of Garduend.

As the dragon moved on, she could see another large track where Andwyrdan had been. She peered over and the dragon tilted gliding to the ground. She made her way down, careful not to disturb the marks as she went. Saranon examined the pattern, tracing the markings back to their original location. First she went to where Hollie had stood, the struggle still showed on the ground. She tried not to step on the scuff marks as they lay all around. Then she went further ahead, following the tell-tale signs that lead to where Deandra had been. She turned, looking over the whole landscape, there was an odd sensation. Yet she could not describe it.

She glanced around, a spark glinted in the ground and she reached down. The small remains of a seal shone, only it was unlike any she had seen. The air was calm and still. It cleared her head from the rough night before as the last aches left her body. She found herself standing where Andwyrdan had been. A familiar sound thudded behind her. Katholomu rolled on his side in the charred dirt. His tail swished flicking clumps everywhere. Before she had time to yell at him he had rolled over the area where she had been.

Saranon ran forward. The dragon darted over the top, landing where Andwyrdan had been. 'Katholomu get here now,' she yelled, but it was too late.

He had already rolled and rubbed his back straight over the top of the site. She wanted to throttle him and used a small amount of energy to shift him sideways. The dragon pounced in one massive leap. He rolled in another patch of charred earth. She ran after him, the dragon flicked his tail and moved again. It had turned into a game, as she realised that chasing him would remove all sign of the attack.

She shouted and the dragon gave her a quizzical look. Then he ignored her while scratching an itch. She stood closer staring him in the face. Kat pretended to ignore her, without a care in the world at what he had just done. She could only hope that no one would notice the dragon's work. It would be impossible to miss the trail and Katholomu wore the evidence. As she stared at the ground Kat nudged her with his grimy chin, showering a spray of ash over her. She was too angry to be upset as she shook her head in disbelief.

Saranon brushed her shoulder then stared down at the remnants in her hand. Then she smiled as the attack made sense. She hugged the dragon and Kat looked astounded not expecting her response. The Razen sorcerers were making it difficult. They would not be able to fight them without the Orb of Garduend.

A voice called out from over the edge of the hillside. It bellowed so loud she jumped with fright as Gallagher yelled out again. She stood frozen behind the dragon hoping not to be noticed. It was a lame attempt. He yelled out again, 'I leave you alone and look what you do.'

Saranon's face went pale as she met Gallagher. He continued, 'Not you,' then he stared at Katholomu, 'You.'

The dragon sat upright looking rather skittish from the accusation. The great beast glanced sideways in a bid to avoid his gaze.

Gallagher leaned over to pat the great beast and Kat snorted in a cool response. 'Wreaking havoc on the land, I see,' Gallagher said.

He spoke in a softer tone near the dragon's ear. He turned to Saranon adding a firm comment, 'You need a tighter grip.'

He climbed on Katholomu's shoulders, 'I'm taking the dragon. How are you getting to Validain?'

'Are you forgetting something?' She asked.

Gallagher leaned down, 'You are as good as the Lord at keeping secrets. You are not the only one.'

She could feel her face grow warm. 'We thought the Armythral were hiding something,' he offered to help her up.

She clambered aboard. Gallagher spoke, 'You've got a lot to learn if you want to fly with me.'

With that he moved his leg and the great dragon flew into the sky. All she could do was cling on and she did not trust her odd companion. They circled around the grandest sorcerer Keep she had ever laid eyes on. The pearl Keep glowed through the night. In stark contrast to the rough sorcerers who wore light armour. The same colour of darkness. The image took her breath away and she gasped in astonishment. They descended into the main courtyard as the lights flared an audience greeted them.

The balconies were full as all eyes followed the dragon. The Keep was the largest she had seen. It appeared out of place in the hands of the Vandragamond. They were renowned for holding out against the Dreshan Occupation. As she glanced around she could sense why the Dreshans feared them. Her legs trembled as she held her gaze. The great sorcerer warriors parted as Lord Shakar marched through the crowd. She saw the horns on his helmet and rough dark fur around the shoulders of his cape. She stared into his eyes. The high Lord had a menacing glare even at peace and this was the closest it would be.

Saranon followed as the Lord swept through. The crowds parted in a wave of strength and respect. This was not a place for the weak as the glances held steady. Gallagher closed the great doors behind them with a bang. The sound reverberated through the enormous chamber. The light from the Keep bounced off the pale walls. The thick columns reached to the high ceiling looming in a tall arch overhead. Lord Shakar turned to face her. As he reached the centre of the grand chamber, 'This is where the last Angeon stood. She forced my predecessor to his knees. If you ever do the same I will make you wish you had died at Antavagon.'

Gallagher began clapping behind her, the sound echoed through the chamber. 'Welcome to the clan,' he said. 'Now what will we do about the other Angeon.'

'Kill him,' Lord Shakar said.

'Merrick is in Serenphel,' Saranon spoke.

'He will come and I will deal with him,' Lord Shakar answered without a hint of doubt. 'Daughter of mine, the call of Angeon will grow. You will be given a choice, one chance and if you miss it, all will be lost. Then, I will kill you.'

Saranon gasped and Gallagher spoke as he circled around her. 'The high Lord Vandragamond will kill the Angeon who chooses the wrong path.'

'How will I know?' She asked.

Lord Shakar bellowed with a hollow laugh that rang out, echoing in her ears. 'If it was that easy I would tell you.

I could rule Zyanthia with an Angeon,' he said.

The conversation left her feeling cold. Gallagher led her away from the grand chamber. Validain was vast by any standard for a Keep. The building stretched on over the rocky hill taller than any other. The ambient lights glowed filling the night sky. Gallagher grinned before opening the door to the largest bedroom she had ever seen. The floor half-filled the space creating a mezzanine. She glanced over the edge and there in the dark below was her dragon. Katholomu had his belly showing as he relaxed in the dragon pen. 'You can keep an eye on your dragon,' Gallagher said before leaving.

The room filled a high tower on the same level as the grand chamber. It stood several floors above the fields below. The wind swept around the building reminding her of how tall the Keep was. The hour was late and she could not relax. She did not expect the Lord to be the one who would know about the Angeon. Yet the Vandragamond never fell to the Dreshans. They had a complete history and the Lord did not fear her. Saranon's mind held onto the thoughts, long after she went to sleep.

A crash in the dragon pen below woke her in the morning light. Katholomu gave a low growl as he bashed into the gate again. 'Hold on,' she sang out and slid down the small staircase. 'Wait for me.'

Kat glared at her as though it were her fault he had been shut in. The gate sprang open with a rush to the surprise of onlookers. The courtyard and walkways were filled with people. Gallagher shouted from the balcony,

'You are late.'

Before she could answer Katholomu hurled himself into the air and flew off. She asked, 'What's going on?'

'This,' he opened his arms, 'is Validain, welcome to the chaos. Your wizard has arrived.'

'Pardon?' She asked.

'The one you attached yourself to,' Gallagher smirked.

Saranon went red with embarrassment.

The great hall filled with voices, shattering the peace, as she opened the door. Lord Shakar eyed her from the head table located in the centre of the hall, 'There you are. You can tell my administrator that he has nothing to fear.'

Edred Heath the administrator explained, 'Andwyrdan is in possession of the Orb of Garduend.'

Saranon went pale, 'Ah…'

'He will be fine,' Lord Shakar reassured the administrator.

'Ah…,' she continued.

'He will be fine,' Lord Shakar stated to her.

'It's twice the size of an ordinary Orb,' she spoke.

The Lord threw his metal chalice at the administrator's head. Edred held his book up blocking it without flinching, as though he had done it before. The chalice bounced off and Gallagher caught it. 'This is your fault,' Lord Shakar pointed at Edred.

The administrator responded, 'Yes sire.'

'Why can't I have an Orb like that?' Lord Shakar asked. 'Oh well, he will find out soon enough. Now, your wife…'

'My ex-wife sire,' Edred the administrator responded.

'Your wife…' Lord Shakar repeated. 'Is a…'

'A difficult person to deal with,' Gallagher spoke.

'…A wretch,' Lord Shakar said. 'Can I burn her at the stake?'

The administrator went pale. Gallagher interrupted, 'That was taken off the list a while ago.'

'Who removed it?' The Lord asked.

'You did sire,' Gallagher responded, 'As part of reconciliation with the wiccan.'

'Oh, well you can think of something,' the Lord spoke. 'Garridan, take Saranon to her wizard.' Lord Shakar then turned to her. 'Next time you visit I would prefer that your wizard was not attached,' he said.

Gallagher shook his head when he saw that she was about to respond. Saranon took the hint and followed Garridan out of the great hall. He was as tall as the high Lord, yet his youth showed behind his small beard. He wore the uniform of his station with a plain dark fur covering his broad shoulders. The bond-breaker on his belt shone in the light and he grinned when he caught her staring at it. 'You are not the only one who can make a bond-breaker. He held it out with pride and Saranon took it. The dark blade of heart stone shone the colour of burnt blood and she gave it back. 'Were you weak when you bonded the wizard?' Garridan asked.

He waited for a reply then laughed. 'You won't last long with a wizard.'

'I will be fine,' she retorted.

Garridan opened the door then left. Saranon glanced through to a large room with tall glass windows. They opened up to the balcony overlooking the inner courtyard. The balcony stretched onward. It joined up to the many walkways that wrapped around the towers. Mitch sat as he spoke to Commander Iona. She appeared formidable even for a sorceress. Her uniform wore the heavy toll of a life in the harsh terrain. Iona spoke first, 'I hear my daughter Faeryn and Andwyrdan have the Orb.'

The Commander did not look old enough to be Faeryn's mother. Yet she did not doubt the resemblance. Iona was a dark haired beauty with a trace of grit on her cheek from the night's travel to the Keep. Mitch gave an expression as though he had been picked up from Kaythar. The Commander answered the unspoken question, 'We found your wizard not far from Validain.'

'I was looking for you,' Mitch clarified.

'The wizard can stay with you, try not to lose him,' the Commander left them in peace.

Mitch relaxed, 'I was outside Kaythar. Andwyrdan took the Orb before it had been sealed within the Keep.' He continued. 'What are you doing here?'

'I'm not sure,' Saranon said as shouts reached them.

The door burst open. Gallagher entered, 'You have been invited to the central core.'

She asked, 'Pardon?'

'It is an instruction from Lord Shakar. All Vandragamond meet Validain as a curtesy,' He explained.

'The custom dates back more than a thousand years,'

Mitch said.

'Do I have too?' She asked.

'Yes,' replied Mitch and Gallagher at the same time.

'You are not supposed to agree,' she remarked.

The last thing Saranon wanted to do was visit the central core yet it intrigued her. A Keep of such grandeur would have a spectacular core by any standard.

While they spoke the walkways around the tall windows filled with spectators. A slow chant rose through the crowd. 'Really,' she whispered, and glanced at Mitch.

Lord Shakar's voice boomed from outside the open door, 'Saranon.'

She asked, 'Now?'

'You will meet the central core…now,' the Lord's voice boomed above the noise.

She did not see what the urgency was, 'You want me to meet the core now?'

'Yes,' the Lord replied.

Saranon raised her arms catapulting her energy downward into the depths of the Keep. Validain answered with a rising surge of stallic energy. It melted through the floor creating a vortex. The vapours spun around in a tight whirlwind gaining speed. 'Not now,' Lord Shakar shouted.

Mitch stepped back as the vortex grew, the central core was no place for a wizard.

'Stop, wait,' the Lord's voice carried above the whirlwind.

The energy from the central core crashed into her. It flooded up through the whirlwind that held her. The vortex began to close and the core took her deep beneath the ground. Validain whirred with an electrifying storm in the deep as she peering above her. Gravity had no place in the central core, the magnitude of the core made its own. Validain whirred in the darkness, it sped raising the energy from the deep. Faster and faster it sped as the energy coiled up from the giant rod and into the core. She reached out to the core and it accepted.

In that moment Saranon was Vandragamond, she was Validain and she was the Angeon. The energy ran through her, concentrating as the central core whirred in the deep. The storm in the heart of the central core began to move with a rapid pace. It wrapped around her with a droning sound. The deep rumbling of the core began to fade, in the centre of the storm began a calm that filled her soul. She focused outward toward the sky. With a deafening roar the central core answered. The outer shell of the core opened creating a funnel to the sorcerer's stone above. The vacuum pressed against her and Saranon brought the might of the Keep with her.

The sorcerer's stone stood above the grand chamber. It formed a platform above the heart of the Keep. Saranon, the Angeon, rose into the sky and Validain with her. The brilliant light from the energy shone, radiating throughout the Keep. She locked onto her target, the old Keep that once was Garduend. A thunderous pounding erupted from the deep and she waited in anticipation. The central core drove the raw energy with such force it flew up into the air. All sound was lost as she focused the energy on the old

Keep.

The stallic energy catapulted across the sky in a giant arc. Sparks sprayed through the air. Then it landed deep in the ground of Tordoren. The energy formed the seed of hope that would give rise to a new Keep. Validain rumbled from beneath and Tordoren awakened. They both sensed the new central core forming a Keep from deep below. She floated down until her feet touched the sorcerer's stone. Garridan stood beside her, 'Most sorcerers flare the shield. They don't create a new Keep.'

Mitch ran onto the sorcerer's stone toward her, 'The Lord wants to see you.'

'I bet he does,' Garridan replied.

Saranon made her way down the elegant tower that wrapped around the grand chamber. It was not what she had expected, yet Garduend did not deserve to die. The Asdenard wizards needed their Keep. Lord Shakar greeted her. They strode towards the great hall as the cheering around her began. The Lord reached the great hall, 'This is why we are Vandragamond. We are the greatest sorcerers to walk Tordoren and nothing will break us.'

A great cheer rose up and the Lord welcomed her to the main table at the centre of the room.

He leaned over, 'If you ever make a wizard Keep again do not use Validain.'

'Now where were we,' the Lord spoke aloud.

'Sire,' Gallagher interrupted.

'Yes,' replied the Lord.

'Andwyrdan has attacked Ardaguar Keep,' Gallagher

said.

'What? Well he had better succeed,' the Lord spoke. 'Send the troops, if he flags, fall to plan B.'

Saranon tried to interject. The Lord remarked, 'This is Andwyrdan's fight do not intervene.'

'But…' She began.

'We do not interrupt a Vandragamond in battle. The last time involved removing the Dreshan Occupation from Zyanthia. That will not happen again,' Lord Shakar glared at her.

The Lord repeated, 'That will not happen again.'

'I am the Angeon,' she stated.

Lord Shakar raised his hand. Saranon blocked his sorcery before it hit and he was caught off-guard. The Lord stumbled and fell, slamming into the floor on his knees. 'Leave,' he shouted. 'Leave Validain and do not come back.'

Saranon ran from the great hall. Mitch grabbed her arm and they fled toward the courtyard. 'Jump,' he said.

'What?' She asked.

Katholomu swooped from the sky. They both jumped landing on the dragon as he sped into the sky.

CHAPTER SEVENTEEN

A wizard out of place

The dark mood clung in the air long after the midday sun shone bright over the Darkonian sky. Katholomu flew north to the border then turned left toward the fledgling Keep. 'What are doing?' Saranon asked the dragon.

'We cannot fly to Ardaguar in the light,' Mitch explained.

It was not what she wanted to hear, Andwyrdan was at Ardaguar and so was the Orb. She wanted to scream, as the dragon landed in the shelter of the building. Mitch helped her down and she glanced around, 'Wow.'

The new Keep had the immediate structure emanating from the ground. The building reached above the lower chambers in places stretched far apart. It showed the true size of the central core below. She gasped in astonishment, 'Did I make that?'

'Yes,' Mitch opened the main door to the great hall.

The place felt empty. With little more than the great hall spreading back into the hillside. The columns continued up to the high ceiling above. Facing the great doors at the opposite end a platform loomed. The size and scale dwarfed them as they glanced around.

The hum of the central core warmed the Keep with a radiant glow as the sun sank in the afternoon sky. Mitch went to the platform and opened a panel, glancing at the inner workings of the Keep. 'It's a wizard Keep,' he shouted with delight.

He took her by the hand and swung her round in the excitement. 'Yes,' she stared at him wondering what the fuss was about.

'You made a wizard Keep,' Mitch repeated.

'I still don't get it,' she said.

'That's impressive,' Mitch explained.

Saranon sat on the platform gazing out the high windows. The frustration showed plain on her face. She wanted to be at Ardaguar, yet as she waited, the exhaustion set in. Validain and making the Keep had been draining. 'Have you thought of a name?' Mitch asked.

She gave him a puzzled look, 'Pardon?'

'You need to name the Keep,' he replied.

'Oh no,' she shook her head, 'You can name it.'

'Angore,' Mitch responded.

'Really,' she stood on the platform and raised her arms, 'I name you Angore.'

The Keep hummed in response. 'I think he likes it,'

she said to Mitch.

They rested through the afternoon in the darkness of the great hall. They waited for the cover of the night sky. Saranon took out her small sova bag. It changed size and she opened it laying her bedding on the platform. The exhaustion of the day sank in and she slept.

As her dreams settled in, a figure stood over her and she recognised her old friend. Tasha was insistent trying to say something, yet no sound came out. In her dream she reached out, the more she reached the further away Tasha appeared. Her friend's eyes were filled with a solid determination. Saranon moved and every part of her body felt heavy, weighing her down. She fell over and could not get up.

The dream had crippled her. It frustrated her as every time she tried to lift herself she failed. It should have been easy, yet something was weighing her down. She shouted out to let Tasha know. The figure of her old friend stood there without emotion, her eyes looking past. Saranon gazed over her shoulder and there was nothing. She turned back and a different face appeared it was Hollie. She tried to wake up but she could not move, she tried to shout out and the sound was muffled. She screamed over and over again, yet the dream did not stop.

She screamed louder and louder. Until the sound filled her head to the point where she thought she would burst. Then it broke out into the silence, into the void, into the nothing. It reached beyond the dream that held her tight in its grip. Angore reassured her in the dark as she woke. Mitch was ready and Katholomu had his head through the door. The dragon snorted warm air into the room as he watched with impatience. 'We have to go,' Saranon scrambled to her feet.

'Andwyrdan has not breached the shield, we have time,' Mitch said.

'How do you know?' She asked.

Pennie answered, 'Because I told him. You made a Keep and didn't tell me.'

She was about to apologise, 'It's okay, the Glyrondagar need you.'

Galven appeared beside her in the great hall glancing around in amazement, 'She's beautiful.'

'Angore is a he and a wizard's Keep,' she explained.

'Next time I want a sorcerer's Keep,' Pennie stated with a hint of amusement. 'The Asdenard will be pleased. You make a solid Keep.'

'I saw Tasha, I have to leave,' she said.

Pennie eyed her with suspicion, 'You still see her?'

'Yes,' she remarked.

Pennie was not impressed, 'We will talk later.'

Saranon climbed up on Kat's shoulders with Mitch behind her. The dragon was itching to fly, and took off in the cover of the night sky. She clung on hoping they were not too late. They had to save Ardaguar from Andwyrdan and the Orb of Garduend. The fiery haze wafted through the air as they flew close, yet it was not the sight she expected. The Glyrondagar held out strong attacking in the night sky. The great weapons built into Ardaguar made the

Vandragamond look easy prey. The sorcerers hung back. 'He doesn't know how to use the Orb,' she remarked.

'It's just as well,' Mitch spoke.

Katholomu veered behind the Keep avoiding the main thrust of battle. Mitch sent up a wizard light for the Glyrondagar to know who they were. At first there was no response then a welcome flare sparked through the dark. Kat glided in with no more than hand's width for grace between the walls of the building. She closed her eyes as he passed through. 'Show off,' she exclaimed and the dragon roared with amusement. Zara came into the dragon pens to greet them, 'You took your time.'

'What do you mean?' She asked.

'We were expecting you a few days ago,' she explained while leading her to the great hall.

The air simmered with the dark mood that had fallen over the Glyrondagar. Lord Dackren gave a grim smile as she strode toward his table, 'We have a problem.'

'Yes,' she responded thinking he meant Andwyrdan.

'Andwyrdan does not have the Orb,' the Lord said.

'What?' She exclaimed.

'…and we have to pound him into the ground before we can find who has it. Do you care to join me?' Lord Dackren asked.

All eyes in the great hall fell on her and waited. 'I will fight with you,' she answered. Applause erupted through the crowd and Mitch spoke, 'Are you sure?'

'We have to end this and get the Orb,' she replied.

He nodded in acknowledgement. The air was thick

with smoke from the Keep. It was mixed with wizardry from the battlements. She made her way up to the sorcerer's stone. Where Lord Dackren's finest soldiers stood. Ben Waterworth glanced her way, 'I thought you were going to stand me up.'

'Never,' she humoured him.

'How do you want to do this?' Ben asked.

Saranon went toward the centre where Ben stood. The sweat ran down his face, yet he managed a smile. A wave of sorcery aimed toward them in the night sky. Screeching as the sparks ripped through the air. She sensed the central core below, Ardaguar wanted vengeance. 'Wait,' she answered.

The stallic energy from the core surged below. She summoned it forward calling to the Keep. The sparks grew ever closer and she repeated her words, 'Wait.'

The sparks flung down toward them. 'Now,' she shouted.

Ben and the wizards gathered around the stone. She attacked with the full might of the Keep. The stallic energy raged into the air like a cloud enveloping the night sky. The sparks evaporated and the shield shone a brilliant fiery golden haze. It flared out toward the sorcerer clan. The Vandragamond hesitated at the sight, then a small group at the rear ran. The rest followed, breaking off in sections as they went. Shouting rang out below as the dragon riders disappeared into the darkness.

'We must do that again some time, when the Keep is not under attack,' Ben peered over the low wall. Watching as the Vandragamond clan scattered in disarray. His great marmoz dragon Thrack flew down from the sky and Saranon climbed on. 'Hey, he doesn't fly without me,' Ben spoke as he climbed on. 'I could get used to this.'

She said nothing as she focused on the Vandragamond below. 'Andwyrdan is in the sky,' Ben responded as though reading her thoughts. Thrack plunged in the darkness he flew hard then turned looping around. 'What is he doing?' She asked.

'Hang on,' Ben clung on low to the dragon as Thrack sped faster making tight turns, as he went. Her heart thudded, they were gaining ground as she spotted Andwyrdan's dragon up ahead. Thrack dived in close, as the dragon swooped and sped toward the border.

Thrack beat his wings hard and dived again on his prey. This time he knocked into the other dragon. His claws ripped through flesh and the dragon screamed on its descent. Saranon watched on in horror. The dragon plunged to the ground with a screech that pierced through her. They flew down hitting the earth hard. She rolled off summersaulting along the grass. Above her stood Edred the administrator. He turned his attention to Andwyrdan, 'Where is the Orb?'

'You cannot have it,' he fumed.

Commander Iona hit him to the ground, 'The administrator asked you a question.'

'You won't get it,' Andwyrdan spat the words out.

Edred hurled his sorcery at Andwyrdan who let out a horrible scream. 'Stop, he doesn't have it,' Saranon shouted.

From the darkness Faeryn spoke, 'We lost the Orb to the north of Validain.'

Commander Iona stared at the administrator. 'I bet your former wife knows where it is,' she said.

Edred glared down at Andwyrdan, 'You had to take the Orb from Kaythar.'

'You attacked Ardaguar with no Orb,' Commander Iona yelled. 'Wait until Lord Shakar hears of this.'

Ben watched in a silence stance as the band of wizards grew around him. After the sorcerers had left he spoke, 'That is how the Vandragamond apologise. Andwyrdan will be punished for his actions.'

'Now can we find the Orb?' She asked.

Captain Edevon strode through the crowd, 'You have permission to search for the Orb.'

Ben glanced at her, 'That was meant for me.'

She grew impatient as the Captain waited for a response, 'Are we going to Kaythar?'

'Ah, that would be splendid,' the Captain replied. Ben shrugged then climbed on Thrack.

'Oh no, this time I'm directing the dragon,' she said.

She did not want to fall off the dragon again. They followed Captain Edevon through a silent sky and made their way toward Kaythar. The Keep appeared as she had last seen it, standing solid in the night.

Thrack touched the ground with a smooth glide much to her relief. A great thud landed next to them. Katholomu pounded against the ground with Mitch riding high. The dragon riders took it as their que to follow them into the dragon pens. The day's events had caught up with them. Saranon almost tripped as she fell backward into Ben. 'I think you need to rest,' he said in a serious tone.

She was not about to argue as time slipped away, the Orb was still out there somewhere. Again it would have to wait.

Captain Daina Ressinden showed her to a small cosy room. The wizardess wanted to talk then refrained from doing so. Saranon could not relax so she invited the Captain to sit by the fireplace. 'Did you bring Lord Shakar to his knees?' The Captain asked.

'It was an accident,' she replied.

'The Vandragamond are comparing you to the Angeon of old. They say you made a wizard Keep.' Captain Daina said.

'I did. Angore stands where Garduend fell. Mitch named him,' she replied.

The Captain smiled, then she added, 'Sleep well.'

Tasha came haunting her dreams, the Orb held in her hands near the black ocean. The grass moved in the wind and Saranon ran toward her. The Orb of Garduend gave a blinding flash and she could not see. The ground changed and she found herself in a cave with no way out. She yelled and no one heard. The dream racked at her thoughts as she slept through the night. Mitch appeared in the morning light and startled her. Even with the bond the wizard could still sneak up. 'Captain Edevon has a lead on the Orb,' he said.

'Of course he does,' she did not think much of the

Captain.

She raced down to the dragon pens, and Mitch ran after her, 'Not that sort of lead.'

'What do you mean?' She asked and he pointed outside.

In the courtyard stood Jack Heath, she had not seen him since her first trip to Ardaguar. The Vandragamond sorcerer gazed at her. His eyes confirmed her thoughts, he knew who had the Orb of Garduend. Gallagher patted her on the back and she almost jumped. 'Now you just need to humiliate Garridan,' he said.

Her face went red and he laughed.

After Andwyrdan she had not wanted to be among the sorcerer clan. Yet there in the courtyard a garrison from the clan made themselves ready. To her amazement the Asdenard prepared with them. It was the first time she had seen the wizard and sorcerer clan talk with ease, united by a common foe. Gallagher asked, 'What of your dragon?'

Saranon turned her head. To her embarrassment Katholomu was scratching his back. He pelted the outer wall of the dragon pens. He paid her no attention as she called his name. Gallagher whistled and Kat scurried over rubbing his head against the sorcerer.

Kat glanced at the two clans getting ready to leave. He stared at her with a silent expectation. She was dreading the word before he spoke, 'Coward.'

Jack gaped in astonishment, 'I didn't know he could talk.'

'Yes,' she answered.

'Your dragon has a point,' Gallagher spoke, 'You have done nothing to prepare.'

She dreaded the thought of having to meet the Razen again, yet they had the Orb. 'I am ready,' she replied.

The dragon scoffed at her. 'I am,' she repeated.

Captain Daina Ressinden came up to meet them, 'We are set to go.'

Kat glared at her in a grump, as her dragon riders began to take to the sky. 'No, you can wait,' she said.

Katholomu beckoned, yet he nudged Jack instead. 'I know who you're riding with,' Ben said to the dragon then he climbed up on Thrack.

Before she could decide Kat flew into the air with a giant leap. She climbed up next to Ben who spoke, 'You need to earn your dragon's respect. He'll keep flying off otherwise.'

'Thanks,' she gave a flat response.

They followed Katholomu through the air at a steady pace. The clouds grew thick in the hazy sky. She reached out her hand then the dragon swooped down. The thin sprawl of trees changed into a rocky hillside rising above. They landed as Jack waited, 'We are close.'

Saranon could sense the dampening of sorcery emanating from the ground. It gave an eerie sensation, one that filled her with dread. Jack's stony face showed his determination. Yet there was no sign of the other dragon riders.

She held her bond-breaker Corsavere in the form of a sword. He glanced at it and their eyes locked. Ben drew his bond-breaker, an elegant blood red the colour of the Glyrondagar. Ben quickened his pace, taking the lead, as Jack stepped aside. She followed the wizard and he ran. The dark sorcery made it difficult to sense anything below the surface. A glowing ball grew in the distance the light filled their vision making it hard to see. Ben yelled out in pain, the dark sorcery caught her off-guard. The strength of the blast pelted down, knocking the air out of her lungs and she began to choke.

She charged forward attacking with her energy. It was just enough to block the blow. She reached Ben sheltering him as he regained his composure. He ran forward and she shouted, but he did not stop. More than one blast headed toward them and Saranon had to choose. She took out the blast to the right and held up a shield as the second came shattering down. Ben dived back under the shield as the blast hit. Sparks pounded with a fiery eruption above them. He pointed to the left and she nodded. They ran and she blasted her energy forward. Ben ran past the flames that lapped along the ground. His blade hit the shield of a figure in the haze up ahead, she could almost make them out.

A blast hit her from behind, it pummelled her to the ground. Pain seared as the air sparked and she dived for cover. She lost sight of the wizard Ben. In the distance the figure stepped forward, Hollie glared at her. The dragon riders broke through the sky from the clan Vandragamond. In the confusion Ben Waterworth rushed toward Hollie. He knocked the Orb of Garduend out of the Razen's hands. It rolled as it hit the ground. A scream pierced the air as Ben held Hollie tight. The hold was broken when he was flung backward. The dark sorcery seared and Saranon blocked the blast as she stood in front of Ben.

Deandra picked up the Orb as the Vandragamond sorcerers closed in. The shadows of the swooping dragons dimmed the sun's light. Then the blasts hit the ground toward the Orb. Deandra ran from the fight leaving Hollie alone. As the dragons landed Saranon turned to help Ben. A surge of pain ran across her back and she fell to the ground, as the air caught in her lungs. She looked around, but only darkness greeted her. She realised her vision had blurred. Yet she could still sense Hollie as she gathered her energy to block the Razen. Hollie took aim again and the fractured remnants broke through knocking her back.

She heard the Vandragamond rallying around her, as she stood regaining her strength. Before she could take aim Hollie hurled another blast straight toward her. Saranon managed to absorb the impact and regain her stance. She sent a massive flare of energy hurling across the open ground. The blast hit its mark, yet Hollie did not falter to her amazement. The Razen kept on going as the energy drew back toward Hollie. She gasped as she felt the vacuum pull around her in the void. She was missing something, but it was too late.

She braced herself as the blast flared. It raged through the air with a mighty strength. Every breath she took stung, as she just managed to hold on through the attack. A movement caught her eye, and she squinted in the haze.

A figure stood where it should not have and she gasped trying to reach out. Yet the blast was too great and she held on trying to battle her way forward. Another blast rang out thick and strong, yet it was not her as she sensed Jack up ahead. She tried to reach him through the thick haze.

Hollie struck again and she managed to hold it back. As the sparks flew with a deep roar and the blast hit her energy. Jack ran toward Hollie as Saranon struggled to hold on. Then a deep loud thunderbolt cracked along the ground. It roared with a pounding against her ears, blocking out every other sound. She hurled her energy forward and had lost sight of Jack. She ran forward as another blast struck her. She fell as the remainder of the blast cascaded over head with a fiery rage.

She reached out her hand and caught his. The sparks dimmed in the grey sky and she stood over him. He looked up with the last gasps fighting for every breath and it was too late. Tears welled in her eyes flooding down her cheeks and she wanted to scream. A sound rang out, but it was not her not this time. As the last breath of air left his lips, Jack Heath's head sank to the ground. She clung on not knowing what to do. As the haze cleared Hollie's hysterical screams filled the air and Gallagher moved in. He swung his bond-breaker deep. Saranon hung her head as Hollie's final scream cut through the air. Gallagher stood silent as the Vandragamond sorcerer's ran through the hillside. They ran past with one goal, to find the Orb. Gallagher gazed down and did not speak.

She stared down in disbelief, her arms were numb, yet

they would not relax. She stared down into Jack's dull eyes and the tears blurred her vision. She wanted to scream, but no sound would come out. Her voice had gone hoarse from the pain. Yet she felt numb inside as she knelt down and she let him go. She trembled as she stood trying to make her legs work as the exhaustion set in. The tears continued to creep down her cheeks. A constant reminder of what had been lost.

Saranon stared down at the lifeless body. She touched Jack's face closing his eyes from the unseen world. She was in too much shock to be angry. Before she could say anything Gallagher patted her shoulder. With a reassuring tone asked her to leave. She felt numb, every muscle in her body ached as she walked away. She turned back one last time it was all over. She felt completely drained as exhaustion set in. The darkness of night covered them and all she could do was cry.

Katholomu waited, his face was hard, the dragon showed no sympathy as she wept. He backed away before letting her climb on. 'Okay Kat you have your wish, find Deandra.'

The dragon's ears tilted back realising what he was being asked. It was the only hesitation he gave as he pelted into the dark sky blending into the cover of night. The image of Jack Heath stayed with her as she clung on to Katholomu.

CHAPTER EIGHTEEN

Vengeance with a cost

The night covered them as Kat flew through the sky. Saranon felt like the only one who was trapped in a cloud of unease that clung in her mind. She was caught in the middle of something she did not understand. The loss of her Orb only made it worse. The dragon swooped low along the hill side, he almost stopped. Mitch ran out of the darkness joining her on Kat's shoulders. 'Validain,' he ordered the dragon.

Saranon was not impressed as Katholomu did as he was told. They took off into the sky. 'I asked Kat to find Deandra,' she said.

'She's heading to Validain,' he replied.

She asked, 'How do you know?'

'Deandra carved through a legion of Asdenard on her way,' he replied.

He was almost out of breath. Saranon gasped, 'We are in trouble.'

'You have to stop her,' he said.

'Don't tell me what to do,' she retorted.

'If she gets Validain she could do more damage than you,' he responded.

'Thanks,' she said in a flat tone.

She not sure she wanted to be compared to a Razen sorceress with an Orb. Kat flew straight for the Keep. The dragon blended in as he swooped low and she saw the first signs of the attack on the outer rim. The Vandragamond were clustered around the perimeter near the damage. It took her a moment to realise Kat was taking her to an end node. A barrier beamed faint around the low tower at the perimeter. The dragon tilted away in frustration. His claws carved into the ground catapulting both riders into the scrub nearby. She wanted to shout at him, but there was no time.

Validain called out creating a void. That sucked her in as she moved backward toward the end node. As she touched the sorcerer's stone it flared. She realised it was not the Keep that dragged her in. She wanted to scream as the air left her lungs. Mitch read her thoughts and he went to lunge forward onto the node. She shouted in her mind, 'Don't.'

Katholomu tilted his ears back and leaped straight over the top of Mitch. He plunged his claws into the top of the sorcerer's stone. It broke releasing the pressure. The dragon screeched in pain. He hurled himself away from the stallic energy as it shot into the sky.

The raw energy of the Keep coursed through piercing her skin. The energy of the Validain was more than she had ever known. The Razen appeared on the outskirts surrounding Mitch and Kat. All she could do was look on as the stallic energy held her above the ground. In the distance the Issola came, she sensed Pennie and Galven riding on the misquew. The riding cats rustled through the trees. That clung around the grounds of the Keep. Silent and deadly. Katholomu roared as he joined the fight, and Mitch followed. Validain was beginning to seal the sorcerer's stone beneath. The tide turned and the stallic energy fell into the closing void.

Saranon rushed down with it and the sorcerer's stone closed above her. It blocked out the night sky and the noise above. She landed with a thud, hitting the floor as the stallic energy drained away. The ledge broke off at a sharp angle. She peered over into the depths as sparks flew up from the stallic energy. The void closed and a rumble resounded through the Keep. The sound echoed through her mind jarring at her senses and her eyes grew wide. She ran down toward the central core as the doors began to close in the imbenik chamber. 'No,' she spoke her thought aloud.

The Keep was being sealed off she ran using her energy to speed up. The doors were closing and she ran down toward the middle of the Keep. She had to make it to the centre, but the path was blocked. She thumped her hands against the sealed path, 'No.'

The sound began to fade as the doors below sealed off

the central core. One last strand remained in the middle, but she was standing on the wrong side. The Keep would not let her in. She sensed movement along the tunnels, the Razen were coming and she was trapped.

The Keep was trapped, and she had to get through she pounded her fists on the wall. The Razen approached, a blast rang out and she blocked it. The dark sorcery disintegrated shattering back through the tunnel buying her time. There was only one way to get to Validain in time and she did not want to use her energy. The Razen were closing in and she had a moment of grace before they would descend. The way to the central core was blocked and her options were fast running out. 'You left me no choice,' she whispered toward the oncoming Razen.

She let Validain in and the Keep dragged her into the centre. The stallic energy wrapped around her and she was in, but at what cost? The energy from the Orb trickled down as the Keep repulsed against it, not wanting to let it in. It clung to her, using her to block the Orb from creating a connection. Saranon winced she would have to block the Orb of Garduend from below. The Orb pounded from the other side of the sorcerer's stone. The stone sealed the floor of the grand chamber above. The energy seared through as giant fractures creased along the stone. The fractures let the energy of the Orb seep in and with it the dark sorcery.

Deandra held control of the Orb and her sorcery flared in the darkness, it was not her own. The sorcery stolen from her victims leaked through into the stallic energy. Saranon reached out weaving the stallic energy around the walls. A whirlwind picked up from the depths as Validain took the hint. It created a void to prevent the dark sorcery from connecting with the energy of the Keep. Then a jarring sound split the air as the sorcerer's stone shattered. Sending shards down in the vacuum created by the whirlwind. The shards flared, hitting her shield as she protected herself from the damage.

The blasts of sorcery filled the ceiling of the void. The Razen and the Vandragamond fought above. The whirlwind kept the dark sorcery from reaching the stallic energy in the void. She hoped it would be enough, yet Deandra still had the Orb. She tried to reach up but the sorcery surging downward was too great blocking her path. Validain called to her and she hesitated. The Orb of Garduend shone bright through the damaged floor. She tried again and could not make it, Validain called out even stronger. She had to get access to the grand chamber. Lord Shakar's shouts filled the air. He was flung into the void held over the damaged floor.

Validain called out and she relented before the Lord's screams filled the void. She may not be able to enter the grand chamber, but someone else could. In that moment she gave the Keep something more than it could ever have on its own. She gave it life. The Angeon joined with the stallic energy melding into the flow. The embodiment of the Keep appeared above, an exact imitation of her. 'There is just one thing I need to tell you,' she said to the Keep. 'Just one thing, Deandra cheats.'

The Keep knew what she meant in the void, then the

screams rang out from above. She wanted to block them out, but they ran through her mind. Such was the cost of being part of the Keep.

***

She stood near the wall. Lord Shakar's screams filled the air as Deandra used the Orb against him. The Razen sorceress held it in her hands as she laughed. The Razen followers stood surrounding the fallen Lord. Saranon froze and Lord Shakar shouted at Deandra. The sorcerer's stone on the floor had been blown to pieces. The damage lay in the centre where Lord Shakar floated. Deandra turned to face Saranon giving her captive a small reprieve. The Razen directed the Orb at her. The energy emanating from the Orb crackled through the air so close that it hissed.

She waited holding out her arms as the energy from the Orb hit. The pain split her skin before she was ready and the Angeon began to show. Deandra hit with the Orb's energy again. The skin ripped away showing more of the Angeon underneath. The Razen sorceress screamed, 'Die.'

Deandra aimed again and again, yet more of the Angeon showed through. The Razen made the Orb shine bright. Then she sent the sorcery toward her in one giant blast taking the last of her old self away. The Angeon stood before the Razen. If she held out her hand she could touch Deandra but instead she touched the Orb.

Her hands racked with pain as the Angeon held on, and Razen sorceress would not let go. Then Angeon pushed Deandra toward Lord Shakar. Deandra screamed, 'Why won't you die?'

The Razen sorcerers tried to attacked, but the Angeon had locked on to the Orb. Just as Deandra tapered on the edge of the gaping hole in the floor Andwyrdan attacked. The blast broke Saranon's lock on the Orb and the Razen sorceress attacked him. The blast from the Orb sent Andwyrdan flying and he hit the wall of the grand chamber hard.

Lord Shakar shouted at him for interfering. The Razen sorceress laughed, as she began her attack on the Lord. He was struggling to hold on as Deandra floated toward the void. Then the Angeon melted the sorcerer's stone closing the gap. Lord Shakar laughed dragging Deandra down with him. She screamed through the darkness as the gap began to close over. The last remnant sealed them in. Deandra's screams could still be heard echoing from below the chamber.

The Razen sorcerers closed in. The Angeon raised the Orb of Garduend through the sorcerer's stone. It hung in the air above the centre connected to Validain. The Keep used it to attack the sorcerers. The Angeon watched as they disintegrated. Andwyrdan gazed at the Orb she did not want him running off with it again. He placed his hand so close then pulled it away as though taunting her. Deandra's screams echoed up through the walls. She shivered as the Lord held the Razen sorceress in a tight grip. It was all she could do to remain calm, as he bled the sorcery from Deandra down in the void.

Saranon could sense the pain of the Razen sorceress. She leaned over clutching her stomach as it showed on her face. She clenched her jaw tight as the screaming continued. Andwyrdan studied her face, 'You can feel it.'

She wanted the pain to cease but the screaming continued as the Lord attacked. The Orb glowed as Deandra reached out. Saranon gripped the Orb and held it steady. The Lord attacked from below and amidst the pain came sweeping relief. It was so sudden, she fell back.

Lord Shakar melded through the floor. She waited for him to emerge before stepping through the Orb. When she passed through her old self returned. A fine web of deception covering what lay beneath the surface. Andwyrdan tried to remove the Orb and it would not budge. Saranon wanted to berate him but it had taken all her strength not to succumb to an old trick, that Deandra had used to gain the advantage. She was not sure if she would ever thank Lord Dackren for his effort by cheating with the disc. The knowledge had been invaluable.

Lord Shakar gazed at the Orb with open awe, 'Can I have it?'

She reached over, then hesitated, I think there is someone else you need to ask. Saranon placed her hand on top of the Orb. The lady that was the embodiment of the Keep stood where she was. Lord Shakar gaped, 'Validain.'

'Yes my Lord,' Validain spoke.

'Can I…' He stammered, 'Can I have the Orb of Garduend.'

Validain smiled and gave the Orb to the Lord, 'You can have the Orb, but you will always be mine.'

Lord Shakar nodded in agreement as the embodiment

of the Keep vanished. 'Where is Saranon?' Andwyrdan asked.

The question brought Lord Shakar back to reality. 'Saranon,' he yelled.

His voice boomed in the grand chamber but no answer came.

***

She heard their voices from above and did not answer. It had taken all her strength to stay out of the fight with the Razen sorceress. Deandra was gone. The Keep had asked her not to intervene. All she wanted to do was block the memory of the screams from her ears. She waited for Validain to settle. Then she disentangled herself from the flow of stallic energy. Letting go was much harder than she realised. The exhaustion hit as she floated in the void. She had given all she could to take back the Orb of Garduend. Her muscles pounded with the lasting pain. She made it to the ledge forming the opening to a tunnel.

She gasped as the air filled her lungs and cradled her head against the wall. Down far below, the Keep had destroyed the last remnants of Deandra. Part of her wanted to be normal, yet then the Keep would not have stood a chance and that frightened her even more. Validain hummed away in the silence content with the outcome. Saranon glanced toward the sealed tunnel. She murmured under her breath, 'The least you could do is open it.'

The Keep seemed amused by the request.

It was all the warning she had before Validain opened the sealed tunnel. The blasts from the Razen sorcerers

800

rushed in. She blocked and answered them with a thunderous catapult of energy, that whirled around as it swept the length of the tunnel. The Angeon rose to the surface as the pain faded. She ran after the few Razen, who were brave enough to remain in the Keep. The blasts flew along the walls. Cascading through the air with thousands of sparks as the sorcery clashed up ahead. She did not hesitate as she ran through to the open sky raising her arms in an open embrace. The night air met her in a cool stance as the Angeon slipped away.

Pennie greeted her, 'You always did make an exit.'

Saranon turned with great reluctance to face Validain, 'I have to go back.'

They stood in silence before Pennie asked, 'Will you stay.'

'No,' she exclaimed and her friend laughed.

'Where is the Orb?' Pennie asked.

'Lord Shakar has it,' she was doubtful, but the Keep was certain the Lord would look after it.

Pennie left her comment unsaid, as they walked toward the Keep.

The sky lit up with the fires still raging around the rim, yet the walls held strong. Commander Iona came out to greet them, her garrison close by. 'Lord Shakar is looking for you,' the Commander said.

The lights from the energy of the Keep glowed fierce. They revealed the signs of the attack along the walls and the internal courtyard. The Vandragamond appeared at ease with the last remnants of their opponents almost gone.

Pennie stayed close as the sorcerer clan stared at them.

The grey sky waned before the sun rose over the hillside giving the first hint of dawn. The doors of the great hall were wide open as shouts rang out through the air. Lord Shakar chose not to notice her. She approached the main table in the centre of the hall. A sense of disarray and exhaustion hung over the atmosphere in the great hall. The sorcerer clan re-grouped after a long night. Edred the administrator stood. The only one who gave a sense of calm as his heavy brow revealed the toll of losing a son. The Orb of Garduend rolled on the thick wooden table and she stopped it with her hand.

'We need to talk,' Saranon stared at the Lord who had drowned his sorrows in a bottle of wine.

'You are too late,' the Lord replied with a broad smile, 'the war is won.'

An exhausted round of cheers went up through the crowd gathered in the great hall. All eyes were on her. 'You were too late,' Saranon spoke the words with a sense of finality. 'You let Garduend fall and I helped you destroy Deandra.'

Lord Shakar stood and the crowd went silent, he moved toward the Orb and she held it out of reach. 'The new Keep Angore goes to the Asdenard,' she spoke.

Before the Lord could answer Edred did, 'You have an agreement.'

The Lord glared at Edred, 'You…'

'You can have the Orb,' Saranon interrupted.

'Validain gave it to me,' Lord Shakar stated.

'Yes we did,' she replied. 'We both did. I took control of Validain, perhaps next time you won't be so careless.'

'That is not possible,' Lord Shakar spoke in an even tone.

'I am the Angeon,' she said taking a deep breath. 'I have the power to make or break the world, and I took control of your Keep.'

The Lord's face changed with an expression of anguish. 'You were there when I killed Deandra,' he said.

Saranon wanted to scream out, but she had made an agreement with Validain. The cost of retrieving the Orb had been to watch Deandra die. She avoided his unspoken question, 'The Orb stays with you. Angore goes to the Asdenard.'

Lord Shakar looked into the Orb perplexed by the choice before him. Losing a new Keep was difficult to fathom. 'You drive a hard bargain the Asdenard may have the Keep,' he said.

'But…' Andwyrdan began.

'Silence,' the Lord shouted in disgust. 'A wizard Keep is for the weak.'

Lord Shakar became pensive and was almost about to say something. He changed his mind at the last moment. 'I will place it near the other one,' he said.

Saranon asked, 'Pardon?'

'You are not the first to make a large Orb,' he replied.

He strode through the enormous doors of the great hall and into the waiting crowd. A cheer rose up as the flames burned near the outer rim of the Keep. Lord Shakar turned to her, 'That is how I will kill you.'

The words sent a chill through her. She froze watching the Lord walk into the gathering crowd. The thankless sun rose over the new day. Showing the marks spread across the fine pearl building. It stood strong with minimal damage below the surface, as though mocking the Razen. The Vandragamond paid no attention to the burning flames, that shot up around the perimeter. The sun shone bright as it rose in the morning sky warming the air.

Saranon glanced up and the wings of Katholomu spread across the light. The beast cast a shadow deep along the walls of the Keep. The great marmoz dragon let out a stomach curdling roar that bounced off the walls. She walked toward him and he lowered his head. She wanted to cry, she wanted to let all the pain out, but it stayed inside. She patted the dragon's head and he rubbed his chin against her. Deandra's screams still filled her ears, she wanted to cry and could not. The memory lay like an open wound on her mind. Mitch climbed up on the great beast. He held out his hand, 'I think it's time you told the Asdenard they have a new Keep.'

'How often do you read my mind?' She asked.

He laughed, 'You confronted Lord Shakar I didn't need to.'

Katholomu took to the sky in the full light of day casting a shadow deep on the ground. The breeze caught her hair and she smiled, the dragon knew how to ease her mind. Kaythar Keep shone with a brilliant glow in the sun. The large fortress had a soft edge that blended into the background. The dragon swooped low before gliding into the courtyard. The Keep was calm with no sign of the previous events. Ben Waterworth ran to greet them the wizard appeared out of place so far into Darkonia.

'I should warn you, the Asdenard are not impressed about losing the Orb,' Ben said. 'They had the opportunity to take care of it,' her voice held a bitter edge.

She was not about to argue with the Darkonian wizards over the Orb of Garduend. Captain Edevon strode toward them, his face an image of stone. She prepared herself but before he could speak Captain Daina did. 'Welcome back to Kaythar. You cannot stay long. The Arthrose know you are here,' the Captain continued. 'I'm not sure how that happened.'

Captain Daina glared at Captain Edevon as she spoke.

'The Orb of Garduend is with Lord Shakar. In return he has agreed for the new Keep Angore to go to the Asdenard,' Saranon said.

'The Lord does not enter into agreements,' Captain Daina spoke.

'This time he did,' she replied.

Bells rang out around the Keep breaking the silence. She found herself at the centre of a growing crowd. The official word had been given from the Vandragamond. The new Keep Angore belonged to the Asdenard.

In among the cheers she collapsed with exhaustion, Mitch held onto her as she fell. 'Mitch,' she whispered and he took her through the crowd into the Keep. 'I thought the Angeon was not supposed to sleep,' he spoke.

The joke was lost on her as she tried to stay awake. It did not take long to make her way to a warm cosy bed. She could just keep her eyes open long enough to settle as sleep stole her away. As she rested the Angeon crept into her dreams towering over her thoughts. The inner turmoil had taken its toll as she struggled with the Angeon within. It gripped her even still as the energy moved restless. It waited just beneath the surface. The energy dragged her into its depths as she fought against who she was. Validain appeared and in her dream she sank down below the surface. She fell into the heart of the Keep. She was not the first person to arrive. The figure turned and she came face to face with her old friend Tasha.

Tasha's fawn coloured curls flowed down her shoulders. Each time her old friend grew older as though still in the world of the living. She reached out her hand and Tasha stepped back shaking her head, not yet. The Keep disappeared and she was left alone standing on an open plain. A worn path trailing along the ground led to one place. She stepped on the path and Tordoren shuddered. It called, weighing her down as she tried to clear her thoughts. Yet the disturbance remained long after the thought was gone.

A sharp light broke through the slit between the curtains. She ignored it and went back to sleep. She opened her eyes again and sat up. Realising she had slept a full day to the following morning. Faint shouts from the courtyard below and the building shook. Katholomu blocked out the sun as he peered through the window. She shouted at him but he would not leave. Shouting rang out below and she rushed downstairs to the impatient dragon.

CHAPTER NINETEEN

A faded memory

Katholomu bowed his head scooping her up onto his shoulders. He moved before she had time to argue. He leaped into the sky as she wrestled to stay on. She shouted in his ear to no effect as he flew on with a purpose. The great beast refused to take any notice. Kat began a slow decent as he circled before touching the ground. She slid down as he dropped his shoulder to let her off. Saranon took a step back before facing the large marmoz dragon. He lowered his head nudging her with a rugged kindness and the anger she held, ebbed away.

She found it difficult to stay angry with the beast. She patted the dragon with a mingled frustration. The dragon nudged her again and she hugged his thick neck. He nudged her again and she patted his cheek. He nudged her sideways and she took a step back. The small rocks slipped underfoot. Before she could blink she toppled over the unseen edge. Her arms flew up in the air, with only a moment to use her energy to soften her landing. Still the hard ground felt real as she picked herself up glaring up at the stunned dragon. Katholomu did his best imitation of being meek as she shouted at him. His gleaming fangs gave his silent chuckle away.

The ground had given way years before leaving a small hole. It led down into a labyrinth of tunnels on the outskirts of Validain. The grass had covered the sloping earth that led down to where she stood. She strode toward the path when something moved and she froze. The dry air whooshed with a hollow beckoning drone. It called in an uneven tone from the labyrinth. The dragon had a habit of getting her into trouble and this felt no different. She made her way along the old tunnels and a musty smell filtered through. She crept forward to a sealed door. Without thinking, she placed her hand up, and melded through the solid frame.

The acrid stench from inside the room lay thick in the air. She pried around a dismal mess left behind. All the signs told her it had been abandoned by the Razen, yet something was still there. She could feel it on the edges of her senses, when she focused, it slipped away staying out of reach. A small tapping caught her attention and she turned to find nothing. In her haste she knocked a glass tube off the bench and it hit the floor with a shattering jolt. A thin haze shrieked out of the shards as she stumbled back in fright. She caught her breath while the last wisps evaporated in the dank air. Saranon let out a gasp and covered her mouth. She stepped around the remnants lying on the floor, as a chill crept down her spine.

She hesitated, not wanting to admit what she had seen. Her heart thudded in her ears filling the uneven silence. A draft rippled past from beyond the room. She froze in place as the hair on the back of her neck stood on end. She willed herself to move, yet the message only just made it to her limbs. A rising panic gripped her, almost holding her back with a frightening numbness. Saranon counted the seconds in a silent whisper as she opened her eyes. She moved in a fluid motion as she kept the panic at bay.

She steadied herself against the rising sensation, warning her to stay away. Still her heart thudded louder. She held out her hand trying not to tremble and pushed against the door. It was stuck, she should have known. She belted against the door in a rush and it would not budge. The door slid away as she melded through with an uneasiness that would not settle. The floor was slippery underneath, as she made her way forward, staying away from the edge.

The narrow walkway wrapped around the centre leading down into the great void below. She could not sense anyone. Yet the uneasiness still remained as she peered into the murky darkness. She stepped closer and almost slipped grasping the railing in front. A whirling motion caught her eye. Instead of running away the panic vanished in the shock of what lay in the deep. She made her way down standing on the edge of the murky glow.

She was mesmerized by the slow moving whirlpool. Its stream edged off into the darkness leading straight toward Validain.

Saranon took out Tellembre, awakening the bond-breaker into the form of a sword. The heart stone blade shone like steel in the dim light. She held it above her head and the blade shimmered with an internal glow. She pitched it down hard into the dark liquid. It hit the ground below before she had time to cease the plunge. It gave a short acknowledgement before sinking in. She waded in making her way along the tunnel as it lead ever closer to the Keep. It was high enough if she did not stand tall. The draft grew stronger with a stagnant smell, creeping into her lungs.

The tunnel began to widen and she peered straight into a large cavern on the edge of the Keep. At the far end lay the outer wall thick and strong. The barrier stood impenetrable. Yet lapping at its door in great volume, the dark, unstable liquid lurked. She was standing in it. She had to move. She held Tellembre up and its light gave a soft glow. It was enough to make her way across to a narrow set of stairs hidden near the edge of the wall. A sense of relief swept over her as she lifted herself out of the liquid.

She clambered up the slippery steps to a small alcove. She began to meld through the thick outer door and stopped. She glanced back at the liquid below. The volume was too great, enough to break apart the wall of the Keep. She trembled as she put Tellembre away. If she left the unstable liquid, it could be used to break into the Keep.

She could not leave Validain helpless, not after all it had done. The ledge of the small alcove extended back into the open cave. She peered down staring into the silent gloom. She had to make a choice, yet the choice had been made for her. The resentment sank in as the Angeon rose to the surface.

The energy of the Angeon bounced off the walls. The vast space of the cavern revealed itself in the light. Saranon waited for the sorcery to strengthen like a rising tide and held it in. The walls glowed radiating from the sorcery held within. The web of sorcery criss-crossed the room in an uneven maze, that glistened in the light. One spark, just one spark and she held her breath. 'Forgive me Validain,' she spoke into the blinding flame.

The Angeon ignited the web. A thunderous blast rang out and the result was instant. She melded through the sealed door guarding the Keep. 'Forgive me for what I have done,' she whispered into the darkness.

Validain shook and she ran as the liquid trapped in the cavern evaporated. The immense volume managed to shake the building. She kept running not wanting to turn back. The impact resounded through the lower levels of the Keep. Echoing above, as the commotion flooded in. Saranon rushed through not wanting to turn back. She ran until she reached the surface. The midday sun pelted down as a shadow of dust rose up through the air and she this time she turned back. A giant dust cloud rose out of a deep hole in the ground. Arcing its way around the wall where she had stood. The crevasse gaped like an open wound staring up at the sky.

She stood in astonishment as panic rose and she glanced around for Katholomu. She had forgotten about the great dragon. She gazed along the hillside for sign of his presence. Her head sank as she realised what she had done. The dragon did not deserve such a fate even if she was angry with him. The tears welled in her eyes and a booming voice shouted, 'Saranon.'

Andwyrdan charged toward her in a fit of rage. He pushed his way through the crowd, yet she did not move. He ran driven by a steady anger as he came toward her, 'You endangered Validain.'

He hurled his energy toward her with precision. Saranon put her hand up to block at the last moment. Andwyrdan continued as she edged out of his way. The blows were unrelenting, yet she could only block the sorcery. When all she could think of was Katholomu.

She had grown fond of the dragon and now it was too late. All she wanted to do was leave. It showed on her face as Andwyrdan forced her farther away. She moved toward the edge of the courtyard. She had no desire to stay, yet Andwyrdan would not let her go. She moved away from the Keep, and he kept at her with a steady ferocity. Forcing her back and still she would not strike out. They were alone as the crowd stayed well out of the way. Andwyrdan struck out again and again.

She kept her eyes locked on him as she moved backward. Then she trod on something soft, and fell. The world went hazy and for a moment she lost her bearings as she scrambled to refocus. A loud snort rumbled from above. The stench from the dragon's breath wafted past. She shouted with excitement, 'Katholomu.'

The haze lifted and her smile disappeared. Andwyrdan was still standing there waiting for her.

This time she struck, he flew back and stumbled. Saranon did not waste time as she rushed toward him. Andwyrdan shouted at her, but she did not listen. She blasted him as she held her ground. A roar of laughter shot up from the balcony above. Lord Shakar watched on with a small audience and she gaped in astonishment.

Andwyrdan turned his back on her. He rushed into the haven of Validain away from the crowd that had gathered. Saranon was so mixed with emotions it was hard to know what to feel. She smiled up at the great dragon that still wore the dust from his ordeal. Before she had a chance to speak the beast shook his coat. He poured the grimy dust straight over her. Then he rubbed the side of his chin on her shoulder. He gave a loud grunt of satisfaction and jumped over her head. He flew straight up into the clear blue sky spreading his wings to the sun's warm rays.

She had managed to stifle most of the blast, but the crevasse still showed. She made her way back to the Keep. Her limbs ached as she stood, trying not to let her annoyance show. The Vandragamond set to work restoring the Keep. She coughed from the dust and used her sorcery to remove the rest of the grime. Her head continued to rush with the thought of almost loosing Kat. The great beast had shrugged it off far quicker than she. Saranon had no idea how the dragon had survived.

The crevasse ran deep in the earth leaving part of Validain exposed. The Keep could not stay vulnerable for long. Voices travelled along from the open courtyard. She hastened her step trying to avoid Andwyrdan who spotted her. He announced to Lord Shakar that he would mend the damage. Saranon refrained from speaking, while Andwyrdan made a glorious exit. He rode high on the back of Dregora. The great dragon paid no attention as he flew in one fluid motion. The beast headed straight to the edge of Validain and the deep crevasse.

'You shouldn't let him get to you,' Tom Heath spoke beside her.

Saranon jumped. She had been so busy glaring at Andwyrdan that she had not noticed Tom right next to her. His sad eyes still showed the pain from the loss of his brother. He invited her up to the main platform to watch the display. She hoped Andwyrdan would fail in his attempt. The sorcerer's stone shone with a brilliant darkness in the full light of day. She took care making her way around the edge of the raised floor.

The view was spectacular and awful at the same time. She stared down at the full extent of the damage. The crevasse carved deep into Tordoren, Andwyrdan flew toward it on Dregora. She fumed as she recognised the Orb of Garduend. He held the Orb high floating it above the dragon. Saranon gripped the low wall so tight her fingers began turning white. The Orb shone a brilliant pale blue in the clear sky. Andwyrdan's sorcery spun around the outside strengthening the glow. The sight was impressive though she was reluctant to admit it. Calm fell across the land. He directed the sorcery toward the crevasse in a widening arc. The blast flared across the sky hitting hard near the edge of the gaping hole.

Andwyrdan blasted the crevasse again and again. Yet the wall of the Keep remained exposed. The blasts of sorcery became desperate and with a great reluctance he ceased. He flew Dregora straight for the platform. The dragon swooped in at speed causing her to duck out of the way. The talons in the hind legs almost hooked her as the great beast landed. He threw the Orb at her and she caught it, passing it to Tom. Andwyrdan shouted, 'This is your problem, deal with it.'

Tom turned to her, 'Are you going to leave that unanswered?'

Saranon took a moment to realise what he meant. A smile crept across her face as she ran to the centre of the sorcerer's stone. The Angeon flowed in with the void. Taking her high above the platform as the energy surged from deep inside. The circle beneath her shone with a fiery embrace. The energy resonated through the Keep. The central core stirred from deep within. The raw stallic energy flowed up to the surface. The sparks caught the last glimpses of light. It raged across the golden sky with a brilliant white shimmer. It flowed through the sorcerer's stone.

The Angeon absorbed the energy and compounded it. Until it grew into a giant fiery ball above, glowing red hot.

As the last ray of light ebbed across the ground, she severed the connection. The flaming ball stood there in a void of reality. The Angeon hurled the raging sphere toward the open wound. A great roar of thunder shook the Keep as the sphere sank into the damaged ground. Pulling the wound shut as it melted into Tordoren. The shockwave pummelled its way back. Saranon stood strong, shielding the Keep from the blast. The waves rushed overhead in a storm of energy as the sparks flew in every direction.

The Angeon held on with a renewed purpose as the land below healed. She covered the exposed Keep to the world. The last crackles of energy simmered along the shield in a final wave. Then it ebbed away. She floated above the circle for one last moment before the stallic energy disappeared. The Angeon slipped away leaving her drained and she descended onto the sorcerer's stone. The circle once again returned to its brilliant darkness. It lay dormant once more in the shadows of the early night. Tom smiled, 'That was not what I meant, but it will do.'

Saranon took one last glance over the low wall to admire her handy work. It was hard to see, even though she could sense it in the dim light. Music filled the walls inside as she headed down to the great hall where a feast was underway. Ben Waterworth waved her over, he had already made a start. The wizard looked better than he had for days, with no sign of his earlier struggle. As he spoke, 'I guess you'll want to head back to Ardaguar after all this. You're welcome to stay if can you deal with this lot.'

Commander Iona sat at the other side of the table,

'Are you saying you don't like my company?'

'No,' the wizard sighed.

Saranon smiled and took no noticed as she dug in to a hearty feast. She could sense the humming of the Keep in the background, it was content at last. She took a moment to answer Ben, 'I have somewhere else I need to go.'

Ben responded between mouthfuls, 'You will always be welcome.'

As the night grew dark the exhaustion from the day set in. She took one last glance back at the hall filled with song and laughter. The shadows danced across the wall from the glow of the Keep's energy. She made her way to a soft warm bed. The night filled her head with a myriad of dreams, yet one returned over and over again. It called out from a distance with a shimmering white glow. All her dreams turned to a white soft silence. Someone was trying to reach out calling across the void.

Saranon woke with a pounding head as the light crept in. She peered over the sweeping staircase to check on Katholomu. The dragon was stretched out in a relaxed sleep with his belly showing. The warm sun beat down with the last days of summer as she made her way downstairs. The morning was still early and the sounds of life began to trickle through the Keep. She took a deep breath and steadied herself. There was something she had been meaning to do. She had been running away from the inevitable.

The sunlight sparkled glowing across the dry grass. She descended down the steps with a heavy heart. She wanted to run away. It would be easier than facing the truth as she walked along the stone path. There was just one thing that remained, as she felt her breath catch in the morning air. She found him, his name engraved in the stone above. Saranon knelt on the grass peering down at the sewn earth.

She hung her head with the weight of all that had happened. She wondered if it could have been different. It was all she could do to stand and whispered the words. 'Goodbye Jack,' and touched the grave stone one last time.

She walked away as though leaving would somehow make Jack Heath's passing final. She took one last glimpse back as she closed the gate and a figure caught her eye. Standing at the edge of the open field, as she gazed up, stood the silhouette of an elegant sorceress.

The lady removed a scarf from around her shoulders. She uncovered long golden locks that shone in the light. Oriana wore a beautiful pale dress in stark contrast to her dark grimy garments.

'Saranon,' Oriana's soft voice froze her to spot.

'Do I know you?' Saranon asked.

'You are my daughter,' Oriana's eyes welled with tears.

She stood in disbelief, as though moving would make the image disappear. Oriana placed an arm around Saranon for the first time in years. She gazed into the eyes of the mother she hardly knew and stood spellbound by the moment. Not sure if she should look away in case it was a dream. Yet the dream was real enough, as the tears escaped down her face.

CHALLENGING THE FIRES OF CHAOS

THE LEGACY OF ZYANTHIA BOOK FOUR

CHANTELLE GRIFFIN

CHAPTER ONE

Facing the consequences

No matter how much Saranon tried the taste of blood would not leave. It had been days since her half-brother had challenged her. She smiled at the thought of humiliating him. The victory had been sweet even if she had lost her temper. It had been worth every moment. Her mess of brown hair blew across her face in the wind. Somehow it always managed to break free of the tie. She blew it out of the way and the great black dragon crashed onto the deck mid-flight. She jumped clear swinging over the balcony, clinging to the narrow ledge. 'Kat,' she shouted in disgust.

The dragon moved his large frame overhead as he nimbly sat beside her. His deep dark eyes remained level with hers. A flight of dragon riders swept across the edge of the Menna Range. The dragon nudged her and she clambered up before being squashed. He bolted into the air picking up speed and she clung on. He swooped down without slowing and she shouted at him. Instead the dragon sped up skimming dangerously close to the ground. Saranon shouted again, but he would not listen. Kat began to rise skyward and she let go. For a brief moment she was air born. She flung her arms wide catching the breeze. Then fell, sensing the world Tordoren below. Yet she refrained from using sorcery as the wind caught her. A great whoosh reached upward as a bellowing gust of wizardry softened the blow.

She landed on the damp mossy ground and Mitch ran over. His shadow loomed blocking the sun. He towered over her at the ready with every muscle in his neck showing. Mitch glared at her as she brushed off the dirt. 'You were supposed to stay at the Temple.' He said.

It was difficult to take him seriously with those soft brown eyes. The former guard still had a hard edge, but she ignored it. 'It was getting stuffy,' she retorted.

Before he could respond. The great black marmoz dragon thudded into the side of the mountain. Katholomu was at home in Alveron.

She had stolen the dragon more than year ago, when his rider had attacked Odana Temple. The dragon only listened to her when it suited him. He was watching the dragon riders, daring them to fly closer. The Menna Range was home to the Otturin sorcerer clan. They were renowned for training dragons. Odana Temple had once been theirs, before it was abandoned during the Dreshan Occupation. The temple rose above the mountain and ran deep beneath the rocky ground. Mitch stayed by her side. The temple pass was calm and deceptive. The road that let through was one of the most volatile. Travellers would often disappear or be found days later with tales of horrible creatures.

She stared with intrigue. As several figures in the distance made their way from the pass to the Menna Range. One turned looking straight at her. 'You are asking for trouble.' Mitch said and she waved.

Katholomu glared at her as though she had committed an offence. She wondered if he ever thought of returning to the Otturin. The clan that had trained him and attacked Odana Temple. She watched as a dragon rider broke from the flock, skimming close to the pass. Kat tensed, it was the only warning before he heaved his full weight into the side the dragon. Both dragons and the rider tumbled in a haphazard motion to the ground. The great black dragon growled with his back arched. Mitch grabbed her by the shoulder before she could run toward them. A searing pain ran along her sore muscles and she glared at him. The rider was tall and slim. His dark robes were dishevelled, but his manner was cool and calm. He raised his arms to Katholomu. 'Let go.' She said to the wizard, but Mitch held on with a firm grip.

The dragon lifted his full bulk forward and ploughed in the shield of sorcery. The sorcerer flew backward and she began to laugh until the dragon honed in. The Otturin glared at her and lashed out with his sorcery. To her amazement Mitch strode in front of the volatile dragon. He twisted the Otturin's arm in a firm grip. 'You can let go,' she said in an amused tone.

Mitch now held both her and the Otturin with the dragon growling overhead. She recognised the dragon rider, he had flown Kat toward the Temple. 'You!' She shouted and tried to wrestle free. 'That's him,' she said to the wizard.

She managed to shove the Otturin to the ground and Mitch lifted her in the air. They both fell as the Otturin attacked, Mitch clamped him to the dirt. At least she was free. 'Who are you?' She asked.

The dragon answered, 'Kail.'

Saranon tried to hide her surprise, 'He only says one word, 'Coward'. Is that what your name means?'

She pranced around as Mitch strained to keep Kail from lashing out. 'You hurt my friends.' She said.

The dragon placed the weight of his paw down on the Otturin and Mitch made a hasty retreat. 'I don't like people that hurt my friends.' She said.

The dragon began to move and crush his prey. 'He belongs to me.' Kail sputtered.

'I think Katholomu is done listening.' She responded.

'The clan is coming,' Mitch said. 'You have done enough.'

She pretended to ignore him as the Otturin sorcerers approached from the Menna Range. 'You owe Kat an apology.' She waited for Kail to speak.

He was still trying to wriggle free, but the dragon had him pinned. He reached out with his sorcery and pulled her toward him. The dragon fell back in surprise. The

Otturin clan had reached them and Kail followed with the utmost obedience. The great dragon stood by her side. It was the first time he had ever adhered to her command. She wondered how long it would last. The beast looked down at her with a piercing cold gaze. At least they had one thing in common, they both disliked Kail.

The frustration played in her mind as she followed Mitch. The silence only broke when they reached the temple. The solid formation of the monumental structure provided its own climate. With the warmth of the central core emanating from beneath. She should have dealt with the sorcerer while she had the chance. Saranon glared at Mitch. His face was cold and unforgiving. The expression told her the matter was done, but it only enraged her. 'I had him,' she seethed.

The wizard stood firm, 'You were meant to stay here.'

His words opened a verbal tirade as she shouted at him. 'I had that pathetic weasel, if it wasn't for you...'

His expression changed and she turned to see a crowd watching. Shaun approached them. His broad shoulders and stocky build looked out of place among the guards. He eyed Mitch with a keen interest, 'Did you run into trouble?'

'Kail,' she said. 'The sorcerer went for my dragon.'

'Is that all?' He asked.

She almost exploded in anger, 'Do you care nothing for what they did?'

'The matter is settled,' he said.

The calm air shown by the wizards was infuriating as

she struggled to contain her rage. 'How can you…' She shouted and stormed off letting the thought trail.

Her mind was a blur and she was getting nowhere. She was expected to forget that the Otturin attacked the temple. It did not sit easy on her mind.

The breeze was cool and she closed her eyes, leaning back against the wall. The image replayed in her head. Shaun had been focused on Mitch, but why? Then it dawned on her, the wizard was her hilazen. She never did understand the strange rules that wizards bestowed on their own. She peered around the corner to find Mitch. His expression was caught between wanting to say something, then he let it be. 'It would be best if you forgot Kail.' He said.

She could feel the firm gaze of his stare and the coldness that ran underneath. It was not the first time they had argued, but he always remained calm. The irritation plagued her. As she swung from the balustrade sliding down the narrow staircase. There were many ways to find the dragon pens. An angry dragon required an easy escape route, yet that did not bother her. At Odana the pens opened to the morning sun, capturing the warmth of the day. Noise scattered through the large open arches holding up the mountainous keep. Clara ran up to greet her and they almost collided. Her face as red as her bright fiery hair. 'Kat,' she said in a huff, trying to catch her breath.

The commotion reached her as she glanced across the broken stalls. Two young dragons were cowering in the corner and a voice boomed orders. She dashed through the maze of people clearing up the mess. There was no sign of

Katholomu. 'He's gone to the Menna Range.' Clara said.

'How do you know?' The sight of the great beast in the distant sky answered her question.

Her heart sank. 'If father finds out we're in trouble,' Clara spoke.

'Quick,' she said scrambling onto the nearest dragon.

Holdvar would not budge without his wizard. Where was Mitch? She tried again and the great beast's muscles held like stone. She had no luck with dragons and they were losing time.

She scurried down into the heart of the Keep. The wizard had to be somewhere. She ran ahead through the winding corridors careful not to knock anyone over. The tight corners made it almost impossible. She caught someone's shoulder and spun around as Anthony held her. The last time she had seen him, it had been when she stomped on him. Anthony wore the uniform of a Alveronian soldier, but he was not much older than she. His rugged tone softened as he let go. 'Where are you headed?' He asked in steady tone.

'I lost my wizard,' she said.

'Really?' He exclaimed.

'Really,' she retorted before running off.

Sometimes wizards could be no help. Before she was able to ask again he had left. Was it so hard to find Mitch? He had warned her not to go near the Otturin, but that did not apply to the dragon. She extended her sorcery through the Keep in the hope of finding him. The only noise that returned was the low dull hum of the central core below.

She rushed down the stairs, the thick round columns ebbed out from the solid walls. Not many people ventured underneath the habitable area. It was said the spirits of the people trapped during the Dreshan Occupation still remained. Silent whispers filled the void. She could sense movement, but the sound failed to filter through the air. Saranon ran into the opening between the columns. A group of wizards huddled round. Shaun, the gruff old man had his back turned to her. He turned to face her and she caught sight of Mitch. He was huddled near the floor. It took all her strength to hold back her sorcery and not send Shaun flying across the room. 'That's my wizard,' she shouted into the silence. 'My wizard.'

She stood her ground facing the one who blocked her path. It was all she could do to stay calm. All she wanted to do was rush forward and take Mitch with her. Yet there was a shield of wizardry holding her back.

She fought her way through, yet the shield held tight. 'Let him go,' she was losing patience.

The shield began to weaken and she took a chance. Saranon plunged in, shoving the wizard to the side. A searing pain wrapped around her when she gripped Mitch, but refused to let go. He returned her hold. They ran toward the stairs before she gathered her thoughts. Shouts echoed spiralling upward. The stench from the dragon pens hit them. Mitch leaped onto Holdvar and the dragon lunged forward with a sprint. Pounding his paws hard against the ground. She clung tight as the great beast swayed, his whole body flying into the sky. The air rushed in a wild motion as she gripped close to stay on. A steady beat of the wings gave a calm rhythm. She gazed ahead to the Menna Range, looming ever closer along the horizon.

'I thought you wanted to avoid the Otturin,' she said.

'I asked you to avoid them,' he replied.

She was unsure how this was any different, but kept the thought silent. They swept above the open pass and onto the rising mountains. The air grew thin as every breath made her head feel light. Mitch drove the beast down into a gliding circle as an explosion arced through the air. No one noticed as they landed. The few Otturin were scattered around the raging inferno. Engulfing a building that had once contained dragons. The former occupants gathered among the valley providing an ideal coverage.

Saranon stayed beside a flock of juvenile dragons while gazing across the darkening sky. The blaze lit up the night with an ominous crackle and she turned. Kail stood so close and the anger she felt earlier diminished. His eyes were haunting in the uneven light. While his face showed nothing but exhaustion. Without thinking she gripped his hand, a small welcome gesture. Smoke gathered from the dying blaze sweeping overhead. A great rush of air broke as Katholomu swooped low. She began to shout at the beast and Kail laughed. Another dragon swooped down from the sky, it was identical. She glared at the sorcerer and he only smiled. 'Katholomu,' she shouted.

Both dragons responded. 'Is this some sort of trick?' She asked.

'I swear there is no trick,' Kail replied.

The smirk stayed on his face far too long, 'You can take Kat if you know which one.'

She glared at him and the smirk turned into an open laugh. 'All right, one is Kat's brother.'

'Really?' She asked in amazement and he nodded. 'I should be able to tell them apart.'

'Yes, you should,' he lingered on the final word to her annoyance.

'Do you enjoy being irritating?' She asked.

He snorted with laughter, 'Only to you.'

The dragons began to stir, they both eyed her. There was a glint of amusement as they synchronised their movement. A breeze swept through and she saw the scarring across the other dragon's shoulder. She stifled a gasp, ' What happened?'

'Gormeron survived the Dreshans,'he replied.

The great beast lowered his head and nuzzled her. The tension left his muscles as he sank to the ground. Kat remained close, not wanting to leave his brother. 'You had better come inside,' Kail spoke with a great reluctance.

It was the most affection he had shown and Saranon treated it with suspicion. The charred walls stood well, but the contents had been obliterated. This did not worry the dragons who curled up on the remnants. No one was surprised that a fire had taken hold in the dragon pens. 'You have no idea how to look after Katholomu,' he said.

The cold remark hit home and she glared at him. 'You bite so easy,' he added.

'So do you,' she retorted and he smiled.

'Kat stays with me,' she said.

'Then why don't you take him,' he taunted.

Saranon gazed out into the night, the dragon was going nowhere. 'He's sleeping,' she replied.

Kail burst out laughing, tears rolling down his cheeks. She began to feel her face go red. 'You can stay here until Kat wakes,' he said.

She managed to hold back her anger. Long enough for Mitch to interrupt, 'We accept your gracious hospitality.'

She glared at him, it was going to be a long night. The air carried with it the many rumbles and growls from the hoards of dragons. A thud shook the building. She shouted at Katholomu before realising where they were. Kail gave her a disapproving glance. Before Gormeron hit the building with a resounding thud. She peered over the balcony as both stared back, daring her to say something. 'Did you teach them to do that?' She asked Kail.

'No,' he replied in a sullen tone.

'How did you end up with that?' She pointed at Kat.

'I am a first grade rider,' he answered.

'I was not questioning your ability,' she mused, eyeing him up and down. 'I meant the dragon.'

He let out a sigh of frustration. No answer was forthcoming, but his shoulders relaxed. The dragons slept below and the hour was getting late. Smoke lingered in the air. It was a small reprieve as the occupants were busy settling the dragons.

As she prepared for the night Mitch leaned over. 'I'll take the first watch,' he said.

Saranon was about to protest, but the wizard had been through much. There remained an uneasy feeling from being so close to the Otturin. 'Stay out of trouble,' she replied.

His composure relaxed but he kept an eye on her. Her dreams were filled with dragons, so many of them. Mitch woke her and it was still dark. She peered out to see the moonlight and movement caught her eye. Dragons and their riders filled the sky. There had been a time when she would have given anything to be the one flying on a majestic beast. Saranon gazed, longing to be in the sky rather than stuck on the ground.

The sleeping wizard was the only reason why she fought the urge to climb out the window. That and the fact that she had lost sight of Katholomu. The morning light burst across the mountain range filling the room with warmth. She almost tripped over the wizard who was still half asleep and ran downstairs. Gormeron greeted her. The dragon's scars stretched across the surface of his thick skin. His head lowered and she could not resist the temptation. Shouts rang out as they took to the sky. A sense of exhilaration came over her and she ignored the protests. Gormeron had a graceful peace hidden underneath the rough surface. His movement turned into one fluid motion as he raced for the sky.

The fine shrill of air rushed past the dragon's wings, chilling her face as they went. The elegant beast spiralled before descending to the ground. Her head spun with excitement and she waited as the beast lowered his shoulders.

Katholomu greeted her, his tail curled in a relaxed pose. As Saranon slid away a silence fell. She stood between the two great dragons. Kat moved first, bowing his head in recognition. She reached out and the dragon stepped away. He eyed her, daring her to come closer. 'Would you rather stay here?' She asked.

The giant beast purred and she glared at him. Kail grinned with satisfaction savouring the moment. Mitch patted her on the shoulder, 'We need to go.'

There was a finality in his voice that made her hesitate. The Otturin went about their day as though she and Mitch did not exist. The familiar warm glow of the lay-line enveloped them. She took the lead through the shortcut. The silence surrounding her compounded by the absence of her dragon. Odana Temple loomed up ahead. The thought of having to explain Kat's absence weighed on her mind. She hesitated as her stomach churned and glared at Mitch. His pace never faltered and she ran to catch up. 'Did you plan that?' She asked.

A silence hung in the air before he answered. 'Do you want bloodshed?'

'You let them take Kat,' she said.

He stopped, 'No one takes a full grown marmoz. He chose to leave.'

His stare cut through her and she wondered if he would leave to. Once, she would have done anything to be on her own. Once, she had shed blood to be free. Perhaps later she would find a reason to return. The temple boundary walls clung to the earth. With faint remnants from a distant past. She wanted to be mad at the wizard, but Mitch had stayed by her side through more than she cared to admit. The morning sun warmed the stone floor as it gleamed in the strong light. Clara swept down the spiral stairs, 'Are you ready?'

Her eyes lit up with excitement, 'Took long enough.'

Saranon did not want to say she had lost the dragon. She hoped no one would notice. As she stuffed her belongings into the large sova bags, shrinking them down. She would have to sort out all the trinkets, but that could wait. The sloping valley hid the narrow treacherous path to the Pearl Castle. She took one last glimpse of the artefact. Before Clara wrapped the remnant of an elaborate hilt away from prying eyes. The bond-breaker had belonged to Zeralden Hadenvar, Queen of Darkania and the last Angeon. The sphere of heart stone at the centre had not a scratch. It still held a faint glow from the sorcery trapped within.

CHAPTER TWO

A risk worth taking

A matted dark hide rolled down toward Saranon at a steady pace. As the dragon took full advantage of the dry dirt, rubbing it well into his coat. She managed to leap over onto his giant belly as Katholomu halted in mid-motion. Turning his head to look her square in the eye. She stumbled while trying to stand. The great beast let out a warm snort of smelly sulphur. As she managed to cover her mouth in time.

'Kat!' Saranon shouted in disgust.

The dragon could be annoying at times. It was a relief to see the great beast that had snubbed her earlier, even if he was unhelpful. When she closed her eyes she could still see Kail glaring at her. Her friend Clara laughed in delight. As Kat gently moved her out of the way and kept on rolling down the hill. She had met Clara the on the first visit to

Odana Temple. It had been too long, it felt wonderful to relax in the moment. She watched as the dragon pretended to make chase. The deep red hair of the sorceress, Clara, trailed past tickling Kat's nose. He sneezed and slumped to the ground. Saranon could feel her face grow hot as he managed to flatten several trees in the process. The dragon merrily used his tail to squash down a patch of shrubs before curling up to rest. It felt good to have Mitch around, the wizard towered over her in comparison. As she stood on her toes and frowned. He smiled and said nothing which made her even more suspicious. As the sun set the cool breeze of autumn followed with a distant reminder of the days to come. Saranon made herself at home by the open fire as a scurry sent a spray of dirt overhead

She looked up and the dragon loomed over her. Katholomu's eyes shone with a purpose as he sniffed the open air. Before she could blink. The great beast leapt over their small campsite and into the shadows of dusk. Filling the sky with the last of the sun's golden rays. If anything she was glad he was gone, the dragon had been fidgeting all day. Clara filled the void with talk of the next step of their journey toward the army barracks. As the sounds of the distant wildlife echoed in the background. Saranon fell into a peaceful sleep. Finally the troubles of Darkonia were beginning to fade from her mind. They were all too real, but for now she could pretend they did not exist. Once again away from her homeland. A place that she longed for and loathed at the same time.

A tiny brush near the edge of her sleeping bag brought

her awake as the dawn crept in. The dull black outer shell of the giant millipede. Crawling unhindered as she watched in amazement. Its body seemed to be never ending. She crouched forward taking care as she picked it up. The creature appeared unafraid as she held it out of curiosity. She took it over to Clara. As the creature caught her friend's attention and screamed. It was then that Saranon realised it was not the greatest idea to pick up the creature and let it go.

Mitch stared at her in disbelief, 'That's a malicor.'

She tried to apologise to Clara who begrudgingly let the matter go. As they set out on their journey toward the Pearl Castle. The day shone bright as they made their way up the rugged hillside. This was as far as she had seen on the last visit. Odana Temple had magnificent sweeping views of the land. Travelling was exciting and rewarding at the same time. Her friend was intent on their mission. Saranon sighed and followed. Somehow she had been conned into helping. Yet the truth was she did not need much convincing.

Facing the wrath of the Darkonian Army again was less appealing than making the journey to the Mercidian Council. She wanted to say something, but all she caught sight of was a mass of fiery red hair. Clara shook her head, 'You had to pick it up.'

She apologised again and this time her friend relaxed. Saranon breathed a sigh of relief. She was so used to Clara talking that the silence was unbearable.

Before long her friend's voice filled the air with the

history of the great tomb of the old King. She stared ahead to where her friend was pointing. All she could see was the same dry brown grass and rocky ground. Still she did not want to dampen her friend's enthusiasm. Making a sound that resembled excitement. Mitch chuckled, then held back to join them. The wizard took great delight in joining the conversation.

She glared at him hoping he would change the subject, but the wizard was having none of it. Mitch extended out his wizardry as she watched in amazement. The images outside of the tomb glowed faintly through the ground. She glared at him in annoyance as the wizard showed off. The group walked on and Saranon stayed behind to watch the image fade. There was so much of the world she longed to know. She tried to imitate the wizard as her sorcery rose to the surface, yet it was too much. She grimaced as it scorched the edge of the grass.

Clara was moving way ahead and Mitch kept glancing over his shoulder. She let out a heavy sigh and she ran to catch up. She was not about to be left behind. As they cleared the edge of the ridge the trail led down. A whooshing noise caught her attention overhead. She gazed up at the shadowy underbelly of a marmoz dragon. The great beast flew without a care for the travellers below. They were nearing the edge of the great dragon colony at the centre of Alveron. Still, it did not make her feel any easier as several more dragons flew in the distance. Yet again she was being left behind. She rushed ahead and tripped, using her energy to block the fall. She bent down and wiped her tunic. Then as she moved forward the ground gave way underneath. It was all she could do to hang on as the earth slipped beneath her. She reached out with her senses, yet she could not hang on. As she fell further away from the distant light above. She screamed. All that came back in the darkness was a scattering of meaningless noise. She tried to focus using her energy to soften the blow. As the rugged floor of an old tunnel revealed itself. She continued to hold onto her energy lighting a path in the dark.

As she peered up, all sign of the outside world was lost. A scurrying sound ran behind her along the wall. Yet she could see nothing as she made her way through the tunnel. The ceiling had broken in patches worn with age as she made her way along. A scurrying noise caught her ear and she turned. The light reflecting back off the tunnel showed nothing. Saranon moved further down the passage searching for a way out. If there was one she could not see it. It was as though Tordoren had closed up trapping her in. She reached for her talik, but the small circular device was useless as she opened it. She was too far away from a Keep for it to work and she let out a sigh.

The grime coated the walls so heavily that it was hard to tell what lay underneath. She wiped away a small patch and extended her senses along the tunnel. She jumped as a faint signal returned like a tiny hum in the distance. It was not what she had expected as she strode toward the source. She moved out into the room and a faint sensation sent shivers up her spine. As something brushed against her arm. She peered in the darkness and held the light above her. Only the shadows playing tricks on her spun to life as she glanced around. The hairs on the back of her neck stood on edge. As the air grew cold and her heart thudded in her ears.

She froze as a soft breath filtered down the back of her neck. She swallowed, taking a deep breath and turned around. The giant creature that loomed in the dark, caught her attention with its piercing yellow eyes. The ockren stood still as its face drew back into a snarl. Before the she had time to leap out of the way a hollow growl rumbled through its belly. The giant magical cat that stood higher than she, leaped forward. She let out a soundless scream before her voice caught up. She blocked the creature, but all it did was slow it down. As she ran, hurtling through the nearest tunnel.

Somehow the creature managed to squeeze through. As it pounded the ground behind her with a speed that made the panic rise in her chest. She ducked through another tunnel, losing track of where she was going. As the ockren rounded the corner kicking the dust up in the air. The ground shook and it growled as the sound echoed around her in the tight space. Saranon summoned her energy as she tried to hold. Yet her mind could not focus. The attempt appeared feeble as the ockren gained speed. She headed further down as the trail tapered off. Skidding to stop before the edge of a giant void.

She peered down into a great hole in the ground swallowed by the darkness and gulped. Behind her the creature ran and her heart thudded hard as she tried to think. She peered up to the worn edges of the old wall poking out. Without a second thought she grasped the rough edge and heaved herself up out of the way. She clung above the opening trying not to use her sorcery. As the only form of light went out. It was pitch dark, yet she could sense the creature below and clung on. Sweat poured down her brow and she hoped the magical creature could not sense her. The ockren sniffed as it waited below in the darkness. She tried not to make a sound.

Saranon clung on hoping the creature could not sense her. As she held on hoping to stay hidden. The panic welled up inside her as she managed to keep her mind clear. Below she could sense the creature turning away. Then a thought filled her mind. How was she going to get out? While trying to remain calm she moved her hand down grasping the rock as her leg slipped. It was enough to send to send a clump of loose rubble rattling down the wall. Saranon cringed and held on hoping it would not attract the ockren. Yet at the same time a rush of air ran across her back. She flinched as her energy lit up the space.

She was caught in the beast's great paw as it yanked her away from the wall. She scrambled to hold on using her energy, but it was no use. As the ockren flung her into the abyss. She screamed as the realisation hit and she was sent into the air. The panic rose up through her stomach as her mind raced. Before she could think, her sorcery surged within. She used the energy to slow her descent. Until she found herself floating in midair. Her heart thudded in her chest as she managed to right herself from an awkward angle. As she stared upward a faint hint of daylight glimmered taunting her from above.

A deep low growl rang out. It echoed around her and without any hesitation she hauled herself upward. She hoped that it would be enough. As she strengthened the flow of energy while steadily rising. The glow became larger as she headed upward and out of the old tomb. As she reached the narrowest part. The strength of her energy threw her out with such speed that it took her a moment to hold back. She spun into the air before slowing near the dry brown earth. As the sun's rays beckoned in the distance. For a moment she saw no one as she searched around. Then a voice called from behind the clearing. 'We're over here,' Mitch said.

Her shoulders slumped with the reassurance of the wizard's voice. She found them waiting near the edge of the lay-line. 'Where have been?' Clara scowled in frustration.

Saranon tried to catch her breath. Before she could talk her friend had already entered the lay-line. Mitch reached over patting her on the shoulder as he urged her on. A frown crossed his face as he stared at her, 'We'll talk later.'

She was not about to argue. Her mind was still racing and she could not wait to get as far away from the tomb as possible.

The faint glow of the lay-line lit up in a circular fashion as they entered. A wave of relief spread over her as they made up time toward the barracks. Mitch eyed her occasionally with a look that said he wanted to say something. She was in no mood to talk as the image of the ockren stayed fresh in her mind. The travel did well to clear her head as she settled into her usual grumpy self. Almost stubbing her toe more than once on hidden rocks in the long dry grass. After a while she realised it was easier to let Mitch go first and he chuckled. She gave out a long sigh.

Her journey moved quickly as she stopped for a moment. Gazing down at a scattering of old carvings hidden in the long grass. She held the broken stone in her hand before taking care as she placed it back. They were near the end of the lay-line. She turned to find the others had gone ahead. She could make out Mitch near the opening. His hands were held high above his head and Saranon realised he was in trouble. As the faint sound of voices trickled her way. She held out her energy to the side of the lay-lines. It sparked before forming a hole and ran though. Her legs misjudged the ground as they crumpled beneath her. Panic began to rise as she lost sight of the wizard, then her senses indicated where he was.

He was some way off in the distance. As she found herself behind the wiccan who had cornered her friends. Her mind raced as she hoped Clara would provide an indication. Saranon felt lost without her friend. Clara would know what to do, but then her friend was the one who needed help. She tried to think as she listened to the voices. A rustle sounded close. As her heart sank at the realisation, she had been discovered. The wiccan cornered her in semi-circle as she froze, not knowing what to do. For all Clara's conversations she had not mentioned wiccan. A young man's voice shouted above the crowd, 'This is the one.'

She gaped in surprise as Oswin held out his hand in a welcoming gesture. Without knowing what else to do, she exchanged the greeting. He smiled, 'Jedd said we might see you.'

Saranon had completely forgotten her first encounter with wiccan community in Normisia. That did not explain how someone in the heart of Alveron knew. Her bewilderment was written all over her face as the strange misunderstanding melted away. Before she could ask, Clara whispered in her ear, 'Just go with it.'

She was not about to argue as their new friends led them to their town through the clearing. The place was sheltered and well protected with wards, yet the wiccan appeared nervous. As she remembered how unusual was for a sorceress to visit Bellington Castle. For a moment she forgot all about being a sorceress. As the small town reminded her of the castle in Normisia. Juren was less grand, but it was well-kept and full of life. She smiled breathing in the smell of fresh bread. Her stomach rumbled, a reminder it was lunchtime. As they sat down to eat the sorceress was too content to worry over the initial hostility.

She scoffed several mouthfuls before noticing Clara's calm gaze. She looked at Oswin, 'How do you know Jedd?'

It was a question she should have asked sooner, yet the thought had not crossed her mind. Oswin explained about the trade route between Alveron and Normisia. She listened while finishing the meal. The wiccan gazed intently.

As though there was something he wanted to say, 'You have been in the tomb.'

Clara gasped in astonishment as Saranon wondered what the fuss was about. She was still unsure as to how she had fallen in.

She began going red with embarrassment and spoke of the ockren chasing her. Clara's expression only made her feel worse. Oswin politely interrupted, 'The ward's have been giving unusual readings.'

He did not say any more, but then he did not need to. It was the first time Saranon had been chased by an ockren. She had the distinct feeling the creature had been grumpy. Well before she had fallen into its home. As the afternoon sun lowered over the hillside. She followed Oswin as he showed them around. Pointing out the wards on the outskirts. It had been over a year since she had taken a close look at the type of wards that circled the township. She place her hand on the stone and it tingled. She had spent half her life getting to know the wards from the camps. This one was similar as it shone with a faint glow.

The air above moved with a mild hum. She watched with a steady silence, as though waiting for something to happen. Clara had grown bored of the exercise as she began to talk away. Suggesting they move on when a fine wisp of magic broke in the air just above the ward. Her friend stopped mid-sentence as they gazed on. Yet whatever it was had fallen silent. She moved her hand just above the stone. It was as though nothing unusual had happened, even though they had all seen it. Mitch waited for the group to ponder in amazement before he added, 'It's sorcery.'

'Don't be silly,' Clara said, unsure of herself.

'I've seen it before,' Mitch replied.

Saranon looked at the expression on his face. She could not read his thoughts, but the seriousness of his tone made her cautious. As she stepped away from the ward. She was not sure if she wanted to know what was causing it. The hour was growing late as they welcomed the invitation to stay at the tavern. That looked almost exactly like the one she had stayed at in Normisia. She unpacked her belongings and Mitch sat down next to her, 'We have a problem.'

'What do you mean?' She asked.

'The ward,' the wizard spoke.

She sighed with resignation. That she was not going to get much sleep tonight, 'I'll take a look.'

There was no point arguing with the wizard. Since Jedd was friends with Oswin she felt obligated to at least do one check. The wizard offered to wake her later so she could get some sleep. Even though her mind was racing, she drifted off.

A hand waved in front startling her as the faint glow of light shimmered in the distance. Mitch looked on expectantly as he waited. She had not planned for the wizard to join her, yet she was not about to argue. As they crept downstairs trying not to make a sound she closed the door behind her. The place was even more beautiful at night. As the faint glow of lights sparkled throughout the buildings. Mitch stood behind her ready for action.

She could sense his irritation as they made their way out beyond the wards. They cleared the boundary as she peered back and froze. A faint green vapour emanated from the ground on the outskirts of the wards.

'Wow,' she spoke in complete surprise. As a horrible tingling sensation shivered down her spine. 'What is it?'

'I was going to ask you,' Mitch said as he stood beside her.

The two stayed there not knowing what to do as they watched and waited in the dark. She had not seen anything like it and wondered if had anything to do with the ockren.

CHAPTER THREE

The ancient sword

The lay-line led to the barracks. The last part of their journey before Saranon could ride a dragon again. The land was Katholomu's home. The dragon had hardly paid her attention since they arrived. A great roar loomed overhead as they peered up to the sky. A group of marmoz dragons flew in formation. She could sense no riders. As they made their way across without any fear of being seen in the light.

She stayed close to the wizard this time and he grinned. Mitch was amused by her acceptance of him. Clara had been unnerved to learn that Saranon had bonded a wizard as her companion. Her friend maintained a respectful distance. As the scenery changed from dry brown to patches of green. Along the edge of the forest the sounds of the creatures that lived there reached her ears. Before she knew it, the first sight of the barracks was revealed up ahead. She stopped in awe as the great building loomed out of the hillside.

The clearing led to a well-worn path and without thinking she walked towards it. A booming voice towered over her as a wizard stood close and jumped out of the way in surprise. She remembered to breathe as Gannon stood in her way. The wizard was accompanied by a small group.

Mitch spoke up behind her, 'She's with me.'

Gannon nodded and stepped aside to let them pass. A hub of life emerged as they drew near the barracks. Adeyorn revealed itself to be a full fledged wizard keep and she laughed. It did not matter where she travelled she always managed to end up at a wizard keep.

Saranon had not ridden a dragon for days, but it felt like ages as her eyes lit up with excitement. She was looking forward to the ride. Mitch placed a hand on her shoulder, 'The Shalough live near the colony.'

Her excitement caught in her throat as the words sank in. The Shalough could have helped her train and chose not to. Her mood dampened, yet she was determined to ride. She longed for the open sky and the wind in her hair. It would be nice to ride again after travelling from Odana Temple on foot.

She could smell the dragons before she saw them even though they were clean. Their hides glistened in the afternoon light. She reached out her senses to the one closest. As the great beast lowered its head and rubbed a cheek along her side in recognition. A great roar thundered from behind as she turned her head. In time to witness

Katholomu puffing out his chest in a grand stance. 'Are you jealous?' Saranon asked with an amused smile.

The dragon lowered his head until he was face to face. Then snorted blowing his fowl breath all over her. She coughed as she waved her hand in annoyance, 'You need a bath.'

She cringed at the thought knowing full well she would be the one having to clean him. Kat's coat was covered in dirt and the smell was not much better. The dragon ran ahead of her into the dragon pens. Hurling himself forward with huge leap into the shallow pool. The affect was instant as water sprayed everywhere except on the dragon. Saranon sighed, this was not the grand entrance she had hoped for. As great beast ruined any chance of making an impression. Perhaps next time would be different. Yet she doubted it as she managed to find a brush and started scrubbing. At least Katholomu would be clean.

As the air grew dark around her the glow from the lights in the keep illuminated her path. She watched the sun slowly set over the rugged rambling landscape. That marked the edge of civilisation. The heart of Alveron was a place that could turn. Even the most adventurous gave it a second thought. 'Are you sure you want to do this?' Mitch asked as he stood ready to go.

Saranon gave him a puzzled look, she had not expected him to be so keen.

They strode out toward the dragons. As the last of the sun's golden raise shone out from above the hill. The autumn breeze swept through her hair. Yet there was still warmth in the day as the memory of summer remained.

As she clambered aboard her dragon. Gannon climbed up beside her, 'What are you doing?'

The wizard said, 'You won't make it on your own.'

She could feel her anger rise and was tempted to say something. Katholomu was too excited to pay the new rider any interest. As he worked up to a mighty run before leaping into the shadowy sky. The cool breeze whipped along her cheeks. As she glanced downward over the approaching dragon colony.

The heart was home to much more than dragons. As her eyes caught sight of some unfamiliar creatures. The wizard directed Kat with an experienced ease. As he used his wizardry to search the ground. At first she could not understand what Gannon was looking for. Yet as he continued she could see the occasional flare striking back. 'Does that really work?' She asked in amazement.

'Most of the time,' Gannon answered.

As she gazed on watching the wizard work a surge of energy prickled along her senses. 'We need to return,' Gannon spoke.

The walls were full of laughter echoing up from the large rooms. Where the occupants of the keep gathered. A warm fire crackled away near the middle of the room. As she approached to take the chill from her hands. Mitch leaned down as he picked up a small parcel and presented it to her, 'Happy Birthday.'

She looked up rather embarrassed and accepted the gift. She had forgotten about her birthday. She felt much older than seventeen. Even though Mitch took great joy in reminding her how young she was. The parcel held a small book. It was not much to look at as she turned it over before opening the dark leather cover. Inside she saw a map of Alveron with details about the creatures that lived there in. She smiled and hugged the wizard.

As Saranon curled up in bed after a long evening she held the book illuminated by a tiny ball of light. She flicked through the pages and found the malicor. Mitch entered the room. He snuffed out her light with his wizardry and the room fell into darkness. 'Hey,' she exclaimed, but the wizard had already gone to bed.

She snuggled down. The Keep hummed away merrily underneath as she drifted off to sleep. Her dreams were filled of the strange land. As images of the creatures crept through. Then her thoughts turned. As the image changed and she could see the wizards from the barracks. They were running away from something. Every time she looked her eyes would not focus. All she could see was the cold grey sky looming behind, as they fled toward her.

A clap of thunder loomed outside and woke Saranon from her slumber. It was still dark as she rushed downstairs. The Keep sang with every step. It was speaking in amongst the hum, but not to her. She reached out her senses, yet all she could find was emptiness. The noise reached her ears as she opened the door. light filtered through from the dragon pens.

Before anyone could stop her. She was out in the courtyard with the grey sky looming overhead. The rain stopped short of the courtyard. She looked on as the wizards darted toward the Keep. A voice rang out behind them. The voice of a sorcerer and before anyone could stop her she answered. As the rain poured down, she answered with the strength of the Keep. The energy lit up the ground blocking the sorcerer out. This time she could sense the sorcerers. Saranon stood strong using the Keep to seal off any access.

She remained so focused that she had not seen the rain stop as the sky cleared. She remained locked in a trance waiting to be challenged, yet none came. It was then that she looked up at the building and saw the damage for the first time. The Keep had already begun repairing itself as the walls held strong.

Before she had time to ask what happened. Flynn rushed toward her, 'We need to get the artefact to the Pearl Castle.'

He did not elaborate anymore as he stayed. For a sorcerer, Clara's father had spent much time among the Athgar wizards. He held a rough and weary look with a well-worn coat that made him blend in. They had split up for the journey. To draw less attention from prying eyes and avoid the ire of sorcerer clans. She could do that on her own, yet had been asked to take the artefact. Her tummy rumbled, a reminder that she had not eaten. The fresh bread smelled delicious as the butter melted down the side. She scoffed down a mouthful as Mitch found her. The wizard looked like he had just woken up. Her head began to ring with the early thumping of a mighty headache.

Mitch smiled and spoke, 'That's what you get for showing off.'

'That's harsh,' Gannon interrupted,'Besides the keep did most of the work.'

Saranon lowered her head as she rubbed her forehead and the pain sank in. Gannon gently grasped her head in his hands. She could sense his wizardry and the pain numbed. She stared straight at Mitch with irritation, 'Why didn't you do that?'

Her companion was not showing any sympathy as he evaded the question. She gazed in annoyance at Mitch who would have let her suffer all day. An awkward silence fell over the room as the last of the early morning events were swept away. She stood not far from the opening to the dragon pens as Katholomu stuck his head out and gazed at her. The dragon had an unusual look on his face as he strained his head sideways and lowered his body. He managed to squeeze out the opening. Kat relaxed his muscles and scratched himself as though nothing had happened. She patted his hind leg and he jumped, gazing down.

The dragon was being difficult. As she searched for a way to climb on his back, Kat side stepped. Ever since they had entered Alveron the beast had been out of sorts.

A scorching sensation hit her shoulder before she had time to think. The pain creased through her body igniting the Angeon within. The sorcery of old soaked through her thoughts. As she blocked the blast from behind. Her mind raced, the attacker was heading straight for Clara. A shiver ran down her spine as she ran ahead. The corridor appeared empty even though she could sense someone.

Turmoil ruptured through the walls as she went, following a faint trace. It ricocheted off the stallic energy travelling upward. She ran further away from Clara and any sign of life. The only thing audible was the distant hum of the Keep. Saranon rounded a corner. Stopping short of an open chasm falling into the hidden depths. A flash crossed the great divide and she honed in, striking across the distance. A sound echoed from within the Keep pulsing as it went, getting louder with every step. She lost sight of the figure as the stallic energy swept up through the floor. From the edge of her vision a strange tinge crept into view. The hum of the Keep began to strain. Something else was there making its way through.

She leapt into the darkness. As the energy flowing up from the central core webbed around, hauling her down. There in the darkness the green tinge began to show. Her hand gripped the hilt. She held it, but the blade was gone. A shock ran through Saranon as she gripped the artefact. The ancient hilt felt warm in her grasp. The embedded heart stone gave a brilliant glow piercing into the void. As she floated downward the light wrapped around protecting her. It extended, evaporating the green tinge as it went. A deafening boom thundered along the outer edges as the light shielded her. Then it closed in melding into the hilt, forming the blade anew. Nothing could have prepared her as she held the bond-breaker. Once belonging to the last Angean, Zeralden Hadenvar. She gazed in awe as the Keep led her down toward the central core. For a moment she stayed transfixed watching the blade as it shone.

Her decent slowed as she reached the outer shell of the central core. A rim almost impenetrable. The words of the Keep Adeyorn were clear. Filtering through the immense void, use the blade. Saranon trembled as her knuckles went pale. She had only used her bond-breakers and this was Zeralden's. It was unfamiliar and cold, showing no sign of recognition. She willed it to work, but her nerves sank in. Stopping any attempt to use the blade. Adeyorn called out, waiting as she faltered. She cleared her mind, thinking of the central core and the pressure around it. Focusing on the heart stone as her sorcery surged. Still the blade remained cold, blocking her out. The frustration grew, she had to protect the Keep.

A tremor shimmered down the side of a giant conduit attached to the central core. It brought a sorcery that she had not sensed in a long time. The memory took her back to the detention camps and her friend Tasha whom she had lost. The central core shuddered. She had to act fast, but the thought of Tasha clung on as she opened her eyes. Her friend was standing there. Tasha reached out, holding the bond-breaker. As they both grasped it the heart stone flared. The blade came to life and her sorcery flowed through. This time it was the energy of the Angeon that filled the void. Sealing the fractures that had enabled the attack.

No trace was left as the blade did its work. Tasha's image faded and then vanished, leaving her feeling hollow inside. The burden crashed down on the emptiness as she stowed the blade away. The Keep lifted her upward once more. She was not ready to face the world and longed for the moment to continue. A sweeping silence greeted her. Before the activities of the habitable area echoed from above. She was so close. A numbness settled on her thoughts. It had been so long since she had truly seen her old friend. A sadness welled up and she tried not to show it, as she made her way through the corridors. The artefact held snug in her belt. She wondered if anyone would notice the short blade.

A smile crept across her face. It was reassuring to know that she was meant to be the Angeon. So many people shunned her and few had accepted. She hesitated as a hint of wizardry caught her senses. She held her hand to the wall of the Keep and extended her energy. The wall gave way to make an opening and it was then that the smell hit. She almost vomited. She entered alone as the sorcery bled through and melded into the barrier. Saranon hesitated as her mind mulled over the detail. Her heart thudded as the panic rose from within, she had to find Gannon.

Her sorcery strengthened and she turned toward the source. Yet still it would not focus. The frustration showed on her face. Her senses prickled as she made her way out toward a large open room and almost slipped. As she gazed down the trail of blood glistened in the light. Saranon's heart sank, she had to find Gannon. A sound rang out in the corridor and she ran toward it. Time slowed, yet at the same time it sped up. She could see Gannon lying on the ground. He was using the last of his energy so that she could see the intruders.

'No,' Saranon cried out.

As the Angeon rose without warning and she realised the wizard could not hold on. The energy rose around the Angeon, whirling as it gained momentum. The intruders placed all their efforts toward her as they forgot about Gannon. Her energy expanded through the melded wall, blocking the energy of the central core. It creaked with a massive deep sound that reverberated through the Keep. Saranon's anger welled inside her. The Keep answered as the wall disintegrated behind her. The Keep thrust the energy from the central core. Through the building with such harshness that she hesitated. The air around her froze with a stillness she could not contemplate.

She held out her hand in a void of calm as she stood in the eye of the storm. She remembered Gannon and ran toward him. The void of calm followed her as she crouched down. The wizard was so weak as he held on. He tried to speak and the words would not come out. She reached over. As the last of the Angeon withdrew deep beneath the surface, she healed the wizard.

CHAPTER FOUR

A dragon's greeting

Saranon stayed with the wizard as the energy thundered throughout the Keep. She closed her eyes as Adeyorn took over, until only she and Gannon remained. She shielded him from the stallic energy flowing out from the Keep. As it smoothed over the damaged walls. As the dust settled, sound returned in an inharmonious wave. It took her a while to make out someone approaching them. For a moment she thought it was Flynn, but as he came closer she could sense Mitch. There was a sense of urgency in his voice as they ran. The wizards of the Keep were heading down toward them.

Mitch found a small escape and they climbed through. Before she could utter a word. He used his wizardry to clean off the last remnants of dust from the attack. 'Now you help me,' Saranon grumbled as she used her energy to close the exit.

'This is not the time for talk.' Mitch whispered.

'Really.' She spoke with a hint of sarcasm.

He glanced around to make sure no one was following, 'The sorcerers were Shalough. If they find out it was the Angeon they will come after you.'

Saranon was not impressed, 'They ignored me.'

Mitch looked as though he was going to burst with frustration, 'You were not a threat.'

'Oh,' she exclaimed.

It did not make sense, but she did not like to say so. She could not understand how anyone would perceive her as non-threatening. When she last visited Alveron. She had always been the Angeon and nothing had changed.

The wizard could tell he was not getting through. He spun a fine ball of wizardry that floated in front of Saranon. The wizardry wrapped around itself as the energy ran around the sphere. She watched mesmerised. Mitch explained while the first ball of wizardry spun in on itself and dissipated. Then he made a new one and as the energy grew it shone brighter than before. 'Wow,' she gasped in amazement, 'I didn't know you could do that.'

The wizard gazed at her in disbelief. 'All right, I get it,' she frowned.

It was not the first time Mitch had taken great delight in explaining something to her. Clara's voice rang out behind them. Saranon was still dazed and found an excuse to leave. She sighed as she turned the corner.

The shock of the event clung on as she made her way

to bed. She closed her eyes, yet her mind did not want to rest. The door creaked open she stared at Mitch. He was moving slowly while trying not to disturb her. 'Are you awake?' He asked.

'You know I am.' She retorted.

'Gannon made it.' He spoke.

She could see the worry on Mitch's face. The former soldier hardly ever showed fear. 'The Shalough know you are here.' He spoke.

'How?' She asked.

'They blocked the pass to the south.' Mitch explained before he bid her goodnight.

This was not what she had expected. Saranon had a terrible feeling. She had been dragged into something that everybody else knew more about than her. With that her mixed dreams carried her away into an uneven sleep.

The building shook with a thud as the dragon misjudged the wall. The sound of a loud grunt crept in through the window. Katholomu grew impatient as she yelled at him for waking her up. The great beast took a step back, then as she leaned closer he picked her up on the edge of his nose. She let out an impulsive scream, before she could tell where the ground was. Mitch came running from below and called out, 'Quick, jump on.'

She was about to say something. When she caught sight of a fleet of dragons heading their way in the morning sky.

She gaped in astonishment. There would be no time to waste. As Katholomu ran in pursuit of the dragon riders as they launched into the sky. Saranon held her breath as Kat manoeuvred so close. His wing almost clipped another dragon, then let out a heavy sigh. Her stomach grumbled. This was not a good start to the morning and the dragon was picking up speed. She grumbled into the wind as all hope of staying in the background faded.

The dragon drove hard through the early morning frost. That hung in the air as the wind swept past. She wanted to call Kat back, but it was too late. They were heading straight for the attacking riders. Sorcery surged inside her as it reacted to the blast heading their way. The dragon swooped, almost knocking her off as she tried desperately to cling on. She yelled, only to find her voice carried away in the wind. Kat was travelling too fast and all she could do was hang on. The great beast ceased turning. Saranon peered over the top of his bulky head only to see yet another blast of sorcery. Before she could answer Kat exhaled at a phenomenal rate. A great roar from deep within his belly ignited in front of them.

She froze with fright, the result was instant as the dragon riders scattered. They had not expected the dragon to breathe fire and neither had she. The dragon chuckled. No one had warned her about Katholomu and she was not sure whether to scold or praise him. Given the fact that she was still sitting on his shoulders she opted to reassure him. He snorted and swooped over one last time, then stumbled into a rough landing.

She made her way down and stepped out of his way. Kat lowered his head as he coughed up the last of his fiery breath on a poor unsuspecting tree. The dragon promptly sat on it and curled up to go to sleep in the morning sun. Saranon stood in astonishment. Staring at the beast when Captain Trevell crept up behind her. 'You need to declare fire breathing dragons,' he stated.

'Do I look like I knew?' She responded, 'What do I do?'

The Captain smiled, 'You could boast about it.'

She frowned in bewilderment. She had known the dragon almost two years and not once had he breathed fire.

The captain broke her thoughts, 'We will be sad to see you go. Flynn is ready to leave.'

She could feel the exhaustion set in even though Kat had done most of the work. She trudged back to the barracks as two dragons waited in the courtyard. She began climbing on the one with Mitch, as Katholomu bounded through the clearing. The dragon nudged her onto his shoulder.

She hoped he did not breathe fire again as she held on tight. Kat was the last to launch into the sky and this time he stayed behind travelling at a steady pace. She breathed a sigh of relief and the dragon chuckled. The sound did nothing to reassure her. The Pearl Castle rose over the hillside as it came into view. The pale stone shone in the midday light as the sun warmed her back. It had been rebuilt after the Dreshan Occupation. In much the same image and towered over the land.

As Katholomu flew into the lower side of the castle she stayed close. The dragon pens took up a majority of the lower ground level. It opened up into the courtyard. Where the main level began further up the hillside. Saranon was astounded by the sheer scale, Clara had not mentioned it. She peered up into the void that led to the main floor. It would be easy to become lost as she tried to stay out of the way. A loud snort behind her sent the air whooshing down her neck. Kat snorted again as the sorcerers on the main floor stopped. Before she knew it, they had become the centre of attention.

She tried to nudge the dragon back into the pens. He was having none of it and ignored her attempts. Edelyn peered down over the balcony. The lady was everything Saranon expected a sorceress to be. As she realised her travelling clothes were worn and grubby. 'Your dragon does not belong in here,' Edelyn spoke with a firm tone.

Saranon's face grew hot and she spoke to the dragon as she tried again to nudge him toward the door.

Instead the great beast sidestepped her and lifted himself up to the main floor. The colour drained from her face as she gaped in astonishment.

She used her sorcery and nothing happened. A shock crept up her spine as she began to panic and nervously swallowed. She tried again, this time with greater strength and without success. She could not work out what was blocking her. The sounds of chaos rang out from above. As Katholomu moved without a care for anyone that came too close. Edelyn stood mortified. Saranon summoned the Angeon hidden deep inside. The energy surged within like a violent flood with no way out. A voice shouted near her in an attempt to restore calm. As the dragon keepers ran toward Katholomu.

A thunderous roar heaved its way up through the Keep. As she realised it was not her who had answered. She became lost in the haze of the Angeon as it swept over her. The energy thundered through after the mighty roar from the Keep. A shimmer of tiny sparks of light flowed like rain from the ceiling. 'Wow,' Saranon gasped in amazement.

Then the hum of the Keep broke through the silence. She smiled, watching Kat make his way down and out to the open courtyard. He flopped down, lapping up the warmth of the afternoon resting his head on the ground. 'What was that?' Saranon asked and jumped when Clara answered behind her.

Her friend had her arms held out as the last spark of light floated down. 'I've never seen anyone do that,' Clara exclaimed.

Saranon was still trying to work out how the sparks came into the equation. That would have to wait until later. Edelyn made her way toward them. She wanted to hide even though there was no way she could. Her only reassurance came from the Keep. As the central core whirred in contentment below.

Before she could speak, Clara took her hand and they darted away. 'What did you do that for?' Saranon asked.

Clara beamed with excitement, 'I'm so glad you're in Alveron again.'

Her friend's response did not answer the question, but she let it be. The last time they had met was at Odana

Temple when the Keep was under attack by the Otturin. Where she had first encountered Kat. The dragon was fidgeting in the courtyard which looked rather awkward given his size. He belonged to the Otturin before she had claimed him. Or perhaps he had claimed her, she was never really sure.

Clara clambered up on the dragon before Saranon could say no. Kat leaned down and nudged her. She made her way up the thick skin that shielded the great beast from almost anything. By the time she had reached his shoulders she was covered in dirt. She grimaced at the thought of having to clean him again. Kat leaped with a jovial step that made her stomach lurch as he flew into the sky. Autumn was beginning to show as the cool breeze swept past under the afternoon sun. Saranon had no idea where she was going as Kat circled down around Fendugal. The outer barracks marked the beginning of east Alveron.

The warm grey stone walls shone in the sunlight. As Katholomu ran across the open ground along the perimeter. The dragon had a habit of landing at the nearest wizard Keep. Today was no different as her enthusiasm waned. The Keep marked the beginning of the well-built roads leading to the nearest town. Yet she stayed on the western side where the great wilderness faded to a halt at the Keep's door. A familiar face came out to greet them. As Mitch approached she gave him a bewildered glare, 'What are you doing here?'

The wizard only smiled. Saranon shook her head before letting it be. He had braved the journey north all the way to Serenphel. Mitch knew more about Alveron than she did. Which made her feel like the odd one out as they went inside the Keep. The building stood with a simple splendour that continued inside. As they made their way to the large open hall. They sat down to enjoy that the sun streaming through the tall windows. As Clara made enquiries to view further into the Keep. Mitch spoke in a low whisper, 'There's trouble south, we need to stay away.'

He emphasised the word "we" as he stared at her. The wizard could be annoying.

A silent click reverberated in the hum of the central core. Creating a void between sound. Saranon turned her head away. Mitch answered for her, as though reading her immediate thoughts, 'Run!'

She strode toward the windows facing the edge of the wilderness. As the blast bulged through, warping the wall as it went. The great rush of air thundered around her. As she stood still in a silent void where the essence of time lingered. She raised her hands in a hazy trance as her energy rose to the surface. It ripped through the blast with an intense heat, as the air tore apart in a fiery rage. The ground trembled as Saranon stammered back with the shock. The wall stood strong and the shattered glass lay in piles swept back against the edge.

A chorus of rage echoed overhead as the dragon riders leapt into the harsh sky. She had not seen so many dragons take to the sky and looked on in astonishment. Mitch pulled her away from the windows and they ran into the depths of the Keep. She fumed as she realised they were being shut in. Mitch spoke, 'Stay here.'

They had been crammed in, it took a while for the sudden fear to vanish. She could feel the staring grow in abundance. Until a wizard a few years older made his way through the crowd. Clara gave a small bow, before thanking the Regent for his hospitality. Saranon stared in amazement. being crammed in a room full of wizards was not her idea of hospitality. The Regent, Robert of Ashden thanked her. For once she was speechless and could not think of anything to say as the Regent moved on. This was not how she expected to spend the evening.

Loud banging and a rustle came from the other side of the door. Much to her relief the wizards began to leave. Mitch stopped her, 'Do not get involved.'

'I already have,' she exclaimed.

He gave her a stern glare which only added to her frustration. They watched the wizards gather into action, reclaiming the sky. Saranon glanced around trying to make sense of what had happened. A rogue wizard group managed to get past the outer shield. She was not convinced, as she made her way out into the damp evening air. The energy of the Keep lit up the dragon pens and foreground as she made her way into the dark. She could not sense any remnants from sorcery except her own. Still it did not make her feel at ease, as she spotted Katholomu guarding the pens.

The great beast was resting. She was about to pat him when a stench wafted toward her. She coughed as the wizards let her through to the shallow pool. Kat stopped short of the water. She placed her hands on hips as she spoke, 'You need a wash.'

The dragon snorted in disgust as he began to arch his shoulders. A few short shouts rang out behind her. She took no notice as she tried to move the dragon. Instead she succeeded in being stared at with two massive grumpy dark eyes.

The thudding rang out when two dragons ran up behind Kat, racing toward the pool. She just had time to grab onto his leg, as he was shoved into the pool with her clinging on. Water sprayed everywhere and soaked through her clothes. Clara screamed in the background. Saranon managed to raise her hand and wave. She was safe for the moment as the dragons splashed around her. Kat's belly moved in a low growl that made its way to a chuckle. She was not impressed.

She requested a brush. Mitch threw it up as he tried not to laugh. 'See, this is what you get for dragging me in,' she told the dragon as she scrubbed his ears.

Finally she managed to make her way down, as he leaned his head forward. He splashed her one last time as he heaved his body out of the pool. Saranon used her energy to dry her clothes. At least the dragon was clean.

'You're not supposed to get in the pool,' Clara exclaimed.

She sighed. They made their way up to the hall where a wonderful aroma of the evening meal met her. The smell of food made her tummy rumble. She picked up a cup of soup and sat near the fireplace as it warmed her hands.

'You did well today,' Robert of Ashden spoke.

Saranon peered up and glanced around. Mitch and Clara were nowhere to be seen and she was unsure what to do. The Regent smiled. 'When you are at the Pearl Castle I would like you to meet the Oracle. Tell me what you make of him.'

She was rather puzzled by the request and nodded her head, 'Yes... your highness.'

Robert of Ashden was called away before she could think of anything else. Clara spoke behind her. She jumped using her sorcery to stop the soup from going everywhere. Clara giggled. 'I just meant to tell you we are leaving.'

Saranon made her way outside, where Mitch greeted her in darkness of the courtyard. 'I hear you made an impression.'

That was not the word she was looking for, as she told him about Robert's request. Mitch went quiet. 'You need to meet the oracle.'

'Why?' She asked out of suspicion.

'Let me know what you think,' he added.

Saranon had the distinct feeling she would be walking into trouble. She gave the wizard a disapproving glare before clambering aboard the sweet smelling dragon. If only Katholomu could stay clean, but that would be too much to ask. She held on tight as Mitch waved goodbye. Clara sat in front as she directed Kat toward the Pearl Castle. By the time they arrived only the night watch greeted them. The dragon needed no encouragement as he spotted a warm cosy bed. He did not let them down until he had curled his tail around and closed his eyes to rest. She could hear the hum of the Keep in the background, as it guided her up toward her room. Sleep was far from her mind, but it had been a busy day and exhaustion set in.

The room was large enough to look spacious without being extravagant. It made her wonder if the Mercidian picked the most average room in the whole Keep. She took out the sova bag and waited for it to expand before rummaging through her belongs. A knock at the door held her attention. Saranon opened the door a fraction. As she glanced up into the dark eyes of a sorcerer almost the same age. The familiar smell of dragon told her more about him than she needed to ask.

'What has Katholomu done this time?' She asked, dreading the reply.

Madoc spoke, 'We had to move him because he can breathe fire.'

Saranon's face went pale as the sorcerer tried to explain that nothing happened. She was not convinced and Madoc kept glancing over her shoulder. 'Would you like to come in?' She asked as he eyed the bond-breakers lying on the table.

She should have known someone would be interested, as she let him in. He held the blade before transforming it from a dagger into a sleek sword that would fit well in his hand.

She had made the bond-breaker Corsavere at Odana Temple. The old heart of Zyanthia in the north-west corner of Alveron. The heart stone shone with a warm glow of recognition at the sorcerer's strength. 'Will you make one here?' He asked with a hint of excitement.

'Is that a request?' Saranon asked.

'Maybe,' Madoc spoke, as he placed the bond-breaker back in its sheath.

After the sorcerer had left she settled down for the night. The central core of the Keep hummed away beneath. Her thoughts turned to the Oracle she had not met. The Pearl Castle was giving nothing away which made her wonder even more.

CHAPTER FIVE

The wizard lord

Creaking sounds made their way through a dreamless sleep. As Saranon stirred with the fresh morning light. The Pearl Castle had a different rhythm. A little slower, like it was dragging its heels. Yet the hum was strong. She held Corsavere to the light before attaching the bond-breaker to her belt. The corridor was quiet as she ducked away. A few people hesitated, glancing her way. Clara was further up the tower. She gave a knock as her friend opened the door and the two giggled, as they ran down the stairs. She had a task and Clara knew where to find the Oracle. They raced toward the courtyard.

Clara stopped in the middle of the gathering, 'That's odd.'

'What is?' Saranon asked.

'He isn't here,' Clara dismissed the thought, dragging

her through the Keep.

They darted to the courtyard on the upper level, as a crowd gathered. They hesitated, but the crowd parted letting them through to a manicured garden. Still they could see no sign of the elusive Oracle and Clara became worried.

'This is not supposed to happen,' Clara spoke aloud.

She was beginning to think the Oracle did not want to be found. The idea made her nervous as she glanced around. 'I know,' Clara said without explanation.

They made their way into a small foyer. Clara vanished around the doorway and Saranon hesitated before peering in. Her friend held out a Mercidian robe and urged her to try it on. Saranon sighed, she did not think it was going to make any difference. Clara gave her a look of approval before they made their way toward the great chambers. She followed through the stream of people, keeping sight of Clara. Then her friend shoved her back into the crowd.

Saranon gasped as she lost her balance and fell backward. Standing right behind her was the one person that had been avoiding her. The Oracle was a tall man, his eyes soft and sombre. Her voice had escaped her as she bowed and backed away into the crowd. Her cheeks grew hot as she leaned on the wall away from Oracle. 'Well?' Clara asked, startling her friend.

'Don't do that,' she exclaimed.

They managed to make their way out through the door. Clara was not going to let her be.

'What do you think?' Clara was itching to know as

they returned the robe.

'I don't think you want to know,' Saranon exclaimed.

The look on Clara's face turned into one of utter disappointment. As her shoulders slumped. Her friend looked like she was about to cry, then reassured herself, 'It's okay.'

Clara did not sound convincing, but there was not much Saranon could do. The man she had seen was not the Oracle. There was no spark of life that she had witnessed with the Prophet at Indarin. If anything there was an unexpected emptiness she could not explain.

The sensation stayed with her long after the image was gone, as she made her way toward the dragon pens. The place was almost empty as the afternoon sun shone through the high windows. The large arches led out to the courtyard where she could make out Kat's tail. As he waved it across the ground in irritation. The great beast turned his head to meet her. Yet he appeared reluctant to leave his cosy spot in the sun. She patted his smooth cheek and the dragon nudged her over his head and onto his shoulders. Saranon steadied herself as she turned around. The great beast leapt too close to the side of the building. She cringed as the angry shouts rang out behind them.

Fendugal came into view as the a cool breeze swept across the open plain. The Keep showed no sign of the attack and she breathed a sigh of relief. Lord Nemard Halleron stood in the doorway of the dragon pens. He was a tall brute of wizard with a face to match. 'What would a sorceress be doing here?' he enquired with a hint of interest.

Saranon had not expected to be greeted by the Lord and found herself lost for words. As she mumbled, 'I was... wondering if I could see the Regent?'

'Really,' he eyed her with an amused smile that was more menacing than friendly. 'Now why would you need to see the Regent?'

'He gave me a task,' her voice became meek.

Lord Halleron rubbed his chin, 'Well then, I will take you to see the Regent.'

She was not sure if she wanted to follow the overbearing wizard. That looked more at home in a tavern than the Keep. He glanced over to make sure she was following. As he led her up to the large drawing room with great windows. That looked in the direction of the capital Terrare. Voices travelled in a low murmur and stopped as she entered. The Regent, Robert of Ashden, was just as she remembered. His face showed the last traces of youth, yet his eyes were far older. The wizards around him parted to let her through. The Regent looked up with patient expectation.

Saranon tried to find her voice, yet it escaped her as she fumbled to find the words. She gave up and shook her head. 'He isn't the one,' she spoke softly.

'Are you sure?' The Regent asked.

'Ulrich is not the Oracle, not even close.' She may as well have been shouting.

Her words had the same effect. She could offer no hope to the Regent. It was not what she had expected, as she became disheartened. Lord Halleron gave a chuckle as he grinned. 'I am amazed Ulrich has lasted this long.'

With a hint of amusement the atmosphere in the room changed before she realised. It felt as though she had been left out of a silent conversation. Saranon politely bowed, her head spun and she longed for fresh air. She rushed out into the open courtyard where Kat waited. With his arms stretched out showing his shiny belly for all to see. The dragon moved sideways. While opening one eye then lied back with an air of contentment.

Mitch met her with relaxed smile. 'Stirring up trouble again?'

'Me,' Saranon gasped in annoyance, as she glared at the wizard.

He towered over her. 'I have accepted Lord Halleron's offer to stay at Kallawere... for the both of us.'

The wizard gave her an unwavering stare as she fumed. 'What!' She shouted and a few people turned around from the dragon pens. 'You did what?' She whispered.

'It's the least we can do…' The wizard spoke without finishing the sentence.

Saranon stood close which meant she had to crane her neck and stand on her toes, 'What do you mean?'

Mitch smiled and spoke in such a soft tone, 'You upset the Mercidian.'

She found the wizard rather puzzling and cryptic messages were not her strong point. She glared at him. While trying to figure out what staying with a bunch of wizards had to do with sorcerers.

'I don't think they were expecting you,' Mitch added.

Saranon was not about to argue as the wizard went

inside, because it did not make sense. She shrugged her shoulders and followed. The Keep remained silent underneath the touch of her fingers. A faint wave of energy caught her by surprise. As Fendugal reacted to her and she smiled before catching up to the wizard. Despite all her attempts to quiz him further, Mitch remained silent. She had trouble reading him. The wizard could hide his emotions well. Try as she might his calm mood did nothing to ease her thoughts.

She decided to explore the Keep by herself. She expected a reaction, but the wizard gave little away. The habitable areas were filled with activity. Yet the place had an open vastness that made it feel too large for its tenants. She ran her hand along the wall without thinking and it moved. Saranon froze, then turned and peered into a doorway with a staircase leading down. She had been thinking about going below the habitable area. This seemed like an invitation. She glanced around before darting down the dust covered stairs. The corridor was narrow and crept around as it lead further down.

She hesitated, then made her way into a small room. As she stood in the centre voices travelled from nearby. A wizard waved his hand through the doorway. She glanced around expecting to see someone behind her, even though she was alone. The doorway opened up into the entrance to a substation. A small crew were in good spirits as the exhaustion showed. Saranon wondered why she had not sensed anything. Yet the Keep had guided her here so perhaps that was her answer. Captain Lydia Grace waved in her direction. Words were not needed as the wizardess pointed toward the open conduit. She peered down into the depths. The empty conduit looked more like a long dark cave, which gradually made its way up to the surface.

As she leaned her head down into the conduit a great ball of black fluff growled. She jumped, fumbled and somehow managed to lose her grip all at the same time. She rolled down the side of the circular conduit. Placing her hand in the grimy layer covering the bottom. Captain Grace called out from above and chuckled after realising Saranon was okay. She turned to face the large ball of black fluff and asked, 'What is it?'

'This is Mina. If you are lucky enough you can meet her parents,' Captain Grace answered.

She smiled at the zennigh kitten. She had to admit it was one of the cutest things she had ever seen. The kitten took a tentative step back as Saranon approached. The giant black kitten had claws and teeth as sharp as its parents, so she did not walk any closer. 'There does not appear to be anything wrong with the conduit,' she spoke.

As she climbed back out. 'There isn't,' Captain Grace replied. 'This is supposed to be a routine maintenance check. We found this.'

Saranon wanted to ask what it was as she held out her hand to touch the rough surface of the broken seal. The carving imprinted on the fragments implied that someone had tried to break in. Her frustration grew. It had not been near the central core, it was far too small. 'It was caused by wizardry,' Captain Lydia Grace added.

'What?' Saranon's astonishment showed plain on her face.

'You aren't the only one who can do serious damage,' the Captain replied.

She attempted to hide her astonishment. As the Captain chuckled, 'Keep an eye open, I don't want to look after you too.'

Saranon grumbled, she thought she was able to look after herself. The old tomb in Alveron had frightened her, there was still so much to learn.

She made her way up to the habitable area via the main stairway. That opened into an elegant foyer hidden in the depths of the Keep. The lights along the walls were well lit as the last of the sun faded through the high windows. She peered up at the ceiling. Where the hexagonal frame of the columns flowed upward into the high arches. 'Beautiful isn't it?' The Regent had crept up behind her and she jumped.

He smiled. 'Come, I want to show you something.'

Saranon hesitated, then sprinted to catch up. The Regent waited for no one. She was fumbling for the right words, yet nothing came to mind as they entered a cosy library. A pile of books grew on a table near the centre of the room, as Lord Halleron flicked through them. The wizard was muttering to himself in annoyance. He took a moment longer to search. 'Ah, Robert just the man I want to see. Which one of these would help find the Oracle?'

The Regent, Robert of Ashden, leaned down to pick out a book. As he did so a sharp searing pain ran up

Saranon's leg and she screamed. The blast pounded through, as she created a shield for the Regent. Lord Halleron burst into action, hurtling a blast over Saranon's head. The air crackled as her ears rang and she filled with rage. As she turned all she could see was Lord Halleron taking a flying leap out the door. A series of agonising screams rang out, then a muffled cry and nothing. The silence that followed left an eerie tone. As the gasps to catch her breath filled the void. She brushed her hand along her leg, it felt fine. She looked down in astonishment. After all the pain there were no marks or sign of what had taken place.

A gruff Lord Halleron entered with the look of someone she did not want to anger. His voice came across with a firm certainty, 'It's nothing. I handed them over to the sergeant.'

'Who were they?' Saranon enquired.

'Hmm...' Lord Halleron had an amused look on his face. 'Whoever they were, they will not be doing much.'

She was not sure what he meant, but did not like to ask. The Regent stood up completely unhurt and calm. Which made her wonder if this was the first time he had faced such danger. Before she had a chance to ask. Lord Halleron picked up the book the Regent had given him and studied it in mild thought. He glanced at Saranon, turned back to the book then glanced at her again, 'How old are you?'

'Seventeen,' she replied.

'Hmm... You are rather young for the Angeon,' Lord Halleron remarked.

She frowned, placing her hands on her hips, 'What does that have to do with the Oracle?'

'No reason,' Lord Halleron replied, as he handed the book to the Regent.

She was not going to get any straight answers. As the two wizards idly changed the subject. Knowing full well that she was irritated. She found an excuse to leave and Lord Halleron gave her an amused smile as he bid her goodnight.

Saranon was not sure what to make of the Athgar wizards. Her thoughts were interrupted with the sharp smell of soot. As she entered the corridor, she gasped as her eyes followed a long charred trail up along the wall. It was not the marks that caught her attention. Rather the smudged outlines where the walls remained untouched. The ghostly reminder made her skin crawl, yet she would have done the same. She tried to block the image out of her mind, but the pungent smell clung to her clothes. The autumn cold brought a chill down the outer wall and she rubbed her arms.

The night had well and truly set in. Yet as she peered out into the courtyard a figure caught her attention. She hesitated before opening the outer door, there was something familiar about the figure. As she watched, Katholomu came out to greet the person. Saranon opened the door and reluctantly put on the coat. It reeked of smoke, but it was warm enough. She passed the outer rim of the courtyard. Before realising the sorcerer was Otturin and froze. He was almost the same age and hesitated as they stared at each other. Kat broke the silence as he gently nudged Kail forward. Saranon grimaced at recognising who the Otturin sorcerer was.

She had thrown him off the dragon and flown Katholomu north to Normisia. The dragon was hers by right, Mark Staragen had paid for the beast as a thank you for saving his life. Now she stood face to face with the Otturin, and for the first time he was not attacking her. In fact he seemed rather shy. 'What are you doing here?' She whispered.

'I came to see Katholomu,' Kail spoke, as he patted the great beast.

The dragon purred in return, much to Saranon's annoyance. 'Are you going to attack again?'

As soon as she had asked the question it sounded silly, 'That wasn't quite what I meant.'

Kail answered. 'It's been a long time since there has been an angeon.'

She gaped in astonishment. Another Otturin sorcerer appeared from the distance and called, 'Kail.'

The word was spoken which such a firm voice. That neither questioned the finality of the tone. 'I should go,' he gave a curt nod before retreating into the darkness.

Another voice cut through the air, as Mitch called out in alarm, 'Saranon.'

'It would appear I have to go to,' she spoke to herself, as she cringed.

Mitch held her arm as he led her inside and gave a strange look as he took a whiff of her jacket. 'I'm fine,' she said, not wanting to elaborate.

'Three sorcerer clans in Alveron and you manage to annoy all them,' he exclaimed.

As he peered down the corridor and caught the remnants of the smoke before it settled. 'That wasn't me,' Saranon retorted, before he could accuse her of anything.

She was beginning to wonder if it was too late to go back to the Pearl Castle. When a welcoming voice trailed out from the great hall. The warmth of the open fire greeted them as Lord Halleron shut the door. It made a small clicking noise that held her attention before she saw who stood in front of them.

There in the centre of the room standing not much taller than she was an Otturin sorceress. The Athgar wizards seemed completely oblivious, to the fact their guest was out of place. Mitch for once gave a bewildered glance. As Lord Halleron announced with an air of amusement, 'This is Adeen.'

Before Saranon could think of what to say Lord Halleron left. Making himself comfortable in a grand chair near the fireplace. The light from the Keep flickered as it washed down the walls. She had not expected to meet an Otturin. Welcomed by the wizards after the damage at Odana Temple. Her lips moved, but no sound came out as she tried think of something and stumbled. Adeen smiled. 'Odana recognises you, yet you do not seem like the Angeon of old.'

Saranon remained silent. She was beginning to get used to people not expecting to meet her.

'I have a task for you,' Adeen added as she eyed the Angeon up and down with a fleeting glance. 'Bring me the Oracle.'

Saranon gaped, 'Why would I do that?'

She was beginning to get annoyed with the Otturin. Yet as she stared around the room the wizards appeared calm. She felt as though she had been unwittingly led into a trap. Adeen turned to Lord Halleron and waited. The wizard did not miss his cue, 'The Mercidian and Shalough both want the Oracle.'

It was not an answer to her question. As the memory of pain still lingered from the attack at Odana Temple. Saranon spoke as she stared at Adeen, 'You are not worthy of the Oracle.'

'Neither are you,' Adeen replied with a calm confidence.

'I will not be drawn into this,' Saranon spoke as she closed her eyes.

Odana still held her thoughts. As she remembered the great central core from the deep.

'You already are,' Adeen responded.

She felt the sorcery of the Angeon swirl within her as she opened her eyes. Adeen clambered back as she turned away. In a moment the Angeon was gone, as it receded back inside.

With that a slow swell of darkness engulfed Adeen and she vanished. In disbelief Saranon waved her hand where the Otturin had been. 'That went well,' Lord Halleron said with a hint of sarcasm, as he rose from the chair. He grasped her shoulder and faced the sorceress. 'What do think will happen when we find the Oracle?'

She glared in disgust and Lord Halleron took no notice as he waited. 'Says the man who has not met one,' Saranon spat the words out.

As she stormed outside into the cold night air. Inside she was fuming, the wizards were so focused on the Oracle and she did not see why. Perhaps that was just as well. She was still agitated when a rustle came from the forest near the edge of the Keep. Adeen strode towards her from the darkness, 'Will you consider our offer?'

'It is not that simple,' she spoke and let out an uneasy sigh. 'Have you ever been near an Oracle?'

'We will not harm her,' Adeen answered.

'When I was in Serenphel, I became friends with the Prophet. It is not what you seek,' Saranon spoke in an anguished tone. There was no way she could make Adeen understand. 'I will search for the Oracle. Perhaps then you will understand,' she turned to leave.

There was no use trying to explain. The fake oracle had reinforced a false hope and she was being asked to unravel what was done.

As she entered inside the grand Keep. It felt as though she was the only one who could see the confusion. It would explain why the Oracle had not been found. If everyone was looking for a distorted truth. Chasing shadows of an image that did not exist, except in the pages of fables. The burden weighed heavy on her shoulders, as she slumped down on the bed for the night. The laughter and voices from the great hall echoed underneath the door. In the darkness she cried silent tears. What would become of the Oracle? The person would not live up to expectations, but then neither did she.

CHAPTER SIX

The betrayal

A steady rain ran down the window, the faint light crept through the curtain as she drew it back. Saranon glanced out and a movement caught her eye. There were too many people in the courtyard. She ran out into the foyer and Mitch greeted her warm smile. It was a pleasant change from the night before as she tried to forget the task she had been given. It grated on her mind like a dull headache not wanting to let go. Mitch had met the Prophet in Serenphel ever so briefly. Yet the wizard appeared oblivious to her concerns. She felt a wave of relief when Flynn made his way toward them.

'I thought you would like to ride with us,' Flynn said, as he led her toward the waiting dragons. 'We can meet up with Mitch at Felkrayer.'

'Are you sure?' Saranon asked with a hint of excited

hesitation.

She patted Flynn's dragon, as Katholomu nudged her with his cheek. About the only time Kat would fawn over her was when she paid attention to another dragon. She smiled then made her way up on her dragon, 'I'll follow you.'

'Of course,' Flynn replied, as he wasted no time taking to the sky.

As they made their way through the sky, she noticed Madoc off and waved. She saw no sign of Clara and frowned. It was not like her friend to miss an opportunity for adventure. Still, their journey had ended. When the artefact had been returned to the Pearl Castle. Now she had been lumped with the task of finding the Oracle. She let out a heavy sigh filled with frustration, she had no idea how to find an oracle. Alveron was beautiful with a vibrant greenery even in the middle of autumn. The chill air ran along her cheeks reminding her of the harsh winter to come.

Katholomu darted in and out. Revelling in showing off his homeland as he soaked up the brisk fresh air. The clouds faded to let through a soft sunlight. Filtering down over the trees and cottages spotting the landscape. They made good progress, as Flynn led the small group down under the glow of the midday sun. Saranon felt her stomach rumble. As Kat thudded along the ground in an uneven pattern. He used the slope of the hill to land. She scrambled onto his side, as he rolled over without a second thought for his rider. Of all the places to land, the dragon had managed to find a dry dirt patch. He merrily flicked his tail in the air, as he rubbed his back in the dirt.

She wanted to tell the dragon off, as Madoc's voice caught her attention. 'Where are you going?' He asked, as he hesitated.

She was not sure what to make of the sorcerer whose eyes showed he wanted to ask much more. Saranon glanced toward the waiting group and Madoc's carefree expression changed, 'Take care.'

She smiled at the thought, before climbing on top of the grubby dragon. Kat needed a bath, but that would have to wait.

The cool breeze turned into a sharp wind as it sent chills along her cheeks. She steadied herself close to the dragon's thick coat. Autumn had taken a strong hold over the land as they flew in formation above. The low hills and vibrant woodland reminded her of a homeland she had hardly seen. Katholomu beamed with excitement, he was only too keen to show off. As Flynn signalled for them to stay close. She hesitated then patted the dragon with a wilful encouragement. As he glided close to the ground in a steep dive. She felt alive and loved every moment as she breathed in the crisp air. Mitch was missing out on so much and then she remembered where she was.

She whispered near the dragon's ear and the great beast swooped around. Heading towards the group which had already landed. Katholomu had too much speed and she clung on and gritted her teeth. The dragon swerved into a clearing and as he lowered his wing she saw movement. Without thinking she dug her heel deep. The dragon flung himself upward with an ear piercing screech. A heavy weight fell on Saranon's back and she lost her grip. Falling the short distance to ground. The soft grass and fallen leaves cushioned her blow. As she stared toward a darkening sky, the shadows lingered as her muscles ached. When she moved, her whole body felt awkward and heavy.

As the shadows grew the darkness swept in, she looked up. There was no sign of Flynn and the dragons were long gone. She had lost track of time as the world moved around her and she went with it. A deep rumbling filled her ears, as the sound reverberated through the ground. She held on as the earth slipped. As she gazed skyward for one last time. Her eyes fell upon the stern faces of the Shalough looking down upon her. Saranon tried to say something, but her voice failed. As Tordoren opened up to swallow her. She clung on, yet all the strength she could summon was not enough. She felt tired and the weakness had ebbed its way through her body.

She tried to shout and the words were lost in the rumbling haze. Then the sky darkened, as she lost her grip. Anger seeped in, rising to the surface. It welled inside her as she fell, deep into the timeless tunnel. That sealed in on itself with a thunderous rush. She breathed, fearing what she might find. As her hands found the solid surface beneath. Then it moved and Saranon's heartbeat jumped into her throat with a rising panic. She opened her eyes and peered down holding her breath for a brief moment. There was a faint warmth emanating from the surface. She placed her ear next to it and a great rumble echoed upward, as she jumped bolt upright.

Time passed without the faintest measure, as she sat pondering her predicament. The small glow of light from her sorcery only added to her gloom. As it shone through the unending cave. She peered upward hoping for the answer to come, but this time she had run out of luck. She sat down on floor of the cave, a flat surface with a murky edge. The cave ran deep. As a thought entered her head to find a way out the surface moved with a jolt. Saranon tumbled backward until she managed to steady herself. She was swept down into the cave as the surface moved. As it did so she realised what it was. She was lying on the top of sheal, almost solid but it was still sheal.

The dark murky substance moved gathering speed. As it went hurtling her down deep underneath. Then the blood ran to her feet as the sheal rose with a fathomless might. The earth rumbled above as the tremors cascaded far below. The sudden rush kept her body flat to the surface as she clung on. Fearing what she would see as she peeked out through dusty haze. Then the sheal stopped with such a jolt that she flew up into the air. Saranon used her energy as a shield to soften the fall as her legs found the solid ground. She could smell the fresh damp grass pressing against her face. She breathed a trembling sigh of relief. As the sound in her ears diminished and for first time she noticed the stars above.

She rolled onto her back from exhaustion. She did not understand what had happened in the depths of Tordoren.

Yet her heart filled with an overwhelming gratitude. A silent tear escaped down the side of her cheek. Before she could stop the back of her head was soaked with an overwhelming sense of relief. Perhaps she could disappear and no one would know. Then she remembered Mitch, the wizard would find her anywhere. It was all a mess, the thought clung on as the chill wind numbed the ends of her fingers. A rustling noise caught her attention. As she turned and the dark silhouette of a figure emerged from the shadows.

She could tell straight away the young man was wiccan. She sighed as she called out and let the world in. As she made a small light she stared down at her grubby hands and clothes. Her hair was covered as well. The young man, Liam, smiled. 'We thought you might turn up.'

'Why is that?' Saranon asked, as bewilderment filled her voice.

'The Shalough are saying they trapped the Angeon and well... Here you are,' Liam spoke with a sense of awe and amusement.

She was too tired to ask how that was meant to make sense, she brushed the mud off her arm. 'I could do with bath,' she exclaimed to herself, as the dry mud made her skin itch.

Kylah smiled, the wiccan had stayed in Liam's shadowed. Her eyes shone bright. As she welcomed the opportunity to show the sorceress to their small town. Set in a well protected clearing. Saranon was not about to argue, as she was offered a warm meal and sat in a cosy chair near the fire place. The tavern was bigger than Mrs. Harper's in Normisia. Yet it had the same welcoming vibe that filled the air as she ate. The tavern was rather full for such late hour. As the sound of vibrant music floated out into the night sky. She had forgotten how much she missed the company of her friend's Celia and Jedd. It seemed ages since she had seen them.

It amazed her, how talk of her had travelled to Alveron. Her eyes were growing tired, as she placed the empty bowl down. As she rose to find a room upstairs Liam approached her. 'I need to talk with you, but it can wait until the morning,' he said.

She looked behind him to the open window. As the first rays of sunlight broke over the hillside. 'Perhaps noon,' she suggested.

Liam looked over his shoulder and smiled before nodding in agreement. As she found the door began to open it, it stopped halfway. She hesitated, yet she could not sense anything.

Mitch peering around the door, 'You're late.'

Saranon jumped with fright then pounded his chest with a tired fist. 'Where were you,' she cried in frustration. She pounded him again, before Mitch hugged her tight, 'We're in danger.'

Saranon stopped and glared up at his dark brown eyes, 'You noticed.'

'You were traded,' Mitch explained, 'Only the Shalough did not hand over the Oracle.'

She felt her blood run cold, as she slumped to the

floor. She wanted to scream and held her head in her hands. Her body shook with anger, yet she knew it would do her no good.

The strong sunlight worked its way into her thoughts, as her mind told her it was time to get up. Then the warm smell of hot bread and butter floated by and she sat up. Mitch was finishing off the last of his meal, as he offered her a plate. He said nothing though he did not need to, every sorcerer in Alveron was after the Oracle. She did not understand how she had been caught up in the chase. She sighed in deep thought, as she eyed the wizard. She had forgotten to ask Mitch how he had made it here. The wizard smiled in response, if only she could read minds. Mitch made it look easy and this annoyed her even more.

'Liam may know where the Oracle is,' Mitch spoke.

'I doubt it,' Saranon responded.

She had befriended the Prophet in Serenphel. Theron was almost the same age, it was not the only thing they had in common. She had a feeling the Oracle did not want to be found.

Her anxious gaze made the wizard uncomfortable. Yet Mitch said nothing as they made their way downstairs. 'I was wondering when you would appear,' Kylah ran to greet them. With an enthusiasm that bewildered the sorceress.

Saranon smiled even though the worry showed in her eyes. The tavern was as warm and welcoming as it had been the night before. Karraden was a humble piece of paradise locked away, far from the coast. She strode outside into the cool breeze bringing the autumn with it. Liam made his way toward her, 'I don't think I could ever leave this place.'

Saranon waited, she did not want to ask as she avoided making eye contact. 'I thought you wanted to know about the Oracle,' Liam spoke.

'I think I am only one who doesn't,' she sighed.

Liam smiled. 'Then we understand each other.'

She frowned at the comment, as Liam continued, 'Follow me.'

She did so as the wiccan spoke in a soft kindness barely audible above the breeze. His words withered away in the wind as soon as he had said them.

She was so intent on listening. She almost stumbled into the tiny stream that made its way across their path. Liam pointed toward the heartland. Her heart sank, she did not want to meet the Shalough again, in any form. Yet she followed his gaze and absorbed the meaning of his words. There in the distance, hidden from view. Were a clan of sorcerers that had unnatural luck at seeking the wiccan out. Liam did not speak the words as he gazed at her. She knew where the conversation was leading and a chill tingled down her spine. She nodded with the grim thought of facing the Shalough yet again. Any time would be far too soon.

Her head was still reeling from the dim darkness held far beneath the ground. Somehow she would have to find a way to deal it. The thought stuck in her throat, it was too soon. Yet if she waited it would be too late. She let out a small sigh and Liam gave her a comforting pat on the shoulder. He understood the meaning of such an enormous task. As she made her way back to the tavern Mitch was waiting with an enviable patience. The wizard was not at all keen to go with her. She breathed a sigh of relief, it would hard enough with just her. The sky consumed the warm afternoon light as she watched it fade taking her hopes with it.

The town of Karraden seemed far smaller than its actual size. It was a bustling lively place on the edge of the heartland. A beautiful bubble of serenity with an underlying air of anticipation, that yanked at her inner thoughts of turmoil. The Shalough were the last people in the whole of Tordoren that she wanted to meet. Even the Otturin seemed more appealing, then she let the thought go. Katholomu would be at home among the Otturin, but it would not be her home. She mused over her own silent thoughts, before noticing Kylah, who leaned against the stone wall beside her.

Kylah peered into the distance at the great rolling hills. That marked the home of the Shalough. The peaceful breeze brushed past in stark contrast to her mood. 'The Shalough will not expect you.' Kylah spoke in a soft voice.

She wanted to believe Kylah but then the Shalough knew more about the Angean than she did. She smiled then let out a long sigh, 'Look after Mitch.' She spoke into the breeze as she left.

'I don't think he needs looking after,' Kylah beamed.

Saranon never ceased to be amazed at how Mitch could blend in. Except for the time they were in Balquene. The thought scared her more than anything. She travelled away at a slow pace. All she wanted to do was stay. As she gazed upward she lost her footing and tripped. The soft fur of the misquew moved so that she landed on the hard ground. The large riding cat curled up, resting in the faint warmth of the sun. As she touched the ground she could sense the Keep running. It whirred with a magnificence that took her breath away. Then before she could blink she heard it. The sound was so slight she thought she had missed it. Then it reverberated again, the Keep knew she was here.

Saranon stood in disbelief, the Keep Sturanin had no fear of her. There was no awe or surprise. A great rumble seeped through the ground as the blood drained from her face and she ran. She wished she could leave, but the Keep had warned the Shalough. Without any hesitation she slipped in through the wall. As though it were not there. She could feel the vibrations shuddering along the walls as she ran. She slowed and glanced around, no one was following. In fact not one person was anywhere near her, yet the Keep was brimming with life. The Keep was under attack, but this time it was not her.

She let out a groan filled with frustration, the Keep knew she was there. Yet the occupants, the Shalough, were distracted. She was trying to imagine what could possibly distract the Shalough, then she froze. The Oracle had to be here. A tremor reverberated through the walls and she ran down the stairs toward it. The Keep gave a mild resistance. Letting her know she was not welcome, before allowing her to pass through the barrier. The air filled with the heat of sorcery. Building up with an energy that crawled along her skin. A great flame of sorcery hurled along without aim. She let it pass, as the energy around vanished in the haze.

She could sense the Shalough nearby. Yet none of it made sense, as she stayed in the shadows out of the way. The force of the energy thundered as it pummelled down the narrow passages. Rumbling in frequent succession as the lower Keep remained sealed. Veridan yelled with an almighty bellow that made her jump. The sorcerer was too close for comfort. The haze began to clear as the fighting ceased. To Saranon's disbelief she was standing right in the midst of the Shalough. 'You!' Veridan's voice boomed across the chamber.

She stood frozen to the spot. Then realised, it was she who should be angry with Veridan and glared at him in defiance. 'You will tear Tordoren apart before you are done,' Veridan said.

He struck out with his sorcery and watched as it dissipated into nothing. This enraged him even more, 'You were meant to remain imprisoned.'

'You were meant to handover the Oracle,' Saranon spoke in a flat tone.

Before Veridan had a chance to raise his voice the Keep shook. His gaze shifted back to the sealed entrance. Then to Saranon's astonishment the Shalough began pounding the seal. As though she did not exist.

As she watched, a force of energy struck her from behind and tried to fling her out of the way. It only succeeded in moving her to the side. Her annoyance clearly showed. As she raised her arm the whole group turned on her. A cataclysm of sparks cascaded around her bouncing off the walls. As she let the energy glide around rather. The sorcery flew in every direction. She raised her arm and the sparks ceased to exist. Veridan stepped back and his brow creased. He was not used to be challenged. As Saranon moved forward she stood outside the sealed entrance. Without taking her gaze away she held out her hand and the seal fell away.

A voice spoke from the open doorway and Saranon fumed, 'You!'

Flynn stood in front of her without any sign of remorse. 'I am going to leave you to kill each other.' She spoke with a hint of sarcasm.

Wandering off in the stunned silence that followed. Sturanin rumbled beneath as she made her way out into the darkness of night. The cool air swept by, yet it did not quell her anger. She sat on the damp grass as a fine rain fell from the sky. She stood in the land of the Shalough as her heart pounded in defiance. Sturanin remained silent giving nothing away.

Soft footsteps made their way across the muddy ground. As she waited for the Shalough to appear. She gasped at the sight of Madoc. Yet she had sensed a Shalough and peered behind him, expecting someone else. 'It's me,' Madoc replied, answering her unasked question.

'What are you doing here?' She glared at him in annoyance at being deceived.

'This is my home,' he spoke in a matter-of-fact tone as

he stood beside her.

'I thought the Pearl Castle was your home,' Saranon remarked.

'It was,' Madoc replied in a moment of regret.

They stood in a mutual peace gazing out at the night sky. As the rain eased and clouds let in the light from the stars. She could feel the excess energy she had absorbed burning underneath her skin. 'You wanted a bond-breaker,' she stated as they stood in the cool night air.

'That doesn't matter,' Madoc spoke as though all his dreams had been dashed.

She strode a few paces toward Sturanin then reached out her hands. The Keep hesitated before relenting. In the wind and the rain, with the earth of Tordoren and the fire of sorcery raging inside her. The sorceress wielded the blade made of heart stone as it formed in her grip. Sturanin gave one last rumble as it surged in the darkness. The blade was complete and cold to the touch.

She held out the blade as it shone in the light, then covered it in the sheath. 'This is a reminder of all the misunderstandings. That have happened this night, guard it well.'

Madoc made a humble bow as he received the gift. Staring in utter disbelief at the object he had longed for, 'I will guard it well.'

The sorcerer spoke with a sincere gratitude. Saranon sighed, if only finding the Oracle was that easy. As though answering her curiosity the Keep rumbled once more. In the distance the shadows grew as figures moved towards them. 'You need to leave,' Madoc whispered.

She could sense the Shalough approaching and hesitated. She was still no closer to the Oracle. Yet for all the attention, she was beginning to wonder if she would find the Oracle at all. She gazed over the growing crowd and stayed. She had no reason to run even as the numbers grew around her. Madoc stared at her as though urging her to run and she whispered, 'No.'

Veridan emerged. As he eyed Madoc he caught sight of the bond-breaker, 'What have you done?'

Saranon did not answer his question, 'You owe me an explanation.'

Veridan stared long and hard before standing so close she could feel his breath. 'The Angeon will break the world,' he said.

'Which one?' Saranon asked, 'Do you mean me or Merrick?'

The colour drained from Veridan's face as the horror of Saranon's words sank in. He had not realised there were two Angeon. 'Next time, I expect an explanation,' she spoke.

As the resounding beat of Katholomu's wings rose behind her. The dragon had impeccable timing. She could feel the great snort of warm air rush down her back. To her surprise the Shalough allowed her to leave. Kat wasted no time as he beat his wings hard. Bounding into the sky with such speed. That Sturanin became a mere memory fading into the night.

CHAPTER SEVEN

The Oracle

The safety of Karraden felt small as she mused over what had happened. She was still no closer to the Oracle. Mitch had packed the last of his belongings. While Kat was busy shredding the remains of tree. The dragon had taken a particular interest in sharpening his claws. She could not blame him. Ever since she had left Sturanin she had felt as though they were being watched. After all the attention they had to leave. The wiccan were a peaceful people. No match for the full might of their sorcerer neighbours hidden away in the hills. Kat would be easy to see in the sky and they waited for the brilliant rays of dusk to subside.

She preferred flying at night underneath the stars. The first two broke through and she breathed a sigh of relief as more gleamed overhead. Kat raised his head breathing in the cold wind as it swept past and she leaped on. The dragon's muscles became taut as he took to the sky with an astonishing ease. The great beast had been on edge all day and she did not blame him. She itched to be away, as far away as she could from both the Mercidian and the Shalough. The betrayal still stung, as her thoughts ran wild in her head, not wanting to commit.

Mitch clung on tight behind her, the wizard seemed so certain as she clung on to an all mighty mess. The dragon dipped and her thoughts strayed as she gazed through the night sky. It shone with elegant light as the stars made out their way in the darkness. The great beast flew higher into the thin cold air. As it clung to the sides of her cheeks, chilling her breath as they went. It gave her a thrill to be away from the Shalough and all the confusion. They would soon be after her. It was all a muddle that ran through her mind. As a great bolt of thunder flew diagonally from the ground.

Kat reacted before she did with an awful precision that made her heart skip a beat. The wizard remained silent behind her, but she could feel him tense. From out of the ground came another roar of flame. Only this time, it leaped through the sky behind her. Before she knew it Katholomu was surrounded in a tight formation. Symmetrical and elegant like a black diamond in the night sky. It took her a moment to realise they following Kat's lead. A dull black fleet of marmoz sucking in the light from the stars as they swept across the sky. Saranon felt the thrill surge through as her senses awakened. The dragon was honing in.

Several balls of flames answered from the ground. Lit

up as they headed toward them in the air. Kat accelerated and so did the fleet of dragons with a silent menace. They did not break formation. Then her stomach lurched as he dived. She could feel the pull of the sorcery below as it illuminated. Criss-crossing the ground and she gulped. For a moment she doubted herself as the energy welled inside. Saranon catapulted the blast with such straight aim. She almost singed the top of Katholomu's head. The dragon answered with a low rumble and she hesitated. The blast was not enough to extinguish the shield of sorcery. They headed closer at a steady pace.

The ground whirled into view and she took a deep breath. As the belly of the dragon gave a great roar beneath her. She closed her eyes and listened to the low rumble. Holding on tight as she summoned all she could. In the last few seconds before the shield gleamed below. This time the dragon dipped his head, as she let out one last blast. It shot across the web of sorcery with a grim finality. The sparks lit up the sky, showing the great fleet of dragons. It was only then that Saranon glimpsed the other riders on the dragons. She had no idea who they were. Yet as soon as the shield was down they took over. Moving ahead with a crushing blow and wizardry ignited the air around them.

The display of fiery colours would be brilliant. If it was not for the howling screams that followed. She wished she could block them out. Kat held his head high with pride. Then with a stretch and a flick of his tail. He gently knocked the two riders off and covered them under his wings. She tried to move the wing as it hung down with a heavy weight, but it would not budge. She wanted to hit the dragon, but she was exhausted. The panic still raced through her mind. Saranon knelt down on the grubby dirt covered by damp grass and caught her breath. The damp was soaking though to her knees, yet she did not move. There was so much happening outside, as the confusion set in.

Katholomu weakened his grip and relented. There was no end in sight as she ran through the mess with a blind haste. Not recognising anyone as the wizards fought on, ignoring her in their wake. A few steady eyes fell on her, hesitating then looked past as though she were not there. Then the ground cracked open with a low tremor. Whispering a challenge she did not want to accept. Yet no one came and she wondered if she had misunderstood. A cry caught her off guard. It was weak and she should not have heard it at all. Yet somehow amid all the fighting it pierced through the air and found her.

Another tremor embarked along the ground, as though taunting from the deep. Whoever it was did not want to be found. At the edge of her senses the Angeon waited within. Taunting from inside her thoughts. The energy seeped through her skin transforming her. As it blended in the shadows of the night. For the Angeon recognised the dull tremors more than she. It came as though summoned. It took Saranon a while to hear the whispers that had turned into a flood and filled her ears. She knew what it was. The Angeon came to life from within. With a calling that echoed through her thoughts. A faint sound, yet it screamed out in fear and she ran for all she was worth.

She blocked out the sounds of the battle around her as she raced. Time slowed and she felt her heart beat against her chest. Counting the distance with a mocking tone. Yet it guided her onward with a swiftness that ignited her senses. The cave ahead wrapped around her as she ran through the wall. There was no resistance as she swept through. The darkness wrapped around with a familiarity she did not share. As she moved down into the dim depths. A blast rang out, it curled around the walls and the ceiling in circular arc. The Angeon answered in a cold rage and the sorcery shattered. With shards raining around her before they vanished.

The sound rattled out with an unnatural call. That brought a blast aimed so close she could feel the heat across her neck. Before the protection of the Angeon set in. She ran forward with a rush and charged, there was no time. She could sense the voice calling. It was desperate, as the Angeon drew from the energy within. There was no time for empathy. As she fought ahead. Carving the path hard against the tumult of sorcery that followed. She seared through, not wanting to hesitate as the voice called. Pleading with her and weeping into her thoughts. Saranon wished she could shut it out, but could not. She knew who it was, as the oracle cried out in her mind.

The sweeping grimy corners led her down to a pungent smell. That filled the air and stuck to her clothes as she ran. Moisture trickled in tiny pools on the floor making it hopeless to be silent. Another blast rang out up ahead.

Only this time the wall ahead gave way, heading towards her. She took a deep breath and held her energy around to shield the blow. As she ducked and sped through. Then a mighty crack fled up the outer wall of the chamber and another. The sharp splitting sound made the Angeon freeze on the spot as she glanced around. She had to leave and soon. A cry rang out, only this time it was not in her mind. The wall splintered and she pounded on the web of lines creasing across the wall and floor.

Her energy hit its mark as she managed to break through. She stretched herself upward and held her hand out. As the Oracle clung on with all her might. The Oracle let out a scream, as a chunk of rock and dirt fell on the Angeon's shield. Then the girl, all of twelve, jumped over Saranon's shoulder and ran. Christine needed no convincing. The girl fled with such blind luck that the Angeon struggled to keep up. A great jarring sound rang out behind her and she held her breath. She had alwost reached the exit with the light of the full moon shining the way.

Yet as the sound had finished its dooms day call, the whole tunnel around her collapsed. She bolted through with she a dive and slid at the same time. The might of the cascading dirt sealed the cave behind her. Dust sprayed in a horizontal gush showering her with a dim reminder of how close she had come. Yet the Oracle was no where in sight. Her heart sank. She brushed off the dirt as she clambered upward. The ground rumbled and this time it was not from the sunken cave. The Angeon felt the surge of sorcery. Before she saw it gather strength along the ground. She ran toward it and saw the Oracle with her hands held high in a protective stance. They were being surrounded faster than the Angeon could count.

Anger swelled up inside her as she made the last distance and reached the Oracle. Her hand grabbed the hilt belonging to Corsavere. Her bond-breaker formed from the depths of Odana Temple. It swung high as she grimaced, yet she was not aiming for the group of sorcerers closing in. Christine shrieked. Her look filled with terror as she realised the Angeon was after her. Saranon's steely gaze locked on the Oracle. As she brought the blade down hard with both hands. The bond-breaker struck so close. It sheered through the Oracle's sleeve as the girl froze from fear. The blade landed hard into the stony ground. As the Oracle regained her strength and stood, pale as the moon above.

The Angeon plummeted her energy down seeping far into the ground and Tordoren answered. The Oracle screamed. As she caught glimpses of what was happening and shouted for the Angeon to stop. Yet the deed was already done, as the energy of the Angeon bled her energy to the surface. Creating a wide ring of sorcerer's stone as it expanded around them. The Angeon and the Oracle stood at the centre. With the sorcerer's growing agitated along the outer rim that kept them away. A pattern broke along the surface of the stone. At the last moment the Angeon twisted the blade of the bond-breaker. The pattern changed.

The Oracle barely had time to tell her off for making

a wizard's circle. As a rustle sprang undergrowth from behind them. Mitch leaped forward in open defiance and ignited the energy within the stone. The shield sprang into being. Lord Halleron's voice rang out above the crowd. More wizards ignited the wizard's circle as the shield grew stronger still. The Oracle watched in open disbelief. Then Mitch turned his attention to the left and right as if knowing. The ambient light from another wizard's circle ignited, then another and another. Lord Halleron's troops needed no convincing. To ignite the row of circles set hard in the earth.

As the pulse of the shield strengthened the sorcerer's disappeared into the darkness. Mitch eyed Saranon wearily as the Angeon seeped back within. 'If no one knew you were here, they do now.' he said.

Then gazed at the young Oracle and wrapped a cloak around her defiant shoulders. 'You, on the other hand, need to keep a low profile.'

Christine stomped on the wizard's foot, as she marched past without uttering a word. Mitch turned to Saranon, 'You can deal with that.'

'Me?' She said under her breath.

The wizard replied, 'I am only dealing with one sorceress.'

Saranon glared at him, she was not ready for a babysitting job. In fact, that was the last thing she was concerned about. She made her way to the great beast Katholomu. As she clambered up the Oracle was already there waiting. With an unimpressed look since the dragon would not budge. Saranon clambered on as Mitch shared another ride. He had made it clear the Oracle was one too may. She gave out a reluctant sigh, as she motioned for the dragon to fly. He obediently headed toward Auden, the great Keep of Lord Halleron, in Felkrayer.

As they flew the Oracle moved sideways, as though searching the ground beneath. She was about to say something and then motion in the dark caught her eye. It was not clear, but whatever it was it worried the Oracle. Katholomu swung at a hard angle. As he glided sideways spiralling down around the curve of the Keep. With a flick of his tail he lowered his wings and came to a screeching halt. Skidding across the courtyard toward the dragon pens. Before she had time to steady herself the Oracle had jumped off and was nowhere to be seen. She grumbled as she made her way down. The dragon let out a low rumble as he chuckled with amusement. 'Don't you start,' she spoke as she let the beast be.

Auden was huge and unfamiliar, it did not resemble any Keep she had come across. Like the Lord, the Keep remained silent. Several times she found herself going around in circles. Only to be greet by a friendly chuckle. 'You have passed this foyer three times,' the wizardess said.

Captain Lydia Grace smiled and showed the sorceress up to the great hall. The warmth hit her in a welcome burst as the door opened. Sounds of merriment and too much drink followed. As she attempted to enter unnoticed and the room fell as silent as the Keep. Mitch had positioned himself in a comfortable chair. Well away from the door and out of reach.

She frowned in dismay, the wizard could be rather unhelpful. He was seven years her senior and taller than most men with a frame to match. In comparison she was still an awkward seventeen. Saranon still had her hair out in much the same way a child would. Lord Halleron paused, before he rose to his feet and lifted her off the ground in a warm embrace. He patted her shoulder and moved her toward the head table with a grin. That showed an uneven row of teeth. If she were anyone else, it would be an intimidating sight. This was not the first wizard lord she had encountered.

The food smelled so good as she sat down. That she began piling her plate before the lord had time to sit. He said in a low voice, 'I think the Shalough have it right.'

He stopped to hear her pause with a worried glance. The Lord continued, 'It is you I should fear.'

Lord Halleron turned his gaze to the young Oracle who shouted in disgust. While no one was paying attention. There were a few warm smiles that made the Oracle erupt in another outburst. As she stomped her feet and sight of Saranon. She had time to hide, even though she knew hiding would serve no purpose. Christine, who had changed into a beautiful pale dress. Grabbed hold of Saranon's arm demanding that she go with the Oracle.

When the girl realised her attempt was futile. Christine sat down in a loud humph right next to her, 'Do you know how much trouble is coming? You are wasting time.'

Saranon smiled. 'I am no good to anyone with an

empty stomach and no sleep.'

The Lord chuckled with a big belly laugh as he ate. His large grin was in stark contrast to the Oracle's frown. The night continued on with a range of drunken song. Somehow every wizard managed to avoid Saranon. An act that she found quite impressive given there was more than one brawl. That had begun with an awkward stumble. As she rose to go to bed the Oracle went with her, the girl showed no intention of leaving her side. She let a sigh, then held out her hand as they made their way to bed. Perhaps in the morning the Oracle would find someone else to annoy. For for now she was all the girl had. The company was welcome given she was in a wizard Keep. There were almost no other sorcerers in sight.

Her dreams were filled with the rage of battle as the voices rang out around her. The last sound that came was the thunderous roar of the cave as it collapsed around. A mighty thud woke her as she stared up at Christine who had jumped on her bed. The girl had already begun ordering her out of bed. Saranon attempted to tell the Oracle there was no need to rush as the girl pushed her out of the way. She grumbled as she gathered her things in haste. It was not the start to the morning she had been hoping for, as the late autumn sun broke across the sky. She eyed Mitch in the corridor who showed no intention of intervening. Even under a stern gaze.

The wizard appeared to enjoy leaving her to occupy the Oracle. As everyone stepped out of their way. She held up her hand to block the rays of the morning light. As they ran out onto the courtyard adjacent the dragon pens. Katholomu opened one eye to peer at them, as he remained curled up in a sleepy fashion. Then to her surprise held out his front paw and gave a gentle flick with his claw. Moving the Oracle toward the door. A scream filled the air, then Christine shouted at the dragon in haste. Saranon took a deep breath, but the dragon did not move. She let out a sigh and in that moment Kat decided he had had enough. The dragon let out a fowl warm gust of air from his lungs. It was enough to give the Oracle a start and she ran out into the open field.

'Really?' She gazed at the dragon. 'Well, at least you didn't squash her.'

She chased after the girl, when she would much rather be curled up asleep. In the distance Lady Halleron had found the Oracle and she breathed a sigh of relief. Someone else could look after the girl, at least for the moment. Mitch stood at the end of the courtyard in a solemn stance at his full height as she peered upward. 'There is someone waiting for you,' he remarked.

'Pardon?' Saranon asked.

The wizard held out his hand and gestured without a reply. There in the largest sitting room she had ever laid eyes upon. Stood a tall and nimble sorcerer. His eyebrows raised in a monotone form as she entered. 'The ockren requests your presence,' Halwende spoke as though it was a mere formality.

'What ockren?' She asked with a puzzled expression.

'The one that sits on the last wizard circle. You so

promptly made,' Halwende replied.

Staring in a matter-of-fact tone as he cleared his voice with a cough. As Saranon stood in a baffled silence. Christine's voice rang out across the room, 'I'm coming with you.'

The Oracle announced in a proud stance with her hands on her hips. Halwende bowed his head in a smooth motion, 'And this young lady, would be the Oracle. The one whom we are to teach in the art of sorcery.'

Christine gave him an uneasy stare then announced in a stern voice, 'I am not going.'

Saranon looked at her agape as though she had missed something. 'I am not going,' the Oracle repeated.

Lord Halleron and Halwende gave a knowing smile. As though the arrangement had already been agreed.

Before thinking Saranon exclaimed, 'Do you know what you are getting involved in?'

Halwende gave her a warm smile, 'Why yes, the oracles of old were from this region.'

Lord Halleron arched his back in a fine gesture of grandeur. 'The Fellowyn's know more about the Oracle than anyone else,' he said.

The Lord looked as though he was about to say more. Instead stopped himself short as he left their company. He was a wizard of few words, but what he did say carried weight. She had the distinct feeling he knew far more than he would ever admit.

The day was cool, yet the sky was crystal clear. As they made their way at an easy pace to see an ockren without a

Keep. Saranon had never heard of such a thing, yet it did not surprise her. She grew anxious as they became closer and the great magical beast could be seen up ahead. She stood and took a deep breath near the edge of the wizard circle, as the ockren raised it's head. The faint marking on the beast appeared different and more notable in the light. She stepped with hesitation and made her way forward. Until she was almost level with the ockren's yellow eyes. The giant cat moved in a way that was not quite right. As it spoke in a hollow tone. That rumbled along the ground, 'Angeon, you have passed your second test.'

Saranon stood expecting something else to happen, but the ockren waited. As it's short rough coat moved in way that did not allow for the movement of muscles beneath. She hesitated, 'What do you mean by a second test?'

She had not recalled her first test and the ockren did not make sense. The ockren smiled, if that was at all possible. Then it let out a low rumble of a laugh that clung in the air and chilled her skin. Just as the sound ceased the ockren arched forward. Light criss-crossed along its skin as though breaking through from underneath. The outer layer melting away before she could take a breath. The energy that had been held within sparkled as it cascaded. A strong gust blew toward her. Before she could move the energy contained within the ockren blew through her. The sensation tingled as she blinked and opened her eyes in a different phase.

The world she had been in was swept away by the

sorcery trapped in the ockren. There before her on the wizard's circle, stood Tasha, the only person she could see. The spirit of her old friend glowed with a warm vibrancy. Silhouetted by her fawn coloured hair, waving free of her shoulders. It had been so long since she had seen her old friend, 'Why have you brought me here.'

Tasha smiled, 'Welcome to my world.'

CHAPTER EIGHT

The memory that remains

Tasha stood still as though waiting for the right moment. Then spoke, 'I could not tell you that you had passed the first test. You would not have survived the Shalough.'

The grim reality of what her friend was saying sank in. The Shalough really had tried to kill her. 'What was my first test?'

Tasha appeared amused by the question, 'You encountered the other Angeon.'

Saranon exclaimed, 'Merrick Calthazard.'

The different phase held few people, only those who could travel there. The uneven wind that swept around them made a hollow sound that made her anxious. Yet she knew she had to return. The ground blurred underneath. She was back where she began on the wizard's circle. Mitch gave her a knowing stare and held out his arm to comfort her. The wizard could read her mind at all the wrong times, just when she hoped for some quiet.

The memory of her friend held so much pain, it was hard to let go. They made their way back to the wizard Keep. She sat down, the anguish plain on her face. By all accounts she should be dead. She had been betrayed by one of the few friends she had. Mitch could not stand still. She could not read his mind, but his anxiety showed. She asked, 'What's going on?'

He hesitated before responding, 'Lord Halleron is gathering support. To meet on the edge of the heartland. I told him we would join them.'

Her face grew hot as she fumed. It was not like him to make a decision, but she could not think of an alternative. 'You want me away from the Oracle,' she quizzed.

'I think it's best,' he said.

It was a blunt reply. She did not want to stay near the Oracle, but the choice had already been made. The last night at Felkrayer moved slow as she wrestled in her sleep. Waking too often in the dark. She woke again as Mitch approached. They left before the light reached over the mountains. Katholomu greeted her and they clambered on. She waited as Mitch steadied himself near the thick folds of the dragon's shoulder.

The great beast jolted into the sky, his wings spread and they gathered speed. The chill of the late autumn wind numbed her face and she held on. Guiding Kat through the morning light. 'I passed two tests of the Angeon,' she spoke her thoughts aloud.

He was quiet for a while, 'You are meant to be older.'

She asked, 'How would you know?'

'The Angeons of old did not experience the tests until they were older,' he said. 'Have you read the books you kept?'

'I missed that,' she exclaimed.

It annoyed her when Mitch knew more about the Angeon that she did. 'So what if I'm a bit early,' she retorted.

'You will not be ready,' he responded.

The dragon remained quiet, as he glided above the hills and dense forest below. 'Mitch,' she said, 'I would prefer it if you didn't tell anyone.'

'I am your hilazen,' he answered.

She was not sure if that meant yes or no, but was not about to ask.

A golden sun shone over Hestrel Keep and Katholomu circled down. Gliding too close to the wall and his claw scrapped. She winced at the sound and the dragon took no notice. As he hit the ground, leaning over to warm his back. She slid off as Kat rolled, it was one of his softer landings. Captain Grace headed toward Mitch, 'You took your time.'

Before Saranon had time to ask she was alone in the stone courtyard.

The sun shone along the grey walls. Warming the courtyard that linked around the Keep. Opening up to the garden that buffered them from the thick woodland. She wandered around to the dragon pens, where supplies were being offloaded from the carts. She darted through a gap into the warmth of the pens. An open hearth gave a welcoming glow from the end of the room. She accepted a drink and found a seat as the wizards rested between work. A blanket moved near the hearth and she jumped. Elethea laughed and an infant marmoz dragon poked its head out. The creature was tiny compared to the full grown dragons.

It wandered over and sniffed her holding one paw up, then curled up in her lap. 'You won't be able to move now,' Elethea smiled. 'Kallie will stay as long as you let her.'

The hatchling felt so fragile as she patted it. The seat provided a good vantage point. As she watched the equipment and weapons being hauled into the Keep. She asked, 'What are you preparing for?'

Elethea grew silent and an officer answered. 'Guarding the trade link,' Bayard spoke.

She asked, 'Is that from the Shalough?'

'No,' he replied.

'It's always been a rough journey to travel inland,' Bayard relaxed.

While taking a break. Yet his eyes took in everything watching. As the last of the supplies vanished into the building. A growl shot across the courtyard. Katholomu squeezed his head sideways through the archway. Saranon glared at him, 'Are you jealous?'

He huffed a snort of warm stale air into the room and she placed the hatchling down. She patted his head while nudging him out of the doorway. The pens were a good size and Kat fit comfortably. He flopped on the floor letting her pat his head.

There was something odd about the supplies. The Keep did not appear lacking in anything. Yet she said nothing, as she began to groom the dragon. Her ordeal had taken its toll. Her friend Clara had betrayed her and Alveron was no longer the safe haven it may have been. Katholomu's offered a small respite from the storm inside her head. If two tests were done, how long did she have until the final one? She was lost in her thoughts when Mitch approached. 'The Athgar need our help,' he said.

'Don't include me in this,' she spoke before he had time to answer.

'Wiccan have disappeared,' he explained.

Ever since Mrs Harper's tavern in Normisia the wiccan had welcomed her. It was more than many had done. The night caved in as the clouds drew close, the days were getting shorter. She let the great dragon rest and entered into the Keep. The outer rim turned from a worn rustic appearance. Into sleek hard walls beautifully formed with wide corridors. She held her hand up against the cold stone and Hestrel Keep responded with a vibrant hum. Its strength shone in the lights illuminating the walls. Mitch led her to the control room. Where Captain Lydia Grace studied several maps spread across a broad table.

As Saranon approached she spied the markers highlighting the wicca towns. Close to the trade link to the south of the heartland. There was something else. She leaned forward picking gazing at a mark for the Athgar, yet it was not the same. The Captain read her immediate thoughts, 'The Athgar are divided.'

It was the only explanation Captain Lydia Grace was willing to give. She made her way to the cosy apartment that waited part way up the wizard Keep. The room was a welcome relief as she sat curled up near the fire. A quiet knock came from the door and Mitch let himself in. He sat on the chair next to her. The wizard had been her companion for over a year and she was yet to figure him out. 'Hold out your hands,' he asked.

She did, there was nothing there and he gave a look of dismay. 'If anything appears let me know,' he said.

She asked, 'If what appears?'

'Anything different,' he replied. 'To mark when the final test is near.'

The thought made her shudder and Lord Shakar's words stayed with her. If she chose the wrong path he would kill her. If she chose the right one he could use her to rule Zyanthia. Mitch hugged her before he left. It was little comfort and she hoped that sleep would bring relief. The wind whirred around the Keep, with a sound that penetrated through the walls as she drifted off.

A clamour woke her with the dawn as Mitch opened the door. She glanced out the window, and asked, 'Do you know what time it is?'

He ignored her protest and waited as she hurried. The smell of warm toast wafted from the great hall and she wandered in. Kat had flattened a corner of the garden including two trees. While warming his belly in the sun. His long tail swished in a dangerous carefree motion. Keeping a buffer between him and the trainers. 'Katholomu,' she shouted so loud the dragon stood up to greet her. She exclaimed, 'Can you be discreet?'

The great beast laughed and his body rumbled magnifying the sound into a low growl.

Kat had never been discreet. She thought she would ask before she climbed up on his shoulders. Mitch motioned for the dragon to fly before she had a chance to hang on and almost slid off. The cloud covered sky hid the dragon as the chill wind set in. Her rough coat had been borrowed from the Athgar. It kept her warm as they flew high staying amid the grey sky. Hestrel was well placed. Guarding a fork between the main road to the south and the road east to Felkrayer. Kat swooped low on the verge of the hillside as it met the forest sweeping along either side. The dense woodland parted to form a road held together with worn stone. She gazed along the road yet it vanished darting in and out of view.

A loud crack caught her attention. She turned to find a tree collapsing under the dragon's weight. Kat rested without a care and she exclaimed, 'Did we have to bring the dragon?'

'The road veers close to the heartland. We will draw attention if we don't,' Mitch explained.

Saranon was tempted to ask if they could bring a different dragon, but Kat may not take the hint. She trudged along, her every attempt to avoid the mud muted by the damp ground. Mitch showed her the first marker along the road and she went pale.

The stone marker was too familiar. Identical to the

ones that had trapped her inside the detention camp. He spoke, but the words did not sink in, '...Are you all right?'

She asked, 'Can we leave?'

He hesitated then took her back to the upside down dragon. Kat had managed to stick his tail and hind legs in the air. While rubbing his back against the muddy ground. The great beast turned and grumbled at the sight of her muddy boots. 'Don't you start,' she said.

They travelled in silence, as soon as the dragon landed she slid down. Mitch caught her halfway and she nose planted into the dragon's dirt ridden scales. He let go and Saranon slid down covered in the mud. Mitch began to laugh and she stormed off. It was not the reaction she had expected. Before she had a chance to sit down he found her, 'I can travel alone.'

The frustration showed on her face, 'No.'

He nodded and let her be. She knew the road had to be protected, but the markers still sent a chill down her spine.

The memory of the detention camp had seemed so far away. The glow of the marker dimmed and she moved. The glow returned, and she glanced around trying to figure out what had happened. She reached out her hand yet there was no change. She tried again and the dragon roared with laughter. He gave a firm nudge with his front leg and she fell toward the rock.

Again the glow dimmed and she peered down. All she could find was her bond-breaker. She placed it on the stone marker and the glow dimmed. 'Oh,' she exclaimed.

The dragon gave a loud snort and rumbled. 'I didn't know,' she said.

'Angeon,' he snorted.

'You know I am the Angeon,' she responded.

The forest parted around them as they were met by a group of wizards. Mitch shouted, 'What are you doing?'

'It was him,' she said pointing to the dragon.

'Don't blame this one on Kat. You tampered with the markers,' he accused her.

She glared at him, 'Yes.'

'They protect the road,' he motioned for her to follow.

The Athgar wizards moved with ease through the forest. The branches shook behind them as the great dragon plodded through. 'Now everyone knows we are here,' she exclaimed.

Mitch responded, 'Dragons are common...'

Before he could finish two juvenile dragons ran past. 'All right,' she retorted.

'If you must know, you are the odd one,' he added.

The Athgar wizards checked the stone markers while she stayed at the edge of the group. The glow held too many memories trapped away, she tried not to let it show. The two younger dragons ran close to Katholomu. He leaped out, sending one to the ground. 'No,' she shouted and Kat released his hold.

The juvenile dragon whimpered and scurried away. Kat stood in front of her stomping his front leg hard on the ground. 'I said "no",' she glared at him.

Mitch spoke, 'Saranon.'

Kathomolu jumped straight over her. Every muscle tense as Kat narrowed in on the adult dragon, ripping into the flesh. Kat's opponent backed down screeching in pain. 'Finish the fight,' she yelled at the dragon who glanced at her.

Mitch stared at her in horror. She yelled again, 'Finish the dragon.'

Katholomu heaved and lay down, breathing heavy. Saranon strode toward the dragon, 'You only get one chance to attack me.'

She let the Angeon flow through, the adult dragon hobbled further away.

Her energy flared into a narrow arc, hitting the dragon's heart. It stood for a moment before falling with a heavy thud. Only then did Kat wince in agony. Saranon searched the dead dragon and found a small trace, the mark of the Shalough. She took a closer glance holding back the dragon's thick coat. The second mark below showed the fires of chaos. It matched the mark on her arm, given to her in the detention camp.

'We should go,' Mitch said.

The sun was beginning to set as the breeze deepened its chill and she nodded.

Katholomu let her climb on and she glanced back. Watching as the dead dragon disintegrated. He flew strong and she clung on until they landed in the courtyard near the dragon pens. Kat lowered his head and winced. Bayard rushed to examine the dragon. The wound was little more than a graze, yet a crowd gathered to dote on the giant beast. Saranon eyed the dragon with suspicion when Mitch spoke, 'He defended you.'

Captain Grace added while patting the beast, 'He did a good job.'

She asked the captain, 'Do the Shalough use the symbol for the fires of chaos?'

'Before the Dreshan occupation, you won't see it much now,' the Captain answered.

She waited to make sure Katholomu was snug and warm inside the pens. He rested with a gentle purr that rumbled through his body. She leaned close and whispered in his ear, 'Did you know I was the Angeon?'

The dragon responded by nuzzling his head against her. She stayed long after the night fell and made her way to the great hall. The large room was almost empty and she spotted Mitch by the fire.

He spoke, 'You killed the dragon.'

'I had to,' she responded.

'That is not what I meant,' Mitch said. 'Anyone else would hesitate.'

'Or run away,' she added.

He asked, 'You doubt my ability?'

'No. Well...' She began.

Mitch gave her an annoyed glare. The wizard was seven years her senior and made it clear when he was not impressed.

Hestrel Keep stayed almost silent. As she slipped through the empty corridors to her room. The thick walls made the place feel smaller than it was, but the room was cosy enough. She took out the bond-breaker Corsavere holding it up to the light. The heart stone embedded in the hilt glowed. The device could nullify her oldest fear and she held it in her hand. The fear was long gone, or so she thought before seeing the stone markers. It had been a long time since she had thought of the detention camps in Darkonia. Tasha's death stayed a constant reminder. The loss of her friend and leader had been so great. It weighed on her mind even more.

She took off her coat staring down at the mark on her arm. The fires of chaos were still there, yet her palms were clear. A faint shadow appeared as she stared at her hands and she gasped. The second test was complete. She should have guessed her marks would begin to show. They were so faint if she pretended they were not there no one would know. Saranon let exhaustion take her as she fell asleep. The turmoil of the day crept into her dreams and well into the early morning.

CHAPTER NINE

The price of survival

An awkward atmosphere hung over the room as Saranon failed to find the right words. Mitch interrupted. It was a welcome relief as she followed him into the fading light covering the dragon pens. Hestrel Keep had been silent, there was only one way to find out what had happened. The thought chilled her more than the wind that took hold. She slipped by the wizards. Making her way down to the indolin chambers below the habitable area. The Keep was strong and sturdy, yet it had fallen to the Dreshan Army that had taken Zyanthia. The region had since been reborn into five countries. Armedicia, Taria and Normisia and in the south, Darkonia and Alveron. Hestrel Keep stood near the midway point joining the south to the north. She should have known it had seen war, yet the thought had not occurred to her.

She made her way further down to the imbenik chambers. The hum from the central core rose above the background noise. A solid sorrowful sound that filled the air. She called out in her mind and it spoke. The foundations reverberated she could sense the shudder from the dragon pens and ran. It came again ever so faint, yet it broke through the low hum of the Keep. At first the pens were empty then the great dragon rammed against the side of the building. She shouted mistaking the beast for Katholomu. The dragon glared at her. His features were similar with a scar running down the left side of his jaw.

Kail stood in the cold night air. The Otturin sorcerer gave the same glare as his dragon, 'Where is the Oracle?'

Captain Lydia Grace and the wizards blocked him from entering the Keep. She glanced around, 'Where is Katholomu?'

'Mitch took him with the riders,' Bayard replied.

She was not impressed. Kail stood close, 'You were supposed to return the Oracle.'

'You haven't had much experience with a real Oracle, have you?' She remarked.

He mused, '... And you have?'

'Yes,' she replied and asked, 'Can I ride with you?'

'You are not stealing another dragon,' he spoke, climbing atop Dramakor.

She gazed over the dragons that were left and let them be. A small group of misquew made their home on the edge of the garden. She called to one and it came. The riding cat was well built for speed, yet not for long distance. She made her way to the first stone markers. Highlighting the gateway to the road and let the misquew go. She stood next to the marker, hesitating before reaching out. The sickly glow wavered and she tried not to let go. Her hand slipped, she took a deep breath and tried again.

She let the flow of the Angeon guide her. Gripping onto a remnant of sorcery in the stone and stepped onto the road. The chill wind faded as she dropped out of phase and the world grew silent. The road passed beneath her with no rhythm as she walked. The distance melted as she picked up speed. A dragon broke through the sky shattering the peace. It threw her back into the real world and she hit the ground with a thud. She glanced up in time to watch Dramakor fall, a web of sorcery dragging him down. She ran to the dragon and Kail's scream cut through. The wizards were guarding the Oracle, but the attackers had caught Kail. Their sorcery rose and the small group became twelve Shalough.

The formation began to close and the energy of the Angeon rose. She ripped through the corner of the circle. Her energy scorched a long trail as it blasted the group apart. The last of the Shalough ran. She grabbed Kail. 'No. Leave me,' he cried out.

'He won't make it,' Mitch said.

She exclaimed, 'What?'

Kail held out his arm, his sorcery was bleeding out. No matter how much he tried to make it stop. 'Leave,' he cried.

Mitch opened a small sova bag, as it grew in size he

took out a hyrik. Saranon jumped back. The metal band made of wizardry had been placed around her neck once.

She shouted, 'What are you doing?'

'It will stop the flow,' Captain Grace explained, 'or he will bleed out.'

Her face grew pale, 'Do you have to?'

Kail screamed even more as the hyrik was placed around his neck. To her amazement the sorcery stopped flowing from his arm. 'You can take him back,' Mitch said.

She protested, 'Me? I don't think so.'

He asked, 'Would you rather stay?'

She wanted to stay, a few of the attackers had escaped. Mitch nodded as though reading her immediate thoughts.

She watched as the group left and Katholomu stood watching her. He did not blink as he stared. 'Let us hunt.' She said.

The dragon flexed his shoulders in eagerness and she climbed up. This time the dragon stayed low to the ground and his muscles moved in a fluid motion. Every step calculated, as he ran through the edge of the forest. The rustle of the wind called to her as she sensed the lay of the land. Waiting with the patient dragon. She drew her bond-breaker Corsavere to the length of a sword. This time there would be no survivors. Katholomu honed in through the darkness, it was all she needed.

Saranon slid down his shoulder while her focus stayed transfixed. She rushed forward taking the first sorcerer by surprise. The marks of dark sorcery revealed as the body slumped beside the brittle bark of the tree. Her heart thudded in her ears as the energy of the Angeon flooded through. She ran along the muddy ground with the last of the autumn leaves underfoot. Two sorcerers up ahead were so close. That the energy took them down in the same blast as it lit up the night. She had not meant to worn the others, as the embers glowed throwing shadows past the trees. A sorceress moved in the distance and she ran toward her. A blow of sorcery knocked her from behind, but it was not enough. As the energy of the Angeon shielded her.

She moved forward still catching her breath and hit the sorceress hard. The energy of the Angeon was so great it ripped the dark sorcery from the sorceress. A hideous scream pierced the night. Saranon hesitated taking a step back. The impact frightened her and she tried not to show it. 'We need to go,' Madoc shouted behind her.

The sight of the dragon trainer was enough to snap her out of the trance. Her attacker lied dead on the ground. Madoc's blade glowed from the impact. She asked, 'What are you doing?'

'Same as you. We have to leave,' he said.

They raced toward Katholomu, she climbed on last. The dragon jolted into the sky while she watched for any sign of attack. The great beast made good speed. They were well away as the first signs of sorcerers scattered across the ground. 'They took my brother,' Madoc explained. Saranon knew what that meant after witnessing the attack on Kail. 'Is that why you hid among the Mercidian?'

'Yes,' he replied.

Katholomu glided into the courtyard and flopped

sideways to let them down. Before curling up into a large ball inside the warmth of the dragon pens.

Mitch ran out to meet them. Eyeing Madoc with caution before speaking, 'Kail has sealed himself in the Keep.'

She shouted, 'What?'

'He is below the habitable area,' he answered.

She made her way down the stairs and Madoc ran after her. He asked, 'Can I join you?'

They made their way down, the corridors were silent. The Keep guided her toward Kail. She made her way through the catacomb of tunnels to a simple room. An altar had been carved out of the far wall. Kail still wore the hyrik, the sight of the band made her hesitate. She reached out with her mind, I cannot take your pain but I can share your burden. Kail opened his eyes, it was the look of exhaustion.

'The Oracle is safe,' she said.

'You should not have taken her,' Kail said.

'Madoc and I just saved your hide,' she spoke as she helped him stand.

Saranon waited until they were out of sight, 'The oracle stays at Felkrayer.'

'You steal my dragon and now you steal the Oracle,' Kail said.

'...And save your life,' Madoc added.

The two sorcerers stared at each other in silence before letting the matter lie.

Mitch stormed along the corridor, 'I want a word

with you.'

Madoc and Kail left her alone to face the wizard. The fact that he was her hilazen did not make it any better and she cringed. Mitch took her to the side, 'What are doing?'

'I... I had to go after the Razen sorcerers,' she explained.

'I meant the young men you were flirting with,' he glared at her.

'I was not flirting,' she shouted. 'I was not flirting,' she repeated in a softer voice.

He asked, 'How old are you?'

'Seventeen,' she rolled her eyes. 'I was not flirting.'

'You are going to be a full Angeon soon,' he said.

She could feel her cheeks grow hot. 'Be careful who you choose,' he added.

The change in Mitch's words surprised her as he left. At Balquene the thought of her having a boyfriend had shocked him. It was not the type of conversation she wanted to have.

The thought clouded her mind and she went beneath the habitable area. Hestrel Keep had survived the Dreshan Occupation and the temptation was too great. She made her way down until she stood at the lowest part of the indolin chambers. The last area before the central core. She waited calling out to Hestrel with her mind, yet the Keep was reluctant to let her in. She listened to the hum of the central core whirring underneath.

She was about to speak and the floor slipped away. The central core caught her off guard as it dragged her down into the deep. It barely spoke above the rhythm that reverberated around. The outer shell closed, trapping her inside a thick storm. The current of the winds picked her up as though she was floating through the air. An array of light glowed along the rod, yet the clouds were so thick, she could only just make it out. Then the light was upon her and she crashed with a thud. Clinging on as the clouds whirled around. She held on and moved around to an opening leading into the control room. Saranon fell on the floor as gravity returned. The makeshift room was in immaculate condition. She took a seat at the control panels, trying to remember how it operated.

A lever moved on the floor and the whirring increased. She turned it the other way and the storm began to slow. Hidden behind the whirring clouds was a central core in perfect condition. The outer shell held no signs of stress. The structural frame leading down was sturdy. She peered down at the rod and the surface was smooth. Somehow the central core had survived the Dreshan occupation. She smiled as she gazed. Watching the stallic energy rise at a steady pace charging the central core.

The core rumbled and she made her way out of the enclosed room. Letting go of gravity as she floated upward. The winds that swept around the core caught her. As the outer shell opened guiding her to the surface. Her feet made contact with solid ground and she reached out. Touching the sorcerers stone. The end node was partially covered by the undergrowth of the forest. A fair distance from the main building. Flynn emerged from the edge of the forest in the morning light. Her anger swelled within as more Mercidian sorcerers arrived.

The Mercidian attacked and the shield surrounding Hestrel Keep flared. Bringing the attention of the Athgar wizards. She was too angry. She tried to calm her thoughts as she watched from distance. Madoc ran toward the Mercidian sending a flare into the sky. She should have known he would bring the Shalough.

Saranon shouted to Flynn, 'You have no place here.'

She turned to Madoc, 'You had to make it worse.'

Madoc hung his head and did not answer. Flynn stared at her, 'You were never meant to live.'

Saranon stepped outside the shield protecting the Keep, 'You are too late Mercidian.'

The energy of the Angeon surged within and Flynn backed down. She waited as he left.

'I was trying to help,' Madoc explained.

She headed toward the Keep, 'At least you have a clan.'

The Keep had become silent as she fumed. Captain Grace was the last person she expected see. 'We have a problem,' the Captain said.

'Kail,' Captain Grace continued. The colour drained from her face.

The stairs leading down below the habitable area, opened into a foyer, lit from above. A pool of dark sheal lapped near the rim of the floor as she entered the underground room. The hyrik was removed and Kail remained slumped at the base of a column. His fingers swinging close to the sheal. His sorcery surged and he let it drain into the sheal. 'You cannot stay here,' she said.

He leaped up and shouted, the sorcery surging along his skin. 'You should have returned the Oracle. Get out!'

She stayed and Kail stumbled. She caught him, but he pulled away from her grasp. 'Leave,' he said. 'Leave.'

He stumbled again. 'You are going to fall in,' she said.

He glared at her as he sat on the floor in resignation. 'I need to be with my clan,' he spoke.

Saranon knelt down, 'Stay away from the Oracle.'

She clasped his head in her hands. The energy of the Angeon rose within. It crept through her and entered Kail sealing his sorcery in. He grabbed her hand and saw the faint mark, 'Well, well. You've been keeping that one secret.'

She pulled away, 'That's none of your business.'

He gave a knowing smile of satisfaction and she fought the urge to shove him into the sheal. 'You owe me,' she said.

'You stole my dragon, I call that even,' he replied.

She lunged at Kail before he was able to leave and they rolled close to the edge of the sheal. A heavy hand picked her up and Kail wrestled free. As soon as Mitch placed her back on the ground she turned on him. His expression was cold and firm. Saranon backed away teetering on the edge of the sheal and fell in. The cool liquid began draining the energy from her. She managed to heave herself up on the floor. Mitch's stance was unwavering. 'He...' the words trailed off as she glared at him. 'Do not annoy the Otturin,' Mitch said.

'He's not...' She began.

Nothing she could say would make the wizard understand. Saranon pulled away from his grasp. The impact of the sheal still plagued her senses. She sought refuge below in the depths of the Keep. The walls became silent as she descended far beneath the habitable area. A great chasm loomed at the edge of the floor, marking the decent to the central core. The magical entity that flowed through the Keep. Nothing above had survived the Dreshan Occupation. Yet the floor held the pattern of the Keep. Hestrel had been alone in the dark, cut off from the outside world. She let the low hum sink through and peered over the edge. A dull drone crept up with the warm air weaving its way up the vents.

She took one step reaching out into the void and held out her arms embracing the fall. The darkness wrapped around, hauling her down. The voice of the Keep hummed welcoming her back amid the drone, as she fell ever closer to the core. The descent gave way in a rush as the outer shell came into reach. Each time she hesitated unsure of what to find, yet knowing too much. Hestrel spoke urging her to enter. Only a few could and even fewer dared. She reached out expecting to find the shell solid. Yet it ebbed away beneath pulling her in. A mass of clouds swirled in the haze as the charge crackled through. There was no way up or down as Hestrel waited. The control room revealed again as the haze lifted and she clung on. Gravity took hold in the circular structure secured at the centre of the core.

A man sat at the controls and she froze. It was the embodiment of the Keep. She backed away. He held out his hand and beckoned her. 'Only you can drive the core,' he said.

'You want something,' she eyed him with suspicion.

She waited and the man became agitated. 'When you want to talk let me know,' she moved away.

'Rebuild the Keep,' Hestrel said.

A smile crept across her face as she slipped into the comfortable seat. Hestrel leaned over and she gently blocked him. He did not resist. The Angeon surged through as she waited for the energy of the core to reach them. It ignited along the rod embedded deep in Tordoren weaving its way toward them.

The Keep began to move upward with a slow pace at first. The great structure rising from the ground. The towers of old rose around the end nodes forming the outer rim. The Keep stopped as it moved into its final resting place. It felt like a life time as Hestrel lifted her back through the open void. Her ears still humming with the sound of the Keep.

Mitch whispered, 'You have been gone seven days.'

The exhaustion found a way to creep in as the sun shone through frost. She left while the wizards shouted with excitement. The room was warm inside the thick walls and she soon fell into a deep sleep.

Mitch's voice cut through the dark as she managed to open her eyes, 'We have to leave.'

Saranon asked, 'Why?'

'We will leave before dawn, be ready,' Lord Halleron said as he closed the door behind him.

'Tathen has been attacked,' Mitch said.

She sat bolt upright and rushed to get ready, it was not what she wanted to hear. The frost had thickened in the night. The Athgar wizards prepared the horses for travel. She asked, 'Why not take the dragons?'

Lord Halleron answered, 'Wizards prefer to stay together.'

She hesitated, then went outside to call to the misquew. One answered and she waited as the wizards formed a tight group. Lord Halleron stayed in the centre. The hilt of his bond-breaker gleamed in the dark. The misquew sat lower than the horses. They made their way to the road where stone markers lit the way ahead. Her stomach churned, yet she held on. Lord Halleron waited for the last wizard to enter the road then gave the signal. The road spun past as the wizards used the stone markers to move at a quick pace. A glimmer of faded light broke over the hill and through the trees. Smoke from the chimneys marked the cottages of Tathen. The smooth stone broke into an uneven trail underneath.

A white layer of frost circled Tathen. They exited the edge of the woods to find Captain Drevon waiting. The group continued through the town growing as the wizards gathered. Saranon glanced around. By the time they reached the end of the town the group verged on a small army. She stayed close to the Lord as they picked up speed. Shouts rang from up ahead as a blast rang out from the hillside. The wizards charged leaving her behind. She sensed the wizardry and hesitated, they were fighting their own. Mitch swung around and yelled out, he pointed ahead and her gaze followed. Still she lagged behind. The wizards took the fight into the heart of the group.

Mitch shouted in anguish, 'What are you doing?'

'I can't,' she answered.

He re-joined Lord Halleron as she watched on, trying not to tremble in disbelief. The Lord stormed into the opposition with his soldiers swarming around him. She wanted to run, but a rustle in the woods caught her attention. She turned to see a wicca girl beckoning her to follow. Saranon left the misquew behind and entered the woods losing sight of the girl. Stubbing her toe on a rock. It gave a green glow that faded until she reached out. As soon as she touched the rock it glowed faint green. She gripped it with both hands and turned it over. The mark of the fires of chaos was etched deep in the surface, but that was not what caught her breath.

She dug into the shallow pit grasping a small leather pouch and opened it. The stolen sorcery leaked into the ground. She glanced over at the wizards as the skirmish slowed and the woods fell silent. Mitch ran toward her and stopped, she was still holding the pouch. It took a moment for him to realise what she held. Cheers rang out around them and she spoke, 'We're in trouble.'

He took the empty pouch and they made their way into the town. A cart went by holding some of the wizards who had fought against Lord Halleron. A wizard glared straight through her and a chill ran down her spine. Time had slipped away as the day turned to afternoon. She managed to squeeze her way into a packed inn. Filled with wiccan and wizards who had fought on both sides.

She could not make sense of the rambling scene as beer and hot meals were brought out. The inn keeper Delores held more beer mugs than she imagined possible. Not spilling a drop. Lord Halleron greeted them, he sat at the head of the table. The wizard who had glared at her, sat near the Lord with his hands bound in front of him. 'Do not worry about Irvyn.' The Lord said.

Mitch threw the pouch on the table. 'Ah,' Lord Halleron picked up the pouch with his knife. 'This is what you've been up to.'

Irvyn's face went pale, 'No… my Lord.'

'Give it here,' Delores inspected the pouch. 'You've been running off with my people for this.'

Lord Halleron beamed showing his crooked teeth, 'Perhaps I should leave you two alone?'

Irvyn's eyes grew wide and he hunched his head. The Lord continued, 'What were you promised? Riches beyond your wildest dreams? The crown?'

Lord Halleron did not wait for an answer, 'We may be staying a while.'

Saranon began to speak and Mitch jabbed her with his elbow while thanking the Lord. He led her away to the courtyard. She glared at him, 'Why did you do that?'

'Shush,' he said. 'The Lord needs your help.'

She was not impressed. Delores came out the kitchen door with two large meals. Placing them down on a small bench, 'You will bring my Fergus back, won't you?'

She hesitated. 'He's a good man,' Delores said.

Saranon nodded, she had no idea what to say. Mitch filled the void, 'It's a small town.'

They sat in silence as the shouts and laughter continued from inside. In complete contrast to the fight that had taken place before. The shouting grew louder as a brawl began to flow out into the courtyard and they left. Mitch stayed close as they strode around the outskirts of the town. Saranon searched the ground for another sign of the glowing stone. He waited every time she hesitated, yet there was nothing.

He suggested, 'Maybe it was just the one?'

'I doubt it,' she replied.

The ice chill of the wind set in as the sky grew dark and they made their way to the inn. The door to the barn was open and a crowd gathered around the open fire in the courtyard. A few glanced their way, but let them be. She made her way up the narrow stairs to a warm room overlooking the gathering. Mitch made his bed and tended to a bruise on his arm while she peered out the window. She was exhausted, yet she had gone beyond the point of sleep. The bed made Mitch look like a giant, his feet hung over the edge. She stifled a laugh and continued to watch the wizards below.

As the night wore on she tried to rest, yet the shouts from outside kept her awake. She tip-toed past Mitch and shut the door. The inn filled with voices from downstairs. She darted out the back and slipped past the barn. A frost had settled in and she drew her cloak near. She made her way past the town's edge and into the forest. It had a restful peace. A patch of wet ground lay amid the frost and peered into the shallow cave. In the dark of night a slit opened to reveal the large eye of a dragon. 'Katholumu,' she said.

The great beast looked as stunned as her. Hesitating before stretching out to welcome the sorceress. She curled up underneath his wing and he rested his head beside her.

CHAPTER TEN

Enter the Fires of Chaos

Kat remained in a peaceful sleep as she woke to the sound of thundering hooves. A glimpse over the dragon's wing showed wizards riding toward Tathen. Saranon gazed at the numbers she did not have time to warn Lord Halleron. They were still some way from the town. A gap appeared and she unravelled herself from the sleeping dragon. The battle worn beast was silent, ignoring the world outside. She strode toward the edge of the cave and shouts rang out above. Her heart pounded as she froze, she thought there were no wizards left. If she extended her sorcery it could attract attention. She back-tracked staying close to the dragon. The voice was strong, but she could not place it.

As the last of the wizards disappeared from site. A Shalough sorcerer rode forward on the misquew. She glimpsed his fine dark cloak, on the side it held the emblem of the fires of chaos. It was the only time Katholomu had stayed away from conflict. The giant beast was silent. She could feel her breath in the cold air. The sorcerer stopped while surveying the path toward Tathen. The silence prolonged time and all she could hear was the rustle of the wind. As it whipped along the frost covered grass. His head turned as though sensing something, yet he did not look her way. His thick cloak draped in a fine edge with the emblem for all to see in a silver outline. The sorcerer, Caddell, showed the first wisps of grey through his shoulder length hair.

A glimpse from the bond-breaker on his belt caught in the first ray of light over the hill. He settled back on the misquew. Saranon crouched down careful to draw the bond-breaker. It shone and transformed into a sword. A faint shrill ring broke the silence. Caddell turned, staring straight into her eyes as she charged toward him. Caddell raised his arms sending a circular blast outward. The first impact knocked through her, yet she held her ground. The shield began to crumble inward around the sorcerer. She waited letting the energy of the Angeon rise. Forming an arc, pushing the energy against the shield. The frost melted as the sorcery burnt a sharp edge into the ground. A web of sparks spread across the shield covering the entire sphere. It shattered carrying the sound through the air.

In the void she glimpsed a few figures on the hillside. Her focus remained on the sorcerer. She let the energy of the Angeon rush toward him. Caddell hurled a blast in retaliation. It spiralled in a fiery arc roaring as it gathered speed. She held out her hands and the energy concentrated deflecting around her. The thunderous tone echoed past her ears as it diverged up the hill behind her. Caddell realised what he had done as his companions ran for cover. She struck out and he faltered, kneeling on the ground. She strode toward him and he stood with the bond-breaker at full length. She lunged and he deflected the blow stepping sideways. Her energy shielded her as she ran through, but he was prepared.

The bond-breakers hit the air as the two forces struck created a shield. Each time neither blade struck the other. The compounded air between echoed with each impact. He deflected the blows with a fluid ease. Saranon's frustration showed with every swing. He did not give her time to meet his blade and in shear anguish she slammed down the hilt. The smooth stone in the centre glowed bright and Caddell fell to his knees, his face pale. 'Yield,' he cried out, 'I yield.'

Saranon staggered back as the words filtered through, she glanced around. The entire legion of Athgar wizards from Hestrel Keep gathered. In a semicircle watching in silence. 'Took you long enough,' Lord Halleron's voice boomed.

Caddell stood and greeted the Lord while brushing off the dirt from his robes. 'Of course it was a close fight,' he said.

Katholomu chose that moment to stretch. His forearms reaghing out of the low entrance to the cave. He poked his head out twisting his body through the narrow gap. He flexed his wings after they cleared the opening.

Ruffled his mane towering over the sorcerer. The ground shook as he flopped into the early frost. 'I am sure it was,' the Lord spoke in an amused tone, 'Now, about my wiccan.'

Caddell bowed and invited the Lord to visit. She glared at the sorcerer as he left and asked, 'Why did you do that?'

Lord Halleron remarked, 'You haven't had much to do with bargaining have you?'

'No,' she replied.

'I want my people returned alive,' he said.

Saranon joined the band of wizards as they made their way to Tathen. The signs of battle lay embedded in the thin layer of frost. As the wizards cleared the ground. She was about to wander into the inn when Lord Halleron waved her into the barn.

The large well-built structure had been converted for the wizards. The fire kept the warmth within the thick walls. The Lord began to remove his armour and the wizards shed their weapons. A corner had been set up for the wounded and Irvyn sat on bench against the wall. They made eye contact as the Lord spoke, 'He will offer you a temptation or the wiccan.'

She asked, 'Me?'

The Lord responded, 'Did you think I was going?'

'Yes,' she answered unsure as she said it.

Lord Halleron laughed, 'The invitation was for you.'

He stood over her, 'You will return the wiccan.'

She began, 'But I thought…'

'Make sure you return the wiccan,' he said.

The Lord's voice carried with it a tone that ended the conversation. She wandered out into cold light air, Mitch stood at the edge of the courtyard. 'Show me your bond-breaker' he said.

She took it out and he examined the hilt. 'Caddell has a bond he did not want you to break,' he spoke as he handed it back.

'I thought it was meant to be used at the sharp end,' she exclaimed.

He laughed then the expression changed to a serious one, 'You will have to face your fear.'

She hung her head in thought, 'It's not...'

Mitch had already walked inside and she hurried after him leaving the thought unsaid. The inn was cosy and warm, yet there was a sadness that filled the air. She wondered how many were missing. A thud rattled through the building. She rushed outside as Katholomu used the barn to scratch his back. He gave her a quick glance and continued while the wizards shouted in disbelief. There was nothing subtle about the dragon. He leaned into the courtyard and nudged her onto his shoulders. Mitch climbed up beside her. Kat removed himself from the gathering before taking off into the sky.

Saranon stayed closed to the giant beast, he flew over the edge of the heartland. A tall hill rose above the land covered by the forest floor that wrapped around the slope. She sensed the outer boundary of the Keep. As the dragon glided through swooping to the side. A platform wedged in the slope came into view. Kat lowered his hind legs, slowing the descent. A lone figure greeted them. Caddell was tall and well-built yet Mitch still managed to tower over the sorcerer. The fine robes wore the mark of the fires of chaos and she hesitated. It was the mark on her right shoulder placed there from the detention camps. The reminder made her uncomfortable.

'Welcome,' he said, 'It has been a while since Ledueran has been host to an Angeon.'

The Keep hidden in the great hill made almost no sound. The only person to greet them was the lone sorcerer. If she had hoped for clues there were none, the rooms were simple and sparse. Their footsteps echoed along the narrow corridors. The Keep was stark and silent. The wind echoed from outside as it whirred around the building. It sent a shiver down her spine, the Keep was the last place she wanted to be. Caddell led them into an open drawing room that extended into a gallery. He took his time meandering along talking of everything, but the missing wiccan. The place was almost peaceful if it was not for her anxious thoughts filling the void. She waited for a cue to speak, but it did not come.

The Keep was surrounded by the forest making its way up the steep incline. She glimpsed back to where they came, 'Where is Katholomu?'

She spoke before the thought had time to settle in her mind.

'We thought you were staying,' the sorcerer answered in a smooth tone.

'No,' Saranon responded.

She could see Mitch's expression change, yet its meaning was lost. 'It must be so troubling always on the move, always on the run, always having to hide. How many near escapes have you had? It would be so nice to have somewhere to stay. We are in the company of many great sorcerers. You are not alone.' Caddell's voice was soothing.

If it was not for Mitch's expressionless face she would not hesitate. She asked again, 'Where is Katholomu?'

A bell chimed echoing along the corridor. 'We will be late for the meeting,' he hurried down out of the room. 'Come we will be late, and you don't want to be late do you?'

She bellowed down the corridor, 'Where is my dragon?'

Caddell said, 'You didn't think there would be a price did you?'

Saranon ignored his remark, 'You had three chances. It's time we found out what you were so afraid of.'

She held out her bond-breaker, but it would not glow. 'We do not permit such devices here,' his voice was calm, yet the threat was there.

Saranon seethed underneath the surface. The possibility of rescuing the wiccan faded. She was not prepared to leave the dragon. Caddell turned and had almost disappeared. Mitch whispered, 'You need to follow.'

She glared at him, the memory of the fire mark from the camp burned in her mind. She rubbed the permanent symbol on her right arm. It was a constant reminder, one she would rather forget. Mitch pushed her forward and she stood firm. 'We will lose the wiccan,' he said.

The energy of the Angeon rose from within. She sensed the stallic energy of the Keep trickling along the walls. It clung in a weblike fashion through the uneven pattern. Ledueran stayed silent. The flickering traces showed in the gaps spread across the walls. Her energy slipped through. She could sense Kathomolou and the wiccan. Her anger flared with the memory of Tasha searing to the forefront of her mind. She peered down at her hands, Tasha's blood was still there. Mitch's voice faded in and out, as the memory took her back to Antavagon. Tasha's lifeless body flashed before her eyes and the anger of the Keep. A faint voice called out from afar. At first she thought it was Tasha, but then the voice became clear.

Antavagon called to her from the depths of Tordoren, break the core. The image left, Saranon stood in a cold sweat. Mitch was staring at her, yet the words did not filter through. Caddell was about to close the door up ahead. The last link to Antavagon slipped away. As Ledueran blocked out the Darkonian Keep, yet the damage was done. Time lapsed into eternity as she raised her hands. The first Keep to embrace the Angeon had summoned her and she answered. The energy flooded through so hard the floor around her shattered upward. Ledueran howled, the rage from beneath thundered along the heavy walls. For a moment the void held her gripped in an unenviable calm. As the stallic energy rose from the deep.

Saranon held out her arms waiting for energy of the Keep to reach out. Mitch shouted through the turmoil,

'No.'

The stallic energy ruptured as the sound became deafening. Yet it could not grip her as she fell toward the central core. Ledueran's angry shouts rang through her mind. Yet the only words she could hear belonged to Antavagon. 'Break the core,' her voice was lost in a cataclysm of fire.

The Angeon held strong against the stallic energy. Yet the searing edges of the shield closed around her. It was a race to the central core and she could not lose. Her hold shrank and when she reached her farthest point she pushed onward.

Stallic energy pressed around her taking the shield ever closer. Yet it was the central core that caught her attention. The outer shell's rugged surface was just beyond reach. Ledueran laughed, it reverberated through the stallic energy. Her rage hit the surface before she had time to think. The blast slammed into the shell protecting the central core. All momentum was lost as the stallic energy flung her upward. A great thunderous roar bellowed from underneath. As the blast from the Angeon found its mark. She smiled with reassuring confidence until the momentum stopped, leaving her in mid-air. The great black marmoz dragon broke through the building. His magnificent wings stretching full length and taking him straight into the sky.

Saranon glanced beneath her to the gaping jaws and let out a scream. The dragon flew into her with a thud. She began tumbling over his thick skull, clinging onto his mane as her legs dangled in the wind. Kat flew so hard it was all she could do to hold on. As the great beast slowed to a comfortable speed. She brought her leg around to sit between his shoulders. The moment was short lived as gravity disappeared. Katholomu swooped straight at the Keep. His lungs sucked in the cold air and his belly grew warm. 'Wait,' she cried out.

It was too late. The flames licked the side of the building and she covered her face from the heat.

The air crackled overhead, she could hear the dragon's powerful wings swooping low. A whirlwind of sorcery spiralled upward. Mixed with the dust and broken shards from the building. Ledueran Keep stood, yet the creases lining the grounds showed. Cheering rose catching her off-guard. She could feel Kat tense his shoulders, as he turned toward the noise. The small group of wiccan swarmed around, their weary faces filled with excitement. Caddell's stone voice cut through the air from the balustrade. The Shalough sorcerer stood parallel to the dragon's gaze. She tried to speak, but the dust caught in her throat turning her voice to a whisper. 'Our offer is no more,' Caddell spoke, 'Take the wiccan and be gone.'

Katholomu took his time as he turned to stare straight into the sorcerer's glare. The great beast said one word, 'Coward.'

Caddell's face went pale as the rage washed over him. Saranon responded, 'Your offer was never there.'

She tilted and the dragon turned with her. Lord Halleron broke through woods bringing his troops with him. The wizards spread forming an arc around the wiccan in a protective stance. At the first sign of movement away from the Keep, Katholomu leaned down. He bounded off the broken stone courtyard spreading his wings high into the sky. The chill wind caught her hair and cooled the dragon.

They flew in a great arc veering to the heartland. Home of the largest dragon colony in Zyanthia. It stretched farther than the eye could see. The great beast made his way to a rocky side, swooping just below the ridge. The dragon stopped with a jolt and she slid down. He wheezed gasping for air and his body shuddered. A lump began to make its way up the dragon's neck. She just had time to jump out of the way as Kat coughed up a pile of charred remains. The smell made her gag and she ran upwind. Before she could look, she heard the crunch as Katholomu ate his own vomit and she winced. Perhaps Caddell would think twice before capturing the dragon again. She made her way down the rocky hill forming the ridge line. The sun began to set as dragons swooped low to perch.

Kat glanced down then rubbed the side of his head against her shoulder. She only just had time to hold her breath. The great dragon rumbled with deep affection as though sensing what she had done. Finally she gave in breathing the smell, with a violent cough, as he moved out of the way. Mitch's voice rose from the valley, 'There you are.'

'Don't come any closer,' she said waving her arms.

The wizard, Mitch, did not change his stride until the smell hit. He pointed to a shallow stream and she headed toward it. 'Not you, the dragon,' he said.

Her cheeks grew red with embarrassment and she called the dragon over. Kat hesitated wiggling from side to side then flopped into the ice cold water. A jet of steam rose around him and he let out a comforting sigh. She sat by the water's edge. Mitch created a small ambient light. She watched as it flickered across the dragon's thick skin. As Katholomu stood up he took half the pool of water with him. She held her arms up as he shook his body, the water dripped off her shield in mid-air. Mitch ran toward her with his hair soaked and she laughed. The dark night covered them as the dragon curled his great body. Making a warm shelter from the frost gathering on the ground.

Mitch sat with his back against the dragon. His pensive gaze gave away his thoughts, 'You did not accept the offer,'

It was a statement more than a question. Saranon removed her coat, the fire mark still showed on her right arm. 'There was only one chance to accept the Angeon.'

The mark remained a stark reminder of her days in the detention camps. Any trust for the sorcerers had vanished long ago. She rested near Katholomu's chest listening to the faint rumblings as he slept. 'You damaged the Keep,' Mitch said.

She glared at him, 'It was the least I could do.'

He did not look impressed. 'Antavagon helped me escape the camp and he asked me to,' she responded.

He said, 'Would you take on the clan if it asked you to?'

She did not answer and the silence became deafening.

Finally she gave in, 'Yes.'

She had never seen Mitch's jaw drop so fast. She asked, 'What did you think I was going to say?'

'Anyone else would have said no,' he replied.

The wind droned around the rocky hillside. As a clear night sky let the frost settle and she tried in vain to calm her mind.

Caddell's image loomed when she closed her eyes. Keeping her awake long after Mitch had fallen asleep. She climbed out of the warm cocoon underneath Kat's wing. Making her way along his shoulders. The dragon's eyes opened with a thin slither and he let out a gruff snort. She stroked his matted coat and he went back to sleep. The moon shone bright over the tops of the trees as the branches swayed in the bellowing wind. A glimmer of light broke through the shadows and she followed. A silhouette formed among the trees holding out a beckoning hand. The spirit of her friend Tasha stood in a flowing white dress. Her fawn coloured hair caught in the light. Tasha moved further away and Saranon ran, not wanting to lose sight.

She ran on through the chill night air leaving marks on the frost covered ground. She moved faster, yet Tasha remained out of reach. The silhouette faded and the woods grew dark around her. She wrapped her cloak around and made her way back. The branches whistled in the dark as the wind picked up speed and she ran to find Mitch waiting. He stood not far from the dragon. His tall muscular frame held a firm stare. 'Chasing shadows,' he remarked.

She nodded and climbed into the warm makeshift camp as Katholomu rested. Mitch watched as her eyes grew heavy.

A wisp of the cool breeze woke her. The dragon had long moved, yet his imprint remained in the shallow snow. She jumped up and breathed in the crisp chill air. Mitch laughed, 'Took you long enough.'

She stood beside him watching a tiny trail of smoke in the distant horizon. 'What's that?'

'Nothing,' he replied.

She was not so sure. 'I saw Tasha in the woods,' she said.

Mitch hesitated before walking in the direction she had seen her old friend. She asked, 'Did you see her?'

He nodded in reply.

The snow had stopped. The early chill of winter held it in place underneath the morning sun. Mitch strode with a purpose and she followed. He moved through the forest with ease. As she clambered through avoiding the low lying branches. The first warm rays broke over the hillside and the dragons began to stir taking to the sky. She glanced back to see Katholomu settled beneath the ridge line, lazing in the sun. 'Mitch,' Clara cried out.

The sound sent a chill through Saranon. She had not been expecting to find the Mercidian sorceress. Astonishment held her in disbelief. Clara was pale and ragged, nothing like the proud cheerful person she knew.

Mitch stiffened at the sight he voice held firm, 'What are you doing here?'

Clara's eyes were red, 'I didn't know, I swear. They've taken the Oracle.'

'No,' the words escaped Saranon's lips.

'I didn't know what to do,' Clara had tears running down her face. 'I didn't mean for any of this.'

'We have to return to the Keep,' she waited for Clara who whispered thank you.

Katholomu uncurled his tail and stretched as they approached. The dragon was slow to accommodate them. He flew toward Hestrel Keep in a silent gesture and the trail of smoke grew closer.

Kat veered sideways and a dragon broke into flight so close she could feel the air rush past. The woods came to life as a fleet of dragons followed with their riders. She glanced toward the Keep. There on the horizon. She could make out the faint line of dragons spreading their wings. They were caught. Clara screamed into the air, 'No!'

Saranon could sense Flynn and her anger rose to the surface. She flew Kat close to the ground and held the thought in her mind hoping that Mitch would read it. He tapped her shoulder then grabbed Clara and they rolled along the soft undergrowth. Katholomu heaved back into the sky rising above the oncoming dragons..

The first blasts of sorcery hurled from both sides aimed at each other. The blazing inferno barely missed the great dragon's tail as he swung upside down. The void of weightlessness held a moment of calm, then she reached out into nothing. Her arms flung wide as the sorcery gravitated around her. Turning into a swirling array as neither side hit. The blast engulfed her in mid-air and she reached out absorbing the energy. The air broke into a crystal blue sky and the Angeon rose from within, the Angeon of old. Shouts rang out as both fleets of dragons dived for the ground. To escape the energy pulsing from the Angeon. She could feel it intensifying as she held on waiting, her heart beat thudding in her ears.

A lone sorcerer broke the silence, just one. Flynn stood on the grounded dragon. He held the blade of the bond-breaker raising it toward her. The Angeon released her energy in a circular arc. It reached Flynn and he fell instantaneously. The blade fell away and he stood alone on the dragon. The Angeon neutralised the flow of sorcery and shouted, 'Leave.'

CHAPTER ELEVEN

Stand strong against the darkness

The Mercidian sorcerers wasted no time making their exit before she found Mitch. She asked, 'Where is Clara?'

'Gone,' he replied.

It hurt, but it did not surprise her. Clara had only found her to help Flynn. Katholomu purred with a giant rumble and rubbed his head against her. Mitch climbed on sitting at the front, he flew the dragon in a wide arc around the Keep. The pillars of smoke rose from the damage along the outer walls.

She could tell Mitch was not impressed and said nothing. The damage revealed itself as the dragon made a smooth descent lowering his head. For once, Katholomu did not fumble as he landed. There was no one to greet them and the panic began to rise. She ran into the building to find Bayard he sat near the fire. She glanced around at the tell-tale signs sprawled along the walls. 'We lost eighteen good wizards,' Bayard said.

Madoc greeted them, 'You should have been here.'

He shouted the last words in disgust. Saranon did not know what to say.

Madoc spoke, 'I'm leaving.'

'No,' she said.

It was a hollow threat, yet she treated the words with the weight by which they were spoken. 'I have to deal with this,' she told him.

'Make them pay,' he said.

She did not answer as she gazed around the dishevelled room and left. The Athgar wizards were still shaken by the event as they began to repair the building. She had not thought the Mercidian would attack. Yet Flynn had been willing to sacrifice her for the Oracle.

Kail gave her a cold glare and she chose to ignore it as she made her way through the corridor. The wizards had team work down to a fine art. The process of rebuilding and strengthening the outer walls was underway. Captain Lydia Grace called out, 'We will not last another attack. Not while the barrier is down.'

She asked, 'What?'

'We changed the connections to hold the shield. It won't last,' the Captain explained.

The shock showed as the colour drained from her face. 'I have to go down,' she said the thought aloud.

'Be careful it's a wreck,' the Captain said.

Saranon hoped Captain Grace was wrong. Smoke

wafted up from below as she avoided the wizards working away to fix the damage. A chunk had been taken out of the wall and a voice called out, 'Mind your step.'

She glanced down and part of the floor was gone. The cavity exposed a broken conduit. The sight in the dark depths far below was almost nauseating and she looked away. Bronwyn, the wizardess, made her way up the ladder. Her head level with the gaping hole in the floor.

'Ever wondered why the sorcerers want the Oracle so bad?' Bronwyn asked.

'Because they don't know what she is,' she answered in a flat tone.

'Christine can stop the Angeon,' Bronwyn said.

Saranon burst out laughing, then stopped when an awkward silence fell. 'Let's get this Keep back up?'

She clambered down to the lower levels. The building was sturdy and the attack had been aimed directly for the shield. Hestrel fared well, she just needed to bring the shield up. Debris littered her way. As she trailed her fingers along the walls listening for the rhythm of the Keep.

All her focus went to the hum emanating from below. She strode passed the wizards until the corridors became empty. The imbenik chambers sat above the pathways leading down to the central core. The hum from the core grew audible as she made her way to the altar. The stone was warm to the touch. She braced herself clearing the thoughts raging inside. As her head lowered the stone altar began to soften and the Keep reached out to greet her. It melded to her skin and her sorcery linked with the energy rising from the central core. She gave all her concentration to guiding the stallic energy in place. Along the damaged walls that had stood against the attack.

She reached out her hand and Mitch held it. Almost breaking the connection with the Keep. Her eyes opened in a haze and she sensed him. She could feel his warm breath on her ear. The connection broke and she stared at him. 'Were you expecting war?' Mitch asked.

'No,' the word escaped before she had time to think.

He led her up toward the light. The stone spread across the floor of the chamber. As the sun shone from the high arches overhead. The pattern embedded in the stone swirled in the same fashion as the temple in her dream. If Saranon closed her eyes she could reach out and see Tasha. The image was gone all too soon. She could almost hear the dark stream. There was just one thing missing as she gazed into the centre of the chamber. A tear fled down her cheek, it still hurt knowing her friend did not make it. 'I appear to have rebuilt the Keep,' she said.

'It's more than that,' Mitch replied.

He waited for her to follow through the high arch doors. She had been expecting to walk out into the courtyard. Stopping at the balustrade around on the balcony. The courtyard was at least three stories below. She eyed Mitch with an amused gaze, 'Maybe.'

'You have lost eight days,' Mitch watched her expression change.

She glanced around, the Keep was calmer than it had been since they arrived. She made her way toward the dragon pens. Katholomu lowered his head out through the open archway. He grumbled as he squeezed out and hit the arch as he went. The Athgar wizards ignored the thud as they worked, preparing the dragons for flight. She stayed on the stone courtyard beside the great beast as he nudged her. A small group stood around the long wooden table near the hearth. The room had access to the dragon pens and the wizard stronghold. The high windows kept out prying eyes and kept in the warmth. Captain Lydia Grace surveyed the map strewn over the table.

Saranon strode toward the group and the Captain lifted her gaze. 'The supplies are not getting through. We have had to resort to the dragons.'

The words were spoken in a matter of fact manner, as though the element of surprise had gone. She asked, 'Who?'

'Our own,' the Captain spoke as she rolled up the map.

Saranon wanted to ask but no more was said as the Captain left the room. Madoc stood by the door, 'I think there is something you should see.'

She was not sure whether to trust the Shalough sorcerer. The wizards paid him no attention.

She followed him down the corridor. Around the edge of the wizard stronghold to the warden's quarters. She hesitated at the threshold, the last time she had been near a prison it had not ended well. Madoc waited as she walked through. Banging resonated from the cells. She stayed in the foyer and backed into Hobson. The wizard towered over her, he carried a band of keys on a thick leather belt. 'You want to see the traitor,' he said.

Hobson walked on before she had time to say otherwise. Saranon glared at Madoc for dragging her to the last place she wanted to be. He smiled and followed behind.

The cells were clean and light shone through from overhead. A wizard sat in the last cell and she spoke his name, 'Bayard.'

The word escaped her lips and took away her breath in the moment of horror. She had never dreamed that there could be a spy from within. Madoc left and she turned hoping for an answer as he left her alone with the wizard. Saranon hated being in the place. The bars and silt covered floor brought back the memory of Antavagon. A memory she tried to forget. Bayard's expression changed as he mistook her sad gaze. 'You heard,' was all he said.

She did not want to admit she had no idea. As she responded, 'Yes.' The awkward silence grew between them until she asked, 'Why?'

He leaned in close wrapping his hands around the bars. 'You know what it's like, when you get the offer. What did he offer you?' He asked.

She flinched and took a step back as their eyes met. She felt the fire mark on her right arm and stepped further away. Her words were bittersweet, 'He offered me a place to belong.'

Mitch had urged her to accept and she almost had. The air was growing stuffy and she backed away avoiding the urge to run.

The corridor filled with light from the high windows across the rough walls. There was not a person in sight, yet voices carried along interrupting the silence. There had been so much damage caused by the sorcerer clans. Yet as she made her way around the Keep, all she could see were familiar faces. The fire from the hearth warmed the great hall together with the central core. Bronwyn waved her over to a plain wooden table where they ate, 'I like what you did with the Keep.'

She felt her face grow red. It had been Hestrel more than she who had restored the building. Making it strong enough to withstand an attack. The ease at which the wizards chatted made her relax as she sat to eat the evening meal. The sky grew dark through the high windows along the far wall, carved into the thick stone. The fire beckoned as she held out her hands to warm them near the hearth. A ripple of air move in a vertical wave and the chairs around the hearth became vacant. She blinked and the room filled with the chatter of voices once more. She scouted the grand hall gazing on the faces and turned to leave. Mitch followed and she spoke, 'I'm all right.'

He waited a moment, 'Perhaps.'

It was no use lying to the wizard. He could read her immediate thoughts, but she was trying to convince herself. Saranon made her way to the sorcerer quarters. The lights were low. Darkness hovered over the edges of the corridor leading to her room. She rolled her coat down her arms and folded the thick worn leather that had kept her warm. The woollen rug was a welcome relief from from the stark wooden floor. The furniture was plain, yet beautifully carved with a smooth finish. She rubbed her fingertips along the thick stone wall. The Keep hummed from beneath. The wind swept around the outer wall keeping her awake. The last of her thoughts drifted away into sleep.

A bell tolling in the distance broke through. Disturbing her as she woke to darkness. The Keep hummed away in the silence as she glanced around. She did not recall seeing a bell and wrapped her coat tight. making her way down the narrow circular stairs. A light shone in a long thin band up the corridor and she walked toward it. The carved wooden door creaked as it opened. A dim light flooded the great chamber from above. The sorcerer stone that covered the floor, showed the trails of a faint carving along the surface. Saranon made her way to the columns marking the large dome in the centre. A lone figure in a long white dress stood with her back turned. The flowing fawn coloured wavy hair could only belong to one person, Tasha.

Saranon moved further into the chamber until she stood beside her old friend. The bell tolled in the distance and Tasha spoke, 'There can only be one Oracle.'

She asked, 'What should I do?'

Mitch shouted from the doorway and Tasha's image faded in the light. She was exasperated, 'Did you have to?'

He took hold of her arm and urged her to follow. Voices entered the chamber as they ducked to the side. She was about to speak. Until she heard Captain Grace's voice trail past the outer columns. Mitch stayed close, she could feel his warm breath. The scraping of the chains etched its way along the floor. As Bayard was brought to the centre kneeling to the ground with his head hung. A whisper of light from the morning sun escaped down the length of the columns. Surrounding the circular dome. It shone along the bond-breaker as the Captain raised it. Saranon let out a gasp and Mitch held her tight as the blade fell. She whispered Tasha's words. As though they would be forgotten, 'There can only be one Oracle.'

She had to leave and Mitch ran after her. 'I did not have time to warn you,' he said.

It broke her out of the frame of mind, 'I was not thinking of Bayard.'

'You should be, he was Corathy,' he said it.

As though it had an important meaning and she gave him a blank stare. 'A wizard from the south,' he explained.

She did not want to be caught up with the Athgar wizards. Hestrel was strong enough to keep the Oracle safe, that was what mattered. She strode out to the courtyard to find Kat and hesitated. The dragons were being readied to enter the sky waiting for their riders. The closest dragon barely acknowledgement her as she wandered through.

Bronwyn glanced up from handing out supplies. Saranon asked, 'Where is Katholomu?'

'He left last evening. No one has seen him since,' Bronwyn answered while continuing her task.

'You can take Holdvar,' Mitch offered.

'No,' she snapped, 'I need to find Kat.'

After the encounter with the Fires of Chaos the

missing dragon made her uneasy. She made her way across the courtyard along the pebble path. Until she found a group of misquew. She patted one of the riding cats and it lifted its head. The grounds of Hestrel kept the harshness of winter at bay, with the energy rising from the central core. The grass was wet underneath. It did not share the covering of frost glistening on the outer edge. She pulled her cloak tight as the misquew made its way along the path. Almost invisible in the fallen snow. Mitch rode beside her. His misquew was a little taller making him appear larger still.

She glanced around, but the snow covered the hillside. In a white blanket hiding any trace of the great dragon. She motioned for the misquew to speed up. It ran into the clearing marking the entrance to the main road. The stone markers gave the frost a pale green glow yet the road remained clear. The well-trodden stone shone in the pale light. Mitch went to turn back. Facing the direction they had come, 'We won't find anything.'

It was not the answer she wanted to hear and rode on. He turned to follow, but his face was stern. He had made his point. As Saranon headed onto the road. The faint glow reminded her of the detention camp, Tasha had been alive then. If only her friend had made it out.

A grumble shook the frost from the trees surrounding the heartland. Kat rose above the branches. His eyes peered just high enough to stare at her as she called his name. She slumped down in the snow and ran through the trees avoiding the branches as she went. The cold wind whipped at her cheeks as she raced ahead. On the ground beneath the great beast, the white snow ran red. It seeped out from where he rested. He lifted his weight to show his thick scales revealing a dark mass below. She had to ask, 'Did you sit on someone?'

The dragon tilted his ears in disgust. The great beast had squashed the metal plate armour of the soldier beyond recognition. She grimaced.

Mitch took one look, 'We have to get out of here.'

He held her arm and she stood firm, 'Wait. If they were heading to Hestrel we would have seen them.'

Mitch was about to argue, his chest heaved. 'I will check where they went.'

She had a better idea, 'Kat, where did the soldiers go?'

The dragon pointed north to the Pearl Castle and Temare. Mitch gave her an exasperated glare and climbed onto the great beast.

She hesitated, 'You go, someone needs to warn the Regent.'

He nodded, 'Don't get caught."-

She laughed and Mitch gave her a stern glare, 'A lone sorceress will be an easy target.'

Saranon wondered if sometimes he forgot that she was the Angeon, 'I will be fine.'

She stood back as Katholomu jolted into the sky. His wings spread wide casting a shadow along the ground. The woods were covered in a layer of thin snow and a rocky path edged its way around. She stepped onto the path and it glimmered pale amid the snow. The lay-line was weak underneath. It would speed up the journey, but the wizards would know. There would be no surprise.

A chill settled through the calm blue sky. As the morning held over the frost covered ground. She trudged along the path. As the wet snow melted underneath from the magic in the lay-line. The trees with their bare branches clung in a tight ring around the edges. Blocking any hope of a view from the road and the hills that hid Hestrel Keep. The path led her deeper into the heartland. As the dragons came into view melting the snow as they rested. The frost tapered away and she glanced around, up ahead the lay-line ended. It touched the edge of a grassy field that appeared out of place amid the white covered hills.

The path ended in a low valley, where she walked there were signs across the rocks on the ground. She leaned down near one and touched the rough surface, her senses prickled. A great raging fireball gleamed overhead. The shield from her own energy protected her. Saranon glanced into the fiery blaze. The heat hurtling overhead with barely a fraction protecting her. At the farther end, deep in the heartland, three figures stood. Behind them, the marks around the building shaped the edge of the Keep. Hidden deep in the hillside.

As she strode closer a Shalough sorceress, not much older, hesitated. A sorcerer stood off to the side. For a moment she thought they were going to turn and run. The sorceress held out her arms and Saranon braced herself. She could sense that buildup of energy and was still far away. she chose not to run and instead waited, watching to see what would happen.

The energy flared into a heavy storm crackling with lightning through the sky. It arched in a random pattern. Saranon watched it all, but the pattern broke. Shattering around her before it approached. The fog lifted as she walked closer at a steady pace. The two sorcerers were aghast as she approached in silence. 'I'm Bridget,' said the sorceress. Not knowing what to say. 'And this is Troy,' she added.

'This is not the right place for that type of sorcery,' Saranon said. 'Is there somewhere else?'

'There's the stadium,' Troy pointed toward the building.

Bridget glared at him and he shrugged his shoulders. Saranon followed the two sorcerers inside, past the field leading to a stone entrance. It was small and humble, but large enough to welcome them inside. The rooms were plain and simple with grey whitewashed walls. As they moved in deeper she noticed the colours change and become more vibrant. At the end of the corridor, around the architrave was a carving of leaves and dragons. Marking the entrance to a grand room.

Deep inside the building the light from the Keep shone. The floor sloped down at a gradual pace toward the centre of the lower stands. The great columns held another row of stands above, arcing around the central stadium. At the end was a heavy wall, sturdy enough to absorb great sorcery. She had travelled far, all the way to Indarin in Serenphel. To be able to learn the art of sorcery so that she could control what she had. Saranon felt sorry for Bridget whose sorcery was not under control. At her age it should have been.

Saranon made an offer to teach as she stood on the floor of the stadium. The two sorcerers looked at her hesitantly. Troy said, 'How can you teach another?'

'I finish my training at Indarin,' she replied.

With such certainty that he backed down. She stood at an even pace. Allowing for a buffer between her and the immense wall that could absorb sorcery. She beckoned for Bridget to begin and the sorceress was hesitant.

'Focus,' she said.

The air blurred in front as the sorcery swelled. She could see it emanating from Bridget as the air heated. The great blast shattered around the stadium.

The energy took up the space with a glow that threw shadows from the columns. It headed toward her uneven swirl, she held her hands and stood steady for the embrace. It swirled overhead and to the sides. She disappeared in the maze and swirl of sorcery. Yet behind remained a gap visible between. Where she stood near the wall there was no rebound from the Keep. No reverberation and instead it dissipated. A ranger shouted from above commanding them to stop. His voice boomed around the last crackles of sorcery. The three sorcerers stood pale and she was about to speak, but the ranger stopped her.

He made his way down from the stand, each footstep echoed in the grand stadium. His presence was felt as he stood tall over the three. He stared at her and said, 'What are you doing here?'

She was about to speak, but Troy said something odd and she stayed silent. She did not understand what completing her training would do. Yet the explanation made the ranger's shoulders relax and he welcomed her. It was an awkward moment. He was not sure how to respond and neither was she.

CHAPTER TWELVE

The path of a guardian

Sounds echoed from the entrance to the stadium saving any need for a reply. The ranger, Korben, followed as they entered the dining area. The room captured the light from the narrow windows spanning from floor to ceiling. The tables were spread around the walls with chairs wrapping around an open hearth. The large opening where a fire would have been, let warm air from the central core flow into the room. Saranon held out her hands, yet the Keep remained silent. A bellowing wind thrust against the windows, 'You are welcome to stay the night.'

'No. I really...' Her words trailed off.

As the soldiers of the Shalough rode across the distant fields. Their steeds kept in a close formation. Only the golden emblem glinting from the uniforms gave them away as sorcerers. 'Perhaps,' she said.

Bridget gave a knowing smile, 'Commander Meghan is enough to scare anyone.'

Saranon caught a glimpse shimmering near Bridget's shoulder. The different phase drew her in with a rush that took the breath from her lips. She stood out of time with the world. Three sorcerers stood around her all bearing the same eyes. Those of the Keep Serensa. Why are you here? The Keep spoke through a sorceress, yet she could hear the words in her mind. Saranon hesitated, she was unsure.

'You know Bridget better than I. How long does she have?' She waited for the answer.

We do not interfere, a sorcerer mouthed the words of the Keep. 'Then why do you ask?' She responded.

Are you only here for the girl? The Keep asked. 'I was on my way to the Pearl Castle. I was going to leave...'

You are welcome on one condition, show yourself. The sorceress who spoke for the Keep held out her hand. Saranon knew what it meant. She had kept her sorcery hidden for so long, creating boundaries to fit in.

If she broke down the boundaries it would warn the Shalough before she attacked. Then it would reveal more than that. 'Only here,' she said waiting for the Keep to answer.

We accept, the words of the Keep clung in her mind. She reached out and the image faded around her. She fell out of phase hitting the floor. Voices floated around as her hearing returned. Someone reached out. 'Don't,' she shouted.

She stood up and Troy stepped back hitting the bench.

The dizziness slipped away leaving a numb resonance. She glanced at the small lights above glowing with the Keep's energy, as did the Ranger. A difference in the faint glow gave away everything in one small detail.

Footsteps echoed along the corridors. Commander Meghan rushed in and the Ranger held up his hand. The Commander stopped, her cloak giving away the impulse of her action. As it fluttered through the doorway. Korben shook his head and the Commander bowed. Her shouts could be heard down the passage. A queasy sensation gripped her. 'What are you?' Korben spoke then hesitated. Her voice was lost as she coughed. She tried again to speak, 'Not the myth you were expecting.'

Her thoughts cleared as the cloudy haze from the conversation with the Keep lifted. The energy of the Angeon pulsed under her skin. It was barely visible, but she could feel its rhythm.

As the Keep settled for the night a storm swept across the grounds. She had wanted to leave earlier. Serensa's request had made a world of difference. The Shalough sorcerers stayed at a distance allowing her to pass through. Yet they watched, conscious of the recognition the Keep had given her. The snow faded as the cold set in carried by the wind lashing at the trees through the forest. Stars shone bright overhead. Dimmed only by the low lights around the walls of the building. The glimmer gave a faint glow through the soft haze as she peered upward. The Keep was nestled tight in the hillside, rising in a manner that belonged. Perhaps she was wrong about the Shalough.

Shouts emerged as she made her way through the foyer. It remained open, but kept the cold outside shielded by the energy from the Keep. Troy grabbed her hand and they darted away as he spoke, 'We have to find Bridget.'

'Why?' She asked.

'That's why they're angry,' he pointed back where the shouting came from.

The response did not answer her question, but he had already run ahead. If she did not catch up he would soon be out of sight. The stairs lead higher and she gripped the rail. Glancing out the narrow window before continuing on.

Shadows fell along the floor. From the beams framing the space tacked away between the walls. Bridget sat gazing out into the darkness covering the frozen land. She stayed a moment longer before acknowledging them. 'I won't go back,' Bridget said.

Troy urged her and she refused. Saranon felt out of place and asked, 'Why not?'

'I'm not supposed to hit the wall,' Bridget said.

Saranon burst out laughing and they both gave her an uneasy look. 'You are supposed to hit the wall,' she said.

'But what if it breaks?' Bridget said.

'That could happen,' Saranon replied, 'Let me show you.'

'You're going to break the wall?' Troy asked in astonishment.

'Maybe,' Saranon said.

She dashed down the open stairs leading into the

stadium. The solid wall at the end stood as a continuous plain form as high as it was wide. Reaching the edges of the main floor that curved around in an arch. The Shalough sorcerers were scattered around the area in front of her. She thought of asking them to move, but it was not necessary for what she intended to do. Saranon felt the energy close to the surface. It came willingly, building up as she held it in place. A loud crack boomed as it flew through the open gaps hitting the wall. The reverberation echoed carrying the thunderous tones around with clear precision.

For a moment silence fell and she raised her arms again for the second blast that hit the wall. As the sorcerers fled to the sidelines. It crackled again and again, each time the reverberation echoed. She continued almost relentlessly until it was clear the wall would not fail. Then she stood to one side and beckoned Bridget to follow her lead onto the stadium floor. Bridget hesitated, her face pale, 'I cannot do that.'

'That is what it's for,' Saranon said.

Korben began to interrupt, but he was cut off mid-sentence by the blast as it hit the wall. Bridget tried again with a renewed sense of certainty. Concentrating all her efforts on the wall.

By the time Bridget was done she had honed the blast and her stance. Silence clung in the air as their audience inspected the wall. The hour was growing late, yet Saranon stayed. Long enough for the Shalough to be assured that the wall would not crumble. 'How did you know?' Korben asked standing by her side.

'There are many like it at Indarin,' she replied.

Her answer appeared to satisfy him. They made their way back to the outer rim of the building, that formed the Ranger's quarters. The wind howled around the stone surface of the walls. It was enough to keep her awake, but she needed to sleep and closed her eyes.

The shudder of the morning bell broke through her dreams and she woke. It had been filled with vague images none of which made sense. She peered out the small window to the icy blanket below. The wind was still, at least for time being. The wooden door creaked loud enough to the let the Rangers know she was there. As she strode into the dining room. An aroma filled the air with the smell of warm bread. Without hesitation she joined them for breakfast. Bridget gazed at her and the silence began to make her uneasy. 'I was told the wall would break,' Bridget finally said.

'Only if your intention was untoward,' Saranon answered. 'There is a difference between lack of control and attacking the Keep.'

She hesitated before adding, 'You should have been told that.'

Her words were harsh and they were meant to be. Bridget had learned fast and the sorceress should have been farther ahead than she. Korben rose to make a start with the days' work. 'One day we will be Rangers looking after the heartland,' Bridget spoke.

Saranon almost choked. Korben and the entire room filled with sorcerers glared at her. 'You are no Ranger,'

Saranon said as Bridget tensed.

'I meant that is not your specialisation,' she added.

'My path has already been chosen,' Bridget said growing confused.

'Not well enough,' Saranon said. 'If you really want to know where your path lies I can show you.'

She was hoping the answer would be no. Especially with the stunned look on Bridget's face. 'I think you should,' Korben replied.

She waited for Bridget to accompany her and pulled her cloak around. 'Where are we headed?' Bridget asked.

'Serensa, though he may be outside by the time we get there,' she answered.

Troy tagged along as the Keep let them pass. The small lights glimmered revealing the way. The stairs opened up leading higher and the cold air hit as they strode near the outer wall. Saranon could not see him, yet the Keep was sure he was there. The walkway trailed into a large open platform. The sorcerers stone underneath lay almost hidden. In the faint clumps of snow drifting down. Commander Meghan turned to greet them. It was then that Saranon pointed ahead to a solitary figure overlooking the great building. He glanced then returned to his silent vigil. Bridget drew in a sharp breath, 'That's Dargon.'

She went no closer and began to leave. 'Are you sure?' Troy asked and she nodded in reply. A deep firm voice shouted across the open space as Dargon locked eyes with her. 'Angeon. Why are you here?'

He closed the distance fast in a motionless effort. His

face carried the scars of an unknown battle and his brow deepened as he towered over her. 'Perhaps we had better go,' Troy tugged her arm. 'It is not for the Guardian of Gate, but for your successor,' she answered.

The Commander stared at Troy. 'Not me,' he explained pointing at Bridget who appeared frozen to the spot.

'A girl,' Dargon spoke the words too soon.

Bridget ran from site, Troy followed after her. 'A Guardian of the Gate is no job for a girl,' Dargon said.

'You cannot choose,' Saranon said.

She ran down into the Keep as the wind set in overhead. Footsteps followed behind her on the staircase, the Guardian's shadow swept over floor. 'A Ranger does not have the makings of a Guardian and you are not a full Angeon,' he said.

She was about to find Bridget and hesitated, 'How did you know?'

'Bridget's path has been chosen,' Dargon said.

It was the answer she was looking for, but she did not want to delay finding Bridget. Serensa led her toward officer quarters. At first she thought the Keep may have misled her. As she made her way through the corridor it opened up to a stadium hidden inside the building. The benches were wrapped around one side, with a second tier in the balcony above. The walkway had a gentle slope down to a floor half the size of the one she had seen near the entrance. The great wall that protected the Keep from sorcery appeared twice. One at either end. The columns surrounding the floor were thick and sturdy made with heavy stone. The small group of Shalough sorcerers training finished their session. They gave her an uneasy glance.

She walked straight past Bridget sitting on the bench and waited. As the sorcerers left the main floor. The space was ideal for sparring and she invited Bridget onto the empty stadium. 'Do you want to spar?' She asked.

There was a moment of hesitation and Saranon removed her cloak. Flinging it on the bench. She reached down and removed her bond-breaker from the belt. 'I thought we already had?' Bridget said.

'No,' she replied.

Before there was time to answer she opened her arms the energy crept along, but it was enough. Bridget deflected the blow and responded. Saranon gave her a chance to warm up and held the energy strong. As the Keep absorbed the remainder around them. The air stayed clear from the sparks of energy. She watched as Bridget skirted around the space, becoming more confident with every move. She kept her pace steady giving time between each attack. Showing the actions before using her sorcery. She stayed close to the centre and Bridget was beginning to show frustration. As they fought the sorcerers began to group around the benches and the balcony.

The strain showed plain on Bridget's face and she came in for the attack. Saranon held strong and answered the blow knocking her opponent down. The fight was over and the Shalough sorcerers clapped their hands in unison. Making beats of noise echoing in the space. 'I failed,' Bridget stood up and they shook hands.

'When you fail you know who you are,' she replied.

Saranon stepped back as the crowd clapped in a rhythm, 'They cheer for you.'

'I didn't do anything,' Bridget said.

'You sparred with an Angeon,' she answered.

Dargon peered down from the balcony and she gathered her belongings. She had lost much time and her mind returned to the task her old friend Tasha had given. She made her way up the walkway and Dargon met her. His heavy cloak still settled around his shoulders. 'Congratulations. You found a Guardian,' He said.

She was about to head toward the Ranger's quarters. 'It is quicker if you go that way,' he pointed north to the main entrance.

It would reduce her time. Yet it would also take her deeper into the territory of the Shalough. She followed his lead through the corridors. As the sorcerers stepped away to let them pass. The grounds were laden in white snow. Not enough to hide the wide paths leading away from the Keep. It was the furthest she had been among the clan, where the Shalough had permitted her to be. Dargon strode as far as the outer gate. The ruin of a heavy stone wall protruded from the earth. As a remnant from a battle long forgotten. Its walls had been lowered, but the sections that lasted still conveyed the perimeter. The two columns stood with a stone bowl filled with a fire. An ornament marking the emblem of the clan. 'Zeralden Hadenvar was one of us,' Dargon spoke as the wind caught the edge of his cloak.

'What?' Saranon exclaimed.

'You are Vandragamond. The blood of the Angeon has abandoned our clan. There are many who would go to great lengths to see it return,' Dargon said.

'I thought it was random,' she said.

'Nothing with sorcery is random,' he said.

With that Dargon turned. All sight of the Shalough sorcerers vanished in the light. As though the Keep had been abandoned. She watched as the wind blew along the ground, yet all that appeared was the building. She let the energy of the Angeon go, falling deep within. The agreement had only been with Serensa. She would rather avoid meeting anymore Shalough.

The path grew narrow as it veered out along the hills. The rocky slope provided an alcove for her to rest. A sacra seal shielded her from the wind. She warmed the air as the trees rustled with a hollow sound. The small seal the same size as a coin sat secure atop the rock's surface. Saranon opened a sova bag, when it had grown large she pulled out a thick cloak. To keep away the last of the cold that crept through the shield. A patter of feet scampered past and the cloak moved. The infant dragon ran underneath. Its eyes poked out and she patted the tiny creature. 'I am not sharing my bed,' she said in a stern voice.

The hatchling did not move.

She took the cloak and the infant began to shiver. 'You are not cold,' she said.

She reached out a hand to make sure and the infant dragon dived in the cloak. It stared out into the white forest and back up at her. 'It's not the cold that makes you shiver,' Saranon spoke her thoughts aloud.

A great thud landed from the sky skidding down the hill. The huge dragon turned to stop and stuck his head next to the alcove. 'Kat,' she said and the dragon snorted.

He flopped down covering the alcove leaving a small gap. The hatchling curled up in the cloak to rest and she did the same.

Katholomu shook off the melted snow as the shield from the sacra seal kept her dry. The spray of water ran down and she stayed wrapped in the warm cloak. The great black dragon edged his claw near the sacra seal. 'Don't you dare,' she said.

He flicked the sacra seal toward the hill and the chill air came in with a rush. She ran out into the thin layer of snow and the dragon laughed as she shouted at him. She gathered her cloak leaving a patch of cloth for the infant dragon who refused to let it go. The hatchling was the same size as a cat. Albeit a rather pudgy one with wings and a tough underbelly. Its tiny sharp teeth glistened with content at claiming the cloth as a prize.

'You returned early,' she spoke as she approached the great dragon.

Katholomu snorted in disgust and stepped back. 'Fine, I'll take the lay-line if you don't want a rider,' she exclaimed.

A line of wizards appeared along the ridge of the low hill. The southern emblem of the Corathy flew from their flags and shone on their cloaks. A ball of flame similar to the emblem worn by the Shalough. The line grew thick as the troops gathered, flanking the front lines. The hooves of the horses at the rear could be heard through the silence. The great beast beside her lied down and purred as his tail swung from side to side.

'A warning would have been nice,' she glared at the dragon.

Kat glanced at her. If the great beast could appear amused he certainly did. 'We have your wizard,' shouted the Captain.

His thick cloak and heavy helmet gave him a broad stance. 'Are you sure?' she asked.

The wizards shoved Mitch to the front row for a brief glimpse then hid him among their ranks. '...And I am expected to do what?' Saranon asked.

'You will surrender,' Captain Harkin said.

'The trouble is I'm not feeling so inclined,' she answered.

Kat stopped his gracious purr and stared at her. '...And I don't think it would be much of a fight,' she said.

The great dragon pricked his ear back. The Captain lifted his hand and the wizards responded. Kat flew away as the wizardry flared striking straight for her. She stood, letting the wizardry pass through the energy of the Angeon. It hurled through into the heartland, home of the Shalough. The sorcerers responded rushing with their troops to meet the wizards. Panic took hold and Captain Harkin's troops began to run. As they broke scattering into the forest she caught sight of Mitch. He used his wizardry, desperately trying to break the chains that held him.

A wizard turned, took one look at her and ran. Mitch broke through before she reached him. Screams carried along the wind as the sorcerers clashed with the wizards, then silence. The Shalough stood around the edge waiting. The wizards stepped forward as a large group. Using their wizardry in unison and the Shalough retreated. 'You think you can take on that?' Mitch asked.

She was about to leave their hiding place and he placed a hand on her shoulder. He shook his head to warn her and she glared at him. The sound from the horses veered close and she could sense the rider. He was Shalough. She went to move and Mitch held her in silence.

Rustling branches filled the void. As the wind swept through creeping into the edges of her clothes. A great thud hit the ground and Kathomolu gave a low growl. She scurried up the embankment as the air around heated. A blaze of sorcery swept overhead. Singeing the wisps of her hair before managing to shield herself. The sorcerer held his gaze then fled a moment before the dragon stampeded. Kat ran so hard he went straight over Saranon's head. She lost sight of the sorcerer before he vanished from view. The woods moved as the wizards of the south revealed themselves. Captain Harkin strode forward, his cape bellowing in the icy chill.

The wizards circled in forming a tight arc as Saranon held her ground. Around her she could see the Captain's troops had taken damage. Yet they stood strong. She steadied herself and a great vacuum of air pulled her cloak back. As Kat ran to greet Captain Harkin. The dragon rolled over showing his belly and rubbed his head against the wizard. 'How do you know my dragon?' She asked.

The Captain nudged the great beast. Kat would not move and instead began a deep purr that rumbled through the ground. Captain Harkin let out a laugh, 'When he listens to you, you can say he's yours.'

She glared at the wizard who was beginning to be as annoying as Mitch. 'Kat!' She shouted.

For once the dragon raised his head and somehow managed to stay lying on his back. Before shaking melted snow on everyone. His ears pricked up in the direction of Sturanin Keep. An uneasy silence fell on the wizards of the south. 'Who was the sorcerer?' She asked.

'It does not concern you,' the Captain said.

'His name is Devaughn,' Meredith spoke up.

The Captain gave her a sideways glance. The wizardess, Meredith, stepped back in line.

The great dragon had dozed off between them giving out a loud snore that rumbled on the wind. The day had been wasted as the night fell early behind the clouds. 'I have a more pressing matter than you,' Saranon held his gaze.

'How quaint?' The captain spat the words out.

Meredith spoke, 'Forgive him, he doesn't know when to quit.'

The two wizards shared a discussion without words, it was over almost as soon as it had begun. The troops relaxed in a visible wave of relief. They gave her a cautious welcome into their midst. 'Your wizard is welcome if he can restrain himself,' Meredith said.

Gazing in the direction just below the ridge. Saranon ignored the cold edge to the comment, 'I have to make it to the Pearl Castle.'

The Captain managed to contain a laugh, 'Only a fool travels in this weather.'

As he spoke a storm settled above. The shield from the wizards kept the icy flakes from breaking through. Mitch joined her, staying close to her side. 'The bear makes an appearance,' Meredith said as she eyed him. The wizards worked around her, ignoring her existence. She stared up at the hills to the north as the last light faded. 'You really want to take on the Pearl Castle?' Meredith asked.

'There is much more at stake,' she left the last unsaid.

The troops would descend on Temare and she had no way to warn the Regent. The Pearl Castle was closer, yet it would still take some time to reach. There were many questions she wanted to ask Mitch, but it would have to wait. The storm set in over the wizards' shield wiping away all hope of travel. She strode over to the sacra seals keeping the troops warm. When a heavy wind broke through the shield dumping an icy blast of snow on her shoulders. 'I'm going to regret this,' she muttered aloud.

Using her energy to strengthen the shield. 'It is a pity you are not going the same way,' Meredith said.

'Do you really want an Angeon meddling with wizards?' She snapped.

'The Shalough do not share your sentiment,' the

Captain said.

CHAPTER THIRTEEN

A worthy foe

Saranon felt the dragon's breath on her back keeping them warm. Mitch glared at her, but his words were calm as he suggested they sleep for the night. She watched the storm skim over the wizard shield, rest was the last thing she could think of. He made his bed as close to Katholomu as he could manage. 'You have a volatile hilazen,' Meredith remarked of the bonded wizard.

It was a word she was used to hearing, but not for Mitch. 'What makes you say that?' She asked.

'He is too ready to fight,' Meredith spoke.

'People say that of me,' she replied.

'You are a sorceress,' Meredith gave her response as though it explained everything.

She changed the subject, 'How do you know Katholomu?'

'He grazes on our herds,' the Captain said. 'And eats the kultier that stray too close.'

'I thought he belonged to the Otturin,' she said.

Meredith laughed, 'No one can keep that dragon. What do you want with the Pearl Castle?'

She remained silent as the wizards watched on, 'The false Oracle.'

A hush fell over the group. 'So it's true,' Meredith said.

'Yes,' she answered and left for bed.

Kat nudged in close as he slept, as did Mitch giving little room to rest. Caught between the dragon and the wizard she fell into a broken sleep. Filled with dreams carrying the great rumble of the snoring beast.

She woke during the night dipping in and out of sleep. Listening to the wizards' voices blend into the wind. That whirled above the still air inside the shield. Once she woke to see Meredith staring straight into her eyes. Over the head of the dragon as he slept. 'Do you sleep?' She asked and the wizardess only smiled.

The morning took hold through the shattered sky. As the shield fell with the fading storm. The last remnants of energy dwindled low into the ground. Until there remained no trace. She breathed in the fresh air. Then the dank sulphur smell of the dragon's coat caught in her lungs. Katholomu glared at her as though daring her to give him a bath. 'You stink,' she said.

'There's a hot spring toward Sturanin,' Meredith explained, 'It's a short walk.'

The troops took their time. Still settled in the slope

and gathering equipment as they went. It was a good excuse to stray from the camp and she could not stand the smell for much longer.

Mitch led the way with an eager step and she hurried to catch up. 'Are you all right?' She asked, but he did not answer.

The spring was long enough for Katholomu to lie in while she did her best to scrub his thick skin. She used her energy to dry him before the chill took the last of the waters' warmth away. A rustle came low from the edge of the woods and she turned, yet there was nothing. Mitch could sense her unease, but the dragon paid no heed. The crunch of snow from heavy boots crept along the breeze and Madoc appeared. 'What are doing here?' Saranon asked, she thought he had stayed at Hestrel Keep.

He held the deep red blade of the bond-breaker free. 'You are in Shalough territory,' he said with a firm grip on the hilt.

She touched her bond-breaker tucked away in the form of a dagger. 'No. I meant...' Madoc explained, 'Sturanin...'

Tiny flecks rose from the ground and Madoc's words were swept in a great catalyst. As the air whipped violently toward Keep Sturanin. Her arms felt the heavy weight dragging. As she moved through the pain to raise one blade, Corsavere. The deep sea green of the heart stone shone with the energy of the Angeon as it swung through the air.

She transformed letting the façade fall to the unnatural wind. The sky began to fill with the swarm of dragon riders. A heavy thud reverberated through the ground. Madoc lost his calm and stumbled back. Katholomu waited for the riders to come closer. As he stood strong, spreading his wings in anticipation. The rumble of the outer edge of sorcery kicked up the fresh snow and shallow earth in its wake. A low cloud hung in the air racing toward them with a crackling sound, that followed as it tore up a path reducing the distance at speed. She strode out facing the edge of the oncoming rush of sorcery. As the sound thickened through the air. Madoc found his strength and stood beside her. 'Brace yourself,' he said as it came ever closer.

Saranon held up her sword arm and called to the bond-breaker she had so readily given up. It pierced the heart of the raging storm. Creating a wedge that cut a gaping hole in the flowing sorcery. As it burst into the air the remnants of sorcery vanished. Madoc let out a harsh rush of air from the breath he had been holding. The Shalough appeared and she could make out Devaughn in the distance. 'I'll handle it,' Madoc said and he went to meet them.

'Do you trust him?' Mitch whispered.

She was about to answer and changed her thought, 'Are you jealous?'

'No,' he said.

The response was not convincing and she smiled. Madoc made his way toward the group of sorcerers and Devaughn let his cape flow in the wind. She could almost hear them. The way the group stood their ground told her all that was required. 'I should have sent you,' she exclaimed.

Mitch strode toward the small group and a shadow crossed the hill behind them. As it extended forward the group made their leave. The horses galloped through the narrow path. The clear markings of the riders shone in the light. Their armour hidden underneath their cloaks, shown by the helmets they wore. Mitch went out to meet the Commander and she waited.

She took her time to meet them taking in the entire band, their sword hilts gleaming. They were calm, but ready and watched her at every step. The Commander gazed down with a casual stance. Yet the alertness in his eyes remained. Saranon stayed where she was until the sorcerer invited them to follow. At each step she could feel the Commander judging her, almost waiting. Every time she turned, his eyes locked onto hers with an even gaze. His cropped grey hair escaped from the edges of his helmet. His skin was worn, yet his poise was strong. The wrought iron gates opened to the grounds surrounding the fort. The entrance was for display with the wall trailing low. The Shalough sorcerers were enough to keep people away.

The inside of the building was plainer than she had anticipated. Commander Regner saw her disappointment, 'We're you expecting something else?'

'Perhaps,' she said.

'It has been a while since our fort has seen an Angeon, more than 200 years. When Queen Zeralden graced her ancestral home,' the Commander said.

Saranon glanced around at the stone walls. With the

thick timber frame breaking the monotony. 'Was the last Angeon a Shalough?' She asked.

'All the Angeon were,' he said with a calm interest. 'I have a question for you. Why would Tordoren choose a Vandragamond?'

The room fell silent and Mitch backed away. Madoc spoke first breaking the Commander's gaze, 'Perhaps it is the Tethaweir?'

She was about to speak when the Commander snapped, 'What would you know?'

He turned to Saranon, 'Stay here until the Athgar have had their unrest.'

'I'm not...' She was interrupted while Madoc shook his head.

Commander Regner raised his voice, 'I will not have anyone interfere with the wizards. If the Armythral had taught you properly you would not be so eager to break the Uvalen Code.'

They were left in an awkward silence. As the Shalough tried to accommodate them after the Commander had gone. 'What is the Tethaweir?'

Cassidy spoke up before Madoc could answer. 'It is when Tordoren disadvantages a sorcerer clan to create balance.'

'That might be, but I have to be somewhere,' Saranon said.

'If you want to take on the Commander go right ahead,' Cassidy replied.

Madoc finally got a word in, 'The Shalough Council

will not cross him.'

'Are you serious?' Saranon asked in exasperation.

'Do not argue with the Commander,' Mitch said.

'Lord Shakar lost to him,' Cassidy added. 'Not that the Lord would admit it.'

Saranon could feel her mission slipping away as she was stifled yet again. An idea occurred to her, 'I thought the Vandragamond stayed at Validain.'

'You are here,' said Cassidy, 'but then the weak can travel freely.'

'I am not weak,' she snapped.

'If you want to prove it. There are many here who would be willing to spar with you,' Cassidy replied.

The sorceress, Cassidy, showed them along the path. That the led through the open grounds. The officers that stood around the perimeter glanced their way. The courtyard was protected by a faint shield that kept the harsh chill of winter at bay. Saranon peered through the tall windows as the sorcerers inside stirred. Madoc grinned, 'I don't think they were expecting us.'

'Perhaps,' she replied as an uneasy feeling rose.

Mitch stayed close, his silence and short glances spoke for him. The air filled with the spray of snow and ice. As Katholomu thudded against the boundary wall. The dragon held his wings wide blocking out the last rays of sun. Enveloping the courtyard in shadow.

He flicked the melted ice with a rapid shake and bounded into the courtyard. For a moment Saranon thought the great beast would stop. Instead he reach over them and scratched his claws down the side of the stone wall.

'I'll show you around,' Madoc said.

She hid her surprise at realising he had been at Melacront. The barracks seemed simple enough and worn with age.

When she stepped across the threshold of the main building. The image fell away revealing a Keep with thick sturdy walls. 'Wow!' She exclaimed showing her astonishment.

'Cool, huh?' Madoc said.

She had not expected to find the Keep wrapped in secrecy. It felt like her chance of a short stay was starting to vanish. They followed him through the building that wrapped around the hill side. He led them up a narrow stairway to the tower overlooking where they had been. The chill broke through as they made their way above the shield and she held her cloak tight. Mitch pointed to a glimpse of the Pearl Castle from a distance.

She waited until Madoc left and asked, 'Did we just gain him entry?'

Mitch nodded in reply. 'I thought so,' she said.

They made their way down as the guards changed. The Commander brushed the last of the chill from his coat. The thin wisps of hair remained straight after the helmet was removed. 'It is not fitting for an Angeon to have a wizard,' the Commander said.

As he glanced toward Mitch. 'The wizard stays,' she replied.

It was not the first time she had heard the remark and she stood close to Mitch to prove her point. The Commander brushed it off as he made his way inside. The place was cosy for a sorcerer Keep and the corridors were small. It was almost impossible to move through without walking into someone. The wizard with his broad shoulders managed to glide along unnoticed. Yet she had to dart around. For a moment she stood in a completely unfamiliar place. Hello, Chronasett's voice trailed through her mind. She jumped back slamming against the wall. Saranon followed Mitch into a decorated lounge. With thick woollen carpet and finely carved chairs. The low table was laden with food and drink.

The Commander sat behind a desk with a heavy stain and leather bound folder to one side. He took a moment to breathe in the warm air. 'I will discuss the terms with the clan. In the meantime do not stray far,' he said.

'What terms?' She asked.

'Your surrender,' The Commander said.

Saranon could feel her anger rise. Mitch reached out and gave a curt reply while leading her toward the door. When they were in the corridor she whispered, 'Why did you do that?'

Mitch waited until they were far enough away, 'Not now.'

She glared at him, the wizard could be infuriating. They were stuck within the grounds of a building barely large enough to be a Keep. It was impossible to find a quiet moment with Shalough watching her. She strode through the courtyard and gazed up at the tiny flecks of snow falling. The flakes melted on the surface of the shield, yet the wind found a way to sneak through. Whipping at the edge of her cloak. She stared at the hills blocking her view. Over the ridge and far off in the distance stood the Pearl Castle. Home to the one whom she had been asked to deal with. For all the desire to find Christine. There was an absence of concern for Ulrich, the false Oracle.

A festive cheer rose up through the corridors as she made her way in for the evening meal. The open friendliness took her by surprise. She had to remind herself that she was a prisoner. As darkness fell the lights of the Keep lit up the space with a warm glow. The sound of the wind sweeping past echoed with a steady drone. Above the faint voices that reached her from outside. The decoration in the large room made up for its lack of size. She struggled to find a spare moment as the sorcerers strode by.

The iron lever holding the thick wooden door creaked as the wind caught it and she went out. Mitch ducked through before it had a chance to close. The night sky shone clear as the clouds hastened their journey. The chill worked its way to the edge of her fingers and across her cheeks. The courtyard opened with an archway above. A night watchman called out and Saranon heard the swooping of giant wings. She gazed up to the underbellies of the dragons. Flying low over the turrets, marking the roof top of the Keep. She ran to the outer yard in time to watch the dragon riders circle and land. The first rider came in too fast. A flurry of fresh snow sprayed across the guards that stood close.

Commander Meghan greeted her with a wry smile, 'I didn't think you would get far.'

Saranon's face went red, though it went unnoticed in the chill night air. 'Follow me,' Mitch whispered behind her. He ran ahead creating a distraction as he let out a blast toward the guard tower, 'Run.'

She watched as the guards went for Mitch and could not let the wizard fight alone.

She let her energy rise outward and it met against a heavy shield from the Keep. Saranon narrowed the source and aimed for the guards. The surprise of an attack stunned them more than the impact. She ran passed grabbing hold of Mitch. Guards swarmed around the way out. They darted to the side through a small courtyard. The shield still held at the outer barrier and she ran through. No one followed and she turned. Mitch was stuck inside the shield with no way out. The Shalough were closing in. 'Leave,' he said.

'No,' she cried out.

She stepped back gathering the energy of the Angeon. As it welled up inside the Keep gave ground, at the last moment it let the wizard through.

Sorcery prickled within and she managed to aim the blast upward. To avoid hitting the Keep head on. The energy crackled engulfing the shield. The sound followed echoing, so loud, that all stood stunned. The shield shivered in an array of bright colours, then finally it fell. Mitch took hold of her and they ran. She glanced back as the first flakes of snow wilted down onto the rooftops. They trudged off the wayward paths. Their boots squelched through the layer of snow. She lost sight of Mitch, but he reappeared. Beckoning her through the darkness of the hillside. It was a tiny slither of an opening just wide enough to pass into an archway. He braced the worn flat wall of the rocky hill and it gave a soft glow.

Shouts rang out in the ice cold wind and she could sense the Shalough. She placed enough energy in the old gateway for them to meld through. Mitch went first. As she glanced back a faint glow of energy streaked through the night sky. Her foot lost the ground while stepping back and Mitch caught her. They clung to the wall and she peeked over the edge. It was a long drop down into the destroyed foundations of an old Keep, piled on the cavern floor. The ledge was narrow and she glanced ahead, 'There's a path.'

Mitch jumped from the ledge. His lower half disappeared and he reached over to help her down. The steps were worn and crumbled, but sturdy enough. She ran, gaining speed and he shouted after her. The stone slipped away and she landed with a thump as the dust scattered. Mitch ran toward her and she held on. He bent over and went pale as the pain showed on his face. 'You didn't tell me,' she gasped.

'There wasn't time,' he said.

He collapsed against the wall. A corridor remained intact opening up to a small set of rooms. Yet all she could hear was a faint droning of the wind above. She opened a sova bag and pulled out some bedding as it expanded. It was an excuse to get a closer look at Mitch's leg, but he kept her away. 'I need to look at it,' she said.

There was blood trickling from the wound. He flinched and pulled away, the shock of blood on her hands made her pale. She rinsed them then ripped the cloth before he had a chance to protest.

Underneath, the wound was small and beginning to heal. Saranon glared at him and put her hand above the deep gash. Her energy coursed through the wound. It closed leaving only the dried blood on the surface. 'I appreciate what you did,' she said.

'That's all right,' he responded.

She made sure he was warm for the night. They were below ground, but the air carried with it a chill.

The odd sounds that creaked from every direction broke her sleep. Mitch had rolled over, his face pale with sweat. He coughed and his eyes held pain. She placed a hand on his chest and reached out her senses. 'Why didn't tell me?' She asked.

'You were supposed to leave me,' he whispered.

'I'm not going to leave you,' she said in an angry tone, trying to concentrate.

She managed to block the wizard's pain so he could sleep. She reached out with her energy finding the damage left behind by the Shalough. As the wound healed he gently removed her hand. Her back ached and she stayed close while he rested. The sounds of the distant wind filled the darkness. She wondered why Mitch would conceal his injuries. Then it occurred to her, he did not expect to live.

She reached over and glared at his sleepy face as he woke. 'Don't you ever do that,' she said.

'Do what?' He asked half asleep.

'I didn't ask you to die,' she said.

'I'll try not to,' he said and rolled over.

'I'm serious,' she said.

'So am I,' he answered.

'Mitch,' she said, 'If anything happens to you Captain Mirshendy will never forgive me.'

He put an arm around her and drifted off to sleep without saying a word. As she closed her eyes she slipped into a strange dream with the Captain chasing after her. Through winding corridors that wrapped around with no end. A tiny strand of light broke through from above. She reached over to find an empty spot where Mitch had been. She glanced around becoming frantic and called out.

He appeared with a makeshift breakfast of dried food they had been carrying. 'We need to keep moving,' he said as they ate.

She eyed him carefully watching every strain to see if the wizard was struggling. He hid his injuries well and she did not like being duped. 'It can wait,' she said.

He was about to argue and she glared at him. 'You aren't going anywhere after I healed you,' she continued.

Knowing full well the effort could be undone. A silence clung in the air and Mitch shrugged his shoulders. They spent the morning wandering through the ruins at a casual pace.

A few paths had led to dead ends, but they made their

forward deeper into the hillside. All signs of natural light faded. She cupped her hands until a faint glow lifted above them. Offering a soft light in the mountain of darkness. 'I should've told you,' he said.

The words were yet another reminder that the wizard could read her immediate thoughts. It was a gift that somehow missed the sorcerer clans, much to her annoyance. 'Come on, I suppose we need to find a way out,' she spoke.

With reluctance not wanting to follow his advice. He grinned and ran ahead leaving her to catch up, before disappearing from sight.

CHAPTER FOURTEEN

Race through the ruins

A thin light beamed onto the rubble of the fallen Keep. Saranon steadied herself on the cold hard surface where the frost marked the outside. They were high up with a view that stretched along the valley. Mitch stayed close as the wind picked up carrying the chill through a clear blue sky. To the east in the distance shone a small glimpse of the Pearl Castle. She strode out into the open and the chill ran across her face. They continued, staying close to the hillside. To the far north loomed the Menna Range, home to the Otturin. The hills remained quiet giving the impression that no one lived there. Yet hidden away were several towns, that traded with the sorcerer clans across the region.

The empty branches of the trees allowed the wind to pass through. The valley between the three sorcerer clans remained barren. A land that few crossed as it kept the old ruins of Zyanthia. The resting place of Galdamore, a once great city where the sorcerer clans met. The stone remnants broke free of the path. Offering a glimpse of the vast buildings that had once stood. A faint green tinge spread in the morning light across the pale white snow. She hesitated, yet as the sun's rays strengthened it began to fade. Mitch caught her gaze and pointed toward the Pearl Castle. Where the haze lingered before it disappeared. 'Do you think...?' She asked, lost in thought.

A horn blew sharp in the distance behind them. Carrying its sound through the clear sky and they turned. Back across the ridge the Shalough on horseback made their way ever closer. 'Run,' Mitch said.

This time he stayed with her. Saranon caught the glimmer of a lay-line up ahead. 'There,' she said.

The Shalough were in the valley. She could make out Devaughn near the lead. They rode in a diamond formation over the ridge. The sound absorbed in the icy snow as they made their way toward the narrow path. She ran for the lay-line, but the gap was closing. She hesitated knowing it would not be long.

Mitch stood his gaze held on the riders. She peered up at the sky and it was still clear. They were on the edge of the heartland, yet the sky remained clear of the dragons. It made no sense. She glanced around for a vantage point and her foot went through the soft layer of snow. She cried out as her arms flailed, clinging onto the ice cold layer as it chilled her hands. Mitch leaned over to help and the fragile layer gave way. She stifled a scream as the air whooshed out her lungs and she slid along the sodden earth. He jumped down, managing to brace himself along the sides of the tunnel.

The cold seeped in with the melting snow and a numb sensation sent a sharp chill down her spine. Mitch patted her on the back, 'You can get up.'

She opened her eyes, the cave worn with age had carvings of the sacra seals. Decorating the crumbling layer on the walls. 'Don't do that,' she exclaimed.

'You were the one who fell,' he said.

She glared at him and edged her sorcery to the surface. Enough to dry her clothes and steal away the chill. The cave floor revealed a scattering of stone work. Amid the rubble leading down to a gentle stream.

Carved archways marked the entrance and exit at either end. With the water flowing freely. 'Do you think if we...?' She asked while peering underneath the arch.

The horn blew above ground. It gave her a greater chill than the icy snow and she went pale. Mitch shifted a large wooden shell near the water's edge. He placed it in the stream watching as it floated. 'Grab the ores,' he said.

She reached over where the boat had been. The ores were hidden underneath. The rubble shifted as she pulled them free. 'Will it work?' She asked.

The voices carried down from above. 'Do you want to stay?' He asked.

She moved at the edge of the stone floor before it dipped away and held on to the boat. It wobbled and she fell in with a thud. Mitch steadied the small wooden craft as the stream took them in its grip. The low arch was thicker than the length of the boat. The stone was worn at the edges. The flow of water took them away. She tried to move and the boat wobbled. Mitch pulled her back down. He kept a look out with the ores ready to help steer. The stream grew wider and dipped at a gradual angle. As they entered an underground lake, the dark engulfed them and she made a soft light. It shone above the boat, yet the air around them remained in a heavy black shadow.

A movement caught her eye. Mitch raised the ores and neither of them dared to speak. After a while she said, 'Should I dim the light?'

'No,' he whispered in concentration.

'What is it?' She asked

He did not answer as the ripples broke the surface once more. They remained in silence waiting as the next ripple broke the surface. Then a dull grey tail followed. The width spread along the tip of the water then vanished. 'Quadmar,' she whispered.

The massive underwater beast had a grey thick skin and two fins that morphed into arms. The head and neck appeared partially human. The creatures were far longer than their tiny boat. Mitch pulled the ores close and they stayed low. She had encountered the Quadmar once before. When they had blocked her only way of escape. The lake had become calm. Mitch dipped the ores into the water keeping the movement shallow. The boat crept forward toward the centre of the lake. She peered up at the hollow of the cavern rising into the darkness. Tunnels wrapped around the edges offering a possible way out. One at the far side rose to a low embankment.

The ores creaked as they rubbed against the side of the boat. Mitch kept the strokes steady as they made their way along. She fought the urge to speak, not wanting to do anything that would draw attention. A cold chill sank through her cloak. Every time she thought to speak Mitch gave her a knowing glare. Her muscles ached as she lied close to the hard wooden shell. A tall long spiky edge swam through the water from a large tunnel. It was unrecognisable from a distance and she pointed. Mitch rowed hard creating ripples through the surface. She sat up gazing at the water as the spiky edge disappeared into the depths.

She fought back the urge to use her sorcery. The boat tilted to the side as a large quadmar was flung high into the air. A spray of water thrashed over them as the tail whipped around. It hit the surface at a flat angle and drenched them as they clung to the wavering boat. The quadmar rose again. She spotted the dragon's great jaws gripping it with blood streaming down. 'Kat!' She shouted as the claws came out holding his prey close.

The great beast ate while floating on his back, showing off his prize to her horror. She took the ores and began steering the boat toward the shore. The movement was hard on her arms. She was not about to be a captive audience. While the dragon munched down on his magnificent prize.

'What did you think he ate?' Mitch spoke with a hint

of amusement.

'That's not funny,' she retorted.

'Would you like me to row,' he said.

'No,' she replied.

Saranon hurried as she rowed toward the shore, Mitch jumped out and she followed. The ice cold water sent a chill through her. She clasped the boat with her numb fingers. Helping to drag it along the rocky embankment.

Katholomu moved through the water with the last of his morsel in his jaws. He reached the shore and glanced their way. Then shook the water out, it sprayed everywhere. The dragon waited then threw the remains of the quadmar away. He bowed his head managing to round them up and pushed them into a tunnel. The great beast proceeded to curl up at the opening to lake and began to purr. Sunlight streamed from above marking the way out. She glanced around at the worn carvings and the uneven stone stairs. 'Where are we?' She asked out loud.

'The Ridge,' Mitch said.

Her heart sank, she had hoped to bypass the stronghold of the Mercidian.

She turned to him, 'If you want to leave...'

'After last time,' he said.

The encounter with the Corathy wizards had not been a pleasant one. She gave a reluctant nod and they moved on. Her clothes dried with her sorcery, but the memory of the chill remained. A breeze swept from the open hillside. The afternoon sun gave the last of its glow as it began to ease its way toward the ground. 'Have we travelled that long?' She asked.

Her weary muscles answered for her and she wondered how Mitch was fairing.

The thought of staying near the quadmar made her uneasy. She glanced around, finding another alcove with columns partially visible along the walls. She set the sacra seals around and created a small glow for warmth. Then rested against the wall. They were both exhausted and she closed her eyes as the shadows grew in the fading light. The wind picked up and she stirred not realising she had fallen asleep. The sky was dark and Mitch watched as he stood. 'I was going to wake you earlier,' he said.

She used her sorcery to search out in the darkness. A slow sensation reached her, it was the Shalough. She thought she had lost them.

The wind whirred around the hillside bellowing along the edges of her cloak. She removed it and the chill fell through the gaps in her coat. She breathed in the sharp chill air. 'I'm going out to meet them,' she said and ran up the rocky slope.

She sensed her way underneath the glinting stars. The wind whipped across her face and she made her way to the path. The night clouded her vision. Yet she could make out the dark forms heading toward her on horseback. She watched as a small group stayed close to the path. Her sorcery rose just underneath. Keeping her warm from the howling chill echoing down the valley.

She could make out six riders, yet she was certain there had been more. The faint sound of the horses reached her through the cold clear air. A shadow on the hillside moved out of the corner her eye. 'Down,' shouted Mitch as he ran past her.

The air knocked out of her before she hit the ground and rolled. The wizard had taken the brunt and it reverberated through her senses. She glanced around and he was gone. Panic rose and caught in her throat as faded shapes shifted around the periphery. She had lost Mitch. Her sorcery broke through the surface pulsing out in waves. Bouncing off the Shalough where they stood. She unsheathed Tellembre the pearl white blade forged at the temple of Ollanthia.

The bond-breaker shone at the centre from the heart stone embedded in the hilt. She began to wield it, but the bond-breaker trembled and refused to swing. In frustration she slammed the hilt against the closest Shalough. The sorcery protecting the Shalough flared and she screamed. If the blade would not wield then she would use the hilt. Slamming it against another sorcerer. This time the sorcery flared outward into the dark. In horizontal sparks leaving a trail that played with her sight. She used her senses to hone in on the group and slammed the hilt hard. The third time met with a clap of thunder from the release of energy. It threw her back to the hillside with a thud. The cracks of energy shattered through the air. The group of sorcerers were exposed.

The resistance in the bond-breaker faded as the Shalough scattered, fleeing the site. She held Tellembre and waited, yet this time the Shalough fled. Saranon glanced around, there was no sign of Mitch. She reached out her senses and found a trace leading below the path. She made her way down and saw him. He lied still against the rocky alcove. She called his name and he glanced up. 'Don't do that,' she said with relief.

He gazed at Tellembre. 'How did you break the bond?' He asked.

'The what?' She asked.

'You used the blade to break the bond,' he answered.

'Isn't that what it's for,' she asked.

'I've only seen it used as a sword,' he said.

She eyed him with suspicion. The night was still dark and she was hoping to get some sleep. They strode further on and found a location a short distance off the path. She hoped it would be enough as she laid the sacra seals out again. The warmth from her sorcery kept the cold away. Mitch stayed close and put his arm around her. It was comforting to know the wizard was with her as she fell asleep. Her dreams were filled with the remnants of the old Keep Galdamore. The once great city had rivalled Indarin in Serenphel, the home of the Prophet.

The winter sun caught her off-guard as it streamed into the valley floor. She rubbed the sleep from her eyes. The Ridge stood strong and silent. Turrets rose giving a glimpse of the building that hid beneath. She wrapped her cloak tight as they made their way down the slope. In the fallen snow it was difficult to tell where they had been. The thought of encountering the ockren in a long dead Keep left her with a sense of unease. They stayed along the low part of the hill. It gave less visibility, but she did not want to take the risk. The valley floor evened out into a well-trodden pebble road that trailed off. The lower Ridge opened up into a narrow band of structures and columns. Jutting out to emphasise the Keep that lay covered underneath.

Saranon gathered her thoughts before noticing the outskirts were absent of Mercidian. When every detail suggested they should be there. 'It's very quiet,' she said.

Mitch stood behind her. She hesitated then walked forward taking care to look around. A movement came from the outer wall then disappeared. She wondered if the Mercidian would choose to protect the false Oracle. There was only one way to find out. She approached the outer rim of the Keep and a faint sound became audible. It emanated from the ground, but was not from the central core. Saranon hesitated close to the boundary. She could sense the end nodes and the energy shielding the perimeter.

A battle cry rang out and Saranon grabbed Mitch, breaking out of phase with the real world. The first line of sorcerers became visible as they ran. Then there was silence. The sky was black and the ground pale. As distance and time moved in a disproportionate fashion. They made their way up the stairs carved into the hill. Saranon was halfway there. Up ahead a group of Mercidian waited. Standing still in the courtyard that wrapped around. Her concentration slipped and they fell back into the real world. The Mercidian were pulled through with them and sunlight fell where they stood. Commander Sedgewick lost his footing. He glared at her, 'State your business Vandragamond.'

The words were hollow after the Mercidian had blocked her way. Dragons flew into view, circling in the sky. The wizards of Adeyorn charged across the open field. While the Mercidian barricaded their Keep. 'Let me pass,' she said.

'Is this your doing?' He asked.

She wanted to yes, but shook her head. 'I will deal with you later,' he said and made his way across the Ridge. Taralynn stood keeping guard. 'Did I just get fobbed off?' She asked aloud. 'Don't try anything,' Taralynn said.

She gazed down watching Captain Lydia Grace lead the charge. At the last moment the Athgar veered to the side running parallel to the shield. The energy in the Keep wavered and dimmed.

The Commander shouted to the sorcerers below as the shield pulsed. Captain Grace spurred onward with the Athgar wizards in close formation. Ignoring the blasts of the Mercidian as the wizards formed one group. Mitch tapped her on the shoulder, 'They cannot hold out for long.'

She understood as the Mercidian began another attack. The blows began to hit the shield and the wizard group was starting to break apart. She had kept the power of the Angeon close after the faint marks surfaced on her hands. If she did not permit the Angeon to rise, the Athgar wizards would be lost. The scene below them began to merge into chaos.

The burning sensation creased across her skin. As the energy of the Angeon rose to the surface. It surged outward crumbling the shield around the Ridge. Commander Sedgewick turned with a look of horror set deep in his eyes. She raised her arms and the energy flowed forward. The ground began to tremble. A crevasse opened, it ran back to the hill and branched out over the hillside. The mound of earth crumbled from the top. Both sorcerers and wizards alike ran from the site. The rubble fell into the open crevasse. Until an entire vertical section had fallen, creating an artificial pass. She reached out to the Keep mending the great walls on either side. At its centre formed a giant archway high above linking the building and the Keep.

Saranon made her way down to the newly formed pass. Sorcerers stone covered the floor with a smooth hard edge. The markings whirled in a majestic spiral. Captain Grace approached, 'I can't go with you.'

'How do you know?' She asked.

'I wouldn't be much of wizard if I didn't,' she said as she glanced at Mitch.

'What about Commander Sedgewick?' She asked.

Captain Grace smiled, 'He's used to me turning up.'

The energy of the Angeon faded away. She heard the Commander's voice boom across the void. 'Angeon, I hope you know what you're doing.'

'Ignore the old prat,' Captain Grace said as she waved them goodbye.

She glanced back to see the Commander speaking with the Captain. As though they were old friends. A puzzled look crossed her face. 'They know each other,' Mitch answered her unspoken question.

'How did the Captain know where we're going?' She asked.

'It's been obvious for a while,' he said.

'You told her,' she accused.

He did not answer. 'You did,' she exclaimed.

Again he said nothing. She had no idea how Mitch had managed to contact Captain Grace, but she was sure he had. The Ridge dropped at a steep angle to meet the rolling fields. That swept around a scattering of buildings. When they had made a good distance away she turned back to gaze at the Ridge. 'Wow!' The word slipped from her lips as she stood in awe.

The large gateway dividing the Keep above ground reminded her of Odana Temple. Its great columns and archway was truly Zyanthian, harking back to the fallen empire.

'I wonder what it would have been like,' she spoke.

Mitch met her with a calm gaze, 'That is where my ancestors would travel to meet the Angeon.'

'I am not staying there,' she said.

A forest along the lower hills from the Menna Range arced around the edge of the plain. The well-trodden path strayed toward the barren trees. That provided protection from the wind as it gathered speed. The sun lowered in the afternoon, but she wanted to keep going. Her body was weary and she walked through the pain.

Mitch placed a hand on her shoulder and pointed to a hut in the woods. He went ahead and invited her in. The wooden hut was simple with a large stone fireplace.

It had been built for wanderers with the royal crest carved into the frame around the door. She dropped the long iron handle holding the door in place. The floor was made of rough stone. With low wooden benches wrapping around the walls. A warm fire in the hearth spread the heat around the room. As night fell and the wind bellowed outside. She stood listening unsure, a sensation reached her that made her uneasy. A noise crept out from behind the door and the long iron handle rose.

She froze as the door creaked open. Adeen lifted the thick hood of her dark cloak as she entered. The Otturin sorceress warmed her hands by the fire and Mitch stepped out of her way. Silence clung in the air as the wind howled outside.

'Where is the Oracle?' Adeen asked.

Saranon glanced at Mitch, 'I do not know.'

'I asked you to bring the Oracle,' Adeen spoke in a firm tone.

'Do you know what happens to people who hunt the Oracle?' She asked.

'You do not know what you are talking about?' Adeen said.

'What happened to the sorcerers who harmed Christine?' She asked.

Adeen drew a sharp breath and Saranon took a step back. She had taken a guess from her conversations with the Prophet in Serenphel. She hoped there was not much difference between the two. 'I will give you one more chance,' Adeen said.

Before she could respond the sorceress vanished. She thought the Otturin had understood that she did not want to be part of their game. 'She's gone,' Mitch said.

Saranon tried to relax, but her heart was thudding in her ears. The scowl remained as she seethed. Mitch held up part of a cooked rabbit skewered on a stick.

She sat down and ate, not wanting to admit defeat. 'I found a lay-line, but the glow had turned green,' he said.

'What do you mean?' She exclaimed.

'It doesn't work,' he said.

At first it was a sense of relief then the true meaning sank in. 'I'm going to take a look,' she said. Mitch followed as the chill wind whipped through his cloak. It was freezing compared to the warm hut, but she had to see for herself. They trudged through the snow staying close to the path. The bright stars shone giving a faint light. She was about to call on her sorcery then recognised the faint green glow.

Her numb fingers reached out and there was nothing. The lay-line remained silent. She let her mind roam using her sorcery around the edges. The rough surface of the green glow appeared. She extended her energy further. The sorcery strangling the lay-line dropped down toward the Pearl Castle. She lost her balance and fell. Mitch helped her up and they went inside. She warmed her hands by the fire and snuggled down to sleep. 'You need a plan,' he said after waiting a while.

'I need a whole lot more,' she replied, gazing into the open fire.

CHAPTER FIFTEEN

A key to enter

The hut had grown cold as they packed their belongings and shrank the sova bags. They fitted well inside the leather pouch that hung on her belt. The forest gave no sign of the Otturin, but Saranon knew they would be watching. The thought annoyed her as they made their way to the Pearl Castle. She could make out the flags along the turrets fluttering in the breeze. A crystal clear sky greeted them as the sun shone across the pale layer of snow. The path came to an abrupt end close to the lay-line and they made their way down to the open field. A silence hung in the air as a lone falcon flew overhead.

The path widened as it met with the cobble road leading toward the buildings. A thin trail of smoke wafted from a stone cottage on the outskirts. As they neared Mitch hesitated. She glanced around and the buildings appeared to be deserted. The side of the barn made a thunk as a hard object hit and they ran from it. A shadow began to block out the light. As the air around grew hazy with sorcery seeping from the Mercidian. She ran through the unnatural fog, yet the only person she could find was Mitch. He became uneasy as the shadows grew.

A storm gathered along the ground. As the shards of sorcery broke through, crackling deeper into the fog. Snow pummelled into them and she held out her arms. Saranon skidded backward. As her sorcery hit the wall of ice splaying through the air. The wind from the blast loosened her cloak letting the chill take hold. Movement caught her eye near the building and she ran after the sorcerers. 'Wait,' Mitch yelled out.

She darted around the corner and slipped as the impact from the blast hit. The sorcery bellowed in a ferocious blaze melting away the unnatural fog.

She turned as the energy rose. It catapulted in a blinding arc cutting the air apart. A scream pierced her ears and she glanced up. Clara ran toward her. 'Stop! Please Stop!' Clara cried out.

Flynn stumbled, the blaze had hit along his side. Saranon hesitated, but in that moment he signalled to the Mercidian and they attacked. She held out against them, blocking each blow as they came. Each time the force knocked her back taking away the ground she had made. She fell back into Mitch and he stood strong. The sorcerers were closing in and all she could do was react. Mitch reached out creating a barrier with his wizardry. She raised her arms as the energy rose from within. This time she held the blast strong aiming it straight into the middle of the group.

The impact shook the buildings and dust whirled along the edges. It was enough to clear the way as two sorcerers fell. She could not tell if they were injured, but that was not her target. She strode toward Flynn standing so close she could feel his breath. As his unwavering gaze followed her. 'I told you the next time we met...' She left the last words unsaid.

'Go on then,' he dared her.

She lunged forward gripping his chest as the sorcery ran through and he fell. It was enough to wound him. Clara ran screaming at her, and a blast of sorcery pelted through the air.

Saranon blocked it and Clara continued until the two met. Flynn reached out, but there was nothing he could do. 'This is not about you,' she said.

'Don't you dare,' Clara shouted. 'Don't you dare say that. How could you? I wish we'd never met.'

The words cut through Saranon and she hesitated. 'I didn't want this,' she said.

Flynn let out a groan and they both turned. An icy chill ran along the ground and a silence clung in the air. 'Ulrich is after the Pearl Castle and you would let him have it,' she said. 'What deal did you make?'

The question was directed to Flynn. Yet Clara answered, 'He has access to the imbenik chambers.'

'You gave him the Keep,' Saranon spoke to Flynn.

There was no angry tone, the energy that held her frustration was gone. 'Wait,' Flynn called out. 'You won't get inside the Castle on your own.' He held out his hand, 'Take this.'

She hesitated before accepting the small sacra seal. It had a pearl finish that matched the flawless surface of the Castle. The thin circle glowed in the light as it lay in her hand. She saw the catch, it was only made for sorcery to pass. Mitch saw her expression change and she explained, 'You will have to stay here.'

For a wizard he conveyed no hint of dismay at being left behind. She glanced around them and could see why. If there had been a threat it had faded as the sky cleared. The Mercidian gathering around the building. Letting down their guard in admission that the fight was over. She hesitated, not wanting to leave the wizard behind. Clara waited expecting her to speak. Saranon wondered if she would regret her words before they were spoken. 'Look after Mitch,' she said.

Clara beamed with delight.

The flags atop the Pearl Castle rippled in the distance. She braced herself for what she would find. The path trailed along the hillside and she gazed toward it. The great marmoz dragons of the Menna Range stared down. On the opposite side the dragons of the Heartland gathered. The dark unwavering eyes followed her every step as she left the field far behind. The narrow path opened to meet a lay-line and she remembered Mitch's warning. The opening looked well enough, but she hesitated and took the long way.

The dragons watched on. As the morning vanished into a low light covering the valley floor. The trees thickened into a forest that spread across the hills with their branches. Letting the harsh unbroken wind howl through. She gripped her cloak tight and the hood flew back. An icy chill whipped through her hair and she drew the hood close. The path met another turn. As her boots stepped across the cobble road hidden underneath the snow. It was growing dark and soon there would be no place to hide. The attack from the day had made her weary and her muscles ached.

If she went any further the danger of encountering the Mercidian would be great. There would be no rest if that happened. She held the white pearl seal in her hand. Then with reluctance found a place hidden in the woods to rest. She kept her sorcery close not wanting to draw attention. The chill settled and she managed to use the sacra seal to hide the heat. The sorcery was enough to warm the edges as the wind travelled past. She drifted into an uneven sleep waking during the night. Each time she heard the rustle from the dragons in the distance.

The light had yet to appear over the hillside. Her muscles had stopped their constant ache. A dragon flew over and she gazed up into the darkness of the early morning sky. Its great wings spread whooshing with a hollow drone into the wind. A voice shouted in the distance. A light glowed from the outer boundary of the Pearl Castle. She packed the long cloak away into a sova bag, it shrank down and she hid it. Her sleeves let the harsh edge of the wind trickle in. Yet this time she let her energy rise below the surface. It kept the ice in the wind at bay.

More than once she questioned herself flipping the white sacra seal in her hand. The stone emblem was no bigger than a coin and cool to the touch. An owl hooted above in the branches and she made her way down the hillside. The end nodes were hidden with the fresh snow. The sorcerers stone marking them gave a faint hum. The edge of the Keep would not be far away, yet she hesitated. The darkness stirred and she clung to the hilt of Tellembre. The owl fluttered into the sky and a voice spoke close by. She froze, not knowing what to do and waited as the footsteps trudged away.

It was too soon. If she encountered the Mercidian at the boundary they would have fair warning. Ulrich could not know she was here, not yet. She crept around staying close to the edge of the boundary. Careful not to pass through. She almost stepped on the end node hidden at the edge of the snow. The sacra seal was warm recognising the energy from the Keep. She leaned down taking great care not to touch the surface of the sorcerers stone. She held the sacra seal above the surface, her heart pounding in her chest. There would be no going back.

The energy flooded inside and the small pearl seal made contact with the Keep. Her sorcery moved through the seal tracing the swirling pattern carved atop the stone. It glowed underneath the layer of snow as the sorcery spread out. The surface gave way as a thin crease appeared, then it widened to expose a staircase. A voice called out and she ran down the stairs as the opening closed behind. A dull glow lit in a trail along the edge of the stairs carved in the ground. The narrow entrance transformed, as it widened to meet the stone outer walls of the foundations.

The bulk of the great columns holding the weight of the Castle above, formed a maze as they merged with the rough cut walls. A grey pattern embedded in the stone gave it a dull ashen colour. In stark contrast to the pearl finish that shone across the land. Saranon called to the Keep and it did not answer. She could feel the hum as she glided her finger tips over the cool surface of the stone. It gave a calm sensation, yet as her hand lifted a faint green tinge remained. It rippled along the wall before it disappeared. Not a sound changed in the Keep and a shiver ran up her spine.

The outer paths circled around forming an underground labyrinth. Taking her deeper toward the main building. Steps wrapped close to the thick stone column many times wider than she. Tiny decorations glinted from the light trimming the lower wall. A low howl came from the distance and she hesitated, steadying her thoughts. If the Keep was trapped she could not falter. Saranon ran as the path doubled back and hit a dead end. She almost slammed into the wall and stopped short. A load grunt echoed, she was not alone.

She held her hand against the stone wall and attempted to meld through. Nothing happened. Saranon would have to go back. The place went silent once more as she followed the curved edges of the columns and walls. The corridors wrapped around and she went further toward the indolin Chambers. It was all that stood between her and the habitable area above. The walls carried no sign of the faint green glow as she brushed past them. The hum of the Keep was almost gone in a place where it should have been strong.

She peered upward at the crack running across the seal above the door. Saranon placed the tip of her boot on a narrow ledge and leaned up. Her energy ran through the seal and it healed. The energy ebbed toward the ground then dissipated. A shadow moved in the distance from the doorway. She lost her footing and slammed into the floor. When she reached out with her senses there was nothing. The imbenik chambers were well laid out. Yet the corridors created a maze of uncertainty.

Saranon kept an open gaze watching for movement. A gruff low grumble came from close by and she hesitated. There was still no sign of sorcery, but someone was there. She moved her hand along the cool surface of the stone. Not a peep came from the depths of the Keep. It was not until the darkness moved that she noticed the shadow waiting. It glinted in the soft light behind the column at the far end. As it moved saranon could see the outline of a figure taller than she. It disappeared and she ran after it as fear set it. There was something wrong about the outline, it niggled at the edge of her mind.

She slowed down letting caution dictate her moves, keeping a safe distance. Saranon veered to the left and moved away from the centre. Soon she would have to return. Silence fell as she came closer to the seals bordering the main building. The columns thickened spreading out into long stone walls. Holding the beautiful pearl stone above. She reached out and the image emerged from the shadows. The minotaur stood almost twice her height. His dark shoulders covered in the hide of a bull.

She was so close and hesitated as the minotaur charged. It came to an abrupt stop as it stood level with the sealed entrance. Saranon's heart thudded so hard she could feel it beat in her ears. She caught her breath as she hid behind a column. The minotaur gave a snort and she hesitated. The beast made a move and she bolted back into the labyrinth. Her heart thudding in her ears. All the corridors appeared the same and she stood not knowing which one to take. The minotaur rammed into the wall with too much speed. It jolted with a thud, its deep black eyes glared at her.

She ran through the nearest doorway without thinking. It opened up into an array of columns offering a refuge to escape. She breathed a sigh of relief, but the sound of the angry minotaur reached her. Saranon took off, regaining her senses. Her energy flowed along the walls guiding the way. She could see the way out and ran for the narrow stairway. The minotaur ran behind storming through the great columns. She hastened up the stairs and the beast rammed into the narrow entrance at speed. Its head made it through the threshold of the stairway, then it stopped.

For a moment she wondered if it would squeeze into the narrow space. Instead it relaxed and turned away. She leaned against the stone wall catching her breath, her lungs hurt. 'So much for an easy way in,' she said.

The cold air rushed around the sorcerers stone marking the end node. As she made her way to the surface. Mitch hauled her out of sight before she could ask what he was doing. He held a finger to his lips for silence. They waited near the forest covering the low hillside. She wanted to speak, but her lungs hurt. She crouched down as Mitch peered overhead. When he gave the signal she followed him to a hideaway in the hillside that led to an old ruin. The walls stood and part of the roof, the inside opened into an alcove. Before she could speak Clara appeared.

It was not the person she wanted to see after being chased by a minotaur. 'Wait. I didn't know,' Clara said. 'Did you meet Haig?'

'Yes, I did,' Saranon spoke too loud. Then whispered, 'It would have been nice if someone warned me.'

'I thought you were going through the Castle, not underneath,' Clara replied.

'The green haze is there,' she said. 'I need to get in.'

She peered at the Keep through the remnants of the old building. The outer wall was still intact, but the windows and doors had long gone. The end crumbled where the roof dipped down into the broken structure. Snow covered the edges of the rubble floor.

Clara asked, 'How was he?'

Saranon glared at her in disbelief, 'You want to know how the minotaur is?'

'You probably scared him,' Clara said.

She tried to comprehend how a beast twice the size

would fear her. 'It was running at me,' she exclaimed.

'You scared him,' Clara said.

Mitch kept a look out as the guards made their rounds. They were some distance away from the Pearl Castle, but it was too close if they were found. She could not rest, 'We have to get in,' she said.

Clara responded, 'Now it's "we" is it?'

'You know... Haig,' she said.

'Oh no. I am not going in there with you,' Clara glared at her.

'I'll go,' Mitch said.

Silence fell on the small group. It was not what she had expected, but he knew the danger. 'All right, I'll go,' Clara said.

They waited as the wind hurled flecks of ice and snow in swirls along the ground. The warmth provided by the sacra seal was enough to keep out the chill in the air. Anything more could give them away. Mitch stayed watch while she rested. There was no sign that the Mercidian knew she was close, but a sensation kept niggling at her. It was too late to turn back and if the Pearl Castle was in danger then she had to find Ulrich.

The memory of the minotaur sent shivers down her spine. She listened as the guards made their way along the path through the forest. Mitch shook her and she woke, not realising she had been asleep. He rested while she crouched against the old stone wall. The gaping whole that had once held a window. Somehow she had to make it past the minotaur. Clara stirred from her rest as the low afternoon light fell over the valley. 'Why did you come back?' She asked.

'You aren't the only one that wants Ulrich gone,' Clara replied. 'You should have handed Christine over.'

She remained silent. 'Fine, don't talk to me,' Clara said.

'I didn't want to find the Oracle... Not like that,' she said. 'An Oracle will rise when ready, if not...'

She left the last words unspoken as she watched the guards making their rounds. 'If not then what?' Clara asked.

'No good will come from forcing the hand of an Oracle,' she said.

She glanced down at the palm of her hand, there was only a faint trace. Yet she hid it from view. 'Christine would have been safe,' Clara explained.

'With three clans wanting the same thing? She would have been better alone,' Saranon said.

'Like you at Antavagon,' Clara responded.

There was silence and Clara backed away. The lights of the Keep began to glow along the outer rim. Marking the fading sky as the winter sun set below the hills. The chill deepened in the air breaching her thick coat, yet she had to wait. 'We have to go now,' Clara said.

'What?' She asked.

'That only works until the sun sets,' Clara explained.

'Now you tell me,' she remarked.

They followed Mitch, the wizard had impeccable timing. He moved to the edge of the boundary between the movement of the guards. She stayed close and he waited crouching low. He gave her a gentle nudge forward and she ran toward the end node. The sacra seal fell in place. A hiss of escaping air broke the surface as the narrow stair case opened. Mitch ran ahead into the darkness. She and Clara made their way down. As the sorcerers stone forming the entrance sealed them in the labyrinth.

Mitch was amid the columns spread along the outer section of the Keep. The minotaur was nowhere and Clara ran ahead. An uneasy feeling welled at the pit of her stomach and she hesitated. The minotaur, Haig, was out in the darkness amid the great columns. Try as she might she could not catch up. The frustration showed as she gazed around glimpsing at shadows. Clara called from up ahead. She ran to catch up forgetting where she was and tripped, sliding along the floor.

A figure moved from behind the column. She caught sight of the large shoulders and called out to Mitch. A gruff snort bellowed from the shadows. She jumped up to face the minotaur. Her heart thudding in her ears. 'Haig,' she whispered.

The beast moved into the soft light of the Keep emanating from the walls. His expression impossible to read as his eyes focused on her. 'Saranon,' he spoke the word in a gruff tone and she froze.

'You can speak,' she gasped.

Haig gave a deep chuckle that made her spine tingle. 'You can do magic,' he said.

'Yes,' she answered.

'You can do magic for me,' he said.

Before she could reply Haig held out his hands. Each wrist was bound by a band with a seal. 'Break them magic user,' he said.

She hesitated. 'Break them,' he told her.

Clara came running. 'Don't,' she cried out.

It was too late. The bands crumbled and the minotaur was free. Haig rubbed his wrists, 'I have waited a long time Angeon. You may pass.'

No one was about to argue as the beast towered over them. She ran toward the centre hoping to find a way in. 'You freed a minotaur,' Clara said in amazement.

She took no notice. 'You freed a minotaur,' Clara repeated. 'How did you do that?'

Saranon had not thought about how and the expression showed on her face. Clara shook her head in disbelief, 'This way.'

'But...' She said.

'The guards are that way,' Clara said.

She wondered if Haig had stopped her from going in the wrong direction. The corridors were silent, but something nagged at the back of her mind. It was emanating from deep underground. 'The Keep,' she spoke aloud.

A tapping echoed up the walls, it barely audible. 'What's happening?' Clara asked.

She wished she knew, 'We have to help the Keep.'

'This way,' Clara rushed toward a sealed door.

They stopped in the archway. The two heavy doors were carved with a seal over the entire frame. Clara stepped back to let her pass, 'It's the central chamber.'

Saranon placed a hand on the door, it was warm to the touch. The stallic energy from the Keep emanated through and a green glow flared. 'Stand back,' she said.

She steadied herself unsure of what would be behind the heavy doors. Her sorcery rose and she hesitated as the green glow ran along the carvings in wood. It linked up with the detail surrounding the frame and engulfed the entire archway. Time was running out as the sorcery built up inside. It hit the frame with a thud and the glow faltered. It was not enough. She rammed the door with the energy from her outstretched hands. The glow halted, but still it was not enough. She gathered her strength and held on. Keeping the blast steady and unrelenting. She held on as the blast continued. A great rush of air shot back as she hit the floor. 'You did it,' Clara cried out.

She glanced up to see the charred remains of the heavy wooden doors. The seal had broken and all she could hear was the Pearl Castle screaming out.

CHAPTER SIXTEEN

The raging Keep

The voice of the Keep struck through Saranon's mind and she struggled to hold it back. The energy raging inside cascaded down the walls. Flooding the lower area and seeping across the floor. 'Wait,' Clara shouted through the noise.

She halted at the lower step watching the stallic energy cross the floor. Heading toward them. 'There is sheal under there,' Clara said.

'I know,' she answered.

The pale glow of stallic energy moved closer. A slim fluid line making its way along the smooth cold surface. Somewhere underneath lay the toxins of the Keep embedded in the sheal. The glowing liquid sparkled as it splattered underfoot. Clara ran along the balcony wrapping around the outer wall. The surface underneath disappeared.

Saranon twisted back holding onto the edge hidden below the liquid. 'Hold on,' Mitch shouted.

He lowered a rope. The stallic energy lapped around her and she tried to concentrate. Her foot hit something hard, 'I found the floor.'

She waded through sensing the outline of the conduit and stopped. There was no way around it, she would have to go in. The liquid wrapped around her arms and prickled along her senses. Her energy held it back, but she had to find the conduit. She dived under and the shock made it hard to think. The pain seared across her arms. She scrambled to break free of the surface. Sending a spray of stallic energy through the air. She gasped for air, 'Sheal.'

The pain numbed and she dived again, ready for the shock of the sheal against her skin. Her energy guided her as she relied on her senses. Making out the line of holes running along the conduit. Her energy waned under the pressure, yet she held on. The weight wrapped around her limbs. Gripping her strength as the energy rippled through her mind. The rough surface of the broken conduit stopped her and she clung on. Her energy spread around the weakened outer wall. Saranon had to concentrate as the sheal closed around. Trapping her in the depths beneath the surface.

The conduit heated with her energy and she could sense the gap closing. Her head broke the surface as the liquid caved away dragging her down. She slipped and reached out finding her grip on the conduit. Clara called out and the energy rushed in her head blocking the words.

The stallic energy disappeared as Keep sealed the opening. She glanced down, still hanging on to the conduit. The liquid sheal swirled well below, leaving her hanging in mid-air. Saranon tried to pull herself up, but there was nothing to hang onto. A thudding sound ran along the surface and a rope swayed close to her shoulders. Mitch lowered himself with the rope using his feet to kick off the side.

He took hold off her and they made it the balcony. Saranon dropped on the floor to catch her breath. Her head was spinning so fast and all she could hear was the Pearl Castle thundering in her mind. Mitch stayed by her side as the Keep rumbled. Clara panicked and ran toward the archway. The Keep closed it, melding the wall into the gap. 'No,' she shouted in a hoarse voice.

Clara was caught between rushing for the opening as it closed and staying. The Keep made the decision for them as the wall solidified. The central core was thudding from deep beneath and it called out. Mitch shouted and she gazed up to see them both. 'You passed out,' Clara said.

'What?' She asked, trying to get up.

Her head spun. Mitch caught her before she fell again, his steady arms wrapped around her. 'You need to lie down,' he said.

'I'm fine,' she said while making another attempt to stand.

The floor went sideways. 'I don't feel so good,' she said.

Mitch stopped her before she hit the hard surface. 'I'll check on the conduit,' Clara spoke in a firm voice.

She was about to argue, but the look on Clara's face was so stern she did not dare. Saranon leaned back in Mitch's arms as they rested. He held on tight in the silence. While her mind raced between the rumbling of the central core hidden in the depths. The energy creased up through the walls and pulsed along the conduit below them. The balcony opened into the upper level revealing a control room. Soft rays of light glowed across a screen matching the patterns of the Keep. She tried to move and Mitch refused to let go. 'It's her Keep,' he whispered.

She watched with a great reluctance for not being able to help. Yet it was Clara to whom the Pearl Castle responded.

'It's not always about you,' Mitch said.

She glared at him, the wizard could be infuriating. Saranon's head spun as she rested against him. 'What are you doing?' She asked.

'We thought we lost you,' he said.

His answer made no sense, but she was too exhausted and drifted in and out of sleep. She could sense the Keep moving. Reaching out to the connections that still held it. The frustration broke through in a hollow thudding clambering throughout the building. The faint noise became audible above the control room. Clara hesitated, 'If I increase the power everyone will know.'

'How long will it take?' She asked.

'I can delay the last stage until morning,' Clara replied.

Her muscles were sore when she moved, 'That will do'

Clara made the preparations adjusting the controls as

the Keep responded. Saranon drew the blade Tellembre. The light pearl bond-breaker gave a soft glow in the dim light from the walls. She had created the blade from Ollanthia in her homeland. It seemed so long ago. The Keep was older than the Pearl Castle from a time Zyanthia had long forgotten. Clara hesitated. Yet the bond-breaker Odayour she had given as a gift stayed by Clara's side. 'I will not follow,' Mitch said breaking the silence.

'I would not expect you to,' she replied.

Saranon tried to hide the fact that she had overlooked the wizard. He did not appear to be amused.

The control room wrapped around into several corridors. She found a small room and began to change. A faint banging noise echoed into the chamber as she emerged. Yet the Keep remained calm. 'It's the guards,' Clara said.

She stumbled hitting the bench and Clara glared at her. 'I need you to distract them. I'm not ready.'

Saranon brushed herself off and strode toward the edge of the chamber. Heat radiated off the walls. The columns of the corridors encircled a colourful mosaic embedded in the floor.

Sorcery pulsated in creases through the sealed archway as the doors began to give. The surge trickled in small flashes flowing out along the corridor. A crack let off a thunderous sound as a broken line edged its way diagonally across the seal. The doors still held, but it would not be long. Saranon steadied herself on the mosaic circle at the centre of the columns. A fine spray of shards flew across the space and she blocked it with her shield. The break line in the door widened and she heard muffled shouts through the gap. The Mercidians pounded at the doorway and she waited. Her heart thudding in her ears. Every blow to the seal reverberated through the Keep. The air heated around her, yet still she waited.

A jarring crack hit the archway and the doors flung open in a hail of dust and fumes. The sorcery struck through the air. Her energy surged, she could feel it rise to the surface shielding her from the blow. The explosion hit the shield with a deafening force. The air cleared revealing the Mercidian guards. Commander Felina stood firm as her guards hesitated. An awkward silence hung in the air and Saranon drew the blade Tellembre. She waited to see what the Commander would do.

Behind her the open passage led to the control room. The Commander's eyes shifted and stayed on the bond-breaker. A haze rippled in waves through the air sweeping around the room as the dust scattered. The stone in Tellembre's hilt shone. The Keep sealed in the passageway behind her. Closing off her only link to the control room. The haze evaporated as the Mercidian guards surrounded her. 'I am here for Ulrich,' she said holding the blade firm.

'This is my Keep,' the Commander responded.

It was the only warning Saranon had as the first blow struck. Tellembre swung as it glided in the air sinking deep into the guard. She let the blade slide free and in one swift blow carried the sword around to meet the next guard. The blade plunged and the guard stumbled back.

Ormond grasped his wound as the blood fell. A silence fell as the guards stood back. He healed the open wound and staggered to his feet. 'You don't know what you do,' Ormond said.

'The Pearl Castle is being bled dry, soon you won't have Keep to protect. All I want is Ulrich,' she said.

'What do you mean?' Ormond asked.

The pain of the Keep surrounded her as it broke through the connections. There were many woven around the building. She held the blade down and the stone at the centre of the hilt shone bright. The sword slammed into the mosaic floor as she let her energy ripple into the Keep. The screams emanating from central core seeped into the space flowing up the columns. An awful low sound filtered through. She gazed upon the guards watching their expressions.

A voice came through from the depths, a voice meant for her. Break them, break them all. The Pearl Castle stirred underneath, Break the Fires of Chaos.

Saranon forgot they had an audience. 'As you wish,' she said.

Felina, the Keep said.

She was stunned, realising the Keep had spoken to the Commander. 'The Pearl Castle is speaking to you,' she said.

'I told you, this is my Keep,' the Commander said.

It was a sharp tone that sent chills down her spine yet she did not show it. 'Then protect it from the real threat,' her words lingered as no one spoke.

The central core rumbled beneath her feet as a warning.

The walls reverberated the deep sound upward. For a moment all stood still, waiting. She could hear Ormond's heavy breathing from the wound. It was still troubling him after he had tried to heal it. She held his shoulder and he relented. As she used her energy to complete the healing process. Her eyes stayed transfixed to the body on the floor. Yet there was only emptiness where her emotions should have been. One more thread from the Fires of Chaos fell and the Keep cried out.

It was enough to send a panic through the Mercidian in the Keep. Edolyn rushed into the room and set eyes upon the body of the fallen soldier. She let out a howl of rage and threw up her arms as the seal opened to the control room. Clara shouted out, but she did not answer. Saranon dared not take her gaze from Edolyn. Ormond reached out to grab her and she elbowed him in the freshly healed wound. He let out a yelp from the pain. The air began to creep in a tidal flow toward Edolyn. Clara appeared at the other end from the corridor. She saw the flicker in Edolyn's eyes. Before the air electrified in an array of sorcery culminating in a great ball.

Clara's scream hit the void. Saranon had no time to wonder why. As the Angeon rose from deep within breaking through the creases in her skin. Her eyes glowed as the energy of old took hold. With every effort she pulled the ball of sorcery toward her. It flexed in the air as time slowed. A rush of energy caught her off-guard and Clara's screaming hit her ears. It was Saranon who fell. The weight of hauling the sorcery out midstream knocked her across the floor. A cackle broke from Edolyn's lips. 'Next time you will think before breaking into the Pearl Castle. I do not know what the Shalough thought you were.'

The words cut deep as Saranon glanced toward her friend.

Edolyn spoke to Commander Felina, 'Take them out of here.'

'Your eminence,' the Commander hesitated.

'You heard me,' Edolyn reiterated.

Before Ormond could move Saranon had melded through the floor. Clara gave a smile before she disappeared into the structure of the Keep. It guided her through to a secret passage and let go. She lost her balance and sprawled across the floor. It was not the graceful movement she had expected, but it gave her a way out. The passage had two doors. One led back the way she came and the other would take her closer to the great hall. It was so tempting to head further into the Keep, her legs moved before she realised. She came to a stand still as the thought of her friends niggled away at the edge of her mind. She could not leave Clara and Mitch.

With a heavy heart she strode toward the door that would take her back. Light gleamed along the crease as the door swung with a soft movement. The polished tiles glinted. As the low winter sun shone from the tall narrow windows. The walls reflected the light with a warm glow. It was not the place she expected to be. Saranon glanced around in a daze. Footsteps approached and it brought her back to reality. As an aged sorcerer with long greying hair entered. 'What has the world come to when it chooses a Vandragamond?'

'Pardon?' She asked.

'Permitting one from the strongest clan to walk the land,' he continued. 'And the most reckless. I suppose you are pleased with what you have done?'

Saranon stood in open astonishment. 'The Oracle...'

'It is not your place...' He interrupted.

'Can destroy world!' She shouted at him.

The words thundered in the open space. 'Can destroy the region,' she corrected. 'Christine is my equal, not Ulrich.'

Her rage boiled beneath the surface, she had to find Ulrich and stop him. Commander Felina spoke in the silence, 'The Fires of Chaos are linked to the Keep.'

The sorcerer's face went a livid red, 'Abominations of treachery.'

'Thurlow,' the Commander said, waiting for the sorcerer to settle.

'You know what to do,' he said and left without any further acknowledgement.

'Did I just get dismissed?' She asked.

'Think yourself lucky,' Commander Felina answered. 'He only has time for those who stray from the Code.'

She had almost forgotten about the Uvalen Code. That governed sorcery in the world of Tordoren. 'Follow me,' the Commander said as she began to leave.

'Where?' She asked.

'To find Ulrich,' the Commander replied.

A smile creased across her face, finally she would meet the false oracle. A wave of relief swept through as the anticipation built underneath. Every step leading her closer as she stayed behind the Commander. 'Don't get any ideas back there,' Commander Felina glanced her way.

They reached a hollow alcove in the central building. She hesitated as a thin vapour of sorcery trickled along the walls. A crack thundered in a stark bold sound hurting her ears. She shouted out to the Mercidian guards. The sorcery blasted through escaping as the remnants shattered. She answered the pulsing blasts that ricocheted outward. Raising her energy and wrapping it around the guards. She skidded against the outer wall with the sudden impact crushing into the shield. The pulse rippled again and she staggered forward under the weight. Before the next blast hit, shattering against the frame of the arch. The pain seared through webbing its way closer with each impact. She glanced at the devastation inside, there was no trace of Ulrich.

A rage swept over her, cascading down the edges of her vision. The blasts evaporated in a hollow silence. A howl escaped her lips filled with all the frustration welling beneath. Her fists slammed down on the charred table and it crumpled under the pressure. 'I will tear him apart and send the pieces to the far reaches of Tordoren.'

A hush met her as the Mercidian guards fell into silence. 'Spoken like at true Vandragamond,' the Commander said in flat tone.

She could not tell if the remark was serious or sarcasm

and let go of the energy of the Angeon. 'He tapped straight into the conduit,' she said.

A flash of fear swept over the Commander. The sorceress stepped back, 'I would hate to be Ulrich when you find him.'

She gazed around the damage, the smoke still rising from the charred furniture. 'Take care of the Keep,' was all she could say.

Commander Felina nodded in agreement. The Pearl Castle hummed. It was tiny, but this time the tune was different. It was one of contentment. In stark contrast to the seething anger framing her mind.

CHAPTER SEVENTEEN

The artefact

A cold chill hit in the open courtyard, it failed to calm Saranon's temper. The dragon Katholomu raised his giant head over the stone perimeter. The beast's eyes pierced through her and came almost level with her gaze. He was waiting, waiting for her to make the call. Fight or Flee? This time she gave into the dragon's wish and a wicked smile creased along his jaw. His belly rumbled under the dark thick layer of leathery skin and scales. She raised her hand and whispered, 'If you do not want a coward find me Ulrich.'

The rumble turned into a low growl of delight as she clambered up his shoulders. She could feel the warmth through his thick skin. Mitch ran out and climbed up beside her. 'Are you sure?' She asked.

Knowing that where ever the dragon took them it lead

to danger. The wizard waited for the dragon to rise into the stirring gale, 'I am coming with you.'

She did not understand, but as the great beast swerved in a tight arc all she could do was cling on. The howling winds wrapped around them. As they toward the empty valley that held the remnants of an ancient empire. The mountain ridge that held the last of the long fallen Keep Galdamore rushed by. The white snow hid any sign from below the icy clouds. The wind whipped across her face and she stayed close. The bellowing streams of air turned into a gale. That brought with it the flecks of snow scattering across the dragon. They melted against the heat of Katholomu's skin. The stench of wet dragon filled her lungs. She gagged on the smell.

Mitch drew a deep breath in, but said nothing. A gust blew the great beast off course and he hastened back to the direction. He was flying straight and true for Sturanin. She held on tight. Hoping with every passing moment that Ulrich was somewhere still out in the valley. If they headed to Sturanin Keep she would have to face the Shalough. Yet she had asked the dragon to find Ulrich. The slope of the hillside steepened as they flew up the valley. Along the same path she had taken to reach the Pearl Castle. The gale passed as the sun set and Kat lowered his wings dropping from the sky in a fluid motion. Swooping low as his belly skimmed the ground. He came to a sudden stop and Saranon lost her grip. She hurtled onto the dragon's head and stared down at his deep black eyes.

He moved his brow and rested on the ground as

she fell. Mitch caught her before she hit the cold layer of snow. The last of the light dimmed as night fell and she began to set up camp. The wizard hesitated with a hint of amusement creasing across his smile. 'What's so funny?' She asked.

'There is a camp up ahead,' he answered.

'I can't see it,' she spoke as she gazed upon nothing but the snow covered valley.

'Turn around,' he took her shoulder and pointed.

A tiny seal glowed marking the entrance to an alcove, it was so faint. He let go and it disappeared. 'Why can't I see it,' she asked.

'It's for wizards,' he said as he led her through the invisible shield.

A chorus of out of sync voices flooded through the air and a warmth that took the chill from her bones. A pain seared up her arms as feeling returned from the cold. Before she could ask, Anthony spotted her with a keen eye. She cringed at the sight of the guard from Qwezkin Fort. There was a nodding glance between wizards as Mitch left her. 'What are you doing here?' She asked as she eyed him with suspicion.

'I might ask you that,' he said in a gruff tone.

He was almost the same age as Mitch, but he missed nothing. 'I seek Ulrich,' she said.

'Then our goal is the same,' he replied.

'Why would you seek out a sorcerer?' She asked.

'Why do you think?' he said.

'Uh...' Her expression carried so much doubt.

'He endangered the trade line,' Anthony said. 'You haven't changed.'

She could feel her cheeks go hot and crimson. 'Now...' She stumbled for words and fumed at the wizard.

The warm glow of wizard lights threw shadows across the open space. A remnant of an old Keep long gone. Yet the stone outline and heavy columns remained. Worn with time and filled with modifications made by the Athgar wizards. She strode near the troops bustling around the space with Anthony following behind. His hair was filled with grit from a long travel. One hand touched the hilt of a blade as he moved with ease. The sun had tanned his olive skin, yet he blended in well with Athgar who roamed the borders. It was odd to see them again. Riddley and Jameson nodded as they saw her. Each wizard had a task and she felt out of place.

Low voices emanated up ahead and she went to made her way closer. Anthony placed a heavy hand on her shoulder and shook his head. It was polite, but she knew what it meant. Jane lifted the hood from her cloak. As she entered from the shield bringing a damp chill inside. The lights wavered in an unseen breeze bringing a deep silence over the troops. 'It's done,' Jane said.

'What is?' She asked.

The wizards went about their work ignoring the question. She glared at Anthony who pretended not to notice as he sat near Riddley.

She was about to leave and Anthony pulled her back with too much strength. She knocked over a barrel and fell to floor with a clatter. The short swords sprawled across the ground as she rolled out of the way. A hush tone fell, as she glanced around there were nervous stares. A lone cough broke through. Anthony steadied the barrel, 'This is not for you.'

Saranon gazed up into his dark eyes, 'You don't have to go after Ulrich.'

'You haven't seen wizards hunt a sorcerer have you?' He said in a cold tone.

She thought back to the time. Captain Mirshendy and Mitch had chased her through the streets of Rededere. The wizards had cornered her with ease, even though she did not like to admit it.

CHAPTER EIGHTEEN

The battle awaits

Saranon wrapped the thick cloak around her shoulder. Yet the winter's chill crept through steeling the warmth from within. The wizards blended into the frost laden landscape. With an ease that scorned her clumsiness. Mitch was nowhere to be seen. 'Where are you?' She yelled.

A flicker crossed her vision, but nothing more. There was a reason why she detested wizards when they showed off. Dragons flocked high along the far ridge line across the valley. She gazed as they watched, but what were they waiting for? She did not have time to think. As the light glistened into the heart of the long valley whisking the shadows away.

The sky cleared and movement caught her eye. A small group in the distance ventured toward the Keep Sturanin. She freed the hilt of her bond-breaker as the blade sung.

Her numb fingers fumbled over the dagger. A whoosh of air sped past. 'They've gone,' she said.

As the crowded feeling left. 'Yes,' whispered Mitch.

The voice from nowhere made her jump as he remained hidden from view. He was no help and she scrambled to keep up. The snow covered ground slowed her down. She was falling even further behind. She stumbled onto a rocky path and gained pace over the hillside. She was catching up when a thin dark line appeared along the horizon.

The horses and their riders made a tight formation. With the flags of the Shalough bellowing in the wind. An eerie silence fell as she gazed at them. The line of riders marched toward the group of sorcerers swarming onto the plateau. 'No,' she cried out into the wind. 'No,' she said again.

Almost willing them to stop. It was too much to bear as the Shalough closed the gap to the sorcerer group and Ulrich with them. His heavy cape bellowing in the wind.

A horn blew out in the crisp chill air and the horses followed gathering speed. Their hooves kicking up flecks of ice creating a white cloudy haze. He rode high and his tall stature with greying hair made him stand out. From the gleaming metal helmets worn by the soldiers. They flanked around in a tight circle as the first line moved forward. Forming a barricade with their shields. As the wizards hedged closer with a wide buffer in between.

There fell a momentary silence on the land. As Ulrich disappeared behind a wall of safety. Concealed by the ever growing numbers. Aas the Shalough swarmed onto the pale snow covering the terrain. The sun shone glinting off their armour and shouts rang out across the plain. Captain Trevell led the Athgar wizards riding from the heartland. They rode hard and the Shalough closed the distance with a sweeping ease. The first blaze let loose from the sorcerer clan. It flared across the shield protecting the wizard riders. The Shalough sorcerers edged in. Forming an arc wrapping around each end, swords and spears ready.

As the first blade plunged its way through the shield. A whooshing noise came from overhead. Faint dots outlining the bright clear sky merged. First from the south as the dragon riders came into sight. Then the east coming in hard and low to the ground. Then from the north the dragons without riders gathered across the ridge line. Waiting in anticipation. The wizards from the sky struck down with a force that shed the snow from the land. The sodden muddy earth squelched beneath the horses hooves. As chaos ensued across the plain. Devaughn held his rank at the lead. Narrowing in on Captain Trevell as the shield lay in tatters.

The Captain outstretched his arms to the sky before he fell. Blood ran where his body hit the ground. A cry went up through the ranks of Shalough soldiers and they spurred on. The wizards rode their dragons circling in with a continuous attack from the air. It was enough to splinter a few from the tight formation of the Shalough. A sorcerer screamed in agony as the blast hit true. A merging line flew into the sky from the Keep Sturanin. As the sorcerers joined the dragon riders. They were but a faint line and the distance was soon closing when they could take aim. A silence drew in the skies above as the wizards angled their dragons ready for the attack. Both troops hesitated. As the rush of swooping wings filled the air with a harrowing sound.

A cry rang out from above as the largest dragon of them all took to the sky. His wings spread the full length casting a shadow wide along the weeping ground. The deep whoosh droned lower than the other dragons circling through the air. The great underbelly was thick and hard with age. As his head faced straight for the Shalough his big cunning eyes honed in. The jaw dropped to show the jagged line of teeth and a gush of air rushed in to fill his belly. Cries rang out as the wizards made quick work to retreat. Before the sight of the fire breather. A crackling spray gushed out of its gaping mouth down upon the sorcerer soldiers. Their screams just audible above the hurtling flames.

Atop the Angeon rode and what the dragon did not finish she came for. Katholomu dug his claws in deep as the earth spewed forth with a heavy landing. Saranon circled in on Devaughn. Before he could flee with the soldiers who were edging back. The dragon riders from Sturanin were almost in reach. It would not be long before they could join the fight. The two faced off as their bond-breakers struck. The echo of the swords spread across the open plain. The great dragon kept the area around them clear. His glaring eyes enough to stir a primal fear in the most foolhardy. A crack, as metal and bone split deep, filled the air and it was Devaughn who lowered to his knees.

The dragon riders from Sturanin were in sight, yet no blast hit the ground. They landed with grace between the Angeon and the troops of the Shalough. Only a few remained on contested ground. Lord Halleron lowered his dragon. Strategically placing it beside Katholomu the dragon of the Angeon. To a hush of silent awe. Commander Regner of the Shalough clan met the wizard Lord on the bloody field. While the Angeon stayed near the great dragon.

Saranon cleaned her blade on the dragon's claw. The unwanted burden fell to the ground. She had meant to wound her opponent. A tiny flicker of movement caught her eye. She sensed Ulrich disappearing behind the ranks of soldiers. 'He's gone,' she said.

Lord Halleron scratched his chin as he took a steady glance at the surroundings. 'You wouldn't want to disappoint me. By losing your bargaining chip?' The Lord spoke in a soothing tone.

Commander Regner did not take the bait, 'We will find him.'

'It would seem your sorcerers have a habit of losing things,' Lord Halleron said.

'Where is the Oracle?' the Commander asked.

The Lord grinned showing his jagged teeth in a heavy set jaw, 'Wouldn't you like to know.'

'You know where the Oracle is?' Saranon interupted.

'Of course I do,' he said.

'Hand her over,' the Commander said.

'You have no idea…' she said.

Lord Halleron glanced at her. Saranon continued, 'She can absorb your darkest secrets and use them against you. She is better off with the Athgar.'

'Perhaps I should have brought her,' the Lord mused.

'I'm serious,' she said. '...And when she grows up the Fires of Chaos will have nothing hidden from her.'

Saranon thought back to when she had rescued the Christine. It would be a pleasant day when the little Oracle could manipulate the Fires of Chaos. Commander Regner gazed down at the Angeon's blade in thought, 'I will find Ulrich.'

'We will find Ulrich,' Lord Halleron said. 'He damaged our trade line.'

Saranon fought the urge to leave as the sorcerer and wizard spoke. The sky was growing dark and she should have been gone. Instead the wizard made it clear she had to stay. It riled her, but the numbers were so many. If she left the fighting might break out again. It was a sore compromise and her frustration was plain to see. Fires were lit to keep the troops warm. The wizards created dome shields to trap the warmth in and the snow out. The dragons formed a perimeter as they rested. With their tails curling around each other' adding another break from the cold. Song filled the air and Saranon found herself standing alone. She was the only one who seemed to notice that earlier there had been a battle on the open plain.

The shrill of energy ran through her from the fight. It buzzed around her head and clouded her mind. Devaughn had been a pleasant accident. She meant to blast him before the blade had struck. The conversation between Lord Halleron and the Commander drawled on. Saranon itched to leap on Katholomu and take to the sky. She let out a deep sigh and stepped back to rest on the dragon. Mitch tapped her on the shoulder, she had almost forgotten about him. She waited for a lull in the conversation. When no one was looking and sneaked off with the wizard. 'Took you long enough,' said Anthony, waiting for them.

'What's going on?' She asked.

'Stay out of sight,' Anthony said.

He led them in a wide arc. Stretching out into the ranks of wizards huddled around the bonfires. 'I know someone who can get you to Ulrich,' he said.

Without any further explanation. They weaved around the edges of the Athgar clan. Before heading south toward the last group of wizards. Meredith greeted them. She was so shocked to see Corathy that she gaped in astonishment. Captain Harkin sat near the open fire, his face was bruised and he did not stand. 'This is your pass to the south, Angeon,' Anthony said.

He waited with the group issuing instructions in a low voice. Meredith nodded, but Saranon could not make out what they were saying. There was an uneasy edge to the group and she stayed close to Mitch. 'When do we leave?' She asked.

'Patience,' Anthony said as he joined them by the fire. 'You need to clear that head of yours.'

The wizard was a few years older than she, but his words carried the weight of experience. 'If you leave now you will be greeted by every Shalough other than the one you seek,' he said.

His words did not sit easy and her frustration showed as she kicked up the dirt at the fire's edge. Meredith spoke, 'Temper. You are not only one who is disappointed.'

She watched as the fire burned into the late evening. Keeping away from the direct heat. Too many sounds emanated from the far edges of the plain denying her sleep. Every muscle ached, part of her wanted to go back and the other wanted to find the false prophet. Mitch was fast asleep curled up in a cloak behind her. He lay close to the other wizards resting beneath the starry sky. Anthony caught her glancing in the direction of Lord Halleron. 'We can deal with the sorcerer clan,' he said.

'I should have gone after Ulrich,' she thought aloud.

'That one's hard to catch,' Captain Harkin said.

As he sat by the fire mesmerised by the flames. 'I should be searching for him,' she said.

'And bring the entire Shalough clan after you,' Anthony said. 'Get some rest and be patient.'

'Sorcerers always provide an opportunity, they are too quick to stir,' the Captain added.

'What?' Saranon asked.

'You'll see,' Anthony replied. 'It's all about patience.'

She hated mind games, and it felt like the wizards were using the moment to annoy her. If they were it was working. 'How can you be so sure?' She asked.

'For an Angeon you are no different to the other sorcerers,' he grinned.

'Now you're mocking me,' she said.

'He has a point,' the Captain said. 'Ulrich will be harder to find if you rush in.'

Her flickering shadow sprawled across the sleeping wizards. As she stood in the warmth of the fire. Calm spread across the open ground and she made her way in the dark. Mitch grabbed her leg and she froze. 'Don't do that,' she whispered.

He had laid out a makeshift bed and she tucked herself in peering up at the stars. She fought sleep until it took the wafting voices away into a distant dream. One filled with a creeping dread seeping silently through the land. Deep beneath the surface. A whisper edged its way from below. The voice was too soft, but it repeated the same message over and over again. Her palms itched as the voice filtered up from Tordoren. In her dreams she opened her hands. She gasped at the shadowy marks visible to the eye. The camp was resting yet there was movement in the distance. The Shalough were coming. She had to wake up, but the dream held her fast. Mitch was sleeping and she called out, shouting his name. Hoping that he could hear her thoughts.

'Wake up,' a voice shouted overhead.

She tried to break free and light creased through her waking mind. The energy of the Angeon flooded along the surface. She did not remember calling it. The Athgar wizards were standing around, yet no one spoke. She looked up into Mitch's eyes, 'The Shalough.'

'We have to leave,' Anthony said.

Saranon cried out, 'Wait.'

'It's time to leave,' he said and helped her atop a magnificent marmoz dragon. 'This is Striker.'

'You have a dragon?' She asked.

'I do now,' he said.

They lifted into the dark morning sky with a graceful whoosh. Before the light creased along the horizon. She clung onto the base of the dragon's neck. As Anthony guided the beast toward the heartland.

A crimson hue broke across the land carving shadows deep into the hillside. The ground sparked with a wave of sorcery cascading along the ground. She gazed in horror, but the wave stopped short as it hit the shield protecting the Athgar. 'I pity anyone who takes on Lord Halleron,' Anthony spoke.

She remembered the bruises on the Captain, 'Is that what happened to Captain Harkin?'

'That is not for you to ask,' he said in a firm tone, ending the subject.

The hillside swept into a vast valley. Teaming with wildlife roaming the pockets of warm springs breaking through the ice. There were few signs of the dragons, but the lack of snow gave their presence away. Their warm underbellies heating the ground beneath. Patches of grass filled the valley floor. Ensuring an ideal place for dragons to hunt. The sun glistened off the melted snow as they flew past. 'Where are we headed?' She asked.

'Ragnorda,' he answered.

The Keep belonged to the Corathy and she wondered

how they would be greeted. 'Do you think we will really find Ulrich?'

'If Captain Harkin has anything to do with it. The damage to the trade line hurt them,' he said.

The dragons glided through the clear winter's day over the rolling hills and valleys. They veered south from the Summer House. The home of Lady Alvere shone, the garden was beautiful even from the sky. It was not long before Striker eased her pace. The great beast slowed and made a soft landing in the field surrounding Ragnorda. The Keep had a simple elegance with fine lines and curved trimmings. Marking the gates and main entrance. The buttresses rose up to meet an ornamental finish with carved gargoyles. They were the last to arrive and were greeted inside the warmth of the dragon pens. 'Welcome to my home,' said Meredith.

'Where is the Captain?' She asked, glancing around.

'He has business to attend to,' Meredith said.

'Lady Muir?' Anthony asked.

'Yes,' Meredith said.

Saranon had the distinct feeling she had been left out of an unspoken conversation. She went to find Mitch. He was grooming Katholomu who had curled up to rest in the pens. 'How?' She asked in astonishment.

The great beast had his paws and legs sticking out of the pen. He had somehow managed to squeeze the rest of his body in the space. 'He knows something,' Mitch said. 'Show me your hands.'

She was speechless as she held out her palms and froze.

The faint marks were visible with the same shadowy outline that had been in her dream. She could hardly breathe and went pale. Mitch leaned close, 'Don't tell anyone.'

She wanted to crumple onto the floor, but instead nodded in agreement. Rolling down the edges of her sleeves to hide the evidence. 'You didn't know,' he said.

'I...' she stammered.

'It's okay,' he said.

Mitch joined the gathering as though nothing had happened. Her stomach was queasy and she rested beside the dragon. 'How did you know?' She whispered.

Kat peered at her through a small slit as he continued to rest. He chose to ignore her as he watched on and she wondered what the great beast was thinking. The great beast had not been his usual grumpy self. When she reached out to pat his thick leathery skin. Ash covered her hand as she pulled it away. 'What have you done?' She asked, but the dragon remained silent.

Music played rummaging down the corridor from above. It was a joyful tune in contrast to the recent events. 'The supplies made it through,' Meredith answered her puzzled gaze.

'Ulrich is still out there,' she said.

'Do you want to give him a clue?' Meredith asked.

'No,' she answered.

'Then as far as anyone knows we are staying here,' Meredith replied.

'Is this about being patient?' She asked.

Meredith smiled as she led them below the main hall.

'We do not allow many sorcerers at Ragnorda.'

'I'll show you the best part,' Anthony said.

As he entered a chamber with slender columns. The stony walls fell away into an underground stream. A channel that ran around two sides for the room, then disappeared from view. The sound of running water trickled in the background. At the end of the room stood a pale altar. Carved with small replicas of the gargoyles that watched over the Keep. The veins of the stone swirled in a dark pattern breaking up the lighter tone. She stood at the centre of the chamber kneeling down as the pattern on the floor moved. Ragnorda was calling out. Saranon placed her hands on the smooth surface. The water began to seep along the floor being pulled from the open stream. The delicate lines weaved along the surface until they reached her hands.

Her heart thudded in her chest. As she concentrated on the Keep's energy rising up from the floor. A fine dust sprayed off the stone from the Keep. It rose with the stallic energy from the central core. The water and air all combining in the heat beneath her palms. The two bond-breakers began to form as she listened to the rise and fall of the rumbling. That emanated from the central core hidden far below. The blades formed with a deep burgundy wine heart stone. As each hilt shone she held them still caught in a trance with the Keep. The blades sparkled with the light reflecting off the pools of water on the floor. She held her arms steady until the blades were complete.

'You should not have done that,' Meredith gasped.

'It was the Keep who willed it,' she said, her voice sounding hollow.

Ragnorda let go and she held out one of the blades for Meredith. 'It is for you,' she said and held out the other for Anthony. 'Ragnorda wants the false oracle found.'

'I only meant you to meet the Keep,' Meredith said.

Saranon smiled. She had to remember that bond-breakers were uncommon even more so for wizards. The music became louder as they made their way to the great hall. The blades tucked away in dagger form. Tellembre stayed hidden beneath the fold of her coat as they entered. She glanced around and gaped as Mitch sat next to Lady Muir at the head of the table. His goblet was rested too close to hers. She followed Anthony to a table close to the door. It would provide an easy way to slip out unnoticed if they had to leave early. She gazed at Mitch as he whispered in Lady Muir's ear and they laughed. 'You look like a scorned woman,' Meredith said.

She blushed trying hide it, but it was no use. She did not think of herself as a woman, yet she was seventeen. 'Get entangled with a wizard and you'll know about it,' Meredith continued.

'That's half true,' said Anthony as he glanced across the table. 'The reason why wizards…'

Captain Harkin interrupted before she could find out more. 'We have the go ahead,' he said.

The conversation changed to finding Ulrich and for once she was not interested. She glared at Mitch intently at the other end of the great hall. He continued to ignore her and it annoyed her even more.

'You have changed since I last saw you,' Anthony said. 'Have you finished reading the books you copied from Qwezkin Fort,' he asked.

'No,' her cheeks felt hot as she spoke.

'Shame,' he said. 'I was wondering what you thought of the one about connecting with your wizardry.'

She threw a chunk of potato at him and he stifled a chuckle. 'I thought it was quite a good read,' the Captain added.

She glared at all three of them while she finished her meal. 'We don't often get sorcerers in these parts,' Anthony said.

'What about the Shalough?' She asked.

'That would involve work,' he said and she gave him a puzzled look. 'When they come this close to the border your friends in Darkonia get excited. The Shalough would be forced to defend themselves.'

'They are not my friends,' she said.

'I thought you were on good terms with the Vandragamond,' he said.

'They don't come down here,' she said.

The wizards burst out laughing. Saranon could not figure it out. She had understood the Vandragamond to be trapped by their own sorcery. She was one of them, but she was also the Angeon. 'When the Shalough are close to the border. The Vandragamond can greet them,' Meredith said.

'With an axe, a sword, or anything else they can get

their hands on,' Captain Harkin said.

'They wait for the Shalough to use their sorcery. Then they can strike,' Anthony said.

She had not known the Vandragamond could travel, yet she was able to. Captain Harkin rose from the table. 'Sleep well, it may be an early start tomorrow.'

She was left to endure the laughter emanating from Lady Muir's table. With Mitch fawning over the wizardess. It was not the first time, but he usually made an attempt to be discreet and hide it from her.

CHAPTER NINETEEN

Chasing the runaway

The fire burned low into the evening and the warmth from the Keep added to the heat. The air became hot. Although Saranon was reluctant to leave the evening was getting late. Anthony led her to a quiet guest area on the third level overlooking the valley. Several sparse sleeping rooms led off from the sitting area. Her room was large enough to hold two narrow beds, but not much more. She took care to unpack leaning the staff and equipment against the wall. She had no idea what would be needed to track down Ulrich. The sorcerer had a habit of finding a way to escape. The damage at the Pearl Castle had been brutal. If it were not for the size of the Keep the impact would have been far more.

She was too drained to think and curled up on the bed. It sank under her weight as she snuggled down. An element of excitement ran through Ragnorda keeping her from sleep. The door bustled open and Mitch staggered through tripping over her bed. The jolt brought her upright and she pushed him away, 'You're drunk.'

He ignored her and made a clumsy attempt to change in the dark. There was a loud thud as he fell backwards into the bags. The staff clattered on the floor and a soft glow from the orb lit the room. She went to help Mitch and he stepped back. 'You never made me a bond-breaker,' he said.

'You already have one,' she explained.

'It would have been nice if you remembered me,' he said. Mitch fought with the blankets as he tried to lie down on the bed. It was only just able to fit him.

She reached into the bag and brought out a bond-breaker in the form of a dagger. It was sheathed in an elegant pattern. With the dark navy heart stone in the hilt still showing. She leaned over and handed it to him, 'I was going to wait until we were in Normisia.'

He took it and silence filled the room as she slumped into bed. 'Where did you make it?' He asked.

'Greddin Fort. The last time I checked you were Normisian,' she replied. 'Why did you have to drool all over Lady Muir?'

'When you're older you will understand,' he said.

'I'm seventeen,' she said, glaring at him.

'Thanks for the bond-breaker,' he said, placing his hand on the hilt.

'Don't take it out. You just wrecked half the room,'

she said.

Mitch put it down beside the bed. 'Lady Muir was going to execute Captain Harkin,' he whispered.

The response sent a chill down her spine. It had not occurred to her that the Captain had risked everything. The heavy sound of snoring came from the wizard and she crammed her head close to the pillow. There was little chance of sleep. Yet she managed to drift off into dreams filled of nothing.

Movement woke her as Anthony tapped her on her shoulder, 'We have a leave.'

It was still dark and her head ached, 'It isn't morning.'

He had disappeared from the room while she rubbed her eyes. Her muscles were stiff and it took a while to get ready. Mitch packed up the rest. Shrinking the sova bags down to their tiny size before tucking them away. He moved at a clumsy pace down the stairs and she ran ahead. The small band of wizards waited for their arrival. Mitch sat down, head in his hands. His face was pale. Saranon's head was still thumping with a dull ache, but it was beginning to ease. Captain Harkin spoke, 'Stay close, I'll give the signal when you can move in.'

He was staring straight at her and she nodded. They moved out and Mitch did not budge. 'Why do you get to stay behind?' She shouted.

The Captain glared at her and she realised, 'Oh.'

The whistling wind sent a chill through the courtyard as the last of winter clung on. A white layer covered the hills through the valley. Only this time they were headed away from Keep Sturanin. The wizards knew the hillside well and they need not worry about her taking the lead. She could barely keep pace. A tiny glow shone up from the snow marking a faint lay-line and she smiled. The land was full of secrets that only the wizards knew. Anthony waited for her as she struggled. There was no sign of any sorcery other than her own, but she had to trust the Athgar. They had reason enough to seek out Ulrich.

The darkness eased with the rising sun. Revealing the entire valley and the forest below. The heavy frost was broken by patches of green. Marking the land as dragon territory. A few trees had blossomed early giving a magical appearance amid the snow. They had reached the end of the lay-line. All she wanted to do was run into the grass covered valley. Anthony held the hood of her cloak and whispered, 'No.'

She was about to speak. 'He's here,' the wizard said.

She glanced across the hills as the sun sparkled off the ridge line. There was no sign and she gazed longer in search of anything that might give Ulrich away.

Captain Harkin glanced her way, 'I will give the sign.'

She was beginning to get annoyed and almost wished to have gone on her own.

The well trodden path lay bare showing the pebbles below. The hardened ground allowed them to make good distance. Serensa loomed up ahead, the resting giant of a Keep in the hill. A hand full of sentinel dragons watched from above. The great beasts relaxed their wings in a half spread ready at any moment to take flight. Ulrich broke away from a small group. He was riding to Serensa and paying no heed of anyone. She glanced along the hillside where the dragons were forming a line. More gathered maintaining a casual glance down into the valley. Ulrich was mid-way along the winding path when the row of winged beasts increased. They were waiting and she could feel the tension.

The great beasts began to gather in the valley. Melting the snow that fell around the perimeter. Ulrich was gaining speed, soon he would be at Serensa. His horse reared and flung him to the wet muddy ground. The horse ran off, but it was not a person that had sent the steed into a spin. A dragon swooped lower still taunting the horse, it circled back wings spread wide. The animal shrieked galloping in a frightened frenzy for the nearest refuge. Saranon made her move breaking out of phase as light turned into a murky dark. The Angeon crept in with every step, seeping through her thoughts. Then the sun glistened as the real world welcomed her and the dragons watched. She stood on the path ahead, her cloak bellowing in the wind. The hot white glow of her yellow eyes glared at the false oracle and she dropped her hood. Ulrich was facing the Angeon.

He had trouble hiding his surprise and cursed the wizards. A rush of energy began pulling the false oracle into the void. It streamed toward the Angeon. Yet he held on, the Shalough were close. Saranon could feel the hooves of galloping horses hitting the hard ground. Ulrich built up his energy, a smile creased across his wrinkled face. The blasts of sorcery from the Shalough erupted through the air. Shattering the trees and scorching the earth. The Angeon still stood. A blaze of cold fire broke in a wide haze splitting the crisp morning air.

Ulrich shuddered as the shield held. Pelting blasts with bold precision straight for the Angeon. Each Shalough waiting with perfect timing, to keep the sorcery strong as it struck with a hollow drone. Sparks flew in a spray as the Angeon held the blasts back. Ulrich was gaining ground at a slow pace. As she stepped back with each blast that hit true thundering into the shield. It had decreased, but still protected her. Ulrich moved forward keeping pace with the Shalough. He was steadying himself and waited for the sorcerers to attack, but it never came.

He glanced behind him and a moment of panic struck him. The minotaur from the Pearl Castle had escaped. Ulrich turned to face the Angeon. She had regained her original position on the path. He continued to fall in line as blast after blast hit. He was not waiting anymore. A horrible howl emerged as the minotaur attacked and left only Ulrich standing.

The Angeon came closer, there was no gap between each attack. Ulrich held on, but as the sorcery cycled, his strength dimmed and Angeon closed in. He gave the blasts everything he had. The Angeon was nearing the edge of the shield, once that fell it was over. A giant thunderous crack pounded and he plunged backward. The ground met him with a thud.

The Angeon stood over him. He was rasping for every breath. 'You don't know what you've done,' he shouted. 'I was protecting your predecessor. Fool!'

Ulrich coughed up blood. 'You are not the only Angeon in this world,' his last words were faint.

He leaned back, the gurgle of death taking the air from his lungs. 'I was never the only Angeon,' Saranon said.

A cold rage ran through her. Somewhere among the Shalough hid an Angeon. Ulrich had been headed toward Serensa. When she had been there it had offered no sign. Yet Ulrich had made a deal with the Fires of Chaos. Perhaps the Angeon was truly hidden. Haig, the minotaur, was twice her height. Yet in the heartland amid the dragons he appeared small. They both did. 'Thank you,' she said.

'It is you I thank, Ulrich was no friend,' Haig said.

She gazed over the valley, there was no sign of the Shalough.

The wizards held no fear of the minotaur as they gathered around. Anthony patted her on the shoulder, 'Ulrich brought it on himself.'

A mix of feelings welled up within her. She could not speak. They waited in the cold fresh air as Captain Harkin and the wizards wrapped the body. To take it back to Ragnorda. It was the proof the wizards had been wanting. The death marked the end of years of hardship with the trade line. The link between north and south would make the Athgar great once more. Her stomach churned. If there was another Angeon out there, she had to find who it was. 'I have to go,' she told Anthony.

He peered into her eyes, 'We can deal with this.'

'There is something else,' she exclaimed.

Saranon had no doubt the wizards would secure the trade line. 'Do not fall for the Fires of Chaos,' he said.

'I won't,' she had no intention of allowing the Fires of Chaos to win, not this time.

Defeating Ulrich had taken much of her strength. She stayed close to the dragons of the heartland. Hiding in their shadows. The journey took her deeper into Shalough territory. The stream trickled by as she followed along its edge. The warm bellies of the great beast kept the harsh frost of winter at bay. Birds sang on the branches taunting her of spring as the sun began to fall below the ridge line.

The shadows darkened along the ground reaching farther as night fell. Yet she did not stop. The tiny white glow of a lay-line lured her in. She checked letting her energy sense its way along the path. It had not been used for some time. Saranon entered and she could tell why it remained unused. The lay-line took her close to the dragon dens. The great scales and thick skin moved within a fraction of the energy that let her pass at speed. A tail flicked and missed. The fear did not sink in, she had to make it to Serensa and find the Angeon before the Fires of Chaos did. What if they already knew? She was more determined than ever to head straight for the Keep.

Thunder cracked through the sky, it was not safe to be in the lay-line yet the end was in sight. The wind whipped through and she pulled her cloak tight just as the rain drenched her. She could sense the Keep up ahead as the rain pelted from the blackened sky. Saranon waited as the troops rode by making their way to the building rising from the hill. The Shalough sorcerers were a distance away and she watched wondering if they knew. It would be a long night as the howling wind ran through her cloak. There was no sign of the Fires of Chaos yet she could not be sure. She trudged, pacing herself along the muddy ground. What would make a sorcerer ruin the trade line? The question ate away at her mind.

The end nodes marking the boundary of Serensa were but a few steps away. As soon as she crossed the line the Shalough would know. If they did not already. She let the ends of the cloak fly free in the wind as the rain poured on her face. One hand gripped the hilt of Tellembre. The cream pearl blade stayed in its sheath at her side. She was Vandragamond, she did not run from a fight. She was the Angeon. She passed the end nodes and the Keep remained quiet. As the wind bellowed around the building. Lights shone from the energy of the central core and she headed to the brightest one. Steps led to the main entrance and the two heavy doors flung open as she made it to the landing.

Thunder struck along the hillside. Lighting the building as it edged close to the ground. The Shalough were caught off guard. Her eyes blazing with a determination that made her forget the icy chill. As a gush of wind droned through the entrance. 'Where is the Angeon?' She shouted.

Commander Meghan addressed her, 'Stand down Vandragamond.'

'Don't play coy with me. Where is the Angeon?' She demanded.

'Have you lost your mind? Perhaps Veridan should've

dealt with you,' the Commander said.

'Veridan ran away,' she said in an even tone scanning the troops that had come in from the cold.

A 'group of Shalough were gathering in the main entrance. She caught sight of Ranger Korban, but chose to ignore him. Dargon stepped forward blocking her path. 'Where are you hiding the Angeon?' She asked.

'Believe me, we would know if there was an Angeon,' his voice was firm and he did not back down.

She was tempted to take him on, she had to find who it was. Lindford stood beside him, his features similar to Ulrich. His hair greying with age. He stared at her unwavering. She held his gaze and grabbed his right hand turning it over. The grey mark was there, it matched hers.

He forced his arm free of her grip and she revealed the mark on her hands. 'I should have known,' she said.

It was Ulrich's brother who wore the mark of the Angeon. It was not enough to harm her, but to hide her predecessor as well. Her head was filled with a cascade of emotions. She had to leave even with the rain beating down. Serensa 'had become unbearable and the Keep would have known. She strode out to the landing as the wind caught at the edges of her cloak.

'Wait! I didn't know. No one did,' Commander Meghan called out.

She glanced back to find the sorcerers in a state of shock. 'Ulrich did,' she said.

'We didn't know. You cannot blame everyone for what one sorcerer's deeds,' the Commander said.

She hated to admit the Commander had a point. The secret had been concealed well. If she left the Fires of Chaos may show. She strode up to Lindford, 'Come with me.'

She did not wait to see if he followed and made her way toward the centre of Serensa. If the Keep was going to hide an Angeon the least it could do was help train him. The stadium for the soldiers had thick walls close to a main conduit. Leading down to the central core. It offered protection and now it would be an ideal training space. The soldiers practising stopped and silence fell around the two-storey room. A balcony ran along the side above her and benches, in rows lay underneath. She made her way down the isle to the threshold of the stadium.

Lindford spoke behind her, 'Practice is over.'

The Shalough filed out into the benches all eyes were on her. She let her sodden cloak fall on the floor. 'Enter,' she said, when it was clear Lindford would not follow.

'No,' he replied.

She gazed at him and he stood firm. She did not have time for games. 'I killed Ulrich,' she said.

She caught the change in his expression. He entered the stadium as the Shalough sorcerers looked on. Lindford steadied himself at the opposite end of stadium. It was only for a brief moment then the blast came. She was ready, the fight with Ulrich had heightened her senses. Her energy lay below the surface, but this was not about defeat. She had to call the Angeon to the surface or he would be vulnerable. She spread her attack wide with little effort. Yet it vanquished Lindford's attempt with ease. He staggered back and fired again. She kept her attack wide. The energy spreading around the edges rather than in a direct line. It was not enough for the Angeon locked within to rise.

Lindford strengthened his attack increasing the flow of energy every time. She maintained her strategy with a firm patience. The Angeon had to rise to the surface. That was her aim. Serensa absorbed the sorcery in the thick walls as sparks flew. She could make out the glowing crease along his arms, the Angeon was about to rise. She could sense it and kept up the attack. Sweeping her energy around both sides, making him rely on the sorcery of old. She was so close, then came the glow in his eyes and she gave a shout of victory. The Angeon had risen to the surface. The Shalough crowded around the arena in silent awe. She waited for Lindford to return the energy inside, but it stayed on the surface. Dargon rushed into the arena and she held up her hand for him to stop.

Time slowed and it felt as though they waited too long. Then the glow dissipated. The relief on Dargon was visible and he rushed in as Lindford fell to his knees. 'In the morning we spar.' She said.

His face was drained with exhaustion. 'Ulrich was protecting you from something.' She explained.

Saranon picked up her cloak and used her energy to dry it. Instead of returning through the crowd she waited for Commander Meghan. 'I need to speak with Serensa,' she said.

'I don't think…' The Commander began.

A sealed entrance behind them opened onto the

stadium. She took her leave, her head was filled with so many thoughts. Including the Keep that had hidden Lindford from her. She travelled down to the chamber. The dark liquid shaol ran in a slow stream to one side. At the end lay an altar, yet she had no need of it. She expanded a sova bag making a small bed on the floor and rested. Clearing her head of the mess that raged inside. 'What did you think I would do?' She spoke the words aloud.

Serensa answered in her mind, you are Vandragamand always. 'I am the Angeon always. Lindford is my kin, you could have told me,' she said.

Serensa answered, he stays here.

'I was not going to take him. He is too weak,' she said.

There was silence. Perhaps she could have been a bit less blunt with her choice of words. Serensa entered her mind once more, You agree he stays. 'I agree, he should remain,' she said.

Senensa responded, typical Vandragamond. Saranon smiled, 'Typical Keep, always hiding secrets.'

Serensa answered, I am not the only one. Then the Keep fell silent. The chamber was warm and dry. She drifted off to a peaceful sleep filled of nothing. As the central core hummed away in the depths below.

Serensa broke her thoughts. It was early morning and the Shalough were preparing for the day. She made her way to the arena, her muscles were tired and sore. The arena was almost empty. She spotted Lindford who appeared well rested. 'Are you ready to spar?' He asked.

He appeared concerned at her appearance. She was

waking up, but she could still spar. 'I'm ready when you are,' she replied.

'Typical Vandragamond,' he said.

She hesitated, 'Do you hear the Keep?'

'No,' he said.

'She can hear you,' Saranon said.

They entered the arena and Dargon stayed. This time he sat in anticipation and she smiled, 'I think your friend wants a show.'

Lindford shook his head in dismay. It did not stop him from leading as the first blast rang out. She concentrated keeping the same steady pace. Moving ever so slightly to practice what she knew. She could only hope it would be enough. At times the blasts hit their mark, she absorbed the blows just as the Keep did. This was about practice, not the fight.

Bridget entered and they stopped. It had been a long morning and the sun was nearing midday. Dargon spoke, 'Caddell wants to speak with the Angeon at Serensa.'

The Fires of Chaos were here already. She replied, 'Well, then I had better go.'

'He wants to see Lindford,' Dargon explained.

'I am the Angeon at Serensa,' she said in a firm tone.

Dargon bowed, 'Indeed.'

She glanced around the room, 'Shall we go?'

They made their way toward the main entrance. As they did Saranon let the energy of the Angeon rise to the surface. She may be Vandragamond, but she was also the Angeon. It was time to meet the Fires of Chaos. The

Shalough bowed and stepped away letting her pass as she moved ahead. A hush of silent awe fell on the sorcerers gathered in the entrance as all eyes turned to her. For a moment everyone ignored the Fires of Chaos as she entered. Her voice boomed across the great height as light shone through the open doors. Illuminating the pale walls, in stark contrast to her heavy dark cloak. 'I am the Angeon,' she shouted into the silence.

CHAPTER TWENTY

Taking on the Fires of Chaos

Saranon strode with a determined march to face the Fires of Chaos. The sorcerers stayed in a close group near the threshold of the entrance. She grabbed the hilt of the bond-breaker Tellembre. The blade sang as it was released, glowing in the light. It was not the blade that mattered as the sorcerers eyes followed its move. 'You are not the one we seek,' Caddell said.

'I could say the same,' she said.

Her eyes caught on the shadowy movement. Across the skin of the sorcerer behind Caddell. The sign of forbidden sorcery. She spread her energy wide as she had done when sparring Lindford. All bar one of of the group fell in agony. She steadied herself, not wanting to reveal her surprise.

Dark shadows crept across the skin of the Fires of Chaos. Her stomach ached as she realised they had stolen wizardry. She stayed firm as the Shalough gathered in a silent vigil. No one stepped in to help. A long moment passed, before the sorcerers from the Fires of Chaos began to realise they would live. Giselbert distanced himself from the group. 'At least one of you had sense,' she said.

Dargon gave a menacing expression and stood by her side. 'I can either hand them over to the Athgar or you can deal with them. What say you?' Saranon asked him.

Dargon gave a terrifiying grin that sent a chill down her spine. 'We can deal with them,' he said. 'What of that one?' he pointed to Giselbert.

The tall gaunt sorcerer trembled. 'I have no interest in that one,' she said.

'Be gone,' Dargon had no need to say more.

The sorcerer vanished from sight as he darted across the open courtyard. It did not take long for order to be restored to Serensa. She did not want to know what would happen to the Fires of Chaos that had become razen. Dark sorcery was universally detested, even among the Shalough.

The sky darkened and she glanced upward. To see the wingspan of Katholomu as he landed with a great thud near the stairs. He poked his nose through the doorway and she patted him. 'You missed the action,' she told him.

The magnificent beast eyed her and let out a sound of disgruntlement. Mitch ran up the stairs to greet her and she fought the urge to run into his arms. 'If you ever need someone to spar with I would be more than happy to,' she spoke to Lindford.

'Stay out of trouble,' he said.

She smiled and waved. Then followed Mitch, clambering up to the great dragon's shoulder. She waited for him to give the signal and Kat whooshed into the air. His wings spread their full width taking them higher.

'You made some friends,' he said in her ear as the wind rushed past.

'Maybe,' she answered. 'How did you escape Lady Muir?'

'She only had eyes for another,' he said.

She laughed and hugged the dragon tight. It was good to be back in the air. She watched as they flew over the heartland. Dragons joined them at brief intervals darting through the sky. 'Has anyone heard from the battle?' She asked.

'Lord Halleron had an entire league, what do you think happened?' he said.

'Umm…' She said.

'The Shalough retreated,' he answered.

The great beast flew in one direction, the last she had ever expected. 'What are you doing?' She asked.

'I am taking you where you need to go,' Mitch said.

The sun set low on the horizon when Katholomu glided the last distance. The Keep shone golden as the last rays of light beamed off the building. The dragon circled down with a jolt as he hit the ground, still moving. The grass had grown over the fields surrounding Antavagon. The stone markers along with the camps were gone. A wind swept past and she hesitated. 'Why did you bring me here?' Saranon asked.

This time Katholomu answered, 'Home.'

'This is not my home,' she replied.

The great dragon nudged her toward the Keep. Antavagon remained silent as she stood in Darkonia, her homeland. She took a deep breath and ventured in. The place was clean and the morning light swept over the plain walls. She reached out and hesitated. Mitch made a noise as he strode toward her and she jumped. 'You need to let go,' he said and she turned away.

There was so much pain hidden within the Keep. She made her way down to the pale room where the altar lay in the middle. Light streamed through from above. She could still see the blood on the floor and her hands. Tasha's blood. The memory of not being able to save her friend remained etched in her mind.

She touched the altar and a voice spoke. ' I have been waiting,' the lady said.

The lady was taller than Tasha, but she had the same fawn coloured hair. 'Who are you? Saranon asked.

'You know who I am,' the lady answered. 'I am Antavagon.'

'But I thought you were…' She began.

'Your friend. That, I have always been,' the lady answered. 'It is time.'

She pulled her hand away from the altar. 'Katholomu brought you home.'

'But this isn't…' She said.

'I have guided you from the moment you left,' the lady responded. 'Look at your hands, tell me what you see?'

The marks on her palms were stronger, there was no way she could hide them.

CHAPTER TWENTY-ONE

Home eternal

One choice was all it took, the ground trembled from below. Saranon glanced back at Antavagon rising over the land. It remained silent as she left. The Keep that held so much anguish. Yet where there had been pain the memory of her friend Tasha remained. The riding cat took her to the glow of the lay-line. She slid off and the misquew bowed its head. The path led to a rumbling deep within Tordoren, one she could not ignore. Each step took her into the territory of the Arthrose. Once she may have hesitated. Yet she was no longer the child that had grown in the shadows of Darkonia. A breeze hinted the end of winter as it fled along the steep valley carved into the earth.

Keep Kedorenn stood partly visible along the steep cliff. The closer Saranon stepped the more certain she became. That the Arthrose knew she was there. A flicker ran near the edge of her vision, as she made the final step movement caught her eye. The flanks of the Darkonian Army spread across both sides of the terrain. Major Shenoff eyed her, his hand resting on the hilt of his blade.

Two years had passed, yet the Major looked not a day older. His broad shoulders carried the weight of a mask of calm. Greying hair kept neat under the rim of the helmet. A faint noise could be heard and to her dismay Mitch emerged from the lay-line. The wizard had a habit of showing up at the wrong time. Her cringe did not go unnoticed. Barely a word was spoken as they followed toward the Keep.

Glimpses of fresh grass and moss wedged between the rocks gave a hint of the warmer days to come. She stayed close to the Major who had little to say. Yet there was something about his eager stride that set her at ease. It was not long before the path veered into the cliff. Opening into a deep void filled with many outlooks across the land. Pennie stood out with her blonde hair and sparkling eyes. She had been so long away and hesitated in the grip of her friend. 'You are here to find the Prince,' Pennie said.

Whispered into her ear while darting around. Her old friend had always been able to think of a plan. The problem was seeing it through, Saranon had been the one to do that. She smiled and took a deep breath while buying time. A Prince? 'What happened?' She blurted it out, but Pennie beamed with delight.

It felt like old times, Pennie had grown and changed. Her hair was longer and tied neatly back. Saranon realised she was being led away as the door closed behind Mitch. Pennie returned to the friend she knew well, the one that had a greater temper than her. 'Are you mad? This is the largest stronghold the Arthrose has within the Army. If one of the Captain's wants you dead there will be little anyone can do.'

'You are here,' Saranon said.

'I am not the one who destroyed the camps. The only reason why you are here. Is because the deaths of the Arthrose Councillors were investigated. It wasn't you,' Pennie snapped.

She was speechless, the Eye of Escora had been in her hands. Saranon had wanted it so badly. She always thought she had willed it to happen. 'You have to find Prince Demarkos, his companions returned without him. They are shaken, but the details are vague,' Pennie became insistent. 'If he isn't found soon the Arthrose will be looking for someone to blame.'

That glare hid so much fear. Saranon nodded, she could not believe she had returned. To run straight into one of Pennie's schemes. A smile crept across her face. It did not take long for Mitch to merge into the background, she wished it was so easy for her. The Major made himself busy, but she could tell he was finding any excuse to stay nearby. The control room had commanding views that swept along the great ravine. Saranon caressed the wall with her finger tips. A faint movement rumbled from beneath. 'You will not find Kedorenn responsive,' the Major said as he watched her.

She paid him little heed as the Keep sang. It was well loved and hummed away with a vibrant tone through the walls. She lifted her hand and the space fell silent. Except for the officers maintaining the Keep.

No sooner than she gazed back toward the control room, when the door burst open revealing a weary Captain Assinden. Pennie's hylizen drew up short of speaking, staring at her and then the Major. The Major nodded and Captain Jacob Assinden relaxed his guard. At least there were a few familiar faces in Darkonia. 'The trail ends at Lepithia,' he said.

A hushed tone fell over the small group as Major Shenoff stared straight at her. Saranon had no idea what it meant and the Major filled in the silence. 'Lepithia is on its way out. The Keep has been abandoned and we stay well clear. Looks like you bought your ticket home.' There was no joy in the Major's voice.

Captain Assinden spoke, 'We can take you as far as the end node.'

He guided her out of the room. 'Bring the Prince back alive,' the edge in his tone sent a chill down her spine.

Pennie rushed to greet her in the chaos that followed. Everyone wanted the Prince to return regardless of how they felt about her. The wind whipped around the base of the Keep with a terrible drone. It played havoc with the dragons who were grounded. 'We take the misquew,' Captain Assinden said.

No one was prepared to argue. Saranon could sense the change in the flow of energy seeping through the ground.

Before they reached the edge of the Keep. The riding cats would travel no closer and she had to disembark. The wizards remained where they were. Captain Assinden had taken her as far as he was prepared to go. Pennie strode toward the building and she followed. It took them into the hillside and the air prickled. 'Are you sure we should be looking here?' She asked.

Pennie nodded, but waited for Saranon to take the lead. It had always been that way for as long as they had been friends. An echo rang out from within. No hum ran along the walls, but odd sounds drifted up from the depths. Stairs led upward and the sounds grew faint as she glanced around. The place was dust ridden and a cold breeze emanated from the broken windows. There was no sign that anyone had been here, yet she felt the need to check if only for her friend. Saranon made her way down and Pennie volunteered to stay behind. The occasional jarring clunk filtered through the old Keep.

The indolin chambers were mostly intact, but the conduits had been left to decay. Pools of sheal liquid dripped along the floor. She moved further away from the stairs and any sign of the outside world. A faint sound travelled up from below. Merging with the last gasps of the central core hidden deep in Tordoren. A voice reached her ears then it was gone. Her heart pounded as she glanced around. There was no sign of life, but Saranon swore she heard it.

The path to the imbenik chambers was blocked with a myriad of fallen rubble. Doubt filled her mind, but she pressed on. A great rumbling echoed through the walls and she called out. This time the voice was clear. She stood near an open conduit, its contents long gone. Saranon called down into the darkness and a reply sent a chill down her spine. 'I have been waiting for you,' he said in a calm and confident tone.

'I doubt that,' she retorted.

As she climbed into the broken conduit and made her way down. Gloom filled the void with one tiny light shimmering against the darkness. It was not the Prince that waited to greet her. The Host was part wizard and part Keep. He rested on the floor, barely moving. He pointed to a sleeping sorcerer down the corridor and a gaping void in between. 'How long do you have?' Saranon asked.

'Hours, minutes, they are the same,' the Host replied. 'The energy is gone.'

The hairs on the back of her neck stood on end. The Host was calm, he knew his life would end and there was nothing she could do. She made her way into the darkness letting her energy flow. Melding with what remained of the Keep. A ledge extended out to where the Prince slept. At a closer glance he was tall and his frame strong. He woke with a start, he had short curls of fawn brown colour. There was no mistaking his eyes, they were Tasha's.

Saranon held out her hand and the Prince hesitated. 'Now would be a good time to leave,' she said.

He did not move. 'Major Shenoff sent me,' she explained.

'The Major would not send a Vandragamond,' he

rasped.

Saranon handed him a flask and he took gulps of water, letting it drip down his chin. 'I will wait,' Prince Demarkos replied.

She had to fight the urge to thump him. 'You can wait above ground, it will be easier to evacuate,' she suggested in a firm tone.

The Prince gazed around, as though taking in the surroundings for the first time. He was unsteady on his feet and almost fell. Saranon was not impressed, but there was an uneasy sense as she watched him. There was no explanation for the Prince's state, at least none that she could see. She guided him away from the dying Host who lay motionless in the rubble. He leaned against her for support and they glanced at each other. As Prince Demarkos became more aware he grew anxious. Pennie greeted them as light streamed through. The fields outside were empty of life, overgrown and untouched. She slipped back down to where the Host remained. His forehead was cool and he still breathed. He spoke in a whisper, 'You are looking for this.'

The Host clasped her hand and images flooded through. The colour drained from his face and the images faded with his last dying breath. The Prince left behind was no accident.

A terrible clambering climbed up the walls. The Host was gone and no energy remained. A great rumbling moved through the building, roaring up from the cavities. As she entered the broken conduit the sound haunted her from the depths. The sound of the central core straining under the weight. Saranon clambered up, willing her limbs to move faster. As she reached out over the jagged opening. A sound filled her with such dread that she hesitated. The eruption rumbled deep beneath the ground. Making its way up the empty conduits through the walls. She ran to find Pennie, 'Get out!'

Pennie stood there for a moment, not comprehending the danger. 'It collapsed, run!'

Pennie waited. 'Why aren't you going?' Saranon asked.

'I'm not leaving without you,' Pennie replied.

She wanted to shake her friend. 'You have to go now. I will be behind you, but you have to leave now,' She was running out of patience.

A terrible roar emerged from deep below. It steadily grew louder. Pennie hesitated then went with the Prince who was still struggling. The rumble from beneath drowned out all other noise. They were not going to make it. She was in a dying Keep and her friend was not going to make it. Saranon turned to face what remained of Lepithia. She glanced down at the faint marks on her hands. The noise became so loud it almost hurt her ears. Then a silence followed as she reached out to the Angeon. The sorcery of old and the Vandragamond that she knew she was. The others had been Shalough, except for her. Except the one who could break the world, and break Tordoren. The thought filled her with a deep horror and understanding. The blast was erupting deep beneath the surface, heading closer with every passing moment.

Saranon had lost one friend, she was not about to lose another. The Angeon enveloped her very essence. Tordoren had chosen her. It had chosen her above the Shalough, it had chosen a different path. She reached out with the energy of the Angeon letting it flow freely, filling the void. The rumbling from the deep was so loud, yet so far away. She let the energy sink deep. Ripping an opening in the ground that pierced deep into Tordoren. The rumbling swept into the void as it opened beneath. Crashing into the darkness as the building crumbled around her. She held on, keeping the great crevasse open. Tordoren rumbled deep below forcing the void to close.

She held on as the pressure increased, hoping it would be enough. The hollow void filled with a deep warning as it shook. The sides began to give way and finally Saranon let it crumble. The earth swallowed the last of the dying Keep. A shudder sent a fine spray of dirt and dust hurtling through the air. Saranon waited in the shield as the air became thick. She made her way through the haze and a breeze began to creep in. The fine mist dissipated as she made her way to the lay-line. Her hands were sore and the marks were real. This time Tordoren had chosen someone else. Someone the rest of the world had not been expecting. Someone with the strength to choose a different path.

ACKNOWLEDGEMENTS

Life has been a journey filled with many challenges, and the people I would like to thank would not fit on this page. To everyone out there who has been part of this incredible journey thank you, your support has been appreciated.

– Please Leave a Review –

For all the wonderful people who have read the book it would be fantastic if you can leave a review, this helps other readers find it. Thank you.

BOOKS

The Legacy of Zyanthia series:
Made in the Image of the Goddess
Running through the Rising Tide
Deep in the Shadow of the Fallen

AUTHOR

If you love fantasy with adventure and a hint of the unexpected the quest is about to begin. Escape into fantasy, and the mystical world of magic mixed with adventure. You are in good company although chose your company wisely. There are anti-heroes, wizards, and a range of chaotic characters ahead. Not to mention dragons. A fantasy world set in an ancient mythical world has to have dragons. Tales of sword and sorcery captivated Chantelle from a young age. Reading until all hours of the night to find out what would happen to the characters. There was just one problem the story would finish far too soon.

Hidden away in the distant past the life of a fantasy writer began. The real life struggles have been a saga all of their own for author Chantelle Griffin born in Tasmania, Australia. Her dreams haunted her from an early age. Vivid tumultuous dreams carrying adventure and danger. It took the author into a fantasy world filled with sorcery and treachery. The story continues to captivate her writing. If you love fantasy with adventure follow the Legacy of Zyanthia series.

www.chantellegriffin.com

GLOSSARY

ANGEON: 'The Angeon is Darkonia's answer to the Oracle, a sorcerer born with the ability to break down all defences and render a civilisation powerless.' There had been no Angeon since shortly after the Dreshan Occupation ended over 200 years ago with Zeralden Hadenvar the last Angeon who ruled Darkonia (as Queen) by marriage to the King's second son.

BOND-BREAKER: A weapon made by sorcery when dormant resembles a dagger, when activated resembles a sword it acts as a catalyst to magnify and aim the user's energy and can be used equally well by wizards as well as sorcerers. 'The most feared swords a sorcerer could use made of heart stone a melding of the elements to form a solid material that resembled crystal and sharp enough to cut through stone.'

CENTRAL CORE: The working core mechanism which powers the Keep, usually hidden away deep within the earth. It is a large engine created by sorcery which then continues to thrive on a combination of energy drawn from deep within the earth and sorcery. The combination creates a very raw and powerful energy which is difficult to manipulate.

DEAD ZONE: This is created when part of the Keep is not receiving energy from the central core or when energy has been diverted.

END NODE: Last outpost of a Keep's main energy source located at semi-regular intervals around the perimeter.

FERMADICIDE: Dark skeletal creatures.

FIRE MARK: A mark on the right shoulder to, the symbol of the fires of chaos given to the Issola in the camps.

HILAZEN: Bonded wizard.

HOST: Wizard joined with a Keep, it takes 60 hours to complete a union.

HYRIK: Restraint on sorcery, like a collar.

IMBENIK CHAMBER: Near the central core within the Keep, in between the indolin chamber and the central core it contains alters where a sorcerer can meld with the Keep.

INDOLIN CHAMBER: Inside the Keep, in between the habitable area and the central core.

KEDRIL(S): Tools to fix a Keep.

KEEP: A building protected by a central core powered by sorcery and energy from the earth. The tunnels led down to the primary systems and the central core that transferred energy from far below the ground into the core and turned into a usable energy source. Most central cores were located deep in the ground where the temperature was constantly warm…'

KULTIER: Long giant cockroaches.

LAY-LINE: Fast method of travel.

MAZETTE: Small (bird size) dragons.

MISQUEW: Riding cat.

NEFRELLE: Small creature (cat size), part human with very sharp teeth and claws.

OCKREN: Big cat, the soul of the Keep.

PALAFON: Tiny dragon.

QUADMAR: Aquatic creature from the murky depths, larger than a mermaid.

SACRA SEAL: Small, can hold it on your hand.

SHEAL: Liquid inside the Keep, very potent compressed raw energy.

SKADA: Small mechanical creatures that help maintain the Keep, they resemble a large spider.

SOVA BAG: A deceptive small light pouch that can become an enormous bag and hold a lot of objects, it will not hold living things.

STALLIC ENERGY: Energy from the Keep.

TALIK: Communication device. 'The sorceress held up her talik a small round disc that could open small enough to fit in the palm of her hand and placed her thumb on the centre of the outside…'

TRIDEN: Giant crab/spider, dark brown.

UVALEN CODE: '…A complex masterpiece describing the natural laws that governed sorcery.'

ZENNIGH: A large cat that normally lives within a Keep, they are too big to fit in a house but that has not stopped the occasional one from trying and getting their head jammed in the doorway.

ZYANTHIAN REGION: Armedicia, Taria, Normisia, Darkonia and Alveron were formed from one country called Zyanthia.

www.ingramcontent.com/pod-product-compliance
Lightning Source LLC
Chambersburg PA
CBHW070146120726
47909CB00001B/1